# THE
# JANSON
# DIRECTIVE

## Also by Robert Ludlum

*The Sigma Protocol*
*The Prometheus Deception*
*The Matarese Countdown*
*The Apocalypse Watch*
*The Road to Omaha*
*The Scorpio Illusion*
*The Bourne Ultimatum*
*The Icarus Agenda*
*The Bourne Supremacy*
*The Aquitaine Progression*
*The Parsifal Mosaic*
*The Bourne Identity*
*The Matarese Circle*
*The Gemini Contenders*
*The Holcroft Covenant*
*The Chancellor Manuscript*
*The Road to Gandolfo*
*The Rhinemann Exchange*
*The Cry of the Halidon*
*Trevayne*
*The Matlock Paper*
*The Osterman Weekend*
*The Scarlatti Inheritance*

# ROBERT LUDLUM

# THE
# JANSON
# DIRECTIVE

ST. MARTIN'S PRESS    NEW YORK

www.stmartins.com

Library of Congress Cataloging-in-Publication Data

Ludlum, Robert.
    The Janson directive / Robert Ludlum.
        p.    cm.
    ISBN 0-312-25348-6
    1. Terrorism—Prevention—Fiction.    2. Intelligence officers—Fiction.
    3. Kidnapping—Fiction.    I. Title.
    PS3562.U26 J36    2002
    813'.54—dc21

                                                    2002005136

First Edition: October 2002

10  9  8  7  6  5  4  3  2  1

It is easy for him to bestow gifts. Were he to live forever he could never squander all he owns, for he holds the Nibelungs' hoard in his power.

—*Nibelungenlied,*
circa 1200 A.D.

# THE
# JANSON
# DIRECTIVE

# PROLOGUE

*8°37'N, 88°22'E*
*N. Indian Ocean, 250 miles east of Sri Lanka*
*Northwestern Anura*

The night was oppressive, the air at body temperature and almost motionless. Earlier in the evening there had been light, cooling rains, but now everything seemed to radiate heat, even the silvery half-moon, its countenance brushed with the occasional wisps of cloud. The jungle itself seemed to exhale the hot, moist breath of a predator lying in wait.

Shyam shifted restlessly in his canvas chair. It was, he knew, a fairly ordinary night on the island of Anura for this time of year: early in the monsoon season, the air was always heavy with a sense of foreboding. Yet only the ever attentive mosquitoes disturbed the quiet. At half past one in the morning, Shyam reckoned he had been on checkpoint duty for four and a half hours. In that time, precisely seven motorists had come their way. The checkpoint consisted of two parallel lines of barbed-wire frames—"knife rests"—set up eighty feet apart on the road, to either side of the search and administration area. Shyam and Arjun were the two sentries on forward duty, and they sat in front of the wooden roadside booth. A pair of backups was supposedly on duty on the other side of the hill, but the hours of silence from them suggested that they were dozing, along with the men in the makeshift barracks a few hundred feet down the road. For all the dire warnings of their superiors, these had been days and nights of unrelieved boredom. The northwestern province of Kenna was sparsely populated in the best of times, and these were not the best of times.

Now, drifting in with the breeze, as faint as a distant insect drone, came the sound of a gunned motor.

Shyam slowly got to his feet. The sound was growing closer.

"*Arjun,*" he called out in a singsong tone. "*Ar*-jun. Car coming."

Arjun lolled his head in a circle, working out a crick in his neck. "At this hour?" He rubbed his eyes. The humidity made the sweat lie heavily on his skin, like mineral oil.

In the dark of the semi-forested terrain, Shyam could finally see the headlights. Over a revved-up motor, loud whoops of delight could be heard.

"Dirty farm kids," Arjun grumbled.

Shyam, for his part, was grateful for anything that interrupted the tedium. He had spent the past seven days on the night shift at the Kandar vehicle checkpoint, and it felt like a hardship post. Naturally, their stone-faced superior had been at pains to emphasize how important, how crucial, how *vital* in every way, the assignment was. The Kandar checkpoint was just up the road from the Stone Palace, where the government was holding some sort of hush-hush gathering. So security was tight, and this was the only real road that connected the palace to the rebel-held region just to the north. The guerrillas of the Kagama Liberation Front knew about the checkpoints, however, and kept away. As did most everyone else: between the rebels and the anti-rebel campaigns, more than half the villagers to the north had fled the province. And the farmers who stayed in Kenna had little money, which meant that the guards could not expect much by way of "tips." Nothing ever happened, and his wallet stayed thin. Was it something he had done in a previous life?

The truck came into view; two shirtless young men were in the cab. The roof was down. One of boys was now standing up, pouring a sudsy can of beer over his chest and cheering. The truck—probably loaded with some poor farmer's *kurakkan,* or root crops—was rounding the bend at upward of eighty miles per hour, as fast as the groaning engine would go. American rock music, from one of the island's powerful AM stations, blared.

The yelps and howls of merriment echoed through the night. They sounded like a pack of drunken hyenas, Shyam thought miserably. Penniless joyriders: they were young, wasted, didn't give a damn about anything. In the morning they would, though. The last time this happened, several days earlier, the truck's owner got a visit later that morning from the youths' shamefaced parents. The truck was returned, along with many, many bushels of *kurakkan* to make amends for whatever damage had been done. As for the kids, well, they couldn't sit without wincing, not even on a cushioned car seat.

Now Shyam stepped into the road with his rifle. The truck kept barreling forward, and he stepped back. No use being stupid about it. Those kids were blind drunk. A beer can was lobbed into the air, hitting the ground with a thunk. From the sound, it was a full one.

The truck veered around the first knife rest, and then the second knife rest, and kept going.

"Let Shiva tear them limb from limb," Arjun said. He scrubbed at his bushy black hair with his stubby fingertips. "No need to radio the back-stop. You can hear these kids for miles."

"What are we supposed to do?" Shyam said. They were not traffic cops, and the rules did not permit them to open fire on just any vehicle that failed to stop.

"Peasant boys. Bunch of peasant boys."

"Hey," Shyam said. "I'm a peasant boy myself." He touched the patch sewn on his khaki shirt: ARA, it read. Army of the Republic of Anura. "This isn't tattooed on my skin, all right? When my two years are up, I'm going back to the farm."

"That's what you say now. I got an uncle who has a college degree; he's been a civil servant for ten years. Makes half what we do."

"And you're worth every ruvee," Shyam said with heavy sarcasm.

"All I'm saying is, you got to seize what chances life gives you." Arjun flicked a thumb at the can on the road. "Sounds like that one's still got beer in it. Now, *that's* what I'm talking about. Pukka refreshment, my friend."

"Arjun," Shyam protested. "We're supposed to be on duty together, you know this? The two of us, yes?"

"Don't worry, my friend." Arjun grinned. "I'll share."

When the truck was half a mile past the roadblock, the driver eased up on the accelerator, and the young man riding shotgun sat down, wiping himself off with a towel before putting on a black T-shirt and strapping himself in. The beer was foul, noisome, and sticky in the heavy air. Both guerrillas looked grave.

An older man was seated on the flat bench behind them. Sweat made his black curls cling to his forehead, and his mustache gleam in the moonlight. The KLF officer had been prone and invisible when the truck crashed the checkpoint. Now he flicked the COMMUNICATE button on his walkie-talkie, an old model but a sturdy one, and grunted some instructions.

With a metallic groan, the rear door of the trailer was cracked open so that the armed men inside could get some air.

The coastal hill had many names and many meanings. The Hindus knew it as Sivanolipatha Malai, Shiva's footprint, to acknowledge its true origins. The Buddhists knew it as Sri Pada, Buddha's footprint, for they believed that it was made by Buddha's left foot when he journeyed to the island. The Muslims knew it as Adam Malai, or Adam's Hill: tenth-century Arab traders held that Adam, after he was expelled from Paradise, stopped here and remained standing on one foot until God recognized his penitence. The colonial overlords—first the Portuguese and then the Dutch—viewed it with an eye to practical rather than spiritual considerations: the coastal promontory was the ideal place for a fortress, where mounted artillery could be directed toward the threat posed by hostile warships. It was in the seventeenth century that a fortress was first erected on the hill; as the structure was rebuilt over the following centuries, little attention was ever paid to the small houses of worship nearby. Now they would serve as way stations for the Prophet's army during the final assault.

Ordinarily, its leader, the man they called the Caliph, would never be exposed to the confusion and unpredictability of an armed engagement. But this was no ordinary night. History was being written this night. How could the Caliph *not* be present? Besides, he knew that his decision to join his men on the terrain of battle had increased their morale immeasurably. He was surrounded by stouthearted Kagama who wanted him to be a witness to their heroism or, if it should turn out to be the case, their martyrdom. They looked at the planes of his face, his fine ebony features, and his strong, sculpted jaw, and they saw not merely a man anointed by the Prophet to lead them to freedom but a man who would inscribe their deeds in the book of life, for all posterity.

And so the Caliph kept vigil with his special detail, on a carefully chosen mountainous perch. The ground was hard and wet beneath his thin-soled boots, but the Stone Palace—or, more precisely, its main entrance— glowed before him. The east wall was a vast expanse of limestone, its weathered stones and wide, freshly painted gate bathed in lights that were sunk into the ground every few feet. It shimmered. It beckoned.

"You or your followers may die tonight," the Caliph had told the members of his command hours before. "If so, your martyrdom will be re- membered—*always!* Your children and your parents will be sanctified by their connection to you. Shrines will be built to your memory! Pilgrims will travel to the site of your birth! You will be remembered and venerated, *always,* as among the fathers of our nation."

They were individuals of faith, fervor, and courage, whom the West was pleased to scorn as terrorists. Terrorists! For the West, the ultimate source of terror in the world, this term was a cynical convenience. The Caliph despised the Anuran tyrants, but he hated with a pure hate the Westerners who made their rule possible. The Anurans at least understood that there was a price to be paid for their usurpation of power; the rebels had repeatedly brought that lesson home, written it with blood. But the Westerners were accustomed to acting with impunity. Perhaps that would change.

Now the Caliph looked at the hillside around him and felt hope—not merely for himself and his followers but for the island itself. Anura. Once it had taken back its own destiny, what would it not be capable of? The very rocks and trees and vine-draped hillocks seemed to urge him on.

Mother Anura would vindicate her protectors.

Centuries ago, visitors had to resort to the cadence of poetry in order to evoke the beauty of its flora and fauna. Soon colonialism, fueled by envy and avarice, would impose its grim logic: what was ravishing would be ravished, the captivating made captive. Anura became a prize for which the great maritime empires of the West would contend. Battlements rose above the spice-tree groves; cannonballs nestled on the beaches among the conch shells. The West brought bloodshed to the island and it took root there, spreading across the landscape like a toxic weed, nourished on injustice.

*What did they do to you, Mother Anura?*

Over tea and canapés, Western diplomats drew lines that would bring tumult to the lives of millions, treating the atlas of the world like a child's Etch-A-Sketch.

*Independence,* they had called it! It was one of the great lies of the twentieth century. The regime itself amounted to an act of violence against the Kagama people, for which the only remedy was more violence. Every time a suicide bomber took out a Hindu government minister, the Western media pontificated about "senseless killings," but the Caliph and his soldiers knew that nothing made more sense. The most widely publicized wave of bombings—taking out ostensibly civilian targets in the capital city, Caligo—had been masterminded by the Caliph himself. The vans were rendered invisible, for all intents, by the forged decals of a ubiquitous international courier and freight service. Such a simple deception! Packed with diesel-soaked nitrate fertilizer, the vans delivered only a cargo of death. In the past decade, this wave of bombings was what aroused the greatest condemnation around the world—which was an odd hypocrisy, for it merely brought the war home to the warmongers.

Now the chief radio operator whispered in the Caliph's ear. The Kaffra base had been destroyed, its communications infrastructure dismantled. Even if they managed to get the word out, the guards at the Stone Palace had no hope for backup. Thirty seconds later, the radio operator had yet another message to convey: confirmation that a second army base had been reclaimed by the people. A second thoroughfare was now theirs. The Caliph felt his spine begin to tingle. Within hours, the entire province of Kenna would be wrested from a despotic death grip. The shift of power would begin. National liberation would glimmer over the horizon with the sun.

Nothing, however, was more important than taking the Steenpaleis, the Stone Palace. *Nothing.* The Go-Between had been emphatic about it, and so far the Go-Between had been right about everything, starting with the value of his own contributions. He had been as good as his word—no, better. He had been generous to the point of profligacy with his armaments and, equally important, his intelligence. He had not disappointed the Caliph, and the Caliph would not disappoint him. The Caliph's opponents had their resources, their backers and benefactors; why should he not have his?

"It's still cold!" Arjun cried out with delight as he picked up the beer can. The outside of the can was actually frosty. Arjun pressed it to the side of his face, moaning with pleasure. His fingers melted oval impressions in the icy coating, which glinted cheerily in the checkpoint's yellow mercury light.

"And it's really full?" Shyam said doubtfully.

"Unopened," Arjun said. "Heavy with the health drink!" And it *was* heavy, unexpectedly so. "We'll pour off a swig for the ancestors. A few long swallows for me, and whatever drops are left for you, since I know you don't like the stuff." Arjun's thick fingers scrabbled for the pull tab, then gave it a firm yank.

The muffled pop of the detonator, like the sound of a party favor that spews confetti, came milliseconds before the actual explosion. It was almost enough time for Arjun to register the thought that he had been the victim of a small prank and for Shyam to register the thought that his suspicions—although they had remained at the not-quite-conscious level of vague disquiet—had been justified. When the twelve ounces of plastique exploded, both men's trains of thought came to an end.

The blast was a shattering moment of light and sound that instantly expanded into an immense, fiery oval of destruction. The shock waves destroyed the two knife rests and the wooden roadside booth, as well as the barracks and those who slept there. The pair of guards who were supposed to have been on duty as backstop at the other end of the road-block died before they awoke. The intense, momentary heat caused an area of the red laterite soil to crust into an obsidian-like glass. And then, as quickly as it arrived, the explosion—the deafening noise, the blinding light—vanished, like a man's fist when he opens his hand. The force of destruction was fleeting, the destruction itself permanent.

Fifteen minutes later, when a convoy of canvas-topped personnel carriers made its way through what remained of the checkpoint, no subterfuge would be necessary.


There was an irony, the Caliph realized, in the fact that only his adversaries would fully understand the ingenuity of the predawn onslaught. On the ground, the fog of war would obscure what would be obvious from far away: the pattern of precisely coordinated attacks. The Caliph knew that within a day or so, analysts at the American spy agencies would be peering at satellite imagery that would make the pattern of activity as clear as a textbook diagram. The Caliph's victory would become the stuff of legend; his debt to the Go-Between—not least at the insistence of the Go-Between himself—would remain a matter between him and Allah.

A pair of binoculars was brought to the Caliph, who surveyed the honor guards arrayed before the main gate.

They were human ornaments, an accordion of paper dolls. Another instance of the government's elitist stupidity. The compound's nighttime illumination rendered them sitting ducks while simultaneously impeding their ability to see anything in the surrounding darkness.

The honor guards represented the ARA's elite—typically, those with relatives in high places, mannerly careerists with excellent hygiene and a knack for maintaining the crease in their neatly pressed uniforms. The crème de la crème brûlée, the Caliph reflected to himself with a mixture of irony and contempt. They were showmen, not warriors. Through the binoculars, he gazed at the seven men, each holding a rifle braced upright on his shoulder, where it would look impressive and be perfectly useless. Not even showmen. Playthings.

The chief radio operator nodded at the Caliph: the section commander was in position, ensuring that the barracked soldiers would be undeployable. A member of the Caliph's retinue presented him with a rifle: it was a purely ceremonial act that he had devised, but ceremony was the handmaiden of power. Accordingly, the Caliph would fire the first shot, using the very same rifle that a great independence fighter had used, fifty years ago, to assassinate the Dutch governor general. The rifle, a bolt-action Mauser M24, had been perfectly reconditioned and carefully zeroed. Unwrapped from the silk that had enfolded it, it gleamed like the sword of Saladin.

The Caliph found the number one guard in the weapon's scope and exhaled halfway so that the crosshairs settled on the center of the man's beribboned chest. He squeezed the trigger and intently watched the man's expressions—successively startled, anguished, dazed. On the man's upper right torso, a small oval of red bloomed, like a boutonniere.

Now the other members of the Caliph's detail followed suit, loosing a brief fusillade of well-aimed bullets. Marionettes released from their strings, the seven officers collapsed, tumbled, sprawled.

Despite himself, the Caliph laughed. These deaths had no dignity; they were as absurd as the tyranny they served. A tyranny that would now find itself on the defensive.

By sunrise, any free-floating representatives of the Anuran government that remained in the province would be well advised to shred their uniforms or else face dismemberment by hostile mobs.

Kenna would no longer be part of the illegitimate Republic of Anura. Kenna would belong to him.

*It had begun.*

The Caliph felt a surge of righteousness, and the clear piercing truth filled him like a light. The only solution to violence was more violence.

Many would die in the next several minutes, and they would be the fortunate ones. But there was one person in the Stone Palace who would not be killed—not yet. He was a special man, a man who had come to the island in an attempt to broker a peace. He was a powerful man, revered by millions, but an agent of neocolonialism nevertheless. So he had to be treated with care. This one—the great man, the "peacemaker," the man of all peoples, as the Western media insisted—would not be a casualty of a military skirmish. He would not be shot.

For him, the proper niceties would be observed.

And then he would be beheaded as the criminal he was.

*The revolution would be nourished on his blood!*

# PART ONE

# CHAPTER ONE

The worldwide headquarters of the Harnett Corporation occupied the top two floors of a sleek black-glass tower on Dearborn Street, in Chicago's Loop. Harnett was an international construction firm, but not the kind that put up skyscrapers in American metropolises. Most of its projects were outside the United States; along with larger corporations such as Bechtel, Vivendi, and Suez Lyonnaise des Eaux, it contracted for projects like dams, wastewater treatment plants, and gas turbine power stations—unglamorous but necessary infrastructure. Such projects posed civil-engineering challenges rather than aesthetic ones, but they also required an ability to work the ever shifting zone between public and private sectors. Third World countries, pressured by the World Bank and the International Monetary Fund to sell off publicly owned assets, routinely sought bidders for telephone systems, water and power utilities, railways, and mines. As ownership changed hands, new construction work was required, and narrowly focused firms like the Harnett Corporation had come into their own.

"To see Ross Harnett," the man told the receptionist. "The name's Paul Janson."

The receptionist, a young man with freckles and red hair, nodded, and notified the chairman's office. He glanced at the visitor without interest. Another middle-aged white guy with a yellow tie. What was there to see?

For Janson, it was a point of pride that he seldom got a second look. Though he was athletic and solidly built, his appearance was unremarkable, utterly nondescript. With his creased forehead and short-cropped steel-gray hair, he looked his five decades. Whether on Wall Street or the Bourse, he knew how to make himself all but invisible. Even his expensively tailored suit, of gray nailhead worsted, was perfect camouflage, as appropriate to the corporate jungle as the green and black face paint he once wore in Vietnam was to the real jungle. One would have to be a trained observer to detect that it was the man's shoulders, not the customary shoulder pads, that filled out the suit. And one would have to have spent some time with him to notice the way his slate eyes took everything in, or his quietly ironic air.

"It's going to be just a couple of minutes," the receptionist told him blandly, and Janson drifted off to look at the gallery of photographs in the reception area. They showed that the Harnett Corporation was currently working on water and wastewater networks in Bolivia, dams in Venezuela, bridges in Saskatchewan, power stations in Egypt. These were the images of a prosperous construction company. And it was indeed prospering—or had been until recently.

The company's vice president of operations, Steven Burt, believed it ought to be doing much better. There were aspects of the recent downturn that aroused his suspicions, and he had prevailed upon Paul Janson to meet with Ross Harnett, the firm's chairman and CEO. Janson had reservations about taking on another client: though he had been a corporate-security consultant for only the past five years, he had immediately established a reputation for being unusually effective and discreet, which meant that the demand for his services exceeded both his time and his interest. He would not have considered this job if Steven Burt had not been a friend from way back. Like him, Burt had had another life, one that he'd left far behind once he entered the civilian world. Janson was reluctant to disappoint him. He would, at least, take the meeting.

Harnett's executive assistant, a cordial thirtyish woman, strode through the reception area and escorted him to Harnett's office. The space was modern and spare, with floor-to-ceiling windows facing south and east. Filtered through the building's polarized glass skin, the afternoon sunlight was reduced to a cool glow. Harnett was sitting behind his desk, talking on the telephone, and the woman paused in the doorway with a questioning look. Harnett gestured for Janson to have a seat, with a hand movement that looked almost summoning. "Then we're just going to have to renegotiate all the contracts with Ingersoll-Rand," Harnett was saying. He was wearing a pale blue monogrammed shirt with a white collar; the sleeves were rolled up around thick forearms. "If they're not going to match the price points they promised, our position has to be that we're free to go elsewhere for the parts. Screw 'em. Contract's void."

Janson sat down on the black leather chair opposite, which was a couple of inches lower than Harnett's chair—a crude bit of stagecraft that, to Janson, signaled insecurity rather than authority. Janson glanced at his watch openly, swallowed a gorge of annoyance, and looked around. Twenty-seven stories up, Harnett's corner office had a sweeping view of

Lake Michigan and downtown Chicago. A high chair, a high floor: Harnett wanted there to be no mistaking that he had scaled the heights.

Harnett himself was a fireplug of a man, short and powerfully built, who spoke with a gravelly voice. Janson had heard that Harnett prided himself on making regular tours of the company's active projects, during which he would talk with the foremen as if he had been one himself. Certainly he had the swagger of somebody who had started out working on construction sites and rose to the corner office by the sweat of his brow. But that was not exactly how it happened. Janson knew that Harnett held an MBA from the Kellogg School of Management at Northwestern and that his expertise lay in financial engineering rather than in construction engineering. He had put together the Harnett Corporation by acquiring its subsidiaries at a time when they were strapped for cash and seriously underpriced. Because construction was a deeply cyclical business, Harnett had recognized, well-timed equity swaps made it possible to build a cash-rich corporation at bargain-basement prices.

Finally, Harnett hung up the phone and silently regarded Janson for a few moments. "Stevie tells me you've got a real high-class reputation," he said in a bored tone. "Maybe I know some of your other clients. Who have you worked with?"

Janson gave him a quizzical look. Was he being *interviewed?* "Most of the clients that I *accept*," he said, pausing after the word, "come recommended to me by other clients." It seemed crass to spell it out: Janson was not the one to supply references or recommendations; it was the prospective clients who had to come recommended. "My clients can, in some circumstances, discuss my work with others. My own policy has always been across-the-board nondisclosure."

"You're like a wooden Indian, aren't you?" Harnett sounded annoyed.

"I'm sorry?"

"I'm sorry, too, because I have a pretty good notion that we're just wasting each other's time. You're a busy guy, I'm a busy guy, we don't either of us have time to sit here jerking each other off. I know Stevie's got it in his head that we're a leaky boat and taking on water. That's not how it is. Fact is, it's the nature of the business that it has a lot of ups and downs. Stevie's still too green to understand. I built this company, I know what happens in every office and every construction yard in twenty-four countries. To me, it's a real question whether we need a security consultant in the first place. And the one thing I have heard about you is that your services don't come cheap. I'm a great believer in corporate frugality. Zero-based budgeting is gospel as far as I'm concerned. Try to follow me here—every penny we spend has to justify itself. If it doesn't add value, it's not happening. That's one corporate secret I don't mind letting you in on." Harnett leaned back, like a pasha waiting for a servant to pour him tea. "But feel free to change my mind, OK? I've said my piece. Now I'm happy to listen."

Janson smiled wanly. He would have to apologize to Steven Burt—Janson doubted whether anyone well disposed toward him had called him "Stevie" in his life—but clearly wires had got crossed here. Janson accepted few of the offers he received, and he certainly did not need this one. He would extricate himself as swiftly as he could. "I really don't know what to say, Mr. Harnett. It sounds from your end like you've got everything under control."

Harnett nodded without smiling, acknowledging an observation of the self-evident. "I run a tight ship, Mr. Janson," he said with smug condescension. "Our worldwide operations are *damn* well protected, always have been, and we've never had a problem. Never had a leak, a defection, not even any serious theft. And I think I'm in the best position to know whereof I speak—can we agree on that?"

"A CEO who doesn't know what's going on in his own company isn't really running the show, is he?" Janson replied equably.

"Exactly," Harnett said. "Exactly." His gaze settled on the intercom of his telephone console. "Look, you come highly recommended—I mean, Stevie couldn't have spoken of you more highly, and I'm sure you're quite good at what you do. Appreciate that you came by to see us, and as I say, I'm only sorry we wasted your time. . . ."

Janson noted his use of the inclusive "we" and its evident subtext: *sorry that a member of our senior management inconvenienced us both.* No doubt Steven Burt would be subjected to some withering corporate scorn later on. Janson decided to allow himself a few parting words after all, if only for his friend's sake.

"Not a bit," he said, rising to his feet and shaking Harnett's hand across the desk. "Just glad to know everything's shipshape." He cocked his head and added, almost incidentally: "Oh, listen, as to that 'sealed bid' you just submitted for the Uruguay project?"

"What do you know about it?" Harnett's eyes were suddenly watchful; a nerve had been struck.

"Ninety-three million five hundred and forty thousand, was it?"

Harnett reddened. "Hold it. I approved that bid only yesterday morning. How the hell did you—"

"If I were you, I'd be worrying about the fact that your French competitor, Suez Lyonnaise, knows the figures, too. I think you'll discover that their bid will be precisely two percent lower."

"*What?*" Harnett erupted with volcanic fury. "Did Steve Burt tell you this?"

"Steven Burt gave me no information whatsoever. Anyway, he's in operations, not accounting or business affairs—does he even know the specifics of the bid?"

Harnett blinked twice. "No," he said after a pause. "There's no way he could know. Goddammit, there's no way *anyone* could know. It was sent by encrypted e-mail from our bean counters to the Uruguayan ministry."

"And yet people do know these things. Because this won't be the first time you've been narrowly outbid this year, will it? In fact, you've been burned almost a dozen times in the past nine months. Eleven of your fifteen bids were rejected. Like you were saying, it's a business with a lot of ups and downs."

Harnett's cheeks were aflame, but Janson proceeded to chat in a collegial tone. "Now, in the case of Vancouver, there were other considerations. Heck, they had reports from the municipal engineers that they found plasticizers in the concrete used for the pilings. Made it easy to cast, but weakened its structural integrity. Not your fault, of course—your specs were perfectly clear there. How were you to know that the subcontractor bribed your site inspector to falsify his report? An underling takes a measly five-thousand-dollar bribe, and now you're out in the cold on a hundred-million-dollar project. Pretty funny, huh? On the other hand, you've had worse luck with some of your own under-the-table payments. I mean, if you're wondering what went wrong with the La Paz deal . . ."

"Yes?" Harnett prompted urgently. He stood up with unnatural rigidity, as if frozen.

"Let's just say Raffy rides again. Your manager believed Rafael Nuñez when he told him that he'd make sure the bribe reached the minister of the interior. Of course, it never did. You chose the wrong intermediary, simple as that. Raffy Nuñez took a lot of companies for a ride in the nineties. Most of your competitors are wise to him now. They were laughing their asses off when they saw your guy dining at the La Paz Cabana, tossing down tequilas with Raffy, because they knew exactly what was going to happen. But what the hey—at least you tried, right? So what if your operating margin is down thirty percent this year. It's only money, right? Isn't that what your shareholders are always saying?"

As Janson spoke, he noticed that Harnett's face had gone from flushed to deathly pale. "Oh, that's right—they *haven't* been saying that, have they?" Janson continued. "In fact, a bunch of major stockholders are looking for another company—Vivendi, Kendrick, maybe Bechtel—to orchestrate a hostile takeover. So look on the bright side. If they have their way, none of this will be your problem anymore." He pretended to ignore Harnett's sharp intake of breath. "But I'm sure I'm only telling you what you already know."

Harnett looked dazed, panicked; through the vast expanse of polarized glass, muted rays of sun picked out the beads of cold sweat on his forehead. "Fuck a duck," he murmured. Now he was looking at Janson the way a drowning man looks at a life raft. "Name your price," he said.

"Come again?"

"Name your goddamn price," Harnett said. "I need you." He grinned, aiming to disguise his desperation with a show of joviality. "Steve Burt told me you were the best, and you sure as shit are, that's obvious. You know I was just yanking your chain before. Now, listen, big guy, you are not leaving this room before you and I come to an agreement. We clear about this?" Perspiration had begun to darken his shirt in the areas beneath his arms and around his collar. "Because we are going to do a deal here."

"I don't think so," Janson said genially. "It's just that I've decided against taking the job. That's one luxury I have as a consultant working alone: I get to decide which clients I take. But really—best of luck with everything. Nothing like a good proxy fight to get the blood racing, right?"

Harnett let out a burst of fake-sounding laughter and clapped his hands together. "I like your style," he said. "Good negotiating tactics. OK, OK, you win. Tell me what you want."

Janson shook his head, smiling, as if Harnett had said something funny, and made his way to the door. Just before he left the office, he stopped and turned. "One tip, though—gratis," he said. "*Your wife knows.*" It would have been indelicate to say the name of Harnett's Venezuelan mistress, so Janson simply added, obliquely but unmistakably: "About Caracas, I mean." Janson gave him a meaningful look: no judgment implied; he was, speaking as one professional to another, merely identifying a potential point of vulnerability.

Small red spots appeared on Harnett's cheeks, and he seemed stricken with nausea: it was the look of a man contemplating a ruinously expensive divorce on top of a proxy fight he was likely to lose. "I'm willing to talk *stock options*," he called after Janson.

But the consultant was already making his way down the hall toward the elevator bank. He had not minded seeing the blowhard squirm; by the time he reached the lobby, though, he was filled with a sense of sourness, of time wasted, of a larger futility.

A voice from so long ago—another life—echoed faintly in his head. *And this is what gives meaning to your life?* Phan Nguyen asked that, in a thousand different ways. It was his favorite question. Janson could see, even now, the small, intelligent eyes; the broad, weathered face; the slender, childlike arms. Everything about America seemed to engage his interrogator's curiosity, with equal parts fascination and revulsion. *And this is what gives meaning to your life?* Janson shook his head: Doom on you, Nguyen.

As Janson stepped into his limousine, which had been idling on Dearborn just outside the building's lobby, he decided to go straight to O'Hare; there was an earlier flight to Los Angeles he could catch. If only Nguyen's questions could be as easily left behind.


Two uniformed women were standing behind a counter as he entered the Platinum Club lounge of Pacifica Airlines. The uniforms and the counter were both the same blue-gray hue. The women's jackets featured the sort of epaulets to which the major airlines were so devoted. In another place and time, Janson reflected, they would have rewarded extensive battlefield experience.

One of the women had been speaking to a jowly, heavyset man who wore an open blue blazer and a beeper clipped to his belt. A glint of badge metal from his inside coat pocket told Janson that he was an FAA inspector, no doubt taking his break where there was human scenery to be enjoyed. They broke off when Janson stepped forward.

"Your boarding card, please," the woman said, turning to him. She had a powdery tan that ended somewhere below her chin, and the kind of brassy hair that came from an applicator tip.

Janson flashed his ticket and the plastic card with which Pacifica rewarded its extremely frequent fliers.

"Welcome to the Pacifica Platinum Club, Mr. Janson," the woman twinkled.

"We'll let you know when your plane is about to board," the other attendant—chestnut bangs, eye shadow that matched the blue piping on her jacket—told him in a low, confiding voice. She gestured toward the entrance to the lounge area as if it were the pearly gates. "Meantime, enjoy our hospitality facilities and relax." An encouraging nod and a broad smile; Saint Peter's could not have held more promise.

Carved out between the structural girders and beams of an overloaded airport, venues like Pacifica's Platinum Club were where the modern airline tried to cater to the carriage trade. Small bowls were filled not with the salted peanuts purveyed to *les misérables* in coach but with the somewhat more expensive tree nuts: cashews, almonds, walnuts, pecans. At a granite-topped beverage station, there were crystal jugs sticky with peach nectar and fresh-squeezed orange juice. The carpeting was microfiber swank, the airline's signature blue-gray adorned with trellises of white and navy. On round tables interspersed among large armchairs were neatly folded copies of the *International Herald Tribune, USA Today,* the *Wall Street Journal,* and the *Financial Times.* A Bloomberg terminal flickered with meaningless numbers and images, shadow puppets of the global economy. Through louvered blinds, the tarmac was only just visible.

Janson flipped through the papers with little interest. When he turned to the *Journal's* "Market Watch," he found his eyes sliding down column inches of familiarly bellicose metaphors: bloodshed on Wall Street as a wave of profit takers launched an onslaught against the Dow. A sports column in *USA Today* was taken up with the collapse of the Raiders' offense in the face of the rampaging blitzes of the Vikings' linemen. Meanwhile, invisible speakers piped in a song by the pop diva *du jour,* from the soundtrack of a blockbuster movie about a legendary Second World War battle. An expense of blood and sweat had been honored by an expense of studio money and computer-graphics technology.

Janson settled heavily into one of the cloth-upholstered armchairs, his eyes drifting toward the dataport stations where brand managers and account executives plugged in their laptops and collected e-mail from clients, employers, prospects, underlings, and lovers, in an endless search for action items. Peeking from attaché cases were the spines of books purporting to offer marketing advice from the likes of Sun Tzu, the art of war repurposed for the packaged-goods industry. A sleek, self-satisfied, unthreatened folk, Janson mused of the managers and professionals who surrounded him. How these people loved peace, yet how they loved the imagery of war! For them, military regalia could safely be romanticized, the way animals of prey became adornments after the taxidermist's art.

There were moments when Janson almost felt that he, too, had been stuffed and mounted. Nearly every raptor was now on the endangered-species list, not least the bald eagle, and Janson recognized that he himself had once been a raptor—a force of aggression against forces of aggression. Janson had known ex-warriors who had become addicted to a diet of adrenaline and danger, and who, when their services were no longer required, had effectively turned themselves into toy soldiers. They spent their time stalking opponents in the Sierre Madre with paintball guns or, worse, pimping themselves out to unsavory firms with unsavory needs, usually in parts of the world where baksheesh was the law of the land. Janson's contempt for these people was profound. And yet he sometimes asked himself whether the highly specialized assistance he offered American businesses was not merely a respectable version of the same thing.

He was lonely, that was the truth of it, and his loneliness was never more acute than in the odd interstices of his overscheduled life—the time spent after checking in and before takeoff, the time spent waiting in over-designed venues meant, simply, for waiting. At the end of his next flight, nobody was anticipating his arrival except another visored limo driver who would have misspelled his name on a white cardboard sign, and then another corporate client, an anxious division head of a Los Angeles–based light industrial firm. It was a tour of duty that took Janson from one corner office to another. There was no wife and no children, though once there had been a wife and at least hopes for a child, for Helene had been pregnant when she died. "To make God laugh, tell him your plans," she used to quote her grandfather as saying, and the maxim had been borne out, horribly.

Janson eyed the amber bottles behind the bar, their crowded labels an alibi for the forgetfulness they held inside. He kept himself in fighting trim, trained obsessively, but even when he was in active deployment he was never above a slug or two. Where was the harm?

"Paging Richard Alexander," a nasal voice called through the public announcement system. "Passenger Richard Alexander. Please report to any Pacifica counter."

It was the background noise of any airport, but it jolted Janson out of his reverie. Richard Alexander was an operational alias he had often used in bygone days. Reflexively, he craned his head around him. A minor coincidence, he thought, and then he realized that, simultaneously, his cell phone was purring, deep in his breast pocket. He inserted the earphone of the Nokia tri-band and pressed SND. "Yes?"

"Mr. Janson? Or should I say, Mr. Alexander?" A woman's voice, sounding strained, desperate.

"Who is this?" Janson spoke quietly. Stress numbed him, at least at first—made him calmer, not more agitated.

"Please, Mr. Janson. It's urgent that we meet *at once.*" The vowels and consonants had the precision that was peculiar to those who were both foreign-born and well educated. And the ambient noise in the background was even more suggestive.

"Say more."

There was a pause. "When we meet."

Janson pressed END, terminating the call. He felt a prickling on the back of his neck. The coincidence of the page and the call, the specification that a meeting take place immediately: the putative supplicant was obviously in close proximity. The call's background acoustics had merely cinched his suspicions. Now his eyes darted from person to person, even as he tried to figure out who would seek him out this way.

Was it a trap, set by an old, unforgiving adversary? There were many who would feel avenged by his death; for a few, possibly, the thirst for vengeance would not be entirely unjustified. And yet the prospect seemed unlikely. He was not in the field; he was not spiriting a less-than-willing VKR "defector" from the Dardanelles through Athens to a waiting frigate, bypassing every legal channel of border control. He was in O'Hare Airport, for God's sake. Which may have been why this rendezvous was chosen. People tended to feel safe at an airport, moated by metal detectors and uniformed security guards. It would be a cunning act to take advantage of that illusion of security. And, in an airport that handled nearly two hundred thousand travelers each day, security was indeed an illusion.

Possibilities were considered and swiftly discarded. By the thick plate glass overlooking the tarmac, sitting in slats of sunlight, a blond woman was apparently studying a spreadsheet on her laptop; her cell phone was at her side, Janson verified, and unconnected to any earpiece. Another woman, closer to the entrance, was engaged in spirited conversation with a man whose wedding ring was visible only as a band of pale skin on an otherwise bronzed hand. Janson's eyes kept roaming until, seconds later, he saw her, the one who had just called.

Sitting with deceptive placidity in a dim corner of the lounge was an elegant, middle-aged woman holding a cell phone to her ear. Her hair was white, worn up, and she was attired in a navy Chanel suit with discreet mother-of-pearl buttons. Yes, she was the one: he was certain of it. What he could not be certain of were her intentions. Was she an assassin, or part of a kidnapping team? These were among a hundred possibilities that, however remote, he had to rule out. Standard tactical protocol, ingrained from years in the field, demanded it.

Janson sprang to his feet. He had to change his location: that rule was basic. *It's urgent that we meet at once,* the caller had said; if so, they would meet on his terms. Now he started to make his way out of the VIP lounge, grabbing a paper cup from a water cooler he passed. He approached the greeting counter with the paper cup held in front of him, as if it were full. Then he yawned, squeezing his eyes shut, and walked straight into the heavyset FAA inspector, who staggered back a few feet.

"I am so sorry," Janson blurted, looking mortified. "Oh, *Christ,* I didn't *spill* anything on you, did I?" Janson's hands moved rapidly over the man's blazer. "Did I get you wet? God, I'm really, really sorry."

"No harm done," he replied with a trace of impatience. "Just, you know, watch where you're going, OK? There's lots of people in this airport."

"It's one thing not to know what time zone you're in, but—*Jesus,* I just don't know what's wrong with me," Janson said, the very picture of a flustered and jet-lagged passenger. "I'm a wreck."

As Janson made his way out of the VIP lounge and down the pedestrian corridor that led toward Concourse B, his cell phone buzzed again, as he knew it would.

"I don't think you quite understand the urgency," the caller began.

"That's correct," Janson snapped. "I don't. Why don't you let me know what this is about?" In an angled stretch of the pedestrian corridor, he saw a recessed area, about three feet deep, and then the expected steel door to a room that was off-limits to travelers. UNAUTHORIZED PERSONNEL KEEP OUT was emblazoned on a plaque above it.

"I can't," the caller said after a beat. "Not over the phone, I'm afraid. But I'm in the airport and could meet you—"

"In that case, call me back in one minute," Janson interjected, ending the conversation. Now he hit the door's horizontal push bar with the heel of his hand and made his way inside. It turned out to be a narrow room that was lined with electrical panels; LCD displays measured outputs from the airport's heat and refrigeration plant, which was just to the east of the terminal. A rack of pegs held caps and windbreakers for outdoor work.

Three airline employees in navy-blue twill uniforms were seated around a small steel-and-Formica table, drinking coffee. He had obviously interrupted their conversation.

"What do you think you're doing?" one of them yelled at Janson as the door banged closed behind him. "You can't *be* here."

"This ain't the fucking john," another one said under his breath.

Janson smiled without warmth. "You're going to hate me, boys. But guess what?" He pulled out an FAA badge, the item he had lifted from the heavyset man in the lounge. "Another drug-abatement initiative. Random testing for a drug-free air-transport workforce—to quote the administrator's latest memorandum on the subject. Time to fill those cups. Sorry for the inconvenience, but that's why you make the big bucks, right?"

"This is *bullshit!*" the third man yowled in disgust. He was nearly bald, save for a graying fringe around the back, and he kept a short pencil behind an ear.

"Haul ass, guys," Janson barked. "We're following a whole new procedure this time. My team's assembled over at gate two in Concourse A. Don't make them wait. When they get impatient, sometimes they make mistakes with the samples, if you get my drift."

"This is *bullshit,*" the bald man repeated.

"Want me to file a report saying that an Air Transport Association member protested and/or sought to evade the drug audit? Your test comes in positive, better start combing the want ads." Janson folded his arms on his chest. "Get the hell out of here, *now.*"

"I'm going," the bald man grumbled, sounding less sure of himself. "I'm *there.*" With expressions of exasperation and disgruntlement, all three men hastened out of the room, leaving clipboards and coffee cups behind. It would take them a good ten minutes before they reached Concourse A, Janson knew. He glanced at his watch and counted the few remaining seconds until his cell phone buzzed; the caller had waited one minute exactly.

"There's a food court near the ticketing pavilion," Janson said. "I'll meet you there. The table on the far left, all the way to the back. See you in a few." He removed his jacket, put on a dark blue windbreaker and cap, and waited in the recessed area. Thirty seconds later, he saw the white-haired woman walking past.

"Hey, honey!" he called out as, in one continuous movement, he reached an arm around her waist, clamped a hand over her mouth, and hustled her into the now-abandoned service room. There was, Janson had verified, nobody around to see the three-second maneuver; if there had been, his actions, coupled with his words, would have been taken for a romantic embrace.

The woman was startled, and rigid with fear, but she did not even try to scream, displaying a measure of professional composure that Janson found not the least reassuring. Once the door had closed behind them, Janson brusquely gestured her to take a seat at the Formica table. "Take a load off," he said.

The woman, looking incongruously elegant in the utilitarian space, sat down on one of the metal folding chairs. Janson remained standing.

"You're not exactly the way I'd pictured you," she said. "You don't *look* like a . . ." Conscious of his frankly hostile stare, she decided against finishing the sentence. "Mr. Janson, we really don't have time for this."

"I don't look like a *what?*" he said, biting off the words. "I don't know who the hell you think you are, but I'm not even going to list the infractions of protocol here. I'm not going to ask how you got my cell phone number or how you learned whatever you think you've learned. But by the time we're finished here, I'd better know everything I want to know." Even if she were a private citizen legitimately seeking his services, the public nature of the contact was completely inappropriate. And the use of a field legend of his, albeit a long-disused one, was a cardinal violation.

"You've made your *point*, Mr. Janson," she said. "My approach was, let's agree, ill advised. You'll have to forgive me—"

"I will? That's a presumption." He inhaled, detected a faint fragrance about her: Penhaligon's Jubilee. Their eyes met, and Janson's anger diminished somewhat when he saw her expression, mouth drawn with anxiety, gray-green eyes filled with grim determination.

"As I say, we have very little time."

"I have all the time in the world."

"Peter Novak doesn't."

*Peter Novak.*

The name delivered a jolt, as it was meant to. A legendary Hungarian financier and philanthropist, Novak had received a Nobel Peace Prize the previous year for his role in conflict resolution around the world. Novak was the founder and director of the Liberty Foundation, which was devoted to "directed democracy"—Novak's great passion—and had offices in regional capitals through Eastern Europe and other parts of the less developed world. But then Janson had reasons of his own to remember Peter Novak. And those reasons constituted a debt to the man so immense that Janson had occasionally experienced his gratitude as a burden.

"Who are you?" Janson demanded.

The woman's gray-green eyes bore into him. "My name is Márta Lang, and I work for Peter Novak. I could show you a business card, if you thought that would be helpful."

Janson shook his head slowly. Her business card would provide a meaningless title, identifying her as some sort of high-ranking employee of the Liberty Foundation. *I work for Peter Novak,* she had said, and simply from the way she spoke the words, Janson recognized her type. She was the factotum, the point person, the lieutenant; every great man had one. People like her preferred the shadows yet wielded great, if derivative, power. From her name and the barest trace of an accent, it was evident she was Hungarian, like her employer.

"What are you trying to tell me?" Janson said. His eyes narrowed.

"Only that he needs help. As you once did. In Baaqlina." Márta Lang pronounced the name of that dusty town as if it were a sentence, a paragraph, a chapter. For Janson, it was.

"I haven't forgotten," he said quietly.

"Then all you have to know right now is that Peter Novak requires your assistance."

She had spoken few words, but they were the right ones. Janson held her gaze for a long moment.

"Where to?"

"You can throw out your boarding card. Our jet is on the runway, cleared for immediate departure." She stood, her desperation somehow giving her strength and a sense of command. "We must go now. At the risk of repeating myself, *there's no time.*"

"Let *me* risk repeating myself: Where to?"

"That, Mr. Janson, will be our question to you."

# CHAPTER TWO

As Janson followed her up the grip-textured aluminum steps to Novak's Gulfstream V, his eye was caught by a legend that was painted on its side, the white cursive letters in shimmering contrast to the jet's indigo enamel: *Sok kicsi sokra megy.* Hungarian, and meaningless to him.

The runway was a wall of noise, the scream of air intakes layered over the bass-heavy roar of the exhausts. Once the cabin door was closed, however, silence reigned supreme, as if they had stepped into a soundproof booth.

The jet was handsomely appointed without seeming lavish, the cabin of a man for whom price was no object, but luxury no concern. The interior was maroon; the leather-upholstered seats were large, club-sized, one on either side of the aisle; some faced each other, with a low, bolted table between them. Four grim-faced men and women, evidently members of Márta Lang's staff, were already seated farther back in the plane.

Márta gestured for him to take the seat opposite her, in the front of the cabin, and then picked up an internal phone and murmured a few words. Only very faintly could Janson detect the whine of the engine revving up as the plane began to taxi. The sound insulation was extraordinary. A carpeted bulkhead separated them from the cockpit.

"That inscription on the fuselage—what does it mean?"

"It means 'Many small things can add up to a big one.' A Hungarian folk saying and a favorite motto of Peter Novak's. I'm sure you can appreciate why."

"You can't say he's forgotten where he came from."

"For better or worse, Hungary made him who he is. And Peter is not one to forget his debts." A meaningful look.

"Nor am I."

"I'm aware of that," she said. "It's why we know we can rely upon you."

"If he has an assignment for me, I'd like to hear about it sooner rather than later. And from him rather than someone else."

"You will have to make do with me. I'm deputy director of the Foundation and have been with him for many years."

"I don't question your absolute loyalty to your employer," Janson said coolly. "Novak's people are ... renowned for it." Several rows back, her staffers seemed to be huddled over maps and diagrams. What was going on? He felt a growing sense of unease.

"I understand what you are saying, and also what you are too polite to say. People like me are often seen as starry-eyed true believers, I realize. Please accept that we have no illusions, none of us. Peter Novak is only a mortal. He puts his pants on one leg at a time, as you Americans like to say. We know that better than anyone. This isn't a religion. But it is a calling. Imagine if the richest person you knew was at once the smartest person you knew and the *kindest* person you knew. If you want to know why he commands loyalty, it's because he cares—and cares with an intensity that really is almost superhuman. In plain English, he gives a damn. He wants to leave the world a better place than he found it, and you can call that vanity if you like, but if so, it's the kind of vanity we need more of. And the kind of vision."

" 'A visionary' is what the Nobel committee called him."

"A word I use under protest. It's a debased coin. Every article of *Fortune* proclaims some cable titan or soft-drink CEO a 'visionary.' But the Liberty Foundation *was* Novak's vision, and his alone. He believed in directed democracy when the idea seemed a pipe dream. He believed that civil society could be rebuilt in the parts of the world where totalitarianism and strife had eviscerated it. Fifteen years ago, people laughed when he spoke of his dream. Who is laughing now? Nobody would help him— not the United States, not the U.N.—but it didn't matter. *He changed the world.*"

"No argument," Janson said soberly.

"Your State Department analysts had endless reports about 'ancient ethnic enmities,' about conflicts and border disputes that could never be settled, and about how nobody should try. But *he* tried. And time and again, he succeeded. He's brought peace to regions that had never experienced a moment of it for as long as anyone could remember." Márta Lang choked up, and she stopped speaking.

She was obviously unaccustomed to such displays of emotion, and Janson did her the favor of talking while she regained her composure. "I'd be the last person to disagree with anything you've said. Your employer is a man who seeks peace for the sake of peace, democracy for the sake of democracy. That's all true. It's also true that his personal fortune rivals the GDP of many of the countries he has dealings with."

Lang nodded. "Orwell said that saints should be judged guilty until proven innocent. Novak's proved who he really is, again and again. A man for all seasons, and a man for all peoples. It has become difficult to imagine the world without him." Now she looked at him, and her eyes were red-rimmed.

"Talk to me," Janson said. "Why am I here? Where's Peter Novak?"

Márta Lang took a deep breath, as if what she had to say was going to be physically painful. "He's a captive of the Kagama rebels. We need you to set him free. An 'exfiltration' is what I gather you people call it. Otherwise, he will die where he is, in Anura."

*Anura.* A captive of the Kagama Liberation Front. One more reason—the main reason, no doubt—that they wanted him for the job. Anura. A place he thought about nearly every day and had for the past five years. His own private hell.

"I'm starting to understand," Janson said, his mouth dry.

"A few days ago, Peter Novak arrived on the island, trying to broker a peace between the rebels and the government. There had been many hopeful signs. The KLF said they regarded Peter Novak as an honest broker, and a meeting place in the Kenna province was agreed upon. A rebel delegation agreed to many things they had flatly rejected in the past. And a lasting accord in Anura—an end to the terror—would be a very great thing. I think you understand that as well as anyone."

Janson said nothing, but his heart began to pound.

*Their home, furnished by the embassy, was in Cinnamon Gardens, in the capital city of Caligo, and the area was still interspersed with the trees that once forested the land. In the morning breeze, leaves rustled and birds cawed. What roused him from his light sleep, though, was a soft coughing noise from the bathroom, then the running of the faucet. Helene came back from the bathroom, brushing her teeth vigorously. "Maybe you should stay home from work today," he'd said drowsily. Helene shook her head. "It's called morning sickness for a reason, my darling," she told him with a smile. "It vanishes like the morning dew." She started dressing for work at the embassy. When she smiled, she smiled with her whole face: with her mouth, her cheeks, her eyes—especially her eyes. . . . The images flooded his mind—Helene laying out her clothes for a day at the office, proofreading State Department reports.*

*A blue linen skirt. A white silk blouse. Helene opening the bedroom windows wide, inviting in the tropical morning air, scented with cinnamon and mango and frangipani. The radiance of her face, retroussé nose and limpid blue eyes. When the nights at Caligo were hot, Helene was cool against his body. How callused and rough his battered hide always felt next to the velvet of her skin. "Take the day off, my dearest," he'd told her, and she'd said, "Better not, my darling. Either they'll miss me or they won't miss me at all, and either way that's not good." She kissed him on the forehead as she left. If only she had stayed with him. If only.*

*Public acts, private lives—the bloodiest of crossroads.*

*Anura, an island in the Indian Ocean the size of West Virginia, had a population of twelve million, and was blessed with rare natural beauty and a rich cultural legacy. Janson had been posted there for eighteen months, charged with directing an intelligence-gathering task force to make an independent assessment of the island's volatile political situation and to help trace whatever outside forces were helping to foment unrest. For during the past decade and a half, Paradise had been disrupted by one of the deadliest terror organizations in the world, the Kagama Liberation Front. Thousands of young men, in thrall to the man they called the Caliph, wore leather pendants with a cyanide capsule at the end; it symbolized their readiness to give their lives for the cause. The Caliph had a particular fondness for suicide bombings. At a political rally for Anura's prime minister several years ago, one suicide bomber, a young girl whose sari bloused over an enormous quantity of explosives packed with ball bearings, left her mark on the island's history. The prime minister was killed along with more than a hundred bystanders. And then there were the truck bombings in downtown Caligo. One destroyed the Anura International Trade Center. Another, packed into an express courier and freight service truck, had delivered death to a dozen staff members in the U.S. embassy in Anura.*

*Among those dozen was Helene. One more victim of the mindless violence. Or was it two: what of the child they were to have had together?*

*Almost paralyzed with grief, Janson had demanded access to the NSA intercepts, including those of the sat-phone transmissions among the guerrilla leaders. The transcripts, hurriedly translated into English, gave little sense of vocal intonations and context; rapid dialogue was reduced to black type on white paper. But there was no mistaking the exultant tones. The embassy bombing was one of the Caliph's proudest moments.*

*Helene, you were my sun.*

In the jet, Márta placed a hand on Janson's wrist. "I'm sorry, Mr. Janson. I appreciate the anguish this must bring back."

"Of course you do," Janson said in a level tone. "It's part of why you chose me."

Márta did not avert her gaze. "Peter Novak is about to die. The conference in the province of Kenna was nothing less than a trap."

"It was insanity to begin with," Janson snapped.

"Was it? Naturally, the rest of the world has given up, save for those who are furtively promoting the violence. But nothing offends Peter more than defeatism."

Janson flushed angrily. "The KLF has called for the destruction of the Republic of Anura. The KLF says it believes in the inherent nobility of revolutionary violence. How do you negotiate with such fanatics?"

"The details arc banal. They always are. Ultimately, the plan was to move Anura toward a federated government that would grant more autonomy to the provinces. Redress Kagama grievances through a meaningful version of self-rule while offering Anurans genuine civil protections. It was in the interests of both parties. It represented *sanity*. And sometimes sanity prevails: Peter has proved that again and again."

"I don't know what to credit you people with—heroism or arrogance."

"Are the two so easily distinguished?"

Janson was silent for a moment. "Just give the bastards what they want," he said at last, his voice muffled.

"They don't want anything," Lang said softly. "We've invited them to name their price, as long as Peter is released alive. They've refused even to consider it. I don't need to tell you how rare that is. These are fanatics. The answer we keep getting is the same: Peter Novak has been sentenced to death for crimes against the colonized, and the execution decree is 'irrevocable.' Are you familiar with the traditional Sunni holy day of Id ul-Kebir?"

"It commemorates the sacrifice of Abraham."

Lang nodded. "The ram in the thistles. The Caliph says that this year it will be celebrated by the sacrifice of Peter Novak. He will be beheaded on Id ul-Kebir. That's *this Friday*."

"Why? For God's sakes, *why?*"

"*Because,*" Lang said. "Because he's a sinister agent of neocolonialism— that's what the KLF says. Because doing so will put the KLF on the map, gain them greater notoriety than they've achieved in fifteen years of bomb-ings. Because the man they call the Caliph was toilet-trained too soon—who the *hell* knows why? The question implies a level of rationality that these terrorists do not possess."

"Dear Christ," Janson said. "But if he's trying to aggrandize himself this way, whatever the logic, why hasn't he publicized it yet? Why hasn't the media got hold of it?"

"He's canny. By waiting until the deed is done to publicize it, he staves off any international pressure to intervene. Meanwhile, he knows we don't dare publicize it, because it would foreclose even the possibility of a ne-gotiated solution, however remote."

"Why would a major government need any pressure to intervene? The fact is, I still don't understand why you're talking to me. You said it yourself, he's a man of all peoples. Accept that America's the last super-power—why not turn to Washington to help?"

"It's the first thing we did. They provided information. And they were profusely apologetic when they explained that they could offer no official assistance whatsoever."

"That's baffling. Novak's death could be profoundly destabilizing for dozens of regions, and one thing Washington does like is stability."

"It also likes to keep American nationals alive. The State Department believes that any U.S.-identified intervention right now would endanger the lives of dozens of American citizens who are now in rebel-occupied territory."

Janson was silent. He knew how such calculations were arrived at; he had been part of the process often enough.

"As they explained, there are also other . . . *complications*." Márta spoke the word with obvious distaste. "America's Saudi allies, for example, have been quiet supporters of the KLF over the years. They're not particularly enthusiastic about their approach, but if they don't support oppressed Muslims in that Muslim lake called the Indian Ocean, they lose face with the rest of the Islamic world. And then there's the matter of Donna Hed-derman."

Janson nodded. "A Columbia grad student in anthropology. Doing fieldwork in northeast Anura. Which was both foolish and brave. Cap-tured by the Kagama rebels, who accused her of being a CIA agent. Which was both foolish and evil."

"She's been held by them for two months, incommunicado. Lip service aside, the United States hasn't done a damn thing. Didn't want to 'complicate an already complicated situation.' "

"I'm getting the picture. If the United States refuses to intervene on behalf of an American national—"

"—how will it look if it turns around and sends a rescue team for the Hungarian billionaire? Yes. They didn't put it so bluntly, but that's the point they made. The phrase 'politically untenable' got a real workout."

"And then you made all the obvious counterarguments. . . ."

"And some not-so-obvious ones. We pulled out all the stops. At the risk of sounding arrogant, I have to say that we usually get our way. Not this time. Then the other shoe dropped."

"Let me guess. You had what they call the 'terribly quiet chat,' " Janson said. "And my name came up."

"Repeatedly. Several highly placed officials in State and Central Intelligence all strongly recommended you. You're not part of the government anymore. You're a free agent with international connections to others in your line of work, or what used to be your line of work. According to your former colleagues at Consular Operations, Paul Janson is 'the best there is at what he does.' I believe those were the exact words."

"The present tense is misleading. They told you I retired. I wonder whether they told you why."

"The point is, you're a free agent now," she said. "You parted ways with Consular Operations five years ago."

Janson tilted his head. "With the awkwardness of saying good-bye to somebody on the street and then discovering you're walking in the same direction."


Disengaging from Consular Operations had involved more than a dozen exit interviews, some decorous, some frankly uncomfortable, and some outright stormy. The one he remembered best was with Undersecretary Derek Collins. On paper, he was the director of the State Department's Bureau of Intelligence and Research; in reality, he was the director of its covert branch, Consular Operations. Even now, he could see Collins wearily removing his black-framed glasses and massaging the bridge of his nose. "I think I pity you, Janson," Collins had said. "Never thought I'd hear myself say it. You were 'the machine,' Janson. You were the guy with a slab of granite where your heart's supposed to be. Now you say you're repulsed by the thing you're best at. What goddamn sense does that make? You're like a master pastry chef announcing he's lost his sweet tooth. You're a pianist who's decided he can't stand the sound of music. Janson, violence is something you're very, very, very good at. Now you're telling me you've lost the stomach for it."

"I don't expect you to understand, Collins," he had replied. "Let's just say I've had a change of heart."

"You don't have a heart, Janson." The undersecretary's eyes were like ice. "It's why you do what you do. Goddammit, it's why you *are* who you *are*."

"Maybe. And maybe I'm not who you think I am."

A short, bark-like laugh. "I can't climb a hawser, Janson. I can't pilot a blessed PBR, and looking through an infrared scope makes me seasick. But I know people, Janson. That's what *I* do. You tell me you're sickened by the killing. I'm going to tell you what you'll discover one day for yourself: that's the only way you'll ever feel alive."

Janson shook his head. The implication made him shudder and re-minded him why he had to leave, why he should have done so long before. "What kind of man—" he started, and then halted, overcome with re-vulsion. He took a deep breath. "What kind of man has to *kill* to feel *alive?*"

Collins's gaze seemed to burrow through his flesh. "I guess I'd ask you the same thing, Janson."


Now, in Novak's private jet, Janson pressed the point. "How much do you know about me?"

"Yes, Mr. Janson, as you supposed, your former employers explained that you had unfinished business with the Kagama."

"Was that the phrase they used? 'Unfinished business'?"

She nodded.

*Shreds of clothing, bone fragments, a few severed limbs that had been thrown clear. They were what remained of his beloved. The rest: "collectiv-ized," in the grim words of a U.S. forensic technician. A communion of death and destruction, the blood and body parts of the victims impalpable and indistinguishable. And for what?*

*And for what?*

"So be it," Janson said after a pause. "These aren't men with poetry in their souls."

"And, yes, they also understood that your name wasn't exactly unknown to us."

"Because of Baaqlina."

"Come." Márta Lang stood up. "I'm going to introduce you to my team. Four men and women who are here to help you any way they can. Any information you need, they'll have, or know how to find out. We have dossiers filled with signals-intelligence intercepts, and all the relevant information we could gather in what little time we had. Maps, charts, architectural reconstructions. It's all at your disposal."

"Just one thing," Janson said. "I know the reasons you're turning to me for help, and I can't refuse you. But have you considered that those same reasons may be why I'm exactly the wrong person for the job?"

Márta Lang gave him a steely look but did not reply.


The Caliph, attired in brilliantly white robes, walked across the Great Hall, a large atrium on the second floor of the eastern wing of the Stone Palace. All signs of the bloodbath had been rinsed away, or almost all. The intricate geometric pattern on the encaustic tiled floor was disfigured by only a faint rust tinge on the grout where blood had been allowed to rest too long.

Now he took a seat at the head of a thirty-foot-long table, where tea harvested from the province of Kenna had been poured for him. Standing to either side of him were the members of his personal security detail, stalwart and simple men with vigilant eyes who had been with him for years. The Kagama delegates—the seven men who had participated in the negotiations convened by Peter Novak—had already been summoned and would arrive momentarily. All of them had performed their duties well. They had signaled an exhaustion with the struggle, a recognition of "new realities," and lulled the meddlesome mogul and the government representatives with talk of "concessions" and "compromise."

Everything had been executed according to plan by the seven plausible Kagama elders, all of whom had the movement credentials to be accepted as spokesmen for the Caliph. Which was why one final act of service would be required of them.

"Sahib, the delegates are here," said a young courier, keeping his eyes bashfully on the ground as he approached.

"Then you will wish to remain and observe, to tell others what transpired in this beautiful room," the Caliph replied. It was a command, and would be honored as such.

The wide mahogany doors slid open at the other end of the Great Hall, and the seven men filed in. They were flushed with excitement, buoyant with the expectation of the Caliph's gratitude.

"I behold the men who negotiated so expertly with the representatives of the Republic of Anura," the Caliph said, in a loud, clear voice. He rose. "Revered officers of the Kagama Liberation Front."

The seven men bowed their heads humbly. "It was no more than our duty," said the eldest, whose hair was graying but whose eyes shined hard and bright. Anticipation made his smile quiver. "It is you who are the architect of our destinies. What we did was only in the majestic fulfillment of your—"

"Silence!" The Caliph cut him off. "Revered members of the Kagama Liberation Front who have *betrayed* the trust we placed in them." He glanced at the members of his retinue. "Watch these traitors simper and smirk before me, before all of us, for they have no shame. They would sell our destiny for a mess of pottage! They were *never* authorized to do what they tried to do. They are lackeys for the republican oppressors, apostates from a cause that is holy in the eyes of Allah. Every moment they breathe on this earth is an insult to the Prophet, *salla Allah u alihi wa sallam.*"

With the crook of a forefinger, he signaled the members of his guard to proceed as they had been instructed.

The delegates' startled rejoinders and protests were cut short by a burst of tightly clustered gunfire. Their movements were jerky, spasmodic. On white tunics, blossoms of vibrant red appeared. As the low-signature shots echoed through the hall, with the *rat-tat-tat* of celebratory firecrackers, a few of the delegates loosed shrieks of terror before they expired and pitched forward, stacked on themselves like so much kindling wood.

The Caliph was disappointed; they sounded like frightened girls. These were good men: why could they not die with dignity? The Caliph tapped one of his retainers on the shoulder. "Mustafa," he said, "please see that the mess is cleaned up promptly." They had found out what happened to the grout when blood stayed on it too long, had they not? The Caliph and his deputies were masters of the palace now; they had to see to its upkeep.

"Just as you say," the young man replied, bowing deeply and fingering his leather pendant. "Without fail."

The Caliph then turned to the eldest member of his retinue, a man who could always be counted on to keep him informed about matters close at hand. "How fares our ram in the thickets?"

"Sahib?"

"How is the prisoner adjusting to his new accommodations?"

"Not well."

"Keep him alive!" the Caliph said severely. "Secure and alive." He set down his teacup. "If he dies prematurely, we won't be able to behead him come Friday. I should be *very* displeased."

"We will take care of him. The ceremony will proceed as you have planned it. In every detail."

Small things mattered, including the death of small men like the delegates. Did those men understand the service they had just performed in dying? Did they appreciate the love that had propelled the hail of bullets? The Caliph was truly grateful to them and to their sacrifice. And that sacrifice could be postponed no longer, for a KLF communiqué had already been sent denouncing the negotiations as an anti-Kagama plot and those who participated in them as traitors. The delegates had to be shot simply to make the communiqué credible. This was not something he could explain to them beforehand, but he hoped some of them surmised it in the instant before they perished.

It was all of a piece. The execution of Peter Novak, the repudiation of the negotiators, would be guaranteed to strengthen Kagama resolve for complete and unconditional victory. And to give pause to any other outside interlopers—agents of neocolonialism, in whatever humanitarian garb—who might try to appeal to "moderates," to "pragmatists," and so undermine the zeal of the righteous. Such half measures, such temporizing compromises, were an insult to the Prophet himself! And an insult to the many thousands of Kagama who had already died in the conflict. No differences would be split—only the heads of traitors.

And the world would learn that the Kagama Liberation Front would have to be taken seriously, its demands honored, its words feared.

Bloodshed. The immolation of a living legend. How else would a deaf world learn to listen?

He knew the message would be relayed to those it needed to reach among the Kagama. The international media was always another matter. For the bored spectators of the West, entertainment was the ultimate value. Well, the struggle for national liberation was not conducted for their entertainment. The Caliph knew how Westerners thought, for he had spent time among them. Most of his followers were poorly educated men who had traded plowshares for swords; they had never been on a plane and knew little of the world except what they heard on the heavily censored Kagama-language radio stations.

The Caliph respected their purity, but his range of experience was far greater, and necessarily so: the master's tools would be needed to dismantle the master's house. After attending college at the University of Hyderabad, he had spent two years obtaining a graduate degree in engineering from the University of Maryland, in College Park; he had been, he liked to say, to the heart of darkness. His time in the States taught the Caliph—Ahmad Tabari, as he was then called—how Westerners viewed the rest of the world. It introduced him to men and women who grew up in households of power and privilege, where the main struggle was over the remote control, and the greatest danger they faced was boredom. For them, places such as Anura or Sri Lanka or Lebanon or Kashmir or Myanmar had been flattened into metaphor, mere emblems of the pointless barbarity of non-Western peoples. In each case, the West enjoyed the great gift of obliviousness: obliviousness to its complicity, obliviousness to the fact that its barbarity dwarfed any other.

Westerners! He knew they remained an abstraction, ghostly and even demonic, to many of his followers. But they were no abstraction for the Caliph; he could see them and feel them, for he had. He knew what they smelled like. There was, for instance, the bored wife of an associate dean he had met during his school days. At a get-together the administration held for foreign students, she drew out of him his tales of hardship, and as he talked he had noticed how her eyes widened and her cheeks flushed. She was in her late thirties, blond and bored; her comfortable existence was a cage to her. What started as a conversation next to a punch bowl was followed, at her insistence, by coffee the very next day, and then by much more. She had been excited by his stories of persecution, by the cigarette burns on his torso; no doubt she was also excited simply by what she perceived as his exoticism, though she owned up only to an attraction to his "intensity." When he mentioned that electrodes had once been attached to his genitals, she looked both horrified and fascinated. Were there any lasting effects? she had asked solemnly. He had laughed at her ill-disguised interest and said he would happily let her decide for herself. Her husband, with his fecal breath and comical, pigeon-toed walk, would not be home for hours.

That afternoon, Ahmad performed a *salat*, the ritual prayer, with her juices still on his fingers. A pillowcase served as his prayer mat.

The weeks that followed were a crash course in Western mores that proved as valuable as anything else he learned at Maryland. He took, or was taken by, more lovers, though none knew of the others. They spoke dismissively of their pampered lives, but none of them would ever dream of actually leaving the gilded cage. With half an eye on the bluish glow of the TV screen, the spoiled white bitches would watch the events of the day as they waved their hands to hasten the drying of their nail polish. Nothing ever happened that American television could not reduce to a fifteen-second world-news update: slivers of mayhem between segments on new diet fads and pets in peril and warnings about expensive toys for toddlers that could be hazardous if swallowed. How rich in material things the West was, how poor in spiritual! Was America a beacon unto the nations? If so, it was a beacon leading other vessels into the shoals!

When the twenty-four-year-old graduate student returned to his native land, it was with a sense of even greater urgency. Injustice prolonged was injustice magnified. And—he could not say it enough—the only solution to violence was more violence.

Janson spent the next hour going through the dossiers and listening to brief presentations by Márta Lang's four associates. Much of the material was familiar; some of the analyses even reflected his own reports from Caligo, submitted more than five years ago. Two nights earlier, the rebels had taken over army bases, surged through checkpoints, and effectively seized control of the province of Kenna. Obviously, it had all been carefully planned in advance, down to the insistence on holding the summit in the province. In its latest communication to its followers, the KLF had officially repudiated the Kagama delegation at the summit, calling them traitors acting without authorization. It was a lie, of course, one of many.

There were a few new details. Ahmad Tabari, the man they called the Caliph, had gained in popular support during the past few years. Some of his food programs, it emerged, had won him sympathizers even among Hindu peasants. They had nicknamed him the Exterminator—not because of his propensity to murder civilians but because of a pest-eradication campaign he had launched. In the areas controlled by the KLF, aggressive measures were invariably taken against the bandicoot rat, an indigenous species of vermin destructive to poultry and grain. In fact, Tabari's campaign was motivated by an ancient superstition. In Tabari's clan—the extended family to which his father belonged—the bandicoot rat represented death. It did not matter how many Koran verses Ahmad Tabari had committed to memory: that primal taboo was marked indelibly on his psyche.

But the physical realm, not the psychological one, was what commanded Janson's full attention. For the next two hours, Janson scrutinized detailed topographical maps, grainy satellite imagery of the multiphase rebel incursion, and old blueprints of what had once been a colonial governor general's compound and, before that, a fortress—the building on Adam's Hill known by the Dutch as the Steenpaleis, the Stone Palace.

Again and again he stared at the elevation mappings of Adam's Hill and of the Stone Palace, moving back and forth between overhead views and structural blueprints. One conclusion was inescapable. If the U.S. government had declined to send in the SEALs, political considerations were only part of the story. The other part was that any exfiltration operation had an extremely remote probability of success.

Lang's associates knew it. He could see it in their faces: they were asking him to conduct a mission that was essentially doomed from the start. But perhaps nobody was willing to tell Márta Lang. Or she had been told and refused to accede. It was clear that she regarded Peter Novak as somebody worth dying for. She would give her life for him; and people like her were always willing to give the lives of others as well. Yet could he say that she was wrong? American lives had frequently been lost in pursuit of derisory gains—putting up a bridge over the Dak Nghe, for the tenth time, that would be destroyed, for the tenth time, before morning came. Peter Novak *was* a great man. Many owed their lives to him. And, though he tried to put it out of his mind, Janson knew he was among them.

If people were unwilling to put themselves at risk to save such an apostle of enlightenment, what did it say about the ideals of peace and democracy to which Novak had devoted his own life? Extremists scoffed at Westerners and their lightly held beliefs, yet was extremism in pursuit of moderation not itself a moral contradiction? Wasn't Janson's recognition of that fact what had driven him to retire?

Abruptly, Janson sat up straight. There *was* a way—perhaps.

"We'll need aircraft, boats, and most of all, the right operatives," he told Lang. His voice had subtly shifted, from the mode of gathering information to that of issuing orders. He stood and paced silently. The make-or-break factor was going to be the men, not the machinery.

Márta Lang looked at the others expectantly; for the moment, anyway, the look of grim resignation had lifted.

"I'm talking about a crack team of specialists," he said. "Best of breed in every case. There's no time for training exercises—it's going to have to be people who have worked together before, people *I've* worked with and can trust." He pictured a succession of faces, flashing in his mind like so many file photos, and mentally culled the list according to essential criteria until four remained. Each was someone he had worked with in his past career. Each was someone he felt he could trust with his life; indeed, each was someone who owed him his life, and who, temperamentally, would respect a debt of honor. And none of them, as it happened, were American nationals. The State Department could breathe easy. He gave Lang the list. Four men from four different countries.

Suddenly Janson slapped the bolted table. "Christ!" he half shouted. "What was I thinking? You're going to have to scratch the last name, Sean Hennessy."

"He's dead?"

"Not dead. Behind bars. Her Majesty's Prison Service. HMP Wormwood Scrubs. Got embroiled on a weapons charge a few months ago. Suspected of being IRA."

"Was he?"

"As it happens, no. Hadn't been since he was sixteen, but the military police kept his name in its Provo files all the same. In point of fact, he was doing a job for Sandline Ltd.—keeping the Democratic Republic of Congo safe for coltan extraction."

"Is he the best person for the job you want him to do?"

"I'd be lying if I told you otherwise."

Lang punched a series of numbers on what looked like a flat telephone console, and brought the handset to her ear.

"This is Márta Lang," she said, speaking with clipped precision. "Márta Lang. Please verify."

Sixty long seconds elapsed. Finally she spoke again. "Sir Richard, please." The number dialed was obviously not one that was in general circulation; it was unnecessary to specify to whomever had answered that it was an emergency, for that assumption would be automatic. Verification no doubt involved both voice print analysis and a telephony trace to the ANSI signature unique to every North American telephone line, including those that used a sat-com uplink.

"Sir Richard," she said, her voice defrosting slightly. "I have the name of an HMP prisoner by the name of Sean, S-E-A-N, Hennessy, double *n*, double *s*. Probably an SIB apprehension, approximately three months ago. Status: arraigned, not convicted, awaiting trial." Her eyes sought out his for confirmation, and Janson nodded.

"We'll need to have him released at once and on a plane bound for . . ." She paused, reconsidering. "There's an LF jet docked at Gatwick. Get him on board immediately. Call me back within forty-five minutes with an estimated arrival time."

Janson shook his head, marveling. "Sir Richard" had to be Richard Whitehead, the director of Britain's Special Investigations Branch. But what most impressed him was her coolly instructive tone. Whitehead was to call back to let her know not whether the request could be accommodated but *when* the request would be accommodated. As Novak's seniormost deputy, she was obviously well known to political elites around the world. He had been preoccupied with the advantages enjoyed by his Anuran adversaries, but Novak's people were hardly without resources themselves.

Janson also admired Lang's instinctive respect for operational security. No final destination was divulged; the Liberty Foundation jet at Gatwick would just need to provide a proximate flight plan. Only once it had crossed into international airspace would its pilot need to know the rendezvous point Janson had determined, in the Nicobar archipelago.

Now Janson started to go over a list of military equipment with one of Lang's associates, a man named Gerald Hochschild, who served as a de facto logistics officer. To each request, Hochschild responded not with a yes or no, but with a time interval: twelve hours, four hours, twenty hours. The amount of time that would be necessary to locate and ship the equipment to the Nicobar rendezvous.

It was almost too easy, Janson mused. Then he realized why. While human rights organizations held conferences to discuss the problem of the small-arms trade in Sierre Leone or the traffic in military helicopters in Kazakhstan, Novak's foundation had a more direct method for taking the noxious hardware off the market: it simply acquired the stuff. As Hochschild confirmed, as long as the model was discontinued and therefore irreplaceable, the Liberty Foundation would buy it, warehouse it, and eventually recycle it as scrap or, in the case of military transport, have it retooled for civilian purposes.

Thirty minutes later, a green light on the telephone blinked. Márta Lang picked up the handset. "So he's en route? Condition?" There was a pause, and then she said, "We'll assume a departure time in less than sixty minutes, in that case." Her voice softened. "You've been a dear. We couldn't appreciate it more. Really. And you be *sure* to send my love to Gillian, will you? We all missed you in Davos this year. You can be certain that Peter gave the PM an earful about that! Yes. Yes. We'll catch up properly—soon."

A woman of parts, Janson thought admiringly.

"There's a reasonable chance that your Mr. Hennessy will beat you to the rendezvous," Márta told him immediately after she hung up.

"My hat's off," Janson said simply.

Through the windows, the sun was a golden orb, cushioned by white, fluffy-looking clouds. Though they were flying toward the setting sun, the passage of time was keeping pace. When Lang's eyes lowered to her watch, he knew she was looking at more than simply the time of day. She was looking at the number of hours Peter Novak had left. She met his gaze and paused for a moment before speaking. "Whatever happens," she said, "I want to thank you for what you've given us."

"I've given you nothing," Janson protested.

"You've given us something of quite substantial value," she said. "You've given us hope."

Janson started to say something about the realities, the long odds, the abundant downside scenarios, but he stopped himself. There was a higher pragmatism to be respected. At this stage of a mission, false hope was better than none at all.

# CHAPTER THREE

The memories were thirty years old, but they could have been yesterday's. They unspooled in his dreams at night—always the night before an operation, fueled by repressed anxiety—and though they started and ended at different points, it was as though they were from the same continuous loop of tape.

In the jungle was a base. In the base was an office. In the office was a desk. On the desk was a sheet of paper.

It was, in fact, the list for that date's Harassment & Interdiction fire.

*Possible VC rocket attack, launch site grid coordinates AT384341, between 0200 and 0300 this morning.*

*A VC political cadre meeting, Loc Ninh village, BT415341, at 2200 this evening.*

*VC infiltration attempt, below Go Noi River, AT404052, between 2300 and 0100.*

That pile of well-thumbed slips on Lieutenant Commander Alan Demarest's desk was filled with similar reports. They were supplied by informants to ARVN officials, who then passed them along to the Military Assistance Command-Vietnam, MACV. Both the informants and the reports were assigned a letter and a number assessing their reliability. Nearly all the reports were classified as F/6: reliability of agent indeterminate, reliability of report indeterminate.

*Indeterminate* was a euphemism. Reports came from double agents, from VC sympathizers, from paid informants, and sometimes just from villagers who had scores to settle and had figured out an easy way to get someone else to destroy a rival's paddy dike.

"These are supposed to be the basis for our Harassment and Interdiction fire," Demarest had said to Janson and Maguire. "But they're bullshit. Some four-eyed Charlie in Hanoi wrote these for our sake, and piped them through the pencil dicks at MACV. These, gentlemen, are a waste of artillery. Know how I know?" He held up a filmy slip, fluttered it in the air like a flag. "There's no blood on this paper." A twelfth-century

choral work played through the tiny speakers of an eight-track tape system, one of Demarest's small enthusiasms.

"You get me a goddamn VC courier," Demarest went on, scowling.
"No, you get me an even dozen. If they've got paper on them, bring it
back—certified with VC blood. Prove to me that *military intelligence* is
not a contradiction in terms."

That evening, six of them had rolled over the gunwales of the fiberglass-
hulled STAB, the SEAL tactical assault boat, and into the bath-warm shallow water of Ham Luong. They paddled through an eighth of a mile of
riverine silt and landed on the pear-shaped island. "Come back with prisoners, or don't come back," their CO had told them. With luck, they
would do so: the island, Noc Lo, was known to be controlled by Viet
Cong. But luck had lately been in scarce supply.

The six men wore black pajamas, like their foe. No dog tags, no signs
of rank or unit, of the fact that they were a SEAL team, of the even more
pertinent fact that they were Demarest's Devils. They had spent two hours
making their way through the island's dense vegetation, alert to any sign
of the enemy—sounds, footprints, even the smell of the nuoc cham sauce
their enemy doused over their food.

They were divided into three pairs, two of them in front, traveling ten
yards apart; two of them serving as rear guard, in charge of the forty-
pound M60, ready to provide cover.

Janson was on point, paired with Hardaway, a tall, thickly built man
with dark brown skin and wide-spaced eyes. He kept his head close-shorn
with electric clippers. Hardaway's tour of duty was up in sixty days, and
he was getting antsy about returning stateside. A month ago, he had torn
out a skin-mag centerfold and divided it into numbered squares. Each
day, he filled in one of the squares. When they were all filled in, he would
take his centerfold girl back home and trade her in for a real one. That
was Hardaway's idea, anyway.

Now, three hundred yards inland, Hardaway picked up a contraption
made out of tire rubber and canvas, and showed it to Janson with a
questioning look. They were mud shoes. The light-bodied VC used them
to glide tracklessly through swampy terrain. Recently discarded?

Janson called for thirty seconds of silent vigilance. The team froze in
place, alert to any noise that was out of the ordinary. Noc Lo was in the
middle of a free-fire zone, where firing was permitted at any time without
restriction, and there was no escape from the muffled sounds of distant
batteries, mortars booming at half-second intervals. Away from the veg-

etation, one could see the white pulsations on the fringe of the horizon. But after thirty seconds, it seemed evident that there was no activity in the immediate vicinity.

"You know what the mortar fire makes me think of sometimes?" Hardaway asked. "The choir clapping in my church. Like it's religious, some kind of way."

"Extreme unction, Maguire would tell you," Janson replied softly. He had always been fond of Hardaway, but this evening his friend seemed unusually distracted.

"Hey, they don't call it the Holiness Church for no reason. You come to Jacksonville, I'll take you one Sunday." Hardaway bobbed and clapped to a rhythm in his head. " 'Sanctify my lord, *sanc*-tify my lord.' "

"Hardaway," Janson warned, putting a hand on his gear belt.

The crack of a rifle told them that the enemy had learned of their presence. They would have to dive to the ground, to take immediate evasive action.

For Hardaway, however, it was too late. A small geyser of blood erupted from his neck. He staggered forward several yards, like a sprinter who had crossed the finish line. Then he collapsed to the ground.

As Maguire's machine gun began to fire bullets over their heads, Janson scrambled over to Hardaway. He had been struck in the lower outside part of his neck, near his right shoulder; Janson cradled his head, applying pressure with both hands to the pulsing wound on the front of his neck, desperately trying to staunch the flow.

"Sanctify my lord," Hardaway said weakly.

The pressure was not working. Janson felt his shirt becoming warm and wet, and he realized what was wrong. There was an exit wound, at the back of Hardaway's neck, perilously near his spine, from which bright arterial blood was gouting.

In a sudden display of strength, he wrenched Janson's hands from his neck. "Leave me, Janson." He was trying to shout, but it came out as a low rasp. "*Leave* me!" He crawled away a few feet, then used his arms to raise himself, his head swiveling around the tree line as he tried to make out the shapes of his assailants.

Immediately, a blast hit his midriff, slamming him to the ground. His abdomen had been torn apart, Janson saw. Recovery was out of the question. One man down. How many more?

Janson rolled behind a thornbush.

It was a goddamn ambush!

The VC had been lying in wait for them.

Dialing his scope furiously, zooming through the marsh grasses and palms, Janson saw three VCs running down a jungle path directly toward him.

A direct assault? No, he decided: it was more likely that the raking overhead fire from the M60 had caused them to change their position. A few seconds later, he heard the sharp *thwack* of bullets hitting the ground near him.

Dammit! There was no way the fire could be this heavy and well targeted unless Charlie had received advance word of the infiltration. But how?

He shifted his rifle scope rapidly to different directions and focal points. There: a hooch on stilts. And just behind it, a VC aiming a Chicom AK-47 in his direction. A small, skilled man who must have been responsible for the last blast that had hit Hardaway.

In the moonlight, he saw the man's eyes, and just underneath, the bore hole of the AK-47. Each, he knew, had spotted the other, and what AK-47 fire lacked in precision it made up for in volume. Now he saw the VC brace the butt on his shoulder and prepare to squeeze off a fusillade just as Janson located the man's torso in his crosshairs. Within seconds, one of them would be dead.

Janson's universe constricted to the three elements: finger, trigger, crosshairs. At that instant, they were all he knew, all he needed to know.

A double tap—two carefully aimed shots—and the little man with the submachine gun pitched forward.

Yet how many more were out there?

"Get us the fuck out of here!" Janson radioed back to base. "We need backup now! Send a Mike boat. Send whatever the *hell* you've got. Just do it *now!*"

"Just one moment," the radio operator said. Then Janson heard the voice of his commanding officer coming on the line: "You holding up OK, son?" Demarest asked.

"Sir, they were expecting us!" Janson said.

After a pause, Demarest's voice crackled on the radio headphones. "Of course they were."

"But *how,* sir?"

"Just consider it a test, son. A test that will show which of my men have what it takes." Janson thought he heard choral music in the background. "You're not going to complain to me about the VCs, are you? They're just a bunch of overgrown kids in pajamas."

Despite the oppressive tropical heat, Janson felt a chill. "How did they *know,* sir?"

"If you wanted to find out how good you were at shooting paper targets, you could have stayed at camp in Little Creek, Virginia."

"But Hardaway—"

Demarest cut him off. "He was weak. He failed the test."


*He was weak:* Alan Demarest's voice. But Janson would not be. Now he opened his eyes with a shudder as the plane touched down on the macadamized landing strip.

Katchall had for years been declared a restricted, no-entry location by India's navy, part of a security zone that included most of the Nicobar Islands. Once it was rezoned, it became nothing less than a trading post. Mangoes, papaya, durian, PRC-101s, and C-130s all made their way to and from the sun-scorched oval of land. It was, Janson knew, one of the few places where nobody would blink at the sudden arrival of military transport vehicles and munitions.

Nor was it a place where the niceties of sovereign border control were observed. A jeep took him directly from the plane to the compound along the western shore. His team would already be assembling in the olive drab Quonset hut, a structure of ribbed aluminum over a frame of arched steel ribs. The floor and foundation were concrete, the interior pressed wood. A small prefab warehouse adjoined it. The Liberty Foundation had a low-profile regional office in Rangoon, and so was able to move advance men in place to ensure that the rendezvous sites were in order.

Little had changed since Janson had last used it as a base of operations. The Quonset hut he would borrow was one of many on the island, originally erected by the Indian military and now abandoned or commandeered for commercial interests.

Theo Katsaris had already arrived when Janson pulled up, and the two men embraced warmly. Katsaris, a Greek national, had been a protégé of Janson's and was probably the most skilled operative he had ever worked with. The only thing that disturbed Janson about him, in fact, was his tolerance—indeed, appetite—for risk. Janson had known plenty of daredevils from his SEAL days and knew the profile: they typically came from depressed Rust Belt towns, where their friends and parents had led dead-end lives. They were up for anything that saved them from punching the clock at the rivet factory—including another tour of duty in VC-controlled territories. But Katsaris had everything to live for, including a stunningly beautiful wife. Impossible to dislike, he had a charmed life, and yet set little store by it. His very presence would raise morale; people enjoyed being around him: he had the sunny aura of a man to whom nothing bad would ever happen.

Manuel Honwana had been in the nearby hangar but made his way back when he learned of Janson's arrival. He was a former colonel in the Mozambican air force, Russian-trained and unequaled at ground-hugging flight over hilly tropical terrain. Cheerfully apolitical, he had extensive experience with combating dug-in, entrenched guerrillas. And it was very much a point in his favor that he had flown numerous sorties in the fixed-wing rattletraps that were all his poor country could get its hands on. Most American flyboys were PlayStation graduates, used to being surrounded by millions of dollars in digital avionics. Instinct tended to atrophy as a result: they were mere custodians of the machine, less pilots than information-system technicians. But this job would require a pilot. Honwana could reassemble a MiG engine with a Swiss Army knife and his bare hands, because he'd had to. If he had instruments, so much the better; if he did not, he was unfazed. And if an emergency nonstandard landing was required, Honwana would be right at home: on the missions he'd both flown and directed, a proper airstrip was the exception, not the rule.

Finally, there was Finn Andressen, a Norwegian and a former officer in his country's armed forces, who had degrees in geology and had a well-honed instinct for terrain assessment. He had designed security arrangements for mining companies around the world. He arrived within the hour, followed in short order by Sean Hennessy, the remarkably versatile and unflappable Irish airman. The team members greeted one another with hearty shoulder clasps or quiet handshakes, depending on their temperament.

Janson led them through the plan of attack, starting with the broad outlines and descending to details and alternative options. As the men absorbed the mission protocol, the sun grew red, large, and low in the horizon, as if it were getting heavier and its weight were forcing it down toward the sea. To the men, it was a giant hourglass, reminding them how little time remained.

Now they split up into pairs and set about fine-tuning the plan, bringing schematics in line with reality. Leaning over a folding wooden bench, Honwana and Andressen reviewed maps of wind-current and ocean-current patterns. Janson and Katsaris studied a plasticine mock-up of the Steenpaleis, the Stone Palace.

Sean Hennessy, meanwhile, was doing chin-ups from an exposed I beam as he listened to the others; it had been one of his few distractions in HMP Wormwood Scrubs. Janson glanced at him; would he be all right? He had no reason to think otherwise. If the Irishman's complexion was paler than usual, his physique was burlier. Janson had run him through a rough-and-ready field physical and was satisfied that his reflexes were as quick as ever.

"You do realize," Andressen said to Janson, turning away from his charts, "that there will be at least a hundred people based in the Stone Palace alone. Are you sure we have enough manpower?"

"More than enough," Janson said. "If five hundred Gurkhas were called for, I'd have requested them. I've asked for what I need. If I could do it with fewer, I would. The fewer men, the fewer the complications."

Janson now turned from the plasticine model to the highly detailed blueprints. Those blueprints, he knew, represented an enormous effort. They had been prepared in the past forty hours by a task force of architects and engineers assembled by the Liberty Foundation. The experts had been provided with extensive verbal descriptions from visitors, a profusion of historical photographs, and even present-day overhead satellite imagery. Colonial archives in the Netherlands had been consulted as well. Despite the rapidity with which the work was done, Novak's people told him they believed it was "quite accurate" in most of the particulars. They also warned that some of the particulars, the ones pertaining to seldom-used areas of the structure, were "less certain" and that some of the materials analysis was conjectural and "uncertain."

*Less certain. Uncertain.* Words Janson was hearing too often for his taste.

Yet what was the alternative? Maps and models were all they had. The Dutch governor general's compound was adapted from a preexisting fortress, laid out on a promontory three hundred feet above the ocean. Walls of limestone, five feet thick, were designed to withstand cannonballs from Portuguese men-of-war of centuries past. The sea-facing walls were topped with battlements from which hostile schooners and corvettes would be fired upon.

Everyone Janson had assembled in that Quonset hut knew precisely what was at stake. They also knew the obstacles they faced in trying to derail what the Caliph had set in motion. Nothing would be gained by compounding Novak's death with their own.

It was time for a final briefing. Janson stood; his nervous energy made it difficult for him to sit. "OK, Andressen," he said. "Let's talk terrain."

The red-bearded Norseman turned the large, calendared sheets of the elevation maps, pointing out features with a long forefinger. His finger moved along the massif, almost ten thousand feet at the Pikuru Takala peak, and then onward to the plateaus of shale and gneiss. He pointed out the monsoon winds from the southwest. Tapping a magnification of Adam's Hill, Andressen said, "These are recently reclaimed areas. We're not talking about sophisticated monitoring. A lot of what we're up against is the protection offered by the natural terrain."

"Recommended flight path?"

"Over the Nikala jungle, if the Storm Petrel's up for it."

The Storm Petrel was Honwana's well-deserved nickname, honoring his ability to pilot a plane so that it nearly skimmed the ground, the way a storm petrel flies above the sea.

"The Petrel's up for it," Honwana said, his lips parting to reveal ivory teeth in what was not quite a smile.

"Mind you," Andressen went on, "as long as we can hold off until around four hundred hours, we'll be almost guaranteed a heavy cloud cover. That's obviously advisable for the purposes of stealth."

"You're talking about a high-altitude jump through heavy cloud cover?" Hennessy asked. "Jumping blind?"

"A leap of faith," said the Norseman. "Like religion. Like embracing God."

"Begorrah, I thought this was a commando operation, not a kamikaze one," Hennessy put in. "Tell me, Paul, what bloody fool is going to be making this jump?" The Irishman looked at his fellow crew members with genuine concern.

Janson looked at Katsaris. "You," he told the Greek. "And me."

Katsaris stared at him silently for a few moments. "I can live with that."

"From your lips to God's ear," Hennessy said.

# CHAPTER FOUR

Packing one's own chute: it was practically a ritual, a military superstition. By the time one got out of jump camp, the habit was as ingrained as brushing one's teeth or washing one's hands.

Janson and Katsaris had repaired to the adjoining warehouse to do the job. They started by draping the canopy and rigging over the large, flat concrete flooring. Both sprayed silicone over the rip-cord cable, the closing pin, and the closing loop. The next steps were rote. The black canopy was made of zero-porosity nylon, and Janson rolled his body over the loose drapes, pressing as much air out of it as he could. He straightened the stabilizer lines and toggles, and folded the flattened canopy to ensure an in-sequence opening, taking care that the rigging was on the outside of the folds. Finally, he bunched it into the black mesh pack, squeezing the remaining air through the edge stitching before slipping a clasp through the grommet.

Katsaris, with his nimble fingers, was finished in half the time.

He turned to Janson. "Let's you and I do a quick weapons inspection," he said. "Pay a visit to the junk shop."

The premise of a team was that anybody would accept personal risk to reduce a risk borne by another. An ethos of equality was crucial; any sense of favoritism was destructive to it. When they met as a group, Janson therefore dealt with the men in a tone that was at once brusque and friendly. But even within elites, there were elites—and even within the innermost circles of excellence, there is the chosen one, the golden boy.

Janson had once been that person, almost three decades earlier. Just a few weeks after he'd arrived at the SEAL training camp at Little Creek, Alan Demarest had picked him out from the enlisted trainees, had him transferred to ever more elite combat teams, ever more grueling regimens of combat drills. The training groups got smaller and smaller—more and more of his peers dropped out, defeated by the punishing schedule of exercises—until, by the end, Demarest isolated him for intensive sessions of one-on-one training.

*Your fingers are weapons! Never encumber them. Half a warrior's intelligence is found in his hands.*

*Don't squeeze the vein, squeeze the nerve! Memorize the nerve points until you can find them with your fingers, not your eyes. Don't look—feel!*

*I spotted your helmet above that ridgeline. You're fucking dead!*

*Can't see a way out? Take the time to see things differently. See the two white swans instead of the one black one. See the slice of pie instead of the pie with the slice missing. Flip the Necker cube outward instead of inward. Master the gestalt, baby. It will make you free. Firepower by itself won't do it. You've got to think your way out of this one.*

*Yes! Turn your hunter into your prey! You've got it!*

And thus did one legendary warrior create another. When Janson had first met Theo Katsaris, years back, he *knew*—he simply knew, the way Demarest must have known about him.

Yet even if Katsaris had not been so extraordinarily gifted, operational equality could not supplant the bonds of loyalty forged over time, and Janson's friendship with him went far beyond the context of the commando mission. It was a thing compounded of shared memories and mutual indebtedness. They would talk to each other with urgency and candor, but they would do so away from the others.

The two made their way to the far end of the warehouse, where Foundation-supplied weaponry had been stowed earlier that day. Katsaris quickly disassembled and reassembled selected handguns and long-barreled weapons, making sure that the parts were oiled, but not too heavily—combusted lubricant could create plumes of smoke, visual or olfactory giveaways. Imperfectly plumbed barrels could overheat too quickly. Hinges should be tight, but not too tight. Magazines should slide readily into place, but with just enough resistance to ensure they would be held securely. Collapsible stocks, like those of the MP5Ks, should collapse with ease.

"You know why I'm doing this," Janson said.

"Two reasons," Katsaris said. "Arguably the two reasons you shouldn't be doing this." Katsaris's hands moved as he spoke, the clicking and snapping of gunmetal providing a rhythmic counterpoint to his conversation.

"And in my position?"

"I'd do exactly the same," Katsaris said. He raised the disassembled chamber pocket of a carbine to his nose, scenting evidence of excessive lubrication. "The military wing of the Harakat al-Muqaama al-Islamiya never had a good reputation for returning stolen property." *Stolen prop-*

*erty:* hostages, especially those suspected of being assets of American intelligence. Seven years ago, in Baaqlina, Lebanon, Janson had been captured by the extremist group; his captors initially thought they had taken an American businessman, accepting his legend at face value, but the flurry of high-level reactions fueled other suspicions. Negotiations quickly went off the rails, foundering on power struggles within the faction. Only the timely intervention of a third party—the Liberty Foundation, as it later emerged—caused them to alter their plans. After twelve days of captivity, Janson walked free. "For all we know, Novak wasn't even involved, didn't have any knowledge of the situation," Katsaris went on. "But it's his foundation. Ergo, you owe the man your life. So this lady comes up to you and says, Baaqlina has come due. You've got to say yes."

"I always feel like an open book around you," Janson said, his smile crinkling the lines around his eyes.

"Yeah, written with one time pad encryption. Tell me something. How often do you think about Helene?" The warrior's brown eyes were surprisingly gentle.

"Every day."

"She was magical, wasn't she? She always seemed so *free.*"

"A free spirit," Janson said. "My opposite in every way."

Katsaris slid a nylon-mesh brush through the bore hole of another automatic weapon, checking for any cracks, carbon deposits, or other irregularities, and then he looked straight into Janson's eyes. "You once told me something, Paul. Years ago. Now I'm going to tell it to you." He reached over, placed a hand on Janson's shoulder. "*There is no revenge.* Not on this earth. That's storybook stuff. In our world, there are strikes and reprisals and more reprisals. But that neat, slate-cleaning fantasy of revenge—it doesn't exist."

"I know."

"Helene's dead, Paul."

"Oh. That must be why she hasn't been answering my phone calls." His deadpan was masking a world of pain, and not very well.

Katsaris's gaze did not waver, but he squeezed Janson's shoulder harder. "There is nothing—*nothing*—that can ever bring her back. Do what you want to the Kagama fanatics, but know this."

"It was five years ago," Janson said quietly.

"Does it *feel* like five years ago?"

The words came out in a whisper. "Like yesterday." It was not how an officer spoke to those he commanded. It was how a man spoke to the person with whom he was closest in the world, a person to whom he could never lie. He exhaled heavily. "You're afraid I'm going to go berserk and visit the wrath of God upon the terrorists who killed my wife."

"No," Katsaris said. "I'm afraid that on some gut level, you think that the way to wipe the slate clean, the way to honor Helene, is to get yourself killed by them, too."

Janson shook his head violently, though he wondered whether there could be any truth to what Katsaris said. "Nobody's going to die tonight," he said. It was a ritual of self-assurance, they both knew, rather than a statement of probabilities.

"What's ironic is that Helene always had real sympathy for the Kagama," Janson said after a while. "Not the terrorists, not the KLF, of course, but the ordinary Kagama caught in the middle of it all. Had she lived, she probably would have been right by Novak's side, trying to work out a peace agreement. The Caliph is an archmanipulator, but he exists because there are genuine grievances for him to manipulate."

"If we're here to do social engineering, we've been given the wrong equipment." Theo ran a thumbnail against a combat knife, testing its keenness. "Besides, Peter Novak tried that, and look where it got him. This is a strict in-out. Insertion and extraction."

Janson nodded. "If everything goes right, we'll be spending a total of a hundred minutes on Anura. Then again, if you've got to deal with these people, maybe it'll help if you know where they're coming from."

"If we've reached that stage," Katsaris replied grimly, "everything will have gone wrong that can go wrong."


"I won't mind taking this baby out for a spin," Honwana said admiringly. He, Janson, and Hennessy were standing in the gloomy hangar, their eyes still adjusting from the bright sun outside to the shadows within.

The BA609 was a sea-landing-equipped tiltrotor aircraft; like the discontinued Ospreys, it had propellers that enabled vertical takeoffs and landings but that, when tilted to the horizontal position, would enable the craft to function like a fixed-wing airplane. Bell/Agusta had crafted the fuselage of this particular specimen not from steel but from a tough molded resin. The result was an exceptionally lightweight craft that could travel much farther on a liter of fuel than any conventional design—up to four times as far. Its versatility would be important to the success of the mission.

Now Honwana ran his fingertips over the nonreflective surface. "A thing of beauty."

"A thing of invisibility, if the gods are with us," said Janson.

"I'll pray to the ancestors," Honwana said, with no little mirth. A Moscow-educated die-hard atheist, he was sympathetic to neither indigenous nor missionary-spread forms of religiosity.

"There's a full tank. Assuming you haven't put on weight since we worked together last, that should just get us there and back."

"You're cutting things close. The tolerances, I mean." The Mozambican's eyes were serious.

"No choice. Not my timetable, not my locale. You might say the KLF is calling the shots here. I'm just trying to improvise as best I can. This isn't a well-scoured contingency plan we're looking at. More like, 'Hey, kids, let's put on a show.' "

"Mickey Rooney and Judy Garland in a barn," Hennessy put in heavily. "With a whole load of high explosives."


The north coastline of Anura nipped in like a deeply grooved valentine's heart. The eastern lobe was mostly jungle, sparsely inhabited. Honwana flew the tiltrotorcraft low to the ground through the Nikala jungle. Once over the sea, the plane angled upward, banking nearly forty degrees.

Despite the plane's curious trajectory, Honwana's piloting was extraordinarily smooth, anticipating and compensating for wind currents and updrafts. The now-horizontal nacelles emitted a steady noise, something between a hum and a roar.

Andressen and Hennessy were up front with Honwana, part of the crew, providing essential navigational support; separated by a bulkhead, the two paratroopers were left alone on uncushioned benches in the rear of the aircraft, to confer with each other and go through their last-minute preparations.

Half an hour into the flight, Katsaris consulted his shockproof Breitling and swallowed a 100mg tablet of Provigil. It would adjust his circadian rhythms, ensuring late-night alertness, without the excessive stimulation and exaggerated confidence that amphetamines could induce. They were still two hours away from the drop zone. The Provigil would be in maximal effect during the operation. Then he took another small pill, a procholinergic that would inhibit perspiration.

He gestured toward a pair of thick black aluminum tubes that Janson was holding up to his ear.

"Those things are really going to make it?" he asked.

"Oh yes," Janson said. "As long as the gas mixture doesn't leak. The little darlings are going to be full of pep. Just like you."

Katsaris held up a foil strip of Provigil tablets. "Want one?"

Janson shook his head. Katsaris knew what he was doing, but Janson knew that drugs could have unpredictable side effects in different people, and he declined to take substances he had no experience with. "So tell me, Theo," he said, putting away the tubes and shuffling the blueprints, "how's the missus?" Now that they were not around the others, he once more called his friend by his first name.

"The missus? She know you call her that?"

"Hey, I knew her before you did. The beautiful Marina."

Katsaris laughed. "You have no *idea* how beautiful she is. You think you do, but you don't. Because right now she's positively radiant." He pronounced the last word with special emphasis.

"Wait a minute," Janson said. "You don't mean she's . . ."

"Early days, still. First trimester. Touch of morning sickness. Otherwise, she's doing great."

Janson flashed on Helene, and he felt as if a giant hand were squeezing his heart in a crushing grip.

"And we *are* a handsome couple, aren't we?" Katsaris said it with mock swagger, but it was the indisputable truth. Theo and Marina Katsaris were among God's favored, perfect specimens of Mediterranean strength and symmetry. Janson remembered a week he'd spent with them in Mykonos—remembered the particular afternoon when they encountered an imperious Paris-based director of a fashion shoot in pursuit of the ever potent combination of skimpy swimsuits, abundant white sand, and azure sea. The Frenchwoman was convinced that Theo and Marina were models, and demanded the name of their agency. All she saw were their perfect white teeth, flawless olive complexion, glossy black hair—and the possibility that these attributes were not enlisted for some commercial enterprise struck her as a wasteful indifference toward a valuable natural resource.

"Then you're going to be a father," Janson said. The rush of warmth he had felt on hearing the news quickly cooled.

"You don't sound overjoyed," Katsaris said.

Janson said nothing for a few moments. "You should have told me."

"Why?" he returned lightly. "Marina's the one who's pregnant."

"You know why."

"We were going to tell you soon. In fact, we were hoping you'd agree to be the godfather."

Janson's tone was almost truculent. "You should have told me before."

Theo shrugged. "You don't think a dad should take risks. And I think you worry too much, Paul. You haven't gotten me killed yet. Look, I understand the risks."

"*I* don't understand the risks, dammit. That's the point. They're poorly controlled."

"You don't want to orphan my kid. Well, guess what—neither do I. I'm going to be a father, and that makes me very, very happy. But it isn't going to change the way I lead my life. That's not who I am. Marina knows that. You know it, too—that's why you picked me in the first place."

"I don't know that I would have picked you had I realized—"

"I'm not talking about now. I'm talking about then. I'm talking about Epidaurus."

It was only eight years ago when a twenty-man contingent from the Greek army was detailed to a Cons Op–run interception exercise. The objective was to train the Greeks to detect and deter a growing small-arms trade that made use of Greek freighters. A ship a few miles off the coast of Epidaurus was chosen at random for the exercise. As luck would have it, however, the ship happened to be loaded with contraband. Even worse, a Turkish drug merchant was on board, accompanied by his heavily armed private guard. Things went wrong, terribly wrong, in a cataract of misfortune and misunderstanding. Inexperienced men on both sides panicked: the supervisors from Consular Operations could observe—by means of a digital telescope and the remote listening devices on the frogmen's suits—but, agonizingly, they were too far away to intervene without jeopardizing the trainees' safety.

From a small frigate anchored half a nautical mile away, Janson had been horrified by the disastrous unfolding of events; in particular, he recalled the twenty tension-filled seconds in which matters could have gone either way. There had been two bands of armed men, evenly matched. Each individual maximized his own chance of survival by opening fire first. But once the automatic weapons were engaged, the surviving members of the adversary would have no choice but to return fire. It was the sort of suicidal "fair fight" that could easily have resulted in 100 percent fatalities for both sides. At the same time, there was no chance that the Turk's guards would stand down—it would be seen as a treasonous abdication, ultimately repaid by their own compatriots with a swift death.

"Don't shoot!" a young Greek shouted. He lay down his weapon, yet the gesture conveyed not fear but disgust. Janson heard his voice tinnily but clearly through the transmitter unit. "Cretins! Dolts! Ingrates! We work for *you*."

The jeers of the Turks were boisterous, but the claim was sufficiently bizarre that they demanded further explanation.

An explanation arrived, mixing fact and fiction, brilliantly improvised and fluently delivered. The young Greek invoked the name of a powerful Turkish drug magnate, Orham Murat, to whose cartel the merchant on board belonged. He explained that their commanding officers had assigned him and the other soldiers to search suspect freighters but that Murat had paid them generously to ensure that his own vessels were protected from seizure. "A generous, generous man," the young officer had said, in a tone of solemnity and greed. "My children have him to thank for their three meals a day. With what the government gives us? *Bah!*" The other Greeks were silent at first, their reticence interpreted as simple fear and awkwardness. Then they began to nod, as they understood that their colleague was telling this tale for their own sakes. They lowered their weapons and kept their gaze downcast, unchallenging.

"If you are lying..." the seniormost member of the Turkish guard began in a growl.

"All we ask is that you not radio about this—our superiors monitor all maritime communications, and they have your codes."

"*Lies!*" barked a gray-haired Turk. It was the merchant himself who had finally appeared on deck.

"It is the *truth!* The American government has helped our commanders with this. If you radio about us, you might as well shoot us now, because the army will have us executed when we return. In fact, I would *beg* you to shoot us now. Then the Greek army will think we died as heroes and provide pensions to our families. As to whether Orham Murat will be as generous to *your* widows and children when he learns that you destroyed an operation he spent so much time and money on—this you will have to decide for yourselves."

A long, uncomfortable silence ensued. Finally, the merchant broke in:

"Your claims are preposterous! If they had access to our communications—"

"If? *If?* Do you think it is an *accident* that we were ordered to board your freighter?" The Greek snorted contemptuously. "I ask you one question. *Do you really believe in coincidence?*"

With that, the salvation of his unit was secured. No smuggler—none who survived long, anyway—ever believed in coincidence.

The young Greek led the other frogmen back into the water and to the American-run frigate. Loss of life: zero. Seven hours later, a flotilla of maritime security vessels converged on the *Minas:* artillery engaged and aimed. In the face of an overwhelming display of force, the drug merchant and his guard surrendered.

Afterward, Janson introduced himself personally to the young Greek who had the spur-of-the-moment ingenuity to seize upon and invert the one implausible truth—the truth that the drug merchant's freighter had been boarded by accident—and so render his tale plausible indeed. The young man, Theo Katsaris, turned out to be more than just levelheaded, clever, and bold; he was also endowed with remarkable physical agility and had earned top-percentile scores in field-skill tests. As Janson learned more about him, he saw how anomalous he was. Unlike most of his fellow servicemen, he came from a comfortably middle-class background; his father was a mid-level diplomat, once posted to Washington, and Katsaris had attended St. Alban's for a couple of years in his early teens. Janson would have been tempted to dismiss him as merely an adrenaline addict—and that was part of the story, without a doubt—but Katsaris's sense of passion, his desire to make a difference in the world, was genuine.

A few days later, Janson had drinks with a Greek general he knew who was himself a product of the U.S. Army War College, in Carlisle, Pennsylvania. Janson explained that he had come across a youngster in the Greek army who had potential that could not be fully exploited by the routine of the Greek military. What he proposed was to take him under his wing and supervise his training personally. At the time, the leadership of Consular Operations was particularly attuned to "strategic partnerships"—joint operations with NATO allies. Under such auspices, Consular Operations would gain an asset in the short term; in the longer term, Greece would ultimately benefit by having somebody who could pass along skills and techniques in counterterrorism to his fellow citizens. The deal was done by the third cocktail.

Now, in the rear of the tiltrotorcraft, Janson gave Katsaris a steely look. "Marina know what you're doing?"

"Didn't tell her details, and she didn't press." Katsaris laughed. "Come on, Marina has more balls than the Greek army's Eighth Division. You know that."

"I do know that."

"So let me make the decisions. Besides, if this operation is too risky for me, how can you in good conscience ask another person to take my place?"

Janson just shook his head.

"You need me," Katsaris said.

"I could have gotten somebody else."

"Not somebody as good."

"I won't deny that." Neither man was smiling anymore.

"And we both know what this operation means to you. I mean, it isn't just work for hire."

"I won't deny that, either. Arguably, it means a lot for the world."

"I'm talking about Paul Janson, not the planet Earth. People before abstractions, right? That was something else we always agreed on." His brown eyes were unwavering. "I'm not going to let you down," he said quietly.

Janson found himself oddly touched by the gesture. "Tell me something I don't know," he said.


As the zero hour grew near, an unspoken sense of anxiety mounted. They had taken what precautions they could. The aircraft was fully blacked out, with no lights and nothing that might reflect light from another source. Sitting on canvas slings near the plane's greasy ramp, Katsaris and Janson followed the same rule; they wore nothing reflective. As they approached the drop zone, they put on full black-nylon combat garb, including face paint. To have done so too far in advance would have been to risk over-heating. Their equipment-laden vests looked lumpy beneath the flight suit, but there was no alternative.

Now came the first great improbability. He and Katsaris had three thousand jumps between them. But what would be required tonight was beyond anything they had experienced.

Janson had been pleased with himself when he first had the insight that the compound's sole point of vulnerability was directly overhead—that the one possibility of an undetected arrival would be from the night sky to the center of the courtyard. Whether there was a serious chance of accomplishing this, on the other hand, remained purely conjectural.

To arrive undetected, they would have to fall to the ground, silently, through the starless, moonless night that the monsoon season would provide. The satellite weather maps confirmed that at four o'clock in the morning, and extending through the next hour, the cloud cover would be total.

But they were men, not action figures. To succeed, they would have to land with extraordinary precision. To make things worse, the same weather system that provided cloud cover also provided unpredictable winds— another enemy of precision. Under ordinary circumstances, any one of these complications would have led Janson to abort a jump.

It was, in too many ways, a shot in the dark. It was also the only chance Peter Novak had.

Honwana opened the hatch at the altitude they had agreed upon: twenty thousand feet. At that altitude, the air would be frigid, perhaps thirty below zero. But exposure to those temperatures would be relatively brief. Goggles, gloves, and the tight-fitting swimming-cap-like helmets they wore would help, as would their nylon flight suits.

It was another reason they wanted to release off the water, more than a lateral mile from the Stone Palace. As they descended, they would want to be able to discard items like the rip-cord handle and their gloves, and to do so with the assurance that these items would not come raining down over their target like so many warning leaflets.

The high-altitude release would also give them more time to maneuver themselves into position—or to get themselves hopelessly out of position. Without physical rehearsal, it was impossible to know whether this was the right decision. But a decision had to be made, and Janson made it.

"OK," Janson said, standing before the open hatch. "Just remember. This isn't exactly going to be a hop-and-pop. Time to play follow-the-leader."

"No fair," Katsaris said. "You always get to go first."

"Age before beauty," Janson grunted as he made his way down the four-foot aluminum ramp.

Then he leaped out into the inky skies.

# CHAPTER FIVE

Blasted by the aircraft's powerful slipstream, whipsawed by icy crosscurrents, Janson struggled to keep his limbs properly aligned. *Free fall*, it was called, and yet it did not feel like falling. Surrendering to gravity, he felt perfectly still—felt himself to be immobile in the face of powerful, loudly whistling winds. Moreover, free fall, in this case, would have to be anything but free. Four miles below him was a heaving ocean. If he were to achieve the necessary trajectory, almost every second of his fall would have to be carefully controlled. If the next two minutes did not go as planned, the mission would be over before it had begun.

Yet the turbulence made control difficult.

Almost immediately, he found himself buffeted by the wind, and then he began to spin, slowly at first and then faster. *Dammit!* He was overcome by paralyzing vertigo and a growing sense of disorientation. A deadly combination at this altitude.

Facedown, he arched hard, spreading out his arms and legs. His body stopped spinning, and the vertigo abated. But how much time had elapsed?

In ordinary free fall, terminal velocity was reached at about 110 miles per hour. Now that he had stabilized, he needed to slow the descent as much as possible. He moved into spider position, keeping his limbs spread out and rounding his spine into a *C.* All the while, the freezing winds, seemingly angered by his efforts to harness them, whipped at his rig, equipment, and clothing and burrowed behind his goggles and flight cap. His gloved fingers felt as if they had been injected with Novocain. Slowly, he moved his right wrist toward his face, and he peered through his goggles at the large, luminous displays of the altimeter and the GPS unit.

It was high-school math. He had to make it to the drop zone within the forty seconds that remained. An inertial fiber gyroscope would tell him if he was moving in the right direction; it would be less help in figuring out how to correct his course.

He craned his head to see where Katsaris was.

There was no sign of him. That was not a surprise. What was the visibility, anyway? Was Katsaris five hundred feet away from him? Fifty? A hundred? A thousand?

It was not an idle question: two men hurtling blindly through a dark cloud could collide, fatally. The odds were against such a collision. But then the whole operation itself was in defiance of any rational calculation of the odds.

If, at the end of the jump, they were off the destination point by a mere twenty feet, the result could be disastrous. And the same cloud cover that conferred invisibility also made a precision landing immeasurably more difficult. Normally, a paratrooper would land on a well-marked DZ—tracer flares were standard practice—using his vision as he tried to direct himself with the rig toggles. To an experienced sky diver, this became a matter of instinct. But those instincts would be little help in this case. By the time they were close enough to the ground to see much of anything, it could very well be too late. Instead of instinct, they would be forced to rely upon global positioning system devices strapped to their cuffs and, in effect, play an electronic game of Marco Polo.

*Thirty-five seconds.* The window was closing: he had to get into delta position as soon as possible.

Janson swept his arms back and steered himself with his shoulders and hands. No good: a walloping, gale-level crosscurrent struck Janson and pulled him into an overly steep flight path. He immediately realized what had gone wrong. He was consuming altitude swiftly. Too swiftly.

Could anything be done about it?

His only chance was to increase his drag. Yet he had to progress toward the compound as fast as possible if he had any chance of reaching it. To do both would be impossible.

Had he destroyed the mission only seconds into it?

*It could not be.*

But it could.

Lashed by icy winds, Janson found the quiet commands of expertise competing with a din of internal recrimination. *You knew this wouldn't work; it couldn't work. Too many unknowns, too many uncontrollable variables. Why did you accept the mission in the first place? Pride? Pride in your professionalism? Pride was the enemy of professionalism: Alan Demarest had always said so, and here he spoke the truth. Pride gets you killed. There never was a reasonable chance of success. No sane person or responsible military branch would accept it. That's why they turned to you.*

A quieter voice penetrated the din. *Max track.*

He had to move into track position. It was his own voice he heard, from decades back, when he was training new recruits to a special SEAL team. *Maximum track.*

Could he do it? He had not attempted the maneuver in many years. And he had certainly never tracked on a GPS-directed jump. Tracking meant turning one's body into an airfoil, with the humped profile of an airplane's wing, so that one actually acquired some lift. For several seconds, Janson accelerated, with his head down and his limbs spread out slightly. He bent his arms and waist slightly, and rolled his shoulders forward, as if preparing to kowtow; he cupped his hands. Finally, he pulled his head back as he put his legs together, pointing his toes like a ballet dancer.

Nothing happened. He was not tracking.

It took ten seconds of acceleration before he experienced a sense of lift and noticed that his dive was beginning to flatten. In a max track, a human being should be able to reach an angle of descent that was close to forty-five degrees from vertical.

In theory.

In max track, it should be possible to move as rapidly horizontally as one was moving vertically—so that every yard downward took one almost a yard forward, closer to the drop zone.

In theory.

In reality, he was an equipment-laden commando who, beneath his flight suit, had forty pounds of gear hooked to his combat vest. In reality, he was a forty-nine-year-old man whose joints were stiffening in the sub-zero air that blasted its way through his flight suit. A max track required him to maintain perfect form, and it was not clear how long his skeletal muscles would permit him to do so.

In reality, every glimpse he took at his altimeter and GPS unit violated that perfect form he was depending on. And yet without them he was truly flying blind.

He cleared his mind, swept from it all anxieties; for the time being, he would have to be a machine, an automaton, devoted to nothing other than the execution of a flight trajectory.

He stole another glance at his wrist-worn instruments.

He was heading off course, he saw from the blinking of the GPS device. How far off course? Four degrees, maybe five. He angled both hands in parallel, at forty-five degrees, slightly deforming the cushion of air that surrounded him, and was rewarded with a slow turn.

The GPS device stopped blinking, and he felt suffused with a heedless, unthinking sense of hope.

He was tracking, soaring through the inky skies, an air cushion conserving his altitude as he tracked toward his destination. He was black, the sky was black, he was at one with the currents. The wind was in his face, but it was also keeping him aloft, like the hand of an angel. He was alive.

A vibration at his wrist. The altimeter alarm.

A warning that he was reaching the vertical point of no return—the height below which the only sure thing was death on impact. The manuals put it in less dramatic words: they referred to the "minimum altitude for parachute deployment." A high-altitude, low-opening jump established only the rough parameters: if the opening was too low, the ground would hit him like a tractor-trailer in the passing lane of the autobahn.

And yet he was farther away from the DZ than he'd planned to be at this point. He had imagined that he would be in the immediate vicinity of the compound when he opened the chute. For one thing, the difficulties in maneuvering amid shifting currents were immensely greater with an open canopy. For another, slowly drifting downward over the Stone Palace brought with it a greater danger of detection. A man plummeting at 160 miles per hour was harder to see than a man slowly drifting beneath a large rectangular parachute.

There were risks either way. He had to make a decision. Now.

He craned his head around, trying to see something, anything, in the thick blackness. What he felt was, in free flight, an entirely unaccustomed sensation: claustrophobia.

And that decided him: there would be fog. He and his black canopy would not stand out against the starless night. He arched himself into a vertical position, reached for the rip-cord handle, and tugged. There was a brief flutter as the tightly packed chute spread itself in the air and the lines stretched out fully. He felt the familiar jolt, the sense of being gripped at his shoulders and seat. And the noise of the wind ceased, as if a MUTE button had been pressed.

He tossed the rip-cord handle away and peered up to make sure the black nylon canopy was properly flared. He himself had a difficult time making out its outlines in the night sky, just fifteen feet above him. On another occasion, that might have been unsettling; tonight it was reassuring.

Abruptly, he felt himself pushed sideways by another gusting crosscurrent, and there was something almost corporeal about the sensation, as though he were being tackled. He would have to control the rig carefully; if he oversteered, it would be nearly impossible to return to the DZ. He was also acutely conscious of the trade-off between steering and speed: the canopy was at its top forward speed when the steering lines were up all the way and undeployed.

Now his GPS indicator showed that he had drifted significantly off course.

*Oh Christ, no!*

Even as he floundered in the turbulent air, he as well as Katsaris knew that what lay ahead would be even more difficult: they would have to make a silent, unobserved landing in an enclosed courtyard. An error made by either of them would imperil them both. And even if they executed their task flawlessly, any one of a thousand unpredictable complications could be lethal. If a soldier happened to be in the vicinity of the central courtyard—and no law ordained otherwise—they would be dead. The mission would be aborted. And, in all likelihood, the object of the mission would be summarily killed. That much was standard operating procedure for their terrorist friends. One responded to an in-progress rescue mission by destroying the object of rescue—posthaste.

Now he pulled his right steering line down far and fast. He would need to make a fast turn, before another gust sent him beyond the point of recovery. The effect of the pull was almost instantaneous: he found himself swinging out from under the canopy, arcing wildly. And the large, round altimeter told him what he could feel: that his speed of descent had just increased considerably.

Not good. He was closer to the ground than he should be. Still, he had to assume that he had returned to the proper angle of flight, and he raised the steering lines again, allowing the canopy to yawn out to its full 250 square feet and maximize its vertical drag. He was adept at maneuvering around wind cones, but the very unpredictability of the air currents made ordinary calculations irrelevant. All he knew was that he was off the wind line; crabbing across it was the only way to return to it. As he had done hundreds of times before, he fidgeted with the toggles to establish the direction of the prevalent winds; finally, he found that he was able to make gentle S-turns astride the wind line, holding and running every time he drifted off it. The process required complete concentration, especially because the sea was sending up thermals at random, or so it seemed. The Anuran sky was like a horse that did not want to be broken.

His pulse quickened. Like the mast of a ghost ship, battlements and embrasures were becoming visible through the fog, the ancient white limestone reflecting the faintest light seeping through the cloud cover. The vista came as something of a shock; it was the first thing he had seen since the jump. Quickly, he cast off his gloves and flight cap. Now he mentally rehearsed the landing maneuver. Crosswind leg. Downwind leg. Base leg. Final approach.

To minimize landing velocity, it was crucial to approach the destination from upwind. The crosswind jaunt took him a thousand feet to the right. Then he drifted downwind for another five hundred feet, deliberately overshooting the target. He would be traveling 250 feet into the wind for the final approach. It was an elaborate but necessary maneuver. He could slow his forward movement by pulling in the corners of the canopy with both toggles, but the effect would be to increase his rate of descent to an unacceptable speed. He would therefore have to rely upon the wind itself to reduce his horizontal velocity.

He prayed that no sudden turn would be necessary to position himself over the central region of the courtyard, for a fast turn, too, would dangerously hasten his descent. The last fifteen seconds had to be perfect. There was no margin for error; the compound's high walls made a low, shallow approach impossible.

He was suddenly aware how hot and moist the air was—it was as if he had moved from a meat locker into a steam bath. Water was actually condensing on his chilly extremities. His fingers were wet as he reached for the toggles, and he felt a pang of adrenaline; he could not afford for them to slip.

With the toggles fully up and the canopy therefore fully extended, he glided toward the center of the courtyard, which was visible to him only as a play of black hues. As soon as his hands were free, he deactivated his wrist instruments, lest their glow give his presence away.

His heart started to beat hard: he was almost there—if he could only manage, with his wet, slick fingers, the final landing fall.

Choosing the right second was crucial. Now? His boots were fifteen feet above the ground; he could tell because the ground and the canopy seemed just about the same distance from him. No. Even within the walls of the compound, the gusts were too unpredictable. He would wait until he was half that distance from the ground.

*Now.*

He brought both toggles down to shoulder level, and then, in one fluid motion, he turned down his wrists and pulled the toggles down between his thighs, bringing his forward motion to a complete stop. As he sank down the remaining few feet, he tensed his leg muscles and rotated his body in the direction of the fall, bending his knees slightly. Two seconds before he hit the ground, he had to decide whether to make a soft-roll landing—knees and feet together—or try for an upright landing, which meant keeping them apart. In for a penny, in for a pound: he'd go for a standing touchdown.

Keeping his leg muscles flexed, he sank to the ground on the soles of his boots. The soft rubber was designed for silence, and it performed as it was meant to. Soundlessly, he bounced on the balls of his feet, preparing to fall. But he did not.

He was standing. On the ground of the courtyard.

He had made it.

He looked around him, and, in the starless night, he could just make out the contours of a vast deserted courtyard, three times as long as it was wide. A large white structure—the old fountain, as the blueprints had specified—loomed several yards away. He was almost exactly in the center of an area that was approximately the size of half a football field and that was eerily quiet. There was, he confirmed, no sign of movement—no sign that his arrival had been observed.

Now he unhooked his rig, removed his flight suit, and quickly gathered the canopy from the cobblestoned courtyard. It would have to be hidden before further action could be taken. Even a starless night was not wholly devoid of illumination. The black nylon, visually protective against the night sky, contrasted with the light gray cobblestone. It couldn't be allowed to lie on the ground.

But where was Katsaris?

Janson looked around. Had Katsaris overshot the courtyard? Landed on the beach, far below? Or on the hard-packed gravel road that led to the compound? Either mistake could be lethal—to him and to the others involved in the mission.

*Dammit!* Once again, a small fist of fury and fear gathered strength within him. It was the hubris of the planner that he—he, of all people—had succumbed to: the desk jockey's error of thinking that what worked on paper would mesh with tactical reality. The tolerances were too small. Every member of the team knew it; the men were simply too much in awe of his record to drive the point home. The jump required something close to perfection, and perfection wasn't possible in this fallen world.

Janson felt a surge of frustration: who knew that better than he did? It was sheer luck that he himself had made it this far.

His thoughts were interrupted by a faint rustle—the sound of the cells of a nylon canopy gently collapsing overhead. Janson looked up into the black sky. It was Katsaris, floating down slowly, as he flared his chute and landed with a gentle, noiseless roll. He scrambled to his feet and came toward Janson.

Now there were two of them.

Two of them. Two highly experienced, highly skilled operatives.

And now they were in place—in the middle of the Stone Palace courtyard. The last place, he had to believe, where anyone would expect visitors.

There were two of them—against an entire battalion of armed guerrillas.

Still, it was a start.

# CHAPTER SIX

Now Janson activated the communication system and *tsked* into the fila-ment microphone near his mouth, a click and sibilant. Military protocol.

Katsaris followed his lead: he silently removed his flight suit, then gath-ered the canopy into a tight bundle.

The two of them packed the nylon fabric of canopy and suit into the dank basin of the grand stone fountain that stood in the center of the courtyard. Once an impressive feat of sculpture—its marble was finely incised—it now gathered rainwater and algae. A light-absorbing scum adhered to the sides of the wide, circular pool like a black liner. It would do. Black on black: the protective coloration of the night.

Janson's hands groped over his vest and fatigues, his fingers identifying the key items of equipment. Katsaris, standing nearby, was doing the same; each visually inspected the other's camouflage and gear, standard proce-dure for such operations. They had each traveled a long distance in turbulent conditions. A lot could happen in that time. Punched by the slipstream, whipped by crosswinds, a paratrooper could arrive without his full complement of equipment, however securely it had been attached to his combat vest and fatigues. Janson had learned that from his SEAL days; Katsaris had learned it from him.

Janson surveyed his partner. The whites of his eyes were the only bea-cons from his painted face. Then he saw a patch of pale over his right shoulder. Katsaris's shirt had been torn during his landing roll, revealing light skin. Janson signaled him to stand still while he pulled out a few inches of black electrical tape from a spool in his fatigues. He taped the seams together, and the light patch disappeared. *Tailoring in the drop zone,* Janson thought to himself.

And yet such details could make all the difference. Their black garb would help them disappear into the shadows of a deeply shadowed court-yard. By the same token, even a few inches of silvery flesh could spell betrayal in the carelessly roving beam of a guard's flashlight.

As he had emphasized on Katchall, the rebels would not have high-tech perimeter defenses, but they would have defenses of a sort that technology had not yet equaled: the five senses of vigilant human beings. An ability to detect anomalies in the visual, aural, and olfactory fields that surpassed the capabilities of any computer.

The descent had largely been through subzero winds. But on the ground, even at four o'clock in the morning, it was eighty-five degrees and humid. Janson could feel himself starting to sweat—real sweat, not condensation from the atmosphere—and he knew that in time his body's own smell could betray him. His dermal proteins, those of a meat-eating Westerner, would be alien to the Anurans, who subsisted largely on vegetables and fish curries. He'd have to trust that the salt breezes would whisk away any olfactory signals of his presence.

Janson unhooked his night-vision glasses from his combat vest and raised them to his eyes; the large courtyard was suddenly bathed in a soft green glow. He made sure that the black rubber ocular cups were pressed firmly against his face before he dialed up the image luminosity: any light spilling from the NV scope could alert a watchful sentry. He had once seen a member of a commando team killed by a patrol who had caught the telltale glint of green and fired almost blindly. Indeed, he had once seen a man perish because of an illuminated watch dial.

Now he and Katsaris stood back-to-back, each conducting an NV sweep of the opposite quadrants.

On the north side of the courtyard were three orange phosphorescent blobs, two leaning toward each other—a sudden white flare emerging between their spectral forms. Janson depowered the scope before lowering it to view the scene with his naked eyes. Even from twenty yards away, he could clearly see the flickering flame. A match had been struck—an old-fashioned fireplace match, it appeared—and two of the guards were lighting their cigarettes with it.

*Amateurs,* Janson thought. A guard on duty should never provide incidental illumination and should never encumber his most important weapon, his hands.

But then who were these people? There was a vast gap between the Caliph with his top strategists, trained by terror cells in the Middle East, and their followers, typically recruited from villages filled with illiterate peasants.

There *would* be highly trained sentinels and soldiers in place. But their attention would be directed toward the outside world. They would be at the battlements and in the watchtowers. The ones stationed along the inner courtyard would be charged with the relatively trivial chores of internal discipline, making sure that no ganja-fueled carousing disturbed the sleep of the Caliph or the members of his command.

Though they stood only a few feet away from each other, Katsaris whispered into his filament microphone, his voice amplified in Janson's earpiece: "One sentry. Southeast corner. Seated." A beat. "Probably half asleep."

Janson replied in a subwhisper, "Three sentries. The north veranda. Very much awake."

In a hostage exfiltration, as neither had to be reminded, one went where the guards were. Unless an ambush had been laid: the visible guards in one place, the valuables in another, and a further set of guards in wait. Yet there was no room for doubt in this case. The blueprints made it clear that the dungeon was located beneath the northern face of the courtyard.

Janson moved slowly to his left, along the wall, and then beneath the overhang of the western veranda, walking half-crouched beneath the parapet. They could not be overreliant on the darkness: a rod in the human retina could be activated by a single photon. Even in the blackest night, there were shadows. Janson and Katsaris would stay in those shadows as long as possible: they would move along the sides of the courtyard, avoiding the center.

Now, for a few moments, Janson kept perfectly still, not even breathing: just listening. There was the distant, soft roar of the sea, washing at the base of the promontory. A few bird noises—a cormorant, perhaps—and, from the forests to the south, the scraping and buzzing of tropical insects. This was the aural baseline of the night, and they would do well to be aware of it. It was impossible to move with absolute silence: fabric slid against fabric, nylon fibers stretched and contracted around a person's moving limbs. Soles, even those of thick, soft rubber, registered their impact on the ground; the hard shells of a dead beetle or cicada would crunch with a footfall. The night's acoustic tapestry would conceal some noises but not others.

He listened for sounds of Katsaris's movement, straining harder than any sentry would, and heard nothing. Would *he* be as successful in maintaining silence?

Ten feet, then twenty feet, along the wall. There was a scraping sound, then the burst of a tiny combustion: the third guard was lighting up.

Janson was near enough to watch the motion: a thick, self-lighting match struck against brick, its candlelike flame held under what looked like a thin cigarillo. After twenty seconds, the tobacco smell wafted toward him—it was indeed a cigarillo—and Janson relaxed a little. The flare of the match would constrict the sentries' irises, temporarily reducing their visual acuity. The tobacco smoke would render their noses all but useless. And the activity of smoking would compromise their ability to respond, in an encounter where a split second was the difference between life and death.

He was now fifteen feet away from the northern veranda. He took in the rusticated limestone and wrought-iron grille. The terra-cotta mission roof tiles were a late addition and sat oddly on a structure that had been built and rebuilt over centuries. Four stories; the grand rooms on the second floor, where the leaded glass, hood moldings, and arched transoms suggested the transformation of a Portuguese fortress into what a Dutch overlord pretentiously dubbed his "palace." Most of the windows were dark; dim hallway lights seeped through some of them. And where was the Caliph, the architect of death, sleeping tonight? Janson had a pretty good guess.

It would be so easy. A fragmentation grenade, lobbed through the leaded glass. A stinger missile, blasting into the bedroom. And Ahmad Tabari would be dead. No more would remain of his corporeal existence than remained of Helene's. He batted the thought away. It was a fantasy merely, and one he could not afford to indulge. It was inconsistent with the mission objective. Peter Novak was a great man. Not only did Janson owe him his life, but the world might owe him its future survival. The moral and strategic calculus was incontrovertible: the preservation of a great man had to take precedence over the destruction of an evil one.

Janson lowered his gaze from the governor's suite to the northern veranda.

Fifteen feet away from the nearest sentry, he could see the men's faces. Broad, peasant faces, unwary and unsophisticated. Younger than he had expected. But then, the forty-nine-year-old operative reflected, these men would not have looked young to him for most of his career as a field agent. They were older than he was when he was running raids behind the Green Line near Cambodia. Older than he was when he killed for the first time, and when he first escaped being killed.

Their hands were visibly chafed, but no doubt from farmwork rather than martial arts. *Amateurs,* yes, he mused again; but it was not a wholly reassuring thought. The KLF was too well organized to have entrusted so valuable a treasure to the protection of such men as these. They were a first line of defense only. A first line of defense where, logically, no defense at all would have been called for.

And where was Katsaris?

Janson peered across the courtyard, across sixty feet of darkness, and could make out nothing. Katsaris was invisible. Or gone.

He made a quiet *tsk* into the filament mike, trying to modify the sound to echo the insect and avian noises of the night.

He heard an answering *tsk* in his earpiece. Katsaris was there, in place, ready.

The accuracy of his first determination would be crucial: Was it safe to take out these men? Were the men themselves decoys—birds on a wire?

*Was* there a wire?

Janson raised himself from his crouch, peered into the windows behind the iron grille. Perspiration lay on him like a film of mud; the humidity of the air prevented evaporation. Now he envied Katsaris the procholinergic. The perspiration wasn't cooling him; it just adhered to his skin, an unwanted layer of clothing.

At the same time, it concerned him that he was even conscious of such incidentals. He had to focus: *Was there a wire?*

He looked through the NV scope, angling it toward the iron grille behind the smoking peasants. Nothing.

No, *something*. An orange spot, too small to correspond to a body. In all likelihood, it was a hand belonging to a body concealed behind a stone wall.

The men on the veranda, it was a reasonable surmise, were unaware that they had backup; it would have diminished their already doubtful efficacy. But they did.

Did the backup have backup? Had a sequential operation been designed?

Improbable. Not impossible.

From a long thigh pocket, Janson withdrew a blackened aluminum tube, thirteen inches in length, four inches in diameter. Inside, it was lined with a snug steel mesh, which prevented the living creature within from making noise. An atmosphere of 90 percent pure oxygen prevented asphyxiation during the operation schedule.

The time had come for noise, for distraction.

He unscrewed one sealed end, the Teflon-coated grooves moving soundlessly over each other.

By its long, naked tail, he removed the rodent and flung it toward the veranda in a high parabola. It landed as if, in its nocturnal travels, it had lost its purchase and dropped off the roof.

Its glossy black pelt was now standing on end, and the creature made its telltale piglike grunts. The sentries had a visitor, and within four seconds they knew it. The short head, wide muzzle, scaly, hairless tail. One foot long, two and a half pounds. A bandicoot rat. *Bandicota bengalensis* was its formal name. Quite literally, Ahmad Tabari's bête noire.

In their Dravidian tongue, the Kagama guards broke out into short, hushed, frantic exchanges.

"*Ayaiyo, ange paaru, adhu yenna theridhaa?*"

"*Aiyo, perichaali!*"

"*Adha yepadiyaavadhu ozrikkanum.*"

"*Andha vittaa, naama sethom.*"

"*Anga podhu paaru.*"

The animal scurried toward an entryway, following its instincts, while the guards, following theirs, tried to stop it. The temptation was to fire a weapon at the giant rodent, but that would awaken everyone in the compound and make them look foolish. Worse, it could draw attention to a failure, and a crucial one. If the Beloved One, asleep in the governor's suite, were to come across this harbinger of death in his living quarters, there was no telling how he would react. He might, in a black terror, enact its prophecy himself by ordering the death of the sentries who had permitted its entry. They knew what had happened last time.

The consternation had, as Janson had hoped, brought out the others— the second team. How many? Three—no, four.

The members of the second team were armed with American M16s, probably Vietnam-era. They were standard infantry issue during Vietnam, and the NVA collected them by the thousands after the South fell. From there, the M16 entered the international market and became the standard semi-automatic of less-than-well-funded guerrilla movements everywhere—the kind that bought on the installment plan, that scrimped and saved and never splurged on nonessentials. Christmas Club warriors. The M16 would fire short, buzz-saw bursts, seldom jammed, and, with a minimum of maintenance, was reasonably rust-resistant, even in humid climes. Janson respected the weapon; he respected all weapons. But he also knew that they would not be fired unnecessarily. Soldiers in proximity to a resting leadership did not make loud noises at four in the morning without good cause.

Janson withdrew a second bandicoot rat, an even larger one, and, as it writhed and squirmed in his gloved hands, pressed into its belly a tiny hypodermic filled with d-amphetamine. It would produce hyperactivity, thus making the rat even bolder and faster than the other one and, in the eyes of the sentries, even more of a menace.

A low, underhand toss. Its small, sharp claws grabbing at thin air, the rat landed on the head of one of the peasant sentries—who let out a brief but piercing scream.

It was more attention than Janson had been aiming for.

Had he overshot the mark? If the scream drew soldiers who were not assigned to the north wing, the exercise would prove self-defeating. So far there was no sign of that, although the guards who were already present were plainly agitated. Moving his head to the edge of the berm line, he watched the quiet confusion and dismay that had swept through the northern veranda. His destination was the space beneath that veranda, and there was no covered route to it, for the stone walkways that projected from the long east and west walls of the compound stopped fifteen feet before they reached the wall opposite.

That the guards were sitting in the light, whereas he and Katsaris would be in the dark, offered some protection, but not enough: the human visual field was sensitive to motion, and some of the interior light spilled onto the cobbled ground in front of the northern veranda. The mission required absolute stealth: however well trained and equipped, two men could not hold off the hundred or so guerrillas who were housed in the Stone Palace barracks. Detection was death. It was that simple.

Thirty feet away and six feet up, an older man, his leathery brown skin deeply creased, appeared on the veranda, enjoining silence. Silence: so as not to wake the sleeping commanders, who had taken residence in the palace as its proper and rightful inhabitants. As Janson focused on the older man, however, his unease grew. The man spoke of silence, but his face told Janson that it was not his sole, or even primary, concern. Only a larger sense of suspicion could explain the squinted, searching eyes; the fact that his focus moved quickly from the panicked sentries to the shadowy courtyard beyond him, and then to the iron-grilled windows above him. His darting gaze showed that he understood the peculiarities of nighttime vision: the way peripheral vision became more acute than direct vision, the way a direct stare transfigured shapes according to the imagination. At night, observant eyes never stopped moving; the brain could assemble an image from the flickering outlines they collected.

As Janson regarded the man's creased face, he made some other quick
inferences. This was an intelligent, wary man, disinclined to take the incident at face value. From the way the other men deferred to him, his
position of seniority was obvious. Another sign of it was the very weapon
cradled in a sling around his shoulders: a Russian KLIN. A commonplace
weapon, but a smaller and slightly more expensive make than the M16s.
The KLIN was more reliable for tight-cluster shooting, as opposed to the
raking fire to be expected from the relatively untrained.

The others would take their lead from him.

Janson watched him for a few more moments, saw him talking quietly
in Kagama, gesturing toward the darkened courtyard, excoriating a sentry
who had been smoking. This man was *not* an amateur.

Detection was death. Had they been detected?

He had to make the contrary assumption. *The contrary assumption:*
What would Lieutenant Commander Alan Demarest have made of such
reasoning, of the hopeful stipulation that the world would conform to
one's operational imperatives, rather than confound them? But Demarest
was dead—had died before a firing squad—and, if there was any justice
in the universe, was rotting in hell. At four o'clock on a sweltering Anuran
morning, in the courtyard of the Stone Palace, surrounded by heavily
armed terrorists, there was no advantage in calculating the operation's
chances of success. Its tenets were, had to be, nearly theological. *Credo
quia absurdum.* I believe because it is absurd.

And the older man with the creased face: What did he believe? He was
the one to take out first. But had enough time passed? By now, word of
the small commotion would have been spread among those on duty. It
was crucial that an explanation for it—the appearance of the accursed
bandicoot—had spread as well. Because there would be other noises. That
was inevitable. Noises that had an explanation were innocuous. Noises
that lacked an explanation would prompt further investigation, and could
be deadly.

Janson withdrew the Blo-Jector, a twenty-inch pipe of anodized aluminum, from a dangle pouch on his black fatigues. Pockets and pouches
had presented an operational challenge. They could not afford the ripping
sound of Velcro, the clicking noise of a metal snap, so he had replaced
such fasteners with a soundless contrivance. A pair of magnetic strips,
sealed within soft woolen cladding, did the job: the magnets would keep
the flaps shut tightly, yet would release and engage soundlessly.

Janson whispered his plan into his lip mike. He would take the tall man and the guard to his right; Katsaris should aim for the others. Janson now raised the rubber mouthpiece of the blowpipe to his lips, sighting over the end of the tube. The dart was of covert-ops design, a fine, 33-gauge needle and bolus housed within an acrylic-and-Mylar replica of a wasp. The artificial insect would withstand no more than a casual inspection, but if things went right, a casual inspection was all it would receive. He puffed hard into the mouthpiece, then quickly inserted another dart, and discharged it. He returned to his crouching position.

The tall man grabbed at his neck, pulled out the dart, and peered at it in the dim light. Had he removed it before it had injected its bolus? The object had visual and tactile resemblances to a large stinging insect: the stiff exoskeleton, the striped body. But its weight would be wrong, particularly if it still contained the incapacitant fluid, one milliliter of carfentanil citrate. The man with the creased face stared at it furiously, and then he looked directly at Janson. Focusing intently, he had evidently made out his form in the shadowed corner.

The soldier's hand reached for a revolver, holstered on his side—and then he toppled forward off the veranda. Janson could hear the thud of his body hitting the cobblestones six feet below him. Two other sentries slid to the ground, losing consciousness.

A jabbering exchange broke out between two of the younger guards, to his far left. They knew something was wrong. Hadn't Katsaris hit them yet?

The use of the incapacitant was not simply an attempt to be humane. Few human beings had experience with a carfentanil dart; there was a ten-second window when they would assume they had been stung by an insect. By contrast, there was nothing mysterious about gunfire: if a silenced shot didn't cause instant unconsciousness—if it failed to penetrate the midbrain region—the victim would pierce the night with his yells, sounding the alarm for everyone to hear. In stealthy, close-up encounters, garroting would do, choking off air as it did blood, but that was not an option here. If the blow darts were a risky approach, tactical optimization was not about choosing the best possible approach; it was about choosing the best one available.

Janson aimed his blowpipe toward the jabbering two guards and was preparing to send off another dart when the two woozily collapsed; Katsaris had hit them after all.

Silence returned, softened only by the cawing of magpies and gulls, the buzzing and scraping of cicadas and beetles. It *sounded* right. It sounded as if the problem had been dealt with, and the men had returned to watchful waiting.

Yet the safety they had just gained for themselves could vanish at any moment. The information they had distilled from intercepts and sat imagery suggested that the next shift would not arrive for another hour— but there was no guarantee that the schedule had not changed. Every minute was now of immense value.

Janson and Katsaris made a dash for the darkness beneath the northern veranda, sliding between the stout piers that supported it at three-foot intervals. According to the blueprints, the circular stone lid was at the midpoint of the northern wall, just abutting the limestone of the main structure. Blindly, Janson felt along the ground, his hands moving along the rubblework foundations where ground and building met. Suddenly, he felt something poking at his hand, then sliding over it, like a taut rubber hose. He jerked back. He had disturbed a snake. Most varieties on the island were harmless, but the poisonous ones—including the sawscaled viper and the Anuran krait—happened to be quite common. He pulled a combat knife from his fatigues and whipped it in the direction where the snake had been probing him. The knife encountered midair resistance—it had hit something—and he brought it down silently to the stone wall. Something sinewy and dense gave way before the razor-sharp blade.

"I *found* it," Theo whispered, from a few feet away.

Janson turned on a small infrared flashlight and strapped on his nightvision scope, adjusting it from starlight mode to IR mode.

Theo was crouching before a large stone disk. The grotto under their feet had been used for any number of purposes over the years. The storage of prisoners was a principal one. At other points in time, it had been used for the storage of inanimate objects, ranging from foodstuffs to ammunition, and beneath the heavy circular masonry was a vertical passageway that was made to serve as a chute. The lid had been designed to be removed easily, but the passage of years had a way of complicating matters. That it could be removed at all would be sufficient.

The lid was fashioned with handholds on either side. Theo pulled on one, using his powerful legs as he tried to lift the flat round stone. Nothing. The only sound was his stifled grunt.

Now Janson joined him, crouching on the opposite side, placing both his hands on the slot that had been designed for that purpose. Bracing himself with his legs, he flexed his arms as hard as he could. He could hear Theo letting his breath out slowly as he strained himself to the utmost.

Nothing.

"Twist it," Janson whispered.

"It's not a jar of olives," Theo said, but he repositioned himself accordingly. He braced himself with his legs against the perpendicular wall and, locking his hands around the slotted flange, pushed at the lid. On the other side, Janson pulled it in the same clockwise direction.

And there was movement at last: the abrasive grinding of stone on stone, faint but unmistakable. Janson realized what they had encountered. The circular bed where the lid had been seated was made of some sort of fired clay, and over the years, as the limestone had eroded in the tropical moisture, the amalgamated debris from each substance had formed a natural mortar. The lid had, in effect, been cemented in place. Now that the bonds had been broken, the task would be manageable.

He and Theo crouched over the lid again, as before, and lifted in one coordinated movement. The lid was eight inches thick and immensely heavy, meant to be moved by four strong men, not two. But it could be done. Using all their strength, they eased it up and placed it gently on the ground to one side.

Janson peered down into the hole they had uncovered. Just under the lid there was a grate. And through it, he heard a welter of voices drifting up from the subterranean space.

Indistinct, yes, but untroubled as well. Most of what a voice conveyed—anger, fear, merriment, scorn, anxiety—was through *tone*. Words as such were so much garlanding, designed to mislead as often as not. Much interrogation training had to do with learning to hear *through* words to the characteristics of sheer vocality. The sounds that drifted up were not those of any prisoner—Janson knew that much. And if you were stationed in the dungeon area and were not a prisoner, you were guarding the prisoner. These were the guards. These were their immediate enemy.

Lying flat on the ground, Janson placed his head directly above the grate. The subterranean air was cool on his face, and he became conscious of the smell of cigarettes. At first the sounds were like a babbling brook, but now he could separate them into the voices of several different men. How many? He was not sure yet. Nor could one assume that the number of speakers was the number of men.

The chute, they knew, descended through several feet of stone, angled at forty-five degrees for most of the way, then bending and funneling down more shallowly. Though a dim light filtered upward through the grate, nothing could be seen directly.

Katsaris handed Janson the fiber-optic camera kit, which looked like a makeup compact with a long cord attached. Janson, crouching with his back against the rough-carved limestone, threaded the cord down through the grate, inch by inch, taking care not to overshoot the mark. It was the thickness of an ordinary phone wire and had a tip hardly bigger than a match head. Within the cable ran a double-layered glass strand that would transmit images to a three-by-five-inch screen at the other end. Janson kept an eye on the small active-matrix display as he slowly fed the cord down the grate. If anyone down there noticed it and recognized what it was, the mission was over. The screen was suffused with gray hues, which grew lighter and lighter. Abruptly, it filled with a bird's-eye view of a dimly illuminated room. Janson pulled the cord up an inch. The view was now partly occluded, but most of the previous vista was still in the screen. The tip was probably a millimeter from the end of the chute, unlikely to be detected. After five seconds, the device's automatic focusing program brought the visual field into maximal sharpness and brightness.

"How many?" Katsaris asked.

"It's not good," Janson said.

"How many?"

Janson fingered a button that rotated the camera tip before he replied. "Seventeen guards. Armed to the teeth. But who's counting?"

"Shit," Katsaris replied.

"I'll second that," Janson grunted.

"If only there was a sight line, we could just hose the bastards."

"But there isn't."

"How about we drop a frag grenade down right now?"

"All you need is a single survivor, and the prisoner's dead," Janson said. "We've been over all this. Better get your ass over to Ingress A." Ingress A, as it was designated on the blueprints, was a long-disused entrance that would lead to the rear of the dungeon. It was a key part of the plan: while the prisoner was hustled into the bowels of the ancient compound, a silent white-phosphorous grenade would be dropped through the chute, incapacitating his guards.

"Roger that," Katsaris said. "If it's where it's supposed to be, I should be back in three minutes. I just hope you can get some sort of fix on them in the meantime."

"Hurry back," Janson said distractedly. He fine-tuned the image manually, rotating the camera tip occasionally for a new angle.

Through a blue haze of cigarette smoke, he saw that the men were sitting around two tables, playing cards. It was what soldiers did, God knew. Strong, armed men, with the power to make life-or-death decisions, would arm themselves against their most pressing enemy, time, with flimsy, laminated pieces of cardstock. He himself had played more card games while outfitted in combat fatigues than he cared to remember.

Janson studied the casual movements, the pickups and discards. He knew this game. He had played it for hours in the Mauritian jungle once. It was called proter, and was essentially the Indian Ocean's answer to rummy.

And because Janson knew the game, his gaze was drawn by a young man—eighteen, nineteen?—who sat at the larger table and drew glances from the others, half wary, half admiring.

The young man looked around, his acne-dotted cheeks gathering into a smile, revealing even white teeth and a sly look of victory.

Janson knew this game. Not just proter. He knew the game that the young man was playing: take maximum risk for maximum reward. That, after all, was the game they were both playing.

A bandolier of what looked like 7mm rounds was draped over the young man's shoulder; a Ruger Mini-14 was cradled in a sling around his chest. A heavier automatic weapon—Janson could not see enough to verify its make—was propped against his chair and was no doubt the reason for the bandolier. It was a complement of arms suggesting that the young man had some sort of position of leadership, in military as well as recreational matters.

Now the young man rubbed his knuckles against the blue rag tied around his crown and scooped up the entire pile.

Janson could hear a few shouts: card-game incredulity.

This was a bizarrely self-destructive move at this point of the game—unless, that is, a player was certain he could get rid of the cards at once. Such certainty required extraordinary powers of observation and retention.

The game came to a halt. Even the soldiers at the smaller second table crowded around to watch. Each had a rifle, Janson saw as the men stood, and at least one side arm. The equipment looked worn but well maintained.

The young man flipped down cards, one after another, in a string of flawless sequences. It was like the moment in a pool match when a master pockets ball after ball, appearing to play a private game. And when the young man had finished, he had no cards left. He tossed back his head and grinned. A thirteen-card set: evidently his comrades had never seen such a thing, because they burst into applause—anger at having been defeated giving way to admiration at the deftness with which the defeat had been managed.

A simple game. A Kagama guerrilla leader who was also a champion proter player. Would he be as agile with the machine gun by his chair?

Through the fiber-optic spyglass, Janson took in the intent look on the young man's face as another round of cards was dealt. He could tell who would win if the set was ever finished.

He could also tell that these were not simple farmers, but seasoned veterans. It was evident even from the way their weaponry hung on their combat garb. They knew what they were doing. If they found themselves under siege and had only seconds to regroup, any one of them would take out the prisoner. From intercepts he had seen, it was likely to be their standing instructions.

He zoomed in on the acned young man, then swiveled again. Here were seventeen seasoned warriors, at least one of whom had almost supernal powers of observation and retention.

"*We're fucked*": Katsaris on the lip mike, expressionless and to the point.

"I'll be right over," Janson said, retracting the camera by a few inches into the recesses of the chute. His gut clenched into a small, hard ball.

Janson stood up as far as the space allowed, his joints aching from the extended crouch. The truth was, he was too old for this sort of expedition, too old by at least a decade. Why had he chosen to play this role, the most dangerous and demanding of them? He'd told himself that he was the only one who would be willing to do it, to face the odds; or rather, if *he* was not willing to, nobody else would or should. He had told himself, as well, that his experience made him the best one for the job. He had told himself that having devised the plan, he would be the one best prepared to alter it if necessary. But was vanity involved, too? Did he want to prove to himself that he could still *do* it? Or was he so desperate to expunge a debt of honor to Peter Novak that he had made a decision that might ultimately endanger Novak's own life, as well as his own? Doubts came to his mind like a shower of needles, and he forced himself to remain calm. *Clear like water, cool like ice.* It was a mantra he had often repeated to himself during the long days and nights of terror and agony he'd known as a POW in Vietnam.

Katsaris was standing precisely where the blueprints had suggested they would find the second entrance—the entrance that made the entire operation possible.

"The thing is where it's supposed to be," Katsaris said. "You can see the outline of the trapdoor."

"That's good news. I like good news."

"It's been sealed off with cinder block."

"That's bad news. I hate bad news."

"Masonry's in sound shape. Probably not more than thirty years old. There might have been a problem with flooding at some point, and this was the fix. Who knows? All I know is that Ingress A no longer exists."

Janson's gut furled even tighter. *Clear like water, cool like ice.*

"Not a problem," Janson said. "There's a workaround."

But it *was* a problem, and he *had* no workaround. All he knew was that a commanding officer must never let his men sense panic.

They had entered into the situation with sketchy knowledge. There was the information, confirmed by intercepts, that Peter Novak was being held in the colonial dungeon. There was the inference, supplied by common sense, that he would be heavily guarded. There was the necessary recourse to an aerial insertion. But then? Janson had never entertained the idea of a merely frontal approach to the dungeon—running a gauntlet that would equally jeopardize the rescuer and the one to be rescued. What made the plan workable was the prospect of simultaneity: removing the hostage even as the guards were being incapacitated. There was no longer any viable rear entrance. Hence no viable plan.

"Come with me," Janson said. "I'll show you."

His mind raced as he and Katsaris returned to the cargo chute. There *was* something. The realization went from inchoate to merely murky, but something was better than nothing, hope better than no hope.

Manipulating the fiber-optic cuff, he shifted the field of vision away from the seated soldier and toward the worn staircase that rose up at the end of the room. "Stairway," he said. "Landing. Ductwork. Ledge." Projecting out from the midlevel landing was a shelf of poured concrete. "A relatively recent addition—the last few decades, I'd guess, done when the plumbing got modernized."

"Can't get there without being spotted."

"Not necessarily. The period of exposure—going from the landing to the concrete shelf—would be relatively brief, the room is filled with the haze of cigarette smoke, and they're all playing a pretty damn engrossing round of proter. You still get the principle of simultaneity. It's just that we're going to have to resort to the main entrance as well as the chute."

"This was your backup plan?" Katsaris shot back. "You're doing more improvising than the Miles Davis Quintet. Jesus, Paul, is this an operation or a jam session?"

"Theo?" It was a request for understanding.

"And what guarantee is there that there won't be a guard hived off, stationed in the dungeon with the prison?"

"Any close contact with Peter Novak is dangerous. The KLF knows that—they'll guard him, but they'll keep him isolated from any of the Kagama rebels."

"What are they afraid of—that he'll stab a guard with a cuff link?"

"His *words* are what they're afraid of, Theo. In a poor country, the words of a plutocrat are dangerous things—implements of escape more formidable than any hacksaw. That's why the guards are going to be grouped together, and at some distance from the prisoner. Let the prisoner have the opportunity to strike up a relationship with a single guard, and who knows what manipulations might occur? Remember, Theo, the per capita income in Anura is less than seven hundred dollars a year. Imagine a Kagama guard being drawn into conversation with a man worth tens of *billions*. You do the math. Everybody knows that Novak is a man of his word. Suppose you're a Kagama rebel, and he's telling you that he could make you and your family rich beyond the dreams of avarice. You're going to start to think about it—it's human nature. Ideological fervor might immunize some men against that temptation, the way it has with the Caliph. But nobody in command is going to count on it. BSTS— better safe than sorry. So you guard him, but you isolate him, too. It's the only safe way."

Unexpectedly, Katsaris smiled. "OK, boss, just give me my marching orders," he said. Both of them had moved to a place beyond fear; an odd Masada-like serenity had settled in, at least for the moment.

Removing the grate required them both, and the effort needed was doubled by the imperative that it be removed noiselessly. By the time Janson left Katsaris there, his joints and muscles were protesting furiously. He was creaky. That was the truth of it. The Beretta, in its thigh holster, seemed to dig into his flesh. Perspiration beaded up on his water-resistant face paint; rivulets fell into his eyes and burned. His muscular recovery, Janson was learning the hard way, was not what it once was: his muscles remained knotted longer—they ached when the last thing he needed to deal with was bodily pain. Years ago, in the midst of combat, he would feel as if he himself were a weapon, an operational automaton. Now he felt all too human. Sweat was beginning to cause the nylon combat suit to bind around his knees, crotch, underarms, elbows.

A humbling thought crossed his mind: Maybe *he* could have stayed by the chute, and let Katsaris do this part. Now he clambered up the rubblework supporting wall toward the narrow rectangular gap that would lead to the inside edge of the veranda. The rectangular space, one of several along the roofline, served to prevent water from pooling on the first floor during the heavy downpours of monsoon season. As he wriggled through the eighteen-inch-wide drainage port, he found that he was having difficulty breathing: Exertion? Fear? Katsaris had told him he'd come up with a good plan. He was, they both knew, lying. This wasn't a good plan. It was merely the only one they had.

His muscles still spasming, Janson made his way down a service corridor adjoining the stateroom of the north wing. He flashed on the blueprints: down the corridor to the left, twenty feet. The door would be at the end of the hallway. Discreet. Wood-clad stone. The unremarkable-looking door that led to an unspeakable pit. Two chairs to either side were empty. The men, having been summoned by the commotion, would be still unconscious at the foot of the veranda. The same was true of the backup pair of guards, who would have had a clear view of the hallway. Seven down. Seventeen to go.

Janson's pulse quickened as he stood before the door. The lock was many decades old, and more of a formality than anything. If an intruder had got this far, a lock on a door was unlikely to stop him. It was, as a quick inspection confirmed, a wafer tumbler lock, probably of mid-century design. Such locks, Janson knew, used flat rectangles of metal, not pins, and the springs were placed inside the cylinder itself rather than in the lock shell. He produced a small tension wrench; in shape it resembled a dental pick, but was little larger than a matchstick. He placed the bent end of the wrench in the keyway, pushing on its far end, so as to maximize both the torque and his tactile sensitivity. Each would be important. One by one, he pulled each tumbler away from the shear line. After ten seconds, the tumblers had been picked. The lock was not yet ready to open, however. Now he inserted a second tool, a pick of carbide steel, thin yet inflexible, and began applying clockwise torque.

Holding his breath, he kept both instruments in the keyway as he heard the tongue withdraw and used the tension to pull the door toward him, just a few inches. The door swung easily on well-oiled hinges. Those hinges *had* to be well oiled: as it opened, he saw that the door was fully eighteen inches thick. The governor general may have placed a dungeon beneath his feet, but he wished to be spared even the faintest echoes of whatever cries might come from it.

Janson opened the door a few more inches, standing now a foot away from the entrance, in case someone was lying in wait.

Slowly, carefully, he verified that at least the immediate passageway was clear. Now he walked through the door, to a stone landing worn smooth with time, and, using his electrical tape, he secured the brass tongue to the door so that it would not relock.

And he began to make his way down the stairs. At least they were stone, not creaking wood. A few more steps down the landing led to a second impediment, a hinged grate of steel bars.

The portcullis-like grate succumbed to his slim tools without difficulty; unlike the stone door above, however, it was far from soundless.

It opened with a distinct scraping noise, of metal against stone—one that the assembled guards could not have failed to hear.

Astonishingly, they did not react. Why? Another decoy? Birds on a wire—this time a flock of them?

A flurry of thoughts ran though Janson's mind. Then he caught the word *Theyilai!*

Even with his guidebook Anuran, he knew that word: *tea*. The guards were expecting somebody—somebody coming with a samovar of tea for them. That was why they did not start at the noise. On the other hand, if that tea did not arrive soon, they would grow suspicious.

Now he could see directly some of what he had glimpsed through the fiber-cam. A single, naked incandescent bulb provided lighting. He heard the gentle burble of conversation resuming, the card game still at full steam. The smoke that had wafted up through the stairwell suggested at least a dozen cigarettes lighted simultaneously.

Seventeen guards for one man. No wonder they had little worries about the security of their hostage.

Janson thought about the young KLF proter champ, with his high-stakes play, the play that meant either disaster or triumph. Nothing in between.

Everything now was a question of timing. Janson knew that Katsaris was awaiting his command, a silent thermite grenade in his hand. Ordinary combat procedure would have called for a "flash and banger," but an audible explosion might alert others. If the soldiers stationed in the barracks were mobilized, the odds of a successful exfiltration would shift from slim to none.

Katsaris and Janson each had a modified MP5K, a 4.4-pound submachine gun made by Heckler & Koch, with a short barrel, a sling-attachment buttcap, and a sound suppressor. The magazines held thirty hollow-point rounds, for close-quarter, interior use. The 9mm Hydra-Shok bullets were less likely to ricochet; they were also more likely to destroy any flesh they encountered—to tear rather than simply penetrate human viscera. Janson's SEAL comrades had cruelly nicknamed this weapon, which had a firing rate of nine hundred rounds per minute, the "room broom." What could not be silenced was the clamor of its victims. But the massive hallway door would provide substantial acoustic isolation, and several feet of stone separated the grotto from the floor above it.

Janson took six steps down, then swung himself onto the four-foot-deep concrete ledge. It was, as expected, draped with PVC pipes and insulated electrical wires, but he landed without a sound. So far, so good. The soldiers were studying their cards; no one was scanning the ceiling.

Now he flattened himself against the wall and inched along the ledge carefully; the farther he was from the stairway, the less expected his firing position would be—and the sooner he would be able to reach Peter Novak in his cell. At the same time, Janson's sight-line position was far from ideal; soldiers at one end of the larger table would still be able to see him if they looked up and into the shadowed ledge. Yet, as he reminded himself, there was no reason for them to do so.

"*Veda theyilai?*" The proter champion, thumbing his cards at the end of the table, spoke the words in a tone of slight annoyance, and as he did, he rolled his eyes. Had anything registered?

After a beat, he lifted his eyes again, peering into the gloom of the overhead shelf. His hands moved toward his cradled Ruger Mini-14.

Janson had not been wrong about the young man's powers of observation. His scalp was crawling. *He had been made.*

"*Now!*" Janson whispered into his lip mike and slid to a prone position on the farthest recess of the concrete ledge as he put on his polarized goggles. He flipped his weapon's safety down, setting it to full fire.

The young man stood up suddenly, shouting something in Kagama. He fired his gun toward the area where he had seen Janson, and the bullet took a bite out of the concrete just an inch from his head. A second bullet tore into nearby ductwork.

Suddenly, the dimly lit room filled with a flare of eye-searing brightness and heat. The slow-burning thermite grenade had arrived: a small, indoor sun, blinding even those who tried to look away. Its brightness was a multiple of that emitted by a welder's torch, and the fact that the guards' eyes had adjusted to low-light conditions made the blindness all the more complete. Scattered gunfire was directed toward Janson, but the angle made it a hard shot, and the bullets were poorly aimed.

Through his nearly black goggles, Janson saw the soldiers in disarray and confusion, some shielding their eyes with forearms and hands, others firing blindly toward the ceiling.

Still, even a blind shot could be fatal. With the entire room whited out by the preternaturally bright flare, he returned fire, directing the automatic fusillades in tight, carefully aimed clusters. He depleted one thirty-round magazine and snapped in another. Shouts filled the room.

Now Katsaris appeared, bounding down the stairway with polarized goggles and a softly buzzing MP5K, directing bullets at the guerrillas from yet another angle.

In seconds it was over. Few of them, Janson reflected, even had the opportunity to look their opponents in the eye. They had been slaughtered, impersonally, by a smoothly operating magazine-fed weapon that discharged bullets at a rate of fifteen per second. Because of the low-signature sound suppression, the MP5 bursts were not merely lethal but eerily quiet. It took Janson a moment before he realized what the sound reminded him of: the fluttering of a deck of cards being shuffled. *Killing should not sound like that,* Janson thought to himself. It was too trivial a soundtrack for so grave an action.

An odd silence now reigned. As gloom and shadows returned, Janson and Katsaris removed their goggles. The naked, forty-watt overhead bulb, Janson noticed, was still intact. The guards were not so lucky. Bodies were splayed on the floor, as if pinned there by the hollow-point bullets. They had functioned as they were designed to, discharging their entire force to the bodies they hit, coming to a stop several inches into those bodies, destroying all the vital organs they encountered. As Janson came closer, he saw that some of the men were taken down even before they'd had the opportunity to flip the safeties of their M16 carbines.

Were there any signs of movement? It took him a few moments before he saw it. Sliding along the ground was the young man who had played the amazing thirteen-card set—the man who had lifted his eyes to the concrete ledge. His midriff was red and slick, but his arms were out-stretched, reaching for the revolver of the lifeless soldier next to him.

Janson let off one more burst from his HK. Another shuffle of life's deck, and the young man became still.

The grotto was an abattoir, filled with the rich, sickening stench of blood and the contents of ripped-open alimentary canals. Janson knew the stench all too well: it was the stench of life once life was taken away.

Oh Christ. Oh God. It was nothing short of carnage, outright *butchery*. Was this what he did? *Was this who he was?* The words of an old fitness report returned to mock him: Was he indeed "in his element"? Once more, he flashed back to one of his exit interviews.

*"You don't have a heart, Janson. It's why you do what you do. Goddammit, it's why you are who you are."*

*"Maybe. And maybe I'm not who you think I am."*

*"You tell me you're sickened by the killing. I'm going to tell you what you'll discover one day for yourself: it's the only way you'll ever feel alive."*

*"What kind of man has to kill to feel alive?"*

*What kind of man was he?*

Now he felt something hot and acidic splash in the back of his throat. Had he lost it? Had he changed in ways that made him unfit for the task he had accepted? Perhaps it was simply that he had been out of it for too long, and the necessary calluses had softened.

He wanted to throw up. He also knew he would not. Not in front of Theo, his beloved protégé. Not in the middle of a mission. Not now. His body would be permitted no such indulgences.

A coolly remonstrating voice in his head took over: Their victims were, after all, soldiers. They knew their lives were expendable. They belonged to a terrorist movement that had taken a man of international renown and sworn solemnly to execute him. In guarding a civilian unjustly held captive, they had placed themselves in the line of fire. For Ahmad Tabari, el Caliph, they had pledged to give their lives—all of them had. Janson had merely taken them up on the offer.

"Let's go," Janson called to Katsaris. He could rehearse the excuses in his head, could recognize that they were not without some validity, and yet none of it made the slaughter before him any more tolerable.

His own sense of repugnance was the only thing that gave solace. To contemplate such violence with equanimity was the province of the ter-rorist, the extremist, the fanatic—a breed he had spent a lifetime combating, a breed he had feared he was, in his own way, becoming. Whatever his actions, the fact that he could not contemplate them without horror indicated that he was not yet a monster.

Now he moved swiftly down from the concrete ledge and joined Katsaris at the iron-plated gate to the governor general's dungeon. He noticed that the soles of Katsaris's boots were, like his, slick with blood, and quickly looked away.

"I'll do the honors," Katsaris said. He was holding a big, antique-looking hoop of keys, taken from one of the slain guards.

Three keys. Three dead bolts. The door swung open, and the two stepped into a narrow, dark space. The air felt dank, stagnant, suffused with the smells of human sickness and sweat that had passed beyond rancid, to something else. Away from the overhead bulb in the area where the guards had waited, the space was dim, and it was difficult to make anything out.

Katsaris toggled his flashlight from infrared to optical light. Its powerful beam cut through the murk.

In silence, they listened.

The sound of breathing was audible somewhere in the gloom.

A narrow passageway broadened out, and they saw how the two-hundred-year-old dungeon was constructed. It consisted of a row of impossibly thick iron bars set only four feet away from the stone walls. Every eight feet, a partition of stone and mortar segmented the long row of cells. There were no windows up to the ground, no sources of illumination; a few kerosene lanterns had been set in the stone bulkheads; they had provided what illumination there was the last time that the dungeon had been in service.

Janson shuddered, contemplating the horrors of a previous age. What sort of offenses landed people in the governor general's dungeon? Not ordinary aggressions of one native against another: the traditional village leaders were encouraged to deal with them as they always had, subject to the occasional urging to be "civilized" in their punishment. No, the ones who ended up in the colonial overlord's dungeons, Janson knew, were the resisters—those who opposed the rule of foreigners, who believed that the natives might be able to run their own affairs, free from the lash of Holland's rump empire.

And now a new set of rebels had seized the dungeon and, like so many rebels, sought not to dismantle it but only to use it for their own ends.

It was a truth both bitter and undeniable: those who stormed the Bastille inevitably found a way to put it to use again.

The area behind the grate was shrouded in darkness. Katsaris swept his flashlight along the corner of the cages until they saw him.

A man.

A man who did not look glad to see them. He had flattened himself against the wall cell, trembling with fright. As the beam of light illuminated him, he dropped to the ground, crouching in the corner, a terrified animal hoping to make himself disappear.

"Peter Novak?" Janson asked softly.

The man buried his face in his arms, like the child who believes that when he cannot see, he cannot be seen.

Suddenly, Janson understood: What did he look like, with his black face paint and combat garb, his boots tracking blood? Like a savior—or an *assailant?*

Katsaris's flashlight settled on the cowering man, and Janson could make out the incongruously elegant broadcloth shirt, stiff not with a French launderer's starch but with grime and dried blood.

Janson took a deep breath and now spoke words he had once merely fantasized he would be able to say.

"Mr. Novak, my name is Paul Janson. You saved my life once. I'm here to return the favor."

# CHAPTER SEVEN

For a few long seconds, the man remained motionless. Then he raised his face and, still crouched, looked straight into the light; Katsaris quickly redirected the beam, so as not to dazzle him.

It was Janson who was dazzled.

A few feet away from him was the countenance that had adorned countless magazines and newspapers. A countenance that was as beloved as the pope's—in this secular age, perhaps even more so. The thick shock of hair, flopping over his forehead, still more black than gray. The high, nearly Asiatic cheekbones. Peter Novak. Winner of last year's Nobel Peace Prize. A humanitarian like none the world had ever known.

The very familiarity of his visage made Novak's condition all the more shocking. The hollows beneath his eyes were dark, almost purple; a once-resolute gaze was now filled with terror. As the man shakily brought himself to his feet, Janson could see the small tremors that convulsed his body. Novak's hands shook; even his dark eyebrows quivered.

Janson was familiar with this look: it was the look of a man who had given up hope. He was familiar with this look because it had once been his. *Baaqlina.* A dusty town in Lebanon. And captors whom hatred had transformed into something not quite human. He could never forget the anthracite hardness of their eyes, their hearts. *Baaqlina.* It was destined to be his place of death: he had never been so convinced of anything. In the end, of course, he walked away a free man after the Liberty Foundation intervened. Did money change hands? He never knew. Even after his liberation, though, he spent a long time wondering whether that destiny was truly averted or merely deferred. They were deeply irrational, these thoughts and sensations, and Janson had never confided them to anyone. But perhaps the day would come when he would confide them to Peter Novak. Novak would understand that others had been through what he had been through, and perhaps he would find comfort in that. He owed Novak that much. No, he owed Novak everything. And so did thousands, perhaps millions, of others.

Peter Novak had traveled around the world to resolve bloody conflict. Now somebody had brought bloody conflict to him. Somebody who would pay.

Janson felt a welling up of warmth toward Peter Novak, and equally an intense wrath toward those who had sought to bring him low. Janson lived so much of his life in flight from such feelings; his reputation was as a coolly controlled, even-keeled, emotionally disengaged man—"the Machine," as he'd been nicknamed. His temperament made some people uncomfortable; in others, it inspired an abiding confidence and trust. But Janson knew he was no rock: he was merely skilled at internalizing. He seldom showed fear, because he feared too much. He banked his emotions because they burned too hotly. All the more so after the bombing in Caligo, after the loss of the only thing that had made sense of his life. It was hard to love when you saw how easily love could be taken away. It was hard to trust when you'd learned how easily trust could be broken. Once, decades earlier, there was a man he had admired more than any other; and that man had betrayed him. Not just him—the man had betrayed humanity.

Helene had once told him that he was a searcher. *The search is over,* he'd told her. *I've found you,* and he tenderly kissed her forehead, her eyes, her nose, her lips, her neck. But she had meant something else: she had meant that he was in search of meaning, of something or somebody larger than himself. Somebody, he now supposed, like Peter Novak.

Peter Novak: a wreck of a man, by the evidence of his eyes. A wreck of a man who was also a saint of a man. He could have been a brilliant economist, and some of his theoretical papers had become widely cited. He could have been the Midas of the twenty-first century, a pampered playboy, a reincarnation of the Shāh Jāhan, the Mughal emperor who built the Taj Mahal. But his sole interest was in leaving the world a better place than he had found it. And certainly a better place than had found him, born as he was on the killing fields of the Second World War.

"We've come for you," Janson told him.

Taking a tentative step away from the stone wall, Peter Novak pitched his shoulders back as if bellowing his lungs. Even to speak seemed to require enormous effort.

"You've come for me," Novak echoed, and the words were thick and croaky, perhaps the first he had spoken for several days.

*What had they done to him?* Had his body been broken, or his spirit? The body, Janson knew from experience, would heal more quickly. Novak's breathing indicated that the man had pneumonia, a fluid congestion of the lungs that would have come from breathing the dungeon's dank, stagnant, spore-filled air. At the same time, the words he spoke next seemed largely incoherent.

"You work for *him*," Novak said. "Of course you do. He says there can only be *one*! He knows that when I am out of the way, he will be *unstoppable*." The words were intoned with an urgency that substituted for sense.

"We work for *you*," Janson said. "We've come to get you."

In the great man's darting eyes was a look of bewilderment *"You can't stop him!"*

"Who are you talking about?"

"Peter Novak!"

"You're Peter Novak."

"*Yes!* Of course!" He clasped his arms around his chest and held himself straight, like a diplomat at an official convocation.

*Was his mind gone?*

"We've come for you," Janson repeated as Katsaris matched a key from the ring to the grate to Peter Novak's cell. The grate swung open. Novak did not move at first. Janson inspected his pupils for signs that he had been drugged, and concluded that the only drug to which he had been subjected was the trauma of captivity. The man had been kept in darkness for three days, no doubt given water and food, but deprived of hope.

Janson recognized the syndrome, recognized the elements of post-traumatic psychosis. In a dusty town in Lebanon, he had not entirely escaped it himself. People expected hostages to sink to their knees in gratitude, or join their rescuers, arm in arm, as they did in the movies. The reality was seldom like that.

Katsaris gave Janson a frantic look, tapping on his Breitling. Every additional minute exposed them to additional risk.

"Can you walk?" Janson asked, his tone sharper than he had intended.

There was a beat before Novak responded. "Yes," he said. "I think so."

"We have to leave now."

"No," said Peter Novak.

"Please. We can't afford to wait." In all likelihood, Novak was suffering the normal confusion and disorientation of the newly released captive. But could there be something more? Had the Stockholm syndrome set in? Had Novak been betrayed by the famously expansive compass of his moral sympathies?

"No—there's someone else!" he whispered.

"What are you talking about?" Katsaris interrupted.

"Somebody else here." He coughed. "Another prisoner."

"Who?" Katsaris prodded.

"An American," he said. He gestured to the cell at the end of the passageway. "I won't leave without her."

"That's impossible!" Katsaris interjected.

"If you leave her behind, they'll kill her. They'll kill her at once!" The humanitarian's eyes were imploring, and then commanding. He cleared his throat, moistened his cracked lips, and took another breath. "I cannot have that on my conscience." His English was manicured, precise, with just a faint Hungarian inflection. Another labored breath. "It need not be on yours."

Bit by bit, Janson realized, the prisoner was regaining his composure, becoming himself again. His piercing dark eyes reminded Janson that Novak was no ordinary man. He was a natural aristocrat, accustomed to ordering the world to his liking. He had a gift for it, a gift he had used for ends of extraordinary benevolence.

Janson studied Novak's unwavering gaze. "And if we can't . . ."

"Then you'll have to leave me behind." The words were halting, but unequivocal.

Janson stared at him in disbelief.

A twitch played out on Novak's face, and then he spoke again. "I doubt your rescue plans provide for an unwilling hostage."

It was clear that his mind was still blazingly fast. He had played the tactical card immediately, impressing on Janson that no further discussion would be possible.

Janson and Katsaris exchanged glances. "Theo," Janson said quietly. "Get her."

Katsaris nodded reluctantly. Then they both froze.

*The noise.*

A scrape of steel against stone.

A familiar noise: that of the steel grate they had opened to go down there.

Janson remembered the soldier's hopeful cry: *Theyilai.*

The expected visitor, bringing the soldiers their tea.

Janson and Theo strode from the dungeon to the blood-drenched adjoining chamber, where they could hear the jangling of someone's key chain, and then watched as a tray—laden with a teapot of hammered metal and several stacks of little clay cups—came into view.

He saw the hands supporting the tray—remarkably small hands. And then the man, who was no man at all.

It was a boy. If Janson had had to guess, he would have said that the boy was eight years old. Large eyes, mocha skin, short black hair. He was shirtless and wore blue madras shorts. His sneakers looked too large for his slender calves and gave him a puppyish look. The boy's eyes were trained on the next step: he had been entrusted with an important responsibility, and he was going to be as careful as possible about his footing. Nothing would be dropped. Nothing would be spilled.

He was two-thirds of the way down the stairs when he pulled up short. Probably the smell had alerted him that something was out of the ordinary—either that or the silence.

The boy now turned and regarded the carnage—the guards sprawled in pooled, congealing blood—and Janson could hear him gasp. Involuntarily, the little boy dropped the tray. His precious tray. The tray that the guards were to have received with such gratitude and merriment. As it rolled like a hoop, down the stairs, the cups smashed on the steps below him, and the teapot splashed its steaming contents at the boy's feet. Janson watched it all happen in slow motion.

Everything would be dropped. Everything would be spilled. Including blood.

Janson knew precisely what he must do. Left to his own devices, the boy would flee and alert the others. What had to be done was regrettable but inarguable. There was no other choice. In one fluid movement, he leveled the silenced HK at the boy.

A boy who returned his gaze with large, frightened eyes.

A slack-jawed eight-year-old. An innocent, given no choice as to his decisions in life.

Not a combatant. Not a conspirator. Not a rebel. Not involved.

A boy. Armed with—what?—a hot jug of mint tea?

No matter. The field manuals had a name for persons like him: engaged noncombatants. Janson knew what he had to do.

But his hand did not. It refused to follow his command. *His finger would not squeeze the trigger.*

Janson stood stock-still, frozen as he had never been in his life, even as turbulence overtook his mind. His disgust for the casualties of "standard tactical protocol" became absolute, and now paralyzing.

The boy turned from him and scampered up the stairwell, taking the steps two at a time—back up the stairs, back to safety.

Yet his safety was their doom! Recriminations flooded Janson like lava: his two seconds of sentimentality had fatally compromised the mission.

The boy would sound the alarm. By allowing him to live, Janson had signed a death warrant for Peter Novak. For Theo Katsaris. For himself. And quite possibly for the other participants in the mission.

He had made an insupportable, inexcusable, indefensible mistake. He was now, in effect, a murderer, and of far more than one child. His stricken eyes ran from Novak to Katsaris. A man he admired more than any he'd known; another he loved like a son. The mission was over. Sabotaged by an errant force he could never have anticipated: himself.

Now he saw Katsaris streak by, saw Katsaris's footprints in the blood; the man had taken the shortest route to the stairwell, vaulting over corpses and chairs. The boy had to have been within an arm's length of the door to the hallway when Katsaris squeezed off a silenced shot to the heart. Even after the muzzle flashed, Katsaris remained in full precision-firing position: a steadying hand to his firing hand, the stance of somebody who could not afford to miss. The stance of a soldier firing at a person who could not return fire, but whose continued survival was itself a dire menace.

Janson's vision blurred briefly, then focused again, and when it did he saw the child's lifeless body tumble down the stone stairs, almost somersaulting.

And then it lay on the bottom step, like a rag doll carelessly tossed aside.

When Janson moved a few feet closer, he saw that the boy's head lay upon the metal tray he once carried so proudly. A saliva bubble had formed at his soft, childish lips.

Janson's heart pounded slowly, powerfully. He was sickened, at himself and what he had nearly allowed to happen, and at the same time sickened by what needed to have happened. By the waste of it all, the prodigality with the one thing that mattered on this earth, human life. The Derek Collinses of the world would never understand. He remembered why he retired. Decisions like this, he recognized, had to be made. He had no longer wanted to be the one to make them.

Katsaris looked at him with wildly questioning eyes: Why had he frozen? What had come over him?

He felt strangely moved that Katsaris's expression was one of bewilderment rather than reproach. Katsaris should have been furious at him, as Janson was furious at himself. Only the soldier's love for his mentor could have modulated outrage into mere astonishment and incredulity.

"We've got to get out of here," Janson said.

Katsaris gestured toward the stairs, the egress stipulated in the revised plan.

But Janson had devised those plans, and knew when they would have to be altered for the sake of the mission. "That's too dangerous now. We've got to find another way."

Would Katsaris trust his judgment any longer? A mission without a commanding officer was a sure route to disaster. He had to demonstrate his mastery of the situation.

"First things first. Let's get the American," he told him.

Two minutes later, Katsaris fiddled with the lock of another iron gate as Novak and Janson looked on. The gate opened with a groan.

The flashlight played off matted hair that had once been blond.

"Please don't hurt me," the woman whimpered, cowering in her cell. *"Please don't hurt me!"*

"We're just going to take you home," Theo said, angling the beam so that they could assess her physical condition.

It was Donna Hedderman, the anthropology student; Janson recognized her face. Once the KLF had captured the Steenpaleis, they had evidently moved the American woman to its dungeon as well. The two high-profile captives, they must have reasoned, would be easier to guard in one place.

Donna Hedderman was a big-boned woman, with a broad nose and round cheeks. She had once been heavyset, and even after seventy days of captivity, she was not lean. As was the way with terror groups of any sophistication, the KLF made sure that its prisoners were amply fed. The calculation was brutality itself. A prisoner weakened by starvation might succumb to disease and die. To die of disease was to escape the power of the KLF. A prisoner who died could not be executed.

Even so, Donna Hedderman had been through hell: it was apparent from her bleached, fish-belly flesh, her clumped and tangled hair, her staring eyes. Janson had seen photos of her in the newspaper articles about her kidnapping. In the pictures, from happier days, she was round, beaming, almost cherubic. "High-spirited" was a recurrent adjective. But the long weeks of captivity had taken all that away. A KLF communiqué had dementedly called her an American intelligence agent; if anything, she had left-wing sympathies that would have ruled out such employment. She had been singularly sympathetic to the plight of the Kagama, but then the KLF scorned sympathy as a nonrevolutionary sentiment. Sympathy was an impediment to fear, and fear was what the Caliph sought above all else.

A long pause. "Who do you work for?" she asked in a quavering voice. "We work for Mr. Novak," Janson said. A sidelong glance.

After a beat, Novak nodded. "Yes," he said. "They are our friends."

Donna Hedderman got to her feet and made her way toward the open gate. Edema had swollen her ankles, making her stride unsteady.

Now Janson conferred quietly with Katsaris. "There is another way, and right now it looks like the better bet. But we'll need to pool resources. We each have an ounce of Semtex in our kit. We'll need them both." A small wad of Semtex, along with a detonation device, was included in their gear, standard spec-ops equipment for missions into uncertain environments.

Katsaris looked at him closely, then nodded. Janson's tone of voice, the specificity of his instructions, were, for whatever reason, reassuring. Janson had not lost it. Or if he had, it was only a momentary lapse. Janson was still Janson.

"Kerosene lanterns." Janson gestured toward them. "Before the place was electrified, it would have been the primary source of illumination. The governor general's compound would have had a kerosene tank in the basement, something that would be filled from outside. He'd want to have a plentiful supply of the stuff."

"They might have ripped it out," Katsaris noted. "Filled it with cement."

"Possibly. More likely it was left to rust, quietly. The subfoundation level is vast. It isn't as if they would have needed the space."

"Vast is right. How are we going to find it?"

"The blueprint has a tank positioned approximately two hundred meters in from the northwest retaining wall. I hadn't realized what it was for, but it's obvious now."

"That's some distance," Katsaris said. "Is the woman going to be up to it?"

Donna Hedderman gripped the iron bars to help herself stay erect; clearly, the period of relative immobility had weakened her muscles, and her still considerable girth gave them a great deal to support.

Novak looked at her and turned away, embarrassed. Janson understood the kind of relationship that developed between two deeply frightened prisoners who might not be able to see each other but could communicate, whispering through pipes, tapping code on metal bars, passing notes scrawled with grime on scraps of cloth or paper.

"You run ahead, Theo. Let me know when you've located it, and I'll bring the others."

Three minutes elapsed before he heard Katsaris's triumphant words in his earpiece: "Found it!"

Janson looked at his watch: further delay was dangerous. When might the next contingent of guards arrive to relieve the ones who had been on duty? When would they next hear the scrape of the steel grate on the stone landing?

Now he led Peter Novak and Donna Hedderman along the dank subterranean corridor that led to the old kerosene tank. Hedderman held on to Janson's arm as she walked, and even then her gait was slow and painful. These were not the cards he would have chosen, but they were the cards he had been dealt.

The tank, obviously long neglected, had an iron door with lead flanges to maintain a tight seal.

"There's no time," Janson said. "Let's kick the damn thing in. The hinges are already rusting off. They just need help." He made a running start toward the door, throwing up a foot as he reached iron door. If the door did not give way, the result would be a bone-jarring experience. But it did, collapsing in a cloud of dust and oxidized metal.

Janson coughed. "Get out your Semtex," he said.

Now Janson strode through what had once been a storage tank for kerosene. The copper-lined chamber was still suffused with an oily smell. The fill hole was almost hidden by the hardened tarlike residue that covered the walls—impurities of the kerosene, which remained after many decades of disuse.

He hammered the butt of his HK against the outside wall, heard the hollow ring of the copper flashing. This was the area. Probably a four-foot elevation above the ground, unless it had been reduced by the passage of time.

Katsaris packed the ivory-colored putty, about the size of a wad of bubble gum, around the rusting iron bunghole and pressed into it twin silvery wires, filament-thin. The other end of the wires attached to a small, round lithium battery, similar in appearance to those used in many watches and hearing aids. The battery hung low, and Katsaris decided to press it into the Semtex, simply to stabilize it.

As he worked, Janson primed his own wad of Semtex, then took a few moments to determine the optimal position of the second blast. The positioning of plastique was crucial to the desired outcome, and they could not afford to fail. So far, they had been protected by the isolation of the dungeon—the layers of stone protecting it from the rest of the north wing.

Mayhem had occurred, but no sound would have been audible to those who were not its victims. There was no way to make a soundless exit, however. Indeed, the aftershock from the blast would travel almost instantaneously throughout the Stone Palace, rousing everyone in the immense compound. There would be no confusion among the rebels about where the blast had originated, no confusion about where to dispatch soldiers. The escape route had to be hitchless, or their efforts would all be for nothing.

Now Janson pressed his ounce of Semtex to the corner of the far wall where it met the curving top of the copper-lined tank, three feet above Katsaris's ounce.

It fell off, and Janson grabbed it before it hit the ground. The ivory putty would not adhere to the greasy surface.

What now? He took out his combat knife and used it to scrape the gummy residue from the corner of the tank. The blade was soon ruined, but his penlight revealed an area of gleaming, gouged metal.

He pressed the unsoiled side of the Semtex wad to the spot. It hung there, but uncertainly, as though it might drop at any moment.

"Fall back!" Janson called.

Theo and Janson exited the tank, Janson taking one last look to make sure the Semtex was still in position. Once the two rejoined the hostages, around a bend in the corridor, they depressed in unison the radio frequency controllers that activated the batteries.

The explosion was deafening, the reverberation a rumble-roar, like a vast collection of forty-thousand-watt speakers blasting bass-range feedback. The shock waves traveled through their flesh, causing their very eyes to vibrate. White smoke billowed inward, bringing with it the familiar nitrous scent of plastique—and something else, too: the salty tang of the sea breeze. They had a route to the compound's exterior.

If they lived to use it.

# CHAPTER EIGHT

How long would it take before the KLF forces were fully mobilized? A hundred and twenty seconds? Less? How many guards were on duty? How many guards were stationed along the battlements?

They would find out soon enough.

A portion of the heavy stone wall had crumbled under the blast, and thick, jagged metal plates were strewn everywhere. But Theo's penlight confirmed what the moist sea breeze had promised. The opening was wide enough to enable them to clamber out to the exterior of the compound, if they used a push-pull maneuver. Katsaris went first. Janson would go last. Between them, they would help the weakened captives make their way over the rubble and onto the surrounding grounds.

Eighty seconds later, the four of them were on the outside. The sea breeze was stronger, and the night sky was brighter than it had been; the cloud cover was beginning to break up. Stars were visible, and so was a patch of moon.

It was not a good time for the nocturnal glow. They were outside the dungeon. But they were not free.

Not yet.

Janson stood against the limestone wall with the others, determining their precise position. The breeze cleared Janson's nostrils, cleared them of the bloody, clinging stench of his victims, as well as of the fainter animal stench of the unwashed captives.

The area immediately beneath the limestone wall of the compound was safer, in certain respects, than the area farther out. The seaside battlements, he saw, were filled with armed men, some manning heavy artillery. That was why the battlements were constructed—to fire upon the corvettes and schooners of rival colonial empires. The farther out they were, the more exposed they would be.

"Can you run?" Janson asked Novak.

"A short distance?"

"Only a short distance," he said reassuringly.

"I'll do my damnedest," the billionaire replied, jut-jawed and determined. He was in his sixties, had been held in captivity under doubtful conditions, but his sheer force of will would see him through.

Janson felt reassured by his steely resolve. Donna Hedderman he was less certain of. She seemed the kind who might collapse into hysterics at any moment. And she was too heavy to sling over a shoulder.

He put a hand on her arm. "Hey," he said. "Nobody's asking you to do anything that's beyond you. Do you understand?"

She whimpered, her eyes beseeching. A commando in black face paint was not a comforting sight to her.

"I want you to focus, OK?" He pointed to the rocky outcropping, fifty yards away, where the promontory dropped off in a sheer cliff. A low split-rail fence, painted white and peeling, surrounded the cliff, a visual demarcation rather than a physical impediment. "That's where we're going."

For her sake, he did not spell out in further detail what the plan called for. He did not tell her that they would be going over the cliff, dropping down on ropes to a boat waiting on the frothing waters eighty meters below.

Katsaris and Novak now sprinted toward the rocky outcropping at the promontory's rocky overhang; Janson, slowed by the wheezing American, followed.

In the gray scale of nighttime vision, it looked like the very edge of the world. A crag of pale rock, and then nothingness, complete and absolute.

And that nothingness was their destination; indeed, their only salvation.

If they reached it in time.

"Find anchor!" Janson called to Katsaris.

The cliff was largely gneiss, a tough, metamorphic rock, weathered into irregular crags. There were a couple of plausible rock horns near the overhang. Using one of them would be safer and faster than pounding bolts or pitons into crevices. With sure, deft hands, Katsaris wrapped two loops of rope around the more prominent of the solid rock horns, making a double-strand loop beneath it, secured with an overhand knot. If one strand were cut—by friction against a sharp crag, or a stray bullet—the other would hold. Janson had packed dry-coated 9.4mm Beal rope, with some elasticity to control the deceleration rate in a fall. It was compact, but strong enough for the job.

As Katsaris secured the anchor, Janson swiftly trussed Novak in a sewn nylon climbing harness, making sure the leg loops and waist belt were securely buckled. This would not be a controlled rappel: the work would be done by the equipment, not the man. And the equipment could not be elaborate: they had to rely upon devices that could be easily carried. A figure-eight descender would serve as the rappel brake. It was a simple piece of polished steel, smaller than his hand, with two rings on either end of a center stem. One ring was big, the other small. No moving parts. It could be rigged rapidly and easily.

Katsaris passed a bight of the rappel rope through the big ring and looped it around the stem. He clipped the small ring onto Peter Novak's harness with a locking carobiner. It was a rudimentary device, but it would provide enough friction to safely control the rate of descent.

From a corner tower above the battlements, a guard aimed a long burst of gunfire in their direction.

*They had been spotted.*

"Christ, Janson, there's no time!" Katsaris shouted.

But he could buy time—perhaps a minute, perhaps less.

Janson unhooked a stun grenade from his combat vest and threw it toward the watchtower. It arced through the air and into the guard's cabin.

At the same time, Janson tossed the rope coil over the cliff. The sooner Novak followed, the safer he'd be: a single-pitch rappel was his only chance.

Unfortunately, the Kagama in the watchtower was swift and skilled: he grabbed the grenade and hurled it away from him, with seconds to spare. The grenade blew in midair, the flash outlining the four people at the edge of the cliff for attack like a floodlight from a guard tower.

"Now what?" asked Novak. "I'm no rock climber."

"Jump," Katsaris urged. *"Now!"*

"You're *mad!*" Novak cried out, aghast and terrified by the black noth-ingness that seemed to stretch out below.

Katsaris abruptly lifted the great man and, taking care not to lose his own footing, pitched him off the side of the cliff.

It was graceless. It was also the only way. The humanitarian was in no state to absorb and follow even the most elementary coaching: a regulated plumb drop was his only chance. And the overhang meant that the rock face would be a safe distance away from him.

Janson heard the controlled slither of the 9.4mm rope as it fed through the figure-eight brake, confirming that the cord would bear him down to the water-plashed rocks below at a regulated speed of descent. The plunging cliff was now Novak's greatest protection, shielding him from the riflemen on the battlements. Bullets could only shoot past him; they could not reach him. Novak had to do nothing. Gravity would do its part.

The B team, waiting in the boat at the base of the cliff, would do the rest.

The overhang of the cliff had protected the compound from amphibious attack over the centuries, even as the rocks and shoals kept warships from approaching too closely. The location of the fortress had been well chosen. And yet these features could provide the invaders with safety, too.

Peter Novak was almost home.

For the rest of them, it would not be so simple.

Janson and Katsaris could rappel down the cliff easily enough. But what of Donna Hedderman? There was no spare climbing harness and braking system for her use. A long look passed between Janson and Katsaris: wordlessly, a plan was agreed upon, tacitly devised in desperation.

Even as he made a double cord loop around another rock horn, Theo's expression was clear enough. *Damn* the American! But leaving her behind was out of the question.

A burst of gunfire kicked up a painful spray of rock.

*There was no time.*

More and more of the sentinels would direct their raking fire toward the promontory. No doubt the darkness and fog made sighting difficult, for the bursts were aimed with only approximate accuracy, and at forty yards, that was not sufficient for a reliable kill. The rebels were compensating with sheer quantity, however. More fire rained down on them. How much longer before a bullet struck home?

"Rig yourself," Janson ordered Katsaris. Meanwhile, Janson belayed the woman with what was to have been his own harness, the nylon webbing stretching tautly around her thighs and considerable waist. Hastily, he rigged the figure eight. A less-than-gentle push, and she was on her way down.

That left Janson with neither a harness nor a rappelling device. Facing the anchor Katsaris had rigged, he straddled the rope, looping it around his left buttock and across his hip, up across his chest and around his head to his right shoulder, and then over and down his back to his left hand. The rope was now configured in an *S* around his upper body. He would guide with his right hand, regulate speed with his left. Clasping the rope palm up, he could move it off his back to increase speed, and winch it around his hip to slow down. His nylon clothing would provide some protection from rope burns. Still, he was under no illusions. He had body-rappelled once before, in a training exercise; it would be extremely painful.

"Does that really work?" Katsaris asked skeptically.

"Sure it does," Janson said. "I've done it before." And he had hoped he would never have to do it again.

Several buzz-saw-like bursts of gunfire pelted the cliff like a hailstorm of lead. The rock at their feet exploded, only inches away; fragments stung Janson's face. *There was no time.*

"I'm *stuck!*" Donna Hedderman's wailing voice, perhaps thirty feet down the cliff.

"We'll be right there," Janson called to her, as he and Katsaris eased off the overhang. Bending at the waist, the two men kept their legs perpendicular to the sheer surface, "walking down" where it was possible. For Janson, the descent was excruciating; the nylon shell was strong but supplied no cushioning as the cord bit into his flesh. The only way to lessen the pressure was to increase the demands on his already aching muscles.

"Help me!" The woman's quavering voice echoed against the sheer rock.

A third of the way down, they found her and saw what had happened. Her long, matted hair had become entangled in the figure-eight rappel device. It was a hazard they should have anticipated. Katsaris took out a knife and, propelling himself sideways with his feet, approached her. She let out an earsplitting scream. With one slice, her entangled hair was free. But there was more of it, and it could happen again. Katsaris released his brake hand and activated his autoblock, a piece of webbing that now wrapped around his rope and arrested further descent.

"Hold still," he said. Inching farther toward her, he grabbed handfuls of her hair and sliced them off, ignoring her loud squawks of protest. As coiffure it was inelegant; as a safety precaution it was a thing of beauty.

Janson worked hard to keep up with the others, gritting his teeth as the stresses moved along the cord. At one moment, it tightened around his chest like a python, constricting his breath; at the next, it was digging into his gluteus muscles. Body-rappelling was natural, he supposed, in the way that natural childbirth was. The agony was what made it real. His hands were overstrained; yet if he let go of the rope, there would be nothing between him and the rocks below.

He had to hold on just a little longer. He had to keep reminding himself that at the base of the cliff, the other team members would be waiting for them, in the ultralightweight rigid inflatable boat that had been stowed on the BA609. They would be rested and ready. Janson and the others would be safe in their hands. If only they could reach them.

*Clear like water, cool like ice.*

Seconds ticked by like hours. He could hear the sounds of the aquatic team as they untrussed Peter Novak and bundled him into the boat.

This race would go to the swift. If there was any doubt where they had gone, the cable anchors would tell the sentries everything they needed to know. And if those anchors were sliced in the next few minutes, three people would plunge to their death. The darkness and fog were their only allies, time their greatest enemy.

The only hope of survival lay in speed—to get off the ropes and into the boat as fast as possible.

How much time had passed? Forty seconds? Fifty? Sixty?

Just when his muscles had reached the point of total depletion, Janson felt hands reaching up to grab him, and finally he let go of a lifeline that had turned into an instrument of torture. As he took his seat in the flat-bottomed watercraft, he looked around him. There were six of them. Novak. Hedderman. Katsaris. Andressen. Honwana. Hennessy would be piloting the BA609, taking second shift.

The motor whined as the rigid inflatable boat—a Sea Force 490—shot off from the rocks, hugging the shore for half a mile as it moved south, and then out into the mist-shrouded waters. The poor visibility would make it difficult to sight the RIB, and they had chosen a course that would take them out of the way of the rebels' fixed artillery. "All accounted for," Andressen said into his communicator, alerting Hennessy in the BA609. "Plus one guest."

A few bullets pocked the waters some distance from them. They were bullets fired out of desperation, fired for show. But such stray projectiles could sometimes achieve the same result as ones that were carefully guided.

Only when they were half a mile out could they no longer hear the sounds of the rebel forces; KLF gunfire no doubt continued, not least out of sheer frustration, but the reports were lost amid the sound of the restless ocean.

The Sea Force heaved in rhythm with the waves; its powerful motor strained as it competed with the monsoon-roiled waters. As the Anuran coast disappeared in the mists, Janson had a fleeting sense of how insignificant their vessel was, a tiny thing of rubber and metal propelling itself through the vast, empty seas. And yet for those who cared about the future of humanity on this planet, its cargo was significant indeed.

Peter Novak faced the direction in which they were traveling. From the set of his jaw, Janson could see that he was continuing to regain a sense of his identity, a sense of his selfhood. Yet his expression was blank; his mind was elsewhere. The spray and spume of the ocean was glittering in his hair and on his face; his broadcloth shirt was spattered with brine. From time to time, he would run a hand through his bristle-thick hair.

Hedderman's face was buried in her hands. She had curled up into a ball. It would take her a long time to heal, Janson knew. The two had fallen into the KLF's clutches in radically different circumstances and were a study in contrast.

Janson's men, too, were silent, lost in thought, or rehearsing the remaining operational steps.

Would the rebels follow in a speedboat? It was a possibility, though not a probability. If one was not skilled at rappelling, Adam's Hill was a formidable obstacle.

The six people in the RIB could hear the *whomp-whomp* of the rotors before they could see the craft. Another quarter mile of open sea separated them from it. Andressen checked his watch and turned up the throttle. They were in operational overtime: the exfiltration had taken longer than anticipated. The small boat rose and fell with the waves like driftwood while its powerful outboard motor kept them moving in a more or less straight line. Now the aircraft came into view. It was resting on a flotational helipad, an expanse of self-inflating black rubber. The downwash from the rotors caused the sea to bowl around it. Hennessy, who would be piloting the return flight as Honwana rested, was merely readying the hydraulics.

Now the craft's matte resin body was outlined in the first glimmers of the new day, a pink tendril over the horizon. A few minutes later, the tendril had become something indistinct but intense, like an arc light glimpsed through closed fingers. Dawn was breaking, into what was now an almost clear sky. A dark violet, shading swiftly into an intense cerulean. Dawn on the Indian Ocean. The first dawn that Peter Novak had seen for some days.

Hennessy opened his window and called out to Janson. "And who's the woman, now?" he asked, his voice tense.

"Ever hear of Donna Hedderman?"

"Mary, mother of God, Janson. This extraction was for *one*. This craft can't seat another person. Dammit, we're already at the limit of our fuel capacity. We can't take another hundred pounds of cargo without running out of fuel before we reach the landing zone. That's how fine the tolerances are."

"I understand."

"You should. It was your plan, bejaysus. So give me an alternative LZ."

Janson shook his head. "There's no place nearer that's safe, or it wouldn't be an alternative."

"And what does your plan call for now?" the Irishman demanded.

"I'll stay behind," Janson said. "There's enough fuel in the RIB to get me to Sri Lanka." Hennessy looked incredulous, and Janson added, "Using reduced speed, and taking advantage of the currents. Trust me, I know what I'm doing."

"Sri Lanka's not safe. You said so yourself, be the holy."

"Not safe for Novak is what I said. I'll make do. I've prepared contingency plans, in case something like this came up." He was only half bluffing. The plan he had specified would work, but it was not an eventuality he had foreseen.

Now Donna Hedderman, gasping and sputtering, was brought on board the aircraft. Her face was flushed, her clothes drenched from the spray of the ocean.

"Mr. Janson?" The Hungarian's voice was reedy and clear, even through the pulsing rumble of the nacelles. "You're a very brave man. You humble me, and I'm not easily humbled." He clasped Janson's upper arm. "I won't forget this."

Janson bowed his head, then looked straight into Peter Novak's brown eyes. "Please do. In fact, I'm going to have to ask you to do so, for reasons of my security, and that of my team." It was the professional response. And Janson was a professional.

A long pause. "You're a good man," the humanitarian said. Katsaris helped Peter Novak up the ramp and into the aircraft and then walked back down it.

The Greek's face was stern as he faced Janson. "I stay. You go."

"No, my friend," Janson said.

"Please," Katsaris said. "You're needed there. Mission control, yes? In case things go wrong."

"Nothing can go wrong at this point," Janson said. "Novak's in capable hands."

"A hundred miles on the open sea in an inflatable boat—that's no joke," Katsaris said stonily.

"You're saying I'm too old for a little sailing?"

Katsaris shook his head, unsmiling. "Please, Paul. I should be the one." His black hair gleamed in the dawn light.

"Goddammit, *no!*" Janson said, in a burst of anger. "My call, my screw-up, my foul. No member of my team takes a risk that should be mine. This conversation is over." It was a point of pride—of what passed for manhood or honor in the shadowy world of secret ops. Katsaris swallowed hard, and did as he was instructed. But he could not erase the worry from his face.

Janson downshifted the RIB's motor: fuel efficiency would be increased at a more moderate speed. Next he verified his direction with the compass on his watch face.

It would take him three or four hours to reach the coastal plains of southeastern Sri Lanka. There, he had a contact who could put him on a fast lorry to Colombo International Airport, assuming that the place wasn't in the hands of the Liberation Tigers of Tamil Eelam again. It wasn't the ideal; only, once again, the best of the available alternatives.

He watched the small turquoise-bodied aircraft rise into the air, describing something like a ziggurat pattern as it started its ascent to an altitude suited to extended flight, taking advantage of the prevailing winds for the long trip to Katchall.

The early-morning sky was now a beautiful azure, almost matching the resin skin of the rotorcraft, and Janson was filled with a sense of growing calm and relief as the craft glided through the sky.

He allowed himself a brief moment of pride. It had been a triumph against nearly impossible odds. Peter Novak was free. The murderous fanatics would be bereft of their glorious captive and would have gained nothing but humiliation. Janson leaned back in the boat and watched as the aircraft rose a little higher, its three-axis movement making it look almost like a thing of nature, a darting insect.

In the small boat, the approach toward the coastal plains of Sri Lanka would call for some care on his part; there were sometimes unexpected sandbars that made things treacherous. But from Colombo, there was a direct flight to Bombay, and from there the return stateside would be straightforward. He had committed Márta Lang's private telephone number to memory, and so had Katsaris; it would reach her wherever she was. Though the RIB lacked the requisite telecommunications, he knew that

Katsaris would assume command. In a few minutes, Katsaris would notify Novak's deputy that the mission had been accomplished. It was a call that Janson had hoped to be able to make, but Katsaris had every bit as much a right to it: he had been extraordinary, and absolutely integral to the long-odds triumph.

If Janson knew the Liberty Foundation, they would probably have assembled an aerial flotilla by the time the BA609 had returned to Katchall. Janson continued to watch as the aircraft climbed, soaring and magnificent.

And then—*no!* it couldn't be, it had to be a trick of the light!—he saw the flash, the dazzling, fiery blast and plume of a midair explosion. A pulse of white bleached the early-morning sky, followed immediately by a vast secondary flare, the yellow-white of combusted fuel. Small pieces of fuselage began to drift toward the sea.

*No! Oh, Christ, no!*

For several long seconds, Janson felt perfectly numb. He closed his eyes and reopened them: Had he imagined it?

A detached propeller twirled lazily before it crashed into the sea.

*Oh, dear God.*

It was a catastrophe such as none he had ever witnessed. At once, his heart felt squeezed, hard, harder. Theo. Theo Katsaris, the closest thing he had to a son. A man who loved him, and whom he loved. "Let me stay behind," Theo had begged him, and—out of vanity, out of pride—Janson had refused him.

Dead. Incinerated before his eyes.

In a kaleidoscope, he saw the faces of the others. Taciturn, even-tempered Manuel Honwana. Andressen: loyal, methodical, reliable, soft-spoken—easily underestimated precisely because he was so devoid of self-regard. Sean Hennessy, whom he had spirited out of an English prison cell, only to serve with a death sentence. Donna Hedderman, too—the luckless American do-gooder.

Gone. Dead because of him.

And Peter Novak. The greatest humanitarian of a new century. A giant among men. The peacemaker. A man who had once saved Janson's life. And the object of the entire mission.

Dead.

Cremated, three thousand feet above the Indian Ocean.

An incredible triumph had turned, now that day broke, into a nightmare.

All he knew was that it was no accident, no engine malfunction. The double explosion—the blast that preceded, by a few crucial seconds, the burst of combusted fuel—was telltale. What had occurred was the result of craft and design. Such craft and design that four of the best men he knew had been murdered, along with one of the best men anybody had *ever* known.

What the hell had happened? Who could have planned such a thing? When had the plans been laid?

And why? For God's sakes, *why?*

Janson sagged to the floor of the RIB, paralyzed by grief, futility, rage; for a moment, in the open sea, he felt as if he were in a crypt, with a heavy weight on his chest. Breathing was impossible. The very blood that sluiced through his veins seemed to congeal. The heaving sea beckoned, with its antidote of everlasting oblivion. He was harrowed, tormented, and deeply afraid, and he knew just how to put a stop to it.

But that was not an option.

He would have given his life for any of theirs. He knew that now.

But that was not an option.

Only he survived.

And in some calculating part of his mind, a clockwork mechanism spooled with a hard, icy rage. He had taken arms against a compound of fanatics, only to succumb to something far more diabolical. Outrage infused his soul with a near cryogenic frost. Emotions like despondency and grief had to give way before a larger emotion, an absolute and unyielding thirst for justice, and it was that emotion that commanded him not to succumb to the other emotions. He was the one left alive—left to find out what had just happened.

And why.

# PART TWO

# CHAPTER NINE

*Washington, D.C.*

"The prime directive here is secrecy," the man from the Defense Intelligence Agency said to the others in the room. With his thick, dark eyebrows, broad shoulders, and brawny forearms, he had the look of someone who worked with his hands; in fact, Douglas Albright was an intensely cerebral man, given to brooding and deliberation. He held a Ph.D. in comparative politics and another graduate degree in the foundations of game theory. "Secrecy is priority number one, two, and three. There should be no confusion about that."

Such confusion was unlikely, for the imperative even accounted for the unlikely venue for the hastily convened meeting. The Meridian International Center was located on Crescent Place, just off Sixteenth Street on Meridian Hill. A blandly handsome building in the neoclassical style that was the architectural lingua franca of official Washington, it was anything but eye-catching. Its charms were discreet and had much to do with its curious status as a building that was not owned by the federal government—the center billed itself a nonprofit educational and cultural institution—but was almost entirely devoted to very private government functions. The center had an elegant front entrance of carved oak; of greater importance was the side entrance, accessible from a private driveway, which enabled dignitaries to arrive and depart without attracting notice. Though it was just a mile from the White House, the center had significant advantages for certain meetings, especially interdepartmental conclaves that had no formal justification. Meetings here did not involve the paper trail that was necessitated by the security procedures at the White House, the Old Executive Office Building, the Pentagon, or any of the intelligence agencies. They could take place without leaving behind any telltale logs or records. They could take place without ever, officially, having taken place at all.

The five gray-faced men who sat around the small conference table were all in similar lines of work, and yet, given the structure of governmental agencies, they would never have had cause to meet in the ordinary course of things. Needless to say, the program that had brought them all together in the first place was far from ordinary, and the circumstances they now faced were quite possibly cataclysmic.

Unlike their titular superiors, they were not political appointees; they were lifers, tending to programs that extended far beyond the duration of any particular administration. They liaised with, and reported to, the men and women who shuttled in and out in four-year cycles, but the horizons of their responsibilities, as they conceived them, extended much further.

Sitting opposite the DIA man, the deputy director of the National Security Agency had a high scrubbed forehead and small, pinched features. He prided himself on maintaining an outward air of serenity, no matter what the circumstances. That air of serenity was now close to fraying, and with it his pride. "Secrecy, yes—the nature of the directive is clear," he said quietly. "The nature of our subject is not."

"Paul Elie Janson," said the State Department undersecretary, who was, on paper, the director of that department's Bureau of Intelligence and Research. He had not spoken for some time. A smooth-faced, athletic man with tousled, straw-colored hair, he was lent gravitas by heavy black-framed glasses. The undersecretary was a survivor, the other men knew. And because he was a survivor, they took careful note of the way he positioned himself on the issues. "Janson was one of ours, as you know. The documents you've got on him are lightly redacted. Apologies for that—that's the way they come out of the files, and we didn't have much prep time. Anyway, I think they give you the general idea."

"One of your goddamn killing machines, Derek, that's what he is," said Albright, glowering at the undersecretary. Despite Albright's high administrative rank, he had spent a career in analysis, not operations, and he remained an analyst to the core of his being. The ingrained mistrust that men of his ilk had toward their counterparts in operations was too often justified. "You create these soulless pieces of machinery, loose them on the world, and then leave someone else to clean up the mess. I just don't understand what kind of game he's playing."

The man from State flushed angrily. "Have you considered the possibility that someone is running a game on *him?*" A hard stare: "Jumping to conclusions could be dangerous. I'm not willing to stipulate that Janson is a renegade."

"The point is, we can't be certain," the NSA man, Sanford Hildreth, said after a while. He turned to the man seated next to him, a computer scientist who, as a young man, had earned a reputation as a wunderkind when he almost single-handedly redesigned the primary intelligence database for the CIA. "Is there some data set we're overlooking, Kaz?"

Kazuo Onishi shook his head. Educated at Cal Tech, he had grown up in Southern California and retained a slight Valley accent that made him seem looser than he was. "I can tell you we've had anomalous activities, potential breaches of security firewalls. What I can't do is identify the perpetrator. Not yet, anyway."

"Say you're correct, Derek," Hildreth went on. "Then my heart goes out to him. But absolutely nothing can compromise the program. Doug's right—that's the prime directive. Absolute and unyielding. Or we might as well kiss Pax Americana good-bye. It almost doesn't matter what he thought he was doing. All we can say is that this fellow Janson doesn't know what in the world he's blundered into." He raised his coffee cup to his mouth and took a sip, hoping nobody noticed the tremor of his hand as he returned it to the saucer. "And he's never *going* to know." The words were more declaration than observation.

"That much I'll accept," the man from State said. "Has Charlotte been briefed?" Charlotte Ainsley was the president's National Security Advisor and the principal White House liaison.

"Later today," said the NSA man. "But do you see any supportable alternatives?"

"Just at the moment? He's blundered into quicksand. We couldn't help him if we wanted to."

"It'll go easier if he doesn't struggle," the DIA analyst said.

"No argument here," said Derek Collins. "But he will, if I know my man. Mightily."

"Then extreme measures are going to have to be taken," the analyst said. "If the program gets burned, if even one percent of it gets exposed, it doesn't just destroy us, it destroys everything anybody here cares about. *Everything.* The past twenty years of history gets rolled back, and that's a pie-in-the-sky, win-the-lottery, best-case scenario. The likelier outcome looks a hell of a lot more like another world war. Only this time, we lose."

"Poor bastard," said the deputy director of the NSA, paging through the Janson files. "He's in way over his head."

The undersecretary of state suppressed a shudder. "The hell of it is," he replied grimly, "so are we."

*Athens*

The Greeks had a word for it: *néfos*. Smog—Western civilization's gift to its cradle. Trapped by the circle of mountains, set low by atmospheric inversion, it acidified the air, speeding decay of the antiquities and irritating the eyes and lungs of the city's four million inhabitants. On bad days, it lay on Athens like a noxious pall. This was a bad day.

Janson had taken a direct flight from Bombay to Athens, arriving at the East Terminal of the Ellinikón International Airport. He felt a deadness within; he was a besuited zombie going about his business. *You were the guy with a slab of granite where your heart's supposed to be.* If only it were so.

He had called Márta Lang repeatedly, to no avail. It was maddening. The number she had given him would reach her wherever she was, she had told him: it would go directly to her desk, on her private line, and if she did not pick up after three rings, it would bounce to her cell number. It was a number only three people had, she had stressed. And yet all it ever yielded was the electronic purr of an unanswered line. He had dialed various regional headquarters of the Liberty Foundation, in New York, Amsterdam, Bucharest. *Ms. Lang is unavailable,* subalterns with talcum-smooth voices informed him. Janson was insistent. It was an emergency. He was returning her call. He was a personal friend. It was a matter of the utmost importance. It concerned Peter Novak himself. He had tried every approach, every tactic of importuning, and made no headway.

A *message will be conveyed,* he was told each time, in an artfully passive construction that never varied. But they could not convey the real message, the words of a dreadful and destructive truth. For what could Janson tell them? That Peter Novak was dead? Those he spoke to at the Foundation gave no indication that they were aware of it, and Janson knew better than to provide the information.

Walking through the East Terminal, he heard, funneled through the airport sound system, the ubiquitous America pop diva with her ubiquitous hit song from the ubiquitous American blockbuster. That was what it was to be an international traveler these days: it was to be cushioned in sameness, enveloped in a cultural caul.

A *message will be conveyed.*

It was infuriating! Where *was* she? Had she been killed, too? Or—the possibility slashed at him like a straight razor across the eyes—was she herself part of a dire, unfathomable plot? Had Novak been killed by a member or members of his own organization? He could not automatically dismiss the hypothesis, even though it carried a horrific implication: that he himself had been a pawn in the conspiracy. That rather than having saved the man who once saved him, he had served as the very instrument of his destruction. Yet that was *insanity!* It made no sense—none of it did. Why kill a man with a death sentence?

Janson settled into the airport taxi that would bear him to the Mets neighborhood of Athens, to the southwest of the Olympic Stadium. The task before him would be a difficult one. He had to tell Marina Katsaris what had happened, had to tell her face-to-face, and the prospect lay on him like a boulder on his chest.

The airport was six miles from his destination in downtown Athens; seated uncomfortably in a backseat without room for his long legs, Janson wearily glanced around him. The highway that led from the suburb of Glyfada, where Ellinikón was situated, to the hilly sprawl that was Athens was like a conveyor belt of cars, their pooled exhaust replenishing the low-hanging fug of sulfur dioxide.

He noticed the small "2" in a little window on the meter, and his eyes met those of the driver, a squat man whose chin was darkly shadowed with an incipient beard, the kind that could never quite be shaved away.

"Is there somebody in the trunk?" Janson asked.

"Somebody in the *trunk?*" the driver repeated, mirthful. He was proud of his English. "Ha! Not when I last *checked,* mister! How come you ask?"

"Because I don't see anybody else in the backseat. So I was trying to figure out why you have the meter set for a double fare."

"My mistake," the driver said after a beat, his beaming countenance disappearing. Sullenly, he adjusted the meter, which meant not only shifting to a lower rate but wiping out the drachmas he had already accumulated.

Janson shrugged. It was an old trick of Athenian cabdrivers. Its only significance, in this case, was that the driver must have gauged him to be exhausted and inattentive even to have tried out the petty scam.

Athenian traffic meant that the last mile of the trip took longer than the previous five. The streets of the Mets area were built on a steep hillside, and the houses, which dated before the war—and before the city's population had mushroomed—harked to an earlier and pleasanter era. They were mostly the color of sand, with tiled roofs and red-shuttered windows.

Courtyards with potted plants and spiral outdoor staircases sheltered behind them. Katsaris's house was on a narrow street off Voulgareos, just half a dozen blocks from the Olympic Stadium.

Janson sent the driver on his way with 2,500 drachmas, rang the doorbell, and waited, half hoping there would be no answer.

The door opened after only a few moments, and there stood Marina, just as he had remembered her—if anything, she was even more beautiful. Janson took in her high cheekbones, honeyed complexion, steady brown eyes, her straight and silky black hair. The swelling of her belly was barely detectable, another voluptuous curve that was merely hinted at beneath her loose, raw-silk frock.

"Paul!" she exclaimed, delighted. The delight evaporated as she read his expression; the color drained from her face. "No," she said in a low voice.

Janson did not reply, but his haggard countenance held nothing back.

"*No,*" she breathed.

She began to tremble visibly, her face contorted by grief, then rage. He followed her inside, where she turned and struck him on the face. She did so again, lashing out in broad, flailing strokes, as if to beat back a truth that would destroy her world.

The blows hurt, though not as much as the anger and despair that were behind them. Finally, Janson grabbed her wrists. "Marina," he said, his own voice thick with grief. "*Please,* Marina."

She stared at him as if by force of will she could make him vanish, and with him the devastating news he had brought.

"Marina, I don't have words to say how sorry I am." Clichés came out at such moments, no less true for being so. He squeezed his eyes shut, trawling for words of consolation. "Theo was a hero until the end." The words sounded wooden even as he spoke them, for the sorrow Marina and he shared was indeed beyond words. "There was nobody like him. And the things I saw him do—"

"*Mpa! Thee mou.*" She violently disengaged herself from him, ran to the balcony that overlooked the small courtyard. "Don't you get it? I don't *care* about those things anymore. I don't care about those field-agent heroics, those games of cowboys and Indians. They mean nothing to me!"

"They didn't always."

"No," she said. "Because once I played the game also. . . ."

"My God, what you did in the Bosporus—it was extraordinary." The operation had taken place six years ago, shortly before Marina resigned from her country's intelligence services. A cache of armaments en route to the *17 Noemvri* group, the November 17 terrorist group, had been seized, those who purveyed it apprehended. "I know intelligence professionals who still marvel at it."

"And only afterward do you get to ask yourself: Did it make any difference, any of it?"

"It saved lives!"

"Did it? One shipment of small arms seized. To be replaced by another, routed elsewhere. I suppose it keeps the prices high, the dealers well paid."

"Theo didn't see it that way." Janson spoke softly.

"Theo never got around to seeing it that way, no. And now he never will." Her voice started to quaver.

"You blame me."

"I blame myself."

"*No,* Marina."

"I let him *go,* didn't I? If I insisted, he would have stayed. Do you doubt it? But I didn't insist. Because even if he stayed home this time, there'd be another call, and another, and another. And not to go, not *ever* to go—that, too, would have killed him. Theo was great at what he did. I know that, Paul. It's what made him proudest of himself. How could I take that from him?"

"We make our choices."

"And how could I teach him that he might be great at other things, too? That he was a good person. That he was going to be a great father."

"He was a great friend."

"To you, he was," Marina said. "Were you to him?"

"I don't know."

"He loved you, Paul. That's why he went."

"I understand that," Janson said tonelessly. "I do."

"You meant the world to him."

Janson was silent for a moment. "I am so sorry, Marina."

"You brought us together. And now you've broken us apart, the only way we could ever be broken part." Marina's dark eyes looked at him beseechingly, and a dam within her suddenly broke. Her sobs were animallike, wild and unrestrained; over the next few minutes, they wracked her like convulsions. There she sat upon a black lacquered chair, surrounded by the small appurtenances of domesticity she and Theo had acquired together: the flat-weave carpet, the blond, newly refinished wooden floor, the small, pleasant house where she and her husband had made a life— had prepared, together, to welcome another life. In different ways, Janson mused, a war-torn island in the Indian Ocean had deprived both him and Theo of fatherhood.

"I didn't want him to go," she said. "I never wanted him to go." Her face was red now, and when she opened her mouth a filament of saliva stretched between her swollen lips. Her anger had provided Marina her only mooring, and when it collapsed, so did she.

"I know, Marina," Janson said, his own eyes moist. Seeing her begin to slump, he wrapped his arms around her, holding her to him in a tight embrace. "Marina." He spoke her name like a whispered supplication. The view out of the room's picture window was incongruously sunny, and the honking of frustrated motorists was almost a balm, the bleating white noise of the urban late afternoon. A sea of commuters rushing home to their families: men, women, sons, daughters—the geometry of domestic life.

When she looked at him next, it was through a lens of tears. "Did he save somebody? Did he rescue someone? Tell me his death wasn't in vain. Tell me he saved a life. *Tell me,* Paul!"

Janson sat motionless on a wicker-back chair.

"Tell me what happened," Marina said, as if the specifics of the event would provide her a purchase on sanity.

A minute elapsed before he could collect himself and speak, but then he told her what had happened. It was why he had come, after all. He was the only one who knew just how Theo had died. Marina wanted to know, *needed* to know, and he would tell her. Yet even as he spoke, he became intensely aware of how little the explanation in fact explained. There was so much more that he didn't know. So many questions to which he had no answers. All he knew was that he would find those answers, or die trying.


Hotel Spyrios, located a few blocks from Syntagma Square, was built in the bland international-resort style; elevators were trimmed with resin-coated travertine, doors covered with a mahogany veneer, furnishings designed to sparkle in brochures but afford no unnecessary pleasures.

"Your room will be ready in five minutes," the man at the front desk told him carefully. "You have a seat in the lobby and we'll be right with you. Five minutes, no more."

The five minutes, being metered out in Athenian time, were more like ten, but eventually Janson was given his key card, and he made his way to his ninth-floor hotel room. The ritual was automatic: he inserted the narrow key card in the slot, waited for the green diode to blink, turned the latch knob, and pushed the heavy door inward.

He felt burdened, and not simply by his luggage. His shoulders and upper back ached. The meeting with Marina had been every bit as wrenching as he'd expected. They had bonded, in their sense of loss, but only momentarily: he was its proximate cause, there was no getting away from that, and grief, separated, was doubled in intensity. How could Marina ever understand how bereft he himself felt, how harrowed he was by his own sense of guilt?

He noticed a smell of stale sweat in the room, suggesting that one of the cleaners had only just left. And the curtains were drawn, at an hour when they would normally have been left open. In his distracted state, Janson did not make the inferences that he was trained to make. Grief had interposed itself between him and the world like a gauzy scrim.

Only when his eyes adjusted to the light did he see the man who was seated in an upholstered chair, his back to the curtains.

Janson started, reaching for a gun he didn't have.

"It's been a long time between drinks, Paul," the seated man said.

Janson recognized the man's silky, unctuous tones, the cultivated English with just a slight Greek accent. Nikos Andros.

He was flooded with memories, few of them fond.

"I'm hurt, you visiting Athens and not telling me," Andros continued, rising to his feet and taking a few steps toward him. "I thought we were friends. I thought I was somebody you'd look up for a drink, a glass of ouzo. Hoist one for old times' sake, my friend. No?"

The pebbled cheeks, the small darting eyes: Nikos Andros belonged to another era in Janson's life, to a temporal compartment he had sealed off when he left Consular Operations.

"I don't care how you got in here—my only question to you is how you prefer to leave," said Janson, who was past any displays of joviality. "Quickest would be off the balcony, nine stories down."

"Is that any way to talk to a friend?" Andros wore his dark hair severely short; his clothing was, as always, expensive, neatly pressed, fastidious: the black blazer was cashmere, the midnight blue shirt was silk, his shoes a soft, burnished calfskin. Janson glanced at the nail grown long on Andros's little finger, a foppish custom of certain Athenians, indicating a disdain for manual labor.

"A friend? We did *business* together, Nikos. But that's all in the past. I doubt you've got anything to sell I'd be in the market for."

"No time for 'show and sell'? You must be a man in a hurry. No matter. I'm in the charity business today. I'm not here to sell information. I'm here to give you information. Absolutely gratis."

In Greece, Nikos Andros was known as a conservator of the national treasures. A curator at the Piraeus Archaeological Museum and a crusader for preservation programs, he was frequently quoted on the subject of repatriation, regularly urging that the Elgin Marbles be returned to the country from which they were taken. He lived in a neoclassical villa in the leafy Athenian suburb of Kifissía, on the lower slopes of Mount Pendéli, and cut a colorful figure in Athens's elite circles. His connoisseurship and erudition in classical archaeology made him a much-sought-after guest in the drawing rooms of the rich and powerful throughout Europe. Because he lived well, and occasionally made oblique reference to family money, he appealed to the Greek reverence for the *anthropos kales anatrophes,* the man of high breeding.

Janson knew that the soigné curator grew up the son of a shopkeeper in Thessaloníki. He also knew that Andros's hard-won social prominence was crucial to his sub rosa career as an information broker during the Cold War. It was a time when Athens sector was a center for networks run by the CIA and by the KGB alike, when human assets were often smuggled through the Bosporus Strait, when complex gambits involving the neighboring countries of Asia Minor were launched from the Aegean peninsula. Andros was perfectly detached from the larger play of superpowers; he was no more inclined to favor one side over another than a commodities broker was to favor one customer over another.

"If you have something to say," Janson said, "say it and get the hell out."

"You *disappoint* me," Andros said. "I've always thought of you as a man of sophistication, worldliness, breeding. I'd always respected you for it. Transactions with you were more enjoyable than with most."

For his part, Janson recalled his transactions with Andros as being particularly excruciating. Matters were simpler with those who understood the value of the commodity and were content with a straightforward value-for-value exchange. By contrast, Andros needed to be flattered and cajoled, not just paid. Janson remembered well his endless, wheedling requests for rare varieties of ouzo. Then there were his whores, the young women, and sometimes young men, who would accompany him at inappropriate junctures. As long as he himself was taken care of, he cared little whether he was jeopardizing the safety of others, as well as the integrity of the networks with which he made contact.

Nikos Andros had grown rich as a Cold War profiteer; it was as simple as that. Janson had contempt for such men, and though he could never afford to display this contempt when he might still require their goods and services, that time was long past.

"Who sent you?" Janson demanded.

"Oh dear," Andros said. "Now you're behaving like a *koinos eglimatias*, a common thug—a danger to yourself and others. You know, your acquaintances are divided between those who think you have changed since your days in Vietnam . . . and those who know you haven't."

Janson tensed visibly. "You have no idea what you're talking about." His face grew hot.

"Don't I? You've left quite a few enemies from those days, a number of whom went on to pursue similar careers to your own. There are some who find it difficult to forgive you. In my travels, I myself have met one or two who, after a bottle of ouzo or two, will admit that they consider you a monster. It's said that you gave evidence that got your commanding officer executed for war crimes—despite the fact that what you yourself did was as bad or worse. What a curious sense of justice you have, always pointed outward, like the guns of a fortress."

Janson stepped forward, placed a hand on Andros's chest, and slammed him hard against the wall. A clamoring filled his mind—then was silenced by sheer force of will. He had to focus. "What is it that you want to say to me, Andros?"

Something like hatred flashed in Andros's eyes, and Janson recognized, for the first time, that his contempt was not unreciprocated. "Your former employers wish to see you."

"Says who?"

"That's the message I was asked to deliver. They wanted me to tell you that they need to talk to you. They want you to *come in.*"

*Come in:* a term of art, whose significance Andros appreciated as much as anyone. *Come in*—report to stateside headquarters, to submit to analysis, interrogation, or whatever form of debriefing was deemed appropriate. "You're talking nonsense. If Cons Op command wanted me to come in, they wouldn't give the message to a pampered sociopath like you. You're a person who might work for anyone. I'd love to know who your real employer is today, message boy."

" 'Message boy,' you say."

"That's all you ever were."

Andros smiled, and weblike creases formed around his eyes. "Do you remember the story behind the original Marathon? In the fifth century B.C., the Persians launched an invasion, landing at the coastal town of that name, Marathon. A message boy, Phidippides, was tasked with running to Athens to summon troops. The Athenian army, outnumbered four to one, launched a surprise offensive, and what looked like suicide turned out to be astonishing victory. Thousands of Persians lay dead. The rest fled to their ships, to try to attack Athens directly. A secret message had to be sent again to Athens, to tell them of the victory and of the impending assault. Once more, the message boy Phidippides was entrusted with the mission. Mind you, he'd been on the battlefield all morning himself, in heavy armor. No matter. He ran all the way, ran as fast as his feet could carry him, twenty-six miles, delivered the news, and then keeled over dead. Quite a tradition, that of the Greek message boy."

"Surprise attacks and secret messages—I can see why the tale appeals to you. But you're not answering my question, Andros. *Why you?*"

"Because, my friend, I happened to be in the neighborhood." Andros smiled again. "I like to imagine that's what the boy of ancient Greece panted before he collapsed. No, Janson, you've got it all wrong. In this case, the message belongs to the one who can locate its recipient. Thousands of carrier pigeons were sent out—this one happened to arrive. It seems that by the time your old colleagues got word you'd arrived in this country, they'd lost your scent. They needed me, with my network of connections. I know someone in just about every hotel, *taverna, kapheneion,* and *ouzeri* in this part of town. I put word out, I got word back. Do you think any American attaché could work as fast?" Andros revealed an even row of sharp-looking, almost feral teeth. "But then if I were you, I'd fret less about the singer and more about the song. You see, they're especially anxious about talking to you because they need you to *explain* certain matters."

"What matters?"

Andros sighed heavily, theatrically. "Questions have arisen concerning your recent activities that require an immediate explanation." He shrugged. "Look, I know nothing of these matters. I merely repeat lines I have been given, like an aging actor in one of our *epitheorisi,* our soap operas."

Janson laughed scornfully. "You're lying."

"You're rude."

"There's no way that my former employers would entrust you with such an assignment."

"Because I'm an *outheteros?* A nonpartisan? But, like you, I have changed. I am a new man."

"You, a new man?" Janson scoffed. "Hardly new. Hardly a man."

Andros stiffened. "Your former employers . . . are my present employers."

"Another lie."

"No lie. We Greeks are people of the *agora,* the marketplace. But you can have no market without competition. Free market, competition—eh? These things that get so much lip service from your politicos. The world has changed a great deal in the past decade. Once, the competition was lively. Now you have the *agora* to yourself. You own the market, and call it free." He tilted his head. "So what is one to do? My erstwhile Eastern clients open their wallets and only the odd moth flutters out. Their main intelligence concern is about whether there will be enough heating fuel in Moscow this winter. I am a luxury they can no longer afford."

"There are plenty of hard-liners at the KGB who would still value your services."

"What use is a hard-liner without hard currency? There comes a time when one must choose sides, yes? I believe you often said that to me. I chose the side with—what's the charming American expression you have?—the long green."

"That was *always* your side. Money was your only loyalty."

"It wounds me when you talk that way." He arched his eyebrows. "It makes me feel *cheap.*"

"What game are you running, Andros? You trying to convince people that you're on the U.S. intelligence payroll now?"

The Greek's eyes flashed with anger and disbelief. "You think I would tell my friends that I was doing the work of this warm and fuzzy superpower? You imagine a Greek can boast of such a thing?"

"Why not? Make yourself seem important, like a real player. . . ."

"No, Paul. It would make me seem like an *Americanofilos,* a stooge of Uncle Sam."

"And what's so bad about that?"

Andros shook his head pityingly. "From others I might expect such self-delusion. Not from someone as worldly as you. The Greek people do not hate America for what it *does.* They hate it for what it *is.* Uncle

Sam is *loathed* here. But perhaps I should not be surprised at your innocence. You Americans have never been able to wrap your minds around anti-Americanism. You so want to be loved that you cannot understand why there is so little love for you. Ask yourself why America is so hated. Or is that beyond you? A man wears big boots and wonders why the ants beneath his feet fear and hate him—he has no such feelings toward *them!*"

Janson was silent for a moment. If Andros had cemented a relationship with American intelligence, he was not doing so for the bragging rights: that much was true. But how much else was?

"Anyway," Andros went on, "I explained to your old colleagues that you and I had especially cordial relations. An abiding trust and affection established over long years."

That sounded like Andros all right: the glib, at-the-ready lies, the vacant assurances. Janson could well imagine it: if Andros had got wind that a contact was to be made, he might easily decide to angle for the job. *Words coming from a trusted friend,* Andros would have told the Cons Op liaison officer, *are more likely to be received without suspicion.*

Janson stared at the Greek interloper and felt a roiling sense of tension. *They want you to come in.*

But why? Those words were not used lightly among Janson's former employers. They were not words that one could ignore without consequences.

"There's something you're not saying," Janson prodded.

"I've told you what I was instructed to tell you," Andros replied.

"You've told me what you've told me. Now tell me what you haven't."

Andros shrugged. "I hear things."

"What things?"

He shook his head. "I don't work for you. No pay, no play."

"You son of a bitch," Janson exploded. "Tell me what you know or—"

"Or what? What are you going to do—shoot me? Leave your hotel room stained with the blood of an American asset in good standing? That'll clear the air, all right."

Janson looked at him for a few moments. "I'd never shoot you, Nikos. But an agent of your new employers just might. After they learn about your connection to *Noemvri.*"

His reference to Greek's notorious November 17 group, the elusive terrorist cell long sought by American intelligence, provoked an immediate reaction.

"There's no such connection!" Andros snapped.

"Then tell them. They're sure to believe you."

"Really, you're being exasperating. That's a whole-cloth invention. It's no secret that I was opposed to the colonels, but connected to the terrorists? That's preposterous. A slander."

"Yes." Something like a smile played around Janson's lips.

"Well." Andros fidgeted uneasily. "They wouldn't believe you, anyway."

"Only it wouldn't come from me. Don't you think I can still game the system? I've spent years in counterintelligence—I know just how to plant information so that it can never be traced back to me and so that it gains credibility with each remove from its source."

"I believe you're talking out of your ass."

"A member of the Greek parliament unburdens himself to another, who, unbeknownst to him, is on the CIA payroll. Through cutaways and filters, the information ends up on a MemCon, a memorandum of conversation, filed with the local station chief. Who, by the way, hasn't forgotten that the November 17 terrorists assassinated one of his predecessors. Source rating: highly credible. Report rating: highly credible. A question mark goes by your name, in ink. Now your paymasters have quite an unpleasant dilemma. Even the possibility that a *17 Noémvri* associate was receiving U.S. funds would create a scandal within the intelligence community. It would be a career-ender for anyone involved. If you're the case officer, you could order an investigation. But is that an investigation you really want to risk? Because if the result is positive, the intelligence officers will have to cut their own throats. There'll be an internal paper trail showing that American tax dollars lined the pockets of an anti-American terrorist. So what's the alternative?" Janson maintained steady eye contact as he spoke. "What's the *safe* thing? An accident? Maybe one of those whores you bring home has a special toy, and that night you don't wake up. 'Curator, conservator stricken by fatal heart attack'—that's the news item, and everyone's breathing a lot easier. Or maybe it'll look like you're the victim of a street crime, a mugging gone awry. Or rough trade that got rougher than you'd bargained for."

"Ridiculous!" Andros said, with little conviction.

"On the other hand, the decision might be made to remove you from the rolls, erase any record of payment, and leave you alone. In fact, that's entirely possible." A beat. "Is that a chance you're willing to bet on?"

Andros clenched and unclenched his jaw for a few moments; a vein visibly throbbed on his forehead. "The word is," he said, "they want to know why you have sixteen million dollars in your Cayman Islands account. The Bank of Mont Verde. Sixteen million dollars that was not there only a few days ago."

"More of your lies!" Janson roared.

"No!" Andros pleaded, and the fear in his eyes was real enough. "True or false, it's what they *believe*. And that is no lie."

Janson took a few deep breaths and looked at Andros hard. "Get out of here," he said. "I'm sick of the sight of you."

Without another word, Andros rushed out of Janson's hotel, seemingly stricken by what he'd been compelled to reveal. Perhaps, too, he recognized that Janson had ordered him away for his own protection, lest the operative's growing rage seek a physical outlet.

Alone in his room, Janson found his thoughts tumbling over themselves. It made no sense. Andros was a professional liar, but this message—the implication that he had some secret fortune stowed away—was a falsehood of another order. More disturbing still was the unmistakable reference to the Cayman Islands account; Janson did have such an account at the Bank of Mont Verde, but he had always kept its existence hidden. There was no official record of it—no accessible evidence of it anywhere. What could explain a reference to an account that only he should have known about?

Exactly what was Nikos Andros up to?

Janson turned on his tri-band wireless PDA and inserted the numbers that would give him an Internet connection to his bank in the Caymans. The signals would be two-way encoded, using a random string that would be generated by Janson's own electronic device and never used again. No message interception would be possible. The 1,024-bit encryption made the process slow, but within ten minutes, Janson had downloaded his latest account-activity records.

The account had, when he last checked it, contained $700,000.

Now it contained $16.7 million.

Yet how was that possible? The account was safeguarded against unauthorized deposits, just as it was against unauthorized withdrawals.

*They want you to come in.*

The words returned with a knife-sharp edge.

Over the next thirty minutes, Janson combed through a series of transfers that involved his own unique digital signature, a nonreplicable set of numbers entrusted only to him—a digital "private key" that even the bank had no access to. *It was impossible.* And yet the electronic record was irrefutable: Janson had himself authorized the receipt of sixteen million dollars. The money had arrived in two installments, of eight million each. Eight million had arrived four days ago. Eight million had arrived yesterday, at 7:21 P.M. EST.

Approximately a quarter of an hour after Peter Novak's death.

# CHAPTER TEN

The air in the room seemed to grow heavy; the walls were closing in. Janson needed to regain his bearings, needed to get outside. The area surrounding Syntagma Square was a sprawl of kiosks and shops, growing posher in the vicinity of Syntagma Square proper. Even here, though, were the standard-bearers of globalization: a Wendy's, a McDonald's, an Arby's. Janson pushed on, making his way past the neoclassical facades of the nineteenth-century Ottoman buildings, now mostly given over to functions of state. He strode down Herod Atticus Street and then Vassilissis Sofias and paused before the Vouli, or what was now the Greek parliament, a vast, buff-colored structure, the windows relatively small, the portico long. Before it, évzone guards, with their bayoneted rifles and maroon-tasseled caps and kilts, preened. A series of bronze shields honored now forgotten victories.

He sought out the cooler, clearer air of the National Gardens, which the Vouli fronted. There, dingy white statues and small fishponds were tucked away among the bushes and trees. Bounding along the bowers and arbors were hundreds of feral cats, many with leathery, wrung-out nipples protruding from their underbellies. An odd thing: it was possible simply not to notice them. And yet, once you did, you saw them everywhere.

He nodded at a white-haired man on a park bench who seemed to be looking in his direction; the man averted his gaze just a little too quickly, it seemed, given the affability of most Greeks. No doubt it was Janson's nerves; he was jumping at shadows.

Now he circled back to the Omónia, a somewhat seedy neighborhood northwest of Syntagma, where he knew a man who maintained a very specialized business indeed. He walked swiftly down Stadíou, past shops and *kapheneion*. What first caught his attention was not a familiar face but simply a face that, once more, turned too quickly when he approached. Was Janson starting to imagine things? He replayed it in his mind. A casually dressed man apparently had been squinting at a street sign when Janson rounded the corner, then immediately turned his gaze to a shop. To Janson, it seemed that he did so a bit abruptly, like an observer knowing that it was bad form to be seen close-up by the subject of surveillance.

By now Janson had become hyperattentive to his environs. A block later, he noticed the woman across the street peering into the jewelry shop; but, again, something was off about it. The sun slanted fiercely at the plate glass, making it a better mirror than a window. If she were, in fact, trying to make out the necklaces and bracelets displayed in the window, she would have had to stand at the opposite angle, with her back to the sun, creating a shadow through which the window would be restored to transparency. Moments before, another shopper had held out a wide-brimmed hat to block the sun's slanting rays and see into the store. But what if your interest was only in what the glass was reflecting?

Janson's field instincts began signaling wildly. He was being watched: as he thought back on it, he should have picked up on the couple at the florist's counter opposite the hotel, ostentatiously looking at a large map that hid their faces. Incongruously large. Most tourists on foot contented themselves with the smaller pocket-sized versions.

What the hell was going on?

He strode into the Omónia meat market, which sprawled within a cavernous nineteenth-century building with a fretted-iron front. On beds of chopped ice, there were mountains of glistening organs: hearts, livers, stomachs. The intact carcasses of cows, pigs, and improbably large fowl were stationed upright, head to tail, creating a grotesque topiary of flesh.

Janson's eyes darted around him. To his left, several stalls over: a customer, poking at one of the pork bellies—the same man who had averted his gaze in the National Gardens. Giving no sign that he'd made the watcher, Janson strode swiftly to the other side of a veritable curtain of mutton, the meat hooks hanging from a long steel rod. From between two sheep carcasses, he saw the white-haired customer quickly lose interest in the pig. The man walked along the row of hanging sheep, straining for a view of the other side. Janson pulled back one of the larger specimens, grabbing its rear hooves, and then, as the white-haired man was walking past, swung the massive carcass toward him, sending him sprawling into a quivering bed of calves' tripe.

Vociferous exclamations in Greek erupted, and Janson swiftly dodged the commotion, striking out toward the other end of the meat market and onto the street again. Now he made his way to a nearby department store, Lambropouli Bros., at the corner of Eólou and Lykoúrgos Streets.

The three-story building was all glass and waffle-front concrete, stucco simulacrum. He paused in front of the department store, peering into the glass until he noticed a man in a loose yellow windbreaker hovering near a leather-goods store opposite. Then Janson walked into the department store, heading toward the men's clothing area in the rear of the ground floor. He looked appraisingly at suits, keeping an eye on the time and glancing at the small ceiling-mounted mirrors strategically placed to deter theft. Five minutes elapsed. Even if every entrance was guarded, no member of a surveillance team allows his subject to disappear for five minutes. The risk of an unforeseen occurrence is too great.

Sure enough, the man in the yellow windbreaker made his way into Lambropouli Bros., walking across the aisles until he spotted Janson. Then he stationed himself near the glass and chrome display for fragrances; the reflective surfaces would make it easy to spot Janson if he emerged from the back of the store.

Finally Janson took a suit and a shirt to the changing rooms in the far rear. And there he waited. The store was obviously short-staffed, and the salesman had more customers than he could deal with. He would not miss Janson.

But the watcher would. As the minutes ticked by, he would wonder, with growing concern, what could be taking Janson so long. He would wonder if Janson had escaped through an unanticipated service exit. He would have no choice but to enter the changing rooms himself and investigate.

Three minutes later, the man in the yellow windbreaker did precisely that. From the crack of the dressing-room door, Janson saw the man wander through the alcove with a pair of khaki trousers draped over an arm. The man must have waited until there was nobody visible in the narrow aisle of dressing rooms. Yet that was a circumstance that two could exploit. Just as he passed in front of the door, Janson swung it open with explosive force. Now he sprang out and dragged the stunned watcher back to the end of the alcove and through a door that led to an employees-only area.

He had to work fast, before someone who had heard the sound came over to investigate what was going on.

"One word and you die," Janson told the dazed man softly, holding a small knife to his right carotid artery.

Even in the gloom of the storage facility, Janson could see the man's earpiece, a connecting wire disappearing into his clothing. He tore open the man's shirt, removed the thin wire that ran to a ten-ounce Arrex radio communicator in his trouser pocket. Then he took a second look at what appeared to be a plastic bracelet on the man's wrist: it was, in fact, a positional transponder, signaling his location to whoever was directing the team.

This was not an elaborate system; the whole surveillance effort had been hasty and ad hoc, with instrumentation to match. Indeed, the same went for the human capital deployed. Though they were not untrained, they were either insufficiently experienced or out of practice, or both. This was reserve-caliber work. He took the measure of the man before him: the weathered face, the soft hands. He knew the type—a marine who'd been on desk duty too long, summoned with little notice, an auxiliary reassigned to meet an unexpected need.

"Why were you following me?" Janson asked.

"I don't know," the man said, wide-eyed. He looked to be in his early thirties.

"*Why?*"

"They said to. They didn't say why. The instructions were to watch, not interfere."

"Who's *they?*"

"Like you don't know."

"Security chief at the consulate," Janson said, sizing up his prisoner. "You're part of the marine detail."

The man nodded.

"How many of you?"

"Just me."

"Now you're pissing me off." With stiffened fingers, Janson jabbed at the man's hypoglossal nerve, just inside the lower edge of his jaw: he knew the pain would be breathtaking, and he simultaneously clamped a hand over the man's mouth. "How *many?*" he demanded. After a moment, he removed his hand, permitting the man to speak.

"Six," the watcher gasped, rigid with pain and fear.

Janson would have interrogated the man further if there were more time; but if his locator unit did not indicate motion, others would soon arrive to find out why. Besides, he suspected that the man had no more information to offer. The marine had been assigned to his division's counterterrorism section. He would have been suited up with little notice and less explanation. That was the usual way with consular emergencies.

What had Nikos Andros told them?

Tearing strips from the man's Oxford-cloth shirt, Janson bound his wrists and ankles, and fashioned a makeshift gag. He took the transponder bracelet with him.

He was familiar with the transponder protocol; they were used to supplement the Arrex communicators, which were notoriously unreliable, especially in urban terrain. What's more, spoken communication was not always feasible or appropriate. The transponders allowed the team leader to keep track of those in the shift: each appeared as a pulsing dot on an LCD screen. If one person hived off in pursuit of the subject, the others would be able to follow, with or without verbal instructions.

Now Janson put on the man's yellow windbreaker and gray cap and made his way out the department store's side entrance at a trot.

The watcher had been approximately his height and build; from a distance, Janson would be indistinguishable from him.

But he would have to keep his distance. Now he ran down Eólou to Praxitelous, and then Lekka, knowing that his movements would be showing up as a pulsing dot.

*What had Andros told them?*

And what could explain the money in the Cayman Islands account? Had someone set him up? It was a very expensive method, if so. Who could even put their hands on that kind of money? No government agency could. Yet it would not be out of reach for a senior officer of the Liberty Foundation. The ancient question presented itself: *Cui bono?* Who benefits?

Now that Novak was out of the way, who at the Liberty Foundation would gain? Was Novak killed because he was about to discover some sort of immense malfeasance within his own organization, some malfeasance that had previously eluded his and Márta Lang's notice?

A small, fleet feral cat bounded down the sidewalk: Janson was again nearing Athens's feline capital, the National Gardens. Now he raced to catch up with the cat.

A few bystanders looked at him oddly.

"Greta!" he cried, scooping up the gray cat and nuzzling it. "You've lost your collar!"

He snapped the plastic-housed positional transponder around the animal's neck. It was a snug but not uncomfortable fit. When he approached the gardens, he freed the furiously squirming animal, which bounded into the thickets, in search of field mice. Then Janson stepped into the brown wooden cabin where the park's rest rooms were housed, and shoved the cap and yellow windbreaker in a black steel waste canister.

Within minutes, he was on the no. 1 trolley, no surveillance in evidence. The team members would soon be converging on the feline-infested center of the gardens. If he knew the Athens sector, their real ingenuity would go into face-saving reports later.

*Athens sector.* He'd spent more time there in the late seventies than he cared to think about. Now he racked his mind to try to remember someone he might know who could explain what was going on—explain it from the inside. Plenty of people owed him favors; it was time to collect.

The face came to him a moment before the name: a middle-aged desk jockey from the CIA Athens station. He worked in a small office on the third floor of the U.S. embassy, which was on 91 Vassilissis Sofias Avenue, near the Byzantine Museum.

Nelson Agger was a familiar sort. A careerist with a nervous stomach and little by way of larger convictions. He'd graduated from Northwestern with a master's in comparative politics; though his grades and recommendations were good enough to get him into a handful of doctoral programs, they were not good enough to earn him the scholarship or tuition abatement he needed. The support would have to come from an outside source—a State Department–run foundation, in his case.

Once his paper credentials were secure, he became a desk analyst, displaying complete mastery of the unwritten rules of producing analytic reports. The reports—a number of which Janson had seen—were invariably unexceptionable, safe, and authoritative-sounding, their essential vacuity camouflaged by their sonorous cadence. They were festooned with such phrases as *present trends are likely to continue* and made cunning use of adverbs like *increasingly.* Trends were thus identified with no assessments hazarded as to outcome. *King Fahd will find it increasingly difficult to maintain control,* he had predicted each month of the Saudi leader. The fact that the potentate hung on to power year after year until incapacitated by a stroke—a nearly two-decade reign—was only a minor embarrassment; after all, he never said that King Fahd would lose control within any given time frame. Of Somalia, Agger once wrote, "The situation and circumstances have not yet unfolded to the point that the nature of the successor government or the policies that will eventually be implemented can be described with confidence." The analysis was indeed sound—pure sound, unencumbered by meaning.

Thin, balding, gangly, Nelson Agger was the kind of man whom field operatives were prone to underestimate; what he may have lacked in physical courage he made up for by his adroitness at office politics. Whatever else the bureaucrat might be, he was a survivor.

He was also an oddly likable soul. It was hard, in the abstract, to explain why Janson got along with him so well. Part of it surely had to do with the fact that Agger had no illusions about himself. He was a cynic, yes, but unlike the sententious opportunists who populated Foggy Bottom, he never made any bones about it, at least not when he was around Janson. The dangerous ones, in Janson's experience, were those with grand plans and cold eyes. Agger, though no tribute to his profession, probably did more good than harm.

But if Janson was honest with himself, he had to admit that another reason they got along was the simple fact that Agger liked and looked up to him. Desk jockeys, defensive about their role in the system, usually affected a measure of condescension toward the operatives. By contrast, Agger, who once laughingly referred to himself as "the gutless wonder," never bothered to hide his admiration.

Or, for that matter, his gratitude. In years past, Janson had occasionally seen to it that Agger was the first person to receive a particular piece of intelligence; in a few instances, Agger was able to tailor his analytic reports to make them seem prescient by the time the intelligence cables reached their channels. The baseline of mediocrity in intelligence analysis was such that an officer needed only a few such assists to acquire a reputation for excellence.

Nelson Agger was precisely the sort of person who could help him. Whatever Agger's shortcomings in the world of international intelligence, he had extremely sharp ears for intelligence internal to his division—who was in favor, who was not, who was thought to be losing his edge, who was believed to be on the rise. A tribute to his political skills was that he had become a clearinghouse for gossip without ever being known as a gossip himself. Nelson Agger could shed light on what was going on if anybody could. Nothing could take place in Athens sector without the knowledge of the small, tightly knit CIA station.

Now Janson sat in the back of a café on Vassilissis Sofias, just opposite the American embassy, sipping a mug of the strong, sweet coffee the Athenians favored, and phoned the station switchboard on his dual-mode Ericsson.

"Trade protocols," the voice answered.

"Agger, please."

A few seconds, during which three clicks could be heard; the call would be taped and logged.

"May I say who's calling?"

"Alexander," Janson said. "Richard Alexander."

A few more seconds. Then Agger's voice came on the line. "It's been a long time since I've heard that name," he said. His voice was neutral, unreadable. "I'm glad to hear it now."

"Fancy a glass of retsina?" Deliberately casual. "Can you get away now? There's the *tavernos* on Lakhitos. . . ."

"I have a better idea," Agger said. "The café on Papadhima. Kaladza. You remember it. A little farther, but the food's excellent."

Janson felt a small stab of adrenaline: the counteroffer had come too quickly. And they both knew the food at Kaladza was terrible; it had been a subject of their conversation when they last spoke, four years ago. "The worst in town," Agger had said, taking a mouthful of doubtful calamari and looking green.

Agger was telling him that they would both have to take precautions.

"Sounds great," Janson said heartily, for the sake of anyone else who was or would be listening. "Got a cell phone?"

"In Athens, who doesn't?"

"Take it. If I get held up, I'll let you know."

"Good idea," Agger said. "*Good* idea."

From the café on Vassilissis Sofias, Janson observed Agger leaving from a side door and making his way down the street, toward the naval hospital and the street that would lead toward Kaladza.

Then he saw what he feared he might see. In Agger's wake, a woman and a man emerged from the bland, gray-brick office building adjoining the embassy and set off in his direction. He was being tailed.

And the desk man did not have the rudimentary field skills to know it.

Whoever had been listening in on their phone conversation had recognized the legend name and responded immediately. Janson's relationship with Agger had doubtless been taken account of, the possibility of his making contact with the analyst anticipated.

Now Agger joined a crowd of pedestrians heading toward the Parko Euftherias, and the man and woman merged into the sidewalk traffic.

Kaladza was too dangerous; the rendezvous would be on a terrain he chose. Janson slipped a wad of drachmas beneath his coffee mug and left for the Lykavittós. The Lykavittós was the tallest hill in Athens, and its forested crest swelled from the city like a green dome. The Lykavittós was as good a candidate for an off-the-books briefing as any. What made it attractive to visitors was that it afforded a breathtaking view of the city. What made it attractive to him was that the high ground would make it hard for a surveillance team to take up position undetected—especially if he staked it out first. At the moment, he was armed with only a small pair of binoculars. Was he being paranoid to worry that this would not suffice?

The funicular departed every twenty minutes from the top of Ploutár-khou Avenue, in the upscale Kolonáki district. Alert to any sign of pro-fessional interest, Janson rode the railway up the hill past the tiers of well-tended terracing; there was the gratifying sense of leaving the smog behind as they climbed up nearly a thousand feet. The summit was ringed with observation decks and cafés. At the very top was a small white chapel, Agios Geórgios, St. George's, a nineteenth-century edifice.

Now Janson telephoned Agger on his cell phone. "Change of plans, old bean," he said.

"They say change is good," Agger said.

Janson paused. Should he tell him about the tail? The slight tremor in Agger's voice told him that it would be best not to. Agger would not know how to shake his followers, and an uninformed attempt would only make him an easier mark. Besides, being aware of them might overstrain the man's nerves—might spook him, send him scurrying back to the office. Better to give him an itinerary that gave him a shot at shaking his pursuers willy-nilly.

"Got a pen?" asked Janson.

"I *am* a pen," the analyst sighed.

"Listen carefully, my friend. I want you to take this series of street trams." Janson proceeded to detail a complex sequence of transfers.

"A pretty roundabout route," Agger said.

"Trust me on this," Janson said. What would hold back a professional watcher wasn't the physical task of keeping up with him; it was the di-minishing odds of doing so without being noticed. In a situation like this, covert operatives would desist surveillance rather than risk exposure.

"Right," Agger said with the voice of someone who knew he was in over his head. "Of course."

"Now, when you finally get off the cable car to Lykavittós, you'll take the path toward the Theatre of Lykavittós. We'll meet in front of the fountain of Elijah."

"You'll have to give me, what, an hour?"

"See you then."

Janson tried to sound reassuring; Agger's voice was nervous, even more nervous than usual, and that was not good. It would make him cautious in a counterproductive fashion, too attentive to incidentals, too indiscriminate in his vigilance.

Janson wandered past a hillside café—a cheerful-looking spot with lime-colored plastic chairs, peach tablecloths, a slate terrace. Nearby was a sculpture garden planted with marble figures of modern vintage. Wandering through was a pair of teenagers wearing white muscle shirts that draped loosely around their unmuscular chests, whipped this way and that by the breeze. An addled-looking woman clutching a bag filled with stale pita fed already overfed pigeons.

Now Janson stationed himself within a dense copse of Aleppo pine and took an inventory of the others in the area. On sweltering days, many Athenians sought refuge here from the heat and the smarting *nephos*. He saw a Japanese couple, one holding a tiny videocamera in his hand, the size of an old Instamatic, a testament to the ingenuity of consumer electronics. The man was posing his wife against the dramatic backdrop—all Athens at her feet.

As five minutes stretched into ten and then fifteen, more people came and went in a seemingly random procession. Yet not everything was random. Thirty yards below to his left, a man in a caftanlike shirt was sketching the landscape on a large pad; his hand moved over it in large, looping gestures. Janson focused his binoculars, zooming in on his strong, powerful hands. One hand loosely gripped a stick of charcoal and was filling the pad with random squiggles. Whatever he was interested in, it wasn't the landscape in front of him. Janson zoomed in on his face and felt a pang. This man was not like the Americans he had encountered earlier. The powerful neck straining at his collar, the dead eyes—this man was a professional killer, a gun for hire. Janson's scalp began to crawl.

Diagonally opposite, another man was reading the newspaper. He was dressed like a businessman, bespectacled, in a light gray suit. Janson zoomed in: his lips were moving. Nor was he reading out loud, for when his eyes darted off, he continued speaking. He was communicating—the microphone could have been in his tie or lapel—to a confederate, somebody with an earpiece.

Anyone else?

The redheaded woman in the green cotton dress? But no, ten young children were following her. She was a schoolteacher, taking the children on a field trip. No operative would expose herself to the chaos and unpredictability of a group of young children.

A hundred feet above the fountain where Agger and he had arranged to meet at four o'clock, Janson continued to scan the scene. His eyes roved over the gravel paths and the wild, unkempt expanse of grass and scrub.

Conclusion: an inexpert American tag team had been replaced with local talent, people who knew the terrain and could react quickly.

But what were their orders?

He continued to scan the figures on the sloping hill, alert to further anomalies. The businessman was now apparently napping, his chin resting on his chest, suggesting a postprandial siesta. Only the occasional movement of his mouth—murmured communications, if only to keep boredom at bay—betrayed the illusion.

The two figures he'd identified, the businessman with his newspaper and the artist with his sketchbook, were clearly Greek nationals, not American; that much was plain from their physiognomy, attire, even posture. And language, too: Janson was a poor lip-reader, but he could tell it was Greek, not English, that the man spoke.

But for God's sake, why the dragnet? The simple existence of incriminating evidence did not explain the willingness to accept its import. Janson had been an agent of one of America's most secretive intelligence branches for twenty-five years: his profile was as thoroughly scrutinized as anyone's. If he were after a big score, he could have arranged one long ago in a hundred different ways. Yet now, so it seemed, the worst had been assumed of him, no alternative interpretation of the evidence entertained.

What had changed—something he'd done or was believed to have done? Was it something he knew? One of those things made him a threat to the planners in Washington, half a world away from this ancient hill in the center of Athens.

Who else was there? The sun's slanting rays made it hard to see, but Janson scrutinized every patch of ground that was visible to him, dividing it up like a quadrate grid, to the point that his eyes began to ache.

At four o'clock, a worried-looking Agger came into view; he was carrying his navy linen jacket flung over a shoulder, his blue striped shirt dappled with sweat, no doubt a vexing development for the fastidious analyst, who seldom ventured far from the air-conditioned ambit of office and residence.

Now, as Janson could see from his perch in the pines above, Agger sat down on the long marble bench by the fountain, breathing heavily, looking around for his old drinking companion.

Janson lowered himself to the ground

The man with the artist's pad: Muscle? Surveillance only? The fact that he was Greek concerned him. The observers on the street were, he had ascertained, Americans, part of the standard military intelligence detail attached to U.S. embassies. They weren't amateurs, but they displayed no high level of professional skill, either. They were, he had concluded, the best that could be summoned on extreme short notice. Athens sector hadn't had advance word that he'd be in town; after all, he had made the decision himself, at the spur of the moment, only twelve hours previously.

But these Greeks: Who were they? Not CIA employees. These were professionals, to whom a job had been outsourced. The kind of men you kept at arm's length—until you needed them. Often that meant a sanction, an act that no official members of a security detail could be entrusted with.

But Janson was getting ahead of himself, he knew: there was no cause for a sanction order. Not yet, anyway.

Janson crawled on his belly along the untamed arbor, staying close to a long retaining wall made of piled shale. The scrub of *maquis* impeded his progress. Blades of crabgrass tickled his nose; tall weeds sprouted in clumps every few feet, and Janson took care not to flag his presence by disturbing them. Two minutes later, he raised his head quickly above the berm line, verifying that he was within a few feet of the man with the sketchpad. That man was standing now, the stick of charcoal having been carelessly dropped to the ground like a cigarette butt.

The Greek's back was to him, and he could see how powerfully built the young "artist" was. The man's gaze was resolutely on Agger, on the marble bench before the fountain, and his muscles seemed strained for immediate response. Then Janson saw him reach for something under his caftanlike shirt.

Janson lifted a large piece of shale from the rock terrace, taking care to maintain absolute silence; any unexpected noise, such as the sound of two rocks rubbing against each other, would cause the Greek to whirl around instantly. Janson hoisted the rock above his head and flung it with all his strength, aiming for the back of his neck. The man had begun to turn when the shale struck him, and he staggered to the ground. Janson stepped over the low wall and seized the man by his hair, clamping his forearm against his mouth. He flipped him over the wall and onto his back.

He yanked a flat-sided gun—a powerful automatic pistol, a Walther P99—from the man's trouser band and saw that it had a perforated cylinder permanently attached. A silenced weapon: meant to be used, not displayed—a weapon for fulfilling threats, not simply making them. The man was a professional, with professional equipment. Janson ran his fingers along the man's embroidered collar, feeling for the microphone, and made sure that the contactor switch had not been activated. He flipped over the fabric, exposing a small blue-black plastic disk with a copper wire running out from it.

"Tell your friend it's an emergency!" he said, whispering in his ear. He knew that the task would not have been outsourced to people who did not speak English and might misunderstand orders. "Let him know that you have been betrayed! As you have been!"

"*Den omilo tin Aggliki,*" the man said.

Janson pushed his knee against the man's throat until he gagged. "Don't speak English? Then I guess there's no reason for me not to kill you."

The man's eyes widened. "No! *Please,* I do what you say."

"And remember. *Katalaveno ellinika.*" *I understand Greek.* A half-truth, anyway.

Pressing the hidden contactor toward the front of his collar, the Greek activated his microphone and began to speak, the urgency made more intense as Janson gouged his Walther into his temple.

Once the message was relayed, he slammed the Greek assassin to the shale wall. The man's cranium absorbed most of the impact; he would be unconscious for an hour, probably two.

Through his binoculars, Janson saw the businessman in the light gray suit stand abruptly and stride toward the arbor. Something about the way he carried the folded newspaper made it clear that it was serving to conceal something else. The bespectacled businessman looked warily around as he made his way into the arbor, his hand still enveloped by the folded copy of *Eleftherotypia,* the Athens daily.

Janson glanced at his wristwatch. Too much time was passing; Agger could easily be overtaken by anxiety and decide to return to the office. That was standard procedure anyway with a no-show: one was not to wait beyond a limited amount of time.

Quickly, Janson positioned himself at the end of the arborway. As the man emerged, Janson lunged, swinging the Walther P99 into his face, shattering teeth and bone. Blood spewed from his mouth and spattered on his white shirt and jacket; the paper dropped and the silenced weapon it concealed clattered to the stone underfoot. Swiftly Janson turned over the man's lapel, exposing a small blue-black disk, identical to the one worn by the other Greek.

Janson returned the Walther to his waistband and rubbed a small spot of blood from his hand. An inner bleakness was creeping upon him. In the past few days, he had fallen back into everything he had once prayed he'd left behind him—the violence, the gambits, the lethal subterfuge, a career's worth of ingrained habits. Still, this was no time to gaze into the abyss. He had to focus, to analyze, to act.

Were there others? None that he'd detected, but he could not be certain. The Japanese tourist? Possible. Unlikely.

He would have to take the risk.

Now Janson strode over to Agger, who was still on the marble bench, perspiring heavily.

"Paul," Agger said. "Thank God! I was starting to worry that something had happened to you."

"Traffic on the Vas Sofias. I forgot what a bitch it is this time of day." Janson decided it was important not to alarm him just yet. Agger's was a world of cables and keyboards; such a rendezvous was beyond his customary bailiwick, and, in fact, in violation of procedures. The approach even of a member or former member of the U.S. intelligence community, according to the rule book, required a memorandum of conversation to be filed promptly. Agger was already stretching the rules—and probably his nerves—simply in agreeing to the meeting.

"God, with all those crosstown transfers, I was thinking, What am I, a spy?" A wan smile. "Don't answer that. Look, I'm so glad you called, Paul. I'm been worried about you—really worried. You cannot believe the garbage they're talking about you."

"Take it slow, old friend," Janson said.

Agger seemed reassured by Janson's steadiness and composure. "But I know we can get the whole thing straightened out. Whatever it is, I know we can make it go away. Leave those Washington bureaucrats to me. Trust me, nobody knows a pencil pusher like another pencil pusher."

Janson laughed, mostly for Agger's sake. "I guess I first got wind something was up this morning. I walk down Stadíou, and it's like a class reunion of the embassy security detail. I didn't used to be so popular."

"It's crazy," Agger said. "But they're saying that you took a job, Paul. A job you shouldn't have taken."

"And?"

"Everybody wants to know who you did the job for. A lot of people want to know why you took it. Some people think there are sixteen million answers to that one."

"Christ almighty! How could anybody think that? I'm a known quantity."

Agger's gaze was searching. "You don't have to tell me that. Look, they're all wound up about it. But I know we can get this whole thing straightened out." Almost bashfully, he added, "So . . . it's true you took the job?"

"Yes, I took the job—for Peter Novak. His people contacted me. I owed him one, big-time. Anyway, I was a referral. From State."

"See, the thing is, State denies it."

"*What?*"

An apologetic shrug. "The State Department denies it. The Agency, too. It doesn't even know what went on in Anura, exactly. Reports are conflicting, sketchy at best. But the word is that you were paid to make sure Peter Novak never left the island."

"That's insane."

Another helpless shrug. "Interesting you should use that word. We've been told that you may have gone insane, though the actual words are a lot fancier. Dissociative disorder. Post-traumatic abreaction . . ."

"Do I seem crazy to *you,* Agger?"

"Of course not," Agger said quickly. "Of course not." An awkward pause followed. "But look, we all know what you've been through. All those months of VC torture. I mean, Jesus. Beaten, starved—that's got to mess with your head. Sooner or later, it's *got* to mess with you. Christ, the things they did to you . . ." In a quieter voice he added, "Not to mention the things that you did."

A chill ran down Janson's spine. "Nelson, what are you telling me?"

"Just that there are a lot of worried people, and they're way up the intelligence food chain."

*Did* they think he was insane? If so, they couldn't afford to let him wander free, not with everything the former Cons Op agent had in his head—the extensive knowledge of procedures, informants, networks that remained in operation. A security breach could destroy years of work and would simply not be countenanced. Janson knew the chain of official reasoning in a case like that.

Despite the bright hilltop sun, Janson suddenly felt cold.

Agger shifted uneasily. "I'm not an expert in that kind of thing. They said you'd seem to be plausible, cogent, in command. And no matter where your head's at, sixteen million is going to be pretty hard to resist. Maybe I'm just speaking for myself there."

"I have absolutely no explanation for the money," Janson said. "Maybe the Liberty Foundation has an eccentric way of rendering payment. Compensation was referred to. Not negotiated, not specified. Look, that wasn't a principal motivation on my part. It was a debt of honor. You know why."

"Paul, my friend, I want to get all this straightened out, and I'll do whatever I can—you *know* that. But you've got to help me out here, give me some facts. When did Novak's people make their first approach to you?"

"Monday. Forty-eight hours after Novak's abduction."

"And when was the first eight million deposited?"

"Where are you going with this?"

"It was deposited *before* you say these people approached you. *Before* they knew you'd say yes. Before they knew an extraction might be necessary. It doesn't make sense."

"Did anybody ask them about it?"

"Paul, they don't know who you are. They don't know about the abduction. They don't even know the boss is dead."

"How did they react when you told them?"

"We didn't."

"Why not?"

"Orders from the top. We're in the information-collecting business, not the information-dissemination business. Everyone's been given strict orders as to that. And speaking of collection, that's why people are so determined that you come in. It's the only way. If you don't, assumptions are going to be made. And acted upon. OK? Do I have to say more?"

"*Jesus,*" Janson said.

"Paul, you need to trust me on this one. We can put all this shit behind you. But you've *got to come in*. You've got to."

Janson looked at the analyst oddly. He couldn't fail to notice the way he had grown less deferential and anxious in the course of the conversation. "I'll think about it."

"That means no," Agger said blandly. "And that's not good enough." He reached over to his lapel, and fingered the buttonhole, in an overly casual gesture.

*Summoning others.*

Janson reached over and turned up Agger's lapel. On the reverse side was the familiar blue-black disk. All at once, he felt numb.

The Greeks weren't tails. *They were his backup.* Forcible abduction was the next course of action.

"Now I've got a timing question for you," Janson said. "When did the order go out?"

"The retrieval directive? I don't recall."

*"When?"* Standing so as to hide his actions from any bystanders, he pulled out the Walther and aimed it at the analyst.

"Oh *Jesus,* oh *Jesus!*" Agger shouted. "Paul—what are you doing? I'm just here to *help* you. I only want to *help.*"

*"When?"* Janson shoved the silenced Walther into Agger's bony chest.

The words came out in a rush. "Ten hours ago. The cable was time-stamped 10:23 P.M. EST." Agger looked around him, unable to disguise his growing sense of consternation.

"And what were the orders if I refused to report in? Did termination orders go out?" He pressed the revolver harder against Agger's sternum.

*"Stop!"* Agger called out. "You're hurting me." He spoke loudly, as if panicked; but Agger, though scarcely a field agent, was no amateur, and however anxious, he was not given to hysterics. The shout was not meant for him; it was meant to notify others, others within earshot.

"Are you expecting company?"

"I have no idea what you're talking about," Agger lied in a level tone.

"Sorry. I should have mentioned earlier that your Greek friends were unavoidably detained."

"You goddamn bastard!" The words burst from him. Agger was white-faced—not with fear but with outrage.

"They'll send their regrets. As soon as they regain consciousness."

Agger's eyes narrowed. "Christ, it's true what they say. *You're out of control!*"

# CHAPTER ELEVEN

The harborfront tavern was seedy and dark, the planks of the floor warped from years of spilled beverages, the simple wooden chairs and stools nicked and dented from careless use and the occasional brawl. Janson moved slowly toward the long zinc bar, allowing his vision to adjust to the dimness. A sailor sat to the far left, drinking alone, sullenly. He wasn't the only sailor in the place, but he would be the easiest to approach. And Janson could not wait any longer. He had to get out of Greece now.

A short while ago, he had again performed what had become a maddening ritual: he called Márta Lang's personal number. Nothing.

*They don't even know the boss is dead,* Agger had said.

Yet there was one person Janson could think of who would know what there was to be known and would speak to him freely. Of course, first precautions had to be taken—to protect both himself and the man he was going to visit.

Piraeus's Great Harbor was a vast, circular inlet, cupping the ocean, so it seemed to Janson, like an open manacle—or one that was closing. Necessity had drawn him here all the same. He had no intention of signaling his movements to anyone with a professional interest in them.

For the past couple of hours, he had considered and rejected a dozen other ways of leaving the country. Watchers would surely be swarming in and around the Athens airport by now; quite likely agents would soon be mobilized at the major airports at Thessaloníki and elsewhere. In any case, traveling on his own passport was out of the question: given the involvement of the embassy, the chances were too great that a U.S. advisory had been issued to international points of embarkation and arrival. But when he made his way to the one local he knew who specialized in forging official documents—a man who owned a stationery shop near Omónia— he found surveillance agents in position: a visit would have compromised either his contact or him. Hence his recourse to those whose livelihoods taught them the formalities of international transit—and when the formalities might be overlooked.

Janson wore a suit, which make him an incongruous sight in the Per-
igaili Bar, but his tie hung unknotted around his collar, and he looked
adrift, almost despondent. He stepped forward with a weaving gait. *Decide
on a part and then dress for it.* He was a prosperous businessman in dire
straits. If the air of desperation didn't achieve the intended results, two
minutes in the rest room and a square-shouldered shift in demeanor could
erase that impression entirely.

He took the stool next to the sailor and gave him a sidewise glance.
He was solidly built, with the kind of soft, fleshy build that spoke of a
large appetite but often hid considerable muscular strength. Did he speak
English?

"Goddamn Albanian whore," Janson muttered under his breath, just
loud enough to be heard. Imprecations directed at ethnic minorities—
especially Gypsies and Albanians—were, he knew, a reliable conversation-
starter in Greece, where the ancient notion of purity of bloodlines still
ruled.

The sailor turned to him and grunted. His bloodshot eyes were wary,
however. What was a man dressed like him doing in a such a dive?

"She took everything," Janson went on. "She cleaned me out." He signaled for a drink.

"A *shqiptar* whore stole your cash?" The sailor's expression was devoid
of sympathy, but amused. It was a start.

"Cash is about the only thing I've got left. You want to hear this?" He
saw the insignia on the sailor's uniform: U.C.S. UNITED CONTAINER SER-
VICES. Janson called to the bartender. "Get my friend here a beer."

"Why not some Metaxa?" the sailor said, testing his luck.

"That's a plan—Metaxa!" he called out. "A double! For both of us."
Something about the sailor suggested a man who knew the docks and
waterfronts of the Aegean, and the unsavory enterprises that took root
there.

Two glasses of Metaxa arrived, the colorless variety, flavored with anise.
Janson asked for a glass of water on the side. With a disapproving scowl,
the bartender slid an amber-colored glass toward him, with a few inches
of lukewarm tap water. A bar didn't stay in business by filling its customers' bellies with water, unless you counted the water with which it topped
off its bottles of liquor.

Janson began to tell his companion a tale of wandering into an *ouzeri*
while waiting for the Minoan Lines ferry at the Zea Marina. "I'd just
gotten out of a five-hour meeting, you see. We'd wrapped up a deal that

had been dragging on for months—that's why they sent me here person-ally, you see. The local reps, you can't trust them. You never know who they're really working for."

"And what does your company do, if you don't mind my asking?"

Janson's eyes darted around, settling on the glazed ceramic ashtray. "Ceramics," he said. "High-fired nonconductive ceramic struts for elec-trical appliances." He laughed. "You're sorry you asked, huh? Well, it's a filthy job, but somebody's got to do it."

"And the whore—" prompted the sailor, gulping the brandy like water.

"So I'm totally stressed—you know 'stressed'?—and this girl, she's all over me, and I'm thinking, what the hell. You know, I'm talking about release, right? And she leads me to some shithole, a few doors down, I don't even know where, and . . ."

"And you wake up and she's robbed you blind."

"Exactly!" Janson signaled the bartender to bring another round of drinks. "I must have passed out or something, and she went through my pockets. Lucky for me she didn't find my cash belt. Guess that would have meant turning me over, and she was afraid I'd wake up. But she took my passport, my credit cards. . . ." Janson grabbed at his ring finger, holding it close to the sailor's face, drunkenly demonstrating the final indignity of having a wedding band removed. He breathed hard, a senior sales exec revisiting a nightmare.

"Why not tell the *astynomia?* The harbor police here in Piraeus know the whores."

Janson covered his face. "I can't. I can't risk it. I file a report, it could be my ass. Same reason I don't dare go to the embassy. My company is *very* conservative. I can't chance them finding out—we've got reps all over. I know I don't look it, but I've got a reputation to protect. And my wife—oh *Jesus!*" Suddenly his eyes brimmed with tears. "She can't know, ever!"

"So you're a big man," the sailor said, his gaze taking the stranger's measure.

"And a bigger *idiot.* What was I *thinking?*" He drained his glass of Metaxa, filling his cheeks with the sweetened liquor, then swiveled his stool around, agitated, and raised the amber water glass to his lips. Only a trained observer would have noticed that, though Janson's water glass had not been refilled, its level magically kept rising.

"The big head wasn't thinking," the seaman said sagely. "The little head was thinking."

"If I could just get to our regional headquarters in Izmir, I could take care of everything."

The seaman drew back with a jerk. "You are a Turk?"

"Turkish? *God*, no." Janson wrinkled his nose with disgust. "How could you think that? Are *you?*"

The seaman spat on the floor in response.

In Piraeus, at least, the old enmities still simmered. "Look, we're an international company. I'm a Canadian citizen, as it happens, but our clients are everywhere. I'm not going to the police, and I can't risk turning up at the embassy. The thing could destroy me—you Greeks, you're worldly, you understand about human nature, but the people I work with aren't like that. Thing is, if I could just get to Izmir, I could make this whole *nightmare* disappear. I'll do the breaststroke to get there if I have to." He slammed down the thick-bottomed glass on the banged-up zinc bar. Then he waved a fifty-thousand-drachma note at the bartender, signaling for another round.

The bartender looked at the note and shook his head. *"Ehete mipos pio psila?"* A smaller-denomination bill was required.

Janson peered at the note like a drunk with blurred vision. The note was the equivalent of over a hundred U.S. dollars. "Oh, sorry," he said, putting it away and handing the bartender four thousand-drachma notes.

As Janson intended, the error was not lost on his companion, whose interest in his plight suddenly became livelier.

"A long way to swim," the seaman said with a mirthless chuckle. "Perhaps there is another way."

Janson looked at him imploringly. "You think?"

"Special transport," the man said. "Not comfortable. Not cheap."

"You get me to Izmir, I'll pay you twenty-five hundred dollars—U.S., not Canadian."

The sailor looked at Janson appraisingly. "Others will have to cooperate."

"That's twenty-five hundred just for you, for arranging it. If there are other expenses, I'll cover them, too."

"You wait here," the sailor said, a flush of greed sobering him slightly. "I make a phone call."

Janson drummed his fingers on the bar as he waited; if his drunkenness was feigned, his display of agitation required little acting. After a few long minutes, the seaman returned.

"I speak to a captain I know. He says if you come aboard with drugs, he will throw you into the Aegean without a life jacket."

"Absolutely not!" Janson said, aghast. "No drugs!"

"So the Albanian whore took those, too?" the man returned wryly.

"What?" Janson's tone rose in indignation, a humorless businessman whose dignity had been insulted. "*What* are you saying?"

"I joke with you," the seaman said, mindful of his fee. "But I promised the captain I'd give you the warning." He paused. "It's a containerized cargo ship. U.C.S.-licensed, like mine. And it leaves at four in the morning. Gets in at berth number six port of Izmir, four hours later, OK? What happens at Izmir is on you—you don't tell anyone how you got there." He made a neck-slicing gesture. "Very important. Also very important: you pay him a thousand dollars at Pier Twenty-three. I'll be there to make introductions."

Janson nodded and started to peel off large-denomination drachmas, keeping his hands under the counter. "The other half when I meet you in the morning."

The seaman's eyes danced. "Fair enough. But later, if the captain asks what you paid me, leave a zero off. OK, my friend?"

"You're a goddamn lifesaver," Janson said.

The sailor wrapped his fingers around the roll of bills, appreciating their heft and thickness, and smiled. "Anything else I can do for you?"

Janson shook his head distractedly, gripping his ring finger. "I'll tell her I was mugged."

"You tell your wife an *Albanian* mugged you," the seaman counseled. "Who wouldn't believe that?"

Later, at the Izmir airport, Janson couldn't help but reflect on the curious pattern of such ruses. People gave you their trust when you proclaimed just how untrustworthy you were. Someone victimized by his own greed or lust was a readier object of sympathy than someone who came on his bad luck honestly. Standing shamefaced before a British tour guide, he trotted out a version of the story he'd told the seaman.

"You shouldn't have been cavorting with those dirty girls," the tour guide—pigeon-breasted, with shaggy, white-blond hair—was telling him. His grin was less sporting than sadistic. "Naughty, naughty, naughty." The man wore a plastic badge with his name on it. Above it, printed in garish

colors, was the name and slogan of the cut-rate tour company that employed him: *Holiday Express Ltd.—a package of fun!*

"I was drunk off my arse!" Janson protested, slipping into a lower-
middle-class Home Counties accent. "Bloody Turks. This girl promised
me a 'private show'—for all I knew she was talking about *belly dancing!*"

"I'll just bet," the man replied with a leering smirk. "Such an innocent
you are." After several days of having to jolly along his paid-up wards, he
was relishing the opportunity to stick it to a customer.

"But to *leave* me here! It was a packaged holiday, all right—but that
wasn't supposed to be part of the package! Strand me here like they
couldn't give a toss?"

"Happens. Happens. One of the lads goes on a binge or gets lost. You
can't expect the whole group to miss the flight home because of one
person. That's not reasonable, now, is it?"

"Sodding hell, I've been a complete bleedin' idiot," Janson said, remorse
creeping into his voice. "Lettin' the little head do the thinking, not the
big one, if you see."

" 'Who among us?' like the Good Book says," the man replied, his tone
softening. "Now tell me the name again?"

"Cavanaugh. Richard Cavanaugh." Lifting the name from a Holiday
Express manifest had taken him a full twenty minutes at a cybercafé on
Kibris Sehitleri Street.

"Right. Dicky Cavanaugh takes a dirty holiday to Turkey and learns a
lesson in clean living." Needling the hapless customer—one whose mis-
adventures left him in no position to file a complaint—seemed to amuse
him no end.

Janson glowered.

The platinum-haired man called the Izmir affiliate of Thomas Cook
Travel on his Vodaphone and explained the customer's predicament, leaving out the interesting parts. He repeated the name twice. He remained
on the line for ten minutes, doing progressively less talking and more
listening.

He shook his head, laughing, after he hung up. "Hah! They think you've
arrived at Stansted two hours ago, with your group."

"Bloody hell?" Janson looked incredulous.

"Happens," the man said philosophically, savoring his own worldliness.
"Happens. The manifest says a tour group of twenty is arriving, nobody
wants to redo all the paperwork, so the computer thinks all twenty's accounted for. Couldn't happen on commercial service, but charter airlines

are a bit dodgier. Oops—don't tell the boss I said that. 'Cut-rate prices for a top-rate experience,' is what we like to say. If the computer was right, you'd be larking about in your optician's shop at Uxbridge, instead of quaking in your boots in bloody Izmir and wondering if you're ever going to see home and hearth again." A sidewise glance. "Any good, was she?"

"What?"

"The bird. Was she any good?"

Janson was abashed. "That's the tragic part, see. I was too pissed to remember."

The man gave him a quick squeeze on the shoulder. "I think I can fix things for you this time," he said. "But mind you, we're not in the dirty-holiday business. Keep it in your trousers, mate. Like my girl says, careful you don't poke someone's eye out." He roared with laughter at his own coarse wit. "And you with a bloody *spectacles* shop!"

"We prefer to call it a 'vision center,' " Janson said frostily, settling into the role of the proud shopkeeper. "You sure I'm not going to have any problems getting off in Stansted?"

The tour director spoke in a low voice. "No, see, that's what I'm trying to tell you. Holiday Express is going to make sure there's no snags. You take my meaning? We're going to help you out."

Janson nodded gratefully, although he knew what was really motivating the sudden show of altruism—the dismay that the tour guide's call must have precipitated in the firm's offices. Janson's stratagem, as it was meant to, had put the company in a bind: officials of a packaged-holiday company had plainly misinformed British customs that one Richard Cavanaugh, of 43 Culvert Lane, Uxbridge, had arrived in the United Kingdom. The only way to avoid an audit of its activities and a review of its license was to make sure that Richard Cavanaugh did arrive in the United Kingdom, and without the sort of data trail that could lead to awkward questions about careless business practices. The temporary papers that the pigeon-breasted man was drawing up for him—*Urgent Transport/Airline Personnel*—were a crude recourse, normally reserved for transportation involving medical emergencies, but they would do the job. Holiday Express would tidy up an embarrassing little slipup, and "Dickie" Cavanaugh would be home by suppertime.

The tour guide chuckled as he gave Janson the sheath of yellow-orange pages. "Too bloody pissed to remember, what? Makes you want to break down and cry, don't it?"

A small chartered plane took them to Istanbul, where, after a two-hour layover, they changed to a bigger charter plane that would carry three separate Holiday Express tour groups to Stansted Airport, just north of London. At each junction, Cavanaugh waved the yellow stapled pages he'd been given in Izmir, and a representative of the packaged-holiday company personally escorted him on board. The word had plainly come down from the head office: take care of this berk, or there would be hell to pay.

It was a three-hour flight, and the Uxbridge optician, sullied by his offshore adventure, kept to himself, his look of hapless self-absorption repelling any attempts at conversation. The few who heard his story saw only a tight-assed shopkeeper vowing that his indiscretions would be left behind in the Orient.

Somewhere over Europe, eyes shuttered, Janson drowsed, and eventually let himself succumb to sleep, even though he knew well the old ghosts that would stir.

It was three decades ago, and it was now. It was in a jungle far away, and it was here. Janson had returned from the debacle of Noc Lo to Demarest's office in base camp, without even stopping to clean up. He had been told that the lieutenant commander wanted to see him immediately.

The stench and stains of battle still on his clothing, Janson stood before Demarest, who sat pensively at his desk. A medieval plainsong—an eerily simple and slow progression of notes—emerged from small speakers.

Finally, Demarest looked up at him. "Do you know what just happened out there?"

"Sir?"

"If it doesn't *mean* anything, it happened for no reason. That's not a universe you want to live in. You've got to make it mean something."

"As I told you before, it was like they knew we were coming, sir."

"Seems pretty clear, doesn't it?"

"You didn't—don't—seem surprised, sir."

"Surprised? No. That was my null hypothesis—the prediction that I was testing. But I had to know for sure. Noc Lo was, among other things, an experiment. If one were to file plans for an incursion with the local ARVN liaison to Military Assistance Command-Vietnam, what consequences could one expect? What are the information relays that lead back to the local insurgency? There's only one way to test these things. And now we've learned something. We have an enemy that is committed to our root-and-branch destruction—committed with all its heart and soul and mind. And on our side? A lot of transplanted bureaucrats who think they're working for the Tennessee Valley Authority or some damn thing. A few hours ago, son, you narrowly escaped with your life. Was Noc Lo a defeat, or a victory? It's not so easy to say, is it?"

"Sir, it did not taste like victory. Sir."

"Hardaway died, I said, because he was weak. You lived, as I knew you would, because you were strong. Strong like your dad—second wave of the landing on Red Beach, if I'm not mistaken. Strong like your uncle, in the forests and ravines of Sumava, picking off Wehrmacht officers with an old hunting rifle. There's nobody fiercer than those Eastern European partisans—I had an uncle like that myself. War shows us who we are, Paul. My hope is that today you learned something about yourself. Something I determined about you back in Little Creek."

Lieutenant Commander Alan Demarest reached for a dog-eared paperback he had on his desk. "You know your Emerson?" He began to read from it: " 'A great man is always willing to be little. Whilst he sits on the cushions of advantages he goes to sleep. When he is pushed, tormented, defeated, he has a chance to learn something; he has been put on his wits on his manhood; he has gained facts; learns his ignorance; is cured of the insanity of conceit.' I reckon Ralph Waldo was onto something."

"Be nice to think so, sir."

"The battlefield is also a proving ground. It's where you die or where you're born anew. And don't just dismiss that as a figure of speech. Ever talk to your mama about what it was like to give birth to you? Women know this blinding flash of what it all means—they know that their lives, the lives of their parents, their parents' parents, of all human life on this planet for tens of thousands of years, have culminated in this wet, squirming, screaming thing. Birth isn't pretty. A nine-month cycle from pleasure to pain. Man is born in a mess of bodily fluids, distended viscera, shit, piss, blood—and baby, it's you. A moment of incredible agony. Yes, giving birth is a bitch, all right, because that pain is what gives it meaning. And I look at you standing here with the stinking guts of another soldier on your tunic and I look into your eyes, and I see a man who's been reborn."

Janson stared, bewildered. Part of him was appalled; part of him was mesmerized.

Demarest stood up, and his own gaze did not shift. He reached over and put a hand on the younger man's shoulder. "What's this war about? Ivy Leaguers in the State Department have thick three-ring binders that pretend to give an answer. It's a whole lot of white noise, meaningless rationalizations. Every conflict is the same. It's about the testing fields of battle. In the past four hours, you've known more energy and exhaustion, more agony and ecstasy—more pure adrenaline—than most people will ever experience. You're more alive than the zombies in their station wagons who tell themselves how glad they are that they're not in harm's way like you. *They're* the lost souls. They spend their days price-comparing cuts of London broil and boxes of laundry detergent and wondering, should they try to fix the sink or wait around for the plumber? They're dead inside and they don't even know it." Demarest's eyes were bright. "What's the war about? It's about the simple fact that you killed those who sought to kill you. What just happened? A victory, a defeat? Wrong yardstick, son. Here's what happened. You almost died, and you learned what it was to *live*."

# CHAPTER TWELVE

A heavy white lorry carrying a load of semi-finished lumber swung off the busy M11 highway and onto Queen's Road, Cambridge. There it pulled up beside several parked trucks bearing construction equipment for a major renovation project. That was the way with a large and aging university like Cambridge—something was always being rebuilt or renovated.

After the driver pulled in, the man he'd given a ride to thanked him warmly for the lift and stepped out onto the gravel. Instead of going to work, though, the man, who wore a taupe work suit, ducked inside one of the PolyJohns near the building site; the West Yorkshire company's motto, Leading Through Innovation, was molded on the blue plastic door. When he emerged, he was wearing a gray herringbone jacket of Harris tweed. It was a uniform of another sort, one that would render him inconspicuous as he strolled along the "Backs," the wide swath of green that ran along the oldest of the Cambridge colleges: King's, Clare, Trinity Hall, and, his destination, Trinity College. In all, just an hour had elapsed since Paul Janson arrived at the Stansted Airport, now a blurry memory of glass and quilted-steel ceilings.

Janson had spoken so many lies, in so many accents, over the past twenty-four hours that his head ached. But soon he would meet someone who could sweep all the mist and mystification away. Someone he could talk to in confidence, someone who was in a singular position to have insight into the tragedy. His lifeline would be at Trinity College: a brilliant don named Angus Fielding.

Janson had studied with him as a Marshall Fellow back in the early seventies, and the gentle scholar with the amused eyes had taken him on for a series of tutorials in economic history. Something about Fielding's sinuous mind had captivated Janson, and there was something about Janson, in turn, that the savant found genuinely engaging. All these years later, Janson hated to involve Fielding in his hazardous investigation, but there was no other choice. His old academic mentor, an expert in the global financial system, had been a member of a brain trust that Peter Novak had put together in order to help guide the Liberty Foundation. He was also, Janson had heard, now the master of Trinity College.

As Janson walked across Trinity Bridge and over the Backs, memories swept over him—memories of another time, a time of learning, and healing, and rest. Everything around him brought back images of that golden period in his life. The lawns, the Gothic buildings, even the punters who glided along the Cam under the stone arches of the bridges and the branch curtains of the weeping willows, propelling their small boats with long poles. As he approached Trinity, the wind chime of memory grew even louder. Here, facing the Backs, stood the dining hall, which was built in the early seventeenth century, and the magnificent Wren library, with its soaring vaults and arches. Trinity's physical presence at Cambridge was large and majestic but represented only a portion of its actual holdings; the college was, in fact, the second-largest landowner in Britain, after the queen. Janson walked past the library to the small gravel lot abutting the master's lodge.

He rang the bell, and a servant cracked open a window. "Here to see the master, love?"

"I am."

"Bit early, are you? Never mind, dear. Why don't you come round the front and I'll let you in?" Obviously, she had taken him for someone else, someone who had an appointment at that hour.

None of it was exactly high-security. The woman had not even asked his name. Cambridge had changed little since he had been a student there in the seventies.

Inside the master's lodge, the broad, red-carpeted stairs led past a portrait gallery of Trinity luminaries from centuries past: a bearded George Trevelyan, a clean-shaved William Whewell, an ermine-collared Christopher Wordsworth. At the top of the stairs, to the left, was a pink-carpeted drawing room with paneled walls that were painted white, so as not to compete with the portraits that adorned them. Past this room was a much larger one, with dark-wood floors covered with a number of large Orientals. Staring at Janson as he entered was a full-length portrait of Queen Elizabeth I, painted during her life, with meticulous attention to the details of her dress and flatteringly little to her ravaged face. Isaac Newton, on the adjoining wall, was brown-wigged and imperious. A smirking fourteen-year-old, one Lord Gloucester, stared brazenly at both from his oil pigments. All told, here was one of the most impressive collections of its kind outside of the National Portrait Gallery. It was a pageant of a very particular elite, both political and intellectual, that had shaped the country, had directed its history, could claim some responsibility for both its achievements and its failures. The glowing visages belonged largely to bygone centuries, and yet Peter Novak's own portrait would not have been out of place. Like all true leadership, his stemmed from a sense of his own obligations, a profound and profoundly moral sense of mission.

Janson found himself staring, rapt, at the faces of long-departed kings and counselors, and he started when he heard the sound of a man clearing his throat.

"My heavens, it *is* you!" Angus Fielding trumpeted, in his slightly reedy, slightly hooting voice. "Forgive me—I've been looking at you looking at the portraits and *wondering* whether it was possible. Something about the shoulders, the gait. Dear boy, it's been far too long. But, really, this is the most *delightful* surprise I could imagine. Gilly told me that my ten o'clock was here, so I was preparing to talk to one of our less promising graduate students about Adam Smith and Condorcet. To quote Lady Asquith, 'He has a brilliant mind, until he makes it up.' To *think* what you've saved me from."

Janson's old academic mentor was half-haloed in the cloud-filtered sunlight. His face was etched with age, his white hair thinner than Janson had remembered; yet he was still lean and rangy, and his pale blue eyes retained the brightness of someone who was in on a joke—some nameless cosmic joke—and might let you in on it, too. Now in his late sixties, Fielding was not a large man, but his intensity gave him the presence of someone who was.

"Come along, dear boy," Fielding said. He led Janson down a short hallway, past the doughty, middle-aged woman who worked as his secretary, and into his spacious office, where a large picture window gave a view of the Great Courtyard. Plain white shelves on the adjacent walls were filled with books and journals and offprints of his articles, the titles stultifying: "Is the Global Financial System Imperiled?: A Macroeconomic View," "Central Banks' Foreign Currency Liquidity Position—The Case for Transparency," "A New Approach Toward Measurement of Aggregate Market Risk," "Structural Aspects of Market Liquidity and Their Consequences for Financial Stability." A sun-yellowed copy of the *Far Eastern Economic Review* was visible on a corner table; beneath a photograph of Peter Novak was the headline: TURNING DOLLARS INTO CHANGE.

"Forgive all the bumf," the don said, removing a stack of papers from one of the black Windsor chairs by his desk. "You know, in a way I'm *glad* you didn't let me know you were coming, because then I might have tried to put on the dog, as you Americans say, and we'd both have been disappointed. Everyone says I should fire the cook, but the poor dear has been here practically since the Restoration and I haven't got the heart, or perhaps the stomach. Her entremets are agreed to be especially toxic. She's an *éminence grise*, I try to say—*éminence* greasy, my colleagues riposte. The amenities, such as they are, have a curious combination of opulence and austerity, not to say shabbiness, that takes some getting used to. You'll remember it from your stay in these halls, I daresay, but the way you remember playing tag when you were a child, one of those things that were so appealing at the time but whose point now seems utterly elusive." He patted Janson on the arm. "And now, dear boy, you're It."

The verbal flows and eddies, the blinking, amused eyes—it was the same Angus Fielding, by turns wise and mischievous. The eyes saw more than they let on, and his donnish volubility could be an effective means of distraction or camouflage. A member of the economics faculty that produced such giants as Marshall, Keynes, Lord Kaldor, and Sen, Angus Fielding's reputation extended well beyond his work on the global financial system. He was also a member of the Tuesday Club, a group of intellectuals and analysts who had had, and maintained, connections with British intelligence. Fielding had served a stint as an adviser to MI6 early in his career, helping to identify the economic vulnerabilities of the Eastern bloc.

"Angus," Janson began, his voice froggy and soft.

"A bottle of claret!" the college master cried. "A bit early, I know, but *that* we can supply. Look out the window and you see the Great Courtyard. But, as you may recall, there's a vast wine cellar beneath it. It runs straight across the courtyard, and underneath the garden owned by the college. A *catacombs* of claret. A *fluid Fort Knox!* There's a manciple with a great hoop of keys, and he's the only person who can let you into it, the jumped-up tosser. We've got a wine committee in charge of selections, but it's *riven* with factions, like the former Yugoslavia, only less peaceable." He called to his secretary: "I wonder if we might get a bottle of the Lynch Bages eighty-two, I seem to recall there was an unopened bottle left from last night."

"Angus," Janson began again. "I'm here to talk about Peter Novak."

Fielding was suddenly alert. "You bring news from him?"

"*About* him."

Fielding fell silent for a moment. "I'm suddenly feeling a draft," he said. "A rather chilling one." He tugged at an earlobe.

"I don't know what news has reached you," Janson said tentatively.

"I'm not quite twigging . . ."

"Angus," Janson said. "He's dead."

The master of Trinity blanched, and stared at Janson slackly for a few long moments. Then he took a seat on a harp-backed wooden chair in front of his desk, falling into it as if the air had left him.

"There have been false rumors of his demise in the past," the don said feebly.

Janson took the seat next to him. "I saw him die."

Angus Fielding slumped back in his chair, suddenly looking like an old man. "It's not possible," he murmured. "It can't be."

"I saw him die," Janson repeated.

He told Fielding what had happened in Anura, breathing hard when he reached the still-piercing horror of the midair explosions. Angus merely listened, expressionless, nodding gently, his eyes half shut, as if listening to a pupil during a tutorial.

Janson had once been one of those pupils. Not the typical apple-cheeked boarding-school kid, wearing a backpack filled with dog-eared books and leaking biros, pedaling a bicycle down King's Parade. When Janson arrived at Trinity, courtesy of a Marshall Fellowship, he was a physical wreck, sallow and skeletal, still trying to heal his emaciated body and devastated spirit from his eighteen-month ordeal as a POW, and all the brutalities that had preceded it. The year was 1974, and he was trying to pick up where he had left off, pursuing the study of economic history he had begun as an undergraduate at the University of Michigan, Ann Arbor. The SEAL commando was repairing to the groves of academe. He worried, at first, that he would not be able to make the adjustment. Yet hadn't his military training equipped him to adapt to his surroundings, whatever they were? History texts and economic formulas replaced code-books and graded-terrain maps, but he attacked them with the same doggedness, determination, and sense of urgency.

In Fielding's quarters at Neville Court, Janson would discuss his assigned topic, and the don would seem to nod off as he spoke. Yet when the time came, Fielding would open his eyes, blinking, and pinpoint the weakest turn of his argument. Once Janson gave a yeoman's account of the economic consequences of Bismarck's expansionism, and Fielding seemed to rouse himself from his slumbers only after he'd finished. Then the questions rained like arrows. How did he distinguish between expansionism and regional consolidation? What about the delayed economic consequences of the annexation of the Schleswig and Holstein duchies several years prior? About those numbers he relied upon for the premise of his argument, the devaluation of the deutsche mark between 1873 and 1877—they wouldn't be from *Hodgeman's* study, would they, young man? Pity, that: old Hodgeman got the numbers all wrong—well, an *Oxford* man, what could you expect? Hate to order you off your own premises, dear boy. But before you build your edifice, be certain of the ground beneath.

Fielding's mind was razor-sharp; his manner urbane, unflappable, even giddy. He often cited Shakespeare's phrase about the "smiler with the knife," and though he was no hypocrite, it aptly characterized his scholarly style. Janson's assignment to Fielding, as the don cheerfully admitted only a few months after their tutorials began, was not entirely accidental. Fielding had friends in Washington who had been impressed with the young man's unusual profile and demonstrated capabilities; they had wanted him to keep an eye out for him. Even now, Janson was hard put to say whether Fielding had recruited him to Consular Operations or whether he had merely gestured vaguely in that direction and allowed Janson to make the decision that felt right to him. He remembered long conversations about the concept of the "just war," about the interplay of realism and idealism in state-sanctioned violence. In prompting Janson for his views on a wide range of subjects, had the don been merely exercising the young man's analytical skills? Or had the don been subtly *redirecting* those views, prodding a shattered young man to rededicate his life to the service of his country?

Now Fielding daubed his eyes with a handkerchief, but they still glittered moistly. "He was a great man, Paul. It's unfashionable to use those terms, perhaps, but I've never known anybody like him. My God, the vision, the brilliance, the compassion—there was something absolutely extraordinary about Peter Novak. I always felt I was blessed to know him. I felt our century—this new century—was blessed to *contain* him!" He pressed his hands to his face briefly. "I'm babbling, I'm becoming an old fool. Oh, Paul, I'm not one given to hero worship. Peter Novak, though— it was as if he belonged to a higher evolutionary plane than the rest of us. Where we humans have been busy tearing one another apart, he seemed to belong to some race that had learned, finally, to reconcile the brain and the heart, keenness and kindness. He wasn't just a numbers whiz—he understood people, cared for people. I believe the same sixth sense that allowed him to see which way the currency markets would go— to anticipate the tides of human greed—is also what allowed him to see precisely what sort of social interventions would truly matter on this planet. But if you ask why he threw himself at these problems everyone else regarded as hopeless, you have to put reason to one side. Great minds are rare—great hearts rarer still. And this was ultimately a matter of the heart. Philanthropy in its root sense: a kind of love." Now Fielding blew his nose quietly and blinked hard, determined to keep his emotions at bay.

"I owed him everything," Janson said, remembering the dust of Baaqlina.

"As does the world," Fielding said. "That's why I said it cannot be. For my reference was not to fact but to consequence. He must not die. Too much depends upon him. Too many delicate efforts toward peace and stability, all sponsored by him, guided by him, inspired by him. If he perishes, many will perish with him, victims of senseless suffering and slaughter—Kurds, Hutus, Romani, the despised of the world. Christians in Sudan, Muslims in the Philippines, Amerindians in Honduras. Casamance separatists in Senegal . . . But why even begin a list of the *damnés de la terre*? Bad things will happen. Many, many bad things. *They* will have won."

Fielding looked smaller now, not merely older. The vital energy had drained from him.

"Perhaps the game can be played to a draw," Janson said quietly.

A despairing look came over the scholar. "You'll try to tell me that America, in its bumbling way, can pick up the slack. You may even think it is incumbent upon your country to do so. But then the one thing that you Americans have never quite grasped is how very deep anti-Americanism goes. In this post–Cold War era, many people around the world feel that they live under the American economic occupation. You speak of 'globalization' and they hear 'Americanization.' You Americans see televised images of anti-American demonstrations in Malaysia or Indonesia, about protesters in Melbourne or Seattle, hear about a handful of McDonald's being rubbished in France—and you think these are aberrant events. On the contrary. They are harbingers of a storm, the first few spittlelike drops you feel before a cloudburst."

Janson nodded. These were sentiments he had heard before, and recently. "Someone told me that these days, the hostility isn't really about what America does, but about what America is."

"And that is precisely why Peter Novak's role was invaluable, and irreplaceable." Heat entered the don's voice. "He wasn't American, or perceived to be a handmaiden of American interests. Everyone knew that he'd spurned America's advances, that he'd angered its foreign-affairs establishment by steering his own course. His only polestar was his own conscience. He was the man who could stand up and say that we had lost our bearings. He could say that markets without morality could not sustain themselves—he could say these things and be heard. The magic of the marketplace wasn't enough, he was saying: We need a *moral* sense of where we want to go, and the commitment to get there." Fielding's voice started to crack and he swallowed hard. "That is what I meant when I said that this man must not perish."

"Yet he has perished," Janson said.

Fielding rocked back and forth gently, as if he were at sea. For a while he said nothing at all. And then he opened his light blue eyes wide. "What's so very odd is that none of this has been reported anywhere—neither his abduction nor his murder. So very odd. You have told me the facts, but not the explanation." Fielding's gaze drifted toward the overcast skies that hovered over the courtyard's ageless splendor. The fen's low-hanging clouds over the rough-hewn Portland stone of the courtyard: a vista unchanged in centuries.

"I guess I was hoping you'd be able to help me there," Janson said. "The question is, who would want Peter Novak dead?"

The don slowly shook his head. "The question is, alas, who *wouldn't?*" Janson could tell his mental gears were meshing; his fish-pale eyes grew intent, his face taut. "I exaggerate, of course. Few mortals have so earned the love and gratitude of their fellows. And yet. And yet. *La grande benevolenza attira la grande malevolenza,* as Boccaccio has it: outsized benevolence always attracts outsized malevolence."

"Walk me through this, OK? Just now you spoke of 'they'—you said 'they' will have won. What did you mean?"

"Do you know much about Novak's origins?"

"Very little. A child of war-torn Hungary."

"His origins were at once extremely privileged and extremely *not*. He was one of the few survivors of a village that was liquidated in a battle between Hitler's soldiers and Stalin's. Novak's father was a fairly obscure Magyar nobleman who served in Miklós Kállay's government in the forties before he defected, and it's said that he feared, obsessively, for the safety of his only child. He had made enemies who, he was convinced, would try to avenge themselves against his scion. The old nobleman may have been paranoid, but as the old saw has it, even paranoids have enemies."

"That's more than half a century ago. Who could possibly care, all these decades later, what his dad was up to in the forties?"

Fielding gave him a stern, college-master look. "You obviously haven't spent much time in Hungary," he said. "It's in Hungary, still, that you'll find his greatest admirers, and his most impassioned foes. Then, of course, there are the millions elsewhere who feel victimized by Peter Novak's successes as a financier. Many ordinary people in Southeast Asia blame him for triggering a run against their currency, their rage fomented by demagogues."

"But groundless, do you think?"

"Novak may be the greatest currency speculator in history, but no one has more eloquently denounced the practice. He's pushed for the very policies of currency unification that would make that sort of speculation impossible—you can't say he's been an advocate of his own interests. Quite the opposite. Of course, some would say that merry old England bore the brunt of his speculative savvy, at least at first. You remember what happened back in the eighties. There was that great currency crisis, with everyone wondering which European governments were going to lower their rates. Novak leveraged billions of his own money on his hunch that Britain was going to let sterling plunge. It did, and Novak's Electra Fund nearly tripled. An incredible coup! Our then prime minister pushed MI6 to poke around. In the end, the head of the investigation told the *Daily Telegraph* that, and I quote, 'the only law this fellow has broken is the law of averages.' Of course, when the Malaysian ringgit plunged and Novak landed himself another windfall, the politicians over there didn't take it very well. Lots of demagoguery there about the manipulations of the mysterious dark foreigner. So you ask who would like to see him dead, and I must tell you it's a long list of malefactors. There's China: the old men of that gerontocracy fear, above all else, the 'directed democracy' that Novak's organization has been dedicated to. They know he considers China the next frontier of democratization, and they are powerful enemies. In Eastern Europe, there's a whole cabal of moguls—former Communist officials who seized the plunder of 'privatized' industries. The anti-corruption campaigns spearheaded by the Liberty Foundation in their own backyards are their most direct threat, and they've sworn to take action.

As I say, one cannot perform good deeds without a few people feeling threatened by them—especially the ones who prosper from entrenched enmity and systematic corruption. You asked what I meant by 'they,' and that's as good a specification as any."

Janson could see Fielding struggle to sit up straighter, to rally, to keep a stiff upper lip. "You were part of his brain trust," said the operative. "How did that work?"

Fielding shrugged. "He'd solicit my opinions from time to time. Perhaps once a month, we'd talk on the phone. Perhaps once a year, we'd meet face-to-face. In truth, he could have taught me far more than I him. But he was a remarkable listener. There was never a shred of pretense, except, perhaps, the pretense of knowing less than he did. He was always concerned about unintended consequences of humanitarian intervention. He wanted to be sure that a humanitarian gift didn't ultimately lead to more suffering—that, say, helping refugees didn't prop up the regime that had produced those refugees. You can't always call it right, he knew. In fact, he always insisted that everything you know might be wrong. His one article of faith. Everything you know must be critically assessed at all times, and abandoned if necessary."

Long, indistinct shadows began to fall as the cloud-filtered late-morning sun hovered just over the college chapel. Janson had hoped to narrow the field of suspects; Fielding was showing how vast it really was.

"You say you met with him irregularly," Janson prompted.

"He wasn't a man of fixed habits. Not so much a recluse, I would have said, as a nomad. A man as peripatetic as Epicrates of Heraclea, that sage of classical antiquity."

"But the foundation's world headquarters is in Amsterdam."

"Prinsengracht eleven twenty-three. Where his staffers have a rueful saying: 'What's the difference between God and Novak? God is everywhere. Novak is everywhere but Amsterdam.' " He repeated the well-worn jest without humor.

Janson furrowed his brow. "Novak had other counselors, of course. There were those savants whose names were never mentioned in the media. Maybe one of them might know something significant—without even realizing the significance. The Foundation itself has raised the drawbridge as far as I'm concerned—I can't reach anybody, speak to anybody in a position to know. It's one of the reasons I'm here. I need to reach those people who worked closely with Novak, or who used to. Maybe someone who used to be in the inner circle and fell out of it. I can't rule it out that Novak was done in by a person or persons close to him."

Fielding raised an eyebrow. "You might direct that same curiosity toward those who are, or were, close to *you*."

"What are you suggesting?"

"You were asking me about Peter Novak's enemies, and I said they were widely dispersed. Let me, then, broach an awkward subject. Are you so confident about your own government?" Fielding's tone combined steel and silk.

"You're not saying what I think you're saying," Janson replied sharply. He knew that Fielding, as an habitué of the fabled Tuesday Club, spoke of such matters with genuine worldliness.

"I only pose the question," Fielding said gingerly. "Is it even possible that your own former colleagues in Consular Operations have had some involvement here?"

Janson winced: the don's speculations had struck a nerve; the question, though seemingly far-fetched, had haunted him since Athens. "But why? How?" he demanded.

*Was it possible?*

Fielding shifted uneasily in his harp-backed chair, running his fingertips along its alligatored black lacquer. "I don't state. I don't even suggest. I ask. Yet consider. Peter Novak had become more powerful than many sovereign nations. And so he may have, wittingly or unwittingly, sabotaged some pet operation, cocked up some plan, threatened some bureaucratic turf, enraged some powerful player. . . ." Fielding waved a hand, gesturing vaguely at possibilities too hazy to pin down. "Might an American strategist have deemed him too powerful, too much of a threat, simply as an independent actor on the stage of world politics?"

Fielding's speculations were all too cogent for comfort. Márta Lang had met with high-powered people in the State Department and elsewhere. They had urged her to employ Janson; for all he knew, Lang's people had relied on them for some of the instrumentation and equipment. They would have sworn her to secrecy, of course, invoking the "political considerations" that Lang had alluded to with such sardonicism. There was no need for Janson to know the provenance of the hardware; no reason for Lang not to keep her word to the U.S. officials with whom she had dealings. Who were these officials? No names were used; all Janson was told was that they knew him, or of him. Consular Operations, presumably.

And then the inculpating transfers to his Cayman Islands account; Janson had believed that his former employers remained ignorant of it, but he also knew that the American government, when it wished to, could apply subtle pressure to offshore banking institutions when the activities of U.S. citizens were at issue. Who would have been better placed to interfere with his financial records than high-level members of the American intelligence services? Janson had not forgotten the rancor and ill will that surrounded his departure. His knowledge of still-extant networks and procedures meant that he was, in principle, a potential threat.

*Was it possible?*

How had the plot been hatched? Was it simply that a golden opportunity had presented itself to quick-thinking tacticians? Two birds with one stone: kill the meddlesome mogul, blame the noncompliant ex-agent? Yet why not leave the Kagama extremists to carry out their announced plan? That would have been the easy, the convenient thing to do: let murderous fanaticism run its course. Except . . .

There was the muted sound of an old-fashioned brass bell: somebody was at the rear door, which led to a waiting area outside the master's office.

Fielding roused himself from his own rumination and stood up. "You'll excuse me for a minute—I'll be right back," he said. "The hapless graduate student makes an inopportune visit. But so it must be."

The flowchart branched out. In one branch, the United States does nothing, the world does nothing, and Novak is killed. The diplomats and officials that Márta Lang consulted emphasized the hazards of American involvement. Yet there were risks in inaction as well—the risks of political embarrassment. Despite the countercurrents Fielding identified, Peter Novak was a widely beloved man. If he were killed, ordinary people would wonder why the United States had refused to help a secular saint in his hour of need. The Liberty Foundation might denounce the United States—furiously and vociferously—for refusing to provide any assistance whatsoever. It would be easy to imagine the ensuing deluge of congressional hearings, TV reports, newspaper editorials. The old words would reverberate throughout the land: *For evil to triumph, it is enough that good men do nothing.* In the resulting uproar, careers could be ruined. What looked like the path of caution was in fact strewn with broken glass.

But what if there was *another* explanation?

The Liberty Foundation, typical of its go-it-alone ways, assembles its own international commando team in a reckless attempt to spirit away the captive. Who can they blame but themselves if things go badly? Mid-level employees at the State Department would "leak" the word to the beat reporters who had come to rely upon them as unnamed sources: *Novak's people rejected our offers of help out of hand. It seems they were afraid it would compromise his aura of independence. The secretary of state is completely broken up about what happened, of course—we all are. But how can you provide assistance to people who absolutely refuse to accept it? Arrogance on their part? Well, some might say so. In fact, wasn't that the fatal flaw of the Liberty Foundation itself?* The worldly, knowing reporters—for the *New York Times,* the *Washington Post,* the syndicated wire services—would file dispatches subtly infused with what they'd been told on deep background. *Informed sources said that offers of assistance were snubbed. . . .*

Janson's mind reeled. Was the scenario anything more than a fantasy, an invidious fiction? He did not know; he *could not* know—not yet. What he did know was that he could not exclude the possibility.

Fielding's minute stretched to three minutes, and when he reappeared, closing the door carefully behind him, there was something different about him.

"The aforementioned grad student," Fielding assured him, in a slightly piping voice. "Hopeless Hal, I think of him. Trying to unknot an argument in Condorcet. I can't get him to see that in Condorcet the knots themselves are what's interesting."

Janson's spine prickled. Something in the master's demeanor had altered—his tone was brittle, as it had never been, and wasn't there a slight tremor in his hands that had not been there before? Janson saw that something had upset his old teacher, and profoundly.

The don made his way to a rostrum where a fat volume of a dictionary reposed. Not just any dictionary, Janson knew—it was the first volume of a rare 1759 edition of Samuel Johnson's dictionary, *A–G* stenciled in gold along its spine. Janson remembered it from the don's shelves back when his rooms were in Trinity's Neville Court.

"Just want to look up one thing," he said. But Janson heard the stress beneath the pleasantries. Not the stress of bereavement or loss, but of another emotion. Alarm. Suspicion.

There was something about his manner: the slight tremor, the brittle tone—and? Something else. What?

Angus Fielding was no longer making eye contact: that was it. Some people almost never did so, but Fielding was not one of them. When he spoke to you, his eyes swept back to yours regularly, as if to guide the words home. Almost involuntarily, Janson felt one of his own hands reaching behind him.

He stared, mesmerized, as Fielding, with his back to him, opened the tome, and—*it couldn't be.*

The master of Trinity College spun around to face Janson, brandishing a small pistol in a shaking hand. Just behind Fielding, Janson saw the hollowed-out section carved into the dictionary's vellum pages, where the side arm had been secreted. The side arm that his old don was pointing at him.

"Why have you really come here?" Fielding asked.

At last his eyes met Janson's, and what Janson saw in them took his breath away: murderous rage.

"Novak was a good man," Fielding said in a tremulous voice. The scholar sounded far away. "Possibly a great one. *I've just learned that you killed him.*"

# CHAPTER THIRTEEN

The aging don lowered his gaze momentarily and gasped in spite of himself. For Janson, too, was holding a gun in his hand—the gun he had, in a fluid motion, grasped from his rear holster as his subconscious mind registered what his conscious mind had difficulty accepting.

Wordlessly, Janson thumbed the safety up of his snub-nosed weapon. For a few long seconds, the two men stood facing each other in silence.

Whoever Fielding's visitor had been, it was no graduate student in economic history. "Volume A to G," Janson said. "Appropriate enough. *A* for ammo, *G* for guns. Why don't you put that antique in your hand aside? It doesn't suit you."

The economist snorted. "So you can kill me, too?"

"Oh for Christ's sake, Angus!" Janson erupted. "Use that magnificent brain of yours. Can't you hear how crazy that sounds?"

"Bollocks. What I can see is that you were sent here to betray me— eliminate anyone who might know you too well, I've no doubt. 'A killing machine'—I'd heard that said of you, a Homeric epithet favored by some of your controllers. Oh yes, I kept in touch with my American counterparts. But I never credited the characterization until now. Your guile commands the admiration of this old Footlights trouper. You know, you really give excellent grief. Had me completely fooled. I'm not ashamed to say so."

"All I wanted to learn was—"

"The location of Peter's colleagues—in order to hunt them down, too!" the old professor said hotly. "The 'inner circle,' as you referred to it. And once you'd ferreted out this information, you could be sure that Peter's mission on this planet had been destroyed." He smiled, a chilly, terrible smile, showing his discolored, irregular teeth. "I suppose I should have appreciated your wit, asking whom I meant by 'they' and 'them.' But, of course, 'they' and 'them' are whom you work for."

"You just met with someone—tell me who?" Janson was flushed with fury and bewilderment. His eyes darted back to the college master's weapon, a .22 Webley pistol, the smallest and most easily concealed of those in use by British intelligence agents during the early sixties. "*Who,* goddammit?"

"Wouldn't you like to know. I suppose you want to add another name to your bloodstained punch list."

"*Listen* to yourself, Angus. This is *madness!* Why would I—"

"That's the nature of mop-up operations, isn't it? They're never quite finished. There's always another dangling thread to be tied up—or snipped off."

"Dammit, Angus. You *know* me."

"Do I?" The standoff continued as the tutor and his onetime pupil both kept their handguns leveled. "Did any of us really know you?" Despite the don's affected languor, there was no mistaking his fear and revulsion. This was no ploy: Angus Fielding was mortally certain that Janson had become a renegade, and a murderous one.

And there was nothing he could say to prove otherwise.

What were the *facts,* after all?

That he, alone, was witness to what had happened. That he, alone, was in charge of the operation that led to Novak's death. That millions of dollars had been transferred into his account, in a manner that seemed to have no honorable explanation. Powerful interests had clearly been seeking Novak's elimination; was it inconceivable—was it even unlikely—that they would seek to enlist someone like Janson, a disenchanted ex–field agent with undoubted skills?

Janson knew what an expert in psychological profiling would make of his dossier: the early history of betrayal and brutality that he had suffered. How deep did the trauma go, and could it be rekindled? His employers never referred to the possibility, but he could see it in their eyes; the personality inventory tests that he regularly underwent—the Myers-Briggs, the Thematic Apperception Test, the Aristos Personality Profile—were designed to ferret out any hairline fissures his psyche might have developed. *Violence is something you're very, very, very good at:* Collins's arctic assessment. It was what made him invaluable to his employers, but it was also why the top-level planners harbored a lingering wariness toward him. So long as he remained, like fix-mounted heavy artillery, directed toward the enemy, he could be a godsend; but if he were ever to turn against the men who had trained him, the planners who used him, he could prove a nemesis like no other.

A memory from a decade ago returned to him, one of a dozen almost indistinguishable ones. *He's an attack dog who slipped his leash, Janson. He's got to be put down.* A file was handed to him: names, patterns of movement, a list of strictures—to be memorized and placed in the burn bag. Too much was at stake for the formalities of a court-martial or "disciplinary proceedings": the agent had already cost the lives of several good men who had once been his colleagues and cohorts. Severance would be paid out in the form of a small-caliber bullet to the back of his head; the body would be found in the trunk of a car owned by a Russian crime lord who himself had just come to a grisly end. As far as the world was concerned—and it wasn't, really—the victim was just another American businessman in Moscow who thought he could pull a fast one on his *mafiya* partners, and had paid for his mistake.

An attack dog that slipped its leash must be destroyed: standard operating protocol at Consular Operations. Janson—having been tasked more than once with the job of executioner—knew this as well as anyone.

Now he chose his words carefully. "There is nothing I can say to dispel your suspicions, Angus. I don't know who contacted you just now, so I can't speak to your source's credibility. I find it striking that someone, or some group, managed to convey the message to you so swiftly. I find it striking that, with only a few words and reassurances, they persuaded you to direct a deadly weapon toward someone you have known for years, known as a protégé and friend."

"As someone said of Madame de Staël, you are implacably correct. More implacable than correct." Fielding smiled a sickly, Stilton smile. "Don't try to construct an argument. This isn't a tutorial."

Janson looked intently at the aging scholar's face; he saw a man who feared he was confronting a profoundly treacherous opponent. But he also saw a glimmering of doubt—saw a man who was not absolutely certain of his judgment. *Everything you know must be continually reassessed, critically reviewed. Abandoned if necessary.* Their two small-caliber handguns continued to face each other like mirror images.

"You used to say that academic battles are so fierce because so little is at stake." Janson felt, and sounded, oddly calm. "I guess things change. But as you know, Angus, there are people who have tried to kill me for a living. They've tried for good reasons, sometimes—or, anyway, understandable ones. Mostly they've done so for bad reasons. When you're in the field, you don't think very much about reasons. Afterward, though, you do. If you've hurt somebody, you hope to God you've done it for good cause. I don't know exactly what's going on, but I do know that somebody lied to you, Angus. And knowing that, I'm having a hard time staying mad at you. My God, Angus, look at yourself. You shouldn't be standing here with a gun in your hand. Neither should I. Somebody's caused us to forget who we are." He shook his head slowly, sadly. "You want to squeeze that trigger? Then you'd better be surer than sure that you're doing the right thing. Are you, Angus? I don't believe you are."

"You always did have a rash tendency to make assumptions."

"Come on, Angus," Janson went on. There was warmth in his voice, but not heat. "What did Oliver Cromwell say? 'I beseech you, from the bowels of Christ, to consider that you may be mistaken.' " He repeated the old saw wryly.

"Words I always found strangely ironic," Fielding said, "coming from a man who, to the detriment of his country, was essentially incapable of self-doubt."

Without breaking eye contact, Janson extended his gun hand, unfurled his fingers from the pistol grip, and held out his hand, palm up, the weapon lying on it not as a threat but as an offering. "If you're going to shoot me, use mine. That flintlock of yours is liable to backfire."

The tremor in Fielding's hand grew. The silence was nearly unbearable.

"*Take it,*" Janson said in a tone of reprimand.

The master of Trinity was ashen, torn between the humanitarian he had come to revere and a former pupil to whom he had once been devoted. That much, at least, Janson could read from the old man's etched, stricken face.

"May God have mercy on your soul," Fielding said at last, lowering his side arm. The words were something between a benediction and a curse.


Four men and one woman sat around the table at the Meridian Center. Their own secretaries had them down for various out-of-office engagements: they were having their hair cut, going to a child's piano recital, keeping a long-postponed dental appointment. A subsequent inspection of logs and calendars would reveal only the humdrum, commonplace tasks of personal and family maintenance to which even the highest-ranking officials of the executive branch and its allied bureaus must attend. The crisis was carved out of the invisible interstices of overscheduled lives. It had to be. The Mobius Program had changed the world; its discovery, by those of malign intention, could destroy the world.

"We can't assume the worst-case scenario," said the National Security Advisor, an immaculately attired, round-faced black woman with large, probing eyes. It was the first such meeting Charlotte Ainsley had attended since the crisis began, but the deputy director of the NSA, Sanford Hildreth, had kept her up-to-date.

"A week ago, I would have argued the same thing," Kazuo Onishi, the systems engineer, said. In the formal world of Washington bureaucracy, people like the chairman of the National Security Council were many tiers above the CIA computer whiz. But the absolutely covert nature of the Mobius Program, compounded by its current crisis, had created a small, artificial democracy, the democracy of the lifeboat. No one's opinion mattered more than anyone else's by virtue of rank; power lay in persuasion.

"Oh what a tangled web we weave . . . ," Sanford Hildreth, the NSA man, began.

"Spare us," said the DIA's deputy director, Douglas Albright, resting his hamlike forearms on the table. "What do we know? What have we heard?"

"He's disappeared," the NSA man said, massaging his high forehead with thumb and forefinger. "We had him, and then we didn't."

"That's not possible," the DIA man said, scowling.

"You don't know Janson," said Derek Collins, undersecretary of state and the director of Consular Operations.

"Thank God for small blessings, Derek," Albright returned. "He's a fucking golem—you know what that is? My grandmother used to talk about them. It's like a doll you make out of clay and evil spirits, and it turns into a monster. The shtetl version of the Frankenstein story."

"A golem," Collins echoed. "Interesting. We *are* dealing with a golem here, but we all know it isn't Janson."

Silence settled over the agitated spymasters.

"With respect," Sandy Hildreth said, "I think we need to return to basics. Is the program in jeopardy of exposure? Will Janson be the cause of that exposure?"

"And how did we allow ourselves to get into this situation?" Albright exhaled heavily.

"It's always the same story," the National Security Advisor said. "We thought we were getting laid, when we were really getting screwed." Her brown eyes roamed across the faces in the room. "Maybe we're missing something—let's review your man's records again," she said to the undersecretary. "Just the high points."

"Paul Elie Janson," Collins said, his eyes veiled behind his black plastic glasses. "Grew up in Norfolk, Connecticut, educated at the Kent School. His mother was born Anna Klima—an émigré from what was then Czechoslovakia. She'd been a literary translator in the old country, became too closely associated with dissident writers, paid a visit to a cousin in New Haven, and never returned. Wrote poems in Czech and English, published a couple of them in *The New Yorker*. Alec Janson was an insurance executive, a senior vice president at the Dalkey Group before he died. In 1969, hot-to-trot Paul leaves U-Michigan just before graduating and joins the navy. Turns out he's got this gift for tactics and combat, gets himself transferred to the SEALs, the youngest person ever to have received SEAL training. Assigned to a counterintelligence division. We're talking about a learning curve like a rocket."

"Wait a minute," the DIA man said. "A hothouse flower like that—what's he doing joining up with the Dirty Dozen? Profile mismatch."

"His whole *life* is a 'profile mismatch,'" Derek Collins replied, with a trace of asperity. "You really want to get the shrink reports? Maybe he's rebelling against his dad—the two weren't close. Maybe he'd heard too many stories about a Czech uncle who was a hero of the resistance, a partisan who picked off Nazis through the ravines and forests of Sumava. Dad wasn't exactly a wuss, either. During the Second World War, old Alec was in the marines himself, a Semper Fi leatherneck before he became a business executive. Let's just say Paul's got the bloodlines, preppy or no. Besides, you know what they say—the Battle of Waterloo was won on the playing fields of Eton. Or was that a 'profile mismatch,' too, Doug?"

The DIA analyst colored slightly. "I'm just trying to get a handle on somebody who seems to have walked out of a full-force, all-hands CIA stakeout like the Invisible Man."

"We had very little warning—the whole operation was spur-of-the-moment, our boys had minutes to prepare and mobilize," said Clayton Ackerley, the man from the CIA's Directorate of Operations. He had wispy red hair, watery blue eyes, and a fading tan. "Under the circumstances, I'm sure they did the best they could."

"There's always time for recriminations," said Charlotte Ainsley with a severe, over-the-glasses pedagogic look. "Just not now. Go ahead, Derek. I'm still not getting the picture."

"Served in SEAL Team Four, picked up a goddamn Navy Cross in his first tour of duty," said the undersecretary of state. His eyes fell on a yellowing slip from the file, and he passed it around.

*Office Fitness Report Remarks*
*20 November 1970*

   Lieutenant Junior Grade Janson's performance in Joint SEAL/Special
Force Detachment A-8 has been outstanding. His able judgment, tactical knowledge, creativity, and imagination has allowed him to plan
Swift Strike operations against enemy units, guerrilla personnel, and
hostile installations that were accomplished with minimal losses. Lt. j.g.
Janson has demonstrated extraordinary ability to adapt and to respond
to rapidly changing circumstances, and is unaffected by the hardships
of living under the toughest field conditions. As an officer, he demonstrates natural leadership skills: he does not merely demand respect, he
commands it.
   Lieutenant Harold Brady, Rating Officer


   Lt. j.g. Janson demonstrates potential of the highest caliber: his field
skills and ability to improvise in conditions of adversity are nothing
short of stellar. I will personally be keeping a close watch to see whether
his potential is fully realized.
   Lieutenant Commander ███████ ██████████ Endorsing Officer


"There's dozens just like it. Guy serves one tour after another, continuous combat exposure, no breaks. Then a big gap. Hard to build your
resume as a POW. Captured in the spring of 1971 by the Viet Cong. Held
for eighteen months, in pretty abysmal conditions."

"Care to specify?" Charlotte Ainsley asked.

"Tortured, repeatedly. Starved. Part of the time, he was kept in a cage—
not a cell, a cage, like a big birdcage, six feet high, maybe four feet around.
When we found him, he weighed eighty-three pounds. He grew so skeletal
that the manacles slid off his feet one day. Made about three escape
attempts. The last one succeeded."

"Was treatment like that typical?"

"No," the undersecretary said. "But trying so relentlessly and resource-
fully to escape wasn't typical, either. They knew he was part of a counterintelligence division, so they tried pumping him pretty hard. Got
frustrated when it went nowhere. He was lucky he survived. Damn lucky."

"Not lucky he got captured," the National Security Advisor said.

"Well, that's where things get complicated, of course. Janson believed
that he'd been set up. That the VC had been given information about him
and he'd been deliberately led into an ambush."

"Set up? By whom?" Ainsley's voice was sharp.

"His commanding officer."

"Whose own opinion of his darling protégé seemed to have cooled a little." She flipped to the final sheet headed OFFICER FITNESS REPORT RE-MARKS and read out loud:

> *Although Lt. Janson's own standards of professionalism remain impressive, difficulties have begun to emerge in his concept of leadership: in both training exercises and duty, he has failed to demand from his subordinates a similar level of competence, while overlooking obvious shortcomings. He appears to be more concerned with the welfare of his subordinates than with their ability to help execute mission objectives. His loyalty to his men overrides his commitment to broader military goals, as specified and set out by his commanding officers.*

"There's more going on there than meets the eye," said Collins. "The chill was inevitable."

"Why?"

"Because, it seems, he'd threatened to report him to the high command. Crimes of war."

"Forgive me, I should know this. But what was going on here? The warrior wunderkind had a psychotic break?"

"No. Janson's suspicions were correct. And once he'd returned stateside, and got out of medical, he made a stink about it—within channels, of course. He wanted to see his commanding officer court-martialed."

"And was he?"

The undersecretary turned and stared: "You mean you really don't know?"

"Let's cut the drumroll," the round-faced woman replied. "You got something to say, say it."

"You don't know who Janson's commanding officer was?"

She shook her head, her eyes intent, penetrating.

"A man named Alan Demarest," the undersecretary replied. "Or maybe I should say Lieutenant Commander Demarest."

" 'I see,' said the blind man." Her largely suppressed Southern accent broke through, as it did at times of great stress. "The source of the Nile."

"When next we see our man Janson, it's graduate studies at Cambridge University on a government fellowship. Winds up back on board, in Consular Operations." The undersecretary's voice became summary and brisk.

"Under you," Charlotte Ainsley said.

"Yes. In a manner of speaking." Collins's tone said more than his words, but everyone understood his import: that Janson was not the most subordinate of subordinates.

"Rewind a sec," Ainsley said. "His time as a POW in Vietnam had to have been incredibly traumatic. Maybe he never really recovered from it."

"Physically, he got to be stronger than ever. . . ."

"I'm not talking about physical prowess or mental acuity. But psychologically, that sort of experience leaves scars. Fault lines, cracks, weaknesses—like in a ceramic bowl. The flaw you don't see until something else happens, a second trauma. And then you split, or break, or snap. A good man becomes a bad one."

The undersecretary raised a skeptical eyebrow.

"And I'll accept that this is all on the level of conjecture," she continued smoothly. "But can we afford to make a mistake? Granted, there's a great deal we don't know. But I'm with Doug on this one. Comes down to this: Is he working for us or against us? Well, here's one thing we do know. He's not working for us."

"True," said Collins. "And yet—"

"There's always time for 'and yets,' " Ainsley said. "Just not now."

"This guy is a variable we can't control," said Albright. "In an already complex and confusing probability matrix. Outcome optimization means we've got to erase that variable."

"A 'variable' who happens to have given three decades of his life to his country," Collins shot back. "A funny thing about our business—the loftier the language, the lower the deed."

"Come off it, Derek. Nobody's hands are dirtier than yours. Except your boy Janson. One of your goddamn killing machines." The DIA man glared at the undersecretary. "Needs a taste of his own medicine. My English plain enough?"

The undersecretary adjusted his black plastic glasses and returned the analyst's unfriendly look. Still, it was clear enough which way the wind was blowing.

"He'll be hard to take out," the CIA operations man stressed, still smarting from the Athens debacle. "Nobody's better at hand-to-hand. Janson could inflict serious casualties."

"Everybody in the intelligence community has received rumors and reports about Anura, albeit unsubstantiated," said Collins. "That means your frontline agents as well as mine." He glanced at the CIA operations man and then at Albright. "Why don't you let your cowboys have another go?"

"Derek, you know the rules," Ainsley said. "Everybody cleans up his own litter box. I don't want another Athens. Nobody knows his methods like the cadre that trained him. Come on, your senior operations managers must already have filed a contingency plan."

"Well, sure," said Collins. "But they've got no clue what's really going on."

"You think we do?"

"I take your point." A decision had been made; deliberation was over. "Plans call for the dispatch of a special team of highly trained snipers. They can get the job done, and discreetly. Ratings are off the charts. Nobody would stand a chance against them." His gray eyes blinked behind his glasses as he remembered the team's unbroken series of successes. Quietly, he added, "No one ever has."

"Terminate orders in effect?"

"Current orders are locate, watch, and wait."

"Activate," she said. "This is a collective decision. Mr. Janson is beyond salvage. Green-light the sanction. *Now.*"

"I'm not arguing, I just want to make sure people are aware of the risks," the undersecretary persisted.

"Don't tell us about risks," said the DIA analyst. "You *created* those goddamn risks."

"We're all under a great deal of stress," Hildreth interjected smoothly.

The analyst folded his arms on his chest and directed another baleful glare at Undersecretary Derek Collins. "You made him," Albright said. "For everyone's sake, you'd better break him."

# CHAPTER FOURTEEN

The sidewalks of London's Jermyn Street were filled with people who had too little time, and with people who had too much. An assistant bank manager of NatWest was scurrying with as much speed as was consistent with dignity, late for a lunch date with the junior vice president of Fiduciary Trust International's Fixed Income Department. He knew he shouldn't have taken that last phone call; if he wasn't punctual, he could kiss that job good-bye. . . . A beefy sales rep for Whitehall-Robins was keeping an assignation with a woman he had chatted up at Odette's Wine Bar the night before, braced for disappointment. Daylight usually added ten years to those slags who looked so sultry and appetizing in the smoky gloom of the downstairs banquettes—but a chap had to find out one way or another, right? Maybe a stop-off at the newsagent was in order: being on time might make him seem a tad eager. . . . The neglected wife of a workaholic American businessman was clutching three shopping bags filled with expensive but dowdy clothes she knew she'd probably never wear back in the States: charging it all to his Platinum American Express somehow let her vent her resentment for his having dragged her along. Another seven hours to kill before she and her husband saw *Mousetrap* for the third time. . . . The chief assessor of Inland Revenue's Westminster branch was jostling his way through the crowd with an eye on his watch: you never had as much authority with those berks at Lloyds when you showed up late; everybody said so.

Striding down Jermyn Street in a fast lope, Paul Janson was lost among the window-shoppers, bureaucrats, and businessmen who crowded the sidewalks. He was attired in a navy suit, a spread-collar shirt, and a polka-dotted tie, and his look was harried but not nervous. It was the look of someone who belonged; his face and his body alike telegraphed as much.

The jutting signs—the ovals and rectangles overhead—registered only vaguely. The older names of the older establishment—Floris, Hilditch & Key, Irwin—were interspersed with newer arrivals, like Ermenegildo Zegna. The traffic was half congealed, sludgy, with tall red buses and low boxy cabs and commercial vehicles that amounted to wheeled signage. INTEGRON: YOUR GLOBAL SOLUTIONS PROVIDER. VODAFONE: WELCOME TO THE WORLD'S LARGEST MOBILE COMMUNITY. He turned left on St. James's Street, past Brooks's and White's, and then left again onto Pall Mall. He did not stop at his destination, however, but instead walked past it, his darting eyes alert to any signs of irregularity. Familiar sights: the Army and Navy Club, known affectionately as the Rag, the Reform Club, the Royal Automobile Club. In Waterloo Square, the same old bronzes stood. There was an equestrian statue of Edward VII, with a cluster of motor-cycles parked at its pedestal, an inadvertent comment on changing modes of personal transport. There was a statue of John Lord Lawrence, a viceroy of India from Victorian times, standing proudly, as one who knew he was very well known indeed to the few who knew him. And, grandly seated, Sir John Fox Burgoyne, a field marshall who had been a hero of the Peninsular War and, later, of the Crimean War. "The war is popular be-yond belief," Queen Victoria had said of the Crimean conflict, which would become a byword for pointless suffering. To be a hero of the Cri-mean—what was that? It was a conflict whose eruption represented dip-lomatic incompetence and whose prosecution represented military incompetence.

He allowed his gaze to drift to his destination, at the corner of Waterloo Place: the Athenaeum Club. With its large cream-colored blocks, tall col-umned portico, and Parthenon-inspired frieze, it was a paragon of the early-nineteenth-century neoclassical style. On the side a hooded security camera projected from a cornerstone. Above the front pillars stood the goddess Athena, painted in gold. The goddess of wisdom—the one thing that was in shortest supply. Janson made a second pass in the opposite direction, walking past a red Royal Mail truck, past the consulate for Papua New Guinea, past an office building. In the distance, a red-orange crane loomed over some unseen building site.

His mind kept returning to what had happened at Trinity College: he must have stumbled on a trip wire there. It was more likely that his old mentor had been under surveillance than that he had been followed, he decided. Even so, both the size of the net and the rapidity of the response were formidable. He could no longer take anything for granted.

Sight lines were everywhere. He had to be attuned to the kinds of anomalies that would ordinarily pass without notice. Trucks that were parked that should not have been parked; cars that drove too slowly, or too fast. The gaze from a passerby that lingered an instant too long—or was averted an instant too soon. Construction equipment where there was no construction. Nothing could pass without notice now.

Was he safe? Conclusive evidence was impossible. It was impossible even to say that the mail truck was simply what it appeared to be. But his instincts told him that he could enter the club unobserved. It was not a meeting place he himself would have selected. For his immediate purposes, though, it would be helpful to meet Grigori Berman on his own terms. Besides, the venue was, on reflection, a highly advantageous one. Public parks offered freedom of movement—it was what made them popular rendezvous points—but that freedom could also be exploited by observers. At an old-fashioned gentleman's club, it would be difficult to station an unfamiliar face. Janson would be there as the guest of a member. He doubted whether members of a surveillance team could gain similar access.

Inside the club, he identified himself and the member he was awaiting to a uniformed guard who sat at a booth by the front door. Then he proceeded to the polished marble floors of the foyer, which was four-posted with large, gilded Corinthian pillars. To his right was the smoking room, filled with small round tables and low-hanging chandeliers; to his left, the large dining room. Ahead, past a sea of red and gold carpeting, a broad marble staircase led up to the library, where coffee was taken and periodicals from all over the world lay stacked on a long table. He seated himself on a tufted leather bench by one of the pillars, beneath the portraits of Matthew Arnold and Sir Humphry Davy.

The Athenaeum Club. A gathering spot for members of the political and cultural elite.

And the unlikely rendezvous for a most unlikely man.

Gregori Berman was someone who, if he had developed a nodding acquaintance with morality, preferred to keep the relationship at arm's length. Trained as an accountant in the former Soviet Union, he had made his fortune working for the Russian *mafiya,* specializing in the complex architecture of money laundering. Over the years, he had set up a thicket of IBCs—international business corporations—through which the ill-gotten gains of his *mafiya* partners could be cycled, and thus hidden from the authorities. Several years earlier, Janson had deliberately let him slip through a dragnet that Consular Operations had run. Dozens of international criminals had been apprehended, but Janson—to the annoyance of some of his colleagues—let their financial whiz kid go free.

In fact, the decision represented reason, not whim. Berman's knowledge that the Cons Op officer had decided to let him escape meant that he'd be in Janson's debt: the Russian could be converted from adversary to asset. And having someone who understood the intricacies of international money laundering represented a very significant asset indeed. Moreover, Berman was clever in his manipulations: it would be difficult for the authorities to build a case against him. If he was likely to get off anyway, why not let him off with a debt on which Janson could collect?

There was something else, too. Janson had reviewed hundreds of pages of intercepts, had come to know the principals of the scheme. Many were cold-blooded, thuggish, menacing figures. Berman, for his part, deliberately insulated himself from the details; he was cheerfully amoral, but he wasn't *unkind*. He was perfectly happy to cheat people out of their funds but could be quite generous with his own. And somewhere along the line, Janson acquired a trace of sympathy for the high-living rogue.

"Paulie!" the bearlike man boomed, opening his arms wide. Janson stood and allowed himself to be enveloped in the Russian's embrace. Berman fit none of the stereotypes of a numbers man; he was all emotional effusion, mixing a passion for things with a passion for life.

"I hug you and I kiss you," Berman told Janson, pressing his lips to both his cheeks. Classic Berman: whatever the circumstances, he would display not the wariness of a man under pressure but the swagger of a larger-than-life bon vivant.

The fabric of Berman's pinstriped bespoke suit was a feltlike cashmere, and he smelled faintly of Geo. F. Trumpers extract of limes, the scent said to be favored by the Prince of Wales. In his caricatured way, Berman sought to be every inch the English gentleman, and there were many inches of him at that. His conversation was a cataract of Britishisms, malapropisms, and what Janson thought of as Bermanisms. As absurd as he was, though, Janson could not help feel a certain affection for him. There was even something winning about his contradictions, the way he managed to be at once devious and ingenuous—he always had an eye for the next scam, and he was always delighted to tell you about it.

"You're looking . . . sleek and well fed, Grigori," Janson said.

Gregori patted his generous midriff. "Inside I'm wasting away. Come, we'll eat. Chop-chop." He squired Janson to the dining room, with an arm around his shoulder.

Inside, waiters in morning suits beamed and bobbed their heads as the ebullient Russian appeared, ushering him immediately to a table. Though tipping was prohibited by club rules, their bright-eyed attentiveness re-vealed that Berman had found a way to manifest his generosity.

"Their cold poached salmon—the best in the world," Berman said, settling into his cushioned seat. Berman said that a lot of things were the best in the world; he invariably spoke in superlatives. "But have lobster *à la nage*. Never fails. Also recommend roast grouse. Maybe both. You're too thin. Like Violetta in third act *La Traviata*. Must build you up."

He summoned a wine steward with a glance.

"That Puligny-Montrachet we had yesterday? Could we have bottle of that, Freddy?" He turned to Janson. "It's the greatest. You'll see."

"I have to say I'm surprised to find you here, ensconced at the heart of the British establishment."

"A rogue like me, you mean—how could they ever let me in?" Berman roared with laughter, his belly quivering through bespoke broadcloth. In a lower voice, he said, "It's a great story, actually. You see, about two years ago, I found myself invited to house party at Lord Sherwyn's, and ended up playing billiards with very nice gentleman I met there. . . ." Berman had made a habit of helping certain people out of trouble with timely loans, specializing in dissolute scions of venerable baronies. These were people who, Berman imagined, might have influence in the world. It was, in his book, sound investing.

"You'll have to tell me about it another time," Janson said blandly but pointedly. It was all he could do not to drum his fingers.

Berman was undeterred. "I suppose he had bit too much to drink, and he was winning big, big sums off me, and so I invited him to double up. . . ."

Janson nodded. The scenario was predictable. A more-than-pleasantly-buzzed British gentleman, winning outrageous sums from a seemingly sloppy-drunk Russian with seemingly infinite reserves of cash. The sozzled Russian who, all evening, had shown no sign that he knew one end of a cue stick from the other. The last game, when the British gentleman's substantial winnings were just about to become a true fortune. The gen-tleman thinking, perhaps, of acquiring the apartment adjoining his in Kensington; or buying that place in the country he and his family had been renting for so long. Almost unable to believe his luck. You just never knew about these things, did you? An invitation, reluctantly accepted—the scion was disreputable, but with a family name that still opened doors—had led to a laughably easy stack of money.

And then that game, that last crucial game, when suddenly the Russian didn't seem drunk at all and grasped the cue stick with the serene mastery of a concert violinist holding his bow. And watching dreams of free money dissolve into a reality of ruin.

"But Paul, this bloke I played with—you'll never guess who he was. Guy Baskerton, QC." Baskerton was a prominent lawyer, a queen's counselor, who had chaired a commission on the arts set up by Whitehall. A rather self-important man, with a thin, David Niven mustache, and that distinctly *knowing* look common to the more oblivious men of his class, he would have been an irresistible target for Berman.

"I'm beginning to get the picture," Janson said, sounding more relaxed than he felt. He had to ask Berman for a big favor; it would not do to hector. It would not do to appear desperate, either, or Berman would press his advantage, converting debt to credit. "Let me guess. He's a member of the Athenaeum admissions committee."

"Even better. He's club president!" Berman pronounced *club* like "cloob."

"And so he finds himself into you for a hundred-thousand-pound debt of honor, which he can't possibly make good on," Janson said, trying to make Berman's long story shorter. "But that's OK, because you magnanimously insist on forgiving the debt. Now he's so grateful, he doesn't know what to do. Then the next day, you happen to be seated next to him at Sheekey. . . ." As he spoke, Janson's eyes scanned the fellow guests and serving staff for any signs of potential menace.

"Grigori no go Sheekey. No eat fish. Only *drink* like fish! It was Ivy. Can you believe such coincidence!"

"Oh, I'll bet it was a coincidence. It's not like you bribed the maître d' at the Ivy to make sure you were at the next banquette. Any more than you'd pressured your titled friend to make sure that the QC came to his house party in the first place."

Berman raised his hands, touching his wrists together. "You got me, copper!" He grinned widely, because he liked his machinations to be appreciated, and Janson was someone capable of doing so.

"So, Grigori," Janson said, trying to match his levity, "I come to you with an interesting problem. One that will, I think, intrigue you."

The Russian looked at him, brightly expectant. "Grigori is all ears," he said, lifting a forkful of chicken and morels to his mouth.

Janson sketched out what had happened: the sixteen million dollars that had been deposited in a Cayman Islands account without the account holder's knowledge, yet validated by electronic signatures that should have been accessible to him alone. A clever strike. Yet could it also be a *clue?* Was there a chance that, in the cascade of transfer digits, someone had left digital fingerprints that might be uncovered?

As Janson spoke, Berman appeared to be wholly occupied by his food, and his occasional interjections were culinary in nature: the risotto was the world's *greatest,* and the treacle tart simply the *best,* you try it, you see. How unfair that people were so rude about English cooking!

Yet however desultory his conversation, Janson could see Berman's mind whirring.

Finally the moneyman put down his fork. "What Grigori know about money laundering?" he said with a look of affronted innocence. Then he grinned: "What Grigori *not* know about money laundering? Ha! What I know could fill British Library. You Americans think you know—nothing is what you know. Americans live in big house, but termites eat at foundations. As we say in Moscow: situation desperate, but not serious. You know how much dirty money moves in and out of America every year? Maybe three hundred billion. Bigger than GDP of most countries. Bank wire transactions, yes? And how you find this? Know how much moves in and out of American banks every *day?*"

"I expect you'll tell me."

"Two *trillion* dollars. Pretty soon you're talking real money!" Berman slapped the table in merriment. "All bank wire transaction. Where you hide grain of sand so nobody find? On beach. Ten years ago, you round up my old friends. Coldhearted *nyekulturniy,* every one, I shed no tear, but what did you really stop? Grigori Berman founded more companies than American entrepreneur Jim Clark!"

"Phony companies, Grigori. You invented companies that existed only on paper."

"Nowadays, these people move beyond that. Buy real companies. Insurance companies in Austria, banks in Russia, trucking companies in Chile. Cash goes in, cash comes out, who can say where and when? Who stops them? Your government? Your Treasury Department? Treasury Department has Financial Crimes Enforcement Network. In strip mall in Virginia suburb." Once again, Berman's bountiful stomach began to quiver. "They call it Toilet Seat Building. Who takes FinCEN seriously? You remember story of Sun Ming? Comes to America, says he's woodworker. Borrows hundred and sixty million dollars from Bank of China. Easy as sneezing! Print up handful of import contracts, agency approvals, bills of lading, export certificates, and presto-chango, import application authorized, so. Wire transfer authorized, so. Deposits his money in banks. Tells one banker, 'I play Hong Kong stock market.' Tells another banker, 'I sell cigarette filter.' Tells third banker, 'Textiles!' Zip, zip, zip. From China to America to Australia. Blending is everything. You blend into the ordinary commercial flux, so. So, grain of sand on beach. Americans never catch him. FinCEN charged with watching money, but nobody give FinCEN any money! Treasury secretary doesn't want to destabilize banking system! In your country, four hundred thousand wire transfers every day, in and out. Digital message from one bank computer to another. Americans never catch Sun Ming. *Australians* catch him."

"A smaller beach?"

"Better computers. Look for pattern within pattern. See something funny. So bag is out of cat."

"Funny ha-ha, or funny peculiar?"

"There is difference?" Berman asked, his mouth closing around a spoon full of treacle tart. He gave a moan of gastronomic pleasure. "You know, last week I was in Canary Wharf Tower. Have you been? Fifty stories high. Tallest building in London. Practically bankrupted the Reichman brothers, but never mind, not Grigori's money. So I'm there, visiting Russian friend, Ludmilla, you'd like her, the pair of onion domes on this woman, they put Saint Basel's to shame. And we're forty-some floors up and I'm looking out window, bee-yoo-tiful view of this city, and suddenly guess what I see floating through air."

"A bank note?"

"Butterfly." Berman said it with grand finality. "Why butterfly? What butterfly *doing* forty stories high, middle of city? Most amazing thing, ever. No flowers forty stories high. Nothing for butterfly to do, up here in sky. All the same: butterfly." He raised a finger for emphasis.

"Thank you, Grigori. I knew I could count on you to make everything clear."

"Must always look for butterfly. In the middle of nothing, thing that does not belong. In cascade of digital transfer codes, you ask: is there butterfly? Yes. Always butterfly. Flap, flap, flap. So. You must know how to look."

"I see," Janson replied. "And will you help me look?"

Berman looked, downcast, at the ruins of his treacle tart and then brightened. "Join me for game snooker? I know place nearby."

"*Nyet.*"

"Why not?"

"Because you cheat."

The Russian shrugged cheerily. "Makes for more interesting game, Grigori thinks. Snooker is game of skill. Cheating demands skill. Why is cheating cheating?" The logic was quintessential Berman. At Janson's withering gaze, the Russian held up his hands. "All right, all right. I bring you to my 'umble home, *da?* Have fancy IBM machine there. RS/6000 SP supercomputer. And we look for butterfly."

"We *find* butterfly," Janson said, gently but unmistakably applying pressure. Berman was living the high life in London, having amassed with his wits a fortune well beyond that of the criminal associates he began with. But none of this could have happened had Janson allowed him to be prosecuted all those years ago. He didn't have to tap the ledger; Berman knew precisely what the ledger contained. No one had a more finely calibrated sense of debt and credit than the ebullient ex-accountant.

*Fort Meade, Maryland*

Sanford Hildreth was running late, but when wasn't he? Danny Callahan had been his driver for the past three years, and the only thing that would have surprised him was if he had been on time.

Callahan was one of a small pool of men assigned to chauffeur the topmost intelligence officers of the United States. Each was subject to regular security checks, of the most stringent nature. Each was unmarried and childless, and had advanced training in combat as well as executive safety and diversionary tactics. The instructions were emphatic and explicit: *Guard your passenger with your life.* Their passengers were men who carried the nation's secrets in their heads, men upon whom profound matters of state depended.

The black stretch limousines in which these passengers were driven were armored; the side flanks reinforced with steel plates, the darkened glass capable of withstanding a .45-caliber bullet at point-blank range. The tires were designed to be reinflating and resealing, with a cellular design that prevented rapid leakage. But the capabilities of the driver, not the car, were paramount in ensuring the passenger's safety.

Callahan was one of three men who were usually assigned to the deputy director of the National Security Agency, but Sanford "Sandy" Hildreth made no secret of the fact that he preferred Danny Callahan.

Danny knew shortcuts; Danny knew when it was safe to push the speed limit a little; Danny could get him home from Fort Meade ten or fifteen minutes faster than the others. And the fact that he had won combat honors in the Gulf War was probably a recommendation to Hildreth as well. Hildreth had never seen fighting, but he liked men who had. They didn't talk much, he and Hildreth: usually the motorized partition—an opaque and soundproofed barrier—remained up. But once, a year ago, Hildreth was bored, or in search of distraction, and drew Danny out a little bit. Danny told him about playing football in high school, his team reaching the state championship in Indiana, and he could tell that Hildreth liked that, too. "A running back, huh? You still look like one," Hildreth had said. "Sometime you'll have to tell me what you do to stay in shape."

Hildreth was a small man, but he preferred being surrounded by large men. Maybe he enjoyed the feeling that he, the small man, commanded the large men; that they were his myrmidons. Or maybe they just made him comfortable.

Danny Callahan glanced at the clock on the dashboard. Hildreth had said he'd be ready to leave by six-thirty. It was quarter past seven. What else was new? Hildreth often ran forty-five minutes behind. An hour wasn't uncommon.

In his earpiece, Callahan heard the voice of the dispatcher. *"Capricorn descending."* Hildreth was on his way.

Callahan drove the car directly in front of the exit on the left side of the immense glass shoe box that was the National Security Agency. A rain began to fall, just a few small drops at first. Callahan waited until Hildreth came into view, then got out and stood beside the car.

"Danny." Hildreth nodded, the outdoor halogen lights reflecting off his high forehead. His small, pinched features gathered into a perfunctory smile.

"Dr. Hildreth," Callahan said. He once read an article in the *Washington Post* about Hildreth that mentioned he had a doctorate in international relations. Thereafter, he started calling him "doctor," and he somehow got the sense that Hildreth was pleased by the honorific. Now Callahan held the rear door open for him and then shut it with an efficient *thunk*.

Before long, the rain started to come down harder, in sheets that twisted with the wind and made the headlights of other cars look oddly distorted.

Mason Falls was thirty miles away, but Callahan could practically do the trip blindfolded: off Savage Road, down 295, a quick jaunt on 395, across the Potomac, and up Arlington Boulevard.

Fifteen minutes later, he saw the flashing red lights of a police squad car in his rearview mirror. For a moment, Callahan expected the cop to pass him, but it seemed that the cruiser was trying to pull him over.

It couldn't be. And yet—as best as he could see in the rainstorm—he was the only car around. What the hell?

Sure, he was ten miles over the speed limit, but you'd expect the traffic cops to notice the government license plates and fall back. Some newbie with an attitude? Callahan would take pleasure in putting him in his place. But Hildreth was unpredictable: he might get angry with him, blame him for speeding, even though Hildreth had always made it clear that he was grateful that Danny got him home so quickly—appreciated his "celerity." That was the word Hildreth once used; Callahan looked it up when he got home. Nobody liked to be stopped by the police, though. Maybe Hildreth would make sure the blame was clearly the driver's, and have a black mark put on his fitness report.

Callahan pulled over to the paved shoulder. The squad car pulled over immediately behind him.

As the policeman, a blue slicker obscuring his uniform, appeared by his door, Callahan powered down his window.

"You know how fast you were going?"

Callahan displayed two laminated plastic cards. "Check 'em out, Officer," he said. "You really don't want to be here."

"Oh, sorry, man. I had no idea." The officer sounded genuinely abashed, but it was funny—he couldn't have been a rookie. He seemed to be in his forties, with a boxer's squashed-looking nose and a thin scar that ran along his jaw.

"Take a careful look at the plates next time," Callahan said, his tone bored, officious. "You see the prefix SXT, it means it's high-security federal transport."

The officer tore up a slip of paper. "I'm scratching this from my records. You too, huh?"

"It's understood, Officer."

"No hard feelings?" the officer said, sounding slightly panicked. He extended a hand through the window. "I respect the work you guys do."

Callahan sighed, but reached out to shake the cop's hand—which, oddly, extended past his hand to his wrist. He felt a sudden prick. *"Shit!"*

"Sorry, man," the police officer said. "My goddamn signet ring." But he didn't move.

"What the fuck, man?" Callahan protested. All at once, he felt strangely weak.

The man in the blue slicker reached through the window and unlocked the door. Then he pulled on the knob.

Callahan was puzzled, even outraged. He wanted to say something . . . but nothing came out. He wanted to swat the man away . . . but when he tried to move his arm, nothing happened. And when the door opened, he found himself slumping out of it like a sack of gravel. *He could not move.*

"Easy, boy," the man in the slicker said, laughing genially. He caught Callahan before he hit the ground. Now he leaned into the car, lifting Callahan up and over to the passenger seat on the right.

Callahan stared impassively, slack-jawed, as the man settled beside him in the driver's seat.

The intercom light flashed blue, and a voice squawked through a small speaker: "Danny? What the hell's going on?" Hildreth, on the other side of the opaque "privacy window," was beginning to fret.

The man in the blue slicker pressed the driver-override buttons so that the rear doors were locked and could be reactivated only by him. Then he smoothly shifted into drive and made his way toward the Arlington Memorial Bridge.

"I'll bet you're wondering the same thing," the man said to Callahan companionably. "It's called Anectine. A neuromuscular blocker. They use it during surgery. Sometimes people on respirators get it, too, to make sure they don't thrash around. It's a strange sensation, isn't it? You're fully conscious, but you can't fucking move. Your diaphragm goes up and down, your heart pumps away, you can even blink. But your voluntary muscles are out of commission. Plus which, the way it's metabolized, it's damn hard to identify in forensics unless you already know what to look for."

The man pressed the window controls, lowering both rear windows partway. Another squawk came from the intercom, and the man switched the sound off.

"Your passenger can't figure out why we'd lower the windows when it's raining like a mother," the man said.

*What the hell was going on?*

Callahan focused all his mental energy on the task of lifting his index finger. He strained with all his might, as if he were bench-pressing three times his weight. The finger trembled ever so faintly, and that was all. He was helpless. Utterly helpless. He could see. He could hear. But he could not move.

They approached Memorial Bridge, which was almost empty of traffic, and the driver suddenly floored the accelerator. The powerful three-hundred-horsepower engine surged, and the car leaped forward, cutting a diagonal across two lanes of traffic on the bridge. The driver ignored the furious hammering against the opaque partition as the powerful armored vehicle crashed over the railing on the side of the bridge, sailing through the air and into the river.

The impact with the water was greater than Callahan had expected, and he found himself slammed forward against the straining belts. He felt something snap: probably one of his ribs had broken. But the armored car provided the driver's seat with four-point belts, the sort used by racing drivers, and Callahan knew that for the man in the blue slicker, the force of impact would be safely distributed. As the car sank rapidly into the turbid depths of the Potomac, Callahan could see him release his own belts and roll his window down. Then he released Callahan's belts, and dragged him over to the driver's seat.

Callahan felt like a rag doll. Limp and helpless. But he could see. He could think. He knew why the rear widows had been left just slightly open.

Now the cop who was no cop turned off the engine and wriggled through the open window, shooting toward the surface.

Neither he nor Hildreth would have any such options—Callahan because he was paralyzed, and Hildreth because he was locked in the passenger's compartment. The windows would be frozen in place: lowered just enough to speed the inflow of water. Hildreth's ultrasecure conveyance had turned into a crypt.

The car was settling to the riverbed with its front end raised, probably because water had already filled the rear compartment, and now the water was pouring through the window and a dozen unseen vents to fill Callahan's compartment. It was rising fast, to his chest, his neck, his chin. Higher.

He was breathing through his nose, now, but for how many seconds longer?

And then all his questions dissolved into another question: Who would want to do something like this?

The water seeped into his nose and into his mouth, and dribbled into his lungs, and blossoming within him was a powerful sensation, perhaps the most powerful sensation the human body can know, that of asphyxiation. *He was drowning.* He could not get air. He thought of his uncle Jimmy, dying of emphysema, sitting in a chair with oxygen flowing into his nostrils through those clear plastic nasal prongs, the tank of $O_2$ accompanying him everywhere, the way his yellow Labrador once did. He fantasized kicking free with powerful thrusts, kicking himself to the river's surface. Then he tried to imagine himself breathing good clean air, imagined jogging around the cinder track at his high school in West Lafayette, Indiana, though when he did, he found he was only inhaling water faster. Air spilled from his nose and mouth in a pulsing current of bubbles.

And the agony of breathlessness only increased.

The pressure on his eardrums—he was deep, deep—became excruciating, adding a foundation to the horrible sense of suffocation. It meant something, though. It meant he was not yet dead. Death was not painful. What he was feeling was life's final blow, its farewell pangs, its desperate struggle not to leave.

He wanted to thrash, to flail, to lash out. In his mind, his hands began to churn the water: but only in his mind. His extremities twitched feebly, that was all.

He recalled what the man had said, and some things became all too obvious. *Guard your passenger with your life:* a nonissue now. When the car was dredged out, they would both be dead. Both drowned. One driver, stunned by the impact, drowned in his seat. One passenger the victim of security precautions. The only question would be why Callahan had driven over the bridge.

But it was wet, the pavement was slippery, and Callahan was given to pushing the speed limit, wasn't he?

Oh, they'd blame the peon, all right.

*So this was how it was to end.* He thought of everything that had gone wrong with life. He thought about the athletic scholarship to State he didn't get, because he was off his game the day the scout showed up to check out what West Lafayette High School had to offer. And then with his frickin' knee injury, the coach wouldn't give him any playing time in the regional and state championship games. He thought about the apartment he and Irene were going to buy, until it turned out they couldn't scrape together the money they needed for the down payment, and his dad refused to help, steamed that they'd been counting on his chipping in without having consulted him, so they lost the earnest money, too, a loss they could hardly afford. He remembered how Irene left him soon after, and he could hardly blame her, though he sure did his best to. He remembered the jobs he'd applied for, the string of searing rejections. *No-promotion material*, that was what he'd been labeled, and try as he might, the label would never come off. Like the gummy backing of a bumper sticker you'd tried to scrub away, it was somehow just *there*. People took one look at him and they could see it.

Now Callahan lacked even the strength to sustain the fantasy of being elsewhere. He was . . . where he was.

He was cold, and wet, and breathless, and terrified, and consciousness itself was beginning to darken, to flicker, to narrow to a few essential thoughts.

He thought: *Everybody has to die. But nobody should die like this.*

He thought: *It isn't going to last much longer, it can't last much longer, it can't.*

And he thought: *Why?*

# CHAPTER FIFTEEN

Berthwick House—what the Russian had described as his humble abode—was in fact a grand redbrick Georgian mansion abutting Regent's Park: a three-story pile with dormers in the slate roof and three chimneys. Security was both discreet and overt. It was surrounded by a ten-foot black wrought-iron fence, with rods that came to a sharp, spearlike end. A high-mounted videocamera in an enameled hood surveyed the driveway. There was a small gatehouse with a guard . . . who waved Berman's raspberry-colored Bentley through with a respectful nod.

The spacious reception hall was painted coral and was crowded with antique reproductions. There were side chairs, highboys, and chess tables in the manner of Sheridan and Chippendale: but they were glossy with thick shellac and given an odd orange cast by antiquing stain. A pair of large hunting scenes in gilt frames looked, at first glance, like distinguished eighteenth-century canvases: up close, they looked as if they came from a department store—copies done by a hurried art student.

"You like?" Berman was puffed up with pride as he gestured around the jumble of Anglophilic knockoffs.

"I'm speechless," Janson replied.

"Look like movie set, *da?*" Another expansive gesture.

"*Da.*"

"*Is* from movie set," Berman said delightedly, clapping his hands. "Grigori arrive at Merchant Ivory production, last day shooting. Write check to unit production manager. Buy *everything*. Haul off to home. Now live in Merchant Ivory set. Everyone say, Merchant Ivory do English upper class *best*. Best is good enough for Grigori Berman." A contented chuckle.

"From Grigori Berman, I'd expect no less." The explanation made sense: everything was off, exaggerated, because it was designed only to film well with the proper lights, lenses, and filters.

"Have butler, too. Me, Grigori Berman, poor Muscovite, spend childhood in line at government department store GUM, have butler."

The man he referred to was standing quietly at the end of the foyer, dressed in a black four-button long coat and a stiff pique shirt. He was barrel-chested and strapping, with a full beard, and thinning, neatly combed-back hair. His pink cheeks lent an air of joviality at odds with his somber demeanor.

"This is Mr. Giles French," Berman said. "The 'gentleman's gentleman.' Mr. French take care of all your needs."

"That's really his name?"

"No, not real name. Real name Tony Thwaite. Who cares? I not like real name. Give him name from best American television program."

The bewhiskered manservant gave a solemn nod. "At your service," he said plummily.

"Mr. French," Berman said, "bring us tea. And . . ." He paused, either lost in thought or furiously trying to remember what might accompany tea. "Sevruga?" He sounded tentative, and the request prompted an almost imperceptibly subtle head shake from the butler. "No, wait," Berman corrected himself. Once more, he brightened: "Cucumber sandwiches."

"Very good, sir," said the butler.

"Better idea. Bring scones. Those special scones cook makes. With clotted cream and strawberry jam."

"Excellent, sir. Right away, sir."

Berman beamed, a child able to play with an action figure he'd been pining for. For him, Berthwick was a toy house, in which he'd created a bizarre parody of upscale English living, all in lavishly, lovably bad taste.

"Tell me, really, what you think?" Berman said, gesturing around him.

"It's unspeakable."

"Beyond words, you think?" Berman pinched his cheek. "You not just saying that? Sweet pea! For that I should introduce you to Ludmilla. She show you international travel without leaving bed."

Passing by a small room off the main hallway, Janson paused before a large, gleaming, powerful-looking machine with a built-in video monitor and keyboard and two black-grilled squares to either side. He nodded toward it respectfully. "That the RS/6000?"

"That? Is karaoke machine. Computer system in basement." Berman took him down a curved flight of stairs, to a carpeted room that contained several computer workstations; the heat they threw off made the windowless room uncomfortably warm. Two small electric fans stirred the air. The butler arrived with tea and scones, arrayed on Bristol delft plates. He laid them out on a small corner table, along with small ceramic pots filled with clotted cream and jam. Then he glided off.

After glancing longingly at the scones, Berman sat down at a keyboard and started to activate a series of firewall-penetration programs. He studied the results for a few minutes and then turned to Janson. "In cone of silence, tell Grigori what you get me into."

Janson was silent for a while, thinking long and hard before he disclosed the essential elements of his predicament. Garrulous creatures like Berman, he knew, could sometimes be the most discreet of all, depending on the structure of motivation. Grigori listened without comment or any evident reaction, and then, shrugging, typed the values of an algebraic matrix into the program he was running.

Another minute passed. He turned to Janson. "Grigori not encouraged. We let these programs run, then maybe get results in time."

"How much time?"

"Run machine twenty-four hours, coordinate with global parallel-processing network of other computers, then maybe . . ." Berman looked off. "Eight months? No, I think closer nine months. Like make baby."

"You're kidding."

"You want Grigori to do what others can't do? Must supply Grigori with *numbers* others don't have. You have public-key sequence to account, *da*? We use this, we have special advantage. Otherwise, back to making baby—nine months."

Reluctantly, Janson supplied him with the public-key sequence for his bank account—the codes that the bank transmitted upon receipt of information. The public-key sequence was known to both the bank and the account holder.

Within ten seconds after he typed in the public-key sequence, Berman's screen filled with jumbled digits, scrolling down his monitor like the closing credits of a film. "Numbers meaningless," he said. "Now we must do pattern recognition. Look for butterfly."

"*Find* butterfly," Janson stressed.

"Pah!" Berman said. "You, *moy droog,* are like baked Alaska: sweet and soft outside, hard and cold inside. Brrr! Brrr!" He clasped his arms around, pantomiming an arctic chill. But for the next five minutes, Berman studied sequences of confirmation codes with an intensity that shut out everything else.

At last, he read a series of digits out loud. "Butterfly *here*—5467-001-0087. That is butterfly."

"The numbers mean nothing to me."

"Same numbers mean everything to me," said Berman. "Numbers say beautiful blond women and filthy canals and brown café where you smoke hashish and then more women, from Eastern Europe, sitting in storefront window like mannequin wearing pasties."

Janson blinked. "Amsterdam. You're saying you're looking at a transfer code from Amsterdam."

"*Da!*" Berman said. "Amsterdam transfer code—it cycles through too many times to be accident. Your fairy godmother uses an Amsterdam bank."

"Can you tell which one?"

"Baked Alaska is what you are," Berman said reprovingly. "Give him inch, he take isle! Impossible to get specific account unless . . . *Nyet,* impossible."

"Unless what?"

"Private key?" Berman cringed as if he expected to be slapped for even saying those words. "Use digits like sardine key, scroll open can. Twist, twist, twist. Very powerful." Moving funds in or out of the account required a private key, an authorizing sequence of digits known only to the account holder; the key would not appear in any transmission. This separate, ultrasecure digital pathway protected both the customer and the bank.

"You really expect me to entrust you with the private-key sequence?"

"*Nyet,*" he said, shrugging.

"*Can* I trust you with it?"

A booming laugh. "*Nyet!* What do you take me for! Girl Scout? Private key must be kept *private,* from everyone. Hence name. All men mortal. Grigori more mortal than most." He looked up at Janson. "Please, keep key to self." It was an entreaty.

Janson was silent for a while. Berman liked to say he could resist everything except temptation. To provide him with the private key would present him with a tremendous temptation indeed: he could siphon off its contents with a few keystrokes. Yet at what cost? Berman loved his life here; he knew that to make an enemy of Janson would jeopardize everything he had, and was. No threats were necessary to underscore the risks. Didn't this explain the real source of his reluctance? He didn't want the key because he knew he could not allow himself to give in to temptation—and wanted to avoid the anguish of waking up the next day and knowing he had left a sizable pile of money on the table.

Now Janson recited a fifteen-digit string and watched Berman type the sequence. The Russian's face was sickly and tense; he was obviously wrestling with himself. Within moments, however, he had succeeded in establishing connections to dozens of financial institutions, burrowing from within the Bank of Mont Verde mainframe to retrieve the digital signatures that uniquely identified the counterparty to every transaction.

Several minutes elapsed, the silence disturbed only by the soft clicking of keys and the quiet drone of the fans. Then Berman stood up. *"Da!"* he said. "ING. Which stands for International Netherlands Group Bank. Which you perhaps once knew as Nederlandsche Middenstandsbank."

"What can you tell me about it?"

"Beautiful new central office in Amsterdam. So energy-efficient, nobody can bear to work there. Second-largest bank in country. And Amsterdam women—the most beautiful women in the whole world."

"Grigori," Janson began.

"You must meet Gretchen. Play around-the-world with Gretchen, I guarantee you'll rack up frequent flier miles on your back. Or hers. Gretchen is friend of Grigori. Friend of all weary travelers. Out calls only, but *very* reasonable prices. You tell her you are friend of Grigori. I give you her number. Easier to remember than wire transfer codes to ING. Ha!"

"I'm not convinced we've hit a wall here. If you can identify the bank, can't you narrow it even further?"

"Very difficult," said Grigori, biting cautiously into his scone, as if it might bite back. In a tone of troubled confession, he said, "Cook not really make scones. Cook *say* she makes scones. I know she buy premade from Sainsbury's. One day I saw plastic shrink-wrap in the bin, so, so. So bag is out of cat. I not say anything. Everyone must feel they have victory, or nobody happy."

"Let's focus on making me happy. You said getting account info would be difficult. 'Difficult' doesn't mean impossible. Or is there somebody else you'd recommend for the job?"

His bearlike host looked injured. "Nothing impossible for Grigori Berman." He glanced warily around him, then spooned a generous amount of strawberry jam into his cup of tea and stirred. "Must not let butler see," he said in a low voice. "This Russian way. Mr. French would not understand. It would *shock* him."

Janson rolled his eyes. Poor Grigori Berman: a prisoner of his household staff. "I'm running out of time, I'm afraid," he said.

With a hangdog look, Berman stood and padded heavily back to the RS/6000 workstation. "This *very* boring," he said, like an overgrown child dragged away from his toys and forced to work on his multiplication tables. Meanwhile, Janson established a direct connection with the Bank of Mont Verde via his tri-band PDA.

Fifteen minutes later, Berman, sweating with concentration, suddenly looked up and turned around. "All done." He saw the device in Janson's hand. "You change private key now?"

Janson pressed a button and did precisely that.

"Thank God!" He sprang to his feet. "Otherwise I break down and do the bad, bad thing—today, tomorrow, next month, in middle of night while sleepwalking! Who can say when? To have private key and not put to personal use would be like . . ." He adjusted his trousers.

"Yes, Grigori," Janson interjected smoothly, "I've got the general idea. Now talk to me. What have we found out about the payer?"

"Is great joke," Berman said, smiling.

"How do you mean?" Janson demanded, suddenly alert.

"I traced the originating account. Very difficult, even with sardine key. Required nonreusable back-door codes—burned through valuable property to push through. Just like American pop song, 'What I Did for Love,' *da?*" He hummed a few bars as Janson glared. Then he reverted to the matter at hand. "Reversed asymmetric algorithm. Data-mining software go on hunt for pattern, search out signal buried in noise. Very difficult . . ."

"Grigori, my friend, I don't need the *War and Peace* version of this. Cut to the chase, please."

Berman shrugged, slightly miffed. "Powerful computer program does digital equivalent of triathlon competition, Olympic level, no East German steroids to help, but still identified originating account."

Janson's pulse began to race. "You *are* a wizard."

"And all a great joke," Berman repeated.

"What are you saying?"

Berman's smile grew wider. "Man who pay you to kill Peter Novak? Is Peter Novak."

As he arrived with his small convoy at the training camp, Ahmad Tabari felt a glimmering of relief. Traveling hopefully, he had long known, was overrated. Despite the many hours he had spent in a meditative trance, it had been a long journey and felt like one. The Caliph had made his way first by air to Asmara, in Eritrea. No one would have expected to find the head of the Kagama Liberation Front there. Then he had taken a high-speed boat north along the Red Sea coast to land in the Nubian deserts of northern Sudan. A few hours after landing, his Sudanese guides had taken him on the long and bumpy tracks through the desert, up to the camp near the Eritrean border. Mecca was only a few hundred kilometers to the north, Medina only the same distance farther. It pained him to know that he was as close as he had ever been to the holy places and yet could not walk where the Prophet, blessings be upon him, had stepped while he was on earth. He accepted, as always, God's will, and he drew strength from the righteousness of his cause. Despite the recent setbacks in the Kenna province, the Caliph was a leader in the struggle against the corruption of the West, the brutality and depredation of a global order the West imagined to be "natural." He prayed that his every choice, his every act, would move his country closer to the day when its people would rejoin the *ummah,* the people of Islam, and he could be their rightly guided Caliph in more than name.

Welcomed into the camp by smooth-faced boys and gray-bearded eminences alike, he felt the powerful brotherhood of his fellow believers. The desiccated, dun-colored soil was so different from the vibrant tropical vegetation of his native land, yet his brethren of the desert had a pitch of vigilance, zealotry, and devotion that came less naturally to many of his own Kagama followers. Barren land, perhaps, but it bloomed with the righteousness of the Holy One. The desert leaders were enmeshed in their own campaigns, in Chechnya, in Kazakhstan, in Algeria, in the Philippines. But they knew that every one of their conflicts was a skirmish in a greater battle. That was why he knew they would help him, as he had helped them in the past. God willing, they would, by working together, recover the whole earth for Allah one day.

The first order of business was to allow his hosts to impress him with their training school. He had heard about it, of course. Every leader in the worldwide fellowship of struggle knew of this university of terror. Here, while the government in Khartoum turned a blind eye, the members of this secret brotherhood could learn the ways of the new kind of war. In bunkers carved into the rock were computers that stored the plans of electric generator plants, petroleum refineries, airports, railroads, military installations in scores of countries. Every day, they searched the Web for more of the open secrets that the West so carelessly made available. Here, in the model of an American city, you could study urban warfare: how to block roads and storm buildings. Here, too, you could learn the patient arts of surveillance, methods of assassination, a hundred ways to make explosives from materials available in every American hardware store. As he passed from one unit to the next, he smiled his humorless smile. They were treating him like a visiting dignitary, the way they must treat the president of Sudan on his secret visits. They knew, as he did, that he was destined to rule his homeland. It was just a matter of time.

He was tired, of course. But he had no time to rest. The evening prayer was over. It was time for the meeting.

Within a tent, they sat on low cushions on the cloth-covered ground and drank tea from simple clay cups. The conversation was cordial yet shied away from specifics. All knew the Caliph's extremely fraught situation—his astonishing recent gains, and the fact that they were under ceaseless assault by the coordinated forces of the Republic of Anura. There had been reversals, humbling ones. There would continue to be reversals—unless additional assistance could be provided. The Kagama's repeated attempts to enlist the support of the Go-Between were met with frustration. The Go-Between not only declined to provide the needed support but grew emphatic that the Caliph desist in his efforts at exacting vengeance! Oh, the perfidy of the infidel! Then his further attempts to reestablish contact with the Go-Between, to persuade him of the inexorability of the Caliph's will to justice, had failed, utterly and mysteriously. That was why the Kagama leader was here.

Finally, they could hear the sound of a military helicopter, feel the *whomp-whomp* percussion of its propellers. The camp leaders glanced at one another and at their Kagama guest.

It was the visitor they had been waiting for. The man they called Al-Mustashar, the Adviser.

Colonel Ibrahim Maghur was a man of the world, and his connection with the insurrectionists in the camps was necessarily clandestine. He was, after all, a senior member of Libyan intelligence, and Tripoli had officially renounced its direct links to terrorism. At the same time, many powerful members of the regime retained their sympathies for their brethren in the struggle against Western imperialism and did their best to provide discreet assistance. Ibrahim Maghur was one such man. In the course of his secret visits to the camp, he had provided valuable information from Libyan intelligence. He had pinpointed the location of enemies and even provided suggested assassination techniques. He had supplied valuable terrain maps and detailed satellite imagery that gave the freedom fighters significant strategic advantage. And he had provided them with caches of ordnance and small arms. Unlike so many members of Libya's effete and decadent

elite, Ibrahim Maghur was a true believer. He had guided them toward
the lethal satisfactions of their objectives in the past; he would do so again.

Now the colonel strode from the helicopter, emerging from a small
artificial dust storm, and bowed before the leadership of the Islamic Jihad,
which had assembled to greet him.

His eyes met those of Ahmad Tabari, and he bowed again before extending a hand.

The Libyan's gaze was at once penetrating and respectful. "It is truly
an honor to meet you," he said.

"The Prophet smiles upon us both that we two should be introduced,"
Tabari returned.

"Your military successes are astounding, truly brilliant—deserving of
attention in the textbooks," said the colonel. "And I am a student of
history."

"As am I a student of history," said the Kagama rebel chief. His ebony
face looked almost coal black in the dim light of the desert evening. "My
studies tell me that territories swiftly claimed can as swiftly be reclaimed.
What do your studies tell you?"

"They tell me that history is made by great men. And something about
you indicates that you are a great man—a Caliph indeed."

"The Prophet has been generous with his gifts," said the Kagama, who
had little time for false humility.

"Yet great men have great enemies," the Libyan intelligence official said.
"You must be very cautious. You must be very cautious indeed. You are
a threat to powers that will stop at nothing to annihilate you."

"It is possible to be crippled by caution," said Tabari.

"You speak truly," said the Libyan. "A risk for lesser men than you. It
is your very boldness that vouchsafes your greatness, the security and
survival of your cause, its final victory. Your *khalifa* shall be established.
Yet everything will depend upon the timing and the targeting." He looked
around at the rapt faces of the five seniormost leaders of the Islamic Jihad,
and then returned to the fabled leader of the Kagama Liberation Front.
"Come," he said. "Let us go for a walk together, Caliph. Just you and I."

"Al-Mustashar's advice is a treasure beyond price," one of the hosts
told Ahmad Tabari. "Go with him."

As the two men strolled around the desert encampment, a cool wind
began to gust, billowing through the Caliph's long robes.

"I can assure you that your setbacks will prove only temporary," the
Libyan colonel told him in a low voice. "There is much I will be able to

help you with, as will certain of our allies within the Islamic Republic of Mansur. Soon your cause will be coming along *swimmingly*."

"And in what will it swim?" the islander asked the desert warrior with a brooding half smile.

"That's easy," Ibrahim Maghur replied, and his face was utterly serious. "Blood. The blood of the infidel."

"The blood of the infidel," the Caliph repeated. The words were both reassuring and uplifting.


"How the hell can you know such a thing?" Janson demanded.

"Cross-tabulation of wire transfer indices," said Berman, vigorously stirring jam into his tea. "Origination code can't be spoofed."

"Come again?"

"Sixteen million dollars comes from account in name of Peter Novak."

"How? Where?"

"Where I say. Amsterdam. International Netherlands Group. Where Liberty Foundation have headquarters?"

"Amsterdam."

"So no surprise."

"You're telling me that at a time when Peter Novak was locked away in a dungeon in Anura, he authorized a transfer of sixteen million dollars into a blind account I controlled? What kind of sense does that make?"

"Could be preauthorization. Preauthorization possible. Postauthorization not possible."

"No jokes, Grigori. This is crazy."

"I just tell you origination code."

"Could somebody else have laid their hands on the Novak account, got control of it somehow?"

The Russian shrugged. "Origination code just tell me ownership of account. Could be many specifications as to access. This I cannot tell you from here. This information not flow from modem to modem. Legal certification held by institution of origination. Bank in Amsterdam follows instructions established by owner. Account suffix says it's linked to Foundation. Paperwork at bank, paperwork at headquarters." Berman pronounced the word *paperwork* with the distaste he reserved for older financial instruments, directives and stipulations that could not be reduced to strings of ones and zeros.

"This makes no sense."

"Makes *dollars!*" Berman said merrily. "If somebody put sixteen million dollars in Grigori account, Grigori not insist on dental examination of gift horse." He held out his hands. "I wish I could tell you more."

Had Peter Novak been betrayed by somebody near and dear to him? If so, by whom? A high-ranking member of his organization? Márta Lang herself? She spoke of him, it seemed, with genuine affection and respect. Yet what did that prove, aside from that she might have been an accomplished actress? What now seemed irrefutable was that whoever had betrayed Novak was in a position to have earned his trust. And that meant the agent was a master of deception, a virtuoso of the patient arts of craft and deceit and waiting. But to what end?

"You come with me," Berman said. "I show you house." He put an arm around Janson's shoulder and propelled him up the stairs, down the magnificent hallways of the estate, and into the airy, light-filled kitchen. He pressed a finger to his lip. "Mr. French not want us in kitchen. But Russians know that heart of house is kitchen."

Berman stepped toward the glittering stainless-steel sink, where the casement windows looked onto a beautifully tended rose garden. Beyond it stretched Regent's Park. "Take a look—twenty-four hundred acres in the middle of London, like my backyard." He pulled out the sink spray nozzle and held it to his mouth like microphone. "Someone left the scones out in the rain," he sang in a thick Russian basso. "I don't think that I can take it . . ." He pulled Janson closer, trying to form a duet. He raised an expressive hand high in the air, like an opera singer on the stage.

There was a tinkle of glass, and Berman broke off with a sharp expulsion of breath. A moment later, he slumped to the floor.

A small red hole was just visible on the front of his hand. On the upper left quadrant of his shirtfront was another puncture wound, just slightly rimmed with red.

"Jesus Christ!" Janson shouted.

Time slowed.

Janson looked down at Berman, stunned and motionless on the gray tiled kitchen, and then out of the window. Outside, there was no sign of disturbance whatever. The afternoon sun nuzzled well-tended rosebushes, their small pink and white blossoms radiantly emerging from the tight-clustered leaves. The sky was blue, dappled with sparse wisps of white.

It seemed impossible, but it had happened, and his brain raced to make sense of it, even as he heard the approaching footsteps of the butler, obviously roused by his exclamation. On arrival, the butler immediately pulled Berman's supine body out of range of the window, sliding it along the floor. It was the correct response. He, too, scanned the view from the window, holding a P7 sentry pistol in a hand as he did so. An amateur might have fired a shot out of the window for show: the butler did not do so. He had seen what Janson had seen; an exchange of glances revealed his bafflement. Just a few seconds elapsed before the two retreated to the hallway, safely away from the window. From the floor, Berman made rasping, wet noises, as breath forced its way through his injured airway, and his fingers began to scrabble at his chest wound. "Motherfucker," he said in a strangled voice. *"Tvoyu mat'!"*

The fingers of his intact right hand trembled with exertion, as the Russian probed his wound with remarkable single-mindedness. He was fishing for the bullet, and gasping for breath, he yanked a crumpled mass of brass and lead from his chest.

"Look," Janson said to the butler. "I know this has to be a shock to you, but I'm going to need you to stay calm and collected, Mr. . . ."

"Thwaite. And I've had fifteen years in the SAS. This isn't a perimeter breach, we both know that. We're looking at something else."

"SAS, huh?"

"Mr. Berman may be crazy, but he's not a fool. A man like that's got enemies. We've prepared for the usual exigencies. But that shot came out of the clear blue. I can't explain it."

How had it happened?

Janson's mind emptied, and then filled with elliptic curves and right angles. The horrific scene of bloodshed he had just witnessed dissolved into a shifting geometrical schema.

He'd need every fact that was available to him. He connected the point of penetration of Berman's upstretched arm to the upper-left-quadrant chest wound. An elevation of approximately thirty-five degrees from the horizontal. Yet there was nothing visible in the vicinity at that angle.

Ergo the bullet had not been fired from the immediate vicinity.

The mass that Berman had pulled out was confirmation. It had to have been a long-distance shot, toward the end of its trajectory. Had it been fired within a hundred yards, it would have penetrated Berman's body and punched an exit wound. The amount of crumple and the size of the projectile: the crucial information was there.

He stooped and picked up the bullet. What had it been? A six- or seven-hundred-grain, brass-jacketed round. Penetration had been two inches; had it struck Berman's head, it would have been instantly fatal. As it was, the lung hemorrhage made a fatal outcome fairly probable. What had it delivered: a hundred, two hundred foot-pounds of force?

Because of air resistance, impact diminished in a nonlineal relation to distance elapsed. The greater the velocity, the greater the air resistance, or drag force, so it wasn't a simple, linear relation. The velocity-distance matrix involved a first-order differential equation, and Reynolds number— the sort of thing Alan Demarest could solve in his head, maybe Berman, too—but, relying on trained intuition, Janson estimated that the distance traversed would have been twelve hundred yards out, or about two-thirds of a mile.

Janson's mind filled with the skyline of the area, the Palladian roofs of Hanover Terrace, the round dome of the Central London Mosque . . . and the minaret, the tall, slender tower with the small balcony, used by the muezzin to summon the faithful to prayer. Lacking intrinsic value, it was likely unguarded; a professional would have had no problem gaining entry. If Janson's rough calculations were correct, one had.

It was diabolical. A sniper had stationed himself on the balcony of the minaret, a flyspeck from the perspective of Berthwick House, and bided his time, waiting in case his target appeared in the casement windows. He would have had plenty of time to figure out the requisite angles and trajectories. But how many men were even capable of such a shot? Were there forty such in the world? A couple of Russians. The Norwegian sniper who came in first in a worldwide competition hosted in Moscow last year. A couple of Israelis, with their Galil 7.62 rifles. A handful of Americans.

A master sniper had supernal skill, but he had supernal patience, too. He had to be responsive to uncertainties: in a long-range shot, even a slight unexpected breeze could push a flat shot several feet from its intended destination. A subject could move unexpectedly; in this case, Berman had raised his hand *after* the shot was fired. A sniper had to be aware of such possibilities. And he had to be more patient than his target.

And yet who was the target?

The butler had assumed it was his employer, Berman. A natural assumption. And a dangerous one. He recalled Berman's arm around his shoulder, drawing him close. The bullet that hit the Russian was fifteen inches from Janson's head.

Fifteen inches. An uncontrollable variance at two-thirds of a mile. Whether it was a hit or a near miss, the shot's accuracy was incredible. But the sensible assumption had been that Janson was the real target. He was the only new element in the situation.

He could hear the siren of the ambulance Thwaite had summoned. And now he felt a tug on his trouser leg—Berman, from the floor, feebly trying to communicate, to get his attention.

"Janson," he said, speaking as if through a mouthful of water.

His fleshy face had taken on a veal-like pallor. A thin rivulet of blood seeped from the corner of his lips down his chin. Air was sucking through his chest wound, and he pressed his good right hand to the area. Now he raised his bloodied left hand and extended a wagging index finger. "Tell me truth: Turnbull and Asser shirt ruined?" A wet cough came instead of the usual guffaw. At least one of his lungs had filled with blood, and would soon collapse.

"It's seen better days," Janson said gently, feeling a rush of affection toward the ebullient, eccentric maven.

"Get son of whore who did this," Berman said. "*Da?*"

"*Da,*" Janson said huskily.

# CHAPTER SIXTEEN

Thwaite took Janson aside and spoke to him in a low voice. "Whoever you are, Mr. Berman must have trusted you, or he wouldn't have invited you here. But I've got to ask you to make tracks." A wry look. "Chop-chop."

Janson raced down oak parquet floors, past the eighteenth-century French paneling a Woolworth heiress had installed decades ago, and through a rear exit. A few minutes later, he had vaulted over the wrought-iron fence and into the eastern bulge of Regent's Park. "Twenty-four hundred acres in the middle of London, like my backyard," Berman had said.

*Was it safe?*

There were no guarantees—except that it was the only place to which he dared retreat. A sniper on the minaret could easily target anyone emerging from the other exits of Berthwick House. The perch would not afford a sight line to most areas of the park itself.

Besides, Janson *knew* this area; when he was at Cambridge, he'd had a friend who lived in the Marylebone neighborhood, and they had taken long strolls through the great verdant expanse, three times the size of New York's Central Park. Some of it was overlooked by the neoclassical grandeur of Hanover Terrace, with its noble Georgian exteriors and creamy hues, the white and blue friezes adorning its architrave. But the park was a world unto itself. The waterways bustled with swans and odd, imported fowl; they were banked with concrete in some stretches while in others they lapped onto stands of marshy reeds. On the concrete walkway along the embankment, pigeons competed for crumbs with swans. Farther out, trimmed rows of boxwood provided a dense green border. A red lifesaver was mounted on a small wooden kiosk.

To him, it had always felt like a refuge, this vast campus of trees and grass, playing fields and tennis courts. The boating lake stretched like an amoeba, narrowing to a stream that, edged by flower beds, ran under York Bridge in the southern part of the park. And in the inner circle was

Queen Mary's Garden, filled with exotic flora and rare fowl, discreetly penned: a sanctuary for wild birds and lonely, fragile people. Regent's Park, a legacy of the crown architect John Nash, represented an Arcadian vision of an England that, perhaps, never was—the Windermere in the middle of the metropole, at once artfully rusticated and carefully manicured.

Janson jogged toward the boating lake, past the trees, trying to clear his head and make sense of the astounding assault. Even as he ran, though, he was intensely alert to his surroundings, his nerves jangling.

*Was it safe?*

Was he dealing with a single sniper? It seemed unlikely. With such exhaustive preparation, there must have been flanking gunmen in place, covering different wings of the house, different exposures. No doubt, perimeter security was as exacting as Thwaite had indicated. But there were few local defenses against such long-distance marksmanship.

And if other snipers were in the area, where were they?

And *who* were they?

The intrusion of menace in this pastoral redoubt struck Janson as itself an obscenity. He slowed down and looked at the great willow tree in front of him, its branches drooping into the boating lake. A tree like that might be a century old; his eyes must have fallen on it when he visited the park twenty-five years ago. It had survived Labour governments and Tory governments alike. It had survived Lloyd George and Margaret Thatcher, the Blitz and rationing, eras of fear and of boisterous self-confidence.

As Janson approached it, the thick trunk suddenly revealed a rude patch of white. A soft, tapping noise: lead hitting puckered bark.

A shot that had missed him, again, by a matter of inches. The uncanny accuracy of a bolt-action sniper rifle.

He craned his neck around as he ran, but could see nothing. The only sound he had heard was that of the projectile slamming into the tree: there was no sound of the detonation within a rifle chamber. Sound-suppression gear was quite possibly in use. But even with a silenced rifle, a supersonic round produced a noise as it emerged from the muzzle—not necessarily a conspicuous one, but a noise all the same, like the crack of a whip. Janson knew that noise well. The fact that he had not heard it suggested something else: it was another long-distance shot. If the gunman were a hundred yards away, the noise would be lost amid the baffling provided by the tree leaves and the park's ambient sounds. Conclusion: an extremely skilled marksman was in pursuit.

Or a *team* of them.

Where was safety? It was impossible to say. Worms of apprehension writhed in his belly.

Dirt kicked up a couple of feet from him. Another near miss. The shot had been taken from a very great distance, and the subject had been in motion: for a shot to have come within ten yards of him would have represented impressive technique. Yet this shot had come within a couple of feet. It was astounding. And terrifying.

*Keep moving:* confronted with unseen pursuers, it was the one thing he could do to make himself a more difficult target. But movement itself was not sufficient. He had to keep his speed irregular, for otherwise a trained sniper could calculate the "lead" in his sighting. It was a straightforward exercise to fire at a target who was moving at a fixed speed in a fixed direction: taking into account distance and target speed, you measured out a few degrees to the left of the figure in your scope, firing at where the target would be when the bullet arrived, not where it had been when the bullet was fired.

Then there was the crucial matter of the sniper grid. Lateral movement—transverse velocity—was one thing. But movement that took the pedestrian target toward or away from the sniper was of almost negligible importance: it would not prevent the bullet from reaching its target.

Janson had not determined how many marksmen were in position, or where those positions were. Because he did not know the grid, he did not know which movements were transverse, which not. The rules of flanking and enfilading would stipulate an axial array; marksmen as accomplished as these would be conscious of the peril of bullet "overtravel," which could be fatal to a member of the team or a bystander.

The snipers—where were they? The last two shots came from the southwest, where he could see nothing but, a few hundred yards away, a stand of oak trees.

He starting running, his gaze roaming around him. The very normalcy was what was so eerie. The park was not crowded, but it was far from vacant. Here was a young man swaying to whatever was pulsing through his Walkman. There was a young woman with a stroller, talking to another woman, a close friend, from the looks of it. He could hear the distant cries of young children in paddleboats, frolicking in a shallow, fenced-off area of the boating pond. And, as always, lovers walked hand in hand between the copses of oak and white willow and beech trees. They were in their own world. He was in his. They shared a terrain, blithely unaware that anything was amiss. How could there be?

That was the genius of the operation. The sniping was virtually sound-less. The tiny explosions of bark or turf or water were too fleeting and inconspicuous to be noticed by anybody who was not primed for such evidence.

Regent's Park—that serene glade—had been converted into a killing field, with nobody the wiser.

Except, of course, the prospective victim.

Where was safety? The interrogative rose in Janson's head, rose with screechy, needful urgency.

He had the sole advantage of action over reaction: he alone knew his next move; they would have to respond to what he did. But if they could condition his actions, make him act according to a curtailed number of options in reaction to their own actions, that edge would be lost.

He darted this way and that, along what he estimated as a line trans-verse to the axial array of the sniper team.

"Practicing your footwork?" remarked an amused older man, his white hair combed forward and trimmed, Caesar-style. "Looking good. You'll be playing for Manchester United one of these days!" It was the sort of jibe reserved for somebody one took to be insane. What else made sense of Janson's strange, darting movements, his dashes right and left, seemingly random, seemingly pointless? It was the zigzagging of a wingless hum-mingbird.

He put on a sudden burst of speed and plunged through a crowd of pedestrians toward York Bridge. The bandstand beckoned: it would shelter him from the snipers.

He ran along the banks of the boating lake and past an elderly woman who was throwing bread crumbs to ravenous pigeons. An enormous flock of the birds took flight as he pounded through their midst, like an ex-ploding cloud of feathers. One of them, batting its wings just a few yards ahead, suddenly dropped like a stone, landing near his feet. The smudge of red on the pigeon's breast told him that it had caught a stray bullet intended for him.

And still nobody noticed. For everyone but him, it was a perfect day in the park.

A small burst of wooden splinters erupted at waist level, as another shot flicked off the rail of the wooden bridge and into the water. The quality of the shooting was remarkable: it was only a matter of time before one reached the X-ring.

He'd made a mistake when he'd charged toward York Bridge: the two shots they'd just taken was proof of it. It meant, from the vantage of his assailants, that the movement had changed his distance but not his angle, which was harder to correct for. That was another piece of information: he would have to make use of it if he wanted to survive another minute.

Now he made his way around two sides of the tennis courts, which were set off with mesh fencing. Ahead of him was an octagonal gazebo, made of pressure-treated lumber decked out to look rustic and old. It was an opportunity, but a risk as well: if he were a sniper, he would anticipate that his subject would seek temporary refuge there, and cluster his shots in its direction. He could not approach it directly. He ran at an angle, veering away from it altogether; then, when he was some distance past it, he ran jaggedly, bobbing and weaving, to its shadow. He could walk behind it for a bit, because it would serve as a barrier between him and the tree stand where the team of marksmen was based.

An explosion of turf, a yard from his left foot. *Impossible!*

No, it was all too possible. He had been guilty of wishful thinking—assuming that the snipers had restricted themselves to the tall trees behind the boating lake. It made sense that they would station themselves there; professional snipers liked to keep the sun to their backs, partly for viewing purposes, but even more to prevent a visible glare from flashing off their scopes. The spray of dirt suggested that the bullet had arrived from the same approximate direction as the others. Yet the tall gazebo would have shielded him from a tree-mounted marksman. He surveyed the horizon with a sinking feeling.

Farther away, *much* farther away: the steel lattice of a twenty- or thirty-story crane, from a construction site on Rossmore Road. Distance: about three-quarters of a mile.

Christ! Was it possible?

The sight line was direct: with proper optics and perfect zeroing, it *would* be possible, just, for a top-of-the-league marksman.

He scurried back to the gazebo but knew that it was only a very temporary place of refuge. Now an entire team would know his precise location. The more time he spent there, the better coordinated and more effective the sniper fire would be once he tried to leave. They could wait him out. Not that they needed to. They would be able to radio backup—

summon a *stroller,* as pedestrian adjuvants were known in the trade. A stroller in a tweed jacket with an ordinary silenced pistol would be able to pick him off, conceal the weapon, and resume his walk, with nobody alerted. No, the seeming safety of his position was spurious. Every moment increased the risks he would face. Every moment made escape less likely.

*Think!* He had to act. Something like annoyance was welling up in him: he was tired of being used for target practice, dammit! To maximize his safety at this second would be to minimize his safety five minutes from now. Immobility was death. He would not die cowering behind a gazebo, waiting to be picked off from the air or the ground.

The hunted would become the hunter; the quarry would turn predator, or die in the attempt: this was the only option he had left.

Facts: these were marksmen of extraordinary expertise. But they had been deployed in such a way as to put those skills to the test. All the shots were long-range ones, and however extraordinary the shooter, there were dozens of uncontrollable variables—small breezes, an interceding twig—that could put the bullet off its intended trajectory. At great distances, even tiny factors became enormously significant. Nor was the shooting heedless: there clearly was a concern to avoid bystanders. Berman was doubtless seen as an accomplice of his, his possible death of no account, perhaps even beneficial to the mission.

Question: Why was the team stationed at such a remove? What made the pursuit so unnerving was the fact that he could not see his pursuers. They stayed well out of the way. But *why?*

Because they—or their controllers—were risk-averse. *Because they were afraid of him.*

Dear Christ. It was true. It had to be. They must have been commanded to avoid close contact at all costs. Subject deemed unpredictable and dangerous at close quarters. He would be destroyed at long distance.

A counterintuitive conclusion was unavoidable: the reflexive tactic of evasion, increasing the distance between himself and his assailants, was precisely the wrong response.

He had to embrace his enemy, move *toward* his attackers. Was there a way to do so and *live?*

Standing near the Inner Circle, the stone path surrounding Queen Mary's Garden, a stocky woman in a denim skirt was handing a pair of binoculars to her girl. The woman had the sort of complexion, pale but splotchily reddened, that must have had suitors calling her an "English rose" when she was a teenager; but the once becoming blush had coarsened and grown definite.

"See the one with the blue on its wing? That means it's a bluebird."

The girl, who looked about seven, peered through the binoculars uncomprehendingly. The binoculars were the genuine article, a 10×50 by the looks of them: the woman must have been a devoted bird-watcher, like so many Brits, and eager to show her child the wonders of the avian world. "Mummy, I can't see *anything*," the little girl bleated. Her mother, with her trunklike legs, leaned over and adjusted the binoculars so that the eyecups were closer together.

"Now try."

"Mummy! Where's the bird!"

There was another safety factor just now: a breeze was passing through, ruffling the leaves of the trees. A distance shooter would be vigilant about evidence of wind, especially irregularly gusting winds, knowing how much it could disturb the shot's trajectory. If a shot had to be made under such conditions, there were rules for compensation, for "doping the wind." Estimation of wind speed followed rough rules of thumb: a four-mile-per-hour wind was a wind you can feel on your face; between five and eight miles per hour, tree leaves are in constant motion; in twelve-mile-per-hour winds, small trees sway. And then the *angle* of the breeze had to be figured in. A direct crosswind was rare; most winds were at an irregular angle to the line of fire. Moreover, wind zones downrange often varied from the wind experienced by the sniper himself. To complete the necessary calculations before the wind changed was infeasible. And so accuracy was inevitably diminished. If they had any choice, and they did, the snipers would wait until it subsided.

Janson approached the mother and daughter, his heart thudding. Though conscious of his lethal halo, he had to trust to the professional self-regard of the marksmen: snipers of that order prided themselves on their precision; hitting such bystanders would look like unacceptable amateurism. And the breeze was still gusting.

"Excuse me, madam," he said to the woman. "But I wonder if I might borrow your binoculars." He winked at the little girl.

Immediately, the girl burst into tears. "*No*, Mummy!" she screamed. "They're mine, mine, *mine!*"

"Just for a moment?" Janson smiled again, swallowing his desperation. In his head, the seconds ticked off.

"Don't cry, my poppet," the mother said, caressing the girl's purple face. "Mummy will buy you a lollipop. Wouldn't that be nice!" She turned to Janson. "Viola's very sensitive," the mother said coolly. "Can't you see how you've upset her?"

"I'm very sorry. . . ."

"Then *please* leave us alone."

"Would it matter if I said it was a matter of life and death?" Janson flashed what he hoped was a winning smile.

"My *gawd*, you Yanks, you think you own the bloody *world*. Take no for an answer, would you?"

Too many seconds had elapsed. The breeze had subsided. Janson could picture, in his head, the sniper he could not see. Hidden in foliage, or braced on a strong lateral tree branch, or perched on a telescoping boom crane, the steel lattice and base hydraulics minimizing any sway. However positioned, the sniper's main camouflage was his very stillness.

Janson knew the terrible, emptied-out clarity of the sniper's mind first-hand. He had received extensive sniper training in Little Creek, and had been required to draw upon those skills in country. There had been the afternoons spent with a Remington 700 braced on two sandbags, the barrel itself resting on nothing but a cushion of air, waiting for the shimmering motion in his scope that told him his target was emerging. And, on radiophone, Demarest's voice in his ear, coaching, coaxing, reassuring. "You'll feel it before you see it, Janson. Let yourself feel it. Relax into the shot." How surprised he was when he took it and hit his target. He was never in the same league as those who now pursued him, but he did it well and reliably because he'd had to. And his having been on the other side of the scope made his current position that much more nerve-racking.

He knew what they saw. He knew what they thought.

The master sniper's world would be reduced to the circular image through his scope, and then to the relation between the darting body and the scope's crosshairs. His gun is a Remington 700, or a Galil 7.62, or an M40A1. He would have found the spot-weld, the contact point between his cheek and the rifle stock; the rifle would feel like an extension of his body. He would take a deep breath and let it out fully, and then another breath, and let it out halfway. A laser range finder could tell him the precise distance: the scope adjusted to compensate for bullet drop. The crosshairs would settle upon the rectangle that was the subject's torso. More breath would be expelled, the rest held, and the finger would caress the trigger. . . .

Janson dropped to the ground, adopting a sitting position by the crying girl. "Hey," he said to her. "It's going to be all right."

"We don't like you," she said. Him personally? Americans in general? Who could fathom the mind of a seven-year-old?

Janson gently took her binoculars, lifting the straps from around her shoulders, and quickly set off.

"*Mummy!*" It came out somewhere between a scream and a whine.

"What the *hell* do you think you're doing?" the mother bellowed, red-faced.

Janson, clutching the binoculars, dashed toward the wooden bandstand, two hundred yards away. Every time his position changed significantly, the snipers would have adjusted their sightings. The woman ran after him, puffing but determined. She had left her child behind, and now stomped after him with a spray bottle she had extracted from her purse.

An aerosol can of pepper spray. She was striding toward him with a look that combined disapproval and rage, Mary Poppins with mad cow disease. "Damn you!" she shouted. "Damn you! Damn you!" There were countless Brits just like her, their powerful calves stuck into Wellingtons, their bird-watching manuals stuck into bottomless handbags. They invariably collected string and ate Marmite and smelled of toast.

He turned to see her holding the bottle of pepper spray at arm's length, her features twisted into a vicious grin as she prepared to spray a noxious jet of capsicum oleoresin into his face.

There was an odd clang a split second before her bottle burst, and a cloud of pepper exploded around the torn metal of the canister.

A look of utter disbelief passed over her face: she had no experience with what happened when a bullet destroyed a pressurized container. Then the cloud drifted over her.

"Defective, I guess," Janson offered.

Tears streaming from her eyes, the woman spun on her flat-heeled shoes and rushed away from him, gagging and hacking, her breathing now a reedy stridor. Then she threw herself into the lake, hoping for relief from the searing heat.

*Thwack.* A bullet struck the wood of the bandstand, the closest shot yet. Snipers who used high-precision bolt-action rifles paid for greater accuracy with reduced frequency. Janson rolled on the ground until he was under the bandstand, the abandoned concert area, before which plastic chairs were neatly set out for a concert that evening.

The trelliswork of the base would not protect him from bullets, but it would make him more difficult to sight. It would buy him a little time, which was what he most needed right now.

Now he dialed up the binoculars, testing various focal points, avoiding dazzle from the late-afternoon sun.

It was maddening. The sun lit up the boom derrick of the crane like a match; it cast a halo over the trees.

The trees, the trees. Oak, beech, chestnut, ash. Their branches were irregular, the leafy canopies irregular, too. And there were so many of them—a hundred, maybe two hundred. Which was the tallest, and the densest? A rough eyeballing of the arboreal clusters suggested a couple of candidates. Now Janson zoomed the binoculars to maximum magnification and scrutinized just those trees.

Leaves. Twigs. Branches. And—

Movement. The hairs on his neck raised.

A breeze was scurrying through the trees: of course there was movement. The leaves fluttered; the slender branches swayed, too. Yet he had to trust his instinct, and soon his rational mind made sense of what had pricked his intuition. The branch that moved was thick, too thick to have been affected by the passing gust. It moved—why? Because an animal had shifted its weight on it, a scampering squirrel? Or a person?

Or: because it was not a branch at all.

The light made it difficult to make out details; though Janson fine-tuned the scope, the object remained frustratingly indistinct. He imposed different mental images on it, which was an old field trick he had learned as one of Demarest's Devils. A branch, with twigs and leaves? Possible, but not satisfactory. Could it be that it was a rifle, covered in arboreal-camouflage decals, to which small twigs had been attached? When he pictured the optical image according to that mental model, all sorts of tiny irregularities suddenly clicked into place. A gestalt effect.

The reason that the branch seemed unnaturally straight was that it was a rifle. The twigs were attached with furred twist-wires. The tiny area of darkness at the end of a branch was not a tar-healed tree wound, but the rifle's bore hole.

Five hundred yards away, a man was peering through a scope, just as he was, with the settled resolve of sending him to his death.

*I'm coming for you,* Janson thought to himself. *You won't see me when I get there, but I'll get there.*

A team of soccer players were making their way toward the playing fields, and he joined them briefly, knowing that, from a distance, he would be hard to pick out among the dense crowd of tall, athletic men.

The lake thinned into a stream, and as the men crossed the wooden bridge, he rolled off into the water. Had the marksmen seen him? There was a good chance that they had not. He expelled all the air from his lungs and swam through the murky, turbid water, staying near the bottom. If his misdirection succeeded, the sniper scopes would still be trained on the crowd of athletes. High-powered scopes inevitably had a narrow field of vision; it would be impossible to keep an eye on the rest of the terrain and follow the crowd. But how much longer before they realized he was not in it?

Now he crossed the water to the south bank, pulled himself up the concrete basin wall, and dashed over to a copse of beech trees. If he had slipped their purview, the reprieve was only temporary—one mistake could put him in the deadly snare. It was the most thickly forested area of Regent's Park, and it brought to mind training exercises along the ridgelines outside Thon Doc Kinh.

He had studied the formation of trees from a distance and had determined the tallest one. Now he had to turn a distance map into a proximal map, corresponding to the very terrain under his feet.

It was the hour when the park emptied out. This had advantages and disadvantages, and yet *everything* had to be used for advantage: there was no choice. Willed optimism was the order of the day. A sober reckoning of the odds might well lead to defeatism and paralysis, making the dire outcome even more probable.

He sprinted toward one tree, waited, then rushed toward another. He felt a tingle in his stomach. Had he been silent enough? Inconspicuous enough?

If his instincts were correct, he was directly below the tree where at least one of the snipers had positioned himself.

Marksmanship was an activity of intense concentration. At the same time, concentration required shutting out peripheral stimuli, as he knew from experience. Tunnel vision was a matter not merely of the narrowness of field through the scope but of the intensity of mental focus. Now he had to take advantage of that tunnel vision.

The soccer team had crossed the bridge, then made its way past a brick building, Regent's College, a Baptist institution. If he were one of the snipers, that would arouse suspicions, particularly when the crowd spaced out and he discovered that his target was not among them. They would have to entertain the possibility that he had somehow ducked into the brick building. It was not a terribly worrying possibility: they could wait him out.

The marksmen would be intensely scrutinizing every square yard of the park in their purview. But one did not scrutinize one's own feet. Then, too, the snipers would have radiophones to keep them in touch with their coordinator. Yet these would further reduce their sensitivity to ambient sounds. So there *were* elements in Janson's favor.

Now he heaved himself up the trunk, as quietly as he could. Progress was slow but steady. When he reached ten feet, what he saw astonished him. Not only was the sniper rifle brilliantly camouflaged, but the entire apron of branches on which the sniper reposed was fake. It was incredibly lifelike, admittedly—the work of an arboreal Madame Tussaud—but up close he could see that it was an artificial construction attached to the trunk by means of metal rigging, an arrangement of steel-wire rope, rings, and bolts, all spray-painted an olive drab. It was the kind of equipment that no individual had access to, and only a very few agencies. Consular Operations was one.

He reached for the rigging and, with a sudden yank, he released the central eyebolt; the steel cable slithered free, and the sniper's nest was suddenly unanchored.

He heard a muffled curse, and the whole nest dropped through the tree, breaking branches as it tumbled to the ground.

Finally, Janson could make out the green-clad body of the sniper beneath him. He was a slender young man—some sort of prodigy, no doubt, but momentarily stunned by the fall. Janson lowered himself to the ground in a controlled drop, landing with his legs spread over the sniper.

Now he wrenched the rifle from the marksman's hands.

"Damn!" the curse came out like a whisper. It was light in timbre, the voice of a youth.

Janson found himself holding a forty-inch rifle, hard to maneuver at such close distances. A modified M40A1, which was a bolt-action sniper rifle hand made at Quantico by specially trained armorers of the Marine Corps Marksmanship Unit.

"The tables are turned," Janson said softly. He reached down and knotted the sniper's collar around his neck, ripping off the radio communicator. He was still prone. Janson noticed his short, spiky brown hair, his slender legs and arms: not a formidable specimen of manhood at first glance. He started to pat the sniper down, removing a small .32-caliber Beretta Tomcat pistol from his waistband.

"Get your stinking hands off me," the sniper hissed, and rolled over, looking at Janson with a look of the purest venom.

"Christ," Janson said, involuntarily. "You're—"

"What?" A defiant glare.

Janson just shook his head. The sniper reared up and Janson responded with force, shoving the sniper back down to the ground. Then, once more, the two locked eyes.

The sniper was lithe-bodied, agile, surprisingly strong—and a woman.

# CHAPTER SEVENTEEN

Like a wild animal, she lunged at him yet again, frantically trying to re-trieve the Beretta pistol in his hand. Janson deftly stepped back and point-edly pulled back the slide lock with his thumb.

Her gaze kept returning to the Beretta.

"You're overmatched, Janson," she said. "No embassy lardasses this time. See, this time they cared enough to send the very best." Her voice had the twang of the Appalachian backcountry, and though she was trying to sound conversational, the tension showed.

Was the bravado meant for him, or for her? Was she trying to demor-alize him, or ginning up her own courage?

He put on a bland smile. "Now, let me make you a very reasonable proposition: You deal, or I kill you."

She snorted. "Think you're lookin' at number forty-seven? In your dreams, old man."

"What are you talking about?"

"That would make me number forty-seven." When he did not reply, she added. "You've done forty-six people, right? I'm talking sanctioned, in-field killings."

Janson's face went cold. The number—which was never a source of pride and increasingly a source of anguish—was accurate. But it was also a count that few people knew.

"First things first," Janson said. "Who are you?"

"What do you think?" the sniper replied.

"No games." Janson pressed the muzzle of her M40A1 hard into her diaphragm.

She coughed. "Same as you—same as you *were*."

"Cons Op," Janson ventured.

"You got it."

He hefted the M40A1. At three and a third feet and almost fifteen pounds, it was too big and bulky if much repositioning was required; it was for the stationary shooter. "Then you're a member of its Sniper Lambda Team."

The woman nodded. "And Lambda always gets its man."

She was telling the truth. And it meant one thing: a beyond-salvage order had gone out. Consular Operations had sent a directive to an elite squad of specialists: a directive to kill. Terminate with extreme prejudice.

The rifle was obviously well maintained and was, in its own way, a thing of beauty. The magazine held five rounds. He opened the chamber and removed a cartridge. He gave out a low whistle.

A mystery solved. It was a 458 Whisper, a cartridge made by SSK Industries, which propelled a custom six-hundred-grain very-low-drag Winchester magnum. The VLD bullets lost velocity slowly, retaining a great deal of energy even at distances exceeding a mile. But the feature that had made it irresistible was that it launched the bullet at subsonic velocities. It eliminated the cracking noise of the supersonic bullet, while the small amount of powder diminished the internal detonation. Hence the name: Whisper. Someone just a few yards away would hear nothing.

"OK, sport," Janson said, impressed despite himself by her cool. "I need to know the location of the others. And don't bullshit me." With a few quick movements, he stripped the M40A1 of its magazine, and threw it high into the tree's tangled branches, where it lodged, once more a branch among branches to the casual viewer. Then he leveled the Beretta at her head.

She glared at him for a few long moments. He returned her look with complete impassivity: he would kill her, without compunction. Only luck had prevented her from killing him.

"There's one other guy," she started.

Janson looked at her appraisingly. She was an antagonist, but with luck, she could be turned into an asset, someone he could use as a shield and as a source of information. She knew where the fortified positions were, where the members of the sniper team were nested.

She was also a glib and effortless liar.

With his gun hand, he reached over and cuffed her hard on the side of the head.

"Let's not begin this relationship with lies, sweetheart," he said. "As far as I'm concerned, you're just a killer. You almost shot me, and you endangered lives of noncombatants in the effort."

"Bullshit," she drawled. "I knew just what the margin of error was at all times. Four feet in any direction from your torso midline. None of my shots exceeded that error margin, and the field of fire was clean before each trigger pull. Nobody was in jeopardy. Except you."

The geometry she described was consistent with what he had observed: that much was probably the truth. But to achieve that tight a cluster from more than five hundred yards away made her an off-the-charts marksman. A phenomenon.

"OK. Axial formation. It would be a waste of manpower to station another marksman within fifty yards of you. But I also know there are at least three others spread out in the vicinity. Not to mention whoever's on the Wilmut-Dixon crane. . . . Plus at least two others using tree cover."

"If you say so."

"I admire your discretion," Janson said. "But if you're not any use to me alive, I really can't afford to keep you around." He cocked the Beretta, his forefinger curling around the trigger, testing its resistance.

"OK, OK," she blurted. "I'll deal."

The concession came too quickly. "Forget it, baby. There's no trust." He flipped back the safety once more and placed his finger on the trigger, flexing the hardened steel. "Ready for your close-up?"

"No, wait," she said. Any vestige of bravado had evaporated. "I'll tell you what you want to know. If I'm lying, you'll find out and you can kill me then."

"My game, my rules. You give me the location of the nearest sniper. We approach. If you're wrong, you die. If the sniper repositioned himself without notifying the team, too bad. You die. If you give me away, you die. Remember, I know the systems, the protocols, and the procedures. I probably wrote half of them."

She stood up shakily. "All right, man. Your game, your rules. First thing you gotta know is, we're all working as singletons—camouflage require- ments ruled out partners, so we're all doing our own range finding. Sec- ond thing is, we've got somebody stationed on the roof over Hanover Terrace."

He flashed on the majestic neoclassical villa facing the park, where many of England's grandest citizens made their homes. The blue and white frieze over the architrave. The white pillars and cream-colored walls. The marksmen would have to be perched behind the balusters. True? No, another lie. He would have been dead by now.

"You're not using your head, sport," he said. "A sniper on the balus- trade would have already taken me out. He'd also be visually exposed to the crew repairing the roofs on Cumberland Terrace. You considered the position, and rejected it." Once more, he cuffed her hard, and she stag-gered back a few steps. "Two strikes. One more, I kill you."

She lowered her head. "Can't blame a girl for trying," she said under her breath.

"Got anyone stationed by Park Road?"

A beat. She knew he knew; prevarication would be pointless. "Ehren-halt's on the minaret," she admitted.

He nodded. "And who's enfilading to your left?"

"Take my range finder," she said. "You don't trust me, you can see for yourself. Marksman B is in position three hundred yards northwest." It was a low brick structure that housed telecom equipment. "He's on top. The height's not optimal: that's why he hasn't been able to get any good shots yet. But if you had tried to leave via the Jubilee Gate, you'd be a dead man. There are men on foot on Baker Street, Gloucester Street, and York Terrace Way. Strollers with Glocks. Two sharpshooters have a com-plete review of Regent's Canal. And there's a man on the roof of Regent's College. We were hoping you'd try to use it as shelter. Within two hundred yards, all of us are X-circle accurate—head-shot accurate."

*We were hoping you'd try to use it as shelter.* He almost had.

Janson mapped out in his head the vertices she had specified: they made sense. It was how he would have designed the operation.

Keeping the gun securely in one hand, he looked through her Swarovski 12x50 dual range finder scope. The concrete bunker she'd mentioned was exactly the sort of structure that dotted the urban landscape, that people saw without seeing. A good position. Was there really someone there? It was mostly obscured through the leafy canopies, but a few centimeters of concrete were visible. A sniper? He dialed up the magnification until he saw—something. A glove? Part of a boot? It was impossible to say.

"You're coming with me," Janson announced abruptly, grabbing the sniper's wrist. With every lingering moment, the team of marksmen would begin to reevaluate probabilities: if they decided that he had left the pur-view of their axial sight lines, they would reposition, and that would change the ground rules altogether.

"I get it," she said. "It's just like at the Hamas encampment in Syria, near Qael-Gita. You took one of the sentries hostage, forced him to divulge the location of another one, repeated the process, had the perimeter de-fenses peeled off in less than twenty minutes."

"Who the hell have you been talking to?" Janson said, taken aback.

Those operational details were not widely known, even within the organization.

"Oh, you'd be surprised the things I know about you," she said.

He strode down the greenway, dragging her along with him. Her footsteps were noisy, deliberately so. "Soundlessly," he said. "Or I'll start to think you're not cooperating."

Immediately, her footfalls grew careful, picking out landing spots, avoiding leaves and twigs; she had been trained in how to move quietly: every member of her team would have received such training.

As they grew nearer to the boundary of Regent's Park, the noise of traffic and the smell of exhaust drifted toward them. They were in the heart of London, a greensward established almost two centuries before and preserved, lovingly, every year since. Would the carefully trimmed grass end up soaked with his blood?

They approached the concrete bunker, and Janson placed a finger on his lips. "Not a sound," he said. The Beretta remained loosely gripped in his hand.

Now he stooped down, and signaled her to do the same. Atop the low brick structure, the marksman was, he could now see, in prone position, the fore end of his rifle supported by his left hand. No sniper ever let the barrel rest on anything; it distorted the resonance, affecting the shot. He was a picture of complete concentration, peering through the scope, using his left elbow as a pivot as he moved the field of view slightly. His shoulders were level, the rifle butt close to his shoulder pocket. The rifle itself rested in the V of his left thumb and forefinger, its weight resting on the palm. Perfect position.

"Victor!" the woman called out suddenly.

The gunman jerked at the sound, swiveled his rifle around, and squeezed off a shot, wildly. Janson leaped to one side, lifting the woman with him. Then he somersaulted toward the bunker and, with a lightning-fast motion, seized the gun by the barrel and jerked it out of the marksman's grasp. As the man hurriedly reached for his side arm, Janson swung the scoped rifle like a bat, connecting with the man's head. He slumped forward, prone as before but now unconscious.

The woman propelled herself with all her coiled force toward Janson's gun hand. She wanted the Beretta—it would change everything. At the last fraction of a second, Janson dodged her outstretched arms. She seized his wet jacket instead, and hammered her knee toward his groin. As he torqued his pelvis back defensively, she flexed her wrist into a slap block, and sent the Beretta flying through the air.

Both took a few steps back.

The woman assumed the classic military stance: her left arm was out and perpendicular to her body, a barrier to a rush. A blade struck at the arm would hit only skin and glance off bone; the major muscles, arteries, and tendons were on the side facing inward, protected from attack. Her right arm was extended straight down, and held a small knife; it had been boot-holstered, and he had not even seen her draw it. She was good, faster and more agile than he was.

If he lunged forward, her posture made it clear, she would peel his arm with her blade: an effective counter. And straight from the manual.

She was well trained, which, oddly, reassured him. He choreographed the next ten seconds in his head, preparing a counter-response to her probable actions. The fact that she was well trained was her weakness. He knew what she would do because he knew what she had been taught. He had taught enough people those very maneuvers. But after twenty-five years in the field, he had a far richer repertory of moves, of experiences, of reflexes. It would make all the difference.

"My poppa used to tell me, 'Don't bring a knife to a gunfight,'" she said. "Don't know about that. I was never the worse for having a backup blade." She gripped the knife handle like a fiddle bow, loosely but firmly; she was obviously somebody who knew how to wield it with slashing force.

Suddenly, he fell forward, grabbing her extended arm; she raised her knife hand, as he had predicted, and he delivered a crushing blow to its wrist. The median nerve was vulnerable about an inch from the heel of her hand; his precisely directed blow caused her knife hand to open involuntarily.

Now he grabbed the weapon she had released—yet at the same moment, her other hand shot out toward his shoulder. She dug her thumb deep into his trapezius muscle, jolting the nerves that ran beneath and temporarily paralyzing his arm and shoulder. A bolt of agony shot through the area. Her fighting stance was awesome, the triumph of training over instinct. Now he swept his foot toward her right knee, causing intense pain and destabilizing her footing. She toppled backward, but his own leg sweep wrong-footed him, and he ended up falling on top of her.

He could feel the heat of her sweaty body beneath him, feel her muscles tense as she squirmed and thrashed like a practiced wrestler. With his powerful thighs, he pinned her legs down, but her arms were capable of doing him serious damage. He could feel her striking at his brachial plexus, the bundle of nerves that reached from the top of his shoulder to the vertebrae of his neck. He hammered his elbows outward, and pinned her arms to the ground, relying on his greater weight and brute strength.

Her face, inches from his, was contorted in rage and, so it seemed, disgust with herself for having allowed him to gain the stronger position.

He saw the muscles of her neck flex, saw she intended to break his nose by butting with her forehead, and pressed his forehead to her own, immobilizing it. Her breath was warm against his face.

"You really want to kill me, don't you," Janson said, almost with amusement. It was not a question.

"Shit, no," she said with heavy sarcasm. "This is just foreplay as far as I'm concerned." Struggling mightily, she thrashed beneath him, and he only barely maintained his position.

"So what did they tell you? About me?"

She inhaled and exhaled heavily for a few moments, catching her breath. "You're a rogue," she said. "Somebody who's betrayed everything that ever mattered in his life, somebody who murdered for money. Lowest kind of dirtbag there is."

"Bullshit."

"Bullshit's what you are. Double-crossed everything and everybody you could. Sold out the agency, sold out your country. Good agents are dead because of you."

"That right? They say why I went bad?"

"You fucking snapped, or maybe you were always a piece of shit. Don't matter. Every day you live is a day when our lives are in danger."

"That's what they told you?"

"It's the *truth,*" she spat. Another writhing attempt to throw him off her passed through her body like a powerful shudder. "Shit," she said. "At least you don't have bad breath. I should be grateful for that, huh? So what's on the agenda? You gonna kill me, or is it just gonna be a lot of dry humping?"

"Don't flatter yourself," he said. "A sharp cookie like you—you believe everything they tell you?" He grunted. "No shame in it. I did once." Their foreheads were still pressed together, nose to nose, mouth to mouth: the strange and unsettling intimacy of lethal combatants.

Her eyes narrowed to slits. "You got another story? I'm listening. Can't *do* anything else." But she made another convulsive effort to shake him.

"Try this on. I was set up. I served in Consular Operations for over two decades. Look, you seem to know a lot about me. Ask yourself if what they've told you about me really fits the picture."

She said nothing for a moment. "Give me something real," she said. "If you didn't do what they say you did, give me something to show you're telling me the truth. I realize I'm not in any position to negotiate. I just want to know."

For the first time, she spoke without hostility or japery. Was it something in his own voice that gave her pause, that made her wonder if he was the villain she'd been told he was?

He inhaled deeply, his chest expanding next to hers: again, an odd, unwanted intimacy. He felt her relax beneath him.

"OK," she said. "Get offa me. I ain't gonna rear, ain't gonna run—I know you'd get to the rifle first. I'm just going to listen."

He made sure her body was completely slack and then—a crucial decision, a moment of trust in the midst of deadly combat—rolled off her in a quick movement. He had a destination in mind: the Beretta, now nestled under a nearby ash tree. He grabbed it and stowed it in his front waistband.

Looking wobbly and uncertain, the woman rose to her feet. Then she smiled coolly. "Is that a gun in your pocket, or—"

"It's a gun in my pocket," he said, cutting her off. "Let me tell you something. I was once like you. A weapon. Aimed and discharged by someone else. I thought I had an autonomous intelligence, made my own decisions. The truth was otherwise: I was a weapon in the hands of another."

"That's just a bunch of word music as far as I'm concerned," she said. "I'm into specifics, not generalities."

"Fine." He took a deep breath, dredging up an old memory. "A penetration identified in Stockholm. . . ."

He could picture the man now. Blunt, pudgy features, a soft-in-the-middle, sedentary soul. And scared, so scared. Dark smudges under his eyes spoke of sleeplessness and exhaustion. Through Janson's scope, those features formed a rictus of anxiety; the subject made quiet popping noises with his lips, an absurd, nervous tic. Why so scared, if this was a typical contact? He had seen such contacts, men going about their business, making a dead drop, the twentieth or thirtieth dead drop of the year, with a bored and vacant expression. This man's face was different—filled with self-loathing and fear. And when the Swede turned toward the other man, the putative Russian contact, his face read not greed or gratitude but repugnance.

"Stockholm," she said. "May of 1983. You witnessed the subject make contact with the KGB control, and took him out. For a nonspecialist, it was a pretty neat shot: from an apartment rooftop to a park bench two blocks away."

"Stop the tape," he said. Her knowledge of these things was unnerving. "You've described it as I did in my report. Yet how did I know he was a penetration agent? I'd been told he was. And the KGB agent? I recognized the face, but that, too, was a datum I'd been provided with by operations control. What if it were wrong?"

"You mean he wasn't KGB."

"In fact, he was. Sergei Kuzmin was his name. But the man who met with him was frightened, blackmailed into the meeting. He had no interest in providing the KGB with anything useful. He was going to try to persuade the man that he had nothing further to offer, that his diplomatic rank was too low to make him a valuable asset. He was going to tell him to buzz off, damn the consequences."

"How do you know?"

"I spoke to his wife. That wasn't part of my mission instructions."

"That's so *random,* man. And how did you know she spoke the truth?"

"I just did," he responded, shrugging. It was not a question that a highly experienced field agent would have to ask. "Tutored intuition, call it. It's not a hundred percent reliable—but accurate enough."

"How come this wasn't part of your report?"

"Because it wasn't news to those who designed the mission," he said coldly. "The planners had another game in mind. Two objectives, both fulfilled. One, to send a message to any other member of the diplomatic forces that entanglement with the enemy could carry a steep price. I was just ringing up the sale."

"Two objectives, you said. The other?"

"The young Swede had already given dossiers to the KGB. By killing him, we conveyed the message that the information leak was taken seriously—that valuable information had been transferred. In fact, it was planted. Carefully designed disinformation. But it became validated by the man's blood, and KGB analysts bought it."

"So that was a win, too."

"Yes, within narrowly defined parameters. Kuzmin actually got a promotion out of the whole thing. Pull the camera back, though, and you

ask another question: Did it matter? The KGB was misled in this particular, but with what ultimate consequences, if any? And was it worth the
man's life? He had a wife. Had he lived, they would have had children,
probably grandchildren. Decades of Christmases and glögg and skiing va-
cations and—" Janson broke off. "Sorry," he said. "I didn't mean to make
heavy weather of this. None of it will make much sense to you, not at
your age. But there are instances when your instructions amount to a web
of lies. And in some cases, the person giving you the instructions is perfectly unaware of that fact. I expect that's the case here."

"Jesus," she said softly. "No, I do understand. I do. You're telling me
they had you take this guy out—without ever letting you in on the real
reasons for the job."

"They had me kill Kuzmin's contact as part of a manipulation. And
one of the people being manipulated was me. What a directive specifies
and what a directive *signifies* are two different things."

"Jesus, this is making my head swim worse than any goddamn sucker
punch."

"I don't mean to confuse you. Just to make you think."

"Comes to the same thing," she said. "But *why?* Why would they target
you?"

"You think I haven't been asking myself that?"

"You were a legend in Consular Operations, especially among the
younger people. You've got no idea, Janson. No idea how *demoralizing* it
was when they told us you'd turned traitor. They'd never do that on a
whim."

"On a whim? No, that's not how it works. Most people lie to save
themselves, or better themselves, anyway. Maybe they claim credit for an
idea that wasn't really theirs. Or they shift blame from themselves to another. Or they luck out, somehow, and let on that the outcome was the
result of skill. That's not the kind of lie that worries me. The kind of lie
that worries me is the 'noble lie.' The lie spread for higher purposes. The
sacrifice of small men for larger ends." He spoke bitterly. "The liars who
lie in the interest of the greater good, or what they decree to be that greater
good."

"Whoa," she said. She made a whizzing noise, passed a hand over her
head like a discus. "You're losing me. If somebody's scapegoating you,
they've got to have a good reason."

"What they *believe* to be a good reason. A good reason that might strike
others of us as an administrative convenience."

"Lookit," she said. "Earlier, you said something about your profile. That happens to be something I know a lot about. Well, you're right, now that you say it. Something about the story doesn't make sense. Either you weren't as good as you were supposed to have been or you're not as bad as they're saying you are." She took a step closer to him.

"Let me ask you something. Does Lambda have operational authorization from Whitehall?"

"Wasn't time to cross the diplomatic t's. It's all extraterritorial."

"I see," Janson said. "Then you've got a decision to make."

"But our directive . . ."

"It's my life, of course. I have an interest. But it's yours, too. A lesson I learned the hard way."

She looked confused. "OK, take a peek through the range finder again. Marksman C you'll find in the really tall tree near Primrose Hill Gate."

As he lifted the Swarovski dual scope to his eyes, parsing the foliage, Angus Fielding's words echoed in his head. *Are you so confident about your own government?* Indeed, there was a certain logic there. What if Cons Ops, perhaps working with an agent-in-place on Novak's staff, had been responsible for the assassination? Wouldn't that help explain America's official refusal to have any direct involvement in the operation? But then who had set him up with the sixteen million dollars? And if Cons Ops, or some other U.S. government agency, had arranged Novak's death— why? *Why* was Novak seen as such a threat? This, Janson knew, was the crucial piece of the puzzle—a puzzle he had to solve not only for his own sense of justice but for his own physical survival.

His thoughts came to a halt as a crushing blow landed on the side of his head. He reeled backward, stunned, bewildered.

It was the woman. A ridged steel rod in her hand, the kind used in reinforced concrete. On one end it was wet with his own blood. She had wrenched it from the stack of construction materials behind the bunker a few feet away.

"Like the lady says, every tool is a weapon if you hold it right." Another clout, this one just above his ear, the bar bouncing off with the sickening thud of metal against bone. The world around him seemed to waver.

"They warned us about your lies," she growled. His vision was blurred, a red haze, but the expression on her face was unmistakable: pure immaculate loathing.

*Dammit!* At a time when he should have been fully vigilant, he had allowed her to lull him with her lies, her pretense of sympathy; in fact, she had merely been biding her time, awaiting an opportunity. And playing him for a fool.

Sprawled on the ground, he could hear the blood pounding in his head, like a steam engine. Groggily, he reached for the Beretta, but it was too late. She was racing away from him at top speed.

The impact of the rebar had caused a mild concussion at the least; it would take him a few minutes to struggle back to his feet. And by then, she would be gone. An enemy, an asset—gone.

He felt a wave of nausea welling from his gut, and a sense, too, of emptiness. Whom could he trust? Which sides had taken arms against him?

Which side was he on?

At this point, he could only say: his own. Could he expect allies? Did he deserve them? The sniper believed that he was guilty; would he have done anything different in her place?

He glanced at his watch, tried to rise, and blacked out.


"Annunciate radio check."

"Annunciate, annunciate. All secure. Over."

Vietnam was seldom quiet. Combat zones were a cascade of sounds and sights. Artillery pounded, parachute flares whistled as they illuminated the night sky like a hundred kliegs. There was the streak of tracer bullets, the *whomp* of choppers, the winking lights of jets. Soon, it was all as meaningless as the bleating horns and motors of rush-hour traffic. At the same time, their commanding officer had helped them develop a sense of what wasn't routine.

Dialing his scope furiously, zooming through the marsh grasses and palms, Janson saw the clearing with two hutches. There was a cooking fire in front of one, and two VCs squatting in front of them. Were there trip-flares? Three days earlier, Mendez had blundered across one; within seconds, an illumination round was automatically fired—a loudly hissing magnesium flare, which drifted slowly toward earth on a tiny parachute, casting an eerie white glow on them all. They could afford no such mistake now.

Janson radioed Demarest. At least two Victor Charlies identified. Three hundred meters away. Awaiting instructions.

Awaiting instructions.

Awaiting instructions.

There was a crackle of static from the radio headphones, and Demarest's voice came online: "Handle contents with care. You bring them two clicks north of base camp, and pretend they're Waterford crystal. No breaks, bruises, or scrapes. Think you can manage that?"

"Sir?"

"Capture with kindness, Lieutenant. Don't speak English? I can say it in seven other languages if you prefer."

"No, sir. I understand, sir. But I'm not sure just how we'll manage—"

"You'll find a way, Janson."

"I appreciate the confidence, sir, but—"

"Not at all. You see, I know that *I* would find a way. And, like I say, I've got a feeling that you and I are a lot alike."


His finger groped the ground: trimmed grass, not jungle vine. He forced his eyes open again, took in the green vistas of Regent's Park, looked at his watch. Two minutes had elapsed. The retention of consciousness itself would be a supreme effort, yet one at which he must not fail.

The thoughts that had coursed through his brain were drowned out by another, more urgent one: *There was no time.*

The collapse of the axial array must already have been detected, simply by the absence of radio signals. Others would proceed into the area. His vision swimming, his head ringing with pulsing, pounding agony, he crashed through an obstacle course of cone-shaped yews until he had made his way to Hanover Gate.

A black cab was letting out an elderly couple as he staggered to the curb. They were American, and slow-moving.

"No," the bloated and dyspeptic-looking woman was saying, "you don't tip. This is England. They don't tip in England." Garish red-orange lipstick ringed her mouth, drawing attention to the vertical creases of age above and below.

"Sure they do," her husband groused. "What do you know? You don't know *anything*. Always got an opinion, though." He was feebly looking through the unfamiliar currency in his wallet, with the care and deliberateness of an archaeologist prizing apart ancient papyrus. "Sylvia, do you have a ten-pound note?"

The woman opened her purse and, with agonizing slowness, began peering into it.

Janson watched with mounting frustration, for there were no other cabs visible on the street.

"Hey," Janson said to the American couple. "Let me pay for it."

The two Americans looked at him with frank suspicion.

"No, really," Janson said. The American couple kept moving in and out of focus. "It's no problem. I'm in a generous mood today. Just . . . let's get a *move* on."

The two exchanged glances. "Sylvia, the man here said he'll pay. . . ."

"I heard what the man said," the woman replied peevishly. "Tell him thank you."

"So what's the catch?" the old man said, his thin lips drawn into a half frown.

"The catch is, you get out, now."

The two lumbered to the sidewalk, and stood there blinking. Janson slid inside the roomy vehicle, one of the classic black cabs made by Manganese Bronze Holdings PLC.

"Wait a minute," the woman called out. "Our bags. I had two shopping bags. . . ." She spoke slowly and petulantly.

Janson found two plastic bags emblazoned with the Marks & Spencer logo, opened the door, and heaved them at her feet.

"Where you bound, guv?" the driver asked. Then he looked at Janson through the rearview mirror and winced. "Got yourself a nasty gash there."

"Looks worse than it is," Janson murmured.

"You better not get any claret on my upholstery," the driver groused.

Janson pushed a hundred-pound note through the glass partition.

"That's a bit of all right," the driver said, his tone suddenly shifting. "You're the boss, I'm the hoss, crack the whip, I'll make the trip." He seemed pleased with his taxi doggerel.

Janson told the driver the two stops he had to make.

"Bob's your uncle," the driver said.

The pounding in his head had the force and regularity of a jackhammer. Janson pulled out a handkerchief and tied a bandana around his scalp, trying to staunch the seepage of blood. "Can we go now?" He looked out the rear windshield of the cab—which suddenly spiderwebbed in the lower left corner, near his head. A subsonic bullet remained lodged in the laminated glass.

"Mother of *Christ!*" shouted the driver.

"Just floor it," Janson said unnecessarily, hunching down in his seat.

"Bob's your fucking uncle," the driver said, as the engine roared to life.

"He is if you say he is." Janson pushed another hundred-pound note through the partition.

"Am I gonna have any more problems?" the driver asked, looking dubiously at the banknote. They were now at Marylebone Road, merging into fast-moving traffic.

"Not at all," said Janson grimly. "Trust me on this. It's going to be a walk in the park."

She *was* looking at him. He wasn't imagining it.

Kazuo Onishi glanced across the smoky singles bar and then looked back at the sudsy inch of beer remaining in his mug. She was stunning: long blond hair, a pert nose, a mischievous smile. What was she doing alone at the bar?

"Kaz, is that honey on the bar stool hitting on you?"

So it had to be true: even his friend Dexter had noticed.

Onishi smiled. "Why do you sound surprised?" he smirked. "The ladies know a true stud muffin when they see one."

"Must be why you've gone home alone the last half a dozen times we've been here," said Dexter Fillmore, a bespectacled black man whose own luck wasn't much better. The two had known each other since their days at Caltech; now, they never discussed work—since what they both did was classified, that issue simply did not arise—but they had few secrets when it came to affairs of the heart, or just plain affairs. "I'm an eligible bachelor, I make a good living: the ladies should be taking a number and getting in line," Onishi regularly complained.

"Would that be an irrational number or an imaginary one?" Fillmore would snicker.

But now it looked as though Kazuo Onishi had himself a live one.

The woman's third glance definitely had some *linger* to it.

"Call in the referee," Onishi said, " 'cause we're looking at a *knockout*."

"Come on, you're always saying how much a girl's personality matters," Dexter protested playfully. "What could be more superficial than to make judgments from across the room?"

"Aw, she's got a great personality," Onishi said. "You can just tell."

"Yeah," said his friend. "I bet you love the way her *personality* fills that tight sweater of hers."

And now the woman was walking toward him, daintily holding a cosmopolitan. His luck was definitely changing.

"Somebody sitting here?" she asked, pointing to an empty chair near Onishi. She sat down and placed her cocktail next to his beer mug, then signaled a waitress for refills. "OK, I don't usually do this, but I was waiting for my ex-boyfriend who still has issues, if you know what I'm talking about, and I swear, the bartender here starts hitting on me. I mean, what's up with that?"

"I can't imagine," said Onishi, looking innocent. "So where's the boyfriend?"

"Ex," she said pointedly. "Just got a call on my cell phone, said a sudden emergency at work came up. So whatever. Trust me, I wasn't looking forward to it, anyway. I think the only way he's going to stop calling me is for him to get a new girlfriend." She turned to Onishi and smiled a dazzling smile. "Or for me to get a new boyfriend."

Dexter Fillmore finished his beer and coughed. "I'm going to get a pack of Camels. You guys want anything?"

"Get me one," Onishi said.

After Fillmore left, the blonde turned to Onishi and made a face. "You smoke Camels?"

"Not big on smoking, huh?"

"That's not it. But, please, we can do better than that slot-machine shit. You ever try a Balkan Sobranie? Now that's a *real* cigarette."

"A what?"

She opened her handbag and pulled out a metal tin. It contained a row of black unfiltered cigarettes with gold tips. "Fresh from a diplomatic pouch," she said. She handed him one. "Try it," she said. A lighter materialized in her hand as well.

A girl who's good with her hands, Onishi thought as he took a deep drag. Promising. He was also relieved that she hadn't slipped in the what-do-you-do question yet. He always answered that he was a "systems administrator for the government," and nobody ever asked further, though if they did he had a practiced line about "platform interoperability" involving the Departments of Agriculture and Transportation. It was so stupefying that it was guaranteed to repel further inquiries. But the real reason he was glad she hadn't asked was that the one thing he did not want to think about was his job. His real job. In recent days it had become so stressful that his shoulders began to ache as soon as he went to his office. What a string of bad luck they'd had. Fucking unspeakable. All that sweat, all those years—and the goddamn Mobius Program was imploding. He needed to get lucky in some other department of life. Hell, he *deserved* to get lucky.

The beautiful blonde's eyes lingered on his face as the thick smoke filled his lungs. Something about him seemed to fascinate her. A new song came on: the one from the soundtrack of that big new World War II flick. Onishi loved that song. For a moment, he felt he might fly away with happiness.

He coughed. "Strong," he said.

"It's what cigarettes used to be like," she said. She spoke with a very faint accent, but he couldn't tell what kind. "Now be a man. Suck it in."

He took another drag.

"Special, isn't it?" she said.

"A little harsh," he said, tentatively.

"Not harsh, *rich*. I swear with most American cigarettes you might as well be smoking typing paper."

Onishi nodded, but in truth he was beginning to feel more than a little dizzy. It must really be strong tobacco. He felt himself flushing, and starting to sweat.

"Oh my poor dear, look at you," the blonde said. "You seem like you could use some fresh air."

"Might do some good," Onishi agreed.

"Come on," she said. "Let's go for a walk together." He started to reach for his wallet but she put down a twenty, and he was feeling too faint to demur. Dexter would be wondering what happened to him, but he could explain later.

Outdoors, in the cooler air, the dizzy feeling persisted.

She reached out and squeezed his hand reassuringly. In the streetlights, she looked even more beautiful—unless that was more evidence of his dizzy state.

"You don't seem so steady on your feet, you know," she said.

"No," he said, and he knew he had a silly grin on his face but could do nothing about it.

She made a *tsk*ing noise of mock reproach. "Big hunk like you, laid low by a Balkan Sobranie?"

Blondie thought he was a big hunk? That was encouraging. A major positive data point in the multivariate mess that was his sex life. His grin became wider.

At the same time, he found his thoughts growing oddly scrambled, though he also found it hard to care.

"Let's get in my car and go for a drive," she said, and her voice sounded as if it were coming from miles away and something inside him was saying, *Maybe this isn't a good idea, Kaz,* and he found he could do nothing but say yes.

He would go with the beautiful stranger. He would do what she said. He would be hers.

He was only dimly aware of her smoothly shifting the gears of her blue convertible and driving off somewhere with the controlled movements of somebody who had a schedule to keep.

"I'm going to show you the time of your life, Kazuo," she said, her hands brushing his crotch as she reached over to lock his door.

A thought glinted and flashed: *I never told her my name.* It was followed by another thought: *Something is very wrong with me.* And then all such thoughts disappeared into the dark void that was now his mind.

# PART THREE

PART THREE

# CHAPTER EIGHTEEN

The Hasid, nervously clutching his battered hard-sided briefcase, walked over to the railed edge of the upper foredeck in an old man's shuffle. His eyes were vaguely fearful, owing more, it seemed, to his temperament than to his particular circumstances aboard the Stena Line HSS. The giant twin-hull ferry took just four hours to travel from Harwich to Hoek van Holland, where special trains, stationed right alongside the ferry, brought passengers to Amsterdam's Centraal Station. The high-speed ship did all it could to make the trip comfortable: on board were several bars, a couple of restaurants, a number of shops, and a movie theater. The Hasidic man with the battered case did not have the appearance of someone who would avail himself of these diversions, however. He was a recognizable type: the diamond dealer—could there be any doubt of it?—who had no interest in such luxuries as he purveyed, like a teetotaler running a distillery. Other passengers glanced at him and looked away. It wouldn't do to stare. One would not want the Hasid to get the wrong idea.

Now the salty breeze ruffled the man's full white beard and earlocks, his black woolen coat and trousers. The round black hat remained firmly planted on his head as the man continued to take in the pewter sky and the gray-green seas. The vista wasn't inspiring, but the Hasid seemed to find comfort in it.

A figure like him, Janson knew, became invisible by virtue of standing out. If the spirit gum on his cheeks itched, and the woolen cloak was uncomfortably hot, it was easy to produce the low-grade anxiety that his role called for. He let the breeze cool him, dry his sweat. There wasn't any reason to doubt that he was who his passport said he was; from time to time, he took out a small, plastic-encased photograph of the late Rabbi Schneerson, considered by many Hasids to be the messiah, or *mosiach,* and regarded it lovingly. Such details mattered when one was in character.

He turned around slowly, hearing the footfalls of someone approaching him. His stomach dropped as he took in the man's round-brimmed hat and severe black garb. It was a Hasid—a *real* one. A *fellow* Hasid, he told himself urgently. *You are who you pretend to be*—it was an honored koan of spycraft. Another, though, was not to be an idiot about it.

The other man, shorter than Janson, and perhaps in his early forties, smiled at him. "*Voos hurst zich?*" he said, bowing his head a little. His hair was reddish, his eyes a watery blue beneath plastic National Health spectacles. A small leather portfolio was tucked beneath an arm.

Janson bobbed his head, clutching his briefcase, and gave him a cautiously friendly smile, a smile constrained by the imperfect plasticity of the facial adhesive he had employed. How to respond? There were people who had a gift for acquiring new languages, sometimes with uncanny fluency; Alan Demarest was one. Janson, though he had decent German and French from his days as a student, and a certain amount of Czech, gleaned from his Czech-speaking mother, was not among them. Now, he racked his brain, trying to dredge up some scrap of Yiddish. It was an eventuality he should have foreseen. Rather than venture a simpering "sha-lom," he would be safest discouraging any conversation. He had a fleeting fantasy of hurling the inconvenient interloper over the side. After a moment, he gestured toward his throat, and shook his head. "Laryngitis," he whispered, in some approximation of an East End accent.

"*Ir filt zich besser?*" the man said with a kindly look. He was a lonely soul, undeterred in his attempt to bond with someone he took to be spiritual kin.

Janson coughed explosively. "Sorry," he whispered. "*Very* contagious."

The other man took a few steps back, alarmed. He bowed again, clasping his hands together. "*Sholem aleichem.* Peace and blessings be upon you," he said, and shakily raised a hand in farewell, retreating politely but swiftly.

Once more, Janson surrendered himself to the cooling head wind. *We know more than we know,* Demarest used to admonish. Janson believed that it was true in this case—that he could make progress if only he could properly assemble the data points he already had.

He knew that a covert branch of the U.S. government sought his death. That a staggering sum had, through elaborate electronic manipulations, been deposited in his account. That the result was to create a perception that he had been paid to kill Novak.

Could he put that money to use in some way? A voice inside him cautioned him not to—not yet. Not while its true origins remained mysterious. It could prove crucial as evidence. And—the possibility gnawed at him—it could, in some high-tech fashion, be booby-trapped so that any attempt at withdrawal would notify his enemies of his location. Which simply returned him to the question of who these enemies might be.

*Whose side are you on, Márta Lang?* Before boarding, he had once again tried to contact her, without success. Was she part of a murderous intrigue? Or had she been kidnapped, even killed—a victim of the intrigue that had cost Peter Novak his life? Janson had called upon an old friend of his who lived in Manhattan—a veteran of the intelligence services, now retired—to keep a lookout for her at the New York offices of the Liberty Foundation, where Lang ostensibly was based. So far, there had been no sign of her having returned to the Fortieth Street building. She had to be somewhere else—but where?

Then, too, Janson found it as curious as Fielding had that the news of Novak's death continued to go unreported. As far as the general public knew, none of it—not the kidnapping, not the killing—had even happened. Was something afoot, some plan involving insiders at the Liberty Foundation, that made it inopportune to divulge the momentous tragedy? Yet how long did they really think they could conceal such a thing? Janson knew of rumors that Deng Xiaoping's death had been covered up for more than eight days, while the matter of succession was resolved: the regime decided it could not risk even a brief period of public uncertainty. Was something similar at stake with the Liberty Foundation? Novak's enormous wealth, or most of it, was already bound up with the Liberty Foundation. Therefore it was not clear that his passing should directly affect its finances. At the same time, Grigori Berman told him that the wire transfer had originated from Amsterdam, specifically from a Liberty Foundation account of Peter Novak's. Who within the Foundation might have been able to arrange that?

Novak was a powerful man, and his enemies would be powerful as well. He had to accept that Novak's enemies were his enemies, too. And, the most infernal part of the infernal equation, they could be anyone. They could be anywhere. Fielding, before he turned, had spoken incisively about Novak's opponents. The "oligarchs" of corrupt plutocratic regimes, especially those of Eastern Europe, could have found common interest with a cabal of planners within the United States who had regarded Novak's growing influence with dismay and envy. *Ask yourself why America is so hated:* Andros's words. The answers were complex, encompassing the rancor and resentment of those who felt displaced by its dominance. Yet America was no toothless innocent: its efforts to protect its global preeminence could be ruthless indeed. Members of its foreign-policy establishment might well feel threatened by the actions of a truly benevolent figure, simply because those actions were beyond its control. Fielding: *Everyone knew that he'd spurned America's advances, that he'd angered its foreign-affairs establishment by steering his own course. His only polestar was his own conscience.* Who could predict the rage of Washington's planners— shortsighted unilateralists blinded by a zeal for control they mistook for patriotism? This was not America's best face, not the better angels of its nature. But it was sheer naïveté to pretend that the establishment was incapable of such actions. Lieutenant Commander Alan Demarest, he sometimes reflected, believed himself to be a true American. Janson had long considered that a noxious figment of self-delusion. Yet what if the Demarests of the world were right? What if they did represent not *America,* no, but a *strain* of America, an America that foreigners in troubled lands were more likely to encounter than most? Janson closed his eyes but could not banish the piercing, vivid memories that transfixed and haunted him even now.

"No, don't bring them in," the lieutenant commander had told Janson. Faintly, even in the weather-befouled headphones, he could hear choral music. "I'll come out there."

"Sir," Janson replied. "There's no need. They're securely bound, as you requested. The prisoners are unharmed but immobilized."

"Which I'm sure took some doing. I'm not surprised you rose to the challenge, Janson."

"Transport would not present any difficulties," Janson said. "Sir."

"Tell you what," Demarest said. "Take them to Candle Bog."

Candle Bog was what the Americans had named a clearing in the jungle four clicks north of the main army encampment. There had been a skirmish there a month earlier, when American sentinels came upon a couple of hooches and three men they identified as VC couriers. One American was shot in the engagement; all three Viet Cong were eventually killed. An injured member of the American party had corrupted the Vietnamese name of the area, Quan Ho Bok, to Candle Bog, and the appellation stuck.

Transporting the prisoners to Candle Bog took two hours. Demarest was waiting for them when they arrived. He was in a jeep, with his executive officer, Tom Bewick, behind the wheel.

Janson saw that the prisoners were thirsty; because their arms were bound to their sides, he held his canteen to their lips, dividing its contents between the two. Despite their terror and uncertainty, the prisoners slurped the water down gratefully. He let them rest on the ground between the two hooches.

"Good work, Janson," Demarest said.

"Humane treatment of prisoners of war, just like the Geneva Convention says," Janson replied. "If only the enemy followed our lead. Sir."

Demarest chuckled. "You're funny, schoolboy." He turned to his XO. "Tom," he said. "Could you . . . do the honors?"

Bewick's tawny face looked as if it were carved of wood, with crude gashes for eyes and mouth. His nose was small, narrow, and almost sharp in appearance. The overall effect was reinforced by the streaky tan that somehow suggested wood grain. His movements were swift and efficient, but jerky rather than fluid. It added to Janson's sense that Bewick had become a mannequin of Demarest's.

Bewick strode over to the first of the prisoners, withdrew a large knife, and started sawing through the restraints that kept their arms to their sides.

"They need to get comfortable," Demarest explained.

It soon became clear that comfort was not precisely Bewick's objective. The XO fashioned a sling of nylon cord, tightly knotted it around the prisoners' wrists and ankles, and then snaked it around the central beams of each hooch. They were splayed, spread-eagled, their limbs extended outward by the taut rope. They were utterly defenseless, and knew it. That realization of their defenselessness would have psychological effects.

Janson's stomach furled. "Sir?" he began.

"Don't speak," Demarest replied. "Just watch. Watch and learn. It's the old rule: See one, do one, teach one."

Now Demarest approached the prisoner who rested on the ground nearest him. He ran a caressing hand over the young man's cheeks, and said, "*Tôi mén ban.*" He tapped himself on his heart and repeated the words: "I like you."

The two men seemed bewildered.

"Do you speak English? It doesn't matter if you do, because I speak Vietnamese."

The first one spoke, at last. "Yes." His voice was tight.

Demarest rewarded him with a smile. "I thought you did." He ran his index finger down the man's forehead, over his nose, and stopped at his lips. "I like you. You people inspire me. Because you really care. That matters to me. You have your ideals, and you're going to fight until the bitter end. How many *nguoi My* have you killed, do you think? How many Americans?"

The second man burst out, "We no kill!"

"No, because you're farmers, right?" Demarest's tones were honeyed.

"We farm."

"You're not VC at all, are you? Just honest, ordinary hardworking fishermen, right?"

"*Dúng.*" Right.

"Or did you say you were farmers?"

The two looked confused. "No VC," the first man said pleadingly.

"He's not your army comrade?" Demarest indicated his bound companion.

"Just friend."

"Oh, he's your friend."

"Yes."

"He likes you. You help each other."

"Help each other."

"You people have suffered a lot, haven't you?"

"Much suffering."

"Like our savior, Jesus Christ. Do you know that he died for our sins? Do you want to know *how* he died? Yes? Well, why didn't you say so! Let me tell you. No, better idea: let me show you."

"Please?" The word came out like *plis.*

Demarest turned to Bewick. "Bewick, it's downright uncivil to leave these poor young men on the ground."

Bewick nodded, allowing a grin to flicker on his wooden features. Then, rotating a wooden stick twice, he winched the rope tighter. The tension of the rope lifted the prisoners off the ground; the weight of their bodies was supported by their tightly bound wrists and ankles. Each emitted a loud, panicked gasp.

"*Xin loi,*" Demarest said gently. Sorry about that.

They were in agony, their limbs hyperextended, their arms straining at their sockets. The torsion of the position made breathing extraordinarily difficult, requiring a tremendous exertion to arch their chests and extend their diaphragms—an exertion that only increased the torque on their extremities.

Janson flushed. "Sir," he said sharply. "May I have a word with you, alone? Sir?"

Demarest walked over to Janson. "What you're watching may take some getting used to," he said quietly. "But I will not have you interfering with the exercise of executive discretion."

"You're torturing them," Janson said, his face tight.

"You think that's torture?" Demarest shook his head disgustedly. "Lieutenant First Class Bewick, Lieutenant Second Class Janson is upset right now. For his own protection, I need you to restrain him—by any means necessary. Any problems with that?"

"None, sir," Bewick replied. He leveled his combat pistol at Janson's head.

Demarest walked over to the nearby jeep and pressed the PLAY button on his portable tape cassette. Choral music spilled from small, tinny speakers. "Hildegard von Bingen," he said to no one in particular. "Spent most of her life in a convent she founded, in the twelfth century. One day when she was forty-two years old she had a vision of God, and with that she became the greatest composer of her age. Each time she sat down to create, it was always after she had suffered the most excruciating pain—what she called the scourge of God. For only when the pain brought her to the point of hallucination did her work pour from her—the antiphons and plainsongs and religious treatises. Pain made Saint Hildegard produce. Pain made her sing." He turned to the second man, who was starting to sweat profusely. The prisoner's breath came in strangled yelps, like a dying animal's. "I thought it might relax you," he said. He listened to a few bars of the plainsong, pensively.

*Sanctus es unguendo*
*periculose fractos:*
*sanctus es tergendo*
*fetida vulnera.*

Then he stood over the second prisoner. "Look into my eyes," Demarest said. He pulled a small knife from a waist holster and made a small slice in the man's belly. The skin and the fascia beneath immediately sheared, pulled apart by the tension of the ropes. "Pain will make you sing, too." The man screamed.

"Now, *that's* torture," Demarest called to Janson. "What would you like me to say? That it hurts me as much as it hurts them?" He returned to the screaming man beneath him. "Do you think you'll be a hero to your people by resisting me? Not a chance. If you're heroic, I can ensure that nobody ever learns of it. Your bravery will be wasted. You see, I am a very bad man. You think Americans are soft. You think you can wait us out. You think you can watch while we ensnare ourselves with our silly bureaucratic regulations, like a giant tripped up by his own shoelaces. But you think all these things because you've never come across Alan Demarest. Of all Satan's forms of trickery and deceit, the very greatest was persuading man he did not exist. Look into my eyes, my fisherman friend, because I exist. A fisherman like you. A fisherman of men's souls."

Alan Demarest was mad. No: it was worse than that. He was all too sane, too in control of his actions and their controllable consequences. At the same time, he was wholly devoid of the most elemental sense of conscience. He was a monster. A brilliant, charismatic monster.

"Look into my eyes," Demarest intoned, and leaned closer to the man's face, which was already stretched in agony, an agony beyond words. "Who's your ARVN contact? Which South Vietnamese do you deal with?"

"I farm!" the man whimpered, barely able to catch his breath. His eyes were red, his cheeks wet. "No Viet Cong!"

Demarest pulled down the man's pajama trousers, exposing his genitals. "Prevarication will be punished," he said in a bored tone. "Time for the jumper cables."

Janson heaved a few times, leaning forward, and a hot flow of vomit surged up the back of his throat and splattered on the ground before him.

"Nothing to be ashamed of, my son. It's like surgery," Demarest said, soothingly. "The first time you see it done, it's a little rocky. But you'll get the hang of it in no time. It's as Emerson tells us, when a great man 'is pushed, tormented, defeated, he has a chance to learn something.' "

He turned to Bewick. "I'm just going to juice up the motor, make sure there's plenty of jump in the jumpers. We'll give him every chance to talk. And if he doesn't, he'll die the most painful death we can contrive."

Demarest looked at Janson's stricken face.

"But don't worry," he continued. "His companion will be kept alive. You see, it's important to leave somebody to spread the news among the VC: this is what you get when you fuck with *nguoi My*."

And, horrifyingly, he winked at Janson, as if to invite him into the debauchery. How many other soldiers, burned out and callused by too much time in the combat zone, had responded positively to that invitation, finding a club of genuine zealots, losing their souls. An old refrain echoed in the dim recesses of his mind. *Where you going? Crazy—want to come along?*

Want to come along?

Prinsengracht, perhaps the most gracious of the old canal streets of old Amsterdam, was built in the early seventeenth century. The streetfront facades had, at first glance, all the regularity of accordion-folded paper dolls. When one looked more closely, one saw all the ways each tall, narrow brick house had been painstakingly differentiated from its neighbors. The gables atop each house had been carefully designed: step gables, zigzagging to a flat top, alternated with the swooping curves of neck gables and spout gables. Because the staircases within were narrow and steep, most of the houses had projecting ledges that allowed furniture to be brought to higher floors by means of hoists. Many houses boasted fake attics and intricate entablatures. Festoons hung from simple brick. Behind the houses, he knew, discreet *hofjes,* or inner courtyards, were hidden away. To the extent that the burghers of Amsterdam's golden age prided themselves on their simplicity, it was an ostentatious simplicity.

Janson strode down the street, attired in a light zippered jacket and sturdy brogues, like so many of his fellow pedestrians. He kept his hands in his pockets, and his eyes regularly scanned his surroundings. Was he being followed? So far, there was no sign of it. Yet he knew from experience that if his presence was detected, a team could be assembled and deployed with impressive rapidity. *Always have a backup plan:* Demarest had said that, and however appalling its source, the injunction had served him well. File it next to Management Secrets from Genghis Khan, Janson reflected bitterly.

A few blocks from the so-called golden curve, he encountered a cluster of houseboats, anchored on the rust-and-silt-tinctured waters of the canal. These floating domiciles had been a feature of Amsterdam since the 1950s, the result of a housing shortage; a few decades later, the city council passed measures against them, but the existing waterborne dwellings were grandfathered in, tolerated as long as an annual fee was tendered.

Janson kept a sharp eye out, scrutinizing each in turn. The nearest resembled a long, brown-shingled bungalow, with a small turbine vent atop a roof of red corrugated steel. Another resembled a tall, floating greenhouse; inside, the long glass panels were lined with curtains, affording the residents some privacy. Nearby was a houseboat with an intricate trellislike fence around a flat-topped enclosure. A pair of lanterns sprouted out from what looked like stone bird feeders. Boxes of geraniums spoke of a house-proud squatter.

Finally, he saw the familiar blue-painted cabin with an abandoned look. The flowerpots were mainly empty; the windows were small and sooty. On the deck next to the cabin was a bench of age-silvered wood. The boards of the low, wide deck were warped and irregular. It was anchored just next to a small quayside parking lot, and as Janson approached, he felt his pulse quicken. Many years had passed since he had last been there. Had it changed hands? He detected the distinctive resinous scent of cannabis, and he knew it had not. He stepped on board and then walked through the door of the cabin; as he expected, it was unlocked.

In one corner of the sun-dappled space, a man with long, dirty-gray hair was crouched over a large square of vellum. He had pastels in both hands, which veered toward the paper in alternation. A smoldering marijuana cigarette lay next to a red pastille.

"Freeze, motherfucker," Janson said softly.

Barry Cooper turned around slowly, giggling at some private joke. When he identified his visitor, he sobered up a little: "Hey, we're cool, right? You and me, we're cool, right?" There was a fatuous half smile on his face, but the question was tinged with anxiety.

"Yeah, Barry, we're cool."

His relief was visible. He held his arms open wide, his palms speckled with pigment. "Show me some love, baby. Show me some love. How long has it been? *Jeepers.*"

Cooper's speech had long retained an odd mixture of idioms—part stoner, part *Leave It to Beaver*—and the fact that the American had lived abroad for nearly a quarter century served as a linguistic fixative.

"Too long," Janson said, "or maybe not long enough. What do you think?" The history they shared was complex; neither man fully understood the other, but both understood enough for a working relationship.

"I can make you some coffee," Cooper said.

"Coffee would be fine." Janson sat down on a lumpy brown sofa and looked around.

Little had changed. Cooper had aged, but exactly as one would have expected him to. A tangle of graying brown hair had surrendered almost fully to gray. Crow's-feet crowded his eyes, and the lines between the corners of his mouth and his nose were incised now with a fine line; there were vertical creases between his eyebrows, and horizontal creases on his forehead. But it was Barry Cooper, the same old Barry Cooper, a little scary and somewhat crazy, but mostly neither of those things. In his youth, the ratios had been different. In the early seventies, he had drifted from college radicalism to the real thing, a harder, more callous reality, and, by incremental steps, ended up a member of the Weather Underground. *Smash the system!* It was a greeting in those days, a simple salutation. Hanging around the college town of Madison, Wisconsin, he'd fallen in with others who were smarter and more persuasive than he was and who took his inchoate disquiet with the misdeeds of Authority to a crystalline extreme. Small pranks, designed to nettle law enforcement, led to more extreme acts.

One day, in New York, he found himself in a Greenwich Village town house when a bomb one of the members was concocting went off prematurely. He had been taking a shower and, singed and sooty but largely unharmed, walked around in a daze for a while before he was arrested. When he was out on bail, the police determined that his fingerprints matched those found at the scene of another bombing, this one of a university laboratory in Evanston. It had happened at night, and there were no casualties, but that was a matter of luck as much as anything; a night watchman could easily have been in the area. The charges were increased to attempted murder and federal conspiracy, and Cooper's bail was revoked. By that point, however, he had fled the country, making his way first to Canada and then to Western Europe.

And in Europe, another chapter of his curious career began. The exaggerated reports about him circulated by American law enforcement were swallowed whole by the radical groups of Europe's revolutionary left—the circle associated with Andreas Baader and Ulrike Meinhof, known formally as the Rote Armee Fraktion, informally as the Baader-Meinhof Gang; the tight-knit organization that called itself the Movement 2 June; and, in Italy, the Red Brigade. Intoxicated by the romance of urban insurrection, these militants regarded the shaggy-haired American as a latter-day Jesse James, a free rider for the revolution. They welcomed him into their circles and disputatious factions, asking him for advice about tactics and techniques. Barry Cooper was pleased by the adulation, but his visits were also a strain. He knew a great deal about varieties of marijuana— about how Maui sinsemilla differed from Acapulco red, say—but had little interest in, or knowledge of, the practical affairs of revolution. Far from the criminal mastermind of the Interpol advisories, he had been a slacker, along for the ride—for the drugs and the sex. He had been too dazed to comprehend the ferocity of his new comrades—too dazed to comprehend that what he regarded as student pranks, the equivalent of stink bombs in the bathroom, they regarded as prelude to violent upheaval and the

forcible overthrow of the existing order. When he was among the revo-
lutionaries, he kept this to himself, hiding behind gnomic responses. His
reticence and pointed lack of interest in their own activities rattled them:
surely this showed that the American terrorist did not trust them or take
them seriously as a revolutionary vanguard. They responded by revealing
to him their most ambitious plans, trying to impress him by disclosing
the extent of their human and material assets: the safe house in East Berlin,
the front organization in Munich that provided them with financial support, the officer in the Bundesrepublik national guard who kept his radical
lover supplied with quantities of military-grade ordnance.

As time passed, Barry Cooper grew uncomfortable, and not simply with
the masquerade: he had no stomach for the acts of violence they vividly
described. One day, in the aftermath of a subway bombing in Stuttgart
arranged by the Revolutionary Cells, he saw a list of victims in a newspaper. Pretending to be a newspaper reporter himself, he visited the
mother of one of the passersbys who were slain. The experience—coming
face-to-face with the human reality of the glorious revolutionary violence—left him shaken and repulsed.

Janson paid him a visit not long afterward. In the attempt to gain entrée
to the shadowy world of these terrorist organizations, he searched for
people whose fealty to civilization might not have completely eroded—
people who were not yet dead to so-called bourgeois morality. Barry Cooper's association with those organizations always struck him as odd; he
knew his file well, and what he saw was someone who was essentially a
joker, a cutup, a clown, rather than a killer. A get-along go-along guy who
had found himself getting along and going along with some very bad
company.

Cooper was already living in Amsterdam, in the very same houseboat,
making a living selling colorful sketches of the old town to tourists—
kitsch, but sincere kitsch. He had the affect of someone who had smoked
too much pot for too long a time: even when he wasn't stoned, he had a
slightly unfocused and ingenuous manner. The two men did not bond
right away: it was hard to imagine two souls less alike. Still, Cooper finally
appreciated that his visitor from the U.S. government tried neither to
ingratiate himself nor to make threats. He looked like a jarhead but he
didn't come on like one. Oddly low-key in his approach, he played it
straight. When Cooper diverted the conversation to the inequities of the
West, Janson, as a trained political scientist, was happy to follow him.

Rather than jeering at his politics, Janson was happy to concede that there was much to criticize in the Western democracies—but then rejected the dehumanizing simplifications of the terrorists in direct, hard-hitting language. *Our society betrays humanity whenever it doesn't live up to its own expressed ideals. And the world your friends wish to create? It betrays humanity whenever it does live up to its expressed ideals.* Was the choice so hard?

*That's deep,* Barry Cooper had said, sincerely. *That's deep:* the reflexive rejoinder of the shallow. But if Cooper were shallow, his very shallowness had saved him from the worst temptations of the revolutionary left. And his information proved to be the undoing of dozens of violent cells. Their safe houses were shut down, their leaders imprisoned, their sources of funding identified and rooted out. The pothead in the funky blue houseboat had helped to do that. In that respect, the posturing, hard-hearted spokesmen of the revolutionary vanguards had it right: sometimes a small man can make a big difference.

In return, the State Department quietly desisted in its attempts to seek extradition.

Now Janson sipped hot coffee from a mug that still bore smudges of acrylic paint.

"I know you're here just to hang," Cooper said. "I know you don't, like, *want* something from me." It was banter that survived from their first interviews, a quarter century ago.

"Hey," Janson said. "OK if I crash here for a while?"

*"Mi casa es su casa, amigo,"* Cooper replied. He raised the small marijuana cigarette to his lips; Janson was never sure whether it still really affected Cooper or whether the maintenance dose just returned him to what passed as normal. The smoke made his voice pebbly. "I could use the company, tell you the truth. Doris left me, I ever tell you that?"

"You never told me Doris joined you," Janson said. "Barry, I have no idea who you're talking about."

"Oh," Cooper said, and his forehead knit in a moment or two of furious concentration. He was visibly searching for consequence: *And therefore . . . and therefore . . . and therefore.* The engine of reason was turning over but not catching. Finally, he raised an index finger. "Then . . . never mind." He had obviously worked out that someone he hadn't seen in eight years might have little interest in the recent end of a six-week relationship. Cooper was so pleased to have come up with an appropriate response that he leaned back and grinned. "Hey, man, it's really good to see you." He mock-punched Janson's arm. "Roomie," he said. "Be like having a room-mate again. Felix and Oscar."

Janson winced: the side of his arm was still tender from the tussle in Regent's Park.

"You all right, man?" Cooper's eyes filled with concern.

"Fine, fine," Janson said. "But this time, I think we'll keep this little visit between ourselves. *Comprende?*"

"*Comprendo mio maximo,*" Cooper responded, in the made-up lingo he favored—some mishmash of Spanish, Italian, and schoolboy Latin, with moods, aspects, and tenses of Cooper's inconsistent devising. This was someone who was born to be a minor character in a Hunter S. Thompson escapade, Janson reflected on occasion. He'd come a long way in some respects, and seemed almost the same in others.

"Let's go for a walk," Janson said.

"Cool," Cooper said.

The streetlights glowed brightly, holding at bay the evening sky, as the two men walked along the Golden Bend of Herengracht. Once it was the favored address of the shipbuilders and merchants who prospered three hundred years ago, during Amsterdam's golden century. Most of the splendid estates now belonged to banks, museums, publishing houses, consulates. The wash of mercury light made the seventeenth-century dwellings shimmer with a peculiar glamour and seemed to pick out the differences among them. One house had an odd French influence, its sandstone facade adorned with acanthus leaves and volutes; another was a somber affair of dark brick, decorated only by the neck gable. Every-where one found rounded cornices, modillions, finials, decorative con-soles, and bull's-eye windows: there was no end to the nooks and crannies that a hidden observer could exploit. To Janson, even the projecting hoist beams, securely built into the roof timbers, took on a menacing appear-ance by night.

"So you see these streets every day," Janson said.

"Every day, man," Cooper replied. "My art. I draw what's in front of my eyes. Only a little different. Street scenes, or sometimes just one of the mansion houses. Or churches. Tourists really dig churches."

"Could I commission a picture?"

Cooper looked moved. "Really, man?"

"There's a mansion on Prinsengracht, the corner of Leidsestraat. Know the one I'm talking about?"

"You got good taste, man. It's a beauty."

The structure had been made by combining three existing dwellings, but the facade was reconstructed as if it had been built as a single estate. Eight fluted Corinthian pilasters ran under the pediment; seven bay windows faced the street. Red bands of masonry alternated with dressed stone. The world headquarters of the Liberty Foundation had history inscribed on every brick.

"Think you could do that for me now? As detailed as you can make it." A bicyclist whizzed past, going the wrong way down the one-way street, nearly colliding with them.

"Jeepers. You know, I never knew you really grooved to my work. You always were kinda standoffish about it. Thought maybe it wasn't your bag."

"As much detail as you can, Barry," Janson stressed. "Also, if you can get a rear view. Should be visible on Lange Leidsedwarsstraat."

"I'm gonna break out my new pastels," Cooper said. "Just for you."

Bicyclists and street artists: two species who never got a second look in Amsterdam's old town. Cooper could set down on the sidewalk right in front of the place and would not be noticed. He had spent decades doing so. He disappeared into the scenery because he was part of the scenery.

Back in Cooper's houseboat, an hour later, Janson reviewed the sketches. He was not heartened. There were various points of possible egress, but none that were protected from public view. It was likely, too, that sophisticated motion detectors were in use throughout the building. And because the rear faced Lange Leidsedwarsstraat, there would be no surreptitious way to gain entry there, either.

As a rule, there were two ways of achieving security. The more familiar method was through isolation: the castle on the mountainside, the subterranean vault. The other involved proximity and publicity: the building in the town common, where unauthorized entry was inhibited by exposure. The brilliance of the Liberty Foundation headquarters was that rather than relying entirely upon a security detail, it effectively turned hundreds of passersby—the denizens and pedestrians of the city itself—into sentinels. It was protected, ultimately, by being in plain view.

Janson was annoyed at himself: he was thinking inside the proverbial box, was coming up with solutions that had served him in the past but were inappropriate to the situation he now confronted. He needed to think *differently*.

Demarest's words of counsel—echoing from another age—came to him now: *Can't see a way out? Take the time to see things differently. See the two white swans instead of the one black one. See the slice of pie instead of the pie with the slice missing. Flip the Necker cube outward instead of inward. Master the gestalt. It will make you free.*

He closed his eyes for a few seconds. He had to think as they had. Exposure and publicity, they saw, could be the most effective shields of clandestinity—which was a logic that Janson himself would have to embrace. A stealthy entrance was what they were anticipating, what they would be well protected from. He would not arrive stealthily, then. He would arrive as conspicuously as possible, and at the front door. This operation called not for discretion but for brazenness.

Janson surveyed the balled-up papers on the floor near the pastels. "Got a newspaper?"

Cooper padded over to the corner and triumphantly returned with a copy of the latest *De Volksrant*. The front page was smeared with paints and pastels.

"Anything English-language?"

"Dutch papers are in Dutch, man," he answered in a cannabis croak. "They're fucked-up that way."

"I see," Janson replied. He scanned the headlines, and his knowledge of English and German cognates allowed him to get the gist of most. He turned the page, and a small article caught his eye.

"Here," Janson said, tapping it with a forefinger. "Could you translate this one for me?"

"No sweat, man." Cooper looked up for a moment, gathering his powers of concentration. "Not the jukebox selection I'd have gone for. Now wait a minute—didn't you tell me your mother's Czech?"

"Was. She's dead."

"Put my foot in it, didn't I? That's awful. Was it, like, a sudden thing?"

"She died when I was fifteen, Barry. I've had some time to adjust."

Cooper paused for a moment, digesting the fact. "That's cool," he said. "My mom passed last year. Couldn't even go to the goddamn funeral. Tore me up. They'd clap irons on me in customs, so, like, what would be the point? Tore me up, though."

"I'm sorry," Janson said.

Cooper began to read the article, laboriously translating the Dutch into

English for Janson's benefit. It was not, on the face of it, a remarkable story. The Czech foreign minister, having been in The Hague to meet with members of the government, was visiting Amsterdam. There he would meet members of the stock exchange and leading figures of its financial community, to discuss Dutch-Czech cooperative ventures. Another inconsequential trip, by someone whose job it was to make such trips, hoping to raise the level of foreign investment in a country that was pining for it. Holland was rich; the Czech Republic was not. It was the same sort of trip that might have taken place a century ago, or two centuries ago, or three, and probably had. It would, one could safely hazard, solve no problems for the Czech Republic. But it just might solve a problem for Janson.

"Let's go shopping," Janson said, standing up.

Cooper was not taken aback by the sudden change of topic; his cannabis haze made the world as aleatory as a roll of the dice. "Cool," he said. "Munchies?"

"Clothes shopping. Fancy stuff. Top of the line."

"Oh," he said, disappointed. "Well, there's a place I never go, but I know it's real expensive. On Nieuwezijds Voorburgwal, just off the Dam, a few blocks away.

"Excellent," Janson said. "Why don't you come along? I might need a translator." More to the point, if anybody was keeping an eye out for him, they would not be expecting him to be traveling with a companion.

"Happy to," Cooper said. "But everybody understands 'MasterCard.'"

The building that housed the Magna Plaza was erected a hundred years ago as a post office, though, with its ornate stonework, vaulted ceilings, pilasters, string courses, and little round-arched galleries, it seemed overdressed for the purpose. Only after it was converted into a shopping mall did its excesses come to seem appropriate. Now forty stores lined its gallery walkway. At an upscale men's clothing store, Janson tried on a suit, a size 53. It was Ungaro, and its price tag came to the equivalent of two thousand dollars. The regularity of Janson's frame meant that off-the-rack clothing tended to look bespoke on him. This suit did.

A salesman with a stiffly gelled comb-over glided across the floor and attached himself like a remora to his American customer.

"If I may say, the fit is excellent," the salesman said. He was smarmy and solicitous, as no doubt he always was around price tags with commas. "And the fabric is superb on you. It's a beautiful suit. *Very* elegant. Dashing yet understated." Like many Dutch, he spoke English with only a trace of an accent.

Janson turned to Cooper. His bloodshot, unfocused eyes suggested that his mental fog had not entirely dispersed. "He's saying he thinks it looks good on you," Cooper said.

"When they're talking in English, Barry, you actually don't need to translate," Janson said. He turned to the salesman. "I assume you take cash. If you can do up the cuffs right now, you've got a sale. If not, not."

"Well, we have a fitter here. But the tailoring is normally done elsewhere. I could have it sent by courier to you tomorrow. . . ."

"Sorry," Janson said, and turned to leave.

"Wait," the salesman said, seeing his commission on a substantial sale evaporate. "We can do it. Just let me have a talk with the fitter, and give us ten minutes. If I have to walk it across the street, I'll see that it's done. Because, how do you say it in the States, the customer is always right."

"Words to gladden a Yank's heart," Janson said.

"Indeed, we know this about you Americans," the salesman said carefully. "Everywhere we know this."

*Washington, D.C.*

The large man with the maroon tie flagged the taxicab at the corner of Eighteenth and M Streets, near a bar-and-grill with a neon sign in the window advertising a carbonated beverage. The cabdriver wore a turban and favored public radio. His new passenger was a well-dressed man, a little wide around the waist, thick around the haunches. He could bench-press three hundred pounds, but he also liked his beer and his beef, and didn't see why he needed to change his habits. He was good at what he did, had never had any complaints, and it wasn't as if he moonlighted as a catalog model.

"Take me to Cleveland Park," he said. "Four thirty Macomb Street."

The Sikh driver repeated the address, jotted it down on his clipboard, and they set off. The address turned out to be an out-of-business supermarket, boarded up and bleak.

"Are you sure this is it?" the driver asked.

"Oh yeah," he said. "Actually, would you mind driving into the parking lot and around the back? I've got to pick up something."

"No problem, sir." As the cab eased around the low brick-and-glass building, the passenger's heart started to beat harder. He had to do this without making a mess. Anybody could do this. But he was someone who could do it neatly.

"This is great," he said, and sat forward. In a lightning-fast motion, he lowered the garrote over the driver's head and pulled it tight. The Sikh emitted a faint rasp of escaped breath; his eyes widened, and his tongue lolled out. Unconsciousness would come quickly, the passenger knew, but he could not stop there. Another ten seconds of maximum pressure, and the anoxia would result in permanent respiratory cessation.

Now he returned the wooden-handled garrote to his breast pocket, and dragged the limp body of the driver out of the car. He popped the trunk, and arranged the body around the spare tire, the jumper cables, and a surprising number of blankets. It was important to get the man out of the driver's seat as quickly as possible; he had learned this from unpleasant experience. The incontinence that sometimes followed a sudden death could cause a soiled seat. Not something he cared to deal with at a time like this.

His RIM BlackBerry communicator purred from deep in his breast pocket. It would be an update on the location of the subject.

He glanced at his watch. He had little time remaining.

His subject had less.


The voice in his earpiece gave him the precise coordinates of his subject, and as the passenger-turned-driver maneuvered the taxicab toward Dupont Circle he was given regular updates as to her movements. Timing was essential if he was to succeed.

The crowd in front of the department store was sparse; the subject was wearing a navy peacoat, a gold silk neckerchief knotted loosely around her throat, a shopping bag with the elegant logo of the upscale store in one hand.

It was the only thing he was conscious of, the figure of the black woman, growing larger and larger as he gunned the motor of the cab and then, abruptly, swung the steering wheel far to the right.

As the cab lurched onto the sidewalk, shrieks of disbelief filled the air, blending into a sound that was almost choral.

A curious intimacy, again, the woman's startled face coming close and closer to his, like a lover leaning forward into a kiss. As the front bumper smashed into her body—he was traveling at close to fifty miles per hour—

her upper body smashed onto the hood of the cab, and only when he braked did her body fly forward, vaulting through the air and finally landing on the pavement of the busy intersection, where a Dodge van, despite its squealing brakes, left tire tracks on her broken body.

The cab was recovered later that day, abandoned in an alley in Southwest Washington. It was an alley that, in the best of times, was littered with the brown and green shards of broken beer bottles, the clear curved glass of crack vials, the translucent plastic of hypodermics. The local youth treated the cab as just another found object. Before the car was recovered by the authorities, it had been stripped of its hubcaps, its license plate, and its radio. Only the body in its trunk was left undisturbed.

# CHAPTER NINETEEN

Aside from its location, across the street from the Liberty Foundation headquarters, there was little that would draw anyone's eye to the small canal-bank house, or *voorhuis*. Inside, Ratko Pavic regarded its furnishings with a purely utilitarian eye. There was a faint but cloying kitchen odor— pea soup, was it? It must have been from the night before, but the smell was oddly permeating. He wrinkled his nose with distaste. Still, nothing more of that sort would be cooked here. He thought of the two bodies sprawled in the bathtub upstairs, the blood seeping steadily down the drain. He had no feelings about what he had done: the elderly couple, engaged to maintain the house while the owners were in Corfu, were in the way. They were faithful retainers, no doubt, but they had to be dispatched. And it was for a good cause: seated by the small square window in a darkened room, Ratko Pavic had an excellent view of the mansion opposite, and two parabolic microphones conveyed conversations from its front-facing antechambers with reasonable clarity.

All the same, it had been a tedious morning. Administrators and staff arrived between eight-thirty and nine-thirty. The scheduled visitors made their scheduled visits: a senior civil servant from the Netherlands' Ministry of Foreign Affairs was followed by the deputy to the Dutch minister of education, culture, and science. A U.N. high commissioner for refugees was followed by a senior director of the U.N.'s Division for Sustainable Development, and then by another exalted bureaucrat, from its Economic Commission for Europe. Others in Ratko's team had complementary perimeter views. One of them, Simic, was stationed on the very roof of the *voorhuis*, three stories directly overhead. None had glimpsed any sign of Paul Janson. It was not surprising. A daytime infiltration made little sense, although the agent was known to do the unexpected simply because it *was* unexpected.

It was tedious work that required complete concealment, but it was what suited him best since he became a marked man. The jagged, glossy cicatrix that ran from his right eye to his chin—a scar that glowed red

when he allowed himself to become upset—made his visage too memorable for any job that demanded visibility. *He had been marked:* that was
the thought that filled his mind, even as his assailant had lashed out at
him with a knife meant for scaling fish. More punishing even than the
searing pain from his ripped flesh was the realization that he would never
be able to work undercover in the field any longer. As a shooter, of course,
he was as invisible as his Vaime silenced sniper rifle, which was ready for
deployment at any moment. As the hours passed, he began to wonder
whether that moment would ever come.

To keep himself amused, Ratko regularly zoomed in on the petite receptionist, watched the redhead's haunches move as she bent over, and
he felt a warmth in his belly and groin. He had something for her, oh yes
he did. He remembered the Bosnian women with whom he and his fellow
soldiers disported a few years back—remembered faces convulsed with
hatred, remembered how similar the expression was to sexual transport.
It required only a little imagination. As he pounded himself into them,
what thrilled him most was the recognition of how utterly powerless they
were. It was an experience unlike any he had ever had with a woman. It
didn't matter whether his breath was fetid, or if his body stank, because
there was simply nothing they could do. They knew they had to give it
up, to surrender abjectly, or they would be made to watch their parents,
their husbands, their children, shot through the head, before they were
slaughtered themselves.

Fine-tuning his scope, he imagined the redhead roped and pinned to
a mattress, her eyes rolled into her head, her pale softness yielding to the
pistoning of his Serbian flesh.

In the event, Ratko did not need a scope to see the small motorcade of
three black Mercedes-Benzes make its stately way down Stadehouderskade
and onto Leidsestraat, stopping at the Liberty Foundation headquarters. A
uniformed driver of the stretch limo walked around to the rear and held
open the door. A dark-suited man with horn-rimmed glasses and a felt-
brimmed hat came out and stood next to the car for a moment, admiring
the majestic stretch of southwest Prinsengracht. Then the uniformed man—
the minister's personal factotum, it appeared—pressed the buzzer beside
the deeply carved front door. Ten seconds later, the door was opened.

The uniformed man spoke to the woman at the door. "Madame, the
foreign minister of the Czech Republic," the uniformed man said. "Jan
Kubelik." Captured by the twin parabolics, the voices were scratchy but
audible.

The foreign minister spoke a few words of Czech to his factotum and made a gesture of dismissal. The uniformed man turned and stepped away, back toward the limousine.

"You almost look as if you were not expecting me," the man in the elegant navy suit told the receptionist.

Her eyes widened. "Of *course* not, Minister Kubelik. We are most pleased by your arrival."

Ratko smiled, remembering the small panic that had swept through the Foundation's support staff when they received the phone call, thirty minutes earlier, telling them that the recently appointed foreign minister would be keeping his appointment with the executive director. A series of flustered underlings compared notes, for the appointment had gone un-recorded. Nobody wanted to admit to having made a scheduling error, and yet someone must have done so. Through his Schmidt & Bender scope, Ratko had seen the little redheaded woman's consternation. *Just two weeks ago, you double-scheduled the Swedish minister of foreign affairs and the man from the U.N. disarmament program,* the redhead said, be-rating a particularly thickheaded junior secretary upstairs. The junior sec-retary protested that it wasn't her fault, but did so with an air of hesitation that was tantamount to a confession. Another secretary, coming to the other's defense, maintained that the error was probably on the side of the Czech bureaucrats. Yet it would be simply impossible, a hopeless breach of protocol, to tell them so.

Now Ratko watched the red-haired receptionist lead the minister inside to a fancy antechamber, where vision and sound alike grew indistinct. The Serb turned up the electronic light amplification of his scope and switched the microphone to a special signal-enhancement mode so that the input from the parabolics would be further digitally improved—sharpened, with meaningless noise filtered out.

"Our executive director will be with you shortly," he heard the redhead say, as the aural signal was restored.

"You're very kind," the Czech diplomat said airily, removing his hat. "And this is a beautiful estate. Do you mind terribly if I take a look around?"

"Sir, we would be honored," she replied as if by rote.

Silly bureaucrat—searching for decor tips to give to his wife. He would return to the drab presidential palace in Prague and tell his friends about the deluxe details of Peter Novak's Amsterdam lair.

Ratko had done Warsaw Pact exercises with Czech soldiers back when he was in the Yugoslav army, long before the six republics of Yugoslavia struck out on their own, and at each other. The Czechs, he always thought, had a very high opinion of themselves. He did not share it.

A man walking very slowly in front of the house caught his attention: would Janson be so bold? The man, seemingly a tourist, stood against the low railing beside the canal. Slowly, he took out a map.

Ratko directed his scope toward him; the angle was not ideal, but as he took in the tourist's slight build and short hair, he saw how mistaken he had been. No matter how cleverly Janson disguised himself, he could never pass for a twenty-something woman.

Once more, Ratko felt a warmth stirring in his belly.

Janson's eyes swept over the beautifully appointed antechamber. Paintings from the Dutch renaissance were positioned in the center of squares formed by gilt moldings, with obsessive concern for symmetry. The fireplace mantel was of intricately carved marble, veined with blue. It all seemed perfectly in character for a Dutch mansion: far from the public's prying eyes, the vaunted ideal of Nordic moderation was banished.

So far, so good, he thought to himself. Cooper had cleaned up remarkably well, and once attired in that silly uniform, he conducted himself in a manner that did not quite slide into parody. His movements were stiff and official; his expressions imbued with a servile pomposity, every inch the dedicated assistant of a very important official. Janson himself was relying upon the assumption that nobody would have any idea what the Czech foreign minister looked like. The man had been in the job for a mere two weeks, after all. And the country was not high on the Foundation's list of trouble spots.

No disguise was the best disguise: A bit of grease in his hair, a pair of spectacles in a style fashionable in Eastern Europe, the sort of suiting common to diplomats all over the Continent . . . and a manner that was by turns amiable and imperious. The fact that Janson's mother was Czech was helpful, of course, though chiefly in imbuing his English with a persuasive Czech accent. A Czech diplomat would be expected to speak English in a country like Holland.

Janson peered at the red-haired receptionist over his round horn-rimmed glasses. "And Peter Novak? He is here as well?"

The petite woman smiled dreamily. "Oh no, sir. He spends most of his time on the road, flying from place to place. Sometimes we don't see him for many weeks at a time."

When Janson had arrived, he did not know whether a pall of grief would be hanging over the Foundation. But what Agger had told him remained true: they clearly had no idea that anything had befallen their revered founder. "Well!" said Janson. "He's got the whole world in his hands, yes?"

"You could say that, sir. But his wife is in today. Susanna Novak. She helps run the NGO development program."

Janson nodded. Novak was insistent about keeping his family from the public gaze, evidently afraid of kidnapping. His own public stature was necessary for the success of his work; he reluctantly acceded to media coverage for that purpose. But he was not a Hollywood star, and his family was not fair game: that had been the message for years, and by and large the press agreed to abide by those rules. The fact that his primary residence was in Amsterdam made it easier: the *burgerlich* sensibilities of that city served to shield the great man's privacy.

Hidden in plain view.

"And what's over here?" He pointed toward another room, to the left of the main hallways.

"Peter Novak's office," she said. "Where you would surely be meeting Mr. Novak if he were in town—he'd insist on it." She opened the door and pointed to a canvas on the wall opposite. "That painting is by Van Dyck. Remarkable, don't you think?" The portrait was of a seventeenth-century nobleman, rendered in a palette of muted browns and blues, yet curiously vivid all the same.

Janson turned on the overhead lights and strode toward the canvas. He peered closely. "Extraordinary," he said. "He's one of my very favorite artists, you know. Of course, the artistic heritage of the Czech Republic is illustrious indeed. But, between us, we have nothing like this in Praha."

He reached into his pocket and, fingering the side buttons of his Ericsson cell phone, he dialed one of the numbers he had preprogrammed into it. This number went to the receptionist's direct line.

"Would you excuse me," she said, hearing her phone ring.

"Certainly," Janson said. As she hastened to her telephone, he scanned the papers that lay neatly stacked on Novak's desk and credenza. They were from the usual assortment of great and good institutions, with a heavy representation of Dutch ministries. One item of correspondence, however, caused a memory to clang distantly, hazily—a freighter just out of view in foggy weather. Not the brief, innocuous message, but the letterhead. UNITECH LTD. The company name meant something to him—but did it mean something to Paul Janson, corporate security consultant, or to Paul Janson, quondam Consular Operations agent? He wasn't yet sure.

"Minister Kubelik?" A woman's voice.

"Yes?" Janson looked up to see a tall blond woman smiling at him.

"I'm Peter Novak's wife. I'd like to welcome you here on his behalf. Our executive director is still in a meeting with Holland's ambassador to the United Nations. It won't be long at all." She spoke with a neutral American accent.

The woman was beautiful in the Grace Kelly mode, at once voluptuous and patrician. Her frosted, wet-looking lipstick seemed less than businesslike, but it suited her, as did the chartreuse suit that hugged her contours a little more snugly than was strictly necessary.

This was not a woman in mourning. She could not have known. She did not know. Yet how could that be?

Janson strode up to her and bowed slightly. Would a Czech diplomat kiss her hand? He decided that a handshake would suffice. But he could not take his eyes off her. Something about her was familiar. Hauntingly so. The blue-green Côte d'Azur eyes, those long, elegant fingers . . .

Had he seen her before recently? He racked his brain. Where? In Greece? England? Had it been a fleeting glimpse, enough to register on the subconscious mind only? It was maddening.

"You're American?" Janson said.

She shrugged. "I'm from a lot of places," she said. "Like Peter."

"And how is the great man?" There was a catch in his voice as he asked.

"Always the same," she replied, after a pause. "Thank you for asking, Dr. Kubelik." Her gaze was almost playful—verging, he could have sworn, on the flirtatious. No doubt this was simply the way that certain women were trained to make conversation with international eminences.

Janson nodded. "As we Czechs like to say, 'To be the same is better than to be worse.' A certain peasant realism there, I think."

"Come," she said. "I'll take you upstairs to the conference room."

The second floor was less palatial, more intimate; the ceilings were ten feet high, not fifteen, and the decor was much less fustian. The conference room faced the canal, and the late-morning sun slanted through a multipaned picture window, casting golden parallelograms on the polished long teak table. As Janson entered, he was greeted by a man of slightly less than average height with neatly combed gray hair.

"I'm Dr. Tilsen," the man said. "My in-house title is executive director for Europe. A bit misleading, no?" He laughed a tidy, dry laugh. "Our Europe *program*—that would be more accurate."

"You'll be safe with Dr. Tilsen," Susanna Novak said. "A lot safer with him than with me," she added, leaving it up to her visitor whether to read a double entendre in her remark.

Janson sat down opposite the pale-faced administrator. What to discuss with him?

"I expect you know why I wanted to make contact with you," he began.

"Well, I think so," Dr. Tilsen said. "Over the years, the Czech government has been very supportive of some of our efforts, and less so of others. We understand that our objectives will not always mesh with those of any particular government."

"Quite so," Janson said. "Quite so. But I have begun to wonder whether my predecessors have been too hasty in their judgments. Perhaps a more harmonious relationship might be possible."

"That would be most pleasing to contemplate," Dr. Tilsen said.

"Of course, if you provide me with a *tour d'horizon* of your projects in our country, I would be able to make the case more effectively with my colleagues and associates. Really, I'm here to listen."

"Then I shall oblige you, and speak to those very points," Dr. Tilsen said. He smiled, tentatively. Talking was his stock in trade, and for the next thirty minutes, Tilsen did what he did best, describing a battery of initiatives and programs and projects. After a few minutes, the words seemed to form a verbal curtain, woven from the opaque nomenclature and slogans favored by professional idealists: *nongovernmental organizations . . . reinvigorating the institutions of deliberative democracy . . . a commitment to promoting the values, institutions, and practices of an open and democratic society . . .* His accounts were detailed and prolix, and Janson found his eyes beginning to glaze. With a tight, fixed smile, he nodded at intervals, but his mind wandered. Was Peter Novak's wife among the conspirators? Had she herself engineered the death of her husband? The prospect seemed inconceivable, and yet what could explain her conduct?

And what of this Dr. Tilsen? He seemed earnest, unimaginative, and well meaning, if more than a little self-important. Could such a man be part of a nefarious conspiracy to destroy the most important agent of progress the fragile world had? He watched the man talk, watched the small, eroded, coffee-stained teeth, the pleased look with which he punctuated his monologue, the way he had of nodding approvingly at his own points. Was this the face of evil? It seemed hard to believe.

A knock at the door. The petite redhead from downstairs.

"I'm terribly sorry, Dr. Tilsen. There's a call from the prime minister's office."

"Ah," Dr. Tilsen said. "You will kindly excuse me."

"But of course," said Janson.

Left to himself, he examined the relatively spare furnishings of the room, and then he walked over to the window, looking at the busy canal below him.

A feeling of cold ran down his spine, as if it had been stroked with a shard of ice.

Why? Something in his field of vision—once again, an anomaly he responded to instinctively before he could rationally analyze or describe it.

*What?*

Oh Jesus! Behind the bell-shaped gable of the house opposite, there was the shadow of a man crouched upon the tightly imbricated slate tiles. A familiar error: the sun changes position, and shadows appear where there had been no shadows, betraying the hidden observer—or sniper. Which? The glint of sun from the glass of a scope did not settle the question.

His eyes now scrutinized the eaves and attic windows of the house for anomalies. *There*—a small section of a large double-hung window had been cleaned, by someone who wanted to be able to see out of it more clearly.

The hoist beam in front of him: something was odd about it as well. A moment later, he realized what. It was no hoist beam—the beam had been replaced by the barrel of a rife.

Or was his overheated imagination conjuring things into existence, seeing threats in shadows, the way children turned their bedposts into the talons of monster? The bruise on the side of his head throbbed painfully. Was he jumping at ghosts?

Then one of the small square panes exploded, and he heard the harsh splitting of wood as a bullet buried itself somewhere in the parquet floor. Another pane exploded, and then another, shooting splinters of glass through the air, showering the conference table.

Jagged cracks appeared in the plaster of the wall opposite the window. Another pane exploded, another bullet shattered the plaster, this one cracking inches above his head. He sank to the floor, and began to roll toward the door.

Gunshots without shots: they had come from a silenced rifle. He should have been used to it by now.

Then a loud gun blast came from outdoors, an odd counterpoint to the silenced firing. Other sounds ensued: The screeching of tires. The noise of a car door opening and closing.

And from elsewhere in the mansion, panicked screams.

Madness!

A quiet fusillade was loosed, as deadly projectiles snapped though the air, some hitting glass, some traveling uninterrupted through already broken panes. They buried themselves in the walls, ceilings, floors. They pinged off the brass chandelier, ricocheted in unpredictable ways.

The throbbing of his temple had grown so forceful that it required a conscious exertion simply to focus his eyes.

*Think!* He had to think! Something had changed. What made sense of the assault, the contrast in weaponry and approach?

*Two teams were attacking. Two teams that were not coordinated.*

Mrs. Novak must have reported him. Yes, he was certain of it now. She had been onto him the whole time, playing along, playing him. Hence the mischievous look. She was one of Them.

The only place of refuge from the fusillade was deep in the mansion, in one of the inner chambers: yet surely they were counting on him seeking it out, which meant that this refuge was the most dangerous place he could be.

He phoned Barry on his Ericsson.

Cooper was uncharacteristically flustered. "*Jeepers,* Paul! What the hell's going on? It's like the Battle of Midway out here."

"Can you make visual on anyone?"

"Um, you mean, can I see 'em? A glimpse, once in a while. There's a couple of them in military drab. They look mean. The arms-are-for-hugging message hasn't reached these guys, Paul."

"Listen, Barry, we specified that the limo have bulletproof windows when we ordered it. You'll be safest there. But be ready to haul ass at my signal."

Now Janson bolted for the door and raced down the stairs to the first floor. When he reached the landing, he saw the security guard unholster his weapon and approach the front window. Then the gun clattered to the floor.

The guard's mouth sprang open, and a circle of red formed about his left eyebrow. Blood spewed out in a pulsing rush that rolled over the unblinking eye. And all the while, the man stood, upright, as if transmuted into a statue. Slowly, as if in some *danse macabre*, the man's legs started to twitch, then give way, and he toppled onto the ancient Chinese carpet. Janson rushed over and retrieved the man's gun, a Glock pistol.

"Minister Kubelik," the red-haired receptionist cried out. "We've all been ordered to the rear annex. I can't explain what's happening but . . ." She trailed off, stunned and perplexed at the sight of a high government minister in a controlled firing roll.

The roll got him across the hallway and near the front door while remaining within two feet of the ground. It was faster than a crawl, and speed was now of the essence. "Toss me my hat."

"What?"

"Toss me the goddamn hat," Janson yelled. More quietly: "You'll find it's about a meter from your left hand. Throw it to me."

The terrified receptionist did so, as one obeys a dangerous madman, and fled to the rear annex.

The small square in the double-hung window that was cleaner than the rest of it: a sniper would be there.

He had to use the thick wooden door as a movable shield. He jumped up, turned the knob, and opened it a crack.

Two thuds: bullets that dug into the thick wood. Bullets that would have struck him had he continued out the door.

The door was now ajar, just eighteen inches, but it should suffice for a well-targeted shot. That grimeless, sparkling square of glass—with luck, he could hit it from here, even with a mere handgun.

His enemies would be scoped; he would not be. But scopes had their limitations, too. The greater the magnification, the more restricted the field of vision. And it took perhaps ten or twenty seconds to reposition the scope and adjust its optics when the target position changed abruptly.

He crawled to where the security guard lay slain on a pale blue carpet now darkening with his blood and dragged the body toward the foyer, knowing that he would be shielded by the four-foot wall of brick beneath the window. He pulled out a handkerchief and hurriedly wiped the blood from the man's face. He draped his suit jacket on the man's upper body and jammed his felt-brimmed hat on the corpse's head. Firmly grasping the hair on the nape, he positioned the head precisely. In a darting gesture, he pushed the head toward the gap left by the cracked-open door, and swiveled it, emulating the movements of a man cautiously craning to see.

The head would be glimpsed fleetingly, in profile, and from a distance.

A pair of sickening spits confirmed his worst suspicions. The dead man's head absorbed heavy-caliber bullets from two different directions.

Another second or so would pass before the bolt-action rifles would permit a second tap. Now Janson sprang up, to his full height. The snipers' scopes would be trained on the spot where the guard's head had appeared. Janson would expose himself several feet higher. He had to make his sighting and shoot nearly instantaneously.

Time turned to syrup.

He peered out, identified the small, gleaming square of glass, and squeezed out a burst of three shots into it. With luck, he would at least damage the sniper's equipment. The gun bucked in his hand as it sent out its blast, and Janson retreated behind the heavy door. A guttural spray of curses was audible through the broken glass, telling him that he had scored some kind of hit.

One perch may have been deactivated. But how many more remained? He studied the two additional bullet wounds on the guard's head. One projectile had traveled from a steep downward trajectory, evidently from the house opposite. The other, which entered high on a cheek, came at a sharp angle, indicating a sniper from a neighbor to the right.

He could have Cooper pull up in the armored limo, but just the few feet of exposure would, with an active sniper in the vicinity, prove deadly. At least one person would have his rifle aimed directly on the stoop.

Janson heaved the corpse upward in a vaulting movement across the main front room, and studied the reaction.

An unsilenced blast shattered what remained of the window, followed by a cluster of spits, shots that were sound-suppressed but no less deadly. *How many?* How many guns were trained on this house; how many riflemen were awaiting a clean shot? At least five, and the real number could be much higher.

*Oh, dear God.* An all-out assault on Peter Novak's headquarters was in progress. Had he brought this about by his presence? It strained belief, but then little made sense any longer.

All he was certain of was that he had to get out of the house and that he could not use the doors. He charged up the stairs. Another flight up, narrower, brought him to the third floor, where he found himself looking at a closed door. Was there time? He had to check it out—had to *make* time. He tried the handle; it was locked. Janson broke it open with a forceful kick and found himself in a private office.

A desk. A credenza, stacked with cardboard mailers from the ultra-secure, ultra-expensive express-delivery service Caslon Couriers. Beside it, a black metal filing cabinet. Locked, too, but easily forced. Inside was an array of reports about nongovernmental organizations and lending libraries in Slovenia and Romania. And correspondence from Unitech Ltd., content seemingly unexceptional. Unitech: yes, it meant something—but he had no time to think now. Survival was his one goal, and his thoughts had to be directed toward that singular imperative. It had been a thirty-second detour; now he charged up the two remaining flights and clambered up a crude wooden ladder that led to the loft, beneath the roof. It was stifling there, but under the rafters there had to be an opening to a part of the roof that would be hidden by the gables. It was his only chance. A minute later, he had found it and arrived stumbling on the roof. It was steeper than he expected, and he clung to the nearby chimney, as if it were a great tree offering protection in the jungle. It was, of course, nothing of the kind. He scanned the adjoining rooftops, looking for his executioners.

Being at roof level would take him out of range of most of their fixed positions.

But not all.

Perched on a higher rooftop, diagonally opposite to his right, he could make out the deadly brunette from Regent's Park. There she had narrowly missed him from an enormous distance. Now she was a hundred feet away. She could not fail to hit her target. She had not missed when she hit the grotesque puppet he had made of the dead security guard, for he knew now that the diagonal shot was hers.

He turned his head and saw, to his dismay, that there was another rifleman on the adjoining roof, just thirty-five feet to his left.

The rifleman had heard his feet scrambling on the slate roof and was now swiveling his weapon toward him.

Alerted by the drab-suited rifleman, the deadly brunette raised her scope to roof level. His bruised temple flared once again, with almost incapacitating pain.

He was pinned between two sharpshooters, with only a handgun for protection. He saw the woman squinting through her scope, saw the utter blackness of the rifle's bore hole. He was staring at his own death.

It was a shot she could not miss.

# CHAPTER TWENTY

He forced himself to focus on the countenance of his executioner: he would look death in the face.

What he saw was a play of confusion on her face as she swiveled her rifle a few degrees to the left and squeezed off a shot.

The rifleman on the next roof over arced his back and tumbled off the roof like a falling gargoyle.

*What the hell was going on?*

The noisy chatter of a nearby automatic weapon immediately followed—aimed not at him but at *her*. A piece of the ornate cornice behind which she was stationed broke off, leaving a cloud of dust.

Was somebody *rescuing* him, saving him from the Regent's Park executioner?

He tried to puzzle out the complex geometry. Two teams, as he supposed. One using American-issue sniper equipment, the sniper team from Consular Operations. And the other? An odd assortment of weaponry. Irregulars. Hirelings. To judge from the fabric and hardware, Eastern Europeans.

In whose employ?

*The enemy of my enemy is my friend.* If the old saw was true in this case, he was far from friendless. But *was* it true?

The man with the automatic gun, a Russian-made AKS-74, now stood above the parapet, trying to get a better angle on the woman sniper.

"Hey," Janson called out to him.

The man—Janson was near enough to see his coarse features, close-set eyes, and two days' growth of beard—grinned at Janson, and turned toward him.

With his gun set at full fire.

As a raking blast hit the roof, Janson dove into a roll, hurtling down the tiled incline. A fragment of stone whipped past his ear as a noisy fusillade swept the area where he had been moments before. His forehead scraped against another piece of masonry, the palm of his hand stung as it pressed against jagged roof tile. Finally, his body slammed against the balustrade. The impact was jarring, debilitating, yet the alternative would have been worse—a plumb drop from the high roof to the pavement.

He heard shouts, from *there,* and *there.* His dazed brain strove to process the sounds as they raced and echoed and faded.

What had just happened? The woman had him within her sights. *She had him.*

Why didn't she take the shot?

And the other team—who were they? Angus Fielding had mentioned the shadowy enemies Novak had made among corrupt Eastern European oligarchs. Were they a private militia? Everything about them suggested as much.

He was their target. But so was the team from Consular Operations. How could that be?

There was no time. He poked his pistol between the ornamental sandstone balusters and squeezed off two quick shots. The man with the AKS-74 staggered backward, making an odd gurgling sound; one of the bullets had pierced his throat, which exploded in a gush of arterial blood. As he slumped to the tiles, his weapon fell with him, secured by the nylon sling around his shoulders.

That gun could be Janson's salvation—if he could get to it.

Now Janson stood atop the balustrade and leaped the short distance to the adjoining house. He had an objective. The AKS-74. a crude, chattering, powerful submachine gun. He landed imperfectly, and pain shot like a bolt of electricity up his left ankle. A bullet twanged through the air just inches from his head, and he threw himself down on the tiled peak, a few feet away from the man he had just shot dead. The too-familiar smell of blood wafted toward him. He reached out and wrested the submachine gun from its nylon sling, hastily cutting it free with a pocketknife. Without shifting his position, he craned his head around to situate himself.

The planar geometry of the roofs was, he knew, deceptive. Peaks met peaks at what looked like perpendicular angles, but the angles were not truly perpendicular. Parapets that appeared parallel were not truly parallel. Eaves that appeared level were not truly level. Cornices and balustrades, built and rebuilt over the centuries, settled and shifted in ways that the quick glance would not detect. Janson knew that the human mind had a powerful tendency to abstract away such irregularities. It was a cognitive economy that was usually adaptive. And yet when it came to the trajectory of a bullet, small irregularities could make all the difference in the world.

No angles were true; intuition had to be overridden, again and again, with the hard data of range finder and scope.

Now his hands patted down the dead man until he found and retrieved a small device with two angled mirrors attached to a telescoping rod that resembled the antenna of a transistor radio. It was standard equipment for an urban commando. Janson carefully adjusted the mirrors and pulled out the rod. By extending it over the cornice, he would be able to see what threats he still confronted without putting himself in the line of fire.

The weapon that was nestled in Janson's arms was hardly a precision instrument—it was a fire hose, not a laser.

What he saw was far from encouraging. The deadly brunette was still in position, and though he was currently protected from her by the roof-line geometry of the eaves, peaks, and gables, she would be alert to any movement, and he could not reposition himself without exposure.

A bullet *thwack*ed into the chimney, chiseling off a piece of the centuries-old brick. Janson rotated the periscope-like device to see who was responsible. One roof over, standing with an M40 braced against his shoulder, was a former colleague of his from Consular Operations. He recognized the broad nose and quick eyes: an old-school specialist named Stephen Holmes.

Janson moved carefully, sheltering himself from the riflewoman by keeping himself low and behind the projecting brick gable while he snaked himself up the incline of the slate roof. He had to execute his next move perfectly, or he was dead. Now he kept his head down as his hands lifted the muzzle of the AKS-74 over the roofline. He relied on memory, on a fleeting image from the periscope, as he directed a burst of fire toward the long barrel of the rifle. An answering clang—the sound of metal-jacketed bullets striking a long barrel fashioned of a superhard composite resin—told him he had succeeded.

Now he raised his head over the roofline and directed a second, more targeted burst: the steel-tipped bullets tore into the barrel of Holmes's M40 until the green-black shaft shattered.

Holmes was now defenseless, and when his eyes met Janson's it was with the resigned, almost weary look of someone convinced he was about to die.

Janson shook his head disgustedly. Holmes was not his enemy, even if he thought he was. He craned around and, peering through a loophole in the elaborate semicircular pediment, was able to glimpse the brunette diagonally opposite. Would she take him out with one of her trademark double taps? She had seen what had happened, knew that her colleague was out of commission and that she would have to assume responsibility for a larger field. Would she wait until he moved from the protection of the second gable? The slotlike loophole was too narrow and deep to permit a clean shot from a diagonal perch. She would have to wait. Time was a sniper's best friend—and his mortal foe.

He squinted and brought her face into focus. She was no longer in shooting position—had broken from her spot-weld with the rifle and was staring at her colleague with a look filled with uncertainty. A moment later, Janson saw a flicker of movement behind her, and then something more dramatic: an attic door burst open and a giant of a man loomed suddenly behind the slight brunette. He smashed something over her head—Janson could not quite make it out; it could have been the butt of a long firearm. The brown-haired woman slumped limply to the parapet, evidently unconscious. Now the giant seized her bolt-action rifle and squeezed off one, two, three shots to his right. The strangled cry from the adjoining roof told him that at least one had hit its target: Stephen Holmes.

Janson hazarded a quick look, and what he saw sickened him: the shots seemed casual, but were well aimed. The large-caliber bullets had blown off Holmes's jaw. From the destroyed lower half of his face, blood drenched down his tunic; a final breath was expelled like noisy gargle, half cough, half feckless scream. Then Holmes toppled off his roof perch and tumbled down the tiled roof until he slammed into the parapet. Through the ornamental stonework, his lifeless brown eyes stared at Janson.

All that Janson knew was that the giant was no savior. He sprayed a long fusillade toward the hulking man who stood where the Cons Op sniper had been—it would force him into a defensive crouch, at least momentarily—then, using the various stone ornaments as handholds, quickly clambered down the side of the mansion, which was safely out of range. He hit the paved surface of the shadowed alley with as little noise as he could manage and, positioning himself behind two metal trash cans, studied the street scene in front of him.

The giant was *fast*, his agility astonishing for someone of his size. Already he was charging out the front door of the building, dragging the unconscious brunette with him like a sack. The man had a hideous, puckered scar running down his cheek, a grotesque memento of a violent past. His blue eyes were small, piggish but alert.

A second man, attired in similar drab, raced over, and Janson heard them talking. The language was unfamiliar—but not entirely so. Straining, he could make out a fair amount of it. It was Slavic—Serbo-Croatian, in fact. A distant cousin to Czech, but close enough that, by concentrating, he was able to make out the basics.

A small, powerful sedan roared up to them, and after another brief, barked exchange, the two men leaped into the backseat. Police sirens screamed in the distance.

They were leaving the scene because the police were beginning to arrive. Other drab-clad gunmen piled into an SUV and drove off as well.

Battered, bloodied, Janson staggered to the side street where Barry Cooper, sweating and wide-eyed, remained in the driver's seat of the armored limo.

"You need to go to a hospital," Cooper said, shaken.

For a moment Janson was silent, and his eyes were closed. Concentrating intensely, he returned to the words he had heard. *Korte Prinsengracht . . . Centraal Station . . . Westerdok . . . Oosterdok . . .*

"Get me to Centraal Station," Janson said.

"We're going to have half the cops in Amsterdam on our tail." A light drizzle had begun to fall, and Cooper switched on the window wipers.

"Pedal to the metal."

Cooper nodded, and set off north on Prinsengracht, the wheels squealing against the slick pavement. By the time they reached the bridge over Brouwersgracht, it was apparent that they had no police pursuers. But were there pursuers of another kind?

"Serbian irregulars," Janson murmured. "They're mostly mercenaries these days. But whose?"

"Serbian mercenaries? You're harshing my groove, man. I'm gonna pretend I didn't hear that."

Separating Korte Prinsengracht from the Westerdok, where largely abandoned warehouses stood, was the man-made island on which the Centraal Station was built. But that was not where the giant and his friends were headed. They would be heading toward the vast maintenance buildings to the south of the station, which were sheltered from casual observation. At night, heroin addicts went there to score and shoot up; during the day, however, it was almost entirely abandoned.

"Keep going, *straight!*" Janson yelled, jerking to full attention.

"I thought you said Centraal Station. . . ."

"There's a maintenance building to the right, five hundred yards away. Overlooking the wharves of Oosterdok. Now *floor* it."

The limo powered past the parking lot of the train station and bounded down the broken pavement of the derelict yards where, years ago, the business of the wharves had been conducted. Most of the commercial harbors had relocated to North Amsterdam; what remained were phantoms of brick and concrete and corrugated steel.

A gated Cyclone fence suddenly loomed before them. Cooper stopped the car, and Janson got out. The fence was old, the links frosted with oxide. But the knob set, set into a large rectangular metal plate, was bright and shiny, obviously new.

From a distance, he heard shouts.

Frantically, Janson withdrew a small bump key from his pocket and set to work. He positioned the very end of it into the keyway and then, in a sudden, plunging movement, thrust the rest of it into the lock and twisted it in a single continuous motion. The speed of that motion was crucial: the key had to be turned before the lock's spring pressed the top pin down.

His fingers could feel that the top pin had bounced high enough to fly beyond the shear line, that his twist had taken advantage of the split second in which the pin columns had bounced out of alignment. The gate was open.

He waved Cooper through and gestured for him to park the car about a hundred yards away, behind a rusting, abandoned train car.

Janson himself raced over to the side of a huge steel shed and, flattening himself against it, edged swiftly toward the shouts he had heard.

Finally, he could see through the dim light into the vast interior, and what he made out sickened him.

The woman from Consular Operations was roped to a cement pillar with a thick hawser, her clothes crudely torn off her.

"This shit is getting old fast," she growled, but the fear beneath the bravado was all too evident.

Before her, the giant with the glossy, puckered scar loomed. He belted her with his hand, and her head snapped back against the concrete. He pulled out a knife and sliced off her undergarments.

"Don't you touch me, you son of a bitch!" she yelled.

"What are you going to do about it?" The voice was harshly guttural. The giant laughed as he loosened his belt.

"I wouldn't get Ratko mad if I were you," said his companion, who held a long thin blade that glinted even in the gloom. "He prefers 'em alive—but he's not that particular."

The woman loosed a bloodcurdling shriek. Sheer animal terror? Janson suspected that there was more to it—that she was hoping against hope that somebody might hear.

Yet the wind and the rumble of distant barges drowned out whatever sounds might be made.

In the gloom of the warehouse, he could make out the gleaming shape of the powerful sedan the men had ridden in, the engine ticking as it cooled.

The man slapped her again, and then the slaps became rhythmic. The aim was not interrogation. It was, in fact, part of a sexual ritual, Janson realized to his horror. As the killer's trousers dropped heavily to the floor, his organ was silhouetted in the gloom: the woman's death would be preceded by indignity.

Janson froze as he heard a soft Serbian-accented voice from behind him: "Drop the gun."

Janson whirled around and found himself face-to-face with a slender man who had gold-rimmed glasses perched high on an aquiline nose. The man wore khaki trousers and a white shirt, both neatly pressed. He stood very close to him and, with a casual movement, pressed a revolver against his forehead.

*It was a setup.*

"Drop the gun," the man repeated.

Janson let his pistol fall to the concrete. The steady pressure of the man's gun against his forehead admitted no negotiation. Another piercing scream rent the air, this time with a quaver that signified profound terror or rage.

The man with the gold-rimmed glasses smiled grimly. "The American bitch sings. Ratko likes to fuck them before he kills them. The screams turn him on. What is in store for you, I'm afraid, will be far less enjoyable. As you will learn for yourself. He'll be finished shortly. And so will she. And so, if you are fortunate, will you."

"Why? For Christ's sakes, *why?*" Janson demanded in a low, urgent voice.

"Such an *American* question, that," the man replied. His voice was more cultivated than the giant's, but equally devoid of emotion. He was probably the operation's leader. "But we will be the ones asking questions. And if you do not answer them to our satisfaction, you will suffer an excruciatingly painful death before your body disappears in the waters of the *Oosterdok.*"

"And if I do what you ask?"

"Your death will be merciful and swift. Oh, I'm sorry. Were you hoping for more choices?" The man's thin lips twitched with contempt. "You Americans always want things that aren't on the menu, don't you? You can never have enough choices. Only, I am not an American, Mr. Janson. I offer you one choice. Death *with* agony—or death without." His quiet words had the effect of an icy wind.

As the woman released another ear-piercing scream, Janson contorted his face into a look of terror. "Please," he said, in a half whimper. "I'll do anything . . ." Janson reached into a place deep within and began to tremble visibly.

A gratified, sadistic smile came to the man with the gold-rimmed glasses.

Suddenly, Janson's shaking knees buckled, and he dropped down two feet, remaining perfectly erect as he bent his knees. At the same time, his right hand shot straight up, grabbing the wrist of the man's outstretched hand.

The man's smile faded as Janson pulled his arm down in a powerful wrist lock, wrenching it toward his elbow and twisting it at an acute angle. Now the man bellowed in pain as the ligaments in his arm were strained and torn, but Janson was relentless, taking a long step back with his left foot and pulling the attacker to the ground. He yanked on the arm with all his strength and heard a pop as the ball joint was dislocated from the socket. The man roared again, agony mingling with disbelief. Janson fell on him, bringing all his weight down on his right knee, driving it into the man's rib cage. He could hear at least two ribs break. The man gasped, and behind the gold-rimmed glasses, tears rushed to his eyes. The broken ribs would make simply breathing exquisitely painful.

Roused by the nearby footfalls of his companions, the man tried to free his gun arm, despite his dislocated joint, but Janson had it pinned between his chest and left knee. Janson turned his right hand into a claw and clamped it around the man's throat, lifting and slamming his head against the ground until his body was limp. Moments later, when Janson reared up, he had a gun in both hands—

And squeezed off two shots—one at a rough-hewn man rushing toward him with an automatic pistol, a second at a bearded man several feet behind him, with a submachine gun held at his side. Both slumped to the ground.

Janson strode toward where the man they called Ratko stood, only to find the raking fire of an AKS-74 pocking the concrete floor in a storm of sparks and micro-explosions. It had to be directed by a man on a catwalk high above, and it created an impassable zone between Janson and Ratko—who had hastily hiked up his trousers and was turning to face him. A .45 handgun looked small in the Serb giant's enormous hand.

Now Janson ducked behind a concrete pillar. As he expected, the man with the submachine gun overhead repositioned himself to gain an angle on Janson. But in doing so he had exposed himself. Peering around the corner, Janson caught a fleeting glimpse of a short, stocky moonfaced man who held the AKS-74 as if it were part of him. A brief fusillade tore into the pillar he hid behind. Janson snaked a hand around it and squeezed off a blind shot. He heard it twang against steel-pipe railing and knew he had missed. Sudden footsteps on the steel catwalk helped him locate the man in space, however, and he squeezed off three more shots.

Each one missed. *Damn*—what had he expected? And yet he could not visually locate the man with the assault weapon without exposing himself to his deadly fire.

Light briefly flooded the dim warehouse as somebody opened a side door.

He heard footsteps—somebody racing into the cavernous space.

Another burst came from the AKS-74, directed not at Janson but at the unseen arrival.

"Oh shit! Oh *shit!*" It was Barry Cooper's voice.

He couldn't believe it: Barry Cooper had made his way into the abandoned warehouse.

"Barry, what the hell are you doing here?" Janson called.

"Right now, I'm asking myself that. Heard all this gunfire when I was in the car, got scared, and I ran in here trying to escape. Pretty dumb, huh?"

"Truthfully? *Yes.*"

Another fusillade brought up a storm of sparks from the concrete floor.

Janson stepped back from the pillar and saw what was happening. Barry Cooper was huddled behind a large steel drum while the man on the catwalk began to reposition himself.

"I don't know what to *do*," Cooper said in a half wail.

"Barry, do what *I'd* do."

"Gotcha."

A shot rang out, and the short, stocky man on the catwalk abruptly stiffened.

"That's *right*, baby. Make love, not war, *motherfucker*," Cooper yelled as he emptied the entire clip of his pistol into the gunman overhead.

Now Janson could move around the pillar, and he immediately squeezed off a shot at Ratko's companion, who hovered with a knife near the trussed woman.

"*Sranje!* Shit!" the man called out. The bullet had struck his shoulder, and he let the knife drop. The man sank to the ground, moaning and incapacitated.

Janson saw the woman snake a foot out toward the knife, and bring it close to her. Then she wedged it between her two heels and, her legs shaking with the effort, gradually raised it off the ground.

The Serb giant seemed torn between two targets, Cooper and Janson.

"Drop the gun, Ratko!" Janson yelled.

"I fuck your mother!" the giant Serb spat, and he squeezed off a shot at Barry Cooper.

"*Dammit!*" Cooper bellowed. The bullet had penetrated both his arm and his lower chest. His gun fell to the ground and he retreated, in agony, behind a row of steel drums near the side entrance.

"You OK, Barry?" Janson called out, stepping behind another stanchion.

There was a moment of silence. "I dunno, Paul," he replied weakly. "Hurts like a motherfucker. Plus, I feel like I've fallen off the whole Gandhian-pacifist wagon. I'm probably going to have to become a vegan just to get my karma straightened out."

"Nice shooting, though. Weather Underground experience?"

"YMCA summer camp," Cooper said, sheepish. "BB guns."

"Can you drive?"

"Not the Indy 500 or anything, but, yeah, I guess."

"Keep calm and listen to me. Get into the car and drive yourself to a hospital. Now!"

"But what about . . . ?"

"Don't worry about me! Just haul ass."

A bullet from the giant's .45 echoed loudly through the steel enclosure, and a piece of concrete landed near Janson's feet.

It was a standoff now, between the two of them.

Two men, with nothing to lose but their lives.

Janson did not dare shoot blindly, for risk of hitting the man's captive. He took a few steps back until he could make out his target clearly. Ratko, steadying his gun hand with his other hand for precision shooting, had his back to her. A glint of steel told him that the woman was not as helpless as he imagined.

With her one free arm, she had reached down, stretching farther than seemed possible, and grabbed the hilt of the knife, which through extraordinary contortions she had managed to raise to mid-thigh level. Now she was raising it high, keeping the blade horizontal, the better to avoid the ribs, and—

*Plunged* it into the giant's back.

Shock wiped out the menacing expression on his hideously scarred face. As Janson stepped forward, the giant squeezed off another shot, but it went high. Janson had one more bullet left in his magazine: he could not miss.

He assumed the standard Weaver stance and squeezed off his sole remaining shot, aiming for the man's heart.

"I fuck your mother," the Serb rumbled, and then, like falling timber, he pitched forward, dead.

Now Janson strode over to the woman captive. He felt a surge of fury and revulsion as he took in the tattered clothes, the bruised flesh, the red marks left by hands that had groped and grasped her flesh like so much modeling clay.

Wordlessly, Janson withdrew the knife from the Serb's back and sliced through the hawser, freeing her.

She slid to the floor, her back resting against the pillar, seemingly unable to stand. She curled herself up, putting her arms around her knees, drawing them toward her, and resting her head on her forearm.

He disappeared for a moment, returning with the white shirt and khaki trousers that had been worn by the man with the gold-rimmed glasses.

"Take them," he said. "Put 'em on."

Finally, she raised her head, and he saw that her face was wet with tears.

"I don't understand," she said dully.

"There's a U.S. Consulate General at Museumplein nineteen. If you can get there, they'll take care of you."

"You rescued me," she said in a strange, hollow voice. "You came for *me*. What the *hell* would you do that for?"

"I didn't come for you," he snapped. "I came for them."

"Don't lie to me," she said. "Please don't lie to me." A quaver entered her voice. She seemed to be on the verge of collapse, and yet she started to talk, drawling through her tears, desperately clinging to the tattered vestiges of her professionalism. "If you wanted to interrogate one of them, you could have taken one alive and left. You didn't. You didn't, because they'd have killed me if you did."

"Get yourself to the consulate," he said. "File an After-Action Report. You know the regs."

"Answer me, goddammit!" She rubbed the tears from her face desperately, frantically, with the palms of both hands. However traumatized and battered, she remained fiercely ashamed of the display of weakness, vulnerability. She tried to stand up, but the muscles in her legs rebelled and she only ended up sinking to the ground again.

"How come you didn't take out Steve Holmes?" She was breathing heavily. "I saw what happened. You could have taken him out. *Should* have taken him out. Standard combat procedure is, you take the guy out. But all you did was disarm him. Why would you do that?" She coughed, and tried for a brave smile, but it looked like a wince. "Nobody uses a goddamn Havahart trap in the middle of a gunfight!"

"Maybe I missed. Maybe I was out of ammunition."

Her face was red as she slowly shook her head. "You think I can't handle the truth? Well, I don't know if I can. I just know that I can't hear any more lies right now."

"Museumplein nineteen," Janson repeated.

"Don't leave me here," she said, her voice cracking with fear and bewilderment. "I'm scared, all right? These fuckers weren't in the prep book. I don't know who they are or what they want or where they are. All I know is, I need help."

"The consulate will help." Janson started to walk away.

"Don't you turn your back on me, Paul Janson! I almost killed you three times. The least you owe me is an explanation."

"Report back to work," Janson replied. "Go back to your job."

"*I can't.* Don't you understand anything?" Suddenly, her voice became thick; the woman who sought to kill him was choking up. "My job—my *job* is to kill you. I can't do that now. I can't *do* my job." She laughed bitterly.

Slowly, slowly, she struggled to her feet, holding on to the pillar for support.

"Listen to me now. I met this American in Regent's Park who told me some lunatic story that maybe us Cons Op folks had got caught up in some big . . . manipulation. That the bad guy we were supposed to take down wasn't really the bad guy. I ignored that, because if that were true, up was down and down was up. Can you understand that? If you can't trust the people who give you your orders, what's the point of anything? Later, I filed my Memorandum of Conversation about it, just pro forma, and I get a phone call not from my boss, but my boss's boss. And he wants me to remember that Paul Janson is a genius liar, and was I sure he hadn't gotten to me somehow? Now I'm shivering in this godforsaken warehouse and thinking if I ever want to learn what's going on in the world, I'm probably not going to get that from my bosses. Now I'm thinking that the only one who can tell me what time it is is the guy I'm looking at." Trembling, she began to put on the clothes he had brought her. "The same guy I've spent forty-eight hours trying to drill."

"You've just gone through a traumatic experience. You're not yourself. That's all."

"I'm not finished with you, Paul Janson." She licked her cracked lips. Raised welts were beginning to appear on her bruised cheeks.

"What is it that you want from me?"

"I need help. I need . . . to know what's going on. I need to know what's a lie and what isn't." More tears welled up in her eyes, and she wiped them away, mortified. "I gotta get somewhere safe."

Janson blinked. "You want to be *safe?* Then stay the hell away from me. It's not safe where I am. And that's the one thing I am certain of. Do you want me to take you to a hospital?"

An angry stare. "They'd *get* me there. They'd find me, for sure they would."

Janson shrugged uneasily. She was right.

"I want you to tell me what the hell is going on." Her gait was unsteady, but she took a step toward him.

"That's what I'm trying to find out."

"I can help. You have no idea. I know stuff, I know plans, I know faces—I know who's been dispatched to come after you."

"Don't make things worse for yourself," Janson said, not unkindly.

"Please." The woman looked at him forlornly. She had the air of someone who had never experienced a moment's doubt in her professional life before now—someone who did not know how to deal with the uncertainties that now thronged her.

"Forget it," Janson said. "In about a minute, I'm going to steal a car.

This is an act of larceny, and anybody who's with me at the time is legally an accomplice. That put things into perspective for you?"

"I'll steal it for you," she said huskily. "Lookit, I don't know where you're going. I don't care. But if you get away, I'll never know the truth. I *need* to know what's true. I need to know what *isn't*."

"The answer is no," Janson said shortly.

"*Please.*"

His temple began to throb again. To take her with him was madness, self-evident madness.

But maybe there was some sense in the madness.


"Oh Jesus! Oh *Jesus!*" Clayton Ackerley, the man from the CIA's Directorate of Operations, was practically keening, and the sterile phone line did nothing to diminish the immediacy of his terror. "They're fucking taking us *out*."

"What are you *talking* about?" Douglas Albright's voice was truculent but alarmed.

"You don't know?"

"I heard about Charlotte, yes. It's awful. A terrible accident—and a terrible blow."

"You don't know!"

"Slow down and tell it to me in English."

"Sandy Hildreth."

"No!"

"They fished up his limo. Goddamn armored limo. On the bottom of the Potomac. He was in the backseat. Drowned!"

A long silence. "Oh Jesus. It's not possible."

"I'm looking at the police report right now."

"Couldn't have been some sort of accident? Some horrible, horrible coincidence?"

"An accident? Oh sure, that's what they've got it down as. Driver was speeding, eyewitnesses saw the car as it skidded off the bridge. Like with Charlotte Ainsley—some cabdriver loses control of his car, docs a hit-and-run. And now there's Onishi."

"*What?*"

"They found Kaz's body this morning."

"Dear God."

"Corner of Fourth and L Streets in the near Northeast."

"What the hell was he doing *there?*"

"According to the coroner's report, there was phencyclidine in his blood. That's PCP—angel dust. And a lot of other shit besides. Officially, he OD'd on the street corner, outside a crack house. 'We see this all the time,' is what one of the city cops said."

"Kaz? That's *crazy!*"

"Of *course* it's crazy. But that's how they did it. The fact is that these three key members of our program have been killed within twenty-four hours of one another."

"Christ, it's true—they're picking us off, one by one. So who's next? Me? You? Derek? The secretary of state? POTUS himself?"

"I've been on the phone with them. Everybody's trying not to panic and not doing the greatest job of it. Fact is, we're all marked. We just joined the goddamn endangered-species list."

"But it docsn't make any sense!" Albright exploded. "Nobody knows who we are. Nothing connects us! Nothing except the most tightly guarded secret in the United States government."

"Let's be a little more precise. Even if nobody who's not in the program knows, *he* knows.

"Now wait a minute . . ."

"You know who I'm talking about."

"Christ. I mean, what have we done? *What have we done?*"

"He hasn't just cut his strings. He's killing everybody who ever pulled them."

# CHAPTER TWENTY-ONE

The sun filtered through the mulberry trees and tall pines, which spread their boughs protectively over the cottage. It was remarkable how well it blended into its surroundings, Janson noted with satisfaction as he walked through the door. He had just returned from a stroll down the path to the tiny village, a few miles down the mountain, and carried groceries and an armload of newspapers: *Il Piccolo, Corriere delle Alpi, La Repubblica.* Within the cottage, the austerity of the stone exterior was belied by the richly burnished boiserie and warm terra-cotta tiling throughout; the frescoes and ceiling paintings seemed to belong to another age and way of life altogether.

Now Janson entered the bedroom where the woman was still sleeping and prepared a cool, damp compress for her forehead. Her fever was subsiding; time and antibiotics had had their effect. And time had had its healing effect on him, too. The drive to the Lombardy redoubt had taken all night and some of the next morning. She was conscious for little of it, waking up for only the last few miles. It had been picture-perfect northern Italian countryside—the yellow fields of dried cornstalks, the groves of chestnut trees and poplars, the ancient churches with modern spires, the vineyards, Lombard castles perched on crags. Behind them, the gray-blue Alps stood over the horizon like a wall. Yet by the time they arrived, it was clear that the woman had been badly affected by her ordeal, much more so than she had realized.

The few times he had watched her sleep, he saw a woman tossing and turning, in the grip of powerful and disturbing dreams. She would whimper, occasionally lash out with an arm.

Now he draped a cloth drenched in cold water upon her forehead. She tossed feebly, a low moan of protest escaping her throat. After a few moments, she coughed and opened her eyes. He quickly poured water into a glass from the jug at her bedside, and had her drink from it. Before, once she'd taken a drink, she had sunk back into her deep and troubled sleep. This time, however, her eyes remained open. Staring off.

"*More,*" she whispered.

He poured her another glass of water, and she drank it, steadily, without requiring his support or assistance. Quietly, her strength was returning. Her eyes focused, and fell upon him.

"Where?" she said, the one-word question costing her no little effort.

"We're in a cottage belonging to a friend of mine," he said. "In Lombardy. The Brianza countryside. Lago di Como is ten miles to our north. It's a very isolated, very private spot." As he spoke, he saw that her bruises looked even worse; it was a sign of the recovery process. Yet even the livid swellings could not conceal her simple beauty.

"How long . . . here?"

"It's been three days," he said.

Her eyes filled with disbelief, alarm, fear. Then, gradually, her face slackened, as consciousness ebbed.

A few hours later, he returned to her bedside, simply watching her. *She's wondering where she is. She's wondering why she's here.* Janson had to ask himself the same question. Why *had* he taken her in? His decision to do so had been anguishing: cold, hard reason had ensured his survival so far. And there was no doubt that the woman could potentially prove useful to him. But cold, hard reason told him that she could also prove fatal—and that his decision to take her in had been largely a matter of emotion. The kind of emotion that could cost someone his life. What did it matter if she were hunted down in Amsterdam? She had, indeed, repeatedly sought to kill him. *I need to know what's a lie and what isn't,* she had said, and he knew that this much was not a lie.

The woman had endured a shattering experience—made more so, surely, by the fact that she had once imagined herself invulnerable. He knew what that was like, knew it firsthand. What had been violated was not so much her body as her sense of who she was.

He held another compress to her forehead, and after a while she stirred again.

This time, she ran her fingertips over her face, felt the raised weals. There was shame in her eyes.

"I guess you don't remember much since Amsterdam," Janson said. "That's typical of the kind of contusions and concussions you suffered. Nothing helps but time." He handed her a glass of water.

"Feel like shit," was her cotton-mouthed reply.

She drank it greedily.

"I've seen worse," he said.

She covered her face with her hands and rolled over, turning away from him, as if embarrassed to be seen. A few minutes later, she asked, "Did you drive here in the limo?"

"No. That's still in Amsterdam. Don't you remember?"

"We put a 'bumper beeper' on it," she explained. Her eyes roamed across the ceiling, which was covered by an elaborate baroque painting of cherubim gamboling among clouds.

"I figured," Janson said.

"Don't want them to find us," she whispered.

Janson touched her cheek gently. "Remind me how come."

For a few moments she said nothing. Then she slowly sat up in the bed. Anger settled onto her bruised countenance. "They lied," she said softly. "They *lied*," she repeated, and this time there was steel in her voice.

"There will always be lies," Janson said.

"The bastards set me up," she said, and now she was trembling, with cold, or with fury.

"No, I think I was the one being set up," Janson said levelly.

He refilled her glass, watched her raise it to her cracked lips, drink the water in a single swallow.

"Comes to the same thing," she said. Her voice was distant. "When it's your own team does it to you, there's only one word for it. Betrayal."

"You feel betrayed," Janson said.

She covered her face with her hand, and words came out in a rush. "They set me up to kill you, but I don't feel guilty, somehow. Mostly, I just feel . . . so pissed off. So angry." Her voice broke. "And so damn ashamed. Like a goddamn dupe. And I'm starting to wonder about every-thing I think I know—what's real, what isn't. Do you have any idea what that's like?"

"Yes," Janson said, simply.

She fell silent for a while. "You look at me like I'm some kind of wounded animal," she finally said.

"Maybe we both are," Janson said gently. "And there's nothing more dangerous."

While the woman rested, Janson was downstairs, in the room that the house's owner, Alasdair Swift, used as a study. Before him was a stack of articles he had downloaded from online electronic databases of newspapers and periodicals. These were the lives of Peter Novak—hundreds of stories about the life and times of the great philanthropist.

Janson pored over them obsessively, hunting for something that he knew he would probably not find: a key, a clue, an incidental bit of data with larger significance. Something—anything—that would tell him why the great man had been killed. Something that would narrow the field. He was looking for a *rhyme*—a detail that would be meaningless to most people, yet would resonate with something that his subconscious mind had stowed away. *We know more than we know,* as Demarest liked to say: our mind stores the impress of facts that we cannot consciously retrieve. Janson read in a zone of receptivity: not trying to puzzle out a problem but hoping simply to take in what could be taken in, without preconception or expectations. Would there be a fleeting allusion to an embittered business rival? To a particular current of buried animus in the financial or international community? To a conflict involving his forebears? Some other enemy as yet unsuspected? He could not know the kind of thing he was looking for, and to imagine that he did would only blind him to the thing he must see.

Novak's enemies—was he flattering himself to think this?—were *his* enemies. If that were so, what else might they have in common? *We know more than we know.* Yet as Janson read on ceaselessly, his eyes beginning to burn, he felt as if he knew less and less. Occasionally he underlined a detail, though what was striking was how little the details varied. There were countless renditions of Peter Novak's financial exploits, countless evocations of his childhood in war-torn Hungary, countless tributes to his humanitarian passions. In the *Far Eastern Economic Review,* he read:

> In December of 1992, he announced another ambitious program, donating $100 million in support of scientists of the former Soviet Union. His program was designed to slow down that country's brain drain—and prevent Soviet scientists from taking up more lucrative employment in places like Iraq, Syria, and Libya. There's no better example of Novak in action. Even while Europe and the United States were wringing their hands and wondering what to do about the dispersal of scientific talent from the former superpower, Novak was actually doing something about it.
>
> "I find it easier to make money than to spend it, to tell you the truth," says Novak with a big grin. He remains a man of simple tastes.

*Every day starts with a spartan breakfast of kasha, and he pointedly
eschews the luxury resorts and high-living ways favored by the plutocratic set.*

Even Novak's small, homey eccentricities—like that unvarying daily
breakfast of kasha—cycled from one piece to another: a permanent residue
of personal "color," PCBs in the journalistic riverbed. Once in a while,
there was a reference to the investigation of Novak's activities after Great
Britain's "Black Wednesday," and the conclusion, as summarized by the
head of MI6, in the line that Fielding had quoted: "The only law this
fellow has broken is the law of averages." In another widely repeated
quote, Peter Novak had explained his relative reticence with the press:
"Dealing with a journalist is like dancing with a Doberman," he had
quipped. "You never know if it's going to lick your face or rip your throat
out." Testimonials from elder statesmen about his role in rebuilding civil
society and promoting conflict resolution were woven through every profile. Soon, paragraphs of journalistic prose seemed to blend into one another; quotes recurred with only minor variations, as if struck from
boilerplate. Thus, the London *Guardian:*

> *'Time was you could dismiss Peter Novak,' says Walter Horowitz, the
> former United States Ambassador to Russia. 'Now he's become a player
> and a major one. He's very much his own man. He gets in there and
> does it, and he has very little patience with government. He's the only
> private citizen who has his own foreign policy—and who can implement
> it.' Horowitz voices a perspective that seems increasingly common in
> the foreign-policy establishment: that governments no longer have the
> resources or the will to execute certain kinds of initiatives, and that this
> vacuum is being filled by private-sector potentates like Peter Novak.*
>
> *The U.N. Under Secretary-General for Political and Security Council
> Affairs, Jaako Torvalds, says, 'It's like working with a friendly, peace-
> able, independent entity, if not a government. At the U.N., we try to
> coordinate our approach to troubled regions with Germany, France,
> Great Britain, Russia—and with Peter Novak.'*

In *Newsweek,* similar tributes echoed:

> *What sets the Magyar mogul apart? Start with his immense sense of
> assurance, an absolute certainty that you see in both his bearing and*

*his speech. "I don't deal with affairs of state for the thrill of it," says Novak, whose exquisitely tailored wardrobe doesn't distract from his physical vigor. Yet by now he has matched himself against the world markets and won so frequently that the game must not feel like much of a challenge. Helping rebuild civil society in unstable regions such as Bosnia or the Central Asian republics, however, provides as much challenge as any man could hope for, even Peter Novak.*

Hours later, he heard quiet footsteps, bare feet on terra-cotta tile. The woman, wearing a terry-cotton robe, had finally emerged from the bedroom. Janson stood up, his head still a blur of names and dates, a fog of facts as yet undistilled into the urgent truths he sought.

"Pretty swank place," she said.

Janson was grateful for the interruption. "Three centuries ago, there was a mountainside monastery here. Almost all of it was destroyed, then overgrown by the forest. My friend bought the property and sank a lot of money into turning the remnants into a cottage."

For Janson, what appealed wasn't so much the house as the location, rustic and isolated. Through the front windows, a craggy mountain peak was visible, rising from the nearby forest. Streaks of gray, naked stone interrupted its green textures—the distance made the trees look like clinging moss—and the whole was outlined against the azure sky, where small black birds wheeled and circled and plunged, their movements coordinated but seemingly aimless. An iron pergola, draped in vines, stood in the back not far from a centuries-old campanile, one of the few vestiges of the old monastery.

"Where I come from," she said, "this isn't a cottage."

"Well, he discovered a lot of frescoes in the course of renovation. He also installed a number of trompe l'oeil paintings taken from other villas. Went a little wild with the ceiling art."

"Damn bat babies got into my dreams."

"They're meant to be little angels. Think of them that way. It's more soothing."

"Who's this friend anyway?"

"A Montreal businessman. 'Friend' is an exaggeration. If it really belonged to a friend, I wouldn't go near it—the risk would be too great. Alasdair Swift is someone I did a few favors once. Always urged me to stay at his place if I were ever in northern Italy. He spends a few weeks here in July, otherwise, it's pretty much vacant. I figure it'll serve a turn.

There's also a fair amount of high-tech communication equipment here. A satellite dish, high-bandwidth Internet connection. Everything a modern businessman might need."

"Everything but a pot of joe," she said.

"There's a sack of coffee in the kitchen. Why don't you make us a pot?"

"Trust me," she said. "That's a real bad idea."

"I'm not fussy," he said.

She held his gaze sullenly. "I don't cook and I don't make coffee. I'd say it was out of feminist principle. Truth is, I don't know how. No big whoop. Something to do with my mom dying when I was a little girl."

"Wouldn't that turn you into a cook?"

"You didn't know my dad. He didn't like me messing around in the kitchen. Like it was disrespecting my mom's memory, or something. Taught me how to microwave a Hungry-Man dinner, though, and scrape the gunk out of the foil sections and onto a plate."

He shrugged. "Hot water. Coffee grounds. Figure it out."

"On the other hand," she went on, her cheeks aflame, "I am *crazy* good with a rifle. And I'm generally considered hot shit at field tactics, E and E, surveillance, you name it. So if you had a mind to, you probably could put me to good use. Instead, you're acting like you got nothing in your head but boogers and a peanut shell."

Janson burst out laughing.

It was not the reaction she had expected. "That's something my dad used to say," the young woman explained, sheepishly. "But I meant what I told you. Don't sell me short. Like I say, I can come in real handy. You know it."

"I don't even know who you are." His eyes came to rest on her strong, regular features, her high cheekbones and full lips. He had almost stopped noticing the angry welts.

"The name's Jessica Kincaid," she said, and extended a hand. "Make us some joe, why don't you, and we'll sit down and talk proper."

As a pot of coffee made its way into mugs, and into their bellies, accompanied by a few fried eggs and pieces of coarse bread torn from a round loaf, Janson learned a few things about his would-be executioner. She grew up in Red Creek, Kentucky, a hamlet nestled in the Cumberland Mountains, where her father owned the town's only gas station and spent more of his money at the local hunting supply store than was good for them. "He always wanted a boy," she explained, "and half the time he kinda forgot I wasn't one. Took me hunting with him first time when I wasn't any more'n five or six. Thought I should be able to play sports, fix cars, and take down a duck with a bullet, not a cartridge full of shot."

"Little Annie Oakley."

"Shit," she said, grinning. "That's what the boys in high school called me. Guess I had a tendency to scare 'em off."

"I'm getting the picture. Car would break down, boyfriend would start hoofing it for a roadside phone box, and meanwhile you'd be communing with the carburetor. A few minutes after they set off, the motor roars to life."

"Something like that," she said, apparently smiling at a memory his words brought back.

"I hope you don't take offense if I say you're not standard-issue Cons Ops."

"I wasn't standard-issue Red Creek, either. I was sixteen when I finished high school. Next day, I lift a thick handful from the gas station cash register, get on a bus, and keep going. Got a knapsack filled with paperback novels from the wire racks, and they're all about FBI agents and shit. I don't get off until I'm in Lexington. Can you believe, I'd never been there before. Never went anywhere—my daddy wouldn't stand for it. Biggest town I'd ever seen. Go straight to the FBI office there. There's a fat-mama secretary at the front desk. Sweet-talked her into giving me an application form. Now, I'm just a gawky teenager, all skin and bones, mostly bones, but when this young Fed happens by, I'm batting my eyes at him like crazy. He's like, 'Somebody got you in for questioning?' I'm like, 'Why don't you take me in for some questioning, 'cause you hire me, it'll be the best decision you ever made.'" She blushed at the recollection. "Well, I was young. Didn't even know you had to have a college degree to be an agent. And he and another guy in a navy suit are, like, joshing around with me, since it's a slow day, and I tell 'em I can pretty much hit whatever I aim at. And one of them, as a lark, takes me to the shooting range they got in the basement. He's calling my bluff, kinda, but mostly just foolin' with me. So I'm on the shooting range, and they're like, be sure you got the safety goggles on, and the ear muffles, and you sure you've handled a twenty-two before?"

"Don't tell me. You hit in the X-ring."

"Shit. One shot, one bull's-eye. Four shots, four bull's-eyes. No scatter. That hushed their mouths, all right. They kept punching up new targets, I kept hittin' 'em. They went long-distance, gave me a rifle, I showed 'em what I could do."

"So the sharpshooter got the job."

"Not exactly. I got a position as a trainee. Had to get a college-equivalency certificate in the meantime. A pile of book learning. Wasn't all that hard."

"Not for a bright-eyed girl with engine grease beneath her nails and cordite in her hair."

"And Quantico was a piece of cake. I could skedaddle up a rope faster than almost anybody in my class. Hand-over-hand climbing, second-story entrances, first-over-fence, whatever. Buncha football clods, they couldn't keep up with me. I apply for a job at the Bureau's National Security Division, and they take me. So a few years later, I'm on a special NSD assignment, and I catch the eye of some Cons Op spooks, and that's that."

"Like Lana Turner getting discovered on a fountain stool at Schwab's Drugstore," Janson said. "So why do I think you're skipping over the most interesting part?"

"Yeah, well, the details are messy," she said. "I'm in sniper position, in Chicago. A stakeout. It's a funny case, corporate espionage, only the spy actually works for the People's Republic of China. It's Cons Ops' baby, but the Feds are providing local backup and support. My job's pretty much just to keep watch. Things get a little out of hand, though. The guy slips the net. He's got a whole mess of microfiche on him, we know, so we definitely don't want him to escape. Somehow he slipped the lobby cordon, and he's racing down the street to his car. If he gets in the car, he's gone, because we don't have vehicular coverage. Nobody expected him to get that far, see. So I request permission to blow the handle off the car door. Slow him down. Operation manager says no—they think it's too dangerous, that I'll hit the subject, risk an international incident. Shit, the manager's covering his ass. I know what I can hit. The risk's zero. Manager doesn't know me, and he's saying, Hold fire. Stand down. Red light. Desist."

"You squeeze off a shot anyway."

"Pop in a steel-jacketed round, blast off the door handle. Now he can't get into the car, and he's scared shitless to boot, I mean he just *freezes*, saying his prayers to the Chairman, and our guys end up hauling him off. Fellow has beaucoup microfiche on him, technical specs on every kind of telecom device you could name."

"So you save the day."

"And get shit-canned for my troubles. 'Acting in contravention of orders,' that kind of bullshit. Sixty-day suspension followed by disciplinary proceedings. Except these spooks swoop in and say they like my style, and how'd I like a life of travel and adventure."

"I think I've got the general idea," Janson said, and he did. In all likelihood, he knew from his own experience as a recruiter, the Consular Operations team first checked out her scores and field reports. Those had to have been startlingly impressive, for Cons Ops had a generally low estimation of the Feds. Once she was identified as a serious talent, someone in Cons Ops probably pulled strings with a contact at the Bureau and arranged for her suspension—simply to facilitate the transfer. If Cons Ops wanted her, they would get her. Hence they'd take steps to ensure that their offer of employment was accepted with alacrity. The scenario Jessica Kincaid had described sounded accurate, but incomplete.

"That's not all," she said, a little shyly. "I went through heavy-duty training when I joined up Cons Ops, and everyone in my class had to prepare a history paper on something or somebody."

"Ah, yes, the Spy Bio paper. And who'd you pick for Spy Bio—Mata Hari?"

"Nope. A legendary field officer by the name of Paul Janson. Did a whole analysis of his techniques and tactics."

"You're kidding." Janson built a fire in the stone fireplace, stacking the logs and crumpling sections of the Italian newspapers beneath them. The dry logs caught on quickly and burned with a steady flame.

"You're an impressive guy, what can I say? But I also identified certain mistakes you were liable to make. A certain . . . weakness." Her eyes were playful, but her voice was not.

Janson took a long sip of the hot, strong java. "Shortly before Rick Frazier's 1986 match with Michael Spinks, Frazier's coach announced to the boxing world that he'd identified a 'weakness' in Spinks's position. There was a lot of discussion and speculation at the time. Then Rick Frazier got into the ring. Two rounds later, he was knocked out." He smiled. "Now, what were you saying about this weakness?"

The ends of Jessica Kincaid's mouth turned down. "That's why they chose me, you know. I mean, for the hit."

"Because you were a veritable Paul Janson scholar. Someone who'd know my moves better than anybody. Yes, I can see that logic. I can see an operations director thinking he was pretty clever to come up with it."

"For sure. The idea of staking out Grigori Berman's place—that was mine. I was sure we'd catch up with you in Amsterdam, too. Lot of people were guessing you'd be lighting out for the U.S. of A. Not me."

"No, not you, with your graduate-equivalency degree in Janson Studies."

She fell silent, staring into the lees of her mug. "There's one question I've been meaning to ask you."

"Have at it."

"Just something I've always wondered about. In 1990, you had a drop on Jamal Nadu, big-deal terrorist mastermind. Reliable intelligence accounts, from sources you cultivated, identified an urban safe house he was using in Amman, and the car he was going to be transported in. A raggedy, funky ol' beggar approaches the car, gets shooed away, falls to his knees in apology, moves on. Only, the beggar is none other than Paul Janson, our own Dr. J, and while he was kowtowing, he rigged an explosive device under the vehicle."

Janson stared at her blankly.

"An hour later, Jamal Nadu does pile into the car. But so do four high-priced ladies—Jordanian hookers he'd hired. You notify control of the changed circumstances, and the orders are to proceed anyway. In your report, you say that you subsequently attempted to blow up the car but that the detonator failed. Operation foiled by mechanical screwup."

"These things happen."

"Not to you," she said. "See, that's why I never believed the official account. You were always a goddamn perfectionist. You made that detonator yourself. Now, two days later Jamal Nadu is on his way back from a meeting with a group of Libyans when suddenly his brains start to leak down his collar, because somebody, with a single well-aimed shot, had blown off the back of his head. You file a report suggesting that a rival from Hamas did him in."

"Your point?"

"You might have thought what really went down was pretty obvious. Four women in the car—the operative didn't have the stomach to kill 'em. Maybe didn't see why it was necessary. Maybe figured once he had a drop on the sumbitch, he could find another way to do it without a lot of collateral killing. And maybe the Department of Planning didn't see it that way. Maybe they wanted a flashy, fiery end and didn't give a shit about the whores. So you made things happen the way you thought they should happen."

"You did have a point, didn't you?"

"The really interesting question, way I see it, is this. In the world of covert ops, taking out a superbaddy like Nadu would make a lot of people's careers. What kind of man does it, and then doesn't take credit for it?"

"You tell me."

"Maybe somebody who doesn't want the controlling officer to be able to claim a big win."

"Tell me something else, if you know so much. Who was controlling the operation?"

"Our director, Derek Collins," she said. "At the time, he headed up the Middle East sector."

"Then if you have any questions about procedures, I suggest you take it up with him."

She formed a *W* with her thumbs and forefingers. "Whatever," she said, half sulkily. "Truth is, I had a hard time getting a fix on you."

"How do you mean?"

"It's one of the reasons the Jamal Nadu thing was a puzzle. Hard to say what makes you tick. Hard to square what I seen with what I heard. For damn sure, you ain't no choirboy. And there are some pretty brutal stories about the stuff you got up to in Vietnam—"

"There's a lot of bullshit out there," he said, cutting her off. He was surprised at the anger that flared in his voice.

"Well, the rumors are pretty heavy, is all I'm saying. They make it sound like you had a hand in some real sick shit that went down there."

"People make things up." Janson was trying to sound calm, and was failing. He did not quite understand why.

She looked at him oddly. "OK, man. I believe you. I mean, you're the only person who would know for sure, right?"

Janson stabbed at the fire with a poker, and the pine logs crackled and hissed fragrantly. The sun had begun to sink over the far mountain peak. "I hope you won't take offense if I ask you to remind me how old you are, Miss Kincaid," he asked, watching her hard face soften in the glow of the hearth.

"You can call me Jessie," she said. "And I'm twenty-nine."

"You could be my daughter."

"Hey, you're as young as you feel."

"That would make me Methuselah."

"Age is just a number."

"In your case, but not mine, a prime number." He stirred red smoking embers with the poker, watched them burst into yellow flames. His mind drifted back to Amsterdam. "Here's a question for you. You ever hear of a company called Unitech Ltd."

"Well, sure. It's one of ours. Supposed to be an independent corporate entity."

"But used as a front by Consular Operations."

"It's about as independent as a dog's leg," she said, running a hand through her short, spiky hair.

"Or a cat's paw," Janson said. The dim memories were surfacing: Unitech had played a minor role over the years in a number of endeavors; sometimes it helped anchor part of an undercover agent's legend, providing an ersatz employment record. Sometimes it transferred funds to parties that were being recruited to play a small role in a larger operation. "Somebody from Unitech is corresponding with the executive director of the Liberty Foundation, offering to provide logistical support for its education programs in Eastern Europe. Why?"

"You got me."

"Let's imagine that somebody, some group, wanted the opportunity to get close to Peter Novak. To learn about his whereabouts."

"Somebody? You're saying Consular Operations took him down? My employers?"

"Arranged for it to happen, more precisely. Orchestrated the circumstances at a remove."

"But why?" she asked. "Why? Don't make a lick of sense."

Few things did. Had Consular Operations really arranged Novak's death? And why hadn't his passing been reported anywhere? It was growing stranger by the day: people who should have been his close associates seemed completely oblivious of the cataclysmic event.

"What you been reading all this time?" Jessie said presently, gesturing toward the various stacks of printouts.

Janson explained.

"You really think there could be something valuable buried in the public record?" she asked.

"Don't be fooled by the mystique of 'intelligence gathering'—half of the stuff you find in foreign-situation reports filed by agents-in-place they get from reading the local papers."

"Tell me about it," she said. "But you only got two eyes—"

"So says the woman who tried to drill me a third."

She ignored the barb. "You can't read that whole stack at once. Give me some. I'll go through it. Another set of eyes, right? Can't hurt."

They read together until he felt the weight of exhaustion start to press down upon him: he needed sleep, could hardly focus his eyes on the densely printed pages. He stood up and stretched. "I'm going to hit the sack," he said.

"Gets chilly at night—sure you don't need a hot-water bottle?" she asked. She held out her hands. Her tone suggested she was joking; her eyes indicated she might not be.

He raised an eyebrow. "Take more than a hot water bottle to warm these bones," he said, keeping his voice light. "Think I'd better pass."

"Yeah," she said. "I guess you'd better." There was something like disappointment in her voice. "Actually, I think I'll just stay up a little while longer, keep slogging away."

"Good girl," he said, winking, and dragged himself up. He was tired, so tired. He would go to sleep easily, but he would not sleep well.


In the jungle was a base. In the base was an office. In the office was a desk. At the desk was a man.

His commanding officer. The man who had taught him nearly everything he knew.

The man he was facing down.

Twelfth-century plainsong came through the small speakers of the lieutenant commander's eight-track tape system. Saint Hildegard.

"What did you want to see me about, son?" Demarest's fleshy features were settled into bland composure. He looked as if he genuinely had no idea why Janson was there.

"I'm going to file a report," Janson said. "Sir."

"Of course. SOP following an operation."

"No, sir. A report about you. Detailing misconduct, in re Article Fifty-three, relating to the treatment of prisoners of war."

"Oh. That." Demarest was silent for a moment. "You think I was a little rough on Victor Charlie?"

"Sir?" Janson's voice rose with incredulity.

"And you can't think why, can you? Well, go ahead. I've got a lot on my mind right now. You see, while you're filling out your forms, I've got to figure out how to save the lives of six men who have been captured. Six men you know very well, because they're under your command—or were."

"What are you talking about, sir?"

"I'm talking about the fact that members of your team have been captured in the vicinity of Lon Duc Than. They were on special assignment, a joint reconnaissance with the Marine Special Forces. Part of a pattern, you see. This place is a goddamn sieve."

"Why wasn't I notified about the operation, sir?"

"Nobody could find you all afternoon—an Article Fifteen offense right there. Time and tide wait for no man. Still, you're here now, and all you can think to do is find the nearest pencil sharpener."

"Permission to speak freely, sir."

"Permission denied," Demarest snapped. "You do what the hell you want. But your team has been captured here, men who placed their lives in your hands, and you're the person best positioned to lead a force to get them free. Or you would be if you gave a damn about them. Oh, you think I was unfeeling, inhumane toward those Victor Charlies in the boonies. But I did what I did for a reason, dammit! I've lost too many men already to leaks between ARVN reps and their VC cousins. What happened to you in Noc Lo? An ambush, you called it. A setup. Goddamn *right* it was. The operation was vetted by MACV, standard procedure, and somewhere along the lines, Marvin tells Charlie. It happens again and again, and every time it does somebody dies. You saw Hardaway die, didn't you? You cradled him in your arms while his guts were spilling onto the jungle. Hardaway was short, just a few days before his tour was over, and they ripped him open, and you were there. Now tell me how that makes you feel, soldier? Dewy and cuddly and sensitive? Or does it piss you off? You got a pair of balls on you, or did you lose 'em playing football for Michigan? Maybe it's slipped your mind, but we're in counterintelligence, Janson, and I am not going to let my men be horsefucked by the VC couriers who have turned MACV into a goddamn Hanoi wire service!" Demarest never raised his voice as he spoke, and yet the effect was only to reinforce the gravity of his words. "An officer's first imperative is the welfare of the men under his command. And when the lives of my men are at stake, I will do anything—anything consistent with our mission—to protect them. I couldn't give a good goddamn what forms you end up filing. But if you're a soldier, if you're a *man,* you'll rescue your men first: it's your duty. Then pursue whatever disciplinary proceedings your little bureaucratic heart desires." He folded his arms. "Well?"

"Awaiting grid coordinates, sir."

Demarest nodded soberly and handed Janson a sheet of blue paper dense with neatly typed operation specifications. "We've got a Huey gassed and gussied." He glanced at the large round clock mounted on the wall opposite. "The crew's ready to go in fifteen. I hope to hell you are."


Voices.

No, *a* voice.

A quiet voice. A voice that did not wish to be overheard. Yet the sibilants carried.

Janson opened his eyes, the darkness of the bedroom softened by the glow of the Lombard moon. An unease grew within him.

A visitor? There was an active Consular Operations branch based at the U.S. Consulate General in Milan, on Via Principe Amedeo—just a fifty-minute drive away. Had Jessie somehow made contact with them? He got up and found his jacket, felt the pockets for his cellular phone. It was missing.

Had she taken it while he slept? Had he simply left it downstairs? Now he put on a bathrobe, took the pistol from under his pillow, and crept toward the voice.

Jessie's voice. Downstairs.

He stepped halfway down the stone staircase, looked around. The lights were on in the study, and the asymmetry of illumination would provide him with the cover he needed—the bright lights inside, the shadowy darkness outside. A few steps farther. Jessie, he could now see, was standing in the study, facing a wall, with his cell phone pressed to her ear. Talking quietly.

He felt a wrenching feeling in his gut: it was as he had feared.

From the snippets of conversation he made out through the open door, it was apparent that she was speaking to a colleague from Consular Operations in Washington. He edged nearer the room, and her voice grew more distinct.

"So the status is still 'beyond salvage,'" she repeated. "Sanction on sighting."

*She was verifying that the kill orders were still in effect.*

A shudder ran down his spine. He had no choice but to do what he should have done much earlier. It was kill or be killed. The woman was a professional assassin: it was of no account that her profession had once been his—that her employers had as well. He had no choice but to eliminate her; sentiment and wishful thinking, and her own accomplished line of blather, had distracted him from that one essential truth.

As cicadas filled the evening breeze with their rasping—a window was open in the study—he moved the pistol to his right hand, following her pacing figure with its muzzle. The sudden certainty of what he had to do filled him with loathing, self-disgust. Yet there was no other way. *Kill or be killed:* it was the awful shibboleth of an existence he had hoped he'd put behind him. Nor did it mitigate the larger truth, the ultimate truth of his career: kill *and* be killed.

"What do the *cables* say?" she was saying. "The latest signals intelligence? Don't tell me you guys are working blind."

Janson coolly regarded the slightly built woman, the roundness of her hips and breasts offset by the tightly muscular frame; in her way, she was indeed quite beautiful. He knew what she was capable of—had seen, firsthand, her astonishing marksmanship, her extraordinary strength and agility, the swiftness and shrewdness of her mind. She had been built to kill, and nothing would deter her from doing so.

"Are the boys in position, or are they just sitting on their asses?" She kept her voice low, but her intonation was heated, almost hectoring. "*Jesus!* There is no excuse for this. This makes us all look bad. Shit, it's true what they say: when you want a job done right, you gotta do it yourself. I mean, that's how I'm feeling right now. Whatever happened to team efficiency?"

Another dumb, inanimate slug would shatter another skull, and another life would be stricken, erased, turned into the putrid animal matter from which it had been constituted. That was not progress; it was the very opposite. He cast his mind back to Theo and the others, snuffed out, and for what? Some of the rage that filled him was displaced rage at himself, yes. But what of it? The woman would die—die in a five-million-dollar mountainside estate in Alpine Lombardy, a land she had never seen before in her life. She would die at his hands, and that would be their one moment of true intimacy.

"*Where* is he? *Where?* Hell, I can tell you that." Jessie Kincaid spoke again to her unseen interlocutor, after a period of silence. "You big lummox, you mean you guys really haven't figured that out? Monaco, man. There's no doubt in my mind. You know Novak's got a house there." Another pause. "Janson didn't say it in so many words. But I heard him making a joke to his little friend there about playing baccarat—you do the math. Hey, you boys are supposed to be in intelligence, so why don't you try acting intelligent?"

She was lying to them.

Lying *for* him.

Janson returned his gun to his holster, and felt flooded, almost light-headed, with relief. The intensity of the emotion surprised and puzzled him. She had been asked for his location, and she had lied to protect him. She had just chosen sides.

"No," she was saying, "don't tell anybody I called in. This was a private chat, all right? Just me and you, pookie. No, you can take all the credit, and that'll be fine with me. Tell 'em, I dunno, tell 'em I'm in a coma some-where and the Netherlands national health plan is paying for real expen-sive treatment, because I didn't have any identity papers on me. Tell 'em that and I bet they won't be in such a rush to bring me back to the States."

A few moments later, she clicked off, turned around, and was startled to see Janson in the doorway.

"Who's 'pookie'?" he asked, in a bored voice.

"God *damn* you," she erupted. "You been spying on me? The famous Paul Janson turns out to be some kind of goddamn Peeping Tom?"

"Came down for some milk," he said.

"Shit," she said in two syllables, glowering. Finally, she said, "He's a fat-ass desk jockey at State, Bureau of Research and Intelligence. Sweet guy, though. I think he likes me, because when I'm around, his tongue comes out like Michael Jordan doing a fadeaway. Stranger things, right? But what's really strange is what he told me about Puma."

"Puma?"

"Shop name for Peter Novak. And before you ask, you're Falcon. The Puma update is what's freaking me out, though. They don't think he's dead."

"What, are they waiting for the obituary in *The New York Times?*"

"Story is that you took money to arrange his death. But you failed."

"I saw him die," Janson said sadly, shaking his head. "God, I wish it were otherwise. I can't tell you how much."

"Whoa," she said. "What, you trying to claim credit for the kill?"

"I'm afraid your contact is either putting you on or, more likely, just hasn't got a clue." He rolled his eyes. "Your tax dollars at work."

"Mentioned there was a news segment with him on CNN today. We got CNN here? Probably still be showing on the early-morning *Headline News* retreads."

She wandered over to the large-screen television set, and switched on CNN. Then she located a blank videotape atop the connected VCR, popped it in, and hit RECORD.

A special report on the declining power of the Federal Reserve. Renewed tensions between North and South Korea. The latest fashion craze among Japanese youth. Protests against genetically modified foods in Britain. Forty minutes of videotape had been recorded by now. Then came a three-minute segment about an Indian woman who ran a clinic in Calcutta for her countrymen with AIDS. A homegrown Mother Teresa, someone called her. And—the occasion for the segment—the ceremony yesterday honoring the woman's efforts. A distinguished-looking man presenting her with a special humanitarian award. The same man who had helped fund her clinic.

Peter Novak.

The late, great Peter Novak.

Janson watched the large-screen TV with a swirling sense of bewilderment. Either this was some kind of technical trickery or, most likely, it had been filmed earlier, much earlier.

Surely a closer inspection would make this clear.

Together, he and Jessie rewound the recording she had made. There was Peter Novak, the familiar figure, unmistakably so. He was grinning and speaking into a microphone, "There's a favorite Hungarian proverb of mine: *Sok kicsi sokra megy*. It means that many small things can add up to a big one. It's a privilege to be able to honor the remarkable woman who, through countless small acts of kindness and compassion, has given the world something large indeed. . . ."

There had to be an easy explanation. There *had* to be.

Then they watched the segment again, frame by frame.

"Stop there," Jessie said at one point. It was their third viewing. She pointed toward a magazine, fleetingly glimpsed at a cluttered table where Novak was interviewed after the ceremony. She ran to the kitchen and retrieved Janson's copy of *The Economist*, purchased at the newsstand earlier that day.

"Same issue," she said.

The very same image appeared on the cover, which was dated to expire the following Monday. It was not an old tape that had been broadcast. It was filmed, had to have been filmed, *after* the catastrophe in Anura.

Yet if Peter Novak were alive, who had died in Anura?

And if Peter Novak was dead, who were they were watching?

Janson felt his head starting to swim.

*It was madness!*

What had they seen? A twin? An *impostor?*

Had Novak been murdered and . . . replaced with a double? It was diabolical, almost beyond imagining. Who could do such a thing?

Who else knew? He reached for his cell phone, trying Novak's staffers both in New York and in Amsterdam. An urgent message for Peter Novak. Having to do with matters involving his personal security.

He used every code-red word he knew—to no avail, yet again. The response was the familiar one: bored, phlegmatic, unalarmed. A message would be conveyed; no promises of whether it would be returned. No information would be divulged as to Mr. Novak's whereabouts. Márta Lang—if that was even her real name—remained equally elusive.

A quarter of an hour later, Janson found himself clutching his head, trying to order his whirling thoughts. What had happened to Peter Novak? What was happening to Janson himself? When he looked up, he saw Jessie Kincaid staring back at him with wounded eyes.

"I ask only one thing of you," she said, "and I know it's a biggie, but here it is: do not lie to me. I've heard too many lies, hell, I've *told* too many lies, as it is. As for what happened in Anura, I got your word for it, nobody else's. Tell me this, *what* I am supposed to believe?" Her eyes were moist, and she was blinking hard. "*Who* am I supposed to believe?"

"I know what I saw," Janson said softly.

"That makes two of us." She jerked her head at the TV screen.

"What are you saying? That you don't believe me?"

"I *want* to believe you." She took a deep breath. "I want to believe *somebody.*"

Janson was silent for a long moment. "Fine," he said. "I don't blame you. Listen, I'll call for a cab, he'll ferry you down to the Cons Op station in Milan, and you can report back in. Trust me, a crack shot like you, they'll be relieved to have you back. And I'll be long gone by the time you get the cleanup crew here."

"Hold it," she said. "Slow down."

"I think it's best," he said.

"For who?"

"Both of us."

"You don't speak for both of us. You speak for one of you." She was silent for a while, pacing. "All right, you goddamn son of a bitch," she said abruptly. "You saw what you saw. Christ on a raft, you saw what you saw. Shit, now this is what I call a total mindfuck." A mordant chuckle. "Shouldn't do that on a first date, or they won't respect you in the morning."

Janson was lost in his own whirring thoughts. *Peter Novak:* just who was this living legend, this man who emerged from obscurity to global prominence in such a meteoric blaze? Questions crowded his mind, but they were questions without answers. His stomach churning, Janson threw his Deruta mug into the fireplace, where it smashed against the heavy stones. He felt better for a moment, but only a moment.

He returned to the scarred leather chair near the fireplace, settling one battered hide against another. Jessie stood behind him, and began to rub his aching shoulders.

"I hate to add to the tension," she said, "but if we're gonna figure out what the hell's going on, we have got to get out of here. How long do you think it's going to take Cons Ops before they find us? They've got all that eye-in-the-sky data, and believe me, they got technicians working around the clock to identify your car, alternate means of conveyance, whatever. From what my friend told me, the cables so far are worthless, just a lot of false sightings—but there'll be a true one before long. They'll be shaking down known contacts in Europe, following thousands of dangling threads, reviewing video from highway tolls and border crossings. All that cybergumshoe shit. And sooner or later, something's going to lead them here."

She was right. He thought of the philanthropist's motto: *Sok kicsi sokra megy.* Hungarian folk wisdom. Would their own small efforts yield a larger result? Now he recalled Fielding's words: *It's in Hungary, still, that you'll find his greatest admirers, and his most impassioned foes.* And Lang's observation: *For better or worse, Hungary made him who he is. And Peter is not one to forget his debts.*

It made him who he is.

And who *was* that?

It made him who he was: Hungary. That had to be Janson's destination.

It was his best chance at flushing out Peter Novak's blood enemies—the ones who had known him longest and, perhaps, best.

"You look like a man who's just made up his mind," Jessie said, almost shyly.

Janson nodded. "What about you?"

"What kind of question is that?"

"I'm thinking about my next move. What about yours? You going to go back to Cons Ops now?"

"What do you think?"

"Tell me."

"Let me break it down for you. I report in to my operations director, I'd be taken out of the field for at least a year, maybe forever. And I'd be the subject of a very lengthy 'interview.' I know how the system works. That's what would be in store for me, and don't try to tell me otherwise. But that's not even the bigger problem. The bigger problem is, how I am supposed to rejoin this world where I don't know what can be trusted and what can't be. It's like, I know too much and I don't know enough, and for both reasons, I can't go back. I can only go forward. Only way I can live with myself."

"Live with yourself? You don't increase your odds of living by hanging around me. You know that. I've *told* you that."

"Lookit, everything's got a price," she said quietly. "If you let me, I'ma tag along with you. If you don't, I'ma do my darndest to tail you."

"You don't even know where I'm off to."

"Sugar bear, it don't really matter." Jessie stretched her lean, loosely jointed body. "Where you off to?"

He hesitated but a moment. "Hungary. Where it all began."

"Where it all began," she repeated softly.

Janson stood up. "You want to come along, you can. But remember, try to make contact with Cons Ops, and you're as good as deactivated—and not by me. If you're along for the ride, you follow the rules of the road. And I set those rules. Otherwise—"

"Done," she said, cutting him off. "Quit drilling, you struck oil."

He looked at her coolly, appraising her as a soldier and an operative. The truth was, he needed the backup. What would await them was beyond knowing. If she was half as deadly working with him as she had been working against him, she'd prove a formidable weapon indeed.

He had many phone calls to make before he slept, many legends to resurrect. The path had to be prepared.

Where it would lead, of course, was impossible to say. Yet what choice was there? Whatever the risks, it was the only way they could ever penetrate the mystery that was Peter Novak.

# CHAPTER TWENTY-TWO

He was baiting a trap.

The thought did little to calm Janson's nerves, for he knew how often traps caught those who set them. In this phase, his principal weapon would be his own composure. He thus had to steer clear of the pitfalls of anxiety and overconfidence. One could lead to paralysis, the other to stupidity.

Still, if a trap had to be set, he could think of no setting more appropriate. Thirty-five seventeen Miskolc-Lillafüred, Erzsébet sétány 1, was a couple of miles west of Miskolc proper, and the only notable building in the resort area of Lillafüred. The Palace Hotel, as it was now called, stood near the wooded banks of Lake Hámori, surrounded by a sylvan glade that suggested a long-past feudal Europe of parks and palaces. If the place evoked nostalgia, it was in fact a tribute to it. The completion of the faux hunting castle, in the 1920s, was an imperial project of Admiral Horthy's regime, designed as a monument to the nation's historical glories. The restaurant, fittingly, was named for King Matthias, the fifteenth-century Hungarian warrior-sovereign who led his people to greatness, a greatness that gleamed with the blood of their enemies. In the post-Communist era, the place was swiftly restored to its former opulence. Now it drew vacationers and businessmen from all over the country. A project borne of imperial vainglory had been co-opted by a still more powerful dominion, that of commerce itself.

Paul Janson strode through the lavishly appointed lobby and down to the cellar-style restaurant on the level below. His stomach was tight with tension; food was the last thing on his mind. And yet any sign that he was on edge would only betray him.

"I'm Adam Kurzweil," Janson told the maître d'hôtel, in a well-modulated transatlantic accent. It was the sort of language-school English that was common both to educated citizens of the British Commonwealth—Zimbabwe, Kenya, South Africa, India—and to affluent Europeans who had received early instruction in the tongue. "Kurzweil" wore a chalk-striped suit and a scarlet tie, and bore himself with the erect hauteur of a businessman used to being deferred to.

The maître d', dressed in a swallowtail dinner jacket, his black hair oiled and combed into obsidian waves, gave Janson a sharp, appraising look before his face creased into a professional smile. "Your guest is already here," he said. He turned to a younger woman beside him. "She will show you to your table."

Janson nodded blandly. "Thank you," he said.

The table was, as his guest had obviously requested, a discreet corner banquette. The man he was meeting was a resourceful and careful man, or he would not have survived in his particular line of business for as long as he had.

As Janson walked toward the banquette, he concentrated on entering into a character he would have to make wholly his own. First impressions did indeed matter. The man he was meeting, Sandor Lakatos, would be suspicious. As Kurzweil, therefore, he would be more so. It was, he knew, the most effective countermeasure.

Lakatos turned out to be a small, hunched man; the curvature of his upper spine set his head oddly forward on his neck, as if he were tucking in his chin. His cheeks were round, his nose bulbous, and his wattled neck was continuous with his jawline, giving his head a pearlike shape. He was a study in dissipation.

He was also among the biggest arms dealers in Central Europe. His fortunes had risen markedly during the arms embargo of Serbia, when that republic had to seek irregular sources for what was no longer available to it legally. Lakatos had begun his career in long-haul trucking, specializing in produce and then dry goods; his business model, and his infrastructure, required little modification to expand into the armaments trade. That he had agreed to meet with Adam Kurzweil at all was a testament to another factor behind his success: his sheer, unappeasable greed.

Employing a long-disused legend, that of a Canadian principal in a security-services—that is, private militia—company, Janson left calls with a number of businessmen long since retired from the trade. In each instance, the message was the same. A certain Adam Kurzweil, representing a client who could not be named, sought a supplier for an extremely large and lucrative transaction. The Canadian—a legend Janson had created for himself, without notifying Cons Ops—was remembered fondly, his low profile and long periods of invisibility respected. Still, the men he contacted demurred, albeit reluctantly; all were cautious men, had made their fortunes and now had moved on. No matter. In the small world of such merchants, Janson knew, word of a serious buyer would spread; the one who arranged a successful contact could expect a commission on the transaction. Janson would not get in touch with Lakatos; he would contact those around him. When one of the businessmen he spoke to, a resident of Bratislava whose close ties with government officials had kept him safe from investigation, asked him why this Adam Kurzweil did not try Lakatos, he was told that Kurzweil was not a trusting soul and would not use anyone who had not been personally vouched for. Lakatos, as far as Kurzweil was concerned, was simply not trustworthy. He and his clients would not expose themselves to the risk of such an unknown. Besides, wasn't Lakatos too small-time for such a transaction?

As Janson anticipated, the haughty reproach filtered down to the porcine Hungarian, who bristled at being dismissed in those terms. Untrustworthy? Unknown? Lakatos was not good enough for this Adam Kurzweil, this mysterious middleman? Outrage was joined with pragmatic calculation. To allow his reputation to be thus impugned was simply bad business. And there was no more effective way to expunge any lingering aspersions than by landing the elusive account.

Yet who *was* this Kurzweil? The Canadian investor was cagey, obviously unwilling to say what he knew. "All I can say is that he has been a *very* good client of ours." Within hours, Janson's cell phone began chirping with testimonials on the Hungarian's behalf; the man had obviously been calling in favors. Well, the Canadian conceded, Kurzweil would be passing through the Miskolc area, near Lakatos's primary residence. It was *possible* he could be persuaded to meet. But everyone had to understand: Kurzweil was a very untrusting man. If he declined, no offense should be taken.

Despite the tactical pretense of reluctance, Janson's eagerness for the meeting bordered on desperation. For he knew that the one sure way to reach the ancient and entrenched enemies of Peter Novak would be through the Hungarian merchant of death.

Janson, seated at a tall leather chair in the hotel lobby, had observed Lakatos's arrival and deliberately waited ten minutes before joining him. As he approached the Hungarian at the banquette, he maintained a pleasantly blasé expression. Lakatos surprised him by standing up and embracing him.

"We meet at last!" he said. "Such a pleasure." He pressed his breasty upper body to Janson's and reached around, his plump sweaty hands vigorously patting his back and then his waist. None too subtly, the effusive embrace served as a kind of crude security check: any upper-body holster—shoulder, small of back, bellyband—would have been detected easily.

As the two took their seats, Lakatos nakedly scrutinized his guest; avidity vied with no little suspicion of his own. There were, the merchant had learned, opportunities that were too good to be true. One had to distinguish between low-hanging fruit and poisoned bait.

"The *libamaj roston,* the grilled goose liver, is excellent. And so is the *brassói aprépecsenye*—a sort of braised pork." Lakatos's voice was slightly breathless and fluting.

"Personally, I prefer the *bakanyi sertéshús,*" Janson replied.

The Hungarian paused. "Then you know this place," he said. "They told me you were a worldly man, Mr. Kurzweil."

"If they told you anything, they told you too much," he said, a trace of steel in his voice belying his half smile.

"You'll forgive me, Mr. Kurzweil. Yet, as you know, ours is a business based on trust. Handshakes and reputation substitute for contracts and paperwork. It is the old way, I think. My father was a butter-and-egg man, and for decades you'd find his little white trucks up and down the Zemplén range. He started in the thirties, and when the Communists took over, they found it was easier to cede these little shipments to somebody who understood the routes. You see, when he was a teenager he was a truck driver himself. So when his employees would tell him that this or that difficulty—a flat tire, a blown radiator—meant that their route would be delayed by half a day, well, he knew better. He knew just how long it took to fix these things, because he'd had to do so himself. His men came to understand that. They could pull nothing over on him, but this did not breed resentment, only respect. I think maybe I am the same way."

"Do people often try to pull things over on you?"

Lakatos grinned, flashing a row of porcelain teeth, unnaturally white and regular. "Few are so foolhardy," he replied. "They recognize the dangers." His tone wavered between menace and self-regard.

"No one has ever prospered by underestimating the Hungarian people," Janson said soberly. "But then yours is a language, a culture, that few of us can pretend to understand."

"Magyar obscurity. It served the country well when others sought to dominate it. At other times, it has served us less well. But I think those of us who operate under conditions of, shall we say, circumspection have learned its value."

A waiter appeared and filled their water glasses.

"A bottle of your 'ninety-eight Margaux," Lakatos said. He turned to Kurzweil. "It's a young wine, but quite refreshing. Unless you'd like to try the local specialty—one of those 'Bull's Blood' vintages. Some are quite memorable."

"I believe I would, in fact."

Lakatos wriggled his fat fingers at the waiter "Instead, a bottle of the Egri Bikavér, 'eighty-two." He turned again to his companion. "Now tell me," he said, "how do you find Hungary?"

"An extraordinary land, which has given the world some extraordinary people. So many Nobel Laureates, film directors, mathematicians, physicists, musicians, conductors, novelists. Yet there is one laureled son of Hungary who—how shall I say this politely?—has given disquiet to my clients."

Lakatos looked at him, transfixed. "You intrigue me."

"One man's *liberty* is another's tyranny, as they say. And the *foundations* of liberty may be the foundations of tyranny." He paused to make sure that his import was taken.

"How fascinating," Lakatos said, swallowing hard. He reached for his water glass.

Janson stifled a yawn. "Forgive me," he murmured. "The flight from Kuala Lumpur is a long one, however comfortable one is made." In fact, the seven-hour ride from Milan to Eger in the bone-rattling confines of a truck trailer loaded with cured meats had been both uncomfortable and nerve-racking. Even as he dined with the arms merchant, Jessie Kincaid would be using a false passport and credit card to rent another automobile for tomorrow's trip and carefully working out the itinerary in advance. He hoped she would be able to get some rest before long. "But travel is my life," Janson added grandly.

"I can imagine," Lakatos said, his eyes bright.

The waiter, in black tie, appeared with the local red wine; it came in a ribboned bottle without a paper label, the name of the vineyard etched directly on the glass. The wine was dark, rich, seemingly opaque as it splashed into their crystal goblets. Lakatos took a healthy swallow, sluiced it around his mouth, and pronounced it superb.

"As a region for viticulture, Eger is nothing if not robust." He held up his wineglass. "You may not be able to see through it," he added, "but, I assure you, Mr. Kurzweil, you always get value for your money. You made an excellent choice."

"I am pleased to hear you say so," Janson replied. "Another tribute to Magyar opacity."

Just then, a man in a sky blue suit but no tie came over to the table—obviously an American tourist, and obviously drunk. Janson looked up at him, and alarm bells began ringing in his head.

"It's been a while," the man said, slurring his words slightly. He placed a hairy, beringed hand on the white linen tablecloth near the bread basket. "Thought it was you. Paul Janson, big as life." He snorted loudly before he turned and walked away. "Told you it was him," he was saying to a woman who sat at his table across the room.

*Dammit!* What had happened was always a theoretical possibility in covert operations, but so far Janson had been fortunate. There had been an occasion once in Uzbekistan when he was meeting with a deputy to the nation's oil minister, posing as a go-between to a major petrochemical corporation. An American happened to breeze through the office—a civilian, a Chevron oil buyer, who knew him under another name, and in another context, one involving the Apsheron gas and oil fields of Azerbaijan. Their gaze met, the man nodded, but said nothing. For distinctly different reasons, he felt as chagrined at being spotted by Janson as Janson had at being spotted by him. No words were exchanged, and Janson knew he would make no inquiries. But what had happened here was a worst-case scenario, the sort of cross-context intrusion that any field agent hoped he would never encounter.

Now Janson focused on slowing his heartbeat, and he turned to Lakatos with an impassive expression. "A friend of yours?" Janson asked. The man had not made it clear to whom his remarks were addressed: "Adam Kurzweil" would not have assumed he was their subject.

Lakatos looked bewildered. "I don't know this man."

"Don't you," Janson said softly, defusing suspicion by placing the arms dealer on the defensive. "Well, no matter. We've all had such experiences. Between the drink and the dim lighting, he might have taken you for Nikita Khrushchev himself."

"Hungary has always been a land densely populated with ghosts," Lakatos returned.

"Some of your own making."

Lakatos set his glass down, ignoring the comment. "You'll forgive me if I'm curious. I have *quite* a few accounts, as you know. Yours isn't a name I'd come across."

"I'm glad to hear it." Janson took a long, savoring sip of the local wine.

"Or do I only flatter myself about my discretion? I've spent most of my life in southern Africa, where, I must say, your presence is not a noticeable one."

Lakatos tucked his chin deeper into the pillow of fat that was his neck, signaling assent. "A mature market," he said. "I cannot say there has been any great call for my offerings down there. Still, I have had occasional dealings with South Africans, and I've always found you people exemplary trading partners. You know what you want, and you don't mind paying what it's worth."

"Trust is honored with trust. Fairness with fairness. My clients can be generous, but they are not profligate. They do expect to get what they pay for. Value for money, as you put it. I should be clear, though. The assets they seek are not simply material, or matériel. They are equally interested in the sort of thing doesn't come on pallets. They seek allies. *Human capital*, you might say."

"I do not wish to mistake your meaning," Lakatos said, his face a mask.

"Put it however you like: they know that there are people, forces on the ground, who share their interests. They wish to enlist the support of such people."

"Enlist their support . . ." Lakatos echoed warily.

"Conversely, they wish to offer support to such people."

A deep swallow. "Assuming such people are in *need* of additional support."

"Everybody can use additional support." Janson smiled smoothly. "There are few certainties in this world. That is one."

Lakatos reached over and tapped his wrist, smiling. "I think I like you," he said. "You're a thinker and a gentleman, Mr. Kurzweil. Not like the Swabian boors I so often have to deal with."

The waiter presented them with fried goose liver, "compliments of the chef," and Lakatos speared his portion greedily with his fork.

"But I think you understand where I'm going, yes?" Janson pressed.

The American in the light blue jacket was back, with more on his mind. "You don't remember me?" the man demanded belligerently. This time he made it impossible for Janson to pretend he did not know to whom he was speaking.

Janson turned to Lakatos. "How amusing. It would appear I owe you an apology," he said. Then he looked up at the surly American, keeping his face bland and devoid of interest. "It would appear you have mistaken me for someone else," he said, his transatlantic vowels immaculate.

"The hell I have. Why the hell are you talking funny, anyway? You trying to hide from me? That it? You trying to dodge me? Can't say as I blame you."

Janson turned to Lakatos and shrugged, seemingly unconcerned. He worked on controlling his pounding pulse. "This happens to me on occasion—apparently I have that kind of face. Last year, I was in Basel, and a woman in the hotel bar was convinced that she'd run across me in Gstaad." He grinned, then covered his grin with a hand, as if embarrassed by the memory. "And not only that—we'd apparently had an affair."

Lakatos was unsmiling. "You and she?"

"Well, she and the man she took me for. Admittedly, it was quite dark. But I was tempted to take her up to my room and, shall we say, carry on where her gentleman friend left off. I regret that I did not—although I guess she would have realized her mistake at some point." He laughed, an easy and unforced-sounding laugh, but when he glanced up, the American was still there, a drunken sneer on his face.

"So you don't have anything to say to me?" the American snarled. "Shit."

The woman who had been at his table—almost certainly his wife— came over to him and pulled on his arm. She was slightly overweight, and dressed in an inappropriately summery frock. "Donny," she said. "You're bothering that nice man. He's probably on vacation, same as us."

"Nice man? That shitheel's the one got me *fired*." His face was red, his expression frankly choleric. "Yeah, that's right. The CEO brought you in to be his hatchet man, didn't he, Paul? This fucker, Paul Janson, arrives at Amcon as a security consultant. Next thing he's handing in this report about pre-employment screening and employee theft, and my boss is handing me my ass, because how come I let all this happen on my watch? I gave that company twenty years. Did anybody tell you that? I did a good job. I did a *good* job." He scrunched up his crimson face, his countenance radiating both self-pity and hatred.

The woman gave Janson an unfriendly look; if she was embarrassed for her husband, her narrow eyes made it clear that she had also heard plenty about the outside security consultant who cost her poor Donny his job.

"When you sober up and wish to apologize," Janson said, coldly, "please do not concern yourself. I accept your apologies in advance. Such confusions happen."

What else could he say? How would the victim of mistaken identity react? With bafflement, amusement, and then ire.

Of course, it was not a case of mistaken identity, and Janson remembered exactly who Donald Weldon was. A senior manager in charge of security at a Delaware-based engineering firm, he was a complacent lifer who filled his staffing positions with cousins, nephews, and friends, treating the security division as a source of sinecures. As long as no major disaster occurred, who would call his competence and probity into question? Meanwhile, employee theft and the systematic filing of false workmen's compensation claims had become an invisible drag on the operating budget, while a company vice president was doubling his executive compensation by reporting confidential information to a competitor firm. It was Janson's experience that errant executives, rather than blaming themselves and their own dereliction for their dismissal, invariably blamed whoever brought their misconduct to light. In truth, Donald Weldon should have been grateful that he was only fired; Janson's report made it clear that some of the false-compensation claims were made with his complicity, and he provided sufficient evidence for criminal prosecution, one that could easily have resulted in jail time. Janson's recommendation, however, was that Vice President Weldon be relieved of his duties but not prosecuted, to spare the company further embarrassment and prevent potentially damaging revelations at the pretrial and discovery phases. *You owe me your freedom, you corrupt son of a bitch,* Janson thought.

Now the American wagged a finger very near Janson's nose. "You goddamn candy-ass bastard—you'll get yours some day." As the woman led him back to their seats, several tabletops away, his unsteady gait betrayed the alcohol that fueled his fury.

Janson turned brightly to his companion, but a sense of dread filled him. Lakatos had grown cold; he was not a fool, and the drunken American's display could not automatically be discounted. The Hungarian's eyes were hard, like small black marbles.

"You're not drinking your wine," Lakatos said, gesturing with his fork. He smiled an icy executioner's smile.

Janson knew how such people thought: probabilities were weighed, but caution dictated that negative inferences were assumed true. Janson also knew that his protestations could have provided little reassurance. He had been burned, exposed, shown to be someone other than the person as whom he had presented himself. Men like Sandor Lakatos feared nothing more than the possibility of deception: Adam Kurzweil now represented not opportunity, but danger. And, however obscure its motivations, such danger was to be eliminated.

Lakatos's hand now disappeared into the inner breast pocket of his bulky woolen jacket. Surely he was not handling a weapon—that would be too crude a gesture for someone in his position. The hand lingered oddly, manipulating a device. He was, it appeared, thumbing some sort of automatic pager or, more likely, a text-messaging device.

And then the merchant looked across the room, toward the maître d's station. Janson followed his gaze: two dark-suited men, who had been inconspicuously loitering around the long zinc bar, suddenly stood a little straighter. Why hadn't he picked them out earlier? Lakatos's bodyguards— of course. The arms dealer would never have met with a broker he did not personally know without taking such an elementary precaution.

And now, as an exchange of glances suggested, the bodyguards had a new mission. They were no longer simply protectors. They were executioners. Their unbuttoned heavy jackets hung loosely around their torsos; a casual observer would assume that the slight bulge near the right breast pocket was from a cigarette pack or a cell phone. Janson knew better. His blood ran cold.

Adam Kurzweil would not be permitted to leave the Palace Hotel grounds alive. Janson could envisage the scenario all too clearly. The meal would be hurriedly completed, and the two would stroll together out of the lobby, accompanied by the gunmen. At any convenient distance from the crowds, he would be dispatched with a silenced shot to the back of the head, his body disposed of either in the lake or in the trunk of a vehicle.

He had to do something. Now.

Reaching for his glass, he carefully elbowed his fork to the floor and, with an apologetic shrug, bent down to retrieve it. As he reached down, he lifted the cuff of his trousers, released the thumb-break of his ankle holster, and gained a firing grip on the small Glock M26 he had acquired earlier in Eger. Beneath the table, he could use the finger grooves to position his hand on the grip frame. The weapon was now in his lap. The odds had shifted slightly.

"Have you walked around the lake?" Sandor Lakatos asked. "So beautiful this time of year." Another display of his porcelain teeth.

"It's very beautiful," Janson agreed.

"I would like to take you on a walk, afterward."

"Isn't it rather dark for that?"

"Oh, I don't know," Lakatos said. "We'll be able to be alone. That's really the best way to get to know each other, I find." His eyes had an anthracite gleam.

"I'd like that," Janson said. "Do you mind if I excuse myself for a minute?"

"Be my guest." His gaze drifted toward the two suited guards in the bar area.

Janson tucked his Glock into his front trouser waistband before he stood up and wandered to the rest rooms, which were off a short hallway extending from the far corner of the main dining room. As he approached, he felt a sharp pang of adrenaline: before him was another dark-suited man, his posture identical to those at the bar. This man was clearly neither a diner nor an employee of the restaurant. He was another guard of Lakatos's, stationed there for such an eventuality. Janson walked into the marble-floored bathroom, and the man—broad-chested, tall, his face a mask of bored professionalism—followed him in. As Janson turned toward the sinks, he heard the man lock the door. That meant that they were alone. Yet an unsilenced gunshot would only summon the others in Lakatos's employ, who were also armed. Janson's pistol was not the advantage he had hoped. The imperative of visual concealment ruled out the possibility of aural concealment: the bulk of a silenced gun could not have been secreted undetectably in an ankle holster. Now Janson walked to the urinals; in the stainless steel of the knob, he could make out a distorted reflection of the burly guard. He could also make out the long cylindrical shape of the man's weapon. *His* weapon was silenced.

There would be no need to wait for Janson to leave the Palace Hotel; Janson could be dispatched where he was.

"What's he paying you?" Janson asked, without turning around to look at the man. "I'll double it."

The guard said nothing.

"You don't speak English? I bet you speak dollars?"

The guard's expression did not change, but he put away the gun. Janson's very defenselessness suggested a better approach: now the man removed a two-foot loop of cord with small plastic disks on either end serving as handles.

Janson had to concentrate to hear the whisper-quiet sound of the man's jacket stretching as he extended his arms, preparing to loop the garrote precisely around Janson's throat. He could only applaud his would-be executioner's professional judgment. The garrote would ensure not only a soundless death but a bloodless one. In a restaurant like this, particularly given the alcohol consumption patterns in Central Europe, it would take little creativity to escort him out. The guard might well drag him out more or less upright, propping him up with a powerful arm around his shoulder: a sheepish grin, and everyone would assume that the guest had simply imbibed too much Zwack Unicum, the spirit of choice at the Palace Hotel.

Janson bowed deeply, placing his forehead against the marble tiled wall. Then he turned, his stooped body signaling boozy exhaustion. Suddenly, explosively, he surged upward and to the right, and as the guard reeled back from the impact, he smashed his knee into his groin. The man grunted and reared up, throwing his looped cord against Janson's shoulders, and frantically trying to slide it upward, around his vulnerable neck. Janson felt the cord digging into his flesh, searing like a band of heat. There was no way but forward: instead of retreating, Janson pressed closer to his assailant, and dug his chin into his opponent's chest. He thrust a hand into the man's shoulder holster and removed the long, silenced handgun: his assailant could not free up his own hands and maintain the pressure on the cord. He had to choose. Now the man dropped the garrote and struck Janson's hand with an underhand blow, sending the gun skidding along the marble floor.

Suddenly, Janson thrust the top of his head against the man's lower jaw. He heard the clicking sound of the man's teeth banging together as the impact of the head butt traveled from jaw to cranium. Simultaneously, he wrapped his right leg around the man's facing leg and drove forward with all his might until the burly man toppled backward to the marble floor. The guard was well trained, though, and swept his leg toward Janson's feet, knocking him to the floor as well. His spine jangling from the impact, Janson scrambled to his feet again and stepped forward, delivering a powerful kick to the man's groin and keeping his leg planted between his thighs. With his right hand, he pulled out the guard's left leg as, with his left hand, he bent the man's other leg at the knee, folding it so that the ankle went over his other knee. There was a look of fury and fear on the man's face as he thrashed violently against Janson's grip, battering him with his hands: he knew what Janson was attempting, and would do anything to prevent it. Yet Janson would not be deterred. Coldly following *method* when every instinct called for the simplicities of collision or retreat, he lifted the man's straightened leg up and over his own knee for leverage, and wrenched it with all his strength until he heard the joint break. From beneath the wet sheaths of muscle, the sound was not like a piece of wood snapping; it was a quiet popping sound, accompanied by the tactile sense, the sudden *give* as the ligament of a complicated joint tore irremediably.

The man opened his mouth as if to scream, the excruciating pain reinforced by his awareness that he had just been maimed for life. The knee was broken and would never work quite properly again. Combat injuries usually produced their greatest pain afterward; endorphins and stress hormones dampened much of the acute agony at the time the injuries were inflicted. But the figure-four leg lock had its intended consequence, and the agony of the break was, Janson knew, often sufficient to induce unconsciousness by itself. The guard was no ordinary specimen, however, and his powerful arms were forming grapple hooks even as the pain convulsed him. Janson dropped abruptly, pitching forward so that his knees hit the man's face with the weight of his body. It was an anvil blow. Janson heard the man's quick expulsion of breath as unconsciousness overtook him.

He picked up the silenced revolver—it was, he now saw, a CZ-75, a highly effective handgun of Czech manufacture—and shoved it awkwardly into his deep breast pocket.

There was a knock on the door—dimly, he realized there had been such knocks earlier, which the focus of his mind had not permitted to register—and there were urgent Magyar mutterings as well: guests in need of relief. Janson lifted the burly guard and carefully positioned him on one of the toilets, pulling his trousers down around his ankles. The upper body lolled against the wall, but only his lower extremities would be visible to the guests. He latched the door from the inside, slid underneath the partition, and retracted the dead bolt of the rest room. He walked out to the baleful glares of four florid-faced diners and shrugged apologetically.

The bulky revolver was pressed uncomfortably against his chest; Janson buttoned the lowermost button of his jacket, and that one only. At the end of the hallway, he saw the two bodyguards who had been at the bar. From their expressions—dismay turning to congealed hatred—he saw that they had expected to assist their colleague in escorting a "drunk" from the restaurant. As he turned the corner to the dining room, one of them, the taller of the two, stepped directly in front of him.

The man's hatchet face was perfectly expressionless as he spoke to Janson in quiet, accented English. "You'll want to be *extremely* careful. My partner has a gun trained on you. Very powerful, very silent. The rate of heart attacks is very high in this country. Nonetheless, if you are stricken,

it will attract some attention. I should not prefer it. There are more grace-
ful ways. But we will not think twice about dealing with you right here."

Drifting in from the main dining room were the sounds of merriment
and the festive tune that had become universal in the past century, "Happy
Birthday to You." *Boldog szuletesnapot!* he heard. The song lost nothing
in the Hungarian, Janson was sure, recalling the large table filled with a
couple of dozen revelers, a table on which four frosty bottles of champagne
had been assembled.

Now with a look of stark terror on his face, Janson placed both his
hands on his chest, in a theatrical gesture of fright. At the same time, he
slipped his right hand beneath his left hand, stealing toward the handgrip
of the bulky firearm.

He waited another moment for the other sound associated with celebration, at least as much in Hungary as elsewhere: the pop of a champagne
cork. It arrived a moment later, the first of the four bottles that would be
opened. At the sound of the next popped cork, Janson squeezed the trigger
of the silenced revolver.

A soft *phut* was lost among the clamorous festivities, but now a horrifed
look appeared on the gunman's face. Janson was conscious of the tiny
corona of woolen threads puffing out from a barely visible hole in his
jacket as the man collapsed to the floor. An abdominal injury alone would
not cause a professional to plummet as he did. The immediate collapse
could mean only one thing: the bullet had plowed through his upper
abdomen and lodged in his spine. The result was the immediate cessation
of neural impulses, and the resultant paralysis of all muscles of the body's
lower regions. Janson was familiar with the telltale signs of complete cat-
aplexy and numbness, and he knew what the experience uniquely did to
combatants, even hardened ones: they *mourned.* They mourned what they
recognized to be the irreversible loss of their physicality, sometimes even
forgetting to take measures to prevent the loss of their very lives.

"Take your hand from your pocket, or you're next," he told the man's
partner in a harsh whisper.

The authority of his voice, more than the gun in his grip, was his
ultimate weapon here, Janson knew. In theory, theirs was a Mexican standoff, two men with their fingers on short triggers. There was no logical
reason for the other man to stand down. Yet Janson knew that he would.
Janson's actions were unexpected, as was his confidence. Too many factors
could underlie this confidence and they could not be assessed with any
certainty: Did Adam Kurzweil know that he would be able to squeeze off

a shot faster? Was he perhaps wearing concealable soft body armor? Two seconds were not enough to make such an evaluation. And the penalty of guessing wrong was starkly visible. Janson saw the man's eyes dart toward his ashen-faced, immobilized partner . . . and the spreading pool of urine around him. The loss of urinary continence indicated the severing of the sacral nerves caused by an injury to a mid- or lower-spinal vertebra.

The man held out his hands before him, looking sickened, humiliated, scared.

*If your enemy has a good idea, steal it,* Lieutenant Commander Alan Demarest used to say, referring to the wily snares of their Viet Cong adversaries; and it came to Janson's mind, along with a darker thought: *When you gaze too long into an abyss, the abyss will gaze back.* What they had planned for him, he would use on them, including even the burly guard's silenced CZ-75.

"Don't just stand there," Janson said softly, leaning in close to the man's ear. "Our friend has just had a heart attack. Common in your country, as he was just explaining. You're going to lift this man, let him lean against you, and together we're going to walk out of the restaurant." As he spoke, he buttoned the fallen man's jacket, ensuring that the splash of blood was concealed beneath it. "And if I can't see both your hands, you'll find that the attack is contagious. Perhaps the diagnosis will be changed to acute food poisoning. And you two will be shopping for wheelchairs together— *assuming either of you lives.*"

What ensued was ungainly but effective: one man supporting his stricken companion, moving him swiftly out of the restaurant. Sandor Lakatos, Janson saw as they rounded the corner, was no longer at his table. *Danger.*

Janson suddenly reversed direction and dove through the double doors to the restaurant's kitchen. The din was surprisingly loud: there were the noises of meat sizzling in oil, of fluids boiling, of knives rapidly chopping onions and tomatoes, of veal cutlets being pounded, dishes being washed. He paid little attention to the white-coated men and women at their stations as he raced through the kitchen. He knew there had to be some sort of service entrance. It was impossible that the supplies to this kitchen arrived through the exquisitely carpeted lobby.

At the far end, he found the rusty metal stairs, cramped and steep. They led to an unlocked steel panel, flush with the ground overhead. Janson barged through, and the night air felt cool on his skin after the steamy warmth of the kitchen.

He closed the steel panel doors as quietly as he could and looked around him. He was on the rear right side of the Palace Hotel, next to the parking lot. As his eyes adjusted, he saw that twenty yards ahead of him were long-limbed trees and grass: concealment, but not protection.

A *sound*—a scraping noise. Someone moving with his back to the wall, his feet planted firmly on the ground. *Someone who was moving toward him.* The person knew he was armed, and was taking all possible precautions.

He felt the stinging spray of brick and mortar against his face before he heard the cough of the gun. His assailant had gained an angle on him! His assailant was three hundred feet away; accuracy would be paramount. He had, he calculated, four seconds to assume the rollover prone position. Four seconds.

Janson dropped to both knees and extended his left hand in front of him to break his fall as he pitched forward; then he extended his firing arm downrange and rested it upon the ground, rolling up on his right side as he did so. With his left ankle braced against the back of his right knee, he stabilized his position. Now he was able to put his supporting hand on the weapon, the heel of his palm firmly and squarely on the packed-gravel ground: it would provide a solid shooting rest as he placed his forefinger inside the trigger guard of the CZ-75. What the Czech gun lacked in concealability, it made up for in stopping power and accuracy. It would enable far more accurate cluster shooting than his own palm-sized weapon.

He identified his target—it was the suited guard he had just left below—and squeezed off two shots. They were silenced, but the recoil reminded him of just how much force they conveyed. One missed his target; the other struck him in the neck, and the man sprawled to the ground, spouting blood.

A muted explosion came from behind him: Janson tensed until he realized that it was the tire of an SUV ten feet away, abruptly deflating as a bullet struck it. There was another gunman stalking him, it appeared, and the direction of the impact plus the geometry of the building told him approximately where he was situated.

Still in the rollover prone firing position, Janson pivoted thirty degrees and saw Sandor Lakatos himself, holding a gleaming, nickel-plated Glock 9mm. *The preening peacock,* he thought to himself. The shiny surface reflected the light of the parking lot halogens, making him an easier target. Janson aligned the gun's small sights along the man's round torso and he felt his gun buck as he squeezed off another two shots.

Lakatos returned fire spasmodically, the muzzle flash leaving a dark shadow in Janson's night vision, and he heard the thunk of one of the Hungarian's bullets hitting the hard-packed gravel a few inches from his right leg. He was proving a deadly adversary after all. Had Janson missed? Was the man protected by body armor?

Then he heard Lakatos breathing hard, heaving as he slowly sank to the ground. Janson's bullets had struck him in the lower chest and punctured his lungs, which were slowly filling up with the resultant hemorrhage. The merchant of death was too wise not to know precisely what was happening to him: he was drowning in his own blood.

# CHAPTER TWENTY-THREE

"Goddamn you, Paul Janson," said Jessie Kincaid. He was driving the rented car at just under the speed limit while she kept an eye on the map. They were making their way to Budapest, headed for the National Archives, but doing so via a circuitous route, keeping off the main roads. "You should have let me come. I should have *been* there."

Having finally elicited the details of what had happened last night, she was steamed and reproachful.

"You don't know what sort of trip wires there might be at a rendezvous like that," Janson said patiently, his eyes regularly scanning the rearview mirror for any signs of unwanted company. "Besides, the meeting was in an underground restaurant, out of range of any perimeter stakeout. Would you have parked your M40A1 on the bar, or checked it in the cloakroom?"

"Maybe I couldn't have helped inside. Outside's different. Plenty of trees around, plenty of perches. It's a game of odds, you know that better'n anyone. Point is, it would have been a sensible precaution. You didn't take it."

"It represented an unnecessary risk."

"Damn straight."

"To you, I mean. There was no reason to put you at risk unnecessarily."

"So instead you exposed yourself to that risk. That don't seem exactly professional. What I'm saying is, *use* me. Treat me like a partner."

"A partner? Reality check. You're twenty-nine. You've been in the field for how many years, exactly? Don't take this the wrong way, but—"

"I'm not saying we're equals. All I'm saying is, *teach* me. I'll be the best student you ever had."

"You want to be my protégée?"

"I love it when you speak French."

"Let me tell you something. I've had a protégé or two in my time. They've got something in common."

"Lemme guess. They're all men."

Janson shook his head grimly. "They're all dead." In the distance, nineteenth-century church spires were interspersed with Soviet-era tower blocks: symbols of aspiration that had outlived the aspirations themselves.

"So your idea is, keep me at arm's length and you'll keep me alive." She turned in her seat and faced him. "Well, I don't buy it."

"They're all *dead*, Jessie. That's my contribution to their career advancement. I'm talking about good people. Hell, extraordinary people. Gifted as you can get. Theo Katsaris—he had the potential to be *better* than me. Only, the better you are, the higher the stakes. I wasn't just reckless with my own life. I've been reckless with the lives of others."

" 'Every operation with potential benefits also has potential risks. The art of planning centers on the coordination of these two zones of uncertainty.' You wrote that in a field report once."

"I'm flattered by the way you boned up on me. But there are a few chapters you seemed to have skipped: Paul Janson's protégés have a nasty habit of getting killed."


The National Archives were housed in a block-long neo-Gothic building; its narrow windows of intricately leaded glass were set in cathedral-like arches, sharply limiting the amount of sunlight that reached the documents within. Jessie Kincaid had taken to heart Janson's idea of beginning at the beginning.

She had a list of missing information that might help them unravel the mystery of the Hungarian philanthropist. Peter Novak's father, Count Ferenczi-Novak, was said to have been obsessively fearful for his child's safety. Fielding had told Janson that the count had made enemies who, he was convinced, would seek to revenge themselves against his scion. Is that what had finally happened, half a century later? The Cambridge don's words had the keenness of a blade: *The old nobleman may have been paranoid, but as the old saw has it, even paranoids have enemies.* She wanted to retrace the count's movements back in those fateful years when the Hungarian government underwent such bloody tumult. Were there visa records that might indicate private trips that Novak's father had made, with or without his son? But the most important information they could get would be genealogical: Peter Novak was said to be concerned with protecting the surviving members of his family—a typical sentiment among those who had seen such destruction in their tenderest years. Yet who *were* these relations—were there surviving cousins with whom he might have kept in touch? The family history of Count Ferenczi-Novak

might be mired in obscurity, but it would repose somewhere in the vastness of Hungary's National Archives. If they had the names of these unknown relatives and could locate them, they might get an answer to the
most vexing question of all: was the real Peter Novak alive or dead?

Janson dropped her off in front of the National Archives building; he had
some dealings of his own to conduct. Years in the field had given him an instinct for where to find the black-market vendors of false identity papers
and other instruments that could come in handy. He might or might not get
lucky, he told her, but decided he might as well give it a try.

Now Jessica Kincaid, dressed simply in jeans and a forest green polo
shirt, found herself inside an entrance hall, scanning a chart of the Archives' holdings that hung beside a vast and intimidating list of sections.

> *Archives of the Hungarian Chancellery (1414–1848) I. "B."*
> *Records of Government Organs between 1867 and 1945 II. "L."*
> *Government Organs of the Hungarian Soviet Republic (1919) II.*
>     *"M."*
> *Records of the Hungarian Working People's Party (MDP) and the*
>     *Hungarian Socialist Workers' Party (MSZMP) VII. "N."*
> *Archivum Regnicolaris (1222–1988) I. "O."*
> *Judicial Archives (13th century–1869) I. "P." Archives of Families,*
>     *Corporations and Institutions (1527–20th century).*

And the list went on.

Jessie pushed through the next door, where a large room was filled with
catalogs, tables, and, along the walls, perhaps a dozen counters. At each
counter was an archival clerk, whose job was to deal with requests from
members of the public and certified researchers alike. Over one counter
was a sign in English, indicating that it was an information desk for
English-speaking visitors. There was a short line in front of the desk, and
she watched a bored, coarse-featured clerk deal with his supplicants. As
best she could tell, the "information" he dispensed consisted largely of
explanations of why the information sought could be not provided.

"You're telling me that your great-grandfather was born in Székesfehérvár in 1870," he was saying to a middle-aged Englishwoman in a
checked woolen jacket. "How nice for him. Unfortunately, at that time,
Székesfehérvár had more than a hundred and fifty parishes. This is not
enough information to find the record."

The Englishwoman moved on with a heavy sigh.

A short, round American man had his hopes dashed almost as summarily.

"Born in Tata in the 1880s or '90s," the clerk repeated, with a reptilian smile. "You would like us to look through every register from 1880 to 1889?" Sardonicism turned to umbrage. "That is *simply* impossible. That is *not* a reasonable thing to expect. Do you understand how many kilometers of material we house? We cannot do research without something far more specific to guide us."

When Jessie reached the counter, she simply handed him a sheet of paper on which she had neatly written precise names, locations, dates. "You're not going to tell me you're going to have a hard time finding these records, are you?" Jessie gave him a dazzling smile.

"The necessary information is here," the clerk admitted, studying the paper. "Let me just make a call to verify."

He disappeared into an inventory annex that extended behind his counter, and returned a few minutes later.

"So sorry," he said. "Not available."

"How do you mean, not available?" Jessie protested.

"Regrettably, there are certain . . . lacunae in the collections. There were serious losses toward the end of the Second World War—fire damage. And then to protect it, some of the collection was stored in the crypt of St. Steven's Cathedral. This was meant to be a safe place, and many files remained there for decades. Unfortunately, the crypt was very damp, and much of what had been there was destroyed by fungus. Fire and water— opposites, yet both formidable enemies." The clerk threw up his hands, pantomiming regret. "These records of Count Ferenczi-Novak's—they belonged to a section that was destroyed."

Jessie was persistent. "Isn't there some way you could double-check?" She wrote a cell phone number on the paper and underlined it. "If anything turns up, anywhere, I would be just so grateful. . . ." Another dazzling smile. "So grateful."

The clerk bowed his head, his frosty manner beginning to melt; evidently he was unaccustomed to being on the receiving end of a young woman's charms. "Certainly. But I am not hopeful, and neither should you be."


Three hours later, the clerk called the number. His pessimism, he confessed to Jessie, had perhaps been premature. He explained that he had sensed that this was a matter of particular importance to her, and thus made a special effort to ascertain that the records had indeed been lost. Given the vastness of the National Archives, after all, a certain amount of misfiling was inevitable.

Jessie listened to the long-winded clerk with mounting excitement. "You mean to say you've turned them up? We can get access to them?"

"Well, not exactly," the clerk said. "A curious thing. For some reason, the records were removed to a special section. The locked section. I'm afraid access to these files is strictly regulated. It would simply be impossible for a member of the public to be allowed to see this material. All sorts of high-level ministerial certifications and documents of exception would be required."

"But that's plain silly," Jessie said.

"I understand. Your interests are genealogical—it seems absurd that such records are treated like state secrets. I myself believe it to be another instance of misfiling—or miscategorization, anyway."

"Because it would just break me up, having come all this way," Jessie began. "You know, I can't tell you how *grateful* I'd be if you could see a way to help." She pronounced the word *grateful* with infinite promise.

"I think I am too softhearted," the clerk said with a sigh. "Everyone says so. It is my great weakness."

"I could just tell," Jessie said in a sugary tone.

"An American woman alone in this strange city—it must all be very bewildering."

"If only there was somebody who could show me the sights. A real native. A real Magyar man."

"For me, helping others isn't just a job." His voice had a warm glow. "It's—well, it's who I am."

"I knew it as soon as I met you. . . ."

"Call me Istvan," said the clerk. "Now, let's see. What would be simplest? You have a car, yes?"

"Sure do."

"Parked where?"

"At the garage across the street from the Archives building," Jessie lied. The five-story garage complex was a massive structure of poured concrete, its ugliness compounded by the contrast with the splendors of the Archives building.

"Which level?"

"Fourth."

"Say I meet you there in an hour. I'll have copies of these records in my briefcase. If you like, we might even go for a drive afterward. Budapest is a very *special* city. You'll see how special."

"*You're* special," said Jessie.


With a reluctant mechanical noise, the elevator door opened on a floor two-thirds filled with cars. One of the cars was the yellow Fiat she had parked there half an hour ago. It was shortly before the appointed time, and nobody else was around.

Or *was* there somebody?

Where had she parked the car, anyway? She'd come up a different elevator this time, on the opposite end of the lot. As she looked around, she noticed in her peripheral vision a darting motion—someone's head ducking down, she realized a split second later. It was a hallmark of bad surveillance: being noticed by trying too hard not to be. Or was she jumping to conclusions? Perhaps it was an ordinary thief, someone trying to steal a hubcap, a radio; such thefts were prevalent in Budapest.

But these alternate possibilities were irrelevant. To underestimate the risks was to increase them. She had to get out of there, quickly. How? The odds were too great that someone was watching the elevators. She needed to *drive* out—in a different car from the one she had taken in.

She casually walked between an aisle of cars, and suddenly dropped to the ground, cushioning her fall with her hands. She crawled, at tire level, arms and legs moving together. Flattening herself toward the ground, she made her way between two cars to the adjoining aisle and scurried rapidly toward where she had seen the ducking man.

She was behind him now, and as she approached she could see his slender figure. He was not the clerk; presumably, he was whomever the clerk's controller had arranged to send in his place. The man was standing upright now, looking around, confusion and anxiety written on his middle-aged face. His eyes moved wildly, from the exit ramps to the elevator doors. Now he was squinting, trying to see through the windshield of the yellow Fiat.

He had been tricked, knew it, and knew, too, that if he did not reclaim the advantage, he would have to face the consequences.

She sprang up and flung herself at him from behind, throwing the man down on the concrete, vising his neck in a hammerlock. There was a crunch as his jaw hit the floor.

"Who else you got waiting for me?" she demanded.

"Just me," the man replied. Jessie felt a chill.

He was an American.

She flipped him over and dug the muzzle of her pistol into his right eye. "Who's out there?"

"Two guys on the street, right in front," he said. "Stop! Please! You're blinding me!"

"Not yet I'm not," she said. "When you're blinded, you'll know. Now tell me what they look like." The man said nothing, and she pressed the muzzle in harder.

"One's got short blond hair. Big guy. The other . . . brown hair, crew cut, square chin."

She eased up on the pressure. An interception team outside. Jessie recognized the basics of the stakeout. The thin man would have a car of his own on this level: he was here to observe, and when Jessie drove to the exit ramp, he would be in his car, a discreet distance behind her.

"*Why?*" Jessie asked. "Why are you doing this?"

A defiant look. "Janson knows why—he knows what he did," he spat. "We remember Mesa Grande."

"Oh Christ. Something tells me we ain't got time to get into this shit right now," Jessie said. "Now here's what's going to happen. You're going to get into your car and drive me out of here."

"What car?"

"No wheels? If you won't be driving, you won't be needing to *see*." She pressed the pistol into his right eye socket again.

"The blue Renault," he gasped. "Please stop!"

She got into the backseat of the sedan as he got into the driver's seat. She slumped low, out of sight, but kept her Beretta Tomcat pointed at him; he knew that the slug would easily penetrate the seat, and followed her commands. They sped down the spiraling ramp until they approached the glass booth and the orange-painted wooden lever-gate blocking the way.

"Crash it!" she yelled. "Do just what I said!"

The car rammed through the insubstantial barrier and roared out onto the street. She heard the footsteps of racing men.

Through the rearview mirror, Jessie was able to make out one of them—crew cut, square-jawed, just as he'd described. He had been stationed at the other end of the street. As the car hurtled in the opposite direction, he spoke rapidly into some kind of communicator.

Suddenly the front windshield spiderwebbed, and the car started to careen out of control. Jessie peered between the two front seats and saw a large blond-haired man several yards off to the side in front of them, holding a long-barreled revolver. He had just squeezed off two shots.

The American at the steering wheel was dead; she could see blood oozing from an exit wound in the rear of his skull. They must have figured out that what had happened was not according to plan—that the thin man had been taken hostage—and resorted to drastic action.

Now the driverless car drifted through the busy intersection, cutting across lines, rolling into traffic. There was a deafening cacophony of blaring horns, squealing brakes.

A tractor-trailer, its powerful horn blasting like a ship's, missed hitting the car by a few feet.

If she kept down, out of range, she risked a serious collision with onrushing traffic. If she tried to clamber to the front seat and take control of the vehicle, she would likely get shot in the attempt.

A few seconds later, the car, moving ever more slowly, rolled through the intersection, across the four lanes of traffic, and crashed gently into a parked car. Jessie was almost relieved when she felt herself slammed against the back of the bucket seats, for it meant that the car had come to a stop. Now she opened the door on the side nearer the street—and she *ran,* ran along the sidewalk, weaving in and out of groups of pedestrians.

It was fifteen minutes before she was absolutely convinced that they had lost her. At the same time, the requisites of survival had trumped the requisites of investigation. Yes, they had lost her, but the converse was also true, she realized with a pang: she had lost them.


They rejoined each other in the spartan accommodations of Griff Hotel, a converted workers' hostel on the street Bartók Béla.

Jessie had with her a volume she'd picked up somewhere along her wanderings. It was apparently a sort of tribute to Peter Novak, and though the text was in Hungarian, there wasn't much of it: it was basically a picture book.

Janson picked it up and shrugged. "Looks like it's for die-hard fans," he said. "A Peter Novak coffee-table book. So what'd you find out at the Archives?"

"A dead end," she said.

He looked at her closely, saw her face mottled with apprehension. "Spill," he said.

Haltingly, she told him what had happened. It had become obvious that the clerk was on the payroll of whoever was trying to stop them, that he'd sounded the alarm and then set her up.

He listened with growing dismay, bordering on fury. "You shouldn't have done it alone," Janson said, trying to maintain his equipoise. "A meeting like that—you had to have known the risks. You can't go free-lancing like that, Jessie. It's damn reckless. . . ." He broke off, trying to control his breathing.

Jessie tugged on an ear. "Am I hearing an echo?"

Janson sighed. "Point taken."

"So," she said after a while, "what's Mesa Grande?"

"Mesa Grande," he repeated, and his mind became crowded with images that time had never faded.

*Mesa Grande:* the high-security military prison installation in the eastern foothills of California's Inland Empire region. The white crags of the San Bernardino Mountains visible in the near horizon, dwarfing the small, low-slung beige-brick buildings. The dark blue outfit the prisoner had been made to wear, with the white cloth circle attached by Velcro to the center of his chest. The special chair, with a pan beneath it to catch blood, and head restraints that were attached loosely to the prisoner's neck. The pile of sandbags behind, to absorb the volley and prevent ricochets. Demarest had faced a wall, twenty feet away—a wall with firing ports for each of the six members of the squad. Six men with rifles. The wall was what he had protested most about. Demarest had insisted on execution by firing squad, and his preference had been accommodated. Yet he also wanted to be able to see his executioners face-to-face: and this time he had been refused.

Now Janson took another deep breath. "Mesa Grande is where a bad man met a bad end."

A bad end, and a defiant one. For on Demarest's face there had indeed been defiance—no, more than that: a wrathful indignation—until the volley was loosed, and the white cloth circle turned bright red with his blood.

Janson had *asked* to witness the execution, for reasons that remained murky even to him, and the request had reluctantly been granted. To this day, Janson could not decide whether he had made the right decision. It no longer mattered: Mesa Grande, too, was part of who he was. Part of who he had become.

To him, it had represented a moment of requital. A moment of justice to repay injustice. To others, so it appeared, that moment meant something altogether different.

Mesa Grande.

Had the monster's devoted followers gotten together, somehow decided to avenge his death all these years later? The idea seemed preposterous. That did not, alas, mean it could be dismissed. Demarest's Devils: perhaps these veterans were among the mercenaries that Novak's enemies had recruited. How better to counter one disciple of Demarest's techniques than with another?

*Madness!*

He knew that Jessie wanted to hear more from him, but he could not bring himself to speak. All he said was "We need to make an early start tomorrow. Get some sleep." And when she placed a hand on his arm, he pulled away.

Turning in, he felt roiled by shadowy ghosts he could never put to rest, however hard he tried.

In life, Demarest had taken too much of his past; in death, would he now take his future?

# CHAPTER TWENTY-FOUR

It was three decades ago, and it was now. It was in a jungle far away, and it was here.

Always, the sounds: the mortar fire more distant and muffled than ever before, for the trail had led them many miles away from the official combat zones. Immediate proximity made the sounds of mosquitoes and other small stinging insects louder than the immense blasts of the heavy artillery. Cheap ironies were as thick on the ground as punji sticks, the sharpened bamboo stakes that the VC placed in small, concealed holes, awaiting the unwary footfall.

Janson checked his compass once again, verified that the trail had been leading in the correct direction. The triple-canopy jungle left the ground in permanent twilight, even when the sun was shining. The six men in his team moved in three pairs, each spaced a good ways apart, the better to avoid the vulnerability of clustering in hostile territory. Only he traveled without a partner.

"Maguire," he radioed, quietly.

He never heard the response. What he heard, instead, was automatic rifle fire, the overlapping staccato bursts of several ComBloc carbines.

Then he heard the screaming of men—his men—and the barking commands of an enemy patrol party. He was reaching for his M16 when he felt a blow to the back of his head. And then he felt nothing at all.

He was at the bottom of a deep, black lake, drifting slowly along the silt like a carp, and he could stay there forever, swathed in the muddy blackness, cool and close to motionless, but something began to drag him toward the surface, away from his comforting and silent underwater world, and the light began to hurt his eyes, began to sear his skin, even, and he struggled to stay below, but the forces that drew him up were irresistible, buoyancy dragging him up like a grappling hook, and he opened his eyes only to see another pair of eyes upon him, eyes like bore holes. And he knew that his world of water had given way to a world of pain.

He tried to sit up, and failed—from weakness, he assumed. He tried again, and realized that he was tied, roped to a litter, rough canvas stretched between two poles. He was stripped of his trousers and tunic. His head swam and his focus wavered; he recognized the signs of a head injury, knew there was nothing he could do about it.

A harsh exchange in Vietnamese. The eyes belonged to an officer, either of the NVA or the Viet Cong. He was a captive American soldier, and there was clarity in that. From some distance came the static of a short-wave radio, like a section of tuneless violins: the volume waxed and waned until he realized that it was his perception, not the sound, that was shifting, that his consciousness was zoning in and out. A black-clad soldier brought him rice gruel and spooned it into his parched mouth. He felt, absurdly, grateful; at the same time, he realized that he was an asset to them, a potential source of information. To extract that information was their job; to prevent them from extracting it, while keeping himself alive, was his. Besides, he knew, amateur interrogators would sometimes reveal more information than they elicited. He told himself that he would have to use his powers of concentration . . . when they returned. Assuming they ever did.

A bit of the rice gruel caught in his throat, and he realized it was a beetle that had fallen into the pasty substance. A half smile flickered on the face of the soldier who fed him—the indignity of feeding a Yank made up for by the indignity of what he was feeding him—but Janson was past caring.

"*Xin loi*," the soldier said, cruel as a jackknife. One of the few Vietnamese idioms Janson knew: *Sorry about that.*

*Xin loi.* Sorry about that: it was the war in a nutshell. Sorry we destroyed the village in order to save it. Sorry we napalmed your family. Sorry we tortured those POWs. *Sorry about that*—a phrase for every occasion. A phrase nobody ever meant. The world would be a better place if someone could say it and mean it.

Where was he? Some sort of Montagnard hut, was it? Abruptly, a greasy cloth was wrapped around his head, and he felt himself unroped and dragged down, dragged under—not to the bottom of the lake, as in his dream, but into a tunnel, burrowed around and beneath the shallow tree roots of the jungle soil. He was dragged until he started to crawl, simply to spare his flesh the abrasion. The tunnel veered one way and then another; it sloped upward and downward and intersected with others; voices grew muffled and close, then very distant; smells of tar and kerosene and rot alternated with the fetor of unwashed men. When he reemerged into the insect symphony of the jungle floor—for it was the sound of insects that told him he had left the network of tunnels—he was trussed up again and lifted onto a chair. The cloth around his head was removed, and he breathed deeply the clammy air. The rope was coarse, the sort of hemp twine used for tying river sloops to bamboo docks, and it bit into his wrists, his ankles. Small insects hovered around the fretwork of small cuts and abrasions that covered his exposed flesh. His T-shirt and under-pants—that was all he had been left with—were encrusted with dirt from the tunnels.

A large-boned man with eyes that looked small beneath his steel-framed glasses approached him.

"Where . . . others?" Janson's mouth was cottony.

"Members of your death squad? *Dead.* Only you safe."

"You're Viet Cong?"

"That is *not* correct term. We represent Central Committee of the Na-tional Liberation Front."

"National Liberation Front," Janson repeated, his cracked lips forming words only with difficulty.

"Why you not wear dog tags?"

Janson shrugged, prompting an immediate whack with a bamboo stick across the back of his neck. "Must've got lost."

Two guards stood to either side of the scowling interrogator. They each carried AK-47s and a link-belt of rounds around their waists; a Makarev 9.5mm pistol hung just below the ammo belt. One of them had clipped to his belt a U.S. Navy SEALs combat knife, the six-inch blade gleaming. Janson recognized the scars on its Tenite handle; it was his.

"You lie!" the interrogator said. His eyes darted toward the man stand-ing behind Janson—Janson could not see him, but he could smell him, could feel his body heat even through the heat of the moist jungle air—and a crushing blow struck Janson's side. The barrel of a rifle, he guessed. A bolt of agony shot through his side.

He had to concentrate—not on his interrogator but on something else. Through the bamboo struts of the hut, he could see large flat leaves drip-ping with water. He was a leaf; whatever fell upon him would drip off like beads of water.

"We hear about your special soldiers who do not wear tags."

"Special? I wish." Janson shook his head. "No. I lost it. Snagged on a thornbush while I was bellying through your trails."

The interrogator looked annoyed. He moved his chair closer to Janson and leaned forward. He tapped Janson on his left forearm, and then his right. "You can choose," he said. "Which one?"

"Which one what?" Janson asked dazedly.

"Not to decide," the rawboned man said somberly, "is to decide." He glanced up at the man behind Janson and said something in Vietnamese. "We break your right arm," he told Janson, explaining almost tenderly.

The blow arrived with sledgehammer force: a barrel unscrewed from a machine gun deployed as a weapon itself. His wrist and elbow were supported by the bamboo of his chair; the bone of his forearm extended between those two points. It gave way like a dry branch. The bone had split from the blow: he knew it from a soft crunching noise that he felt rather than heard—and from the horrendous pain that surged up his arm, taking his breath away.

He wriggled his fingers, to see whether they would still obey him; they did. Bone but not nerve had been severed. Yet his arm was largely useless now.

The noise of metal sliding against metal alerted him to what was to happen next: a two-inch-thick bar was inserted through the heavy irons around his ankles. Next, the unseen torturer tied a rope around the bar, looped it over Janson's shoulders, and pulled his head down between his knees, even while his arms remained bound to the arms of the chair. The torque on his shoulder was a growing agony, vying with the pulsating pain of his broken forearm.

He waited for the next question. But minutes elapsed, and there was only silence. The gloom turned into darkness. Breathing became even more difficult, as his diaphragm strained against his folded body, and his shoulders felt as if they were in a vise that narrowed and narrowed without end. Janson passed out, and regained consciousness, but it was consciousness only of pain. It was light outside—had morning come? Afternoon? Yet he was alone. He was only half-conscious when his bonds were loosened and bamboo gruel was poured into his mouth. His underpants had been cut off him now, and a rusty metal bucket was placed on the ground beneath the stool. Then the loop was tightened again, the loop that bound his shoulders to the ankle irons, that forced his head between his knees, that threatened to tear his arms from his shoulders. He repeated a mantra to himself: *Clear like water, cool like ice.* As his shoulders burned, he thought about the summer weeks he had spent ice fishing in Alaska as a child. He thought of the emerald beads on the huge flat jungle leaves, the way they dripped away, leaving nothing behind. Later still, two boards were tied to his broken arm with twine, as a sort of makeshift cast.

From the inner recesses of his mind, the words of Emerson that Demarest so often quoted returned to him: *Whilst he sits on the cushions of advantages he goes to sleep. When he is pushed, tormented, defeated, he has a chance to learn something.*

And another day passed. And another. And another.

His innards cramped powerfully: the fly-ridden gruel had given him dysentery. He desperately sought to defecate, hoping he could rid himself of the agony that now convulsed his very guts, but his bowels would not move. They harbored their pain greedily. *The enemy within,* Janson thought mordantly.

It was either evening or morning when he heard a voice, once more, in English. His bonds were loosened, and he could now sit up straight once more—a postural shift that initially caused his nerve endings to scream in renewed agony.

"Is that better now? It soon will be, I pray."

A new interrogator, no one he had seen before. It was a small man with quick intelligent eyes. His English was fluid, the accent pronounced but with clipped, crisp articulation. An educated man.

"We know you are not imperialist aggressor," the voice went on. "You are a dupe of the imperialist aggressors." The interrogator came very close; Janson knew that his smell must be offensive to the man—it was foul even to himself—but he evinced no sign of it. The Vietnamese touched Janson's cheek, rough with stubble, and spoke softly. "But you disrespect us when you treat *us* like dupes. Can you understand this?" Yes, he was an educated man, and Janson was his special project. This development alarmed him: it suggested that they had figured out that he was, indeed, no ordinary soldier.

Janson ran his tongue over his teeth; they felt furry and somehow foreign, as if they had been replaced with a set of choppers carved of an old balsa raft. A noise of assent came from his mouth.

"Ask yourself how it was you were captured."

The man walked around him, pacing like a schoolmaster in front of a class. "You see, we are actually very similar, in a way. Both of us are intelligence officers. You have served your cause bravely. I hope the same might be said of me."

Janson nodded. The thought briefly flickered: *In what demented scheme did the torture of a defenseless prisoner count as bravery?* But he quickly stowed it away; it would not help him now; it would cloud his composure, betray an attitude of sedition. *Clear like water, cool like ice.*

"My name is Phan Nguyen, and I think that, really, we are privileged to know each other. Your name is . . ."

"Private Kevin Jones," Janson said. In his moments of lucidity, he had created a whole life behind that name—an infantryman from Nebraska, a little trouble with the law after high school, a pregnant girlfriend at home, a brigade that had got lost and wandered away from where it was supposed to be. The character seemed almost real to him, though it was cobbled together from snippets of popular novels, movies, magazine stories, TV shows. Out of the thousand tales of America, he could craft something that would ring truer than any true American tale. "U.S. Infantry."

The small man flushed as he boxed Janson on his right ear, leaving it bruised and ringing. "Lieutenant Junior Grade Paul Janson," said Phan Nguyen. "Do not undo all the good work you have done."

How did they know his true name and rank?

"You *told* us all this," Phan Nguyen insisted. "You told us *everything.* Have you forgotten, in your delirium? I think so. I think so. This happens often."

Was it possible? Janson locked eyes with Nguyen, and both men saw their suspicions confirmed. Both saw that the other had lied. Janson had revealed *nothing*—or nothing until now. For Nguyen could tell from his reaction, not of fear or perplexity but of rage, that his identification was correct.

Janson had nothing to lose: "Now it is you who lie," he growled. He felt a sharp, stinging *thwack* of the bamboo stick across his upper body, but it was more for show than anything else; Janson had come to be able to judge these minuscule gradations.

"We are practically *colleagues,* you and I. Is that the word? *Colleagues?* I think so. I think so." Phan Nguyen, as it emerged, often said those words, *I think so,* almost beneath his breath: they distinguished questions that did not require voiced assent from those that did. "Now we will speak candidly to each other, as colleagues do. You will drop your lies and fables, on the pain of . . . *pain.*" He seemed pleased with the English idiom, with the way it could be twisted this way and that. "I know you are a brave man. I know you have a high tolerance for suffering. Perhaps you would like us to test just how high, like an experiment?"

Janson shook his head, his innards churning. Suddenly he heaved forward and retched. A small amount of vomit reached the hard-packed

ground. It looked like coffee grounds. A clinical sign of internal hemorrhage.

"No? Just for now, I'm not going to press you for answers. I want you
to ask *yourself* the questions." Phan Nguyen sat down again, looking intently at Janson with his intelligent, curious eyes. "I want you to ask
yourself how it was that you were captured. We knew just where to find
you—that must have puzzled you, no? What you faced wasn't the response of surprised men, was it? So you know what I say is so."

Janson felt another heaving surge of nausea: what Phan Nguyen said
was true. It may have been wrapped in deceit, but the truth remained,
stony and indigestible.

"You say you did not divulge the details of your identity to me. But
that leaves you with a more troubling question. If not you, who? How is
it that we were able to intercept your team and capture a senior officer
of the legendary American counterintelligence division of the legendary
Navy SEALs? How?"

How indeed? There was only one answer: Lieutenant Commander Alan
Demarest had funneled the information to the NVA or its VC allies. He
was too careful a man for the leak to have been inadvertent at this point.
It would have been extraordinarily easy. The information would have been
"accidentally" revealed to one of the ARVN personnel whom Demarest
knew to have close NVA links; it could have been "hidden" in a cache of
papers "accidentally" left behind at a jungle outpost, too hastily decamped
under enemy fire. The details could have been deliberately transmitted via
a code and radio frequency known to the enemy. Demarest had wanted
Janson out of the way; he had *needed* him out of the way. And so he had
taken care of the matter as only he could. The whole mission had been a
goddamn snare, a subterfuge from the master of subterfuge.

*Demarest had done this to him!*

And now the lieutenant commander was no doubt sitting at his desk,
listening to Hildegard von Bingen, and Janson was trussed to a stool in a
VC compound, foul pus oozing from open sores where the rope cut into
his flesh, his body shattered, his mind reeling—reeling, most of all, at the
realization that his ordeal had only begun.

"Well," Phan Nguyen said. "You must concede that our intelligence is
superior. We know so much about your operations that to hold back
would be pointless, like depriving the ocean of a teardrop. Yes, I think so,
I think so." He walked out of the compound, conferring in a low voice
with another officer, and then returned, taking his seat at his chair.

Janson's eyes fell on the man's feet, which didn't touch the ground, and took in the large American lace-ups, the childlike calves.

"You must get used to the fact that you will never return to the United States of America. Soon, I will tell you about Vietnamese history, starting with Trung Trac and Trung Nhi, the joint queens of Vietnam who ousted the Chinese from our lands in thirty-nine A.D.—yes, as far back as that! Before Ho, there were the Trung sisters. Where was America in thirty-nine A.D.? You will come to understand the futility of your government's efforts to suppress the rightful national aspirations of the Vietnamese people. You have many lessons to learn, and you will be well taught. But there is much you must tell us as well. Are we in agreement?"

Janson said nothing.

At an eye signal from the interrogator, a carbine smashed into his left side: another electric bolt of agony.

"Perhaps we can start with something easier and work up to the more advanced subjects. We shall talk about you. About your parents and their role in the capitalist system. About your childhood. About America's abundant popular culture."

Janson paused, and he heard the sound of metal sliding on metal, as the thick steel bar was inserted between his leg irons again.

"No," Janson said. "*No!*" And Janson began to speak. He spoke about what was shown on television and at the movie theaters; Phan Nguyen was particularly interested in what counted as a happy ending, and what sort of endings was permissible. Janson spoke about his childhood in Connecticut; he spoke about his father's life as an insurance executive. The concept intrigued Phan Nguyen, and he grew scholarly and serious, pushing Janson to explain the underlying concepts, parsing the notions of *risk* and *liability* with near Confucian delicacy. Janson might have been telling a fascinated anthropologist about the circumcision rites of the Trobriand Islanders.

"And he led a good American life, your father?"

"He thought so. He made a good living. Owned a nice home, nice car. Could buy the things he wanted to buy."

Phan Nguyen sat back in his chair, and his broad weathered features were alert and quizzical. "And this is what gives meaning to your life?" he asked. He folded his slender, childlike arms around his chest and tilted his head. "Hmm? This is what gives meaning to your life?"

The questioning went on and on—Nguyen refused to call himself an interrogator; he was, he said, a "teacher"—and each day Janson was permitted more and more mobility. He could walk around a small bamboo hut, although always under watchful guard. Then one day, after an almost good-humored discussion of American sports (Nguyen suggested, as if it were self-evident, that in capitalist societies the class struggle was provided imaginary resolution on the playing field), Janson was given a document to sign. It stated that he had been given good medical care and had been kindly treated by the National Liberation Front, whom the document heralded as freedom fighters devoted to peace and democracy. It called for the withdrawal of the U.S. from imperialist wars of aggression. A pen—a fine fountain pen of French manufacture, evidently a legacy of one of the old colonials—was placed in his hand. When he declined to sign the document, he was beaten until he lost consciousness.

And when he regained it, he found himself chained inside a sturdy bamboo cage, six feet tall and four feet in diameter. He could not stand up straight; he could not sit down. He could not move around. He had nothing to do. A pail of brackish water, strewn with ox hair and dead insects, was placed near his feet by a closed-faced guard. He was a bird in a cage, waiting only to be fed.

It would be, he somehow knew, a very long wait.

"*Xin loi*," the guard taunted. *Sorry about that.*

# CHAPTER TWENTY-FIVE

Molnár. The town that history erased.

Molnár. Where it all began.

It now looked like their last hope of finding any link to Peter Novak's origins. The last hope of unraveling the web of deceit that ensnared them.

Yet what, if anything, remained of it?

The route they took the next morning skirted the major cities and highways, and the Lancia groaned and bounced as they drove through the Bükk Hills in northeast Hungary. Jessie seemed preoccupied for much of the time.

"There's something about those men yesterday," she finally said. "Something about the way they set it up."

"The triangle config?" Janson said. "Pretty standard, actually. It's what you do when you've got just three men on hand. Surveillance and blocking. Straight out of the manual."

"That's what's bothering me," she said. "It's straight out of *our* manual."

Janson did not speak for a few moments. "They had Cons Op training," he said.

"Felt that way," Jessie said. "Sure felt that way. And seeing that blond guy blasting away . . ."

"Like he'd anticipated the possibility of your maneuver and was resorting to the countermeasure."

"Felt like it, yeah."

"Very sound, from a tactical point of view. Whatever his reasons, he had to eliminate you or the hostage. Nearly did both. Shooting a colleague like that meant that a hostage—and therefore the possibility of a security breach—was the one thing he couldn't risk."

"I gotta tell you, it's freaking me out," Jessie said. "The whole Cons Op angle. It's like everything's lined up against us. Or maybe it's more complicated than that. Maybe it's like what that creep at the Archives was saying about how records get destroyed. Something about how fire and water are opposites, but they're both enemies."

The terrain grew increasingly hilly; when even the Soviet-era tower blocks had vanished from the horizon, they knew they were approaching their destination. The village of Molnár was near the Tisza River, between Miskolc and Nyíregyháza. Sixty miles to the north was the Slovak Republic; sixty miles to the east was Ukraine and, just beneath it, Romania. At different points in history, all represented expansionist powers—geopolitical predators. The mountains funneled the river; they also funneled whatever armies wished to proceed from the eastern front to the Magyar heartland. The countryside was deceptively beautiful, filled with emerald-like knolls, foothills ramping toward the low, bluish mountains farther away. Here and there, one of the hills swelled to a lofty peak, lower elevations terraced with vineyards, ceding the higher altitudes to the camouflage drab of forests. Yet the landscape was also scarred, in ways that were visible and in ways that were not.

Now they rolled over a small bridge across the Tisza, a bridge that had once connected two halves of the village of Molnár.

"It's unbelievable," Jessie said. "It's *gone*. Like somebody waved a magic wand."

"That would have been a lot kinder than what happened," Janson said. One winter day in 1945, he had read, the Red Army swept down these mountains and one of Hitler's divisions attempted an ambush. The artillery units had been passing through the road along the Tizsa River when the German and Arrow Cross soldiers sought to head them off, failing, but taking many lives in the attempt. The Red Army believed that the villagers of Molnár had known all along of the ambush. A lesson had to be taught to the rural Hungarians in the area, a penalty paid in blood. The village was torched, its inhabitants slaughtered.

When Jessie had scrutinized maps of the region, she found that on the same spot where the prewar maps showed the small village, the contemporary atlases showed nothing at all. Jessie had pored over the densely printed maps with a jeweler's loupe and a draftsman's ruler; there could be no mistake about it. It was an absence that spoke louder than any presence could.

They pulled into a roadside tavern. Inside, two men sat at a long, copper bar, peering into their Dreher pilsners. Their garb was rustic: tattered, muddy-hued cotton shirts and blue dickeys, or some old Soviet version thereof. Neither man looked up as the Americans arrived. The barkeep followed them with his eyes wordlessly. He wore a white apron and busied himself drying beer steins with a gray-looking towel. His receding hairline and the dark indentations beneath his eyes contributed to an impression of age.

Janson smiled. "Speak English?" he called to the man.

The man nodded.

"See, my wife and I, we've been sight-seeing hereabouts. But it's also kind of an explore-your-roots thing. You follow?"

"Your family is Hungarian?" The barkeep's English was accented but unhalting.

"My wife's," Janson said.

Jessie smiled and nodded. "Straight up," she added.

"Is that so?"

"According to family lore, her grandparents were born in a village called Molnár."

"It no longer exists," the barkeep said. He was, Janson saw now, younger than he had first seemed. "And the family's name?"

"Family name was Kis," Janson said.

"Kis is like Jones in Hungary. I'm afraid that does not narrow your search very much." His voice was cool, formal, reserved. Not a typical rural tavernkeeper, Janson decided. As he took a step back from the bar, a blackish horizontal stripe was visible on his apron where his big belly rubbed against the ledge of the bar.

"I wonder whether anybody else might have any memories of the old days," Jessie said.

"Who else is here?" The question was a polite challenge.

"Maybe . . . one of these gentlemen?"

The barkeep gestured toward one with his chin. "He's not even Magyar, really, he's Palóc," he said. "A very old dialect. I can hardly understand him. He understands our word for *money*, and I understand his for *beer*. So we get along. Beyond that, I would not press." He shot a glance toward the other man. "And he's a Ruthenian." He shrugged. "I say no more. His *forints* are as good as any other's. " It was a statement of democratic sentiment that conveyed the opposite.

"I see," Janson said, wondering whether he was being let in on things by being told of the local tensions, or deliberately frozen out. "And there wouldn't be anybody who lives around here and might remember the old days?"

The man behind the bar ran his gray cloth along the inside of another stein, leaving behind a faint beard of lint. "The old days? Before 1988? Before 1956? Before 1944? Before 1920? I think *these* are the old days. They speak of a new era, but I think it is not so new."

"I hear you," Janson said folksily.

"You are visiting from America? Many fine museums in Budapest. And farther west, there are show villages. Very picturesque. Made just for people like you, American tourists. I think this is not such a nice place to visit. I have no postcards for you. Americans, I think, do not like places that do not have postcards."

"Not all Americans," Janson said.

"All Americans like to think they are different," the man said sourly. "One of the many, many ways in which they are all the same."

"That's a very Hungarian observation," Janson said.

The man gave a half smile and nodded. "Touché. But the people around here have suffered too much to be good company. That is the truth. We are not even good company to ourselves. Once upon a time, people would spend the winters staring into their fireplaces. Now we have television sets, and stare into those."

"The electronic hearth."

"Exactly. We can even get CNN and MTV. You Americans complain about drug traffickers in Asia, and meanwhile you flood the world with the electronic equivalent. Our children know the names of your rappers and movie stars, and nothing about the heroes of their own people. Maybe they know who Stephen King is, but they don't know who our King Stephen was—the founder of our nation!" A petulant head shake: "It's an invisible conquest, with satellites and broadcast transmitters instead of artillery. And now you come here because—because why? Because you are bored with the sameness of your lives. You come in search of your roots, because you want to be exotic. But everywhere you go, you find your own spoor. The slime of the serpent is over all."

"Mister," Jessie said. "Are you drunk?"

"I have a graduate degree in English from Debrecen University," he said. "Perhaps it comes to the same." He smiled bitterly. "You are surprised? Tavernkeeper's son can go to university: the glories of communism. University-educated son cannot find job: glories of capitalism. Son works for father: glories of Magyar family."

Jessie turned to Janson and whispered, "Where I come from, people say that if you don't know who the mark is at the table after ten minutes, it's you."

Janson's expression did not change. "This was your dad's place?" he asked the big-bellied man.

"Still is," the man said warily.

"I wonder if he'd have any recollections. . . ."

"Ah, the wizened old Magyar, swilling brandy and spinning sepia pictures like an old nickelodeon? My father is not a local tourist attraction, to be wheeled out for your entertainment."

"You know something?" Jessie said, interrupting. "*I* was once a barkeep. In my country, it's considered you're in the hospitality business." A trace of heat crept into her voice as she spoke. "Now I'm sorry your fancy degree didn't get you a fancy job, and it just tears me up that your kids prefer MTV to whatever Magyar hootenannies you got for them, but—"

"Honey," Janson interjected, with a warning tone. "We'd better hit the road now. It's getting late." With a firm hand on her elbow, he escorted her out the door. As they stepped into the sun, they saw an old man seated on a canvas folding chair on the porch, a look of amusement in his eyes. Had he been there when they arrived? Perhaps so; something about the old man blended into the scenery, as if he were a piece of nondescript furniture.

Now the old man tapped the side of his head, the sign for "loco." His eyes were smiling. "My son is a frustrated man," he said equably. "He wants to ruin me. You see the customers? A Ruthenian. A Palóc. They don't have to listen to him talk. No Magyar would come anymore. Why pay to listen to his sourness?" He had the uncreased, porcelain complexion of certain elderly people, whose skin, thinned but not coarsened by age, acquires an oddly delicate appearance. His large head was fringed with white hair, scarcely more than wisps, and his eyes were a cloudy blue. He rocked back and forth gently in his chair, his smile unwavering. "But Gyorgy is right about one thing. The people around here have suffered too much to be civil."

"Except you," Jessie said.

"I like Americans," the old man said.

"Aren't you the sweetest," Jessie returned.

"It's the Slovaks and the Romanians who can go hang themselves. Also the Germans and the Russians."

"I guess you've seen some hard times," Jessie said.

"I never had Ruthenians in the bar when I was running things." He wrinkled his nose. "I don't like those people," he added, softly. "They're lazy and insolent and do nothing but complain, all day long."

"You should hear what they say about you," she said, leaning in toward him.

"Em?"

"I bet the bar was packed when you were running things. I bet there were lots of ladies flocking there especially."

"Now why would you think that?"

"A good-looking guy like you? I got to spell it out? Bet you *still* get yourself in a heap of trouble with the ladies." Jessie knelt down beside the old man. His smile grew wider; such proximity to a beautiful woman was to be savored.

"I do like Americans," the old man said. "More and more."

"And Americans like *you*," Jessie said, taking his forearm and squeezing it gently. "At least *this* one does."

He drew in a deep breath, inhaling her perfume. "My dear, you smell like the Tokaj of the emperors."

"I'm sure you say that to all the girls," she said, pouting.

He looked severe for a moment. "Certainly not," he said. Then he smiled again. "Only the pretty ones."

"I bet you knew some pretty girls from Molnár once upon a time," she said.

He shook his head. "I grew up farther up the Tisza. Nearer Sárospatak. I moved here only in the fifties. Already, no more Molnár. Just rocks and stones and trees. My son, you see, belongs to the generation of the disappointed. A *csalódottak*. People like me, who survived Béla Kun and Miklós Horthy and Ferenc Szálasi and Mátyás Rákosi—we know when to be grateful. We never had great expectations. So we cannot be greatly disappointed. I have a son who pours beer for Ruthenians all day, but do you see me complaining?"

"We really should be getting along now," Janson put in.

Jessie's eyes did not leave the old man's. "Well, things used to be a whole lot different, I know that. Didn't there used to be some baron from these parts, some old Magyar nobleman?"

"Count Ferenczi-Novak's lands used to stretch up that mountainside." He gestured vaguely.

"Now that must have been a sight. A castle and everything?"

"Once," he said, distractedly. He was not eager for her to leave. "A castle and everything."

"Gosh, I wonder if there'd be anybody alive who might have known that count guy. Ferenczi-Novak, was it?"

The old man was silent a moment, his features looking nearly Asiatic in repose. "Well," he said. "There's the old woman, Grandma Gitta. Gitta Békesi. Can speak English, too. They say she learned as a girl when she worked in the castle. You know how it is—the Russian noblewomen always insisted on speaking French, the Hungarian noblewomen always insisted on speaking English. Everybody always wants to sound like what they aren't. . . ."

"Békesi, you said?" Jessie prompted gently.

"Maybe not such a good idea. Most people say she lives in the past. I can't promise she's all there. But she's all Magyar. Which is more than you can say for some." He laughed, a phlegm-rattling laugh. "Lives in an old farmhouse, the second left, and then another left, up around the bend."

"Can we tell her you sent us?"

"Better not," he said. "I don't want her cross at me. She doesn't like strangers much." He laughed again. "And that's an understatement!"

"Well, you know what we say in America," Jessie said, giving him a soulful look. "There are no strangers here, only friends we haven't met."

The son, his white apron still stretched around his round belly, stepped onto the porch with a look of smoldering resentment. "That's another thing about you Americans," he sneered. "You have an infinite capacity for self-delusion."


Situated halfway up a gently sloping hill, the old two-story brick farmhouse looked like thousands of others that dotted the countryside. It could have been a century old, or two, or three. Once, it might have housed a prosperous peasant and his family. But, as a closer approach made clear, the years had not been kind to it. The roof had been replaced with sheets of rusting, corrugated steel. Trees and vines grew wild around the house, blocking off many of the windows. The tiny attic windows, beneath the roof, had a cataract haze; at some point glass had been replaced with plastic, which was starting to decompose in the sun. A few fissures ran from the foundation halfway up the side of the front wall. Shutters were encrusted with peeling paint. It was hard to believe that anyone lived here. Janson recalled the old man's amused look, the laughter in his eyes, and wondered whether he had played some Magyar prank on them.

"I think that's what you call a fixer-upper," Jessie said.

They pulled the Lancia off to the side of the road—a road that was hardly deserving of the name, for its pavement was crumbled and pitted by neglect. Proceeding on foot, they made their way down what had once been a cow path, now almost impassable with overgrown brambles. The house was nearly a mile down the slope, the very picture of neglect.

As they approached the entrance, though, Janson heard a noise. An eerie, low rumble. After a moment, he recognized it as the growl of a dog. And then they heard a throaty bark.

Through narrow slot glass set into the door, he saw the white figure springing impatiently. It was a Kuvasz, an ancient Hungarian breed, used as a guard dog for more than a millennium. The breed was little known in the West, but it was all too well known to Janson, who years ago had had an encounter with one. Like other canines bred to be guard dogs— mastiffs, pit bulls, Alsatians, Dobermans—they were fiercely protective of their masters and aggressive toward strangers. A fifteenth-century Magyar king was said to trust only his Kuvasz dogs, not people. The breed had a noble build, with its protruding forechest, powerful musculature, long muzzle, and thick white coat. But Janson had seen such white fur stained with human blood. He knew what a slathering Kuvasz was capable of when roused to action. The incisors were sharp, the jaws powerful, and its light-footed stance could instantly become a pounce that seemed to turn the animal into nothing but muscle and teeth.

Gitta Békesi's animal was not the giant creature spoken of in ancient times; it was three feet tall and 120 pounds, Janson estimated. At the moment, it seemed to be pure hostile energy. Few creatures were as deadly as an enraged Kuvasz.

"Mrs. Békesi?" Janson called out.

"Go away!" a quavering voice replied.

"That's a Kuvasz, isn't it?" Janson said. "What a *handsome* animal! There's nothing like them, is there?"

"That handsome animal would like nothing so much as to clamp its jaws around your throat," the old woman said, her voice gaining resolve. It floated through the open window; she herself remained in the shadows.

"It's just that we've traveled a long, long way," Jessie said. "From America? You see, my grandfather, he came from this village called Molnár. People say you're the one person who might be able to tell us something about the place."

There was a long pause, silent save for the rasping growl of the enraged guard dog.

Jessie looked at Janson and whispered. "That dog's really got you spooked, hasn't it?"

"Ask me sometime about Ankara, 1978," Janson replied quietly.

"I know about Ankara."

"Trust me," Janson said. "You don't."

Finally, the woman broke her silence. "Your grandfather," she said. "What was his name?"

"Kis is what the family was called," she said, repeating the deliberately generic name. "But I'm more interested in getting a feel for the place, the world he grew up in. Not necessarily him in particular. Really, I just want something to remember...."

"You lie," she said. "You *lie!*" Her voice was a wail. "Strangers come with *lies*. You should be ashamed of yourself. Now go! Go, or I will *give* you something to remember." They heard the distinctive sound of a shotgun cartridge being chambered.

"Oh shit," Jessie whispered. "What now?"

Janson shrugged. "When all else fails? The truth."

"Hey, lady," Jessie said. "You ever hear of a Count János Ferenczi-Novak?"

A long silence ensued. In a voice like sandpaper, the woman demanded, "Who *are* you?"


Ahmad Tabari was impressed by the rapidity with which the intelligence chief worked. It was now their third meeting, and already Al-Mustashar had started to work his magic.

"We work in phases," the Libyan told him, his eyes bright. "A shipment of small arms is even now on its way toward your men at Nepura." He referred to the port in the northwesternmost point of Kenna. "These arrangements were not easy to broker. I assume that there will be no difficulties with interception. The Anuran gunboats have created some difficulty for your people, have they not?"

The Kagama warrior was cautious in his reply. "One steps back to step forward. Even the Prophet's struggles did not always go smoothly. Otherwise, they would not have been struggles. Remember the Truce of Hudaybiyah." He referred to the compact that Muhammad had made with the denizens of Khaybar, not far from Medina.

Ibrahim Maghur nodded. "Only when the Prophet's troops were strong enough did he break the pact, overrun the Khaybar rulers, and expel the infidels from Arabia." His eyes flashed. "Are your troops strong enough?"

"With your help, and Allah's, they will be."

"You are a Caliph indeed," said Colonel Maghur.

"When first we met, you told me that history was made by great men," the Kagama said after a while.

"This is what I believe."

"It would follow that history can also be *unmade* by great men. Men of power and prominence whose imperial ambitions masquerade as humanitarian compassion. Men who seek to outmaneuver righteous resistance through preachments of peace—who will do whatever they can to suppress the violence that ultimate justice requires."

Maghur nodded slowly. "Your discernment as well as your tactical genius will guarantee your place in the history books, and the ultimate triumph of your struggles on behalf of *ummah*. I understand whom you speak of. He is indeed a true enemy of revolution. Alas, our attempts to strike at him have so far been futile."

"I cannot forget that he was once my prisoner."

"And yet he slipped from your clutches. He is as slippery as the serpent in the garden."

Ahmad Tabari's face tightened at the memory. All his reverses could be traced back to that humiliating blow. The jewel in his crown had been stolen by a thief in the night. Until then, nothing had marred Tabari's aura of inexorable triumph and serene confidence: his followers believed that Allah had himself blessed the Caliph's every move. Yet just a day shy of Id ul-Kebir came the shocking invasion of the Caliph's newly claimed stronghold—and the seizure of his legendary captive. Nothing had gone smoothly since.

"The serpent must be hunted and killed before progress can resume," Maghur said.

Tabari's gaze was distant, but his mind was furiously engaged. A movement like his depended upon the sense that ultimate success was inevitable: the event had shaken that air of inevitability. The diminishment of morale was subsequently exploited by the incursions of the Republic of Anura's troops—and every successful raid of theirs compounded the loss of confidence among the Caliph's followers. It was a vicious circle. A bold act was essential to break out of it. The Libyan understood that. Now Tabari looked at him closely. "And you will provide support?"

"My position in my government is such that I must operate through many veils. Tripoli *cannot* be connected to your activities. There are others, however, whose hospitality can be turned to your advantage."

"You refer, again, to the Islamic Republic of Mansur," the gimlet-eyed guerrilla said. Mansur had originated as a secessionist movement within Yemen, spearheaded by a charismatic mullah: if the breakaway was not fiercely contested by the Yemeni forces, it was because nothing of value was being lost. Confined largely to the shifting sands of the Rub' al-Khali desert, Mansur was a desperately poor country, with few exports other than *khat* and some paltry handicrafts. The government itself had little to offer to its citizens save a Shiite version of Sharia: piety in medieval garb. Yet if its material exports were scant, it had begun to make a name for itself as an exporter of radical Islam, and the revolutionary fervor it entrained.

Ibrahim Maghur smiled. "On certain occasions, the holy men of Mansur have spoken to me of their security concerns. I have taken the liberty of telling them that I have identified somebody who is both devoted to Allah and truly expert in such matters. You will accompany me to Khartoum, where I have arranged special air transport for you. You will be received in the desert town they call the capital and will, I believe, find them a welcoming people indeed. At that point, you can write your own ticket."

"And they will help me find the serpent?"

Maghur shook his head. "*I* will help you find the serpent. We will remain in close contact, you and I. Your Mansur hosts will merely provide you with the official identity and mobility you will need. In short, Mansur will be the stalking horse upon which you will ride."

A gust of desert air whipped at their loose-fitting garments.

"They say if you strike at a king, you must kill him," the Caliph mused.

"Your enemies will soon learn the truth of that," the Libyan said. "Through his hirelings, Peter Novak struck at you—but failed to kill you. Now you will strike at him. . . ."

"And kill him." The words were spoken as simple fact.

"Indeed," Maghur said. "Allah's own justice demands it. Yet time grows short, for the thirsts of your revolutionary followers are great."

"And what will slake that thirst?"

"The blood of the infidel," Maghur said. "It will flow like juice from the sweetest pomegranate, and with it your cause will regain its life-spirit."

"The blood of the infidel," the Caliph repeated.

"The only question is whom you can trust to . . . extract it."

"Trust?" The Caliph blinked slowly.

"What surrogate will you dispatch?"

"Surrogate?" The Kagama warrior appeared faintly affronted. "This is not a task to be delegated. Recall, it was the Prophet himself who led the onslaught against Khaybar."

The Libyan's eyes widened with what seemed to be even greater respect for the rebel leader.

"The blood of the infidel will indeed flow," the Caliph said, and he held out his hands. "These palms will brim with Peter Novak's blood."

"And it will bear the blessings of Allah." The Libyan bowed. "Come with me now. The stalking horse must be saddled. Mansur awaits you, el Caliph."

# CHAPTER TWENTY-SIX

With supreme reluctance, Gitta Békesi finally agreed to let them enter the decaying farmhouse where she now lived alone with her savage dog. The dog's reluctance seemed greater still: though it obediently stood back, one could tell from its rigid posture that, at the slightest signal from its mistress, it would throw itself at the visitors in a frenzy of bristling fur and snapping teeth.

The old crone shared the decrepitude of her lodgings. The skin hung loosely from her skull; pale, dry scalp showed through her thinning hair; her eyes were sunken, hard and glittering behind loose snakeskin-like folds. If age had softened what had been hard, it had hardened what had been soft, turning her high cheeks gaunt and hollow, her mouth into a cruel slash.

It was the face of a survivor.

From the many articles Janson had digested, he knew that Peter Novak was eight years old in 1945, when clashing forces commanded by Hitler and Stalin essentially liquidated the farming village of Molnár, his place of birth. The population of Molnár had always been small enough—under a thousand, in the early forties. Nearly all perished. Even aside from her age, could someone have experienced such a cataclysmic event and not still bear the impress of the trauma?

In the large sitting room, a fire burned slowly in the fireplace. On the wooden mantel above it, a sepia photograph in a tarnished silver frame showed a beautiful young woman. Gitta Békesi as she once was: a robust peasant girl, exuding rude health, and something else, too—a sly sensuality. It gazed upon them, cruelly mocking the ravages of age.

Jessie walked over to it. "What a beauty you were," she said simply.

"Beauty can be a curse," the old woman said. "Fortunately, it is always a fleeting one." She made a clicking noise with her tongue and the dog came over and sat at her side. She reached down and rubbed its flanks with her clawlike hands.

"I understand that you once worked for the count," Janson said. "Count Ferenczi-Novak."

"I do not speak of these things," she said curtly. She sat in a caned rocking chair, the webbing of the seat half torn. Behind her, resting against the wall like a walking stick, was her old shotgun. "I live alone and ask nothing more than that I be *left* alone. I tell you that you are wasting your time. So. I have let you in. Now you can say that you have sat with the old woman and asked her your questions. Now you can tell everyone concerned that Gitta Békesi says nothing. No, I tell you one thing: there was no Kis family in Molnár."

"Wait a minute—'everyone concerned'? Who's *concerned?*"

"Not me," she said, and staring straight ahead, she fell silent.

"Are those chestnuts?" Jessie asked, looking at a bowl on a small table by the woman's chair.

Békesi nodded.

"Could I have one? I feel so rude asking, but I know you just roasted those, 'cause this whole place of yours smells like it, and it's just making my mouth water."

Békesi glanced at the bowl and nodded. "They're still hot," she said approvingly.

"Makes me think of my grandma somehow—we'd come to her house and she'd roast us some chestnuts. . . ." She beamed at the memory. "And it made every day seem like Christmas." Jessie peeled a chestnut and ate it greedily. "This is perfect. Just a perfect chestnut. This alone was worth the five-hour drive."

The old woman nodded, her manner noticeably less aloof. "They get too dry when you overroast them."

"And too hard when you don't roast them long enough," Jessie put in. "But you got it down to a science."

A small, contented smile settled on the old woman's face.

"Do all your visitors beg you for 'em?" Jessie asked.

"I get no visitors."

"None at all? Can't hardly believe that."

"Very few. Very, very few."

Jessie nodded. "And how do you handle the nosy ones?"

"Some years ago, a young journalist from England came here," the old woman said, looking off. "So many questions he had. He was writing something about Hungary during the war and after."

"Is that right?" Janson asked, his eyes intent. "I'd love to read what he wrote."

The crone snorted. "He never wrote anything. Just a couple of days after his visit, he was killed in an accident in Budapest. The accident rates are terrible there, everyone says so."

The temperature seemed to drop in the room as she spoke.

"But I always wondered," the old woman said.

"He ask about this count, too?" Jessie prompted.

"Have another chestnut," the old woman said.

"Could I really? You don't mind?"

The old woman nodded, pleased. After a while she said, "He was *our* count. You could not live in Molnár and not know the count. The land you worked was his land, or once had been. One of the very old families— he traced his ancestry back to one of the seven tribes that formed the Hungarian nation in the year 1000. His ancestral estate was here, even though he spent a great deal of time in the capital." She lifted her small dark eyes toward the ceiling. "They say I am an old woman who lives in the past. Perhaps it is so. Such a troubled land we lived in. Ferenczi-Novak understood that better than most."

"Did he, now?" Jessie said.

She regarded her quietly for a moment. "Perhaps you will join me in a small glass of *pálinka.*"

"I'm fine, ma'am."

Gitta Békesi stared ahead stonily and said nothing, evidently offended.

Jessie looked at Janson and then back at the old woman. "Well, if *you're* having some."

The old woman slowly rose and walked unsteadily to the glass-front sideboard. There, she lifted an enormous jug filled with a colorless liquid, and poured a small quantity into two shot glasses.

Jessie took one. The old woman settled back into her chair and watched as Jessie had a sip.

Explosively, she sprayed the liquid out. It was as involuntary as a sneeze. "*Jeez,* I'm sorry!" she got out in a strangled voice.

The old woman smiled mischievously.

Jessie was still struggling for breath. "What the . . ." Jessie gasped, her eyes watering.

"Around here, we make it ourselves," the woman said. "A hundred and ninety proof. A bit stiff for you?"

"Little bit," Jessie said hoarsely.

The old woman swallowed the rest of the brandy, and looked more relaxed than she had been. "It all goes back to the Treaty of Trianon, in 1920, and the lost territories. We had to give up almost three-quarters of our land to the Romanians and the Yugoslavs. Can you imagine what that felt like?"

"Like an amputation," Janson offered.

"That's it—there was a ghostly sense that a part of you was there and yet not there. *Nem, nem soha!* It was the national motto, and it means 'No, no never.' It is the answer to the question 'Can it remain like this?' Every stationmaster would inscribe the catechism in flowers in his garden. Justice for Hungary! But nobody in the world took it seriously, this thirst for the lost territories. Nobody but Hitler. Such madness—like riding a tiger. In Budapest, the government makes friends with this man. Soon they are in the belly of the beast. It was a mistake for which this country would suffer so terribly. But nobody suffered more than we did."

"And were you around when . . ."

"All the houses were set on fire. The people who lived here—whose ancestors had worked here as long as anyone could remember—rousted from their beds, their fields, the breakfast tables. Rounded up and forced at gunpoint to walk along the iced-over waters of the Tisza until the ice broke and they fell in. Whole families, walking hand in hand—then, a minute later, drowning, freezing, in the icy waters. They say you could hear the ice cracking all the way up the vineyards. I was in the castle at the time, and it was being shelled. I thought the walls would collapse in on us. Much of it *was* destroyed. But in the cellars, we were safe. A day later, the army had moved on, and I wandered back to the village of my birth, the only home I had ever known, and—*nothing*."

Her voice faded to an inexorable whisper. "Nothing but pillage and destruction. Charred ruins, black embers. The occasional farmhouse on the mountain had escaped destruction. But the village of Molnár, which had survived the Romanian pillage, the Tartars and the Turks, was no more. No more. And in the river, so many bodies were floating, like an ice floe. And among them, naked, bloated, bluish, were the bodies of my very own parents." She raised a hand to her forehead. "When you see what human beings can do to each other, it makes you . . . ashamed to be alive."

The two Americans were silent for a moment.

"How did you find yourself in the castle?" Janson asked after a while.

The old woman smiled, remembering. "János Ferenczi-Novak—a wonderful man, and so was his Illana. To serve them was a privilege, I never forgot that. You see, my parents and my grandparents and my great-grandparents worked the land. They were peasants, but over time, the nobleman deeded them small parcels of land. They grew potatoes, and grapes, and berries of all sorts. They had hopes for me, I think. I was a pretty little girl. It's true. They thought if I worked as a servant at the castle, I would learn a thing or two. Perhaps the count would take me with him to Budapest, where I might meet a special man. My mother nurtured these sorts of dreams. She knew one of the women who helped run Ferenczi-Novak's household, and had her meet her little girl. And one thing led to another, and I met the great man himself, Count Ferenczi-Novak, and his beautiful blue-eyed wife, Illana. The count was spending more and more time in Budapest, in the circles of the government of the Regent Horthy. He was close to Miklós Kállay, who would become prime minister. I think he was some sort of high minister in Kállay's government. The count was an educated man. The government needed such men as he, and he had a strong sense of public service. But even then, he would spend several weeks at a time in his country estates, in Molnár. A tiny village. A tavern owner. The grocer, a Jew from Hódmezövásárhely. But mostly farmers and woodcutters. Humble folk, eking out a living along the Tisza River. Then came the day my mother took me to the castle on the hill—the castle we had somehow imagined, growing up, to be part of the mountain itself."

"It must be hard to remember something that happened so long ago," Jessie ventured.

The old woman shook her head. "Yesterday is sunk into the mists of the past. What happened six decades ago, I can see as if it is happening now. The long, long path, past his stables. The stone gateposts with their worn carvings. And then, inside—the curving staircase, the worn steps. It took my breath away. Drunken guests, people said, would slip on those worn steps. Later, when I joined the household staff, I would overhear Countess Illana talking about such things—she was so funny, and so dismissive about it all. She never liked the staghorns mounted on the walls—did any castle *not* have them? she protested. The paintings, Teniers, Teniers the Younger. 'Like every castle in Central Europe,' I once heard the countess say to someone. The furniture, 'Very late Franz Josef,' she would say. And how dark it was in the main hall. You didn't want to put a hole through the frescoes, you see, to put in electric lighting. So everything glowed with candlelight. In that hall, I remember, there was a grand piano, of rosewood. With the most delicate lace cloth on top, and a silver candelabra that had to be carefully polished every Saturday. And outside it was as beautiful. I was dizzy with excitement the first time I walked through the English-style garden in the back. There were overgrown catalpa trees, with their misshapen limbs, littering pods everywhere, and pollarded acacias and walnut trees. The countess was very proud of her *jardin anglais*. She taught us to call everything by its proper name. In English, yes, English. Another member of her household drilled me in this language. Illana enjoyed addressing people in English, as if she were living in a British country house, and so we learned." She looked oddly serene. "That English garden. The smell of freshly mown grass, the fragrance of roses, and hay—it was like Paradise to me. I know people say I live in the past, but it was a past worth living in."

Janson recalled the ruins that were visible farther up the hill: all that remained of the vast estate were jagged remnants of walls that rose only a few feet from the ground, barely visible through the tall grass. Eroded brick mounts of once grand chimneys protruded through the scrub like tree stumps. A castle that had stood proudly for centuries was reduced to rubble—not much more than a rock garden. A lost world. The old woman had entered an enchanted garden once. Now she lived in the shadows of its ruins.

The wood fire cracked and hissed quietly, and for a minute no one spoke.

"And what about the scampering of little feet?" Jessie asked finally.

"They had only one child. Peter. Would you like a drop more *pálinka?*"

"You're real kind, ma'am," Jessie said. "But I'm fine."

"Peter, you said," Janson repeated, deliberately casual. "When was he born?"

"His naming day was the first Saturday in October 1937. *Such* a beautiful boy. So handsome and so clever. You could tell he was meant to be a remarkable human being."

"Was he, now?"

"I can picture him still, walking up and down the long mirrored hallway in his Peter Pan collar and his little plus fours and his sailor's cap. He loved to watch his reflection reflected back and forth between two facing mirrors, multiplying forever, smaller and smaller." Her smile drew with it a trellis of wrinkles. "And his parents were so devoted to him. You could understand that. He was their only child. The birth was a difficult one, and it left the countess unable to conceive." The old woman was in another place, another world: if it was a lost world, it was not lost to her. "One day, just after lunch, he ate some pastries the cook had made for tea, like a naughty little boy, and the cook berated him. Well, Countess Illana happened to overhear. *Don't you ever talk that way to our child,* she told her. And just the way she said it—little *icicles* hung off her words. Bettina, she was the cook, her cheeks flamed, but she didn't say anything. She understood. We all did. He was . . . unlike other boys. But not spoiled, you must understand. Sunny as the first of July, as we Hungarians say. When something pleased him, he'd smile so hard you'd think his face would split. Blessed, that child was. Magical. He could have been *anything*. Anything at all."

"Peter must have been everything to them," Jessie said.

The old woman stroked her dog's flank again, rhythmically. "Such a perfect little boy." Her eyes lit up, briefly, as if she were seeing the boy in front of her, seeing him in his knickerbockers and sailor's cap swanning in front of the mirrors on both sides of the hall, his reflections trailing off into an infinite regress.

The crone's eyelids fluttered and she closed them hard, trying to halt the pictures in her mind. "The fevers were terrible, he was like a kettle, tossing in bed and retching. It was a cholera epidemic, you know. So hot to the touch. And then so cold. I was one of those who attended him on his sickbed, you see." She put both her hands on her dog's face, gaining comfort from the creature's steadfast strength. "I can never forget that morning—finding his body, so cold, those lips so pale, his cheeks like wax. It was heartbreaking when it happened. He was just five years old. Could anything be sadder? Dead, before he truly had a chance to live."

A heaving sense of vertigo, of utter disorientation, overcame Janson. *Peter Novak had died as a child?* How could that be? Was there some mistake—was this another family the old woman was describing, *another* Peter?

And yet the accounts of the philanthropist's life were all agreed: Peter Novak, the beloved only son of Janós Ferenczi-Novak, had been born in October 1937, and reared in the war-torn village of Molnár. That much was part of the official record.

But as for the rest of it?

There could be no doubt that the old woman was telling the truth as she remembered it. And yet what did it *mean?*

*Peter Novak: the man who never was.*

Amid a growing unease, possibilities fluttered through Janson's mind, like shuffled and reshuffled index cards.

Jessie unzipped her knapsack, took out the picture book on Peter Novak, and opened it to a color close-up of the great man. She showed it to Gitta Békesi.

"See this fellow? *His* name is Peter Novak."

The old woman glanced at the picture and looked at Jessie, shrugging. "I do not follow the news. I have no television, take no newspapers. Forgive me. But, yes, I think I have heard of this man."

"Same name as the count's boy. Sure it couldn't be the same person?"

"Peter, Novak—common names in our country," she said, shrugging. "Of course this is not Ferenczi-Novak's son. He died in 1942. I told you." Her eyes returned to the photograph. "Besides, this man's eyes are brown." The point seemed to her almost too obvious to belabor, but she added, "Little Peter's were blue, like the waters of the Balaton. Blue, like his mother's."

In a state of shock, the two began the long walk back to the Lancia, one mile up the hill. As the house receded into the overgrowth, they began to talk, slowly, tentatively, exploring the deepening mystery.

"What if there was another child?" Jessie asked. "Another kid nobody knew about, who took on his brother's name. A hidden twin, maybe."

"The old woman seemed certain that he was their only one. Not an easy thing to hide from the household staff. Of course, if Count Ferenczi-Novak was as paranoid as his reputation had it, any number of ruses are conceivable."

"But why? He wasn't crazy."

"Not crazy, but desperately fearful for his kid," Janson said. "Hungarian politics was in an incredibly explosive condition. Remember what you've read. Béla Kun took power in March 1919, ruled for a hundred and thirty-three days. A reign of terror. That was followed, once he'd been toppled, by an even more horrifying massacre of the people who helped him gain power. Whole families were slaughtered—Admiral Horthy's so-called White Terror. Reprisals and counter-reprisals were just a way of life back then. The count might have felt that what comes around goes around. That his association with Prime Minister Kállay could be a death sentence, not just for him but for his family."

"He was afraid of the Communists?"

"The Fascists and the Communists both. Hundreds of thousands of people were killed in late forty-four and early forty-five after the Arrow Cross took over. Remember, these Arrow Cross were people who thought Horthy was too *lax!* True homegrown Hungarian Nazis. When the Red Army took control of the country, you had another round of purges. Hundreds of thousands were killed, again. Enemies of the revolution, right? People like Ferenczi-Novak were caught in a pincer. How many instances are there of that kind of ideological whiplash—a country switching from far left to far right to far left again, with nothing in between?"

"So we're back to the old question: How do you bring a child into that world? Maybe these guys thought they couldn't. That any child of theirs would have to be hidden."

"Moses in the basket of bulrushes and pitch," Janson mused. "But that raises a lot more questions. Novak tells the world that these are his parents. Why?"

"Because it's the truth?"

"Not good enough. A child like that would have been raised to be afraid of the truth, to regard the truth as a very dangerous thing—for Christ's sake, he might not even *know* the truth. That's the thing about a child: you can't tell him what he can't deal with. In Nazi Germany, when a Jewish toddler was hidden by a Christian family, the child wouldn't, *couldn't,* be told the truth. The risk was too great: he might say something inappropriate to his playmates, to a teacher. The only way to protect him from the consequences of a potentially deadly truth was to keep him in ignorance of that truth. Only later, when the child was grown, would he be told. Besides, if Novak's parents were who he said they were, this Gitta Békesi would know about it. I feel sure of it. I don't think they had another child. I think she told us the truth: Peter Novak, the count's only son, died when he was little."

Shadows lengthened into long narrow stripes as the sun dipped behind the distant peak. Minutes later, clearings that had been golden suddenly turned gray. On a hillside, sunset came quickly and with little warning.

"This is getting to be a goddamn hall of mirrors, like the one Grandma Gitta talked about. Yesterday, we were wondering whether some impostor had taken on Peter Novak's identity. Now it's looking more and more like Peter Novak himself took on somebody else's identity. A dead kid, a wiped-out village—and, for somebody, an opportunity."

"Identity theft," said Janson. "Beautifully executed."

"It's genius, when you think about it. You choose a village that was totally liquidated in the war—so there's practically nobody around who'd remember a thing about his childhood. All the records, certificates of birth and death, destroyed after the place was torched."

"Making himself an aristocrat's son was a good move," Janson said. "It helps deal with a lot of questions that might have arisen about his origins. Nobody has to wonder how he could be so well educated and worldly without an institutional record of his schooling."

"Exactly. Where'd he go to school? Hey, he was privately tutored—a count's kid, right? Why was he off the radar? Because this aristocrat, this Janós Ferenczi-Novak, had tons of enemies and good reason to be paranoid. Everything fits, real tight."

"Like dovetailed planks. Too tightly. The next thing you know, he's a big-time currency trader."

"A man with no past."

"Oh, he's got a past, all right. It's just a past that nobody knows."

He flashed on the philanthropist's Gulfstream V, and the white cursive letters on its indigo enamel: *Sok kicsi sokra megy.* The same Hungarian proverb Novak had repeated on the news segment. Many small things can add up to a big one. It was a proposition that held for benefaction—and for deception. Márta Lang's words, in that jet, returned to him with a chilling resonance: *Novak's proved who he really is, again and again. A man for all seasons, and a man for all peoples.*

Yet who was he really?

Jessie stepped easily over an immense bough that lay in their path. "Thing I keep going back to is *why?* Why the trickery? Everybody loves him. He's a goddamn hero of the age."

"Even saints can have something to hide," Janson parried, choosing his path more carefully. "What if the man came from a family that had been involved with Arrow Cross atrocities? Again, you've got to imagine a country where people have long memories, where reprisal is a byword, where whole families, including children and grandchildren, were killed or deported because they were on the wrong side. These cycles of revenge were a motive force of twentieth-century Hungarian history. If there was evil like this in your past, you might very well want to escape it, leave it behind you, by whatever means necessary. Grandma Gitta isn't the only person who lives in the past around here. Think about it. Say that this man came from an Arrow Cross family. No matter what he did, it would come up again and again—in every interview, every conversation, every discussion."

Jessie nodded. " 'The fathers have eaten sour grapes, and the children's teeth are set at edge,' " she said. "Like it says in the Book of Jeremiah."

"The motivation could be as simple as that," said Janson. Still, he suspected that nothing about it was truly simple. Something—not an idea, but an inkling of one—hovered indistinctly in his mind, just out of reach, but dartingly present, like a tiny insect. Faint, nearly imperceptible, and yet *there*.

If only he could focus, shut everything else out and focus.

A few moments elapsed before he recognized the sound that drifted up the hill. It, too, was faint and nearly imperceptible, and yet as his senses tuned to the auditory stimulus, he recognized the source, and his heart began to thud.

It was a woman screaming.

# CHAPTER TWENTY-SEVEN

Oh Christ, *no!*

The thorny privet and overgrown vines whipped and scratched at Janson as he raced down the winding hillside path. He was mindful only of his footfalls as he vaulted over boulders and burst through bushes; a misplaced step in the treacherous terrain could result in a sprain or worse. He had ordered Jessie to return to the Lancia posthaste: it would be a disaster if their enemies reached it first. Her trek was uphill, but she ran like a gazelle and would get there soon.

A few minutes later, only slightly winded, Janson arrived at the old woman's dilapidated farmhouse. The screams had ceased, replaced by something even more ominous: utter silence.

The door was ajar, and inside was a spectacle that Janson knew would be forever etched on his mind. The noble Kuvasz lay on its side; it had been disemboweled, and its viscera spilled from its belly onto the flatweave rug, in a glistening, red mound, steaming faintly in the chilly air. Splayed in the nearby rocking chair was Gitta Békesi, a woman who had survived Red Terrors and White, the annihilating clashes of two world wars, the tanks of 1956, outbreaks and plagues of man and nature both. Her face was hidden by her coarse muslin frock, which had been yanked up and over her head, exposing her flaccid torso—and the unspeakable horrors that had been visited upon it. Small, red-rimmed wounds—each corresponding to the plunge of a bayonet, Janson knew—crisscrossed her silvery flesh in a grotesque arrangement. The blades of her assailants had plunged into her dozens of times. On her exposed arms and legs he could see a cluster of red weals caused by the pressure of gripping fingers. The woman had been held down, and tortured with a plunging blade. Were they seeking information from her? Or merely punishing her, sadistically, for the information she had already divulged to him?

What kind of monsters would do such a thing?

Janson's face felt frozen, numb. He looked around, saw spatters of the dead woman's blood on the floor and on the walls. The atrocity had occurred just minutes before. Her visitors had been as swift as they were savage.

And where were they now? They could not be far. Was he meant to be their next victim?

Janson's heart beat in a powerful, slow rhythm. The prospect of confrontation did not fill him with anxiety, but with a strange sense of transport. The old woman might have been easy prey; whoever had done this to her would find that he was not. A convulsing feeling of rage ran through him, familiar and oddly comforting in its familiarity. It would find release.

The half-taunting words of Derek Collins returned to him: *Violence is something you're very, very, very good at, Janson. . . . You tell me you're sickened by the killing. I'm going to tell you what you'll discover one day for yourself: that's the only way you'll ever feel alive.*

It felt true now. For years, he had run from his nature. He would not run from it today. As he surveyed the carnage, one thought ran through his mind like a saber. Those who had inflicted such suffering would themselves know suffering.

*Where were they?*

Close, very close. Because they were looking for him. They would be up the hill. Would Jessie make it to the Lancia in time?

Janson needed elevation if he was to get a proper view of the field of operation. The farmhouse, he saw, was built around a courtyard in the traditional L, with living and working areas under one roof. At right angles to the house was a big portico with a hayloft above and, adjoining it, horse stables. Now he ran into the courtyard and climbed a ladder to the tall hayloft opposite. A hinged door in the rough-planked roof allowed him to clamber to its highest point.

A quarter mile up the hill, he could see, a small party of armed men were making their way toward Jessie Kincaid. Their figures were difficult to make out in the dim light, but broken tree limbs and trampled grass showed their progress. Then Janson saw and heard the flutter of black birds, swooping from the nearby underbrush into the sky, with strident caws; something had disturbed them. A moment later he saw movement in the overgrown trees and bushes surrounding the old farmhouse, and he realized what it meant.

*He had fallen into a trap!*

The men had been *counting* on his overhearing the old woman's screams. They had sought to lure him back to the old farmhouse.

They had him exactly where they wanted him—would do to him exactly what they wanted to! Adrenaline filled his veins, brought a terrible icy focus to his perception.

The farmhouse was itself a gated enclosure, but the armed men had it surrounded on all four sides, and now they showed themselves, edging out of the underbrush and into the yard. They must have seen him enter, had probably been waiting for him to dash out. For there was no way Janson could escape undetected. Kincaid would be intercepted on her way to the Lancia; he would be destroyed or captured in a gated compound that was now his prison.

The spill of their flashlights illuminated each side of the old woman's home; in the light, he could also see their carbines. They would fire at their quarry at the first opportunity. Janson was, at the moment, an easy target indeed—and it would not take them long before their beams sliced toward the hayloft roof and silhouetted him with the clarity of a shooting-range cutout.

Janson lowered himself from the roof with as much speed and stealth as he could manage. Then he let himself down from the loft to the dirt floor. If the men had not rushed the place, it was only because they did not know whether he was armed. They would bide their time, proceed with caution, ensure his death without allowing him to take one of them with him.

Now he darted across the courtyard and back into the woman's parlor. The flickering light from the fireplace cast a ghostly glow on the carnage. Yet he had no choice but to return there. The old woman had a shotgun, hadn't she?

The shotgun was gone. Of *course* it was. It was not the sort of thing that would have escaped their notice, and disarming an octogenarian would have been easy. Yet if the woman kept a shotgun, she must also have a supply of cartridges stowed away somewhere.

A roving beam of yellow light flashed through the windows into the woman's parlor, looking for signs of movement—for signs of *him.* Janson promptly eased himself to the floor. They wanted to locate him, to narrow his mobility progressively. Once they knew for sure which building he was in, they could force the gate of the courtyard and surround the particular structure into which he had retreated. Their uncertainty was his only ally.

Janson crawled toward the kitchen, keeping well out of sight. The shot-gun cartridges—where would the old woman have kept them? By them-selves, they would be useless as offensive weapons against his pursuers. But there might just be another way of using them. He was alive so far only because of their uncertainty about his precise location, but he had to do better than that. He would win only if he could turn uncertainty into error.

He tried several drawers in the woman's kitchen, finding cutlery in one, bottles of condiments and spices in another. It was in a small pantry, next to the kitchen, that he finally found what he was looking for, and in even more plentiful supply that he had hoped. Ten boxes of Biro Super 10-gauge cartridges, twenty to the box. He pulled out a couple of boxes and crawled back to the parlor.

He heard shouts from outside, in a language he could not make out. But there was no missing the larger meaning: more men were arriving to take up perimeter positions.

In the iron pan over the fireplace, where the woman had been roasting chestnuts earlier that day, Janson placed a handful of the long cartridges, the cupped brass on either end connected by a ridged brown plastic tube. Within them was lead shot and gunpowder, and though they were de-signed to be detonated by the firing pin of a shotgun, sufficient heat would produce a similar effect.

The fire was slow, dying, and the pan was a couple of feet above it. Could he depend upon it?

Janson added another small log to the fire, and returned to the kitchen. There he placed a cast-iron skillet on the decades-old electric range, and scattered another handful of cartridges on it. He set the heat on medium low. It would take a minute for the element just to heat the bottom of the heavy skillet.

Now he turned on the oven, and placed the remaining fifty cartridges on the rack, a foot below the top heating element, and set the temperature on high. The oven would surely take the longest to heat of all. He knew that his calculations were crude, at best. He also knew he had no better alternatives.

He crept across the courtyard, past the stables, and climbed the rungs to the hayloft again.

And he waited.

For a while, all he heard was the voices of the men as they grew nearer and nearer, taking positions safely away from windows, communicating to one another with terse commands and flickers of their flashlights. Suddenly, a *bang* shattered the still air, followed, in rapid succession, with four more bangs. Then he heard the return fire of an automatic rifle, and the sound of broken glass. The old warped frames of the front window had to be a scatter of shards and dust now.

To Janson, the acoustic sequence relayed a precise narrative. The cartridges over the fireplace had detonated first, as he had hoped. The gunmen made the logical assumption. Gun blasts from within the parlor indicated that they were being fired upon. They had what they needed: an exact location.

Exactly the *wrong* location.

Urgent shouts summoned the other men to join the apparent gunfight in the front of the farmhouse.

A series of low-pitched blasts told Janson that the cartridges on the rangetop skillet had been heated to the point of detonation. It would tell the gunmen that their quarry had retreated into the kitchen. Through the gap between the slats of the barn wall, he saw that a solitary gunman with a cradled automatic weapon remained behind; his partners had raced to the other side of the compound to join the others in their assault.

Janson withdrew his small Beretta and, through the same gap, aimed it at the burly, olive-clad man. Yet he could not fire yet—could not risk the gunshot being heard by others and exposing the subterfuge. He heard the footfalls of heavy boots drifting in from the main house: the other gunmen were splintering the house with their gunfire as they tried to discover Janson's hiding place. Janson waited until he heard the immense boom-roar of fifty shotgun cartridges exploding in the oven before he squeezed the trigger. The sound would be utterly lost amid the blast and the attendant confusion.

He fired at the exact instant.

Slowly, the burly man toppled over, face forward. His body made little sound as it hit the leafy ground cover.

The position was now unguarded: Janson unlatched a door and strode over to the fallen man, knowing that he would not be seen. For a moment, he contemplated disappearing into the dark thickets of the hillside; he could do so, had disappeared into similar terrains on other occasions. He was confident he could elude his pursuers and emerge safe, a day or two later, in one of the other hillside villages.

Then he remembered the slain woman, her savagely brutalized body, and any thought of flight vanished from his mind. His heart beat hard, and even the shadows of the evening seemed to be glimpsed through a curtain of red. He saw that his bullet had struck the gunman just above his hairline; only a rivulet of blood that made its way down his scalp to the top of his forehead revealed its lethal impact. He removed the dead man's submachine gun and bandolier, and adjusted its sling around his own shoulders.

There was no time to lose.

The team of assailants was now gathered in the house, tramping around heavily, firing their weapons. He knew that their bullets were flying into armoires and closets and every other conceivable hiding place, steel-jacketed projectiles splintering into wood, seeking human flesh.

But *they* were the trapped ones now.

Quietly, he circled around to the front of the farmhouse, dragging the dead man behind him. In the roving beams of light, he recognized a face, a second face, a third. His blood ran cold. They were hard faces. Cruel faces. The faces of men he had worked with many years ago in Consular Operations, and whom he had disliked even then. They were coarse men—coarse not in their manners, but in their sensitivities. Men for whom brute force was not a last resort but a first, for whom cynicism was the product not of a disappointed idealism but of naked avarice and rapacity. They had no business in government service; in Janson's opinion, they reduced its moral credibility by their very presence. The technical skill they brought to their work was offset by a lack of any real conscience, a failure to grasp the legitimate objectives that underwrote sometimes questionable tactics.

He placed his jacket on the dead man, then positioned him behind the sprawling chestnut tree; with the man's shoelaces, he tied his flashlight to the lifeless forearm. He pulled tiny splinters of wood from a dead branch and placed them between the man's eyelids, propping his eyes open in a glassy stare. It was crude work, turning the man into an effigy of himself. But in the shadows of the evening, it would pass on a first glance, which was all Janson needed. Now Janson directed a raking burst of fire through the parlor's already shattered windows. The three exposed gunmen twitched horribly as the bullets perforated diaphragm, gut, aorta, lungs. At the same time, the unexpected burst summoned the others.

Janson rolled over to the scraggly chestnut tree, switched on the flashlight laced to the dead man's forearm, and silently dashed to the boulder ten feet away, where he waited in the gloom.

"There!" one of them called out. It took seconds for the effigy to attract their attention. All they would be able to see was the glare of the flashlight; the spill would illuminate the taupe-colored jacket and, perhaps just faintly, the staring eyes of the crouching man. The inference would be nearly instantaneous: here was the source of the lethal fusillade.

The response was as he expected: four of the commandos directed their automatic weapons at the crouching figure. The simultaneous chattering of their high-powered weapons, set at full fire, was nearly deafening: the men pumped hundreds of bullets into their former comrade.

The noise and the gunmen's furious concentration worked to Janson's advantage: with his small Beretta Tomcat, he squeezed off four carefully aimed shots in rapid succession. The distance was only ten yards; his accuracy was flawless. Each man slumped, lifeless, to the ground, his automatic weapon abruptly falling silent.

One man remained; Janson could see his profile shadowed against the curtains on the top floor. He was tall, his hair cut short but still curly, his bearing rigid. His was one of the faces Janson had recognized, and he could identify him now simply from his gait, the stiff, decisive efficiency of his movements. He was a leader. He was *their* leader, their commanding officer. From what little Janson had seen of their interactions earlier, that much, at least, had been clear.

The name came to him: Simon Czerny. A Cons Op operative specializing in clandestine assaults. Their paths had crossed more than once in El Salvador, during the mid-eighties, and Janson had even then considered him a dangerous man, reckless in his disregard for civilian life.

Janson would not kill him, though. Not until they had had a conversation.

Yet would the man allow himself to put in that position? He was smarter than the others. He had seen through Janson's subterfuge a little quicker than the others, had been the first to recognize the decoy for what it was and called warningly to his men. His tactical instincts were finely honed. A man like that would not expose himself to danger unnecessarily, but would bide his time until an opportunity presented itself.

Janson could not permit him that luxury.

Now the team commander was invisible; out of range of gunfire. Janson ran toward the ruins of the parlor, saw the shattered glass everywhere, saw the splashes of soot around the fireplace mantel from the exploded shotgun cartridges, saw the steel pellets, the ruined glass-front cabinet.

Finally, he saw the gallon-sized jug of brandy, the poisonous *pálinka.*

A hairline crack now ran down the side, no doubt from the pinging of a stray steel pellet, but it had not yet shattered. Janson knew what he had to do. Frisking one of the slain gunmen, he extracted a Zippo lighter. Then he splashed the 190-proof brandy around the room, extending to the hallway that led to the kitchen, and used the lighter to ignite the volatile spirits. Within seconds, a blue fire trail erupted across the room; soon the blue flames were joined by yellow flames as curtains, newspapers, and the canework of the chairs caught on. Before long, the heavier furniture would be flaming, and with it the planking of the floor, the ceiling, the floor above.

Janson waited as the flames grew in strength; leaping and joining one another in a rising sea of blue and yellow. Billows of smoke funneled up the narrow staircase.

The commander, Simon Czerny, would have to make a choice—only, he had no real choice. To remain where he was meant being consumed in an inferno. Nor could he escape the back way, into the courtyard, without exposing himself to a wall of flames: Janson had made sure of that. The only way out was down the stairs and through the front door.

Still, Czerny was a consummate professional; he would expect Janson to be waiting for him outside. He would take precautions.

Janson heard the man's heavy footsteps, even sooner than he had expected. Just as he reached the threshold, though, Czerny loosed a spray of bullets, sweeping around an almost 180-degree range. Anybody laying in wait for him outside would have been struck by the wildly chattering submachine gun. Janson admired Czerny's efficiency and forethought as he watched the gunman's pivoting torso—from behind.

Now he rose up from where he was hidden, by the staircase on the very floor of the burning parlor, perilously near the gathering conflagration—the one place the gunman would not have expected.

As Czerny directed another raking fusillade at the grounds outside, Janson lunged, lashing his arm around the gunman's neck, his fingers hurtling toward the trigger enclosure, tearing the weapon from his hands. Czerny thrashed violently, but rage made Janson unstoppable. He smashed his right knee into Czerny's kidney and dragged him onto the stone porch. Now he scissored the man's waist with his legs and forced his neck into a painful backward arch.

"You and I are going to spend some quality time together," Janson said, his lips close to Czerny's ear.

With an almost supernal effort, Czerny reared up and threw Janson off him. He ran down the yard, away from the burning house. Janson raced after him, taking him down with a powerful shoulder tackle, throwing him to the stony ground. Czerny let out a groan as Janson sharply wrenched one of his arms upward behind him, simultaneously dislocating the arm and turning him over onto his back. Tightening his grip on the man's neck, he leaned in close.

"Now, where was I? That's right: if you don't tell me what I want to hear, you'll never speak again." Janson yanked a combat blade from a holster in Czerny's belt. "I will peel the skin off your face until your own mother wouldn't recognize you. Now come clean—you still with Consular Operations?"

Czerny laughed bitterly. "Goddamn overgrown Eagle Scouts—that's all they were. Should have been selling cookies door-to-door, for all the difference they made, any of them."

"But you're making a difference now?"

"Tell me something. How the fuck do you live with yourself? You're a piece of shit and you always were. I'm talking way back. The shit you pulled—you goddamn traitor. Somebody once tried to help you, a true-blue hero, and how did you repay him? You gave him up, turned him in, pushed him in front of a firing squad. That should have been you at Mesa Grande, you son of a bitch—that should have been *you!*"

"You twisted bastard," Janson roared, sickened and dizzy. He pressed the flat of the man's knife against his lightly bearded cheek. The threat would not be abstract. "You part of some Da Nang revenge squad?"

"You gotta be joking."

"Who are you working for?" Janson demanded. "Goddammit! *Who are you working for!*"

"Who are *you* working for?" the man coughed. "You don't even know. You've been programmed like a goddamn laptop."

"Time to face the music," Janson said in a low, steely voice. "Or you won't *have* a face."

"They've messed with your head so bad, you don't know which end is up, Janson. And you never will."

"*Freeze!*" The abruptly shouted command came from above him; Janson looked and saw the big-bellied tavernkeeper they had spoken to earlier that day.

He was no longer wearing his white apron. And his large, reddened hands were clutching a double-barreled shotgun.

"Isn't that what they're always saying on your crappy American cop shows? I told you that you were not welcome," the beetle-browed man said. "Now I will have to *show* you how unwelcome you are."

Janson heard the noise of a runner, vaulting over boulders and branches, plunging through thickets. But even from a distance, he could identify the lithe, leaping figure. Seconds later, Jessie Kincaid emerged, her sniper rifle strapped to her back.

"Drop the goddamn antique!" she shouted. She held a pistol in her hand.

The Hungarian did not even look in her direction as he carefully cocked the Second World War–era shotgun.

Jessie squeezed one well-aimed shot into his head. The big-bellied man toppled backward like a felled tree.

Now Janson grabbed the shotgun and scrambled to his feet. "I've run out of patience, Czerny. And you've run out of allies."

"I don't understand," Czerny blurted.

Kincaid shook her head. "Drilled four fuckers up the hill." She hocked on the ground near Czerny. "Your boys, right? Thought so. Didn't like their attitude."

Fear flashed in Czerny's eyes.

"And get a load of that barkeep showing up. You'd have thought we stiffed him on the tab."

"Nice shooting," Janson said, tossing her the shotgun.

Jessie shrugged. "I never liked him."

"Eagle Scout," Czerny said. "Collecting your merit badges while the world burns."

"I'll ask you one more time: Who are you working for?" Janson demanded.

"The same person you are."

"Don't talk in riddles."

"Everybody works for him now. It's just that only some of us know it." He laughed, a dry, unpleasant laugh. "You think you've got the upper hand. You don't."

"Try me," Janson said. He placed his boot on Czerny's neck, not yet applying any pressure, but making it clear that he could crush him at any moment.

"You fool! He's got the whole U.S. *government* under his thumb. *He's* calling the shots now! You're just too ignorant to see it."

"What the hell are you trying to say?"

"You know what they always called you: the machine. Like you weren't human. But there's something else about machines. *They do what they're programmed to do.*"

Janson kicked him in the ribs, hard. "Get one thing straight. We're not playing *Who Wants to Be a Millionaire.* We're playing *Truth or Consequences.*"

"You're like one of those Japanese soldiers in the Philippine caves who doesn't know the war's over and they've lost," Czerny said. "It's over, OK? You've lost."

Now Janson bent down and pressed the point of the combat knife to Czerny's face, drawing a jagged line under his left cheek. "Who. Do. You. Work. For."

Czerny blinked hard, his eyes watering with pain and with the realization that nobody would save him.

"Grip it and rip it, baby," Jessie said.

"You'll tell us, sooner or later," Janson said. "You know that. What's up to you is whether you . . . lose face over it."

Czerny closed his eyes and a look of resolve settled itself on his face. In a sudden movement, he reached for the hilt of the knife and, with one powerful twist, wrested control of it. Janson pulled back, away from the blade's range, and Jessie stepped forward with the gun, but neither anticipated the man's next move.

He forced the blade down with shaking muscles and, carving deeply, drew it across his own neck. In less than two seconds, he had sliced through the veins and arteries that sustained consciousness. Blood geysered up half a foot, then ebbed as the shock stilled the pumping organ itself.

Czerny had killed himself, had sliced his own throat, rather than expose himself to interrogation.

For the first time in the past hour, the hard ball of rage within Janson subsided, giving way to dismay and disbelief. He recognized the significance of the spectacle before him. Death had been deemed preferable to whatever Czerny knew was in store for him if he were compromised. It suggested a truly fearsome discipline among these marauders: a leadership that ruled, in no small part, through terror.

Millions in a Cayman Islands bank account. A beyond-sanction order from Consular Operations. A Peter Novak who never was, who died and who came back. Like some grotesque parody of the Messiah. Like some Magyar Christ.

Or Antichrist.

And these men, these former members of Consular Operations. Janson had known them only dimly, but something nagged at his memory. Who were these assailants? Were they truly *former* Cons Op agents? Or were they *active* ones?

# CHAPTER TWENTY-EIGHT

The drive to Sárospatak took only two hours, but they were two hours racked with tension. Janson kept a careful eye out for anyone who might be following them. In town, they made their way past the vast Arpad Gimnazium, part of a local college, with its intricate, curving facade. Finally, they pulled up to a *kastély szálloda,* or mansion hotel, which had been converted from the property of the former landed gentry.

The clerk at the front desk—a middle-aged man with a sunken chest and an overbite—barely glanced at them or their documents. "We have one vacancy," he said. "Two beds will be suitable?"

"Perfectly," Janson said.

The clerk handed him an old-style hotel key with a rubber-ringed brass weight attached. "Breakfast is served from seven to nine," he said. "Enjoy Sárospatak."

"Your country is so beautiful," Jessie said.

"We think so," the clerk said, smiling perfunctorily without showing teeth. "How long will you be staying?"

"Just one night," Janson said.

"You'll want to visit the Sárospatak castle, Mrs. Pimsleur," he said, as if noticing her for the first time. "The fortifications are most impressive."

"We noticed that, passing through," Janson said.

"It's different up close," the clerk said.

"A lot of things are," Janson replied.

In the sparsely decorated room, Jessie spent twenty minutes on his cell phone. She held a piece of paper on which Janson had written the names of the three former Consular Operations agents he had identified. When she clicked off, she looked distinctly unsettled.

"So," Janson said, "what does your boyfriend tell you about their status: retired or active?"

"Boyfriend? If you ever saw him, you wouldn't be jealous. He makes wide turns, OK?"

"Jealous? Don't flatter yourself."

Jessie formed another *W* with her hands and rolled her eyes. "Look, here's the thing. They're not active."

"Retired."

"Not retired, either."

"Come again?"

"According to all the official records, they've been dead for the better part of a decade."

"Dead? Is that what they're telling you?"

"Remember the Qadal explosion in Oman?" Qadal had been the location of a U.S. Marines installation in Oman and a station for American intelligence gathering in the Persian Gulf. In the mid-nineties, terrorists set off a blast that cost the lives of forty-three American soldiers. A dozen "analysts" with the State Department had also been on site, and had perished as well.

"One of those 'unsolved tragedies,' " Janson said, expressionless.

"Well, the records say that all those guys you mentioned died in the blast."

Janson furrowed his brow, trying to assimilate the information. The terrorist incident in Oman must have been a cover. It enabled an entire contingent of Consular Operations agents to conveniently disappear— only to reappear, perhaps, in the employ of another power. But what power? Who were they working for? What kind of secret would motivate a hard man like Czerny to slash his own throat? Was his final deed an act of fear, or conviction?

Jessie paced for a while. "They're dead, but they're not dead, right? Is there any chance—any chance whatever—that the Peter Novak we saw on CNN is the same Peter Novak as ever? Never mind what his birth name might have been. Is it conceivable that—I don't know—he somehow wasn't on the aircraft that exploded? Like maybe he boarded it and then somehow slipped away before takeoff?"

"I was there, I observed everything. . . . I simply don't see how." Janson shook his head slowly. "I've gone through it again and again. I can't imagine it."

"Unimaginable doesn't mean impossible. There must be a way to prove that it's the same man."

On a wood-veneer table, Jessie spread out a stack of Novak images from the past year, downloaded from the Internet back in Alasdair Swift's Lombardy cottage. One of them was from the CNN Web site and showed the philanthropist at the award ceremony they had watched on television, honoring the woman from Calcutta. Now she took out the jeweler's loupe and ruler she had acquired for analyzing the maps of the Bükk Hills region, and applied them to the images spread in front of her.

"What are you trying to do?" Janson asked.

"I know what you think you saw. But it ought to be possible to prove to you that we're dealing with the very same person. Plastic surgery can do only so much."

Ten minutes later, she interrupted a long, unbroken silence.

"Christ on a raft!" she said under her breath.

She turned to look at him, and her face was pale.

"Now you got to take into account things like lens distortion," she said, "and at first I thought that's all I was seeing. But there's something else going on. Depending on the photograph, the guy seems to be slightly different heights. Subtle—no more than half an inch difference. Here he is, standing next to the head of the World Bank. And here he is again, separate occasion, standing next to the same guy. Looks like everybody's wearing the same shoes in both shots. Could be the heels or whatever, right? But—subtle, subtle, subtle—he's got slightly different forearm spans. And the ratio between forearm span and femur span . . ." She jabbed at one of the pictures, which showed him walking alongside the prime minister of Slovenia. The outline of a bent knee was visible against his gray trousers, as was the line where the upper thigh turned at the hip. She pointed to a similar configuration in another photograph. "Same joints, different ratios," she said, breathing deeply. "Something is deeply fucked-up."

"Meaning what?"

She riffled through the picture book she'd bought in Budapest, and busied herself with the ruler again. Finally she spoke. "Ratio of index finger length to forefinger length. Not constant. Photographs can be flopped, but he's not going to switch the hand he's got his wedding band on."

Now Janson approached the array of images. He tapped certain areas of the photographs. "Trapezium to metacarpal. That's another index. Check it out. The ventral surface of the scapula—you can see it against his shirt. Let's look at that ratio, too."

With the loupe and the ruler, she continued to look for and find tiny physical variances. The length of the forefinger in relation to the middle finger, the precise length of each arm, the exact distance from chin to Adam's apple. Skepticism melted as examples multiplied.

"The question is, Who is this man?" She shook her head bleakly.

"I think you mean the question is, *Who are these men?*"

She pressed her fingertips to her temples. "OK, try this on. Let's say you wanted to take everything this guy has. You kill him, and you take his place, because you've somehow made yourself look identical to him, almost. Now his life is your life. What's his is yours. It's genius. And to make sure you can get away with it, you go on some public outings pretending to be the guy, kinda like a dress rehearsal."

"But wouldn't the real Peter Novak catch wind of that?"

"Maybe, maybe not. But say you also had the goods on him, somehow, knew about some secret that he had tried to bury . . . so you could blackmail him some kinda way. Couldn't that make sense of it?"

"When you've got no good explanations, the bad ones start looking better and better."

"I guess." Jessie sighed.

"Let's try another route. I can't get to Peter Novak, or whoever is calling himself that. Who else do we know who might know?"

"Maybe not the people trying to stop you, but whoever's giving the orders."

"Exactly. And I've a strong suspicion I know who that is."

"You're talking about Derek Collins," she said. "Director of Consular Operations."

"Lambda Team doesn't get dispatched without his direct approval," he said. "Let alone the other teams we've seen deployed. I think it's time I paid the man a visit."

"Listen to me," she said urgently. "You need to keep a good safe distance from that man. If Collins wants you dead, don't count on leaving his company alive."

"I know the guy," Janson said. "I know what I'm doing."

"So do I. You're talking about putting your head in the lion's mouth. Don't you know how *crazy* that is?"

"I've got no choice," Janson said.

Heavily, she said, "When do we leave?"

"There's no 'we.' I'm going by myself."

"You don't think I'm good enough?"

"You know that's not what I'm talking about," Janson said. "Are you looking for validation? You're good, Jessie. Top-drawer. Is that what you need to hear? Well, it's true. You're smart as a whip, you're fast on your feet, you're adaptable and levelheaded, and you're probably the best marksman I've come across. The point remains: what I've got to do next, I've got to do alone. You can't come along. It's not a risk you need to take."

"It's not a risk *you* need to take. You're going into the lion's den without so much as a chair and a whip."

"Trust me, it'll be a walk in the park," Janson said with a trace of a smile.

"Tell me you're not still sore about London. Because . . ."

"Jessie, I really need you to reconnoiter the Liberty Foundation offices in Amsterdam. I'll rejoin you there shortly. We can't ignore the possibility that something, or somebody, might turn up there. As far as Derek Collins, though, I can take care of myself. It's going to be OK."

"What I'm thinking is, you're *scared* of putting me at risk," Jessie said. "I'd call that a lapse of professionalism, wouldn't you?"

"You don't know what you're talking about."

"Hell, maybe you're right." She was silent for a moment, averting her gaze. "Maybe I ain't ready." Suddenly, she noticed a small splotch of blood on the back of her right hand. As she examined it more closely, she looked a little sick. "What I did today, in those hills . . ."

"Was what you needed to do. It was kill or be killed."

"I know," she said in a hollow voice.

"You're not supposed to like it. There's no shame in what you're feeling. Taking the life of another human being is the ultimate responsibility. A responsibility I spent the past five years running from. But there's another truth you've got to remember. Sometimes lethal force is the only thing that will defeat lethal force, and though zealots and crazies may twist that precept to their own perverted ends, it remains a truth. You did what had to be done, Jessie. You saved the day. Saved me." He gave her a reassuring smile.

She tried to return it. "That grateful look doesn't become you. We saved each other's lives, OK? We're even-steven."

"What are you, a sniper or a CPA?"

She gave a rueful laugh, but her eyes returned to the dot of dried blood. She was silent for a moment. "It's just all at once I had the thought that, you know, these guys had moms and dads, too."

"You'll find you learn not to think about that."

"And that's a good thing, right?"

"Sometimes," Janson said, swallowing hard, "sometimes it's a necessary thing."

Now Jessie disappeared into the bathroom, and Janson heard the shower run for a long time.

When she returned, a terry-cloth bathrobe was wrapped around her slim yet softly curving body. She walked toward the bed nearest the window. Janson was almost startled at how delicately feminine the field agent now appeared.

"So you're leaving me in the morning," she said after a few moments.

"Not the way I'd put it," Janson said.

"Wonder what the odds of my ever seeing you again are," she said.

"Come on, Jessie. Don't think like that."

"Maybe we'd better seize the day—or the night. Gather ye rosebuds or whatever." He could tell she was afraid for him, and for herself, too. "I got real good eyes. You know that. But I don't need a sniper scope to see what's in front of my face."

"And what's that?"

"I see the way you look at me."

"I don't know what you mean."

"Oh, come on now, make your move, soldier. Now's the time you tell me how much I remind you of your late wife."

"Actually, you couldn't be less like her."

She paused. "I make you uncomfortable. Don't try to deny that."

"I don't think so."

"You survived eighteen months of torture and interrogation from the Viet Cong, but you flinch when I come too close."

"No," he said, but his mouth was dry.

She stood up and moved toward him. "And your eyes widen and your face flushes and your heart starts to race." She reached over, took his hand, and pressed it to her throat. "Same with me. Can you feel it?"

"A field agent shouldn't make assumptions," Janson said, but he could feel the pulse beneath her warm, silky skin, and it seemed to keep rhythm with his own.

"I remember something you once wrote, about interagency cooperation between nations. 'To work together as allies, it is important that any unresolved tensions be addressed through a free and open exchange.' " There was laughter in her eyes. And then something softer, something like heat. "Just close your eyes and think of your country."

Now she stood closer and parted her bathrobe. Her breasts were two perfectly shaped globes, the nipples swollen with tension, and she leaned toward him, cupping his face now with her hands. Her gaze was warm and unwavering. "I'm ready to accept your diplomatic mission."

As she started to remove his shirt, Janson said, "There's an ordinance in the reg book prohibiting fraternization."

She pressed her lips to his, smothering his halfhearted demurrals, "You call this fraternization?" she said, shouldering off her robe. "Come on, everyone knows what a great deep-penetration agent you are."

He became aware of a delicate fragrance that emanated from her body. Her lips were soft and swollen and moist, and they moved across his face to his mouth, inviting his into hers. Her fingers gently stroked his cheeks, his jawline, his ears. He could feel her breasts, soft yet firm, pressed against his chest, and her legs thrust against his, matching his strength with hers.

Then, abruptly, she began to tremble, and convulsive sobs came from her throat even as she gripped him all the more fiercely. Gently, he pulled her face back, and saw that her cheeks were now stained with tears. He saw the pain in her eyes, pain that was compounded by her own fear, and her humiliation that he was now witness to it.

"Jessie," he said softly. "Jessie."

She shook her head, helplessly, and then cradled it against his deeply muscled chest. "I've never felt so alone," she said. "So frightened."

"You're not alone," Janson said. "And fear is what keeps us alive."

"You don't know what it's like to be afraid."

He kissed her forehead tenderly. "You've got it wrong. I'm always afraid. Like I say, it's why I'm still here. It's why we're here together."

She pulled him to her with a savage intensity. "Make love to me," she said. "I need to feel what you feel. I need to feel it now."

Two intertwined bodies rolled over on the still-made bed, flushed with an almost desperate passion, flexing and shuddering toward a moment of fleshly communion. "You're not alone, my love," Janson murmured. "Neither of us is. Not anymore."


Oradea, in the westernmost point of Romania, was a three-hour drive from Sárospatak, and like a number of Eastern European cities, its beauty was a beneficiary of its postwar poverty. The magnificent nineteenth-century spas and Beaux Arts vistas had been preserved simply because there had been no resources available to tear them down and replace them with what Communist bloc modernity would have favored. To glimpse what the city missed out on, one had only to see the faceless, featureless industrialism of its airport, which could have been any one of a hundred just like it found throughout the Continent.

For the purposes at hand, though, it would do just fine.

There, at the fifth terminal, the man in the yellow and blue uniform tucked his clipboard toward his body, preventing the papers from flapping in the breeze. The DHL cargo plane—a repurposed Boeing 727—was preparing to make a direct flight to Dulles, and the inspector accompanied the pilot to the craft. The punch list was long: Were the oil caps properly tightened? Was the engine compartment as it should be, the intake vanes free of foreign materials? Were the cotter pins properly positioned on the landing-gear wheels, the tire pressure normal, the ailerons, flaps, and rudder-hinge assemblies in good working order?

Finally, the cargo area was inspected. The other members of the ground crew returned to service a short-run propeller plane, used to ferry packages from the provinces to Oradea. As the pilot received clearance for takeoff, nobody noticed that the man in the yellow and blue uniform remained within the craft.

And only when the plane had reached cruising altitude did Janson remove his felt-and-nylon inspector's jacket and settle in for the ride. The pilot, sitting next to him in the cockpit, switched on the automatic avionics and turned to his old friend. It had been two decades since Nick Milescu had served as a fighter pilot in the American Special Forces, but the circumstances in which he and Janson became acquainted had produced powerful and enduring bonds of loyalty. Janson had not offered to explain the need for this ruse, and Milescu had not asked. It was a privilege to do Janson a favor, any favor. It did not go far toward the repayment of a debt, but it was better than nothing at all.

Neither of them noticed—could have noticed—the broad-faced man in the food-services truck, idling under one of the loading ramps, whose hard, alert eyes did not quite match the bored and jaded air he affected. Nor could they have heard the man speak hurriedly into a cell phone, even as the cargo plane raised its wheels and angled into the sky. *Visual identification: confirmed. Flight plans: filed and validated. Destination: verified.*

"You want to bunk out, there's a lounger right behind us," Milescu told Janson. "When we fly with copilots, they use it sometimes. Oradea to Dulles is a ten-hour flight."

From Dulles, however, it would be a very short drive to reach Derek Collins. Maybe Jessie was right and he would not survive the encounter. It was simply a risk he had to take.

"I wouldn't mind catching up on some sleep," Janson admitted.

"It's just you, me, and a few thousand corporate memos here. No storms ahead of us. Nothing should disturb your dreams." Milescu smiled at his old friend.

Janson returned the smile. The pilot could not know how wrong he was.


The Viet Cong guard that morning had thought the American captive might already be dead.

Janson was slumped on the ground, his head at an awkward angle. Flies clustered around his nose and mouth, without a flicker of response from the emaciated prisoner. The eyes were slightly open, in a way you often saw with cadavers. Had malnutrition and disease finally completed their slow work?

The guard unlocked the cage and prodded the prisoner with a shoe, hard. No response. He leaned over and put a hand on the prisoner's neck.

How shocked and terrified the guard looked as the prisoner, thin as a wooden jumping jack, suddenly flung his legs around his waist like an amorous lover, then yanked his pistol from his holster and slammed the butt of it against his head. The dead had come to life. Again, with greater force, he crashed the gun into the guard's skull, and this time the guard fell limp. Now Janson crept into the jungle; he figured he could get a fifteen-minute head start before the alarm was raised and the dogs were loosed. Perhaps the dogs would find the dense jungle impassable; he nearly found it so himself, even as he knifed through the thick underbrush with automaton-like movements. He did not know how he managed to keep moving, how he managed to stave off collapse, yet his mind simply refused to acknowledge his physical debility.

One foot in front of the other.

The VC encampment, he knew, was somewhere in the Tri-Thien region of South Vietnam. The valley to the south was dense with the guerrillas. On the other hand, it was a region where the width of the country was especially narrow. The distance from the border with Laos to the west and the sea to the east was no more than twenty-five clicks. He had to get to the coast. If he could get to the coast, to the South China Sea, he could find his way back to safety.

He could get home.

A long shot? No matter. Nobody was coming for him. He knew that now. Nobody could save his life but him.

The land beneath him crested and dipped until, sometime the next day, he found himself at the bank of a wide river. One foot in front of the other. He began to wade through the brown, bath-warm water and found that his feet never left the bottom, even at its deepest. When he was almost halfway across, he saw a Vietnamese boy on the far bank. Janson closed his eyes, wearily, and when he opened them the boy was gone.

A hallucination? Yes, it had to have been. He must have imagined the boy. What else was he imagining? Had he really escaped, or was he dreaming, his mind falling apart in pace with his body in his miserable bamboo cage? And if he were dreaming, did he really want to wake up? Perhaps the dream was the only escape he would ever enjoy—why bring it to an end?

A water wasp alighted on his shoulder and stung him. It was painful, startlingly so, and yet it brought an odd sense of relief—for if he felt pain, surely he was not dreaming, after all. He shut his eyes again and opened them, and looked to the riverbank before him and saw two men, no, three, and one of them was armed with an AK-47, and the muddy water in front of him was blistered by a warning blast, and exhaustion, like a tide, swept over him, and he slowly raised his hands. There was no pity—no curiosity, even—in the gunman's eyes. He looked like a farmer who had trapped a vole.

As a passenger on the Museumboot circle line, Jessie Kincaid looked like all the other tourists, or so she hoped. Certainly, the glass-topped boat was filled with them, chattering and gawking and running their little videocameras as they floated smoothly down Amsterdam's muddy canals. She clutched the garish brochure for the Museumboot—"bringing you to the most important museums, shopping streets and leisure centres of downtown Amsterdam," as it boasted. Kincaid had little interest in shopping or visiting museums, of course, but she saw that the boat's itinerary included Prinsengracht. How better to disguise stealthy surveillance than by joining a crowd of people engaged in overt surveillance?

Now the boat rounded the bend and the mansion came into view: the mansion with the seven bay windows—the headquarters of the Liberty Foundation. It seemed so innocuous. And yet evil, as if an industrial effluent somehow polluted its grounds.

At intervals, she raised to her eyes what looked like an ordinary 35mm camera, equipped with the bulky zoom lens of the amateur enthusiast. This was only a first go, of course. She would have to figure out how to get nearer without being detected. But for the moment she was, in effect, staking out her stakeout.

Just behind her, and occasionally jostling her, were a couple of unruly teenagers who belonged to an exhausted-looking Korean couple. The mother had a shopping bag with sunflowers on them, containing booty from the Van Gogh Museum souvenir shop; her bleary-eyed husband had his headphones plugged in, no doubt dialed to the Korean audio channel, listening to the prerecorded tour guide: *On your left . . . On your right . . .* The teenagers, a girl and a boy, were engaged in one of those private sibling tussles that were both sport and squabble. Trying to tag each other, they would, every so often, bump into her, and their giggling apologies were perfunctory at best. The parents seemed too tired to be embarrassed. Meanwhile, the kids happily ignored her glares.

She wondered whether she should have sprung for the Rederij Lovers cruise, the passengers of which were promised "an unforgettable evening whilst enjoying an outstanding five-course menu." That scene might have been imprudent for a woman on her own, but she hadn't known the choice was between getting hit on by strange men and getting hit by strange children. Once more, she forced her eyes to focus.


Unseen by her, a man shifted slightly from his rooftop perch, high above Prinsengracht's busy streets. The time of waiting had been long, almost intolerably so, but now he had reason to think that it had not been wasted. Yes—*there,* standing in the glass-topped boat. It was her. As he fine-tuned his sniper scope, suspicion settled into certainty.

The American woman's face was now perfectly centered in his scope; he could even make out her spiky brown hair, her high cheekbones and sensual lips. He exhaled halfway, and then held his breath as the crosshairs settled upon the woman's upper torso.

His concentration was unwavering as his fingers caressed the trigger.

# CHAPTER TWENTY-NINE

Less than an hour from Dulles, Janson found himself on small winding roads that took him through some of the most tranquil territory on the Eastern Shore. Deceptively so. He recalled Jessie's words of warning. *If Collins wants you dead, don't count on leaving his company alive.* Jessie believed he was taking an enormous risk, meeting a deadly adversary face-to-face. But a bolus of sheer rage impelled Janson. Besides, Derek Collins gave orders: he did not execute them himself. To do so would be infra dig, beneath him. Those long-fingered hands would not be sullied. Not as long as there were others to take care of matters for him.

Chesapeake Bay covered 2,200 miles of coastline, far more if one counted the 150 tributaries along with all the coves and creeks and tidal rivers. The bay itself was shallow, ranging from ten to thirty feet. Janson knew that all sorts of creatures thrived here: muskrats and nutria, swans, geese, ducks, even osprey. The bald eagle itself bred around the lowlands of Dorchester County, as did the great horned owl. The profusion of wildlife, in turn, made it an inviting place for hunters as well.

And Janson was there to hunt.

Now he drove over the Choptank River at Cambridge, onto 13, and farther south, over another bridge, and finally to the long spit of land known as Phipps Island. As he drove the rented Camry along the narrow road, he could see the water through the salt-marsh grass, the sun glaring off its surface. Fishing sloops were moving slowly along the bay, hauling in nets laden with blue crabs and menhaden and rockfish.

A few miles farther down the road, he entered Phipps Island proper. He saw why Derek Collins had chosen it for a vacation home, a retreat from the pressures of his Washington existence. Though only a relatively short distance from Washington, it was isolated, peaceful; it was also, by dint of the land formation, secure. Janson, approaching the undersecretary's bayside cottage, was feeling distinctly exposed. A long, skinny strip of land connected it to the main peninsula, making a surreptitious land approach difficult. An amphibious arrival would be impeded by the shallowness of the water surrounding the land, much of which had only recently been reclaimed by the steadily erosive sea. The wooden docks for boat landings extended far out, where the depth of the water was sufficient for safe navigation; and the length of those docks, too, rendered potential intruders exposed and vulnerable. Without the need to rely on fallible electronics, Collins had selected an area where nature itself assured him the advantages of easy surveillance and the attendant security.

*Don't count on leaving his company alive.* The director of Consular Operations was a deadly and determined man; Janson had learned that from experience. Well, that made two of them.

The tires of the sedan kicked up dust—beach sand and dried salt— from the surface of the pale gray road, which stretched ahead like a discarded snakeskin. Would Collins seek to kill him before they spoke? He would do so if he believed Janson represented a mortal threat to him. More likely, he would summon backup—the Oceana Naval Air Station, outside Virginia Beach, could send a pair of H-3 Sea King helicopters to Phipps Island in fifteen minutes; an F-18 Hornet squadron could be scrambled in even less time.

The important factors to be gauged had to do with character, not technology. Derek Collins was a planner. That was how Janson thought of such men: the ones who sat in air-conditioned offices as they deployed men on missions doomed to failure, all in the course of some chess game they called strategy. A pawn was moved, a pawn was taken. From the perspective of men like Collins, that was what his "human assets" amounted to: pawns. Yet now Janson had the blood of five former Cons Op agents on his hands, and he was hell-bent on confronting the man who had enlisted them, trained them, guided them, directed them—the man who sought to control his destiny, like a piece of carved boxwood on a playing board.

Yes, Collins was a determined man. But so was Janson, who detested him with a remarkable purity and intensity. Collins was why he had left Consular Operations in the first place. A stiff-necked, cold-blooded son of a bitch, Derek Collins had one supreme advantage: he knew precisely who he was. About himself, anyway, he had few illusions. He was a masterful bureaucratic politician and a thoroughgoing credit-stealing bastard, and such men would always thrive in the marmoreal jungle that was the nation's capital. None of that bothered Janson; he regarded it as nearly humanizing. What incensed Janson was the man's smug certainty that the ends always justified the means. Janson had seen where that led—even seen it, sometimes, in himself—and it sickened him.

Now he pulled off the road, nosing the car into a particularly exuberant growth of bayberries and marsh willows. The remaining mile he would traverse on foot. If Jessie's contacts had provided her with accurate information, Collins should be in his cottage, and by himself. A widower, Collins had a penchant for spending time alone; and here another truth about him was illuminated—that he was a deeply unsociable person who was nonetheless skilled at affecting sociability.

Janson walked through the shoreline grass to the shoreline itself, a jagged tan strip of rocks and sand and battered shells. Despite his thick-soled shoes, he stepped lightly through the dampness of the shore, making little sound. Collins's cabin was built low to the ground, which made it a somewhat more elusive target for anyone with unfriendly intentions. By the same token, however, it assured Janson that as long as he remained on the shoreline, he would not be visible from it.

The sun beat against his neck, and his pale cotton shirt grew dappled with sweat and the salt spray that breezed in from the bay. Occasionally, as the tide gently pulled back the water level, he could make out the silhouette of an intricate tracery upon the water: he realized that flat nets had been stretched from the coastline some distance outward, held afloat by small buoys. The security measures were discreet but not negligible, for doubtless the nets were studded with sensors; an amphibious landing would have been nearly impossible without serving notice of the intrusion.

He heard the sound of heavy boots on the planked walkway just twenty feet away, where the land formed a crown near the top of the beach. A young man in a uniform of green and black camouflage, cinched trousers, a weapons belt: standard-issue National Guard attire. His gait on the boardwalk was a regular tattoo of hard rubber against wood—this was a guard doing a required patrol, not one who was alert to an intruder's presence.

Janson continued to trudge quietly along the wet sand of the shore.

"Hey, you!" The young guardsman had spotted him, and was walking toward him. "You see the signs? You can't be here. No fishing, no shell scavenging, no *nothing*." The man's face was sun-reddened, not tanned; this was obviously a recent posting for him, and he had not yet adjusted to the long hours of exposure to the elements.

Janson turned to face him, stooping his shoulders slightly, *willing* himself to appear older and feebler. A salty waterman, a local. How would a local respond? He recalled his long-ago conversations with one of them, a fellow angler. "Do you have any idea who I am, young man?" He made his face muscles slack, and his voice developed a slight quaver suggestive of infirmity. He spoke with the vowels of the old Eastern Shore regional accent. "Me, my family been living here when you were still eatin' your white bread. Been here through the rubs, been here when things was pretty. Shoreline here is public property. My daughter-in-law's been five years on the Lower Eastern Shore Heritage Committee. You think you're going to tell me I can't go where the law says I can, you got a whole 'nother think come at you. I know my rights."

The guardsman scowled, half amused at the old salt's line of blather and not ungrateful for the interruption of his tedious routine. But his orders were clear. "Fact remains, this is a restricted area, and there's about a dozen signs saying so."

"I'll have you know, my ancestors were here when the Union troops were in Salisbury, and—"

"Listen, Pappy," the guardsman said, rubbing the red and peeling bridge of his nose, "I will frog-march your ass into federal custody at gunpoint if I have to." He stood directly in front of the other man. "You got a complaint, write your congressman." He puffed out his chest, placed a hand near his holstered side arm.

"Why, look at you, you're just breath and britches." Janson limply made a swatting gesture with a hand, indicating dismissal and resignation. "Ah, you park rangers wouldn't know a bufflehead from a widgeon."

"Park ranger?" the guardsman sneered, shaking his head. "You think we're *park rangers?*"

Suddenly, Janson sprang at him, clamping his right hand around his mouth, his left around the back of his neck. They fell together, the sound of the impact muffled by the sand, a quiet *crunch* lost amid the cawing of gulls and the rustling of the salt-meadow cordgrass. Even before they hit the ground, though, Janson had snaked his hand around and grabbed the man's holstered M9 pistol.

"Nobody likes a smart-ass," he said quietly, dropping the accent, jabbing the M9 Beretta into his trachea. The young man's eyes widened in terror. "You got new orders, and you'd better obey them: a sound out of you and you're dead, greenhorn."

With swift movements, Janson undid the guardsman's weapons belt and used it to bind his wrists to his ankles. Next, he ripped narrow strips of cloth from his camouflage tunic and stuffed them in the man's mouth, finally securing the gag with the guardsman's own bootlaces. After pocketing the man's M9 and his Motorola "handy-talky," he lifted him like a heavy rucksack and left him hidden amid a thick growth of cordgrass.

Janson pressed on, and when the beach disappeared, he walked farther up the grass. There would be at least another guard on patrol duty—the undersecretary's weekend house had clearly been designated a federal facility—but there was a good chance that the Motorola TalkAbout T6220 would let him know if any irregularities had been detected.

A fast five-minute walk and Janson found himself on the south side of a sparsely grassed dune, the cottage just out of view. His pace lessened as, with each step, his boots sank into the loose, silty sand, but his destination was not much farther.

He looked out once more and saw the placid water of Chesapeake Bay—misleadingly placid, for it was invisibly swarming with life. In the distant glare, he could just make out Tangier Island, several miles to the south. Now it styled itself the soft-shell capital of the world; yet in 1812, the one war in the country's history where foreign troops were deployed on U.S. soil, it was the base of British operations. The shipbuilding firms of St. Michaels were nearby; blockade-runners circulated around the port. A scrap of military history returned to Janson: it was in St. Michaels that the shorefolk conducted one of the classic ruses of nineteenth-century warfare. Hearing of an impending British attack, the townsmen extinguished their lanterns. Then they hoisted them high into the trees and lit them again. The British fired upon the town but, misled by the lantern placement, aimed too high, their shells uselessly lodging in treetops far overhead.

That was the Eastern Shore: so much serenity hiding so much blood. Three centuries of American strife and American contentment. It was altogether fitting that Derek Collins should have established his private redoubt here.

"My wife Janice used to love that spot." The familiar voice came without warning, and Janson whirled around to see Derek Collins. Inside his jacket, Janson gingerly fingered the trigger to the M9, testing its tension as he looked over his adversary.

The only thing that was unfamiliar was the bureaucrat's garb: a man he had always seen in three-button suits of navy or charcoal worsted was wearing khakis, a madras shirt, and moccasins—his weekend attire.

"She'd set her easel up right there, where you're standing, get her watercolors out, and try to capture the light. That's what she always said she was doing: trying to capture the light." His eyes were dull, his customary bright and scheming avidity replaced by something somber and careworn. "She had polycythemia, you know. Or maybe you didn't. A bone marrow disease, made her body produce too many blood cells. Janice was my second wife, I guess you do know that. A new beginning and all. A few years after we were married, she'd start to feel itchy after she took a warm bath, and that turned out to be the first sign of it. Funny, isn't it? It progresses slowly, but eventually there came the headaches, the dizziness, and just this feeling of exhaustion, and she got the diagnosis. Toward the end, she spent most of her time here, on Phipps. I'd drive down, and there she'd be, sitting at the easel, trying to get her watercolors to make that sunset. She struggled with the colors. Too often, she said, they'd look like blood. As if there was something inside her, wildly signaling to be let out." Collins was standing only ten feet from Janson, but his voice was far away. He stood with his hands in his pockets, looking out at the slowly darkening bay. "She loved watching the birds, too. She didn't think she could paint them, but she loved watching them. You see that one near the Osage orange tree? Pearl gray, white undersides, black mask like a raccoon around the eyes?"

It was about the size of a robin, leaping from one perch to another.

"That's a loggerhead shrike," Collins said. "One of the local birds. She thought it was pretty. *Lanius ludovicianus.*"

"Better known as the butcher bird," Janson said.

The bird trilled its two-note call.

"Figures, you know," Collins said. "It's unusual, isn't it, because it preys on other birds. But check it out. It doesn't have any talons. That's the beauty part. It takes advantage of its surroundings—impales its prey on a thorn or barbed wire before it rips it apart. It doesn't need much by way of claws. It knows that the world is filled with surrogate claws. Use what's there." The bird emitted a harsh, thrasher-like note and fluttered off.

Collins turned and looked at Janson. "Why don't you come inside?"

"Aren't you going to frisk me?" Janson asked, in a tone of indifference. He was surprised at how unruffled Collins seemed, and was determined to match his calm. "See what weapons I might have on me?"

Collins laughed, and his solemnity broke for a moment. "Janson, you *are* a weapon," he said. "What am I supposed to do, amputate all your limbs and put you in a vitrine?" He shook his head. "You forget how well I know you. Besides, I'm looking at somebody who has folded his arms beneath a jacket, and that bulge a foot below his shoulder is quite likely a handgun, aimed at me. I'm guessing you took it off of Ambrose. Young kid, reasonably well trained, but not the sharpest knife in the drawer."

Janson said nothing but kept his finger on the trigger. The M9 would shoot easily through the fabric of his jacket: Collins was a mere finger twitch from death and he knew it.

"Come along," Collins said. "We'll walk together. A peaceable dyad of vulnerability. A two-man demonstration of mutual assured destruction, and the deep comfort the balance of terror can bring."

Janson said nothing. Collins was not a field agent; he was no less lethal in his way, but through more mediated channels. Together, they traipsed over a boardwalk of silvery, weathered cedar and into Collins's house. It was a classic seaside cottage, probably of early twentieth-century construction: weathered shingles, small dormers on the second floor. Nothing that would attract much attention, not at a casual glance, anyway.

"You got a federal-facilities designation for your weekend house," Janson said. "Good going."

"It's a secure, Class A-four facility—completely to code. After the John Deutch debacle, nobody wants to be caught taking office work home, putting classified files on an unguarded bedroom PC. For me the solution was to turn this home into an office. An offsite location."

"Hence the National Guardsmen."

"A couple of kids patrol the area. This afternoon it's Ambrose and Bamford. Make sure nobody's fishing where they shouldn't be, that's what they get up to most of the time."

"You stay here alone?"

Collins smiled wanly. "A suspicious mind would find menace in that question." He wandered over to his kitchen, which gleamed with stainless-steel counters and high-end appliances. "But yes, I've come to prefer it that way. I get more thinking done."

"In my experience, the more thinking you people do, the more trouble you make," Janson said with quiet mordancy. The Beretta was still in his right hand, its butt braced on the counter. When Collins moved behind the exhaust vent of his Viking range, Janson repositioned himself subtly. At no point was Collins ever protected from the 9mm in Janson's hand.

Now Collins set a mug of coffee by Janson. His movements, too, were calculated—calculatedly nonthreatening. A mug of scalding fluid could be a weapon, so he was careful to slide the mugs slowly across the counter. He did not want Janson even to consider the possibility that their contents might be flung into his face, and take countermeasures. It was a way of treating his guest with respect, and it was a way of sparing himself any preemptive violence. Collins had gone through decades clambering to the top of an elite covert intelligence agency without so much as injuring a fingernail; he evidently sought to preserve his record.

"When Janice had all this done"—Collins gestured around them, at the fixtures and furnishings—"I believe she called this a 'nook.' Dining nook or breakfast nook or some such damn thing." They sat together now at the black honed-granite counter, each perched on a high round stool of steel and leather. Collins took a sip of the coffee. "Janice's Faema super-automatic coffeemaker. A seventy-five-pound contraption of stainless steel, plus more computational power than the lunar module, all to make a cup or two of java. Sounds like something the Pentagon might have come up with, doesn't it?" Through his chunky black glasses, his slate-gray eyes were at once inquiring and amused. "You're probably wondering why I haven't asked you to put the gun away. That's what people always say in these situations, isn't it? 'Put the gun away and let's talk'—like that."

"You always want to be the brightest kid in the classroom, don't you?" Janson's eyes were hard as he took a sip of the coffee. Collins had taken care to pour the coffee in front of him, tacitly letting him verify that his coffee had not been spiked or poisoned. Similarly, when he brought the two mugs to the counter, he let Janson choose the one he would drink from. Janson had to admire the bureaucrat's punctiliousness in anticipating his ex-employee's every paranoid thought.

Collins ignored the taunt. "Truth is, I'd probably rather you keep the gun trained on me—just because it'll soothe your jangled nerves. I'm sure it's more calming to you than anything that I could say. Accordingly, it makes you less likely to act rashly." He shrugged. "You see, I'm just letting you in on my thinking. The more candor we can manage, the more at ease you'll be."

"An interesting calculation," Janson grunted. The undersecretary of state had evidently decided he was more likely to escape grievous bodily harm by making it clear and unambiguous that his life was in the field agent's hands. *If you can kill me, you won't hurt me*—so ran Collins's reasoning.

"Just to celebrate Saturday, I'm making mine Irish," Collins said, pulling over a bottle of bourbon and splashing some in his mug. "You want?" Janson scowled, and Collins said, "Didn't think so. You're on duty, right?" He poured a dollop of cream in as well.

"Around you? Always."

A resigned half smile. "The shrike we saw earlier—it's a hawk that thinks it's a songbird. I think both of us remember an earlier conversation we had along those lines. One of your 'exit interviews.' I told you that you were a hawk. You didn't want to hear it. I think you wanted to be a songbird. But you weren't one, and never will be. You're a hawk, Janson, because that's your nature. Same as that loggerhead shrike." Another sip of his Irish coffee. "One day, I got here and Janice was at her easel, where she'd been trying to paint. She was crying. Sobbing. I thought maybe—I don't know what I thought. Turns out she watched as this songbird, that's how she regarded it, impaled a small bird on one of the hawthorn shrubs and just let it hang there. Sometime later, the shrike came back and started to rip it apart with its curved beak. A butcher bird doing what a butcher bird does, the crimson, glistening viscera of another bird dripping from its beak. To her, it was horrible, just horrible. A betrayal. Somehow she never got the nature-red-in-tooth-and-claw memo. That wasn't how she saw the world. A Sarah Lawrence girl, right? And what could I tell her? That a hawk with a song is still a hawk?"

"Maybe it's both, Derek. Not a songbird pretending to be a hawk, but a hawk that's also a songbird. A songbird that turns into hawk when it needs to. Why do we have to choose?"

"Because we do have to choose." He placed his mug down hard on the granite counter, and the *thunk* of heavy ceramic against stone punctuated his shift of tone. "And *you* have to choose. Which side are you on?"

"Which side are *you* on?"

"I've never changed," Collins said.

"You tried to kill me."

Collins tilted his head. "Well, yes and no," he replied, and his nonchalance bewildered Janson more than any emphatic, heated denial would have. There was no stiffening, no defensiveness; Collins might have been discussing the factors contributing to beachfront erosion.

"Glad you're so mellow about it," Janson said with glacial control. "Five of your henchmen who ended their careers in the Tisza valley seemed less philosophical."

"*Not* mine," Collins said. "Look, this really is awkward."

"I wouldn't want you to feel you owe me an explanation." Janson spoke with cold fury. "About Peter Novak. About me. About why you want me dead."

"See, that was a mistake, the Lambda Team dispatch, and we feel terrible about the whole beyond-salvage directive. Big-time product recall on that order—Firestone-tire-size. Mistake, mistake, mistake. But whatever hostiles you encountered in Hungary—well, they weren't ours. Maybe once, but not anymore. That's all I can tell you."

"So I guess everything's squared away," Janson replied with heavy sarcasm.

Collins removed his glasses and blinked a few times. "Don't get me wrong. I'm sure we'd do the same thing again. Look, I didn't institute the order, I just didn't countermand it. Everybody in operations—not to mention all the frontline spooks at the CIA and other shops—thought you'd gone rogue, took a sixteen-million-dollar bribe, all that. I mean, the evidence was plain as day. For a while, I thought so, too."

"Then you learned better."

"Except that I couldn't cancel the order without an explanation. Otherwise, people would assume either I'd lost it or that somebody had got to me, too. Just wasn't feasible. And the thing was, I couldn't offer an explanation. Not without compromising a secret on the very highest levels. The one secret that could never be compromised. You're not going to be able to look at this objectively, because we're talking about your own survival here. But my job is all about priorities, and where you've got priorities, you're going to have sacrifices to make."

"Sacrifices to make?" Janson interjected, his voice dripping with derision. "You mean a sacrifice for me to make. I *was* that goddamn sacrifice." He leaned in closer, his face numb with rage.

"You can remove your curved beak from my torn viscera. I'm not arguing."

"Do you think I killed Peter Novak?"

"I know you didn't."

"Let me ask you a simple question," Janson began. "Is Peter Novak dead?"

Collins sighed. "Well, again, my answer's yes and no."

"God*dammit!*" Janson exploded. "I want answers."

"Shoot," Collins said. "Let me rephrase that: ask away."

"Let's start with a pretty disturbing discovery I've made. I've studied dozens of photographic images of Peter Novak in exacting detail. I'm not going to interpret the data, I'm just going to present the data. There are variances, subtle but measurable, of fixed physical dimensions. Ratio of index finger length to forefinger length. Trapezium to metacarpal. Forearm length. The ventral surface of the scapula, shadowed against his shirt, in two photographs taken only a few days apart."

"Conclusion: these aren't pictures of one man." Collins's voice was flat.

"I went to his birthplace. There *was* a Peter Novak who was born to Janós and Illana Ferenczi-Novak. He died about five years later, in 1942."

Collins nodded, and once more, his lack of reaction was more chilling than any reaction could have been. "Excellent work, Janson."

"Tell me the truth," Janson said. "I'm not crazy. *I saw a man die.*"

"That's so," Collins said.

"And not just any man. We're talking about Peter Novak—a living legend."

"Bingo." Collins made a clicking sound. "You said it yourself. A living legend."

Janson felt his stomach drop. A living legend. A creation of intelligence professionals.

*Peter Novak was an agency legend.*

# CHAPTER THIRTY

Collins slid off the stool and stood up. "There's something I want to show you."

He walked to his office, a large room facing the bay. On rustic wooden shelves were rows of old copies of *Studies in Intelligence,* a classified journal for American clandestine services. Monographs on international conflicts were interspersed with popular novels and dog-eared volumes of *Foreign Affairs.* A Sun Microsystems UltraSPARC workstation was connected to racked tiers of servers.

"You remember *The Wizard of Oz?* Bet they asked you about it when you were a POW. I gather the North Vietnamese interrogators were obsessed with American popular culture."

"It didn't come up," Janson said curtly.

"Naw, you were probably too much of a hardass to give away the ending. Wouldn't want to jeopardize our national security that way. . . . Sorry. That was out of line. There's one thing that divides us: whatever happens, you'll always be a goddamn war hero, and I'll always be a civvy desk jockey, and for some people, that makes you a better man. Irony is, 'some people' includes me. I'm jealous. I'm one of those guys who wanted to have suffered without ever wanting to suffer. Like wanting to have written a book, as opposed to wanting actually to write one."

"Can we move on?"

"You see, I've always thought it's the moment when we lose our innocence. Up there is the great and powerful Oz, and down there is the schmuck beneath the curtain. But it's not just him, it's the whole goddamn contraption, the machinery, the bellows, the levers, the steam nozzles, the diesel engine, or whatever. You think that was easy to put together? And once you had that up and running, it's not going to make much difference who you've got behind the curtain, or so we figured. It's the *machine,* not the man, that matters."

The director of Consular Operations was babbling; the anxiety he displayed nowhere else was making him weirdly voluble.

"You're trying my patience," Janson said. "Here's a tip. Never try the patience of a man holding a gun."

"It's just that we're approaching *la gran scena,* and I don't want you to lose it." Collins gestured toward the softly humming computer system. "You ready for this? Because we're moving toward now-that-you-know-I'm-going-to-have-to-kill-you territory."

Janson adjusted the M9 so that the sights were squarely between Collins's eyes, and the director of Consular Operations added quickly, "Not *literally.* We've moved beyond that—those of us in the program, I mean. We're playing a different game now. Then again, so is *he.*"

"Start making sense," Janson said, gritting his teeth.

"A tall order." Collins jerked his head toward the computer system again. "You might say *that*'s Peter Novak. That, and a few hundred interoperable, omicron-level-security computer systems elsewhere. Peter Novak is really a composite of bytes and bits and digital-transfer signatures with neither origins nor destinations. Peter Novak wasn't a person. He's a project. An invention. A legend, yeah. And for a long time, the most successful ever."

Janson's mind clouded as if overtaken by a sudden dust storm and, just as swiftly, a preternatural clarity set in.

It was madness—a madness that made a terrible kind of sense. "Please," he said to the bureaucrat calmly, quietly. "Go on."

"Best if we sit somewhere else," Collins said. "The system here has so many electronic security seals and booby-traps, it goes into auto-erase mode if you breathe on it hard. A moth once rammed into the window and I lost hours of work."

Now the two settled into the living room, the furniture covered with the coarse floral chintz that, at some point in the seventies, had evidently been decreed by law for seaside vacation houses.

"Look, it was a brilliant idea. Such a brilliant idea that for a long time, people were feuding over credit for who had the idea first. You know, like who invented the radio, or whatnot. Except that the number of people who knew about this was tiny, tiny, tiny. Had to be. Obviously, my predecessor Daniel Congdon had a lot to do with it. So did Doug Albright, a protégé of David Abbott."

"Albright I've heard of. Abbott?"

"The guy who devised the whole 'Caine' gambit, back in the late seventies, trying to smoke out Carlos. Same kind of strategic thinking went into Mobius. Asymmetrical conflicts pit states against individual actors. Mismatched, but not the way you'd imagine. Think of an elephant and a mosquito. If that mosquito carries encephalitis, you could have one dead elephant, and there's really not much Jumbo can do about it. The problem of substate actors is similar. Abbott's great insight was that you really couldn't mobilize anything as unwieldy as a state against baddies of this sort: you had to counter with a matching stratagem: create individual actors who, within a broad mandate, had a fair level of autonomy."

"Mobius?"

"The Mobius Program. Basically, you're talking about what began as a small group at the State Department. Soon it had to extend beyond State, because it had to be interagency if it was going to get off the ground. So there was a fat guy who used to be at the Hudson Institute and ran the operations sector at DIA, those 'committed to excellence' boys. His understudy takes over after he dies—that's Doug. A computer whiz kid from Central Intelligence. Oval Office liaison to the NSC. But seventeen years ago, you're basically talking about a small group at the State Department. And they're tossing around ideas, and somehow they hit on this scenario. What if they assembled a small, secret team of analysts and experts to create a notional foreign billionaire? The more they toss the idea around, the more they like it. They like it because the more they think about it, the more doable it seems. *They can make this happen.* They can *do* this. And when they start to think about *what* they can do with it, it becomes irresistible. They can do *good* things. They can advance American interests in a way that America just can't. They can make the world a better place. Totally win-win. Which is how the Mobius Program was born."

"Mobius," Janson said. "As in a loop where the inside is the outside."

"In this case, the outsider is an insider. This mogul becomes an independent figure in the world, no ties whatever to the United States. Our adversaries aren't his adversaries. They can be his allies. He can leverage situations we wouldn't be able to go near. First, though, you've got to create a 'he,' and from the ground up. Backstopping was a real challenge. For his birthplace, the programmers choose a tiny Hungarian village that was completely liquidated in the forties."

"Precisely because all the records were destroyed, nearly all the villagers killed."

"Molnár was like a gift from the gods of backstopping. I mean, it was terrible, the massacres and all, but it was perfect for the program's purposes, especially when you added to that the short, unhappy career of Count Ferenczi-Novak. Made perfect sense that our boy was going to have a sketchy early childhood. All his peers are dead, and his father's terrified that his enemies are going to take his child from him. So he hides him, has him privately tutored. Eccentric, maybe, but plausible enough."

"There'd have to be an employment record," Janson said, "but that would have been the easy part. You restrict his 'career' to a few front organizations that you can control."

"Anybody makes inquiries, there's always some silver-haired department head, maybe retired, to say, 'Oh yes, I remember young Peter. A little big for his britches, but a brilliant financial analyst. The work was so good, I didn't mind that he preferred to do his work from home. A bit of an agoraphobe, but with that traumatic background, how can you blame him?' And like that."

These men and women, Janson knew, would have been generously compensated for uttering a lie perhaps once or twice to an inquiring reporter, and perhaps never. They would not be aware of what else the bargain would entail: the around-the-clock monitoring of their communications, a lifelong net of surveillance—but what they didn't know couldn't hurt them.

"And the spectacular rise? How could you backstop that?"

"Well, that's where things get a little hairy. But, as I say, there was a brilliant team of experts tasked to the Mobius Program. They—we, I should say, though I wasn't enlisted until seven years into it—caught a number of breaks. And, voilà, you've got a man in charge of an empire of his own. A man who could manipulate global events as we never could ourselves."

"Manipulate . . . ? Meaning what?" Janson demanded.

"I think you know. The Liberty Foundation. The entire conflict-resolution agenda. 'Directed democracy.' All of it."

"So this great humanitarian financier, the 'peacemaker'—"

"It was originally a *60 Minutes* segment that dubbed him that, and it stuck. For good reason. The peacemaker established a foundation with offices in nearly every regional capital in the world."

"And his incredible humanitarian assistance?"

"Isn't this country the best? And isn't it *messed up* that no matter how much good we do, so many people around the world hate our guts? Yes, it meant offering balm to the world's trouble spots. Look, the World Bank is a lender of last resort. This guy's a lender of *first* resort. Which ensured that he would have enormous influence with governments the world over. Peter Novak: your roving ambassador for peace and stability."

"Oil on troubled waters."

"Expensive oil, make no mistake. But 'Novak' could mediate, resolve conflicts that we could never—openly—go near. He's been able to deal effectively and confidentially with regimes that consider us the Great Satan. He has been a one-man foreign policy. And what made him so goddamn effective is precisely the fact that he appears to have no connection to us."

Janson's mind whirled, buzzed, filled with the echoes of voices—confiding, cautioning, threatening. Nikos Andros: *You Americans have never been able to wrap your minds around anti-Americanism. You so want to be loved that you cannot understand why there is so little love for you. A man wears big boots and wonders why the ants beneath his feet fear and hate him.* Angus Fielding: *The one thing that you Americans have never quite grasped is how very deep anti-Americanism goes. . . .* The Serbian with gold-rimmed glasses: *You Americans always want things that aren't on the menu, don't you? You can never have enough choices.* A Hungarian barkeep with a lethal pastime: *You Americans complain about drug traffickers in Asia, and meanwhile you flood the world with the electronic equivalent. . . . Everywhere you go, you find your own spoor. The slime of the serpent is over all.*

A cacophony resolved itself into a single refrain, another kind of plainchant.

*You Americans.*

*You Americans.*

*You Americans.*

*You Americans.*

Janson suppressed a shiver. "But who is—was—Peter Novak?" he asked.

"It was kind of like the *Six Million Dollar Man*—'Gentlemen, we can rebuild him, we have the technology. We have the capability to make him better than he was before. Better. Stronger. Faster.' " He broke off. "Well, richer, anyway. Fact is, three agents were assigned to the part. They were all similar-looking to begin with, very close to one another in build and height. And then surgery made them damned near identical. All sorts of computerized micrometers were used—an exhaustive procedure. But we had to have replicas in place: given our investment, we couldn't afford to have our guy hit by a bus, or drop dead from a stroke. Three seemed like good odds."

Janson looked at Collins strangely. "Who would ever agree to do such a thing? To allow his entire identity to be wiped out, to become dead to everyone he ever knew, his very countenance transformed. . . ."

"Someone who had no choice," Collins replied cryptically.

Janson felt a gorge of anger. He knew Collins's sangfroid was all on the surface, but the heartlessness of the man's reasoning summed everything up: the damnable arrogance of the planners. The damn strategic elites with their neatly trimmed cuticles and their blithe certainty that what worked on the page would work in the real world. They saw the globe as a chessboard, were oblivious to the fact that people made of flesh and blood would suffer the consequences of their grand schemes. He could hardly stand to look at the bureaucrat before him, and his eyes drifted toward the glittering bay, toward the fishing boat that had moved into view, safely beyond the security zone that began half a mile from the shore, marked off by warning buoys. "Someone who had no choice?" He shook his head. "You mean the way I had no choice when you set me up to be killed."

"*That* again." Collins rolled his eyes. "Like I said, calling off the termination order would have raised too many questions. The cowboys at the CIA got credible reports that Novak had been killed and that you had something to do with it. Cons Ops got hold of the same info. The last thing any of us at Mobius wanted bruited about, but you play the cards you're dealt. At the time, I did what I thought was best." The words were mere words, expressing neither sadism nor sorrow.

A scrim of red momentarily suffused Janson's vision: which was the greater insult, he wondered—being executed as a traitor, or being sacrificed as a pawn? Once more the fishing vessel caught his attention, but this time the sight was accompanied by a wrenching sense of danger. It was too small to be a crabber, and too near the shore to be after rockfish or perch.

And the thick staff that extended from the flapping tarpaulin on the deck was not a fishing pole.

Janson saw the bureaucrat's mouth moving, but he could no longer hear him, for his attention was wholly devoted to an immediate and deadly threat. Yes, Collins's bungalow was on a narrow, two-mile-long spit of land, yet the sense of security conveyed by the isolation, Janson realized now, was an illusion.

An illusion that was shattered by the first artillery round that exploded in Collins's living room.


A torrent of adrenaline constricted Janson's consciousness to a laserlike focus. The shell smashed through the window and hurled into the opposite wall, spraying the room with splinters of wood and chunks of plaster and fragments of glass; the blast was so intense that it registered on the ears less as sound than as *pain*. Black smoke began to billow and Janson understood the fluke that had saved them. A howitzer shell, he knew, spun more than three hundred times a second, and the result of its force and spin was that the shell had burrowed far into the cottage's soft-pine and plaster construction before it exploded. Only this had spared them a deadly blast of jagged shrapnel. Seemingly conscious of every millisecond, Janson realized, too, that an artillery gunner's first few shells were fired in order to zero in on the mark. The second shell would not arrive ten feet above their heads. The second shell, if they stayed where they were, would not leave them to ponder shell rotation speeds and detonation times.

The old wood-frame house would offer them no protection at all.

Janson leaped from the couch and raced to the attached garage. It was his only hope. The door was open and Janson took a few steps down to the concrete floor, where a small convertible stood. A yellow late-model Corvette.

"Wait a minute!" Collins called out breathlessly. His face was smudged with soot from the explosion and he was obviously winded from having followed Janson's sprint. "It's my Z-six. I've got the keys right here." He held them out meaningfully, asserting the primacy of property rights.

Janson grabbed them from his hand and jumped into the driver's seat. "Friends don't let friends drive drunk," he replied, shoving the startled undersecretary of state out of the way. "You can come or not."

Collins hastened over to the side, pressed the garage-door opener, and rode shotgun with Janson, who revved the motor in reverse and shot out of the garage with just a millimeter of clearance between it and the lumbering roll-up door.

"Cutting it a little close, are we?" Collins asked. His face was now drenched in perspiration.

Janson said nothing.

Using, in rapid succession, the emergency brake, the steering wheel, and the accelerator with an organist's fluidity, Janson executed a reverse bootleg turn—a J turn—and gunned the car down the narrow macadamized roadway.

"I'm thinking this wasn't such a smart move," said Collins. "We're now totally exposed."

"The flat nets—they extend out all the way around the tip of the island, right?"

"About a half mile out, yes."

"Then use your head. Those nets would entangle any sloop that tried to cut across them. So if the gunboat wants to gain a new line of fire on us, it's got a very wide apex to sail around. It's a slow-moving vessel—it just isn't going to have enough time. Meanwhile, we keep the house itself between us and it: that's concealment and protection."

"Point taken," Collins said. "But now I want you to turn onto the pocket marina we've got a little farther on the right. We get there, we're out of sight. Plus we can take a motorboat to the mainland if we need to." His voice was composed, masterful. "See that little path to the right? Turn on it—*now*."

Janson drove past it.

"Goddammit, Janson!" Collins bellowed. "That marina was our best chance."

"Best chance to get blown to bits. You imagine they won't have thought of it? They'll already have lobbed a time-delayed explosive device there. Think like *they* do!"

"Turn around!" Collins yelled. "Goddammit, Paul, I *know* this place, I *live* here, and I'm telling you—"

A loud explosion from behind them drowned out the rest of his words: the marina had been blown up. Part of a rubber dingy was thrown high into the air and landed on the side of the road.

Now Janson depressed the accelerator pedal farther, barreling down the narrow road faster than would ordinarily be safe. At eighty miles per hour, the tall grass and thorn trees zipped past in the rearview mirror. The roar of the motor seemed to grow ever louder, as if the muffler was cutting out. Now it seemed as if he were floating in the bay, as the spit narrowed to little more than sixty feet across, some beach, some low, scruffy vegetation, and the road, half covered in drifting sand. Janson knew that the sand itself reduced traction like an oil slick, and he reduced speed slightly.

The sound of the motor did not subside.

*It was not the sound of his motor.*

Janson turned to his right and saw the hovercraft. An amphibious military model.

It was skimming along the surface of the bay, a powerful fan keeping it aloft, a couple of feet above the surface of the water and the flat nets stretched beneath. It was unstoppable.

Janson felt as though he had swallowed ice. The lowlands of Chesapeake Bay were perfectly suited for the hovercraft's capabilities. The land would not provide them shelter: unlike a boat, the craft could move almost as easily over dry surfaces as over wet ones. And the powerful engine enabled it to keep pace easily with the Corvette. It was a more dangerous foe than the gunboat, and now it was gaining on them! The sound of the fan was deafening, and the small convertible swayed precariously in its mechanical gale.

He sneaked another glance at the hovercraft. From the side, it had some resemblance to a yacht, with a small forward windowed cabin. Mounted at the other end was a powerful upright fan. Heavy-duty antiplow skirts were mounted to the fore of the craft. As it zipped along the placid waters it gave an impression of fluid effortlessness.

Janson floored the accelerator—only to realize, sickeningly, that the hovercraft was not merely keeping pace; it was passing them. And, perched just below and to the left of the rear fan encasement, someone wearing ear protectors was fumbling with what looked like an M60 machine gun.

Janson aimed his M9 with one hand and emptied the magazine—yet the relative motion of the car and his target made accuracy impossible. The bullets simply clanged off the massive steel blades of the fan.

And now he had no more ammunition.

Bouncing lightly on its bipod, the M60 produced a low, grunting noise, and Janson remembered why it was known as the "pig" when he was in Vietnam. He hunched down as low as he could in his seat without losing control of the car, and the car's body jarred to a jackhammer rhythm as a spray of bullets, two hundred 7.62mm rounds per minute, sledgehammered the yellow Corvette, tearing into its steel body.

There was a momentary pause: A jammed bandolier? An overheated barrel? It was customary to replace the barrel every hundred to five hundred rounds to prevent overheating, and the overzealous gunman may not have realized just how quickly those barrels became hot. Small consolation: the pilot of the hovercraft used the interruption to shift direction. The craft eased back, even with the racing Corvette, and suddenly up onto the beach, and then to the cambered road itself.

It was just a few yards away, and the powerful sucking propellers seemed to loom over the tiny sports car. He heard another noise—a whooshing, bass-heavy thrum. That could mean only one thing: an auxiliary Rotex engine and propulsion fan had just now been activated. In the rearview mirror, Janson watched, bewildered, as the blousing PVC flaps puffed out farther and the entire craft, which had been flying about a foot above the ground, suddenly rose higher—and higher still! The roar of the Rotex engines blended with the howl of the blasting air as a small sandstorm materialized just behind them.

It was increasingly difficult to breathe without choking on the airborne grit. The hovercraft itself was partly obscured in the swirling sand and yet from behind the fore windshield he made out the goggled face of a powerfully built man.

He could also make out that the man was smiling.

Now the hovercraft seemed to jump up another foot into the air, and suddenly it was rearing and bucking like a horse. As the antiplow skirts struck the car's rear fender, Janson had a horrible realization: *It was trying to climb over them.*

He glanced over to his right and saw Collins doubled forward in his seat, his hands over his ears, trying to protect them from the immense din.

The hovercraft bounced and tipped again as the churning blades whipped air into a punishing substance, like water from a water cannon. In the rearview mirror, through the eddying sand, Janson caught a glimpse of the spinning auxiliary propulsion blades mounted on the craft's underside. If the side-strafing from the M60 was not sufficient, the assassins wanted them to know that they could easily lower the powerful blades of the undermounted propeller over them, like a gigantic lawn mower, destroying the car and decapitating its inhabitants.

As the large hovercraft bucked against the rear of the Corvette, Janson swung the steering wheel abruptly to the left, and now the car veered off the paved surface, its wheels spinning into the sand and scrub as it rapidly lost traction and speed.

The hovercraft zoomed past, its motion as effortless as an air-hockey puck, then came to a halt and reversed course without turning around.

It was a brilliant maneuver: for the first time, the man with the M60 had a direct line of fire at the driver and passenger alike. Even as he watched the machine gunner seat a fresh link-belt of ammunition into the M60's drive mechanism, he heard the sound of yet another craft—a speedboat, crazily veering toward the shore.

*Oh Christ no!*

And in the speedboat, a figure, arranged in prone firing position, with a rifle. Aimed at them.

# CHAPTER THIRTY-ONE

The speedboat was equipped with an aircraft turbine engine, for it had to have been traveling at upward of 150 miles per hour. It skimmed along the water, leaving behind a slashing contrail of spume. The small boat became rapidly larger, a mesmeric spectacle of death. Two miles from the cottage, the flat netting was no longer in place; *nothing* protected them from the rushing gunman. Nothing.

Where could he go? *Where was safety?*

Janson turned the wheels of the Corvette back onto the road, heard the chassis scrape as it lurched from the sodden earth to the hard pavement. What if he tried to *ram* the hovercraft, jamming his foot on the accelerator and testing its lightweight fiberglass construction against the steel cage of the Corvette? Yet the odds were slim that he could even reach the craft before the M60 had perforated the engine—and him.

Crouching below the fan, the machine gunner grinned evilly. The link-belt was seated; full-fire mode was activated. Seconds remained before he served them with a lethal fire hose of lead. Suddenly the man pitched forward, slack, his forehead dropping like a deadweight against the bipod-propped gun.

Dead.

There was an echoing sound—on the waters of Chesapeake Bay, it sounded oddly like a cork popping—and then another, and the hovercraft came to a rest just a few feet from the car, half on the road, half on the shoulder. It was not how anyone deliberately parked such a craft.

Like those of many military vehicles and devices, the controls must have been designed to require continual nonpassive pressure—simply put, the grip of a human hand on the tiller. Otherwise, in combat situations, a soldier in command could be killed, and a driverless vehicle—like an unmanned automatic weapon—might inadvertently cause harm to the wrong side. Now the craft depowered, the engines shutting off, the churning blades growing slower and slower, the craft's skids setting firmly on the ground. And as the craft fell to earth, Janson saw that the pilot, too, was sprawled, limp, on the windshield.

Two shots, two kills.

A voice called across the waters of Chesapeake Bay, as the engine of the speedboat sputtered to a halt. "*Paul!* Are you all right?"

A voice from the speedboat.

The voice of a woman who had saved them both.

Jessica Kincaid.

Janson got out of the car and raced to the shore; he saw Jessie in the boat only ten yards away. It was the closest she could bring the speedboat without grounding it.

"Jessie!" he shouted.

"Tell me I did great!" Jessie said, triumphant.

"Two head shots—and from a speeding boat? That's one for the god-damn record books!" Paul said. He felt suddenly, absurdly lighter. "Of course, I had everything under control."

"Yeah, I could see that," she replied drily.

Derek Collins approached. His gait was labored; he was winded, and his sweaty face was coated with a layer of sand and silt that gave him a mummified look.

Janson turned around slowly and faced his adversary. "Your idea of fun?"

"*What?*"

"Were those two your henchmen as well? Or is this another one of those I-had-nothing-to-do-with-it moments?"

"Goddammit, I *had* nothing to do with it! How could you think otherwise! They almost killed *me*, for Christ's sake! Are you too blind and full of yourself to see the truth when it's in front of your face? They wanted *both* us of dead."

His voice rose with the unabated terror that his whole body exuded. He was probably speaking the truth, Janson decided. But if so, who *was* behind this latest attempt?

Something about Collins's manner bothered Janson: for all his candor, he was holding too much back. "Maybe so. But you seem to know who the attackers were."

Collins looked away.

"Goddammit, Collins. If you've got something to say, say it *now!*" Revulsion once more coursed through Janson as he regarded the frightened yet stony bureaucrat, the man with a calculator for a soul. He couldn't forget what he'd learned: that Collins was the one who stood by while the sanction order was processed, unconcerned about sacrificing a pawn for his great game. He wanted nothing to do with this man.

"You lose," Janson said quietly. "Once more. If you want me dead, you're going to have to try a little harder."

"I told you, Janson. That was then. This is now. The game plan has changed. That's why I told you about the program, goddammit—the biggest, most dangerous secret in the entire U.S. of A. And there's a *lot* more I'm not authorized to tell you myself."

"More of your bullshit," Janson snarled.

"No, it's true. I can't tell you what, but there's a lot you *need* to know. For Christ's sake, you've got to come with me to Washington, to meet with the Mobius team. We need you to get with the program, OK?" He placed a hand on Janson's arm. Janson knocked it off.

"You want me to 'get with the program'? Let me ask you a question first—and you'd better give me a straight answer, because I'll know if you're lying."

"I told you, I'm not authorized to reveal—"

"This isn't a big-picture question. It's a little-picture question, a detail. You told me about an ace surgical team that performed three procedures on three agents. I'm just wondering about the members of that surgical team. Where are they now?"

Collins blinked hard. "Damn you, Janson. You're asking a question you know the answer to."

"I just want to hear you say it."

"Security on this operation was mammoth. The number of people who were in the know could be counted on the fingers of two hands. Each and every one with clearance on the very highest level, proven reliability—intelligence professionals."

"But you needed to enlist the services of a top-caliber plastic surgeon. A team of outsiders, by necessity."

"Why are we even talking about this? You understand the logic perfectly well. You said it yourself: each one of them was necessary for the program's success. Each one, inherently, posed a security risk. That simply wasn't supportable."

"Ergo, the Mobius Program followed protocol. You planners had them killed. Every last one."

Collins was silent, bowing his head slightly.

Something burned within Janson, although Collins had done nothing more than confirm his suspicions. They had probably allowed themselves a twelve-month period for the mop-up. It would not have been difficult to manage. A car crash, an accidental drowning, perhaps a deadly collision on a double-diamond ski slope—top surgeons tended to be aggressive sportsmen. No, it would not have been difficult. The agents who arranged their deaths would have regarded each as a task accomplished, another check against a to-do list. The *human* reality—the bereavement of spouses, siblings, sons and daughters; the shattered families, shadowed childhoods, the knock-on effects of desolation and despair beyond consolation—that was not a reality to be considered, even acknowledged, by those who issued the deadly directives.

Janson's eyes drilled into Collins's. "Small sacrifices for the larger good, right? That's what I figured. No, Collins, I'm not going to get with the program. Not *your* program, anyway. You know something, Collins? You're not a songbird and you're not a hawk. You're a snake, and you always will be."

Janson looked out toward the water, saw Jessie Kincaid in the idling craft, saw her short hair ruffled by the gentle breeze, and all at once his heart felt as if it might burst. Maybe Collins was telling him the truth about the role of Consular Operations in what had gone down; maybe he wasn't. The only verifiable truth was that Janson could not trust him. *There's a lot you need to know. . . . Come with me.* That's just the sort of line Collins would use to lure him to his death.

Janson looked again at the gently bobbing speedboat, twenty feet from shore. It wasn't a hard choice. Abruptly, he bolted down the beach, without looking back, first wading into the shallow water and then propelling himself to Jessie's boat with powerful crawl strokes. The water sluiced around his clothing and cooled his body.

As he climbed aboard the boat, Jessie reached for him, took his hand in hers.

"Funny, I thought you were in Amsterdam," Janson said.

"Let's just say its charms ran thin. Especially after a couple of brats almost knocked me over and accidentally saved my life."

"Come again?"

"Long story. I'll explain later."

He put his arms around her, feeling the warmth of her body. "OK, my questions can wait. You've probably got some of your own."

"I'll start with one," she said. "Are we partners?"

He pressed her close to him. "Yeah," he said. "We're partners."

# PART FOUR

# CHAPTER THIRTY-TWO

"You don't understand," said the courier, a straitlaced black man in his late twenties, with lozenge-shaped rimless glasses. "I could lose my job for that. I could face criminal and civil penalties, too." He gestured toward the patch on his navy jacket with the distinctive calligraphic logo of his company: Caslon Couriers. Caslon: the extremely expensive, top-of-the-line, ultrasecure courier service to which select individuals and corporations entrusted highly sensitive documents. A nearly flawless record of reliability and discretion had won it the loyalty of its exclusive clientele. "These brothers don't play."

He was sitting at a small table at the Starbucks on Thirty-ninth Street and Broadway, in Manhattan, and the gray-haired man who had joined him there was politely insistent. He was, he had explained, a senior officer of the Liberty Foundation; his wife was a staff member of the Manhattan office. Yes, the approach was all very irregular, but he was at the end of his rope. The trouble was, he had reason to believe she was receiving packages from a romantic suitor. "And I'm not even sure who the damn guy is!"

The courier grew visibly uncomfortable until Janson began to peel off hundred-dollar bills. After twenty of them, his eyes began to warm behind his glasses.

"I'm on the road about sixty percent of the time, I mean, I can understand how her attention might wander," the gray-haired man said. "But I can't fight off somebody I don't know, you understand? And she won't admit that anything's going on. I see she's got these little gifts, and she says she bought them herself. But I know better. These aren't the sort of things you buy for yourself. These are the kinds of things a guy buys a woman, and I know, because I have. Hey, I'm not saying I'm perfect or anything. But we need to clear the air, my wife and I, and I really mean both of us. Look, I can't believe I'm even doing what I'm doing. I'm not that kind of a guy, trust me."

The courier shook his head sympathetically and then glanced at his watch. "You know, I meant what I said about criminal and civil prosecution. They spell that out when you join up, a dozen ways. You sign all kinds of contracts and if you're found in violation, they'll fry your ass."

The wealthy cuckold was all dignity and caution. "They never will. I'm not asking you to divert anything, I'm not asking you to do anything wrong. All I'm asking is to see copies of the invoice slips. Not to have them, to see them. And if I learn something, if it's the guy I think it is, nobody will ever know how. But I'm begging you, you've got to give Márta and me a chance. And this is the only way."

The courier nodded briskly. "I'm going to get behind on my rounds if I don't get a move on. How about you meet me at the atrium of the Sony Building, Fifty-fifth and Madison, in four hours?"

"You're doing the right thing, my friend," the man told him with fervor. He made no reference to the two thousand dollars he had "tipped" the courier; that would have been beneath the dignity of them both.

At the Sony atrium, hours later, sitting on a metal chair near a poured-concrete fountain, he was finally able to page through the invoices. He had been, he saw, too optimistic: the deliveries lacked a sender's address, being marked only with a code of origination that indicated the general location of pickup. He persevered all the same, looking for a pattern. There were dozens of packages that arrived from all the expected locations, cities corresponding to the major Liberty Foundation branch offices. Yet there were also a handful of packages that were sent to Márta Lang from a location that corresponded to nothing at all. Why was Caslon Couriers making regular pickups from a small town in the Blue Ridge Mountains?

"Yes," he told the courier mournfully. "It's just as I thought." He glanced around the place—an urban terrarium of plants and sluggish waterfalls arrayed in a glassed-in "public space" that some zoning board had demanded in return for a height variance. "She told me they'd broken it off, and maybe they did, for a while. But now it's on again. Well, it's back to couples therapy for us."

Looking mournful, Paul Janson extended a hand, his palm lined with another sheath of slippery large-denomination bills, and the courier grasped it warmly.

"My heartfelt sympathies, man," the courier said.

A little additional research—several hours in the New York Public Library—was suggestive. Millington, Virginia, turned out to be the nearest town to a vast pastoral estate that was built by John Vincent Astor in the 1890s, a place that, by several architectural accounts, rivaled the legendary

Biltmore estate in its elegance and attention to detail. At some point in the fifties, ownership passed into the hands of Maurice Hempel, a secretive South African diamond magnate, since deceased. And now? Who owned it now? Who lived there now?

Only one conclusion suggested itself: a man the world knew as Peter Novak. A certainty? Far from it. Yet there was surely some validity to the inferences that brought the remote spot to his attention. Control *required* communication: if this last surviving "Novak" was still in command of his empire, he would have to be in communication with his top deputies. People like Márta Lang. Janson's plan called for breaching the channels of communication. By tracing the subtle twitchings of the web, he might find the spider.

After spending the following morning on the road, however, Janson felt increasingly unsure of his suppositions. Had it not been too easy? His keyed-up nerves were not calmed by the monotony of driving. For most of the trip, he maintained a near constant speed, shifting from the turnpike, punctuated with blue Adopt-A-Highway signs, to the smaller roads that webbed across the Blue Ridge Mountains like man-made rivers. Rolling green farmland gave way to blue-green hued vistas of rising hills, cresting and ebbing across the horizon. Framed by the windshield, the images straight ahead of him had the beauty of the banal. Battered guardrails stretched along outcroppings of mossy gray shale. The road itself became mesmerizing, an endless procession of small irregularities. Cracks in the road that had been daubed with glossy black sealant; skid marks that formed staccato diagonals; broken white lines that had started to blur from the punishment of a thousand downpours.

A few miles past a camping exit, Janson saw a turnoff marked for the town of Castleton, and he knew that Millington would not be much farther. JED SIPPERLY'S PRE-OWNED AUTO—BUY YOUR NEXT CAR HERE! read a garish roadside sign. It was lettered with white and blue car-body paint on a metal plaque mounted high on a pole. Tear tracks of rust spilled from the corner rivets. Janson pulled into the lot.

It would be the second time he had changed cars en route; in Maryland he had picked up a late-model Altima from its owner. Switching vehicles was standard procedure during long trips. He was confident that he was not being followed, but there was always the possibility of "soft surveillance": a purely passive system of observation, agents instructed to notice, not to follow. A young woman riding shotgun in a Dodge Ram whose eyes flickered from a newspaper to a license plate; the fat man with an overheated car stalled on the shoulder, the hood up, seemingly waiting for AAA. Almost certainly they were as innocent as they appeared, and yet there were no guarantees. Soft surveillance, though of limited effectiveness, was essentially undetectable. So at intervals, Janson changed his vehicle. If anyone was attempting to keep tabs on his movements, it would make a difficult task even more so.

A 120-pound dog lunged repeatedly at a heavy-gauge Cyclone fence as Janson got out of his Altima and made his way toward the low trailerlike office. ALL OFFERS CONSIDERED read a sign in the window. The large animal—he was a mongrel, whose ancestors seemed to include a pit bull and a Doberman, and possibly a mastiff—was penned into one corner of the lot and once more threw himself against the unyielding Cyclone fence. Aside from his size, the wretched mutt was a perfect contrast to the old crone's noble white-coated Kuvasz, Janson mused. But perhaps the animals were only as different as the masters they served.

A thirtyish man with a cigarette tucked into the corner of his mouth sauntered out of the trailer. He thrust out a hand toward Janson, a bit too abruptly. For a split instinctual second, Janson readied himself to deliver a crushing blow to his neck; then he reached out and clasped the man's hand. It bothered him that those reflexes signaled themselves in perfectly civil contexts, but they were the same reflexes that had saved his life on countless occasions. Violence, when it appeared, so often was inappropriate, out of context. What mattered was that such impulses were under Janson's control. He would not be leaving the younger man sprawled on the pavement, howling in pain. He would be leaving him pleased at an advantageous trade-in supplemented with a pocketful of cash.

"I'm Jed Sipperly," the man said, with a showily firm handshake; somebody must have told him that a firm handshake inspired confidence. His face was fleshy but firm beneath a thatch of straw-colored hair; the sun had burned a ruddy crease that started near the bridge of his nose and curved beneath his eyes. Perhaps it was because he had driven for too many hours straight, but Janson suddenly had a vision of what the salesman would look like in a few decades. The meaty lips and padded cheeks would grow loose; the sun-exposed contours of his face would turn into furrows, ravines. What now passed for healthy ruddiness would coarsen into a webbing of capillaries, like cross-hatchings on an engraving. The yellow hair would whiten and retrench to a zone around his nape and temples, the usual follicular fallback.

On the fake-wood table in the shadowed office, Janson could make out an open brown Budweiser bottle and a nearly full ashtray. These things, too, would speed the transformation, doubtless already had started to.

"Now, what kin I do you for?" Jed's breath was faintly beery, and as he stepped closer, the sun picked out his crow's-feet.

There was another cage-rattling lunge from the dog.

"Don't you mind Butch," the man said. "I think he enjoys it. You excuse me for a moment?" Jed Sipperly walked outside to the pavement near the chain-link enclosure and stooped down to pick up a small Raggedy Ann– style cloth doll. He tossed it into the enclosed area. It turned out to be what the mammoth dog was pining for: he bounded over to it, and began to cradle it between huge paws. With a few laps of his floppy pink tongue he cleaned the dust from the rag doll's button-and-yarn features.

Jed returned to his customer with an apologetic shrug. "Look at him slobber on it—dog's so attached to that doll, it ain't wholesome," he said. "I guess everybody's got a *some*body. A real good guard dog, 'cept he won't bark. Which is sometimes a saving grace." A professional smile: his lips curved up in an isolated movement; the eyes remained watchful and without warmth. It was the kind of smile that bureaucrats shared with shop-keepers. "That your Nissan Altima?"

"Thinking of a trade," Janson said.

Jed looked slightly pained, a merchant asked to give to charity. "We get a lot of those cars. I like 'em. Got a weakness for 'em. Be my undoing. Lots of people don't particularly care for those Japan cars, especially hereabouts. How many miles you got on it?"

"Fifty thou," Janson said. "A little more."

Another wince. "Good time for a trade, then. Because those Nissan transmissions start making trouble once you reach sixty. Give you that for nothing. Anybody'll tell you the same thing."

"Thanks for the tip," Janson said, nodding at the patent lies of a used-car salesman. There was something almost endearing about the spirited way he upheld the stereotype of his trade.

"I personally like 'em, mechanical troubles and all. Like the look of 'em, somehow. And repairs ain't a problem for me, because we've got a repair guy on call. If what you're looking for is reliability, though, I can steer you toward one or two models that'll probably outlast *you*." He pointed toward a maroon sedan. "See that Taurus? One of the all-time greats. Runs perfect. Some of the later models all loaded up with special features you never use. More useless features, more stuff to go wrong. This one, it's fully automatic, you got your radio, your A/C, and you're good to go. Change the oil every three thousand miles, gas up with regular unleaded, and you're laughin'. My friend, you are *laughin'*."

Janson looked grateful as the salesman fleeced him, taking the late-model Altima in trade for the aging Taurus and asking for an additional four hundred dollars on top. "A sweet deal," Jed Sipperly assured him. "I just have a weakness for an Altima, kinda like Butch and his Raggedy Ann. It's irrational, but love's not a thing to reason about, is it? You come in with one of those, of *course* I'm gonna let you waltz off with the nicest car on the lot. And anybody else would say, 'Jed, you're crazy. That piece of Jap tin ain't worth the *hubcap* on that Taurus.' Well, maybe it *is* crazy." An exaggerated wink: "Let's do this deal before I change my mind. Or sober up!"

"Appreciate your candor," Janson said.

"Tell you what," the salesman said, signing a receipt with a flourish, "you give me another fiver and you can have the damn dog in with it!" A long-suffering laugh: "Or maybe I should *pay* you to take it off my hands."

Janson smiled, waved, and as he got into the seven-year-old Taurus heard the sibilant hiss of another screwtop Budweiser being opened—this time in celebration.

The doubts Janson had as he traveled intensified upon his arrival. The area around Millington was down-and-out, struggling and charmless. It simply did not feel like an area that a billionaire would have chosen for a country retreat.

There were other towns—like Little Washington, off 211, farther north—where the soul-destroying work of entertaining tourists had over-taken whatever local economy had been left. Those were museum towns, in effect—towns whose white shingled barns were crammed with doubly marked-up Colonial Homestead china and "authentic" milk-glass salt-shakers and "regional" beeswax candles crated in from a factory in Trenton. Farms were converted into overpriced eateries; daughters of woodworkers and pipefitters and farmers—those who sought to stay, anyway—laced themselves into frilly "colonial"-style costumes and practiced saying, "My name is Linda and I'll be your waitress this evening." The locals greeted visitors with manufactured warmth and the wide smile of avarice. *What kin ah do you for?*

That green tide of tourism had never reached Millington. It didn't take Janson long to size up the place. Though scarcely more than a village, it was somehow too *real* to be picturesque. Perched on a rocky slope of Smith Mountain, it regarded the natural world as something to be overcome, not packaged and sold for its aesthetic value. There were no bed-and-breakfasts in the vicinity. The nearest motels were utilitarian, boxy affiliates of downscale national chains, run by hardworking immigrants from the Indian subcontinent: they did just fine by truck drivers who wanted to crash for the night, but had little appeal for businessmen in search of "conference center" facilities. It was a town that was dark by ten o'clock, at which point the only lights you could see came from dozens of miles down the valley, where the town of Montvale sparkled like a flashy, decadent metropolis. The biggest single employer was a former paper plant that now produced glazed bricks and did a side business in unrefined mineral byproducts; about a dozen men spent their working hours bagging potash. A smaller factory, a little farther out, specialized in decorative millwork. The downtown diner, at Main and Pemberton Streets, served eggs and home fries and coffee all day, and if you ordered all three, you got a free tomato or orange juice on the side, though it arrived in something little bigger than a shot glass. The gas station had an attached "foodmart" with racks of the same cellophane-wrapped snacks available everywhere else on the U.S. roadways. The mustard in the local grocery store came in two varieties, French's yellow or Gulden's brown: nothing coarse-grained or tarragon-infused burdened the condiment section of the chipped enameled shelves, no *moutarde au poivre vert* within township limits. Janson's kind of place.

Yet if the decades-old accounts were accurate, there was a vast estate hidden somewhere in the hills, as private a residence as you could hope for—legally as well as physically. For even its ownership was completely obscure. Was it really conceivable that "Novak"—the mirage who called himself that—was nearby? Janson's scalp tightened as he mulled the possibilities.

Later that morning, Janson entered the diner at the corner of Main and Pemberton, where he started a conversation with the counterman. The counterman's sloping forehead, close-set eyes, and jutting, square jaw gave him a slightly simian appearance, but when he spoke he proved surprisingly knowledgeable.

"So you're thinking of moving nearby?" The counterman splashed more coffee into Janson's cup from his Silex pot. "Let me guess. Made your money in the big city and now you want the peace and quiet of the country, that it?"

"Something like that," Janson said. Nailed to the wall behind the counter was a sign, white cursive lettering on black: *Kenny's Coffee Shoppe—Where Quality & Service Rule.*

"Sure you don't want someplace a little nearer to your high-class conveniences? There's a Realtor lady on Pemberton, but I'm not sure you'll find exactly the kind of house you're looking for around here."

"Thinking of building," Janson said. The coffee was acrid, having sat on the hot pad too long. He gazed absently at the Formica-topped counter, its pattern of loose-woven cloth worn to white in the middle of the counter, where the traffic of heavy plates and cutlery was heaviest.

"Sounds like fun. If'n you can afford to do something nice." The man's drugstore aftershave mingled unpleasantly with the heavy aroma of lard and butter.

"No point otherwise."

"Nope, no point otherwise," the counterman agreed. "My boy, you know, he had some dang-fool way he was going to get rich. Some dot-com thing. Was going to middleman some e-commerce gimcrackery. For months he was talking about his 'business model,' and 'added value,' and 'frictionless e-commerce,' and flapdoodle like that. Said the thing about the New Economy was the 'death of distance' so that it didn't make no difference where you was. We was all just nodes on the World Wide Web, didn't matter whether you was in Millington or Roanoke or the goddamn Dulles corridor. He and a couple of friends from high school, it was. Burned through whatever was in their piggy banks by December, was back to shoveling driveways by January. What my wife calls a cautionary tale. She said, just be happy he wuddn't on drugs. I told her I wuddn't so sure about that. Not every drug is something you smoke, sniff, or shoot up. Money, or the craving for it, can be a drug just as surely."

"Getting money is one trick, spending it's another," Janson said. "Possible to build around here?"

"Possible to build on the moon, people say."

"What about transportation."

"Well, you're here, ain't you?"

"I guess I am."

"Roads here are in pretty good repair." The counterman's eyes were on a spectacle across the street. A young blond woman was washing the side-walk in front of a hardware store; as she bent over, her cutoffs hitched a little higher up her thigh. No doubt the highlight of his day.

"Airport?" Janson asked.

"Nearest real airport's probably Roanoke."

Janson took a sip of coffee. It coated his tongue like oil. " 'Real' airport? There another kind around here?"

"Naw. Well. There used to be, back in the forties and fifties. Some sort of tiny airport that the Army Air Force built. About three miles up Clan-gerton Road, a turnoff to the left. The idea is they were training pilots how to maneuver around the mountains in Romania, on the way to bombing the oil fields. So they did some practice flights hereabouts. Later on, some of the lumber guys used it for a while, but the lumber industry pretty near died off. I don't think it's much more than an airstrip anymore. You don't fly masonry if you can avoid it—you truck it."

"So what happened to that airstrip? Ever get used?"

"Ever? Never? I don't use those words." His gaze did not leave the blonde in the short cutoffs washing the sidewalk across the street.

"Reason I ask, you see, is an old business associate of mine, he lives near here, and said something about it."

The counterman looked uncomfortable. Janson pushed his empty cof-fee cup forward to be refilled, and the man pointedly did not do so. "Then you'd better ask him about it, hadn't you?" the man said, and his gaze returned to the vision of unattainable paradise across the street.

"Seems to me," Janson said, tucking a few bills beneath his saucer, "that you and your son both have an eye for the bottom line."

The town grocery store was just down the street. Janson stopped in and introduced himself to the manager, a bland-looking man with light brown hair in a modified mullet. Janson told him what he had told the man at the diner. The store manager evidently found the prospect of a new arrival lucrative enough that he was downright encouraging.

"That is a great idea, man," he said. "These hills—I mean, it's really beautiful here. And you get a few miles up the mountain and look around and it's totally unspoiled. Plus you got your hunting and your fishing and your . . ." He trailed off, seemingly unable to think of a third suitable item. He wasn't sure this man would be a regular at the bowling alley or take much interest in the video arcade recently installed next to the check-cashing joint. Safe bet they had those things in the cities, too.

"And for everyday stuff?" Janson prodded.

"We got a video store," he volunteered. "Laundromat. This store right here. I can do special orders, if you need 'em. Do that once in a while for regular customers."

"Have you, now?"

"Oh yeah. We got all kinds around here. There's one cat—we've never seen him, but he sends a guy down here every few days to pick up groceries. Superrich—gotta be. Owns a place somewhere up in the mountains, some kind of Lex Luthor hideaway, I like to think. People see a little plane touching down near there most every afternoon. But he still uses us for groceries. Ain't that a way to live? Get somebody else to do your shopping!"

"And you do special orders for this guy?"

"Oh for sure," the man said. "It's all real, real secure. Maybe he's Howard Hughes, afraid somebody going to poison him." He chuckled at the thought. "Whatever he wants, it's not a problem. I order it and a Sysco truck comes by and delivers it, and he has a guy come get it, he don't care what it costs."

"That right?"

"You bet. So, like I say, I'm happy to special-order whatever you like. And Mike Nugent at the video store, he'll do the same for you. It's not a problem. You're going to have a great time here. No place like it. Some of the kids can get a little rowdy. But basically it's as friendly as all get-out. You're gonna have a *great* time here once you settle in. My bet? You're never gonna leave."

A gray-haired woman at the refrigerated section was calling to him. "Keith? Keith, dear?"

The man excused himself, and went over to her.

"Is this sole fresh or frozen?" she was asking.

"It's fresh frozen," Keith explained.

As the two carried on an earnest conversation about whether the designation signified a way of being fresh or a way of being frozen, Janson wandered over to the far end of the grocery store. The stockroom door was open, and he stepped into it, casually. At a small metal desk was a stack of pale blue Sysco inventory lists. He flipped through them quickly until he reached one stamped SPECIAL ORDER. Toward the bottom of a long row of foodstuffs in small print, he saw a bold check, from the grocer's Sharpie marker. An order of buckwheat groats.

A few seconds elapsed before it clicked. Buckwheat groats—also known as kasha. Janson felt a stirring of excitement as thousands of column inches from newspaper and magazine profiles whirred through his head in a ribbon of light. *Every day starts with a spartan breakfast of kasha. . . .* A homely detail found in dozens of them, along with the near obligatory references to his "bespoke wardrobe," "aristocratic bearing," "commanding gaze" . . . Such were the stock phrases and "colorful" details of feature writing. *Every day starts with a spartan breakfast of kasha. . . .*

It was true, then. Somewhere on Smith Mountain lived a man the world knew as Peter Novak.

# CHAPTER THIRTY-THREE

In the heart of midtown Manhattan, the bag lady stooped over the Bryant Park steel-mesh trash can with the diligent look of a postal worker at a mailbox. Her clothes, as was usual with derelicts, were torn and filthy and unseasonably heavy—the clothing had to be thick enough to ward off the cold of a night spent in an alleyway, and the warming rays of the sun would not impel her to strip off a single layer, for her clothes and her sack filled with bottles and tin cans were all she had to her name. At her wrists and ankles, grime-gray thermal underwear showed beneath fraying, soiled denim. Her shoes were oversize sneakers, the rubber soles beginning to split, the laces broken and tied together again, in floppy schoolgirl knots. Pulled down low on her forehead was a nylon-mesh baseball cap, promoting not a sports team but a once-high-flying Silicon Alley "incubator" fund that went under the year before. She clutched the grungy satchel as if it contained treasure. Her grip expressed the primal urgency of possession: This is what I have in this world. It is mine. It is me. Time for such as her was meted out by nights she escaped unmolested, by the cans and bottles she collected and traded in for nickels, by the small serendipities she encountered—the intact sandwich, still soft and protected by plastic wrap, untouched by rodents. On her hands were cotton gloves, now gray and sooty, which might once have been a debutante's, and as she rummaged through the plastic bottles and skeins of cellophane and apple cores and banana peels and crumpled advertising flyers, the gloves grew even dirtier.

Yet Jessica Kincaid's eyes were not, in fact, on the refuse; they returned regularly to the small mirror that she had propped against the trash can and that allowed her to monitor those arriving at and departing from the Liberty Foundation offices across the street. After days of a fruitless watch, Janson's confederate, Cornelius Eaves, had called last night excitedly: Márta Lang seemed finally to have made an appearance.

It was not a mistaken sighting, Jessie now knew. A woman matching Janson's detailed description of Deputy Director Márta Lang had been among the arrivals that morning: a Lincoln Town Car with darkened windows had dropped her off at eight in the morning. In the ensuing hours, there was no sign of her, yet Jessica could not risk leaving her post. Attired as she was, Jessica herself attracted almost no attention, for the city had long since trained itself not to notice such unfortunates in its midst. At intervals, she shuttled between two other wire trash baskets that shared a sight line to the office building on Fortieth Street, but always returned to the one nearest it. About midday, a couple of grounds maintenance people in the bright red outfits of the Bryant Park Business Improvement District had tried to shoo her away, but only halfheartedly: their minimum wages inspired no great exertions on the park's behalf. Later, a Senegalese street merchant with a folding stand and a portfolio of fake Rolexes tried to set up shop near her. Twice, she "accidentally" stumbled over his display, bringing it crashing to the ground. After the second time he decided to relocate his business, though not before hurling a few choice epithets at her in his native tongue.

It was nearly six when the elegant, white-haired woman appeared again, striding through the revolving door of the lobby, her face a mask of unconcern. As the woman stepped into the backseat of the long Lincoln Town Car and purred off toward the intersection at Fifth Avenue, Jessica memorized the license plate. Quietly, she radioed Cornelius Eaves, whose vehicle—a yellow taxicab with its OFF DUTY lights on—had been idling in front of a hotel toward the other end of the block.

Eaves did not know the larger purpose of his assignment; he did know enough not to ask whether it was an officially sanctioned job. Jessica Kincaid, for her part, had been stinting with explanation. Were she and Janson pursuing a private vendetta? Had they been assigned to an ultra-secret project requiring the ad hoc enlistment of irregular talent? Eaves, who had been retired from active duty for a few years and was eager to have something to occupy his time, did not know. The only authorization he required was Janson's personal entreaty—and the look on the young woman's face: it was the limpid confidence of somebody who was doing what had to be done.

Diving into the backseat of Eaves's cab, Jessica yanked off her cap, wriggled out of her rags, and changed into ordinary street clothes: pressed chinos, a pastel-colored cotton sweater, penny loafers. She scrubbed the grime off her face with moist towelettes, fluffed her hair vigorously, and after a few minutes was at least vaguely presentable, which is to say, inconspicuous.

Ten minutes later, they had an address: 1060 Fifth Avenue was a hand-some prewar apartment building, its limestone facade grown pearl gray from the city air. A discreet green awning stood before its entrance, which was not on the avenue but around the corner, on Eighty-ninth Street. She glanced at her watch.

All at once, her scalp prickled with apprehension. *Her watch!* She had worn it when she was on her observation post in Bryant Park! She knew that the Foundation's security guards would be alert to any anomalies, any discordant details. Hers was a slim Hamilton tank watch, which had once belonged to her mother. Would a bag lady wear such a watch? Anx-iety burrowed deep within her as she pictured herself the way she had been, trying to figure out whether a guard equipped with binoculars might have dialed in on the glinting object on her wrist. She would have done so in their place. She had to assume that they would, too.

She flashed on the mental picture of her outstretched arms, foraging through the trash like a pauper archaeologist. . . . She saw the image of her gloved hand, and then, overlapping it, the frayed cuff of the long-sleeved thermal undershirt. Yes—the sleeve length of the undershirt was several sizes too big for her: her wristwatch would have been entirely concealed by it. The knot in her stomach loosened slightly. No harm, no foul, right? Yet she knew it was precisely the kind of careless mistake they could ill afford.

"Take me around the block, Corn," she said. "*Slowly.*"


Driving the maroon Taurus up the winding mountain path known as Clangerton Road, Janson found the unmarked turnoff that the counter-man had mentioned. He continued a short distance past it, pulling the car as far off the road as possible, plunging it into a natural cave of greenery, behind shrubs and a stand of saplings. He did not know what to expect, but caution dictated that his arrival be as stealthy as he could manage.

He walked into the woods, a spongy bed of mulched pine needles and twigs beneath his feet, and doubled back toward the small lane he had driven past. The air was filled with the resinous scent of an old-growth pine forest, a scent that recalled nothing so much as the disinfectants and air fresheners that so insistently aped it. Much of the woodland seemed wholly untouched by human habitation, a roadside forest primeval. It was through such a forest that European settlers had journeyed four centuries earlier, establishing themselves on the virgin territory, making their way by flintlock, musket, knife, and barter with an aboriginal people who greatly outnumbered them and were infinitely wiser in the ways of the land. Such were the obscure origins of what would become the mightiest power on the planet. Today, the terrain was some of the most beautiful in the country, and the less it bore the evidence of those who lived there, he reflected, the more beautiful it seemed.

And then he found the airstrip.

It was a sudden clearing in the forest, and disturbingly well maintained: the bramble and bushes had been clipped back recently, and a long oval strip of grass was neatly trimmed. It was a void, empty except for an SUV with a tarpaulin over it. How the vehicle got there was a mystery, for there was no apparent means of access to the strip, save from the skies above.

The strip itself was admirably hidden by the dense growth of trees surrounding it. Still, those trees could serve Janson's own purposes, protecting him as he set up a one-man observation post.

He nested himself in the middle of an old pine tree, largely concealing himself behind its trunk and the profusion of its needle-laden fronds. He steadied his binoculars against a small branch, and waited.

And waited.

Hours chugged past, his only visitors the occasional mosquito and less occasional centipede.

Yet Janson was scarcely aware of the passage of time. He was in another place: the sniper's fugue. His mind, part of it, drifted through the zone of semiconscious thought, even as another module of consciousness remained at a state of acute awareness.

He was convinced that there would be a flight today, not only because of what the grocery-store manager had reported but because a command-and-control structure could not rely solely upon electronic transfers of information: packages, couriers, *people*, would all have to come in and out. Yet what if he was wrong and had been wasting the most valuable commodity of all—time?

He was not wrong. At first it was like the drone of an insect, but when it grew steadily louder, he knew that a plane was circling and slowing overhead for a landing. Every nerve, every muscle in his body strained for complete alertness.

The plane was a new Cessna, a 340 series twin-engine craft, and its pilot, as Janson could tell by the fluid grace with which it touched down and came to a stop, was an extremely skilled professional, not a country doctor playing crop duster. The pilot, dressed in a white uniform, emerged from the cockpit and folded down the hinged, six-step aluminum stairs. The sun glared off the shiny fuselage, obscuring Janson's vision. All he could make out was that a passenger was quickly ushered off the plane by a second assistant, this one in a blue uniform, and brought to the SUV. The assistant yanked the tarpaulin from the vehicle, revealing a Range Rover—armored, he surmised, from the way the body rode low on the chassis—and he held open the backseat for the passenger. Moments later, the 4×4 sped off.

*Damn it!* Janson strained intently through his scope to see who the passenger was, yet the glare of the sun and the car's darkened interior defeated his every attempt. Frustration welled up in him like mercury in an overheated thermometer. Who was it? "Peter Novak"? One of his lieutenants? It was impossible to say.

And then the car disappeared.

*Where?*

It was as if it had vanished into thin air. Janson slid from his perch and peered through his scope from a number of different vantage points before he finally saw what had happened. The lane, only just wide enough to allow passage of the vehicle, was carved into the woods at an oblique angle. The surrounding stand of trees thus rendered it invisible from most points. It was a brilliant feat of landscape design meant to go unnoticed and unappreciated. Now the Cessna's engines revved up, and the small plane turned around, taxied, and took flight.

As acrid fumes of fuel drifted through the woods, Janson set off toward the drive. It was about eight feet wide and was overhung by branches that were about six feet off the ground—just high enough to allow clearance for the armored Range Rover. The tree-sheltered drive was recently paved—a driver who knew the road could make good time—yet could not be seen even from overhead.

It would be an on-foot reconnaissance mission, then.

Janson's task was to follow the drive without walking on the drive; once again, he stayed parallel to it, ten yards away, lest he activate any surveillance or alarm equipment attached to the drive itself. It was a long walk, and soon a strenuous one. He bounded up razorback ridges, pushed through densely wooded patches, and across steep, eroded slopes. After twenty minutes, his muscles started to protest the strain but he never let his pace slacken. As he grabbed another branch for purchase, he was painfully reminded that his hands, once tougher than leather, had lost their calluses: too many years of tending to corporate clients. Pine sap stuck to his palm like glue; splinters of bark worked their way under his skin. As his exertions continued, heat blanketed his upper body and neck like a rash. He ignored it, keeping his attention focused on his next step. One foot in front of the other: that was the only way forward. At the same time, he tried to make his own movements as quiet as possible, preferring rocky outcroppings whenever possible to the crackle of the forest floor. The car was long gone, of course, and he already had a good notion of where the narrow drive would lead, but there was no substitute for direct observation. One foot in front of the other: soon his movements became automatic, and despite everything, his thoughts drifted.

One foot in front of the other.

The skeletal American bowed his head as he surrendered to his new captors. Word of the POW's escape had obviously made it into the surrounding countryside, for the Montagnards and other villagers knew just who he was and where he was to be returned.

He had fought his way through the thick jungle for two full days, straining the very fiber of his existence, and for what? So near and yet so far. For now it would begin all over again, but worse: to the compound's commander, the escape of a prisoner meant a loss of face. The officer would pummel him with bare hands until he had spent his fury. Whether Janson survived the encounter at all depended entirely on how energetic the commander happened to be feeling. Janson began to succumb to a vortex of despair, pulling him down like a powerful riverine current.

*No!* Not after all he had endured. Not while Demarest still lived. He would not cede him that victory.

Two VCs were marching Janson at gunpoint along a muddy path, one in front of him, one behind him, taking no chances. Villagers had gawked at him, perhaps wondering how someone so wasted, so gaunt, could still move. He wondered that himself. But he could not know the limits of his strength until he reached beyond those limits.

Perhaps he would not have rebelled if the VC behind him hadn't reached over and cuffed him around the neck, exasperated by his slow pace. It seemed the final indignity, and Janson snapped—he let himself snap, and let his trained instincts take over. *Your mind does not have a mind of its own,* Demarest had told them in their training days, and he meant to emphasize the ways in which they had to exert control over their own consciousness. Yet after sufficient training, learned reflexes took on the ingrained nature of basic instinct, joining the ropy fiber of one's being.

Janson turned around, his feet gliding along the path as if on ice, and cocked his hip to the right without turning his right shoulder, which would have alerted the guard to what was about to happen: an explosive lunge punch with the fingers of his hand tensed and straight, his thumb tucked down and close to his palm. The spear hand plunged into the guard's throat, smashing the cartilage of his trachea and whipping his head back. Then Janson glanced over his shoulder at the other guard, and gained strength from the man's expression of fear and dismay. He directed a powerful rear snap-kick toward his groin, hammering his heel up and back; the blow's strength came from its speed, and the guard's attempt to rush toward him made it twice as effective. Now, as the front guard doubled over, Janson followed with an arcing round kick, whipping into the side of his exposed head. As his foot connected to the man's skull, jolting vibration traveled up his leg, and he wondered briefly whether he had fractured one of his own bones. In truth, he was past caring. Now he grabbed the AK-47 that had been held by the VC behind him, and used it as a cudgel, beating the still-sprawled soldier until he lay limp.

"*Xin loi*," he grunted. Sorry about that.

He scrambled off, into the jungle and toward the next swell of land. He would struggle on until he reached the shore. This time he was not alone: he had a submachine gun, its buttstock slick with another man's blood. He would persevere, one foot in front of the other, and whoever tried to stop him he would kill. For his enemies there would be no mercy, only death.

And he would not be sorry about that.


One foot in front of the other.

Another hour passed before Janson climbed up the last rocky ledge and saw the Smith Mountain estate. Yes, it was what he had expected to find, yet the sight of it took his breath away.

It was a sudden plateau—encompassing perhaps a thousand acres of rolled Kentucky bluegrass, as emerald as golf-course turf. He got out his binoculars again. The land dipped a little from the ledge where Janson found himself, and extended in a series of ridges that lapped against the sheer stone face of the mountain's summit.

He saw what Maurice Hempel had seen, recognized what had made it irresistible to someone who was as reclusive as he was rich.

Tucked away, nearly inaccessible by ordinary means, was a brilliantly shimmering mansion, more compact than the Biltmore estate and yet, he could see, just as artfully designed. It was, however, the perimeter defenses that inspired Janson's awe. As if the natural impediments surrounding the site were not sufficient, a high-tech obstacle course made the house resistant to any form of intrusion.

Straight ahead of him was a nine-foot chain-link fence, and no ordinary one. The simple existence of the object would discourage the casual hikers. Yet Janson could also see the cunning array of pressure detectors built into the fence: it would repel even a highly skilled burglar. Tensioned wire threaded its way through the chain links, connecting to a series of boxes. Here were two systems in one: a taut wire intrusion-detection system reinforced with vibration detectors. His heart plummeted; fences equipped with vibration detectors alone could often be penetrated with a pair of nippers and a little patience. The taut-wire system made that approach impossible.

Beyond the chain-link barricade, he saw a series of stanchions. These were, at first glance, four-foot-high poles with nothing between them. A closer look revealed them for what they were. Each received and transmitted a microwave flux. In simpler systems, it was possible to clamp a rod on top of a pole and simply climb over it, dodging the invisible beams. Unfortunately, these were staggered, with overlapping beams that protected the stanchions themselves. There was simply no physical way to avoid the microwave flux.

And in the grassy fairway beyond the stanchions? There were no visible impediments, and Janson scanned the grounds until, with a sharp pang, he identified the small box near the graveled driveway with the logo of TriStar Security on it. There, beneath the ground, was the most formidable obstacle of all: a buried-cable pressure sensor. It could not be bypassed; it could not be reached. Even if he somehow surmounted the other obstacles, the pressure sensors would remain.

Infiltration was surely impossible. Logic told him as much. He put down his binoculars, rolled back over the rocky ledge, and sat there in silence for a long moment. A wave of resignation and despair overcame him. So near and yet so far.

———

It was almost dusk by the time he found his way back to the maroon Taurus. His clothing flecked with bits of leaves and many small burrs, he drove back toward Millington and then north on Route 58, keeping a vigilant eye on the rearview mirror.

With the little time he had left, he had to make a number of stops, a number of acquisitions. At a roadside flea market, he bought an electric eggbeater, though all he wanted was the solenoid motor. A strip-mall Radio Shack sufficed for a cheap cell phone and a few inexpensive add-ons. At the Millington grocery store, he bought a large round container of butter cookies, though all he wanted was the steel can. Next was the hardware store on Main Street, where he bought glue, a canister of artist's powdered charcoal, a roll of electrical tape, a pair of heavy-duty scissors, a compressed-air atomizer, and a locking extensible curtain rod. "A handyman, are you?" asked the blonde in denim cutoffs as she rang up his purchase. "My kinda guy." She gave him an inviting smile. He could imagine the counterman across the street glowering.

His final stop was farther down Route 58, and he arrived at Sipperly's car lot just shortly before it closed. From his face, he could tell the salesman was not pleased to see him. The big mutt's ears pricked up, but when he saw who it was, he returned his attentions to his saliva-slick rag doll.

Sipperly took a long drag on a cigarette and walked toward Janson. "You know all sales are 'as is,' don't you?" he said warily.

Janson took five dollars out of his billfold. "For the dog," he said.

"Come again?"

"You said I could have the dog for a fiver," Janson said. "Here's a fiver."

Sipperly laughed wheezily, then he saw that Janson was serious. An avaricious look crept over his fleshy features. "Well, joking aside, I'm really very fond of that dog," he recovered. "He's truly one-of-a-kind. Excellent guard dog . . ."

Janson glanced at the large animal, his muddy coat of black and tan, his short, blunt snout and the curved incisor that jutted outside his lips when his mouth was closed, bulldog-style. A homely creature, at best.

"Except he doesn't bark," Janson pointed out.

"Well, sure, he's a little reluctant in that department. But he's really a great dog. I don't know if I could part with him. I'm kind of a sentimental guy."

"Fifty."

"A hundred."

"Seventy-five."

"Sold," Jed Sipperly said, with another beery grin. "As is. Just remember that. As is. And you'd better take that mangy filth-puppet along with it. The only way you'll ever get the beast in the car."

The mammoth dog sniffed Janson a few times before losing interest and, indeed, got into the vehicle only when Janson tossed the Raggedy Ann into his backseat. It was a tight fit for the enormous animal, but he did not complain.

"Thank you kindly," Janson said. "And, by the way, can you tell me where I can pick up a radar detector?"

"Now, you know those are illegal in the state of Virginia, don't you?" Sipperly said with mock severity.

Janson looked abashed.

"But if you're interested in a sweet deal on one of those babies, all I can say is, you asked the right guy." Sipperly had the grin of someone who knew it was his lucky day.

It was early evening before Janson returned to his motel room; and when he had finished assembling his equipment and loading it into a knapsack, the light had waned. By the time he set out, he and the dog had to walk by the moonglow. Sheer tension made the hike seem to go faster this time, despite the weight of the knapsack.

Just before Janson approached the final ridge, he removed the dog's collar, and scratched him affectionately about the head and neck. Then he scooped up a few handfuls of soil and smeared it around the dog's head and into his already muddy coat. The transformation was not subtle; the collarless dog now looked feral, a particularly large version of the mountain dogs that occasionally roamed the slopes. Next, Janson took the Raggedy Ann doll and flung it over the chain-link fence. As the dog ran after it, Janson stepped back into the dense stand of trees and watched what happened.

The huge dog lunged against the fence, fell back, and sprang forward again, crashing against the vibration sensors and the taut-wire system. They were designed to have a sensitivity threshold that would prevent them from being triggered by a gust of wind or a scampering squirrel; the banging of the enormous canine was far above that threshold. With an electronic chirp, both systems registered the presence of an intruder, and a row of blue diodes lit up, marking out the segment of the fence.

Janson heard the motorized pivot of a closed-circuit videocamera mounted on a high pole within the grounds; it was swiveling toward the disturbance. A cluster of lights mounted over the camera blinked on,

directing a blindingly intense halogen blaze toward the section of the fence
where Butch was launching his repeated assaults. Even sheltered by the
trees, Janson found the light searingly bright, like multiple suns. Time
from initial trigger to camera response: four seconds. Janson had to admire the efficiency of the intrusion-detection system.

Meanwhile, the bewildered canine leaped onto the fence, his front paws
grabbing hold of the wire links: nothing mattered to him but his rag doll.
As Janson's eyes adjusted, he could see the camera's lens elongate. It
seemed that the camera was operated remotely from within one of the
guard stations; having pinpointed the intruder, its operators could zoom
in and make a determination.

That determination did not take long. The halogen light was switched
off, the camera swiveled back to its center position, turned away from the
fence and toward the gravel driveway, and the blue diodes of the section
went black.

Janson heard the springy, clattering noise of the dog lunging once more
against the chain-link fence: Butch making another go at it. Did he think
he would retrieve the doll this way? Was he, in some canine fashion, trying
to show the doll how much he cared? The brute's psychology was opaque;
what mattered to Janson was that his behavior was predictable.

As was the behavior of those who operated the perimeter security systems. The great virtue of the multimillion-dollar system was that it ob-
viated the need to send a guard out in a case like this. You could make a
thorough inspection *remotely*. This time, as the dog sprang against the
fence, no diodes illuminated. The segment was deactivated, the siege of
false alarms forestalled. Janson knew what conclusions had been reached
at the guard stations. No doubt the feral creature was chasing a squirrel
or a groundhog; no doubt its enthusiasm would soon pass.

Now, as Butch crouched for another lunge at the chain-link fence, Janson threw his knapsack over it and started to run toward the barrier
himself. When he was just a few yards away, he *sprang* up into the air, as
the dog had. He caught the fence with the ball of his foot, flattening it
against the vertical as far as he could. With his other foot, he pressed the
toe of his boot into one of the links, and grabbed onto the fence with
both hands. Moving hands and feet in tandem, he swiftly propelled himself toward the top of the fence, which bristled with sharp, pointed spikes.
The way to get over, Janson knew, was to overshoot it, keeping his center
of gravity *above* the fence top before he climbed over: to achieve this, he
imagined that the fence was a foot or so taller than it actually was, and

flung himself over that imaginary point. Maneuvering upside down, briefly, he placed all his fingers into one of the diamonds of the chain links. Then he torqued his body over the fence, pivoting on his clawlike grip. With a flip-twist, Janson righted himself and tumbled to the grass.

There was something soft beneath him as he landed. The rag doll. Janson tossed it back over the fence; the dog gently picked it up with his mouth and crept away somewhere behind the tree line.

A few moments later, he heard the motorized sound of the camera hood repositioning itself, and once again the halogen floodlights blazed.

Was the camera aimed at him? Had he unwittingly tripped some other alarm system?

Janson knew that no buried-cable pressure sensor could be used within fifteen feet of a chain-link fence; the ordinary wind sway of such a large metallic object would produce too great a perturbation in the electromagnetic detection field.

He flattened himself on the ground, his heart thudding slowly. In the dark, his black clothing was protective. Against the powerful beams of light, however, it might help pick him out from the pale gravel and bright green grass. As his eyes began to adjust to the spill of light, he realized that he was not its target. From the play of shadows, it seemed clear that it was aimed, once more, at the segment of fence he had already surmounted. The guards were double-checking the integrity of the barricade before reactivating the segment. Four seconds later, the blazing light was extinguished, and the darkness returned, along with a sense of relief. Faintly blinking blue diodes indicated that the vibration sensors were back online.

Now Janson made his way toward the stanchions. He looked at their configuration once more and felt disheartened. He recognized the model, and knew it was a state-of-the-art microwave protection system. Mounted on each sturdy pole beneath an aluminum hood was a dielectric transmitter and a receiver; a 15 GHz signal was set to one of several selectable AM signal patterns. The system could analyze the signature of any interference—inferring size, density, and speed—and feed it into the multiplex communications modules of the system's central net.

The bistatic sensors were staggered, as he had noticed earlier, so that the beams doubled over each other. You could not make use of one of the stanchions to climb over the flux, because the flux was doubled where the stanchions stood: climbing over one field, you would merely land in the middle of the second field.

Janson looked back to the barricade fence. If he triggered the microwave barrier—and there was an excellent chance that he would—he would have to scramble over the fence before the guards appeared and shooting began. And he would be moving in the glare of the quadruple halogen flood, a device that not only illuminated an intruder sharply for the camera but also, by its very brightness, would tend to blind and so immobilize him. If retreat were necessary, he would retreat: but it would be only a little less risky than proceeding.

Janson unzipped his knapsack and removed the police radar detector. It was a Phantom II, a high-end model meant for motorists who liked to speed and didn't like speeding tickets. What made it so effective was that it was both a detector and a jammer, aiming to make a motorist's car "invisible" to speed-detecting equipment. It worked by detecting the signal and bouncing it back toward the radar gun. Janson had removed its plastic casing, shortened the nub of its antenna, and installed an additional ca-pacitor, thus shifting its radio-frequency spectrum to the microwave band-width. Now he used duct tape to fasten the device near the end of the long telescoping steel rod. If it worked as he hoped, he would be able to exploit an inherent design feature of all outdoor security systems: the necessary tolerance for wildlife and weather. A security system was useless if it regularly issued false alarms. Outdoor microwave systems always used signal processing to distinguish human intruders from the thousand other things that could cause anomalies in the signal—a branch tumbling in the wind, a scampering animal.

Still, he was taking a stomach-plunging gamble. In less exigent circum-stances, he would have field-tested his hypothesis before staking his life on it.

One more time, he studied the configuration of the stanchions. The bistatic sensors could be placed as far as seven hundred feet away from each other. These were merely a hundred feet away—a spare-no-expenses approach that must have gladdened whoever had been paid to install the system. And yet the proximity of the sensors was another factor in Janson's favor. The farther apart they were, the broader the coverage pattern be-tween them. At 250 yards, the coverage pattern would swell to an oval that reached, at the midpoint between the two sensors, a width of forty feet. At thirty yards, the coverage pattern would be tighter and more narrowly focused, no wider than seven feet. That was one of the things that Janson was counting on.

As he had expected, the poles along the second, staggered tier beamed to the alternating pole in the tier closer to him, and vice versa. The point where the two beams intersected, accordingly, was the narrowest possible area of coverage. One stanchion was three feet to the left and two feet behind the other pole; thirty yards to either side, the pattern was repeated. In his head, he drew an imaginary line connecting the pair of adjacent stanchions, then the imaginary line connecting the next pair. Midway between those two parallel lines would be the point where the area of coverage was at its minimum. Janson moved toward that point, or where he intuitively estimated it to be. Holding the steel rod, he moved the Phantom II toward that spot. The system would have instantly detected the appearance of an object, but it would also immediately determine that the waveform patterns did not correspond to that of any human intrusion. It would remain quiet and undisturbed—until Janson himself tried to cross. And that would be the moment of truth.

Would the radar scrambler confuse the signal receivers, preventing them from registering the presence of the very human intruder that was Paul Janson?

He couldn't even be sure that the Phantom II was working. As a precaution, Janson had disabled its displays; there would be no reassuring red light indicating that it was mirroring the signals it received. He would have to proceed on faith. He kept the Phantom II steadily in position, moving himself down the pole, hand over hand, keeping it aloft without shifting its position. Then he rotated the rod and continued to back away from the microwave barrier.

And . . . he was through.

*He was through.*

He was a safe distance on the other side. Which was not a safe place to be at all.

As Janson walked toward the gently sloping fairway toward the mansion, he felt the hairs on the back of his neck bristling, conscious on some animal level that the greatest risks lay ahead.

He looked at the dimly illuminated LCD display of his black Teltek voltmeter, holding it in cupped hands. It wasn't field-caliber equipment, but it would do.

Nothing. No activity.

He traveled another ten feet. The digits began to climb; he took another step, and they surged.

He was approaching the subterranean pressure sensors. Though the voltmeter indicated that the buried cable itself was still a ways off, he knew that the electromagnetic flux of TriStar's buried-cable sensors created a detection field that was more than six feet wide.

The rate of increase in the voltmeter's display suggested that he was nearing the active field. Nine inches beneath the sod, the "leaky" coaxial cable was designed to have gaps in the outer conductor, allowing an electromagnetic flux to escape and be detected by a parallel receiving cable that ran in the same jacket. The result was a volumetric detection field around the coaxial cable, about one foot high and six feet wide. Still, as with other outdoor intrusion-detection systems, microprocessors were tasked with distinguishing one kind of disturbance from another. A twenty-pound animal would not trigger an alarm; an eighty-pound boy would. Intruder speeds, too, could be detected and interpreted. Snow, hail, gusting leaves, temperature changes—all could alter the flux. But the brains of the system would filter out such noise.

Unlike a microwave system, it could not be spoofed. The buried cables were inaccessible, and the TriStar system had redundant tamper protection, so any interruption of its circuits would itself be detected and prompt an alarm response. There was only one way through it.

And that was *over* it.

Janson retrieved the telescoping rod and, twisting the segments counterclockwise, locked it in its fully extended position. He walked some ways back toward the microwave poles and, keeping the rod extended in his hands, raced toward the buried sensor cables, imagining the invisible six-foot-wide band to be a physical barrier.

He held the pole as he ran, then plunged the end of it in the ground, just above where he believed the cable to be buried. Now: a step and drive. He swung his right knee up and forward and jumped, swinging upward with his hips as he held on to the pole. If all went well, his momentum would carry him, and he would land a safe distance from the cable. It need not be a soaring, athletic pole vault, but a broad jump; it was merely necessary to keep his body several feet in the air. The volumetric detector would have been alerted only to the thin pole twitching in the ground—nothing even approaching the volume, or flux disturbance patterns, consistent with a human being. Now, as he kept his eyes on the area of grass where he hoped to land, a comfortable distance from the buried sensor cable, he suddenly felt the metal rod buckling under his weight.

*Oh dear God, no!*

In mid-arch, the rod collapsed and Janson tumbled heavily to the ground, just a few feet from where he'd estimated the coaxial to lie.

He was too close!

Or was he? It was impossible to be sure, and the sheer uncertainty was the most nerve-racking thing of all.

A cold sweat formed on his skin almost instantly as he rolled out of the zone. Any moment now he would know if he had triggered the pressure sensors. The floodlights would blaze; the camera would pivot. And then, as his visage came into focus, a team of heavily armed guards would rush to the site. The barricades and alarm systems to every side would make his chance for escape essentially nil.

With bated breath, he waited, feeling relief budding with each passing second. Nothing. He had cleared it. All three perimeter security systems were now behind him.

Now he stood and looked up at the mansion that loomed before him. Up close, it was breathtaking in its grandeur. To either side of the main house were vast conical turrets; the exterior of the mansion was fashioned from Briar Hill sandstone. The roof was trimmed with an intricate balustrade and topped with a smaller one. The place was an eclectic display of architectural bombast. Yet did it count as ostentation if nobody could see it?

The windows were dark except for a dim glow of what might be standard nighttime illumination; were its inhabitants in the back rooms? It seemed too early for anyone to be asleep. Something about the setup bothered Janson, but he could not say why, and it was no time for turning around.

Now he crept to the left side of the building and over to a narrow side entrance.

Mounted in the stone near the dark, ornately incised door was a discreet electrostatic touch screen, of the kind used by ATMs. If the right numbers were pressed, the entrance alarm would be deactivated. Janson withdrew the small compressed-air atomizer from his knapsack and directed a jet of finely powdered charcoal at the pad. If everything went well, it would alight on fingerprints, and by the pattern he would be able to tell which digits the alarm code used; depending on how light or heavy the oils were, he could make a good guess as to their relative frequency.

A dead end. No pattern was revealed at all. As he had feared, the alarm pad employed a scrambled video display: the numerals were displayed in a random order, never in the same sequence twice.

He cleared his head. *So close and yet so . . .* No, he was not down for the count. Deactivating the alarm would have been enormously helpful, but he had not exhausted his backup plans. The door was alarmed. Accept it. If the alarm system did not detect that it had been opened, however, it would not go off. With the help of a penlight, Janson scanned the dark-stained door until he saw the tiny screws on the topmost section: evidence of the contact switch. Within the door frame, the contacts of a ferrous-metal switch were kept together—the circuit was kept closed—by a magnet recessed in the top of the door. As long as the door was shut, the magnet would keep a plunger within the door frame depressed, completing the electric circuit within the switch unit. Janson withdrew a powerful magnet from his knapsack and, using a fast-drying cyanoacrylate adhesive, fastened it to the lower part of the door frame.

Then he went to work on the door lock. More bad news: there was no keyhole. The door was opened by means of a magnetic card. Could the door simply be forced? No: he had to assume a heavy steel grid inside the wooden door and a multiple door-frame-bolt locking system. You had to *ask* a door like that to open. Unless you meant to take down part of the building, you couldn't force it to.

It was an eventuality he had prepared for; but again, with his rough-and-ready tools, the chances of success were far less than with the kind of instruments he was accustomed to having at his disposal. Certainly, his magnetic picklock was not an impressive-looking piece of equipment, having been jury-rigged with electrical tape and epoxy. He had removed the core of the solenoid and replaced it with a steel rod. At the other end of the rod, he had attached a thin rectangle of steel, which he had cut from a tin of butter cookies using heavy-duty scissors. The electronic part—a random noise generator—was a simple circuit of transistors he had extracted from a Radio Shack cell phone. Once he connected a pair of AA batteries to the apparatus, a quickly oscillating magnetic field was created: it was designed to pulse at the sensors until they were activated.

Janson inserted the metal rectangle in the slot and waited. Slow seconds ticked by.

Nothing.

Swallowing a gorge of frustration, he checked the battery contacts and reinserted the metal card. More long seconds ticked by—and suddenly he heard the click of the lock's own solenoid being activated. The door's bolts and latches were swiftly retracted.

He let out his breath slowly, and opened the door.

As long as the house was occupied, any internal photoelectric alarms would be deactivated. If he'd guessed wrong, it wouldn't take long to find out. Janson quietly closed the door behind him and, in the gloom, proceeded down a long hall.

After a few hundred feet, he saw a crack of light. It was seeping beneath a paneled door to his left.

On examination, it appeared to be a simple swing door, unlocked and unalarmed. What kind of lair was this? Was it an office? A conference room?

Fear slithered through his bowels. Every animal instinct he had was signaling frantically.

*Something was wrong.*

Yet he could not turn back now, whatever the risks. He removed his pistol from a bellyband holster beneath his tunic and, holding it before him, strode into the room.

To eyes that had adjusted to the gloom, the space was dazzlingly bright, illuminated by floor lamps and desk lamps and a chandelier overhead—and Janson squinted involuntarily as an even deeper sense of dread came over him.

His eyes swept the room. He was in the middle of a magnificent drawing room, a textural array of damask and leather and richly burnished antique woods. And in the middle of it, *eight men and women were seated, facing him.*

Janson felt the blood drain from his face.

They had been waiting for him.

"What the heck took you so long, Mr. Janson?" The question was asked with a practiced show of affability. "Collins here told me you'd make it here by eight o'clock. It's practically half past."

Janson blinked hard at his questioner, but the evidence of his eyes remained unchanged.

He was staring at the President of the United States.

# CHAPTER THIRTY-FOUR

The President of the United States. The director of Consular Operations. And the others?

Janson felt flash frozen by the shock. As he stood rooted to the spot, his mind struggled fiercely with itself.

*It couldn't be.* And yet it was.

Men in suits and ties had been waiting for him in the luxurious mansion, and Janson recognized most of them. There was the secretary of state, a hale man looking less hale than usual. The U.S. Treasury Department's undersecretary for international affairs, a plump, Princeton-trained economist. The sallow-faced chairman of the National Intelligence Council. The deputy director of the Defense Intelligence Agency, a burly man with a perpetual five o'clock shadow. There were also a few colorless but nervous-looking technicians: he knew the type immediately.

"Have a seat, Paul." Yes, it was Derek Collins, his slate eyes cool behind his chunky black plastic glasses. "Make yourself at home." He gestured around him wryly. "If you can call this a home."

The room was both spacious and ornate, paneled and plastered in the seventeenth-century English style; burnished mahogany walls gleamed beneath a fine crystal chandelier. The floor marquetry was in an intricate pattern of lighter and darker woods, oak and ebony.

"Apologies for the programmed misdirection, Paul," Collins went on.

*Programmed misdirection?*

"The courier was on your payroll," Janson said, toneless.

Collins nodded. "We'd had the same thought as you about getting access to the incoming documents. As soon as he reported your contact, we knew we had a golden opportunity. Look, you weren't exactly going to respond to an engraved invitation. It was the only way I could bring you in."

*"Bring me in?"* Indignation choked off the words in his throat.

Glances were exchanged between Collins and the president. "And it was the best way to show these other good people that you still have what it takes," Collins said. "Demonstrate that your abilities live up to your reputation. Hot damn, that was one impressive infiltration. And before you get all hurt and sulky, you better understand that the people in this room are pretty much the only ones left who know the truth about Mobius. For better or worse, you're now a member of this select group. Which means we've got an Uncle Sam Wants You situation here."

"God*damn* you, Collins!" He reholstered his pistol and put his hands on his hips. Fury coursed through him.

The president cleared his throat. "Mr. Janson, we really are depending on you."

"With all respect, sir," he said, "I've had enough of the lies."

"Watch it, Paul," Collins interjected.

"Mr. Janson?" The president was looking into his eyes with his famous high-beam gaze, the kind that could be equally mournful or amused. "Lies are pretty much the first language for most folks in Washington. You'll get no argument from me. There are lies and, yes, there will continue to be lies, because the good of the country requires it. But I want you to understand something. You're inside a top-secret ultrasecure federal facility. No tape, no log, no nothing. What does that mean? It means we're at a place where we can all open our kimonos, and that's exactly what we're going to do. This meeting has no official status whatsoever. It never happened. I'm not here, you're not here. That's the sheltering lie, the lie that's going to make all the truth-telling possible. Because here and now, it's all about telling the truth—to you and to ourselves. Nobody's going to shine you on. But it's dead urgent that you get briefed on the situation with the Mobius Program."

"The Mobius Program," Janson said. "I've already been briefed. The world's greatest philanthropist and humanitarian, this one-man roving ambassador, the 'peacemaker'—he's a goddamn fiction, brought to you by your friends in Washington. This latter-day saint is a wholesale creation of . . . what? A task force of planners."

"Saint?" the National Intelligence Council chairman interrupted. "There's no religious valence here. We were *always* careful to avoid anything like that."

"Praise the Lord." Janson's voice was icy.

"I'm afraid there's a lot more going on than you know," offered the secretary of state. "And given that it's the most explosive secret in the history of the republic, you'll understand if we've been a little skittish."

"I'll give you the log line," the president said. It was clear that he was chairing the meeting; a man used to command did not have to make a show of his authority. "Our creature has become—well, not our creature anymore. We've lost control of the asset."

"Paul?" Collins said. "Really, have a seat. This is going to take a while."

Janson lowered himself into a nearby armchair. The tension in the room was palpable.

President Berquist's gaze drifted to the window, which gave a view of the gardens in the rear of the estate. In the moonlight, it was possible to make out the Italian-style formal garden, a rectilinear maze of clipped yew and box hedges. "To quote one of my predecessors," he said, "we made him a god when we didn't own the heavens." He glanced at Douglas Albright, the man from the Defense Intelligence Agency. "Doug, why don't you start?"

"I gather that you've already had the origins of the program explained to you. So you know that we had three extremely dedicated agents who were trained to play the role of Peter Novak. The redundancy was necessary."

"Right, right. Too much of an investment had gone into this to have your Daddy Warbucks hit by a taxicab," Janson said acidly. "What about the wife, though?"

"Another American agent," the DIA man said. "She went under the knife, too, in case she ever encountered anyone who might have known her from the old days."

"Remember Nell Pearson?" Collins said quietly.

Janson was thunderstruck. No wonder there was something about Novak's wife that seemed eerily familiar. His affair with Nell Pearson was brief but memorable. It had taken place a couple of years after he joined Consular Operations; like him, his fellow agent was single, young, and restless. They had both been working undercover in Belfast, assigned to play husband and wife. It didn't take much for them to add an element of reality to the imposture. The affair had been torrid, electric, more an emanation of the body than of the heart. It seized them like a fever, and it proved as evanescent as a fever. Yet something about her had obviously stayed with him. Those long elegant fingers: the one thing that could not be altered. And the eyes: there had been something between them, had there not? Some frisson, even in Amsterdam?

Janson shuddered, imagining the woman he knew being reshaped, irreversibly, by the cold steel edge of a surgeon's #2 scalpel. "But what do you mean you've lost control?" he persisted.

There was an awkward moment of silence before the Treasury Department's undersecretary for international affairs spoke. "Start with the operational challenge: how do you secure the vast funding necessary to sustain the illusion of a world-class tycoon-philanthropist? Needless to say, the Mobius Program couldn't simply divert funds from a closely monitored U.S. intelligence budget. Seed money could be provided, but nothing more. So the program drew upon our intelligence capabilities to create its *own* fund. We put to use our take from signals intercepts. . . ."

"Jesus *Christ*—you're talking about Echelon!" Janson said.

Echelon was a complex intelligence-gathering system comprising a fleet of low-earth-orbit satellites devoted to signals interception: every international phone call, every form of telecommunications that involved a satellite conduit—which was most of them—could be sampled, intercepted, by the orbiting spy fleet. Its mammoth download was fed into an assortment of collections and analysis facilities, all controlled by the National Security Agency. It had the capability of monitoring every form of international telephony. The NSA had repeatedly denied rumors that it used the signal intercepts for purposes other than national security, in its strictest sense. Yet here was the shocking admission that even the most conspiracy-minded skeptics didn't know the half of it.

The jowly Treasury undersecretary nodded somberly. "Echelon enabled us to gain sensitive, highly secret intelligence about central-bank decisions around the world. Was the Bundesbank going to devalue the deutsche mark? Was Malaysia going to prop up the ringgit? Had Ten Downing Street decided to let sterling take a tumble? How much would it be worth to know, even just a few days before? Our creation was armed with that inside information, because the choicest fruits of our intelligence were placed at his disposal. It was child's play. Through him we placed a few massive, highly leveraged currency bets. In rapid order, twenty million became twenty *billion*—and then much, much more. Here was a legendary financier. And nobody had to know that his brilliant intuition and instincts were in fact the result of—"

"The abuse of a U.S. government surveillance program," Janson said, cutting him off.

"Fair enough," President Berquist said soberly. "Fair enough. Needless to say, it was a program that was in place long before I took office. Through extraordinary measures, the Mobius Program had created a highly visible billionaire . . . yet we hadn't counted on the human factor—

on the possibility that access and control to all that wealth and power might prove too great a lure to at least one of our agents."

"Don't you people ever learn?" Janson said, flaring. "The law of unintended consequences—you know it? It sure knows you." His eyes moved from face to face. "The history of American intelligence is littered with ingenious plans that leave the world worse off. Now we're talking about the 'human factor' as if there just hadn't been room for it on your goddamn spreadsheets." Janson turned to Collins. "I asked you, when we spoke earlier, who would agree to play such a role—to have his entire identity erased. What kind of man would do such a thing?"

"Yes," Collins said, "and I answered, 'Someone who had no choice.' The fact is, you *know* that someone. A man named Alan Demarest."

# CHAPTER THIRTY-FIVE

A chill ran through Janson's veins, and for a moment all he could see was the face of his former commanding officer. Alan Demarest. Nausea flooded him, and his head began to throb.

*It was a lie!*

Alan Demarest was *dead*. Executed by the state. Janson's knowledge of that ultimate requital was the only thing that made his memories endurable.

When Janson returned stateside, he filed the lengthy reports that, he had been assured, resulted in Demarest's arraignment. A secret military tribunal had been convened; a decision had been made at the highest levels: the national morale was deemed too vulnerable to permit the public airing of Demarest's activities, but justice would be served all the same. Janson's extensive sworn depositions had made the case open-and-shut. Demarest had been found guilty after just a few hours of deliberation, and was sentenced to death. The man whom one counterintelligence operative dubbed the "Mr. Kurtz of Khe Sanh" had been executed by a military firing squad. *And Janson had watched.*

Mesa Grande. In the foothills of the San Bernardino Mountains. The cloth circle in front of his heart—white, and then bright red.

As Janson stared wordlessly at Collins, he could feel a vein pulsing in his forehead.

"A man who had no choice," Collins said, implacably. "He was a brilliant, brilliant man—his mind an extraordinary instrument. He also, as you discovered, had decided flaws. So be it. We needed somebody with his capabilities, and his absolute loyalty to this country had never been questioned, even if his methods were."

"No," Janson said, and it came out as a whisper. He shook his head slowly. "No, it's impossible."

Collins shrugged. "Blanks, squibs. Basic stagecraft. We showed you what you thought you needed to see."

Janson tried to speak, but nothing came out.

"I'm sorry that you were lied to for all these years. You believed De-marest should have been court-martialed and executed for the things he did, and so you were told that he was, *showed* that he was. Your thirst for justice was totally understandable—but you weren't looking at the big picture, not as far as our counterintelligence planners were concerned. Material like that doesn't come along very often, not in our line of work. So a decision was made. Ultimately, it was a simple issue of human re-sources."

"Human resources," Janson repeated dully.

"You were lied to because that was the only way we could hold on to *you*. You were pretty spectacular material yourself. The only way you'd be able to put it behind you was to be confident that Demarest had suffered the ultimate punishment. So you were better off, and we were better off, too, because it meant that you could go on and do what God made you to do. Totally win-win. It just made sense every which way the planners looked at it. So Demarest was presented with a choice. He could face a tribunal, and the mountainous evidence that you had provided, and prob-ably judicial execution. In the alternative, he essentially had to give his life to us. He would exist at the discretion of his controllers, his very life a revocable gift. He'd accept whatever tasks he was given because he had no choice. It all made him a very . . . singular asset."

"Demarest—alive." It was a struggle to get out the words. "You re-cruited him for the job?"

"The way he recruited you."

"What the hell are you talking about?"

"Probably 'recruit' is too gentle a word," Collins said.

The DIA man spoke up. "The logic of the assignment was unassailable."

"*Damn* you!" Janson cried out. He saw it all now. Demarest had been the first Peter Novak: *primus inter pares*. The others would be matched to the frame of his body. He had been the first because of his redoubtable gifts, as a linguist, as an actor, as a brilliantly resourceful operative. De-marest was the best they had. Had the thought even arisen that there might be risks in giving this responsibility to someone so utterly devoid of conscience—to a *sociopath*?

Janson shut his eyes as the images flooded his mind.

Demarest was not merely cruel, he had an unsurpassed gift for cruelty. He approached the infliction of pain like a four-star chef. Janson recalled the smell of charred flesh as the jumper cables sparked and sputtered at the Vietnamese captive's groin. The look of abject terror in the man's eyes.

And Demarest's almost gentle refrain as he interrogated the young fisherman. "Look into my eyes," Demarest had repeated in a gentle voice. "Look into my eyes."

The prisoner's breath had come in strangled yelps, like a dying animal's. Demarest listened to a few bars of choral music. Then he straddled the second prisoner. "Look into my eyes," Demarest said. He'd pulled a small knife from a waist holster and made a small slice in the man's belly. The skin and the fascia beneath immediately sheared, pulled apart by the tension of the ropes. The man screamed.

And screamed. And screamed.

Janson could hear the screams now. They echoed in his head, amplified by the sickening realization that this man was the one they had chosen to make the most powerful on earth.

Now Derek Collins glanced around the room, as if canvassing opinions, before he continued. "Let me get to the point. Demarest has been able to seize control of all the assets that were created for the use of the Mobius Program. Without getting into the details, I can tell you that he's changed all the banking codes—and foiled the measures we'd taken to prevent just such an eventuality. And they were damn extensive. We had zero-knowledge, top-security cryptosystems in place that required central Mobius authorization for substantial movements of currencies. Codes were changed regularly, divided among the three principals so that no individual could gain control of the whole—one firewall after another. The security measures were damn near insurmountable."

"Yet they were surmounted."

"Yes. He got control."

Janson shook his head, sickened by what he was hearing. "Translation: the mammoth empire of the Liberty Foundation, the financial leverage, all of it—has passed into the control of one dangerously unstable individual. Translation: you're not running him—he's running *you*."

There were no demurrals.

"And the United States can't expose him," said the secretary of state. "Not without exposing itself."

"Just when did you figure out this was happening?" Janson demanded.

The two technicians shifted uncomfortably in the Louis XV chairs, their bulk threatening the slender wooden frames.

"A few days ago," Collins said. "As I told you, the Mobius Program had fail-safe systems in place—what we thought were fail-safe, anyway. Look, we had some of our best minds on this thing—don't imagine we didn't think of everything, because we *did*. The controls were formidable. Only recently did he gain the wherewithal to circumvent them."

"And Anura?"

"His masterstroke," said the chairman of the National Intelligence Council. "We were victims, all of us, of an elaborate ploy. When we heard our man was imprisoned there, we panicked, and acted precisely as Demarest knew we would. We entrusted him with the second set of codes, the ones that would normally have been under the control of the man the guerrillas were about to execute. It seemed necessary, as a stopgap. What we didn't realize was that Demarest had *arranged* the hostage taking. Evidently he used a lieutenant of his named Bewick as the cutout, a cutout the Caliph knew only as the 'Go-Between.' All very, how shall I say, hygienic."

"Jesus."

"For that matter, we failed to realize that he was also responsible for the death of the third agent, a year earlier. We thought our marionette strings were unbreakable. We know better now."

"Now that it's too late," Janson said, and in the faces of tense men and women, Janson saw the acceptance of the rebuke—and its irrelevance. "Question: Why did Demarest bring *me* into it?"

Collins spoke first. "Do you have to ask? The man loathes you, blames you for taking away his career, his freedom, almost his life—turning him in to a government he thought he'd served with incredible devotion. He didn't just want to see you dead. He wanted you to be accused, humiliated, strung up, killed by your own government. What goes around comes around—that's how he must have seen things."

"You want to say 'I told you so'?" President Berquist said. "You're entitled. I've been shown copies of your 1973 reports about Lieutenant Commander Demarest. But you've got to understand where this thing stands right now. Not only has Demarest eliminated his understudies but he's moved into a second, far more deadly phase."

"What's that?"

"The puppet is killing off the puppet masters," said Doug Albright. "He's erasing the program. Erasing Mobius."

"And exactly who is the cast of characters?"

"You're looking at 'em. All in this room."

Janson stared around the room. "There had to have been somebody from the NSA," he objected.

"Killed."

"Who designed the basic systems architecture?"

"A real wizard, from the CIA. Killed."

"And the—oh Jesus . . ."

"Yes, the president's National Security Advisor," said Albright. "Charlotte made the wire services today, didn't she? Clayton Ackerley didn't—officially, he's a suicide, found in his car with the engine running and the garage door closed. Oh, Demarest doesn't like loose ends. He's making a list, he's checking it twice. . . ."

"At this point, most of the people who know the truth about Peter Novak have been eliminated," the secretary of state said, his voice raspy with anxiety.

"Everyone . . . but the men and women in this room," Collins said.

Janson nodded slowly. A global cataclysm loomed, but so did a far more immediate threat to the assembled. As long as Alan Demarest remained in charge of the Novak empire, everyone in this room would be in fear for his life.

"Sorry, Paul. It's too late to get into the dead pool," Collins said wanly.

"Christ, Derek," Janson said, turning to the undersecretary with undisguised outrage, "you *knew* what kind of man Demarest was!"

"We had every reason to think we could *control* him!"

"Now he has every reason to think he can control you," Janson replied.

"It's become apparent that Demarest has been planning his coup d'état for years," the secretary of state said. "As the recent killings have revealed, Demarest has assembled a private militia, recruited dozens of his former colleagues to use as his personal enforcers and protectors. These are operatives who know the codes and procedures of our most advanced field strategies. And the corrupt moguls of the former Communist states—the ones who pretend to be opposed to him—are actually in league with the guy. They've made their own centurions available to him."

"You called it a coup d'état," Janson said to him. "A term usually reserved for toppling and supplanting a head of state."

"In its own way, the Liberty Foundation is as powerful as any state," the secretary replied. "It may soon become more so."

"The fact is," the president said, cutting to the heart of the matter, "Demarest has absolute proof of everything we did. He can blackmail us into doing whatever he demands. I mean, *Jesus.*" The president exhaled heavily. "If the world ever found out that the U.S. had been surreptitiously manipulating global events—not to mention using Echelon to bet against the currencies of other countries—it would be an absolutely devastating blow. Congress would go berserk, of course, but that's the least of it. You'd get Khomeini-style revolutions all over the Third World. We'd lose every ally we have—would instantly become a pariah among nations. NATO itself would fall apart. . . ."

"So long, Pax Americana," muttered Janson. It was true: here was a secret so explosive that history would have to be rewritten if it ever were to come out.

The president spoke again: "He's now sent us a message demanding that we turn control of Echelon over to him. And that's just for starters. For all we know, nuclear codes could be next."

"What did you tell him, Mr. President?"

"We refused, naturally." Glances were exchanged with the secretary of state. "*I* refused, dammit. Against the wisdom of all my advisers. I will *not* go down in history as the person who handed the United States over to a *maniac!*"

"So now he's given us a deadline along with the ultimatum," Collins said. "And the clock is ticking."

"And you can't take him out?"

"Oh, what a *nifty* idea," Collins said dryly. "Get a bunch of angry brothers with a blowtorch and some pliers and get medieval on his ass. Now why didn't we think of that? Wait a minute—we did. God*dammit*, Janson, if we could find the son of a bitch, he'd be dead meat, no matter how well protected he is. I'd plug him myself. But we can't."

"We've tried everything," said the chairman of the National Intelligence Council. "Tried to lure him, trap him, smoke him out—but no go. He's become like the man who wasn't there."

"Which shouldn't be a surprise," Collins said. "Demarest has become a master at playing the reclusive plutocrat, and at this point he's got greater resources than we have. Plus, any person we bring in represents a risk, another potential blackmail threat: there's no way we can expand the number of people involved. That operational logic is self-evident. And sacrosanct. Do you see? *It's just us.*"

"And you," said President Berquist. "You're our best hope."

"What about people who genuinely oppose 'Peter Novak,' the legendary humanitarian? Fact is, he's not without enemies. Isn't there some way to mobilize a fanatic, a faction . . . ?"

"You're suggesting a pretty underhanded ploy," Collins said. "I like how you think."

"This is the place for truth-telling," the president said to Collins with a warning glance. "Tell him the truth."

"The truth is, we've tried just that."

"And...?"

"We've basically thrown up our hands, because, as I say, it's been impossible to locate him. We can't find him, and the crazy terror king can't find him, either."

Janson squinted. "*The Caliph!* Jesus."

"You got it in one," said Collins.

"The man lives for vengeance," said Janson. "Lives and breathes it. And the fact that his celebrated hostage escaped had to have been a major humiliation to him. A loss of face among his followers. The kind of loss of face that can lead to a loss of power."

"I could show you a foot-thick analytic report making exactly the same inference," Collins said. "So far we're on the same page."

"But how are you in a position to steer him at all? *Every* Westerner is satanic, in his book."

The secretary of state cleared his throat, uneasily.

"We're opening our kimonos," the president repeated. "Remember? Nothing that's said in this room leaves this room."

"OK," Derek Collins said. "It's a delicate business. There's somebody high up in Libyan military intelligence who . . . works with us occasionally. Ibrahim Maghur. He's a bad customer, all right? Officially, we want him dead. He's known to have been involved in the German disco bombing that killed two American servicemen. Been linked to Lockerbie, too. He's advised and helped funnel support to all sorts of terrorist organizations."

"And yet he's also an American asset," Janson said. "Christ. Makes a fellow proud to be a soldier."

"Like I said, it's a delicate business. Similar to the deal we had with Ali Hassan Salameh."

A small shiver ran down Janson's spine. Ali Hassan Salameh was the mastermind of the 1972 Munich Olympics massacre. He was also, for a number of years, the CIA's chief contact inside the Palestine Liberation Organization. It was during a period when the United States refused to recognize the organization. Yet the secret liaison afforded real protection to Americans based in Lebanon. A tip-off would arrive when a car bomb or an assassination in Beirut was in the works, and a number of American lives were spared as a result. The math may have worked out, yet it truly was a deal with the devil. A line from II Corinthians came to Janson: *What fellowship hath righteousness with unrighteousness? and what communion hath light with darkness?*

"So this Libyan—*our* Libyan—has been directing the Caliph?" Janson swallowed hard. "Quite an irony if one of the deadliest terrorists on the planet turns out to have been *triply* manipulated."

"I know it sounds preposterous, but we were grasping at straws," said Collins. "Hell, we still are. I mean, if you can think of a way to use him, go for it. But the problem remains: we can't get Demarest in our sights."

"Whereas," the pasty-faced systems analyst put in, "he seems to have no problem getting us in his."

"Which means you're our best hope," President Berquist repeated.

"You were his ace protégé, Paul," Collins said. "Face it. You worked closely with the guy for several tours, you know his wiles, you know the quirks of his character. He was your first mentor. And, of course, there's nobody better in the field than you, Janson."

"Flattery will get you nowhere," Janson said through gritted teeth.

"I mean it, Paul. This is my professional fitness assessment. There's nobody better. Nobody with greater resourcefulness and ingenuity."

"Except . . ." Doug Albright was worrying aloud, then thought better of it.

"Yes?" Janson was insistent.

The DIA man's eyes were pitiless. "Except Alan Demarest."

# CHAPTER THIRTY-SIX

The handsome West African, his silver hair neatly trimmed, gold cuff links glinting in the setting sun, looked pensively out the window of his thirty-eighth-floor office and waited for his calls to be returned. He was the secretary-general of the United Nations, had been for five years, and what he was about to do would shock most of the people who knew him. Yet it was the only way to ensure the survival of everything he had devoted his life to.

"Helga," Mathieu Zinsou said, "I'm expecting a call back from Peter Novak. Please hold all other calls."

"Certainly," said the secretary-general's longtime assistant, an efficient Dane named Helga Lundgren.

It was the hour of the day when he could see the furnishings of his own office reflected in the vast window. The decor had changed little over the years; it would have been sacrilege to replace the modernist furniture custom-designed for the building by the Finnish architect Eero Saarinen. Zinsou had added a few hangings of traditional textiles from his native country of Benin, for a slight flavor of individuality. In addition, gifts from various emissaries were stationed at strategic perches, and there were others, in storage, that could be brought out when representatives of the nation in question came to visit. If the finance minister of Indonesia were keeping an appointment, a Javanese mask might appear on the wall where, earlier in the day, a row of Edo netsuke had greeted the foreign secretary of Japan. Decoration as diplomacy, as Helga Lundgren liked to call it.

The office was positioned outward and away from the bustle of Manhattan. Indeed, when he peered through the ghostly reflections on the glass, he saw straight across the East River to the desolate industrial wasteland that was West Queens: the barnlike brick factory of the Schwartz Chemical Company with its four immense smokestacks, evidently long unused. The yellow-brick remains of an anonymous-looking warehouse. A few wisps of fog rolled over Hunter's Point, the nearest part of West Queens, where an ancient Pepsi-Cola neon sign still blazed, as it had since

1936, atop a now closed bottling plant, like an amulet warding off enemy incursions, or real-estate developers, and notably failing.

The view was not beautiful, but there were times when Secretary-General Zinsou found it oddly mesmerizing. An antique brass telescope was angled from an oak stand on the floor, facing the window, but he rarely used it, the unaided eye sufficed to see what was to be seen. A petrified forest of former manufacturing concerns. Fossils of industry. An archaeology of modernity, half buried, half excavated. The waning sun glittered off the East River, flashed from the chrome of disused signage. Such were the unloved remnants of bygone industrial empires. And what about his own empire, on the banks of Manhattan? Was it, too, destined for the scrap heap of history?

The sun had lowered farther in the horizon, giving the East River a rosy tinge, when the secretary-general's assistant notified him that Peter Novak was on the phone. He picked up at once.

"*Mon cher* Mathieu," the voice said. It had the crystalline clarity of something heavily processed by digital telephony—undoubtedly he was speaking on a top-of-the-line satellite phone. The secretary-general had requested that he and Novak speak on encrypted phones only, and the additional security probably increased the eerily noiseless quality of the signal. After a few pleasantries, Mathieu Zinsou began to hint at what he had on his mind.

The United Nations, the West African told the great man, was a magnificent freighter that was running out of fuel, which was to say, money. It was the simple fact of the matter.

"In many respects, our resources are enormous," the secretary-general said. "We have hundreds of thousands of soldiers seconded to us, proudly wearing the blue helmets. We have offices in every capital, staffed with teams of experts who enjoy ambassadorial status. We're privy to what goes on in these countries at every level. We know their military secrets, their development plans, their economic schemes. A partnership with the Liberty Foundation is simply a matter of common sense—a pooling of resources and competencies."

That much was preamble.

"U.N. officials operate freely in just about every country on the planet," Zinsou continued. "We see the suffering of people victimized by the incompetence and greed of their leaders. Yet we cannot reshape their policies, their politics. Our rules and regulations, our bylaws and systems of oversight—they hamstring us into irrelevance! The successes of your Liberty Foundation have put the United Nations to shame. And meantime our ongoing financial crisis has crippled us in every way."

"All this is true," said Peter Novak. "But it is not new."

"No," Zinsou agreed. "It is not new. And we could wait and, as we have in the past, do nothing. In ten years, the U.N. would be as poverty-stricken as any of its wards. Utterly ineffective—nothing more than a debate club for bickering emirs and tin-pot despots, discredited and ignored by the developed nations of the world. It will be a beached whale upon the shore of history. Or we can take action now, before it is too late. I have just been elected to another five-year term, with the near unanimous support of the General Assembly. I am uniquely in a position to make decisive, unilateral executive decisions. I have the popularity and the credibility to do so. And I *must* do so to save this organization."

"I've always thought your reputation for foresight was well earned," Novak said. "But so is your reputation for strategic ambiguity, *mon cher*. I wish I had a better sense of what you're proposing."

"Simply put, there can be no salvation for us except through partnership with you. A special joint division can be established—joint between the Liberty Foundation and the U.N.—devoted to economic development. Over time, more and more of the U.N.'s institutional resources and responsibilities would migrate to this joint division. It will be a powerful, invisible directorate within the United Nations. I can serve as the bridge between the two empires, yours and mine. U.N. appropriations would continue, of course, but the Liberty Foundation would be able to make intimate use of the U.N.'s extensive assets."

"You intrigue me, Mathieu," said Novak. "But we both know the rules of bureaucratic inertia. You tell me you envy and admire the extraordinary effectiveness of the Liberty Foundation, and I thank you for the kind words. But there's a reason for our record: the fact that I have always retained absolute, top-to-bottom control of it."

"I am deeply aware of that fact," said the secretary-general. "And when I speak of 'partnerships,' I need you to understand my meaning. 'Strategic ambiguity,' as you call it, is something my role at the United Nations often requires. But on one issue there can be no ambiguity. Ultimate control would be exercised by you, Peter."

There was a long moment of silence, and Zinsou briefly wondered whether Novak's phone had gone dead. Then the man spoke again. "You are indeed a man of vision. It's always nice to meet another one."

"It is a grave, an *immense* responsibility. Are you prepared for it?" Zinsou did not wait for an answer but continued to speak, with passion, eloquence, and urgency, elaborating on his vision.

Twenty minutes later, the man who called himself Peter Novak maintained an odd reticence.

"We have so much to discuss," Zinsou said, winding up. "So much that can only be discussed face-to-face, just you and me, together. Perhaps it is grandiose of me to say it, but I truly believe the world is depending on us."

At last, a mirthless laugh came from the phone: "Sounds like you're offering to sell me the United Nations."

"I hope I didn't say *that!*" Zinsou exclaimed lightly. "It is a treasure beyond price. But yes, I think we understand each other."

"And in the short term, my Liberty Foundation people would have ambassadorial rank, diplomatic immunity?"

"The U.N. is like a corporation with a hundred and sixty-nine CEOs. Nimble it is not. But yes, the charter I'll draft will make that quite clear," answered the secretary-general.

"And what about you, *mon cher* Mathieu? You'll be serving out your second term—and then what?" The voice on the phone grew friendly. "You have served your organization selflessly for so many years."

"You're kind to say so," the secretary-general said, catching his drift. "The personal element is an entirely subsidiary one, you appreciate. My real concerns are for the survival of this institution. But, yes, I will be frank. The U.N. job does not exactly pay well. A job as, let us say, a director of a new Liberty Foundation institute . . . obviously with the salary and benefits to be negotiated . . . would be the ideal way to continue my work for international peace. Forgive me for being so forward. The complexity of what I propose makes it imperative that we be absolutely straightforward with each other."

"I believe I'm coming to a better understanding, and find it all very encouraging," said the man who was Peter Novak, now sounding positively genial.

"Then why don't we have dinner. Something *très intime.* At my residence. The sooner the better. I'm prepared to clear my schedule."

"*Mon cher* Mathieu," the man on the phone repeated. A warm glow suffused his voice, the glow of a man who had just been offered the United Nations. It would be a final ornament to his redoubtable empire, and a fitting one. Abruptly, he said: "I'll get back to you." And the line went dead.

The secretary-general held on to the handset for a few moments before returning it to its cradle. "*Alors?*"

He turned to Paul Janson, who had been sitting in the corner of the darkening office.

The operative looked at the master diplomat with frank admiration. "Now we wait," said Janson.


Would he take the bait? It was a bold proposal, yet threaded through with truth. The financial straits of the U.N. were genuinely dire. And Mathieu Zinsou was nothing if not ambitious for his organization. He was also known to be a farseeing man. In his five years at the helm of the U.N., he had reshaped it more vigorously than any SG had ever imagined. Was this next step so unthinkable?

It had been a chance remark of Angus Fielding's that had inspired the ploy, and Janson recalled yesterday's conversation with the man who, not that long ago, had threatened him with a gun. Of course, that was the order of the day, wasn't it—allies and adversaries switching sides with abandon? The conversation had been awkward at first; Fielding had not missed Novak's CNN appearance, and was clearly abashed, bewildered, and humiliated, unaccustomed emotions for Trinity's laureled master. And yet, without so much as hinting at the explosive secret, Janson was able to pick the scholar's agile brain on the question of how one might reach the reclusive billionaire.

There was another element that Janson calculated might lend plausibility to the scenario. Zinsou had for years been dogged by a reputation for benign, small-scale corruption. When Zinsou was a young commissioner at UNESCO, a lucrative contract had been taken away from one medical corporation and awarded to another. The spurned rival put it out that Zinsou had received "special preferments" from the victorious corporation. Had payment been made in a numbered account somewhere? The accusations were groundless, yet in some circles curiously adhesive. The half-remembered hint of corruption would, ironically, make his proposition all the more persuasive.

But what would seal it would be an elemental feature of human psychology: Demarest would *want* it to be true. Intense desire always had a subtle gravitational effect upon belief: we are more likely to credit what we wish to be so.

Now Janson stood at Zinsou's desk and, from a bulky device there, extracted the digital cassette on which the call had been recorded for later study.

"You astonish me," Janson said, simply.

"I'll take that as an insult," the secretary-general said with a small smile.

"The implication being that my expectations were not high? Then I spoke poorly—and you should take it, rather, as proof that there is only one true diplomat in this room."

"The fate of the world should not hang on a lapse of etiquette. I feel that in this case it well may. Have you considered all the things that could go wrong?"

"I have absolute confidence in you," Janson parried.

"An expression of confidence I find dismaying. My confidence in myself is high: it is not absolute. Nor should yours be. I speak, of course, in principle."

"Principles," Janson said. "Abstractions."

"Indulgences, you mean to say." A smile hovered over Mathieu Zinsou's lips. "And this is not the time for them. Now is the time for particulars. Here's one: your plan involves venturing a prediction of somebody who may not be predictable at all."

"There are no absolute predictions that we can make. I take your point. But there *are* patterns—there *are* rules, even for the man who flouts the rules. I do know this man."

"Before yesterday, I'd have said the same. Peter Novak and I have met on a few occasions. Once at a state dinner in Amsterdam. Once in Ankara, in the wake of the Cyprus resolution he brokered—a purely ceremonial event. I was bearing the official congratulations of this organization, announcing the withdrawal of U.N. troops from the partition line. Of course, now I realize I was meeting with a phantom. Perhaps a different man each time—presumably there are files kept by the Mobius Program that could tell us. Yet I must say that I found him both charismatic and affable. An appealing combination."

"And a combination that's been ascribed to you," Janson said carefully.

Zinsou uttered a sentence in the complex tonal language of Fon, spoken by his father's people. Zinsou *père* had been a descendant of the royal court of Dahomey, once a significant West African empire. "A favorite saying of my great-uncle, the paramount chief, which he often repeated to the gaping sycophants who surrounded him. Loosely translated, it means: The more you lick my ass, the more I feel you're trying to slip one past me."

Janson laughed. "You're even wiser than they say—"

Zinsou raised an index finger of mock admonishment. "I can't help wondering. Did Peter Novak believe any of it, or was he just playing along? I ask out of injured pride, of course. It cudgels my sense of amour propre that someone should believe I would, in effect, sell out the organization to which I have devoted my life." Zinsou toyed with his thick Montblanc fountain pen. "But that's just pride speaking."

"Evil men are always quick to think evil of others. Besides, if it works, you'll have plenty of reason for pride. Pull this off, and it will be the greatest feat of your career."

An uncomfortable, lonely silence fell upon them.

Zinsou was not, by habit, a solitary man: after decades spent within the U.N. bureaucracy, deliberation and consultation were second nature to him. His diplomatic skills were most fully engaged in reconciling conflicts among the U.N. divisions themselves—calming hostilities between the Department of Peace-keeping-Operations and the Humanitarian Affairs people, preventing resistance from forming among frontline workers or their superiors in the head offices. He knew the thousand ways that the bureaucrats could stall executive decisions, for in his long career he himself had had occasion to make use of such techniques. The methods of bureaucratic infighting were as advanced and as sophisticated as the techniques of aggression on the world's battlefields. It was a tribute to his own success on the internal battlefields that he had risen as far and as fast as he had. Moreover, the bureaucratic battle was truly won only when those you defeated were led to imagine that they had, in some way, been victorious.

Being the secretary-general of the United Nations, Zinsou had decided, was like conducting an orchestra of soloists. The task seemed impossible, and yet it could be done. When he was in good form, Zinsou could lead a conflict-riven committee to a consensus position that he had planned out before the meeting had begun. His own preferences were masked; he would appear sympathetic to positions he secretly found unacceptable. He would play off the preexisting tensions among the assembled deputy special representatives and high commissioners; subtly lead people into temporary coalitions against detested rivals; guide the discussion through ricochets and clashes, like a pool shark bringing about a complex sequence of carefully planned collisions by a well-aimed cue ball. And at the end, when the committee had worked its way around to the very position he had meant them to reach, he would, with a sigh of resignation and a display of concessive largesse, say that the others in the room had talked him around to their point of view. There were bureaucratic players whose ego demanded that they be seen to have won. But true power belonged to those who wanted to win in actuality, regardless of appearances. A number of people still accepted Zinsou's soft-spoken and courteous demeanor at face value and did not recognize the forceful nature of his leadership. They were losers who imagined themselves winners. Some of those who supported Zinsou did so because they believed they could control him. Others, the smarter ones, supported him because they knew he would be the most effective leader that the U.N. had known for decades, and they knew that the U.N. was in desperate need of such leadership. It was a winning alliance—for Zinsou and for the organization to which he had devoted his life.

But now the virtuoso of manufactured consent had to operate on his own. The secret with which he had been entrusted was so explosive that there was nobody to whom he, in turn, could entrust it. No colloquy, no consultation, no deliberation, real or staged. There was only the American operative, a man Zinsou found himself only gradually warming to. What bound them together was not merely the explosive secret; it was also the knowledge that their countermeasures were likely to end in failure. The so-called Zinsou Doctrine, as the press had dubbed it, endorsed only interventions with a reasonable chance of success. This one failed the test.

Yet what alternative was there?

Finally, Janson spoke again. "Let me tell you about the man *I* know. We're talking about somebody whose mind is a remarkable instrument, capable of extraordinary real-time analysis. He can be a person of immense charm. And even greater cruelty. My former colleagues in intelligence would tell you that men like him can be valuable assets, as long as they are tightly constrained by the situations in which they're placed. The error of the Mobius planners is that they placed him in a context that didn't just permit but actively called upon his skills at fluid and freeform improvisation. A context in which an immensity of wealth and power was placed just out of his grasp. He *played* the world's mightiest plutocrat. Only the rules of the game prevented him from truly *being* that person. So he threw himself into trying to overcome the program's safeguards. Eventually, he did."

"It was not predicted."

"Not by the Mobius planners. Incredible technical prowess combined with extraordinary stupidity about human nature—typical of their breed. No, it *was* not predicted. But it was predictable."

"By you."

"Certainly. But not only by me. I suspect you, too, would have seen the risks."

Secretary-General Zinsou walked over to his enormous desk and sat down. "This monster, this man who threatens us all—you may know him as well as you think you do. You do not know me. And so I remain puzzled. Forgive me if I say that your confidence in me undermines my confidence in you."

"That's not very diplomatic of you, is it? I appreciate your candor, all the same. You may find that I know you a little better than you imagine."

"Ah, those intelligence dossiers of yours, compiled by agents who think people can be reduced to something like an instruction manual—the same mind-set that gave rise to your Mobius Program."

Janson shook his head. "I won't pretend that we were acquainted, you and I, not in the usual sense. But the thrust of world events over the past couple of decades did mean that we ended up patrolling a few of the same rough neighborhoods. I know what really happened in Sierra Leone, that week in December, because I was there—monitoring all communications from the head of U.N. Peace-keeping in the region and the head of the special delegation appointed to coordinate the U.N. response. Not much peacekeeping was happening, needless to say—the bloody civil war was raging out of control. Special Delegate Mathieu Zinsou was asked to relay the commander's report and intervention request to New York. The designee was a U.N. high commissioner who would then present it to the representatives of the Security Council—who would have refused it, forbidden the intervention."

The secretary-general looked at him oddly but said nothing.

"If that happened," Janson continued, "you knew that maybe ten thousand people would have been massacred unnecessarily." He did not need to detail the situation: A cluster of small-arms depots had been identified, freshly stocked by a Mali-based dealer. The U.N.'s on-the-ground commanders had received reliable intelligence that the rebel leader was going to use them to settle a tribal feud—in the small hours of the very next morning. The rebel leader's men would use the arms to launch a deep incursion into the Bayokuta region, shooting his enemies, demolishing villages, amputating the limbs of children. And it could all be prevented by a swift, low-risk sally that would eliminate the illegal arms warehouses. The moral and military calculation was not in doubt. But neither was the bureaucratic protocol.

"Here's where it gets interesting," Janson went on. "What does Mathieu Zinsou do? He's the consummate bureaucrat—just ask anybody. A perfect organization man. A stickler for the rules. Only, he's also a fox. Within an hour, your office sent a cable to the High Commission for Peacekeeping consisting of 123 reports and action items—every insubstantial bit of paperwork you had at hand, I'd guess. Buried in the cable, item number ninety-seven, was an 'Unless Otherwise Ordered' notification, spelling out the proposed U.N. military action in the blandest terms and giving the exact time during which it would be executed. You subsequently told your general stationed outside Freetown that the U.N. central command had been notified of his plans and had voiced no objection. This was literally true. It was also true that the high commissioner's staff didn't even stumble on the relevant advisory until three days after the operation."

"I can't imagine where this is leading," Zinsou said, sounding bored.

"At which point, the event was part of history—an impressive success, a casualty-free raid that averted the death of many thousands of unarmed civilians. Who *wouldn't* want to claim credit for it? A lily-livered U.N. high commissioner proudly told his colleagues that of *course* he had authorized the raid, even intimated that it had been his idea. And as he found himself roundly congratulated, he couldn't help but feel kindly disposed toward Mathieu Zinsou."

Zinsou fixed Janson with a stare. "The secretary-general neither denies nor confirms. But such a story, I submit, would not confirm one's faith in human predictability."

"On the contrary—I came to recognize the hallmarks of your personal style of operating. Later, in the flash-point crises in Tashkent, in Madagascar, in the Comoros, I noticed the extraordinary gift you had for making the best of a bad situation. I saw what others didn't—it wasn't so much that you followed rules as that you'd figured out how to make the rules follow you."

He shrugged. "In my country, we have a proverb. Loosely translated, it means: When you find yourself in a hole, stop digging."

"I also came to recognize your enormous discretion. You had much to boast about privately, and you never did."

"Your comments suggest an unwarranted, invasive, and inappropriate degree of surveillance."

"I'll take that as confirmation of their essential truth."

"You're a man of parts, Mr. Janson. I'll grant you that."

"Let me put a question to you: What do you give the man who has everything?"

"There is no such man," Zinsou said.

"Precisely. Demarest is motivated by power. And power is the one thing that nobody ever feels he has enough of."

"In part, because power creates its own subversion." The secretary-general looked thoughtful. "It's one of the lessons of the so-called American Century. To be mighty is to be mightier than others. Never underestimate the strength of resentment in world history. The strongest thing about the weak is their hatred of the strong." He leaned back in his chair and, for the first time in years, regretted having given up smoking. "But I see where you are going. You believe this man is a megalomaniac. Somebody who can never have enough power. And that's what you have baited the snare with—power."

"Yes," Janson said.

"One of my distinguished predecessors used to say, 'Nothing is more dangerous than an idea when it is the only one you have.' You were quite eloquent in your critique of the premises of the Mobius Program yesterday. Watch that you don't replicate the errors. You are building a model of this man . . ."

"Demarest," Janson prompted. "But let's call him Peter Novak. Better to stay in character, so to speak."

"You're building a model of this man, in effect, and you observe this hypothetical creature move this way and that. But will the real man behave as your model does? Those you angrily dismiss as the 'planners' are happy to assume so. But you? How well founded is your confidence, really?"

Janson looked into the secretary-general's liquid brown eyes, saw the composed face that greeted heads of state by the hundreds. He saw the air of mastery, and as he stared harder he saw something else, too, something only partly hidden. He saw dread.

And this, too, was something they shared, for it arose out of simple realism. "I am confident only that a bad plan is better than no plan," Janson said. "We are proceeding on as many fronts as possible. We may get a lucky break. We may get none. Allow me to quote one of my mentors: Blessed are the flexible, for they will not be bent out of shape."

"I like it." Zinsou clapped his hands together. "A smart fellow told you that."

"The smartest man I ever knew," Janson replied grimly. "The man who now calls himself Peter Novak."

A chill settled, along with another long silence.

The secretary-general swiveled his chair around toward the window as he spoke. "This organization was established by a world that was weary of war."

"Dumbarton Oaks," Janson said. "1944."

Zinsou nodded. "However broad its mandate has become, its central mission has always been the promotion of peace. There are attendant ironies. Did you know that the ground where this very building stands had previously been a slaughterhouse? Cattle were brought up the East River on a barge, then led by a Judas goat to the city's abattoirs, on this very spot. It is something I regularly remind myself: this property was once a slaughterhouse." He turned around to face the American operative. "We must take care that it does not become one again."

"Look into my eyes," the tall black-haired man intoned in a soothing voice. His high cheekbones gave an almost Asiatic cast to his features. The man who called himself Peter Novak hovered over the elderly scholar, who was lying prone on a Jackson table, a large translucent platform that supported his chest and thighs while permitting his abdomen to hang free. It was standard equipment in spinal surgery, for it shifted blood away from the spinal area and minimized bleeding.

Intravenous fluids dripped into his left arm. The table was adjusted so that the old scholar's head and shoulders were propped upward, and he and the man who called himself Peter Novak could commune face-to-face.

In the background, a twelfth-century plainsong could be heard. Slow, high voices in unison; they were words of ecstasy, yet to Angus Fielding it sounded like a dirge.

> O ignis spiritus paracliti,
> vita vite omnis creature,
> sanctus es vivificando formas

A six-inch-long incision had been made in the middle of the old man's back, and metal retractors parted the paraspinal muscles, exposing the ivory-white bones of the spinal column.

"Look into my eyes, Angus," the man repeated.

Angus Fielding looked, could not help looking, but the man's eyes were nearly black, and there was no pity in them whatsoever. They seemed scarcely human. They seemed like a well of pain.

The black-haired man had dropped the cultivated Hungarian accent; his voice was uninflected but distinctly American. "What exactly did Paul Janson tell you?" he demanded once more as the frail old scholar shivered with terror.

The black-haired man nodded to a young woman, who had extensive training as an orthopedic technician. A large, open-bore trocar, the size of a knitting needle, was pushed through the fibrous sheath surrounding the soft disk that separated the fifth and sixth thoracic vertebrae. After less than a minute, the woman nodded at him: the trocar was in position.

"And—good news—we're there."

A thin copper wire, insulated except for the tip, was then inserted through the trocar to the spinal root itself, the trunk through which nerve impulses from the entire body made their way. Demarest adjusted a dial until a small amount of electrical current began to pulse through the copper wire. The reaction was immediate.

The scholar screamed—a loud, bloodcurdling scream—until there was no air left in his lungs.

"Now *that*," Demarest said, cutting off the current, "is a very singular sensation, is it not?"

"I've told you everything I know," the scholar gasped.

Demarest adjusted the dial.

"I've told you," the scholar repeated as pain mounted upon pain, penetrating his body in convulsions of purest agony. "I've told you!" Shimmering and otherworldly, the choral threnodies of joy floated far above the agony that consumed him.

> *Sanctus es unguendo*
> *periculose fractos:*
> *sanctus es tergendo*
> *fetida vulnera.*

No, there was no pity in the black pools of the man's eyes. Instead, there was paranoia: a conviction that his enemies were anywhere and everywhere.

"So you maintain," Alan Demarest said. "You maintain this because you believe the pain will stop if I am persuaded that you have told me the whole truth. But the pain will not stop, because I know that you have not done so. Janson sought you out. He sought you out because he knew that you were a friend. That you were loyal. How can I make you understand that it is me you owe your loyalty to? You feel pain, do you not? And that means you are alive, yes? Is that not a gift? Oh, your entire existence will be a sensorium of pain. I believe that if I can make you understand that, we might begin to make progress."

"Oh dear God *no!*" the scholar shouted as another course of electricity penetrated his body.

"Extraordinary, isn't it?" Demarest said. "Every C fiber in your body— every pain-transmitting nerve—feeds into this main trunk of nerve bundles that I'm stimulating right now. I could attach electrodes to every inch of your body and it wouldn't yield the same intensity of pain."

Another scream reverberated through the room—another scream that ended only because breath itself did.

"To be sure, pain is not the same as torture," Demarest went on. "As an academic, you'll appreciate the importance of such distinctions. Torture requires an element of human intention. It has to be interwoven with meaning. Simply to be eaten by a shark, let us say, is not to experience torture—whereas if someone intentionally dangles you over a shark tank, that *is* torture. You might dismiss this as a nicety, but I'd beg to differ. The experience of torture, you see, requires not only the intention to inflict pain. It also requires that the subject of torture recognize that intention. You must recognize my intention to cause pain. More precisely, you must recognize that I intend you to recognize that I intend to cause pain. One has to satisfy that structure of regressive recognition. Would you say that you and I have done so?"

"Yes!" the old man screamed. "Yes! Yes! Yes!" His neck thrashed this way and that as a bolt of electricity blasted into him once more. He was being raped by pain, felt that the very fiber of his existence had been violated.

"Or would you offer another analysis?"

"No!" Fielding shrieked with pain once more. The agony was simply beyond imagining.

"You know what Emerson says of the great man: 'When he is pushed, tormented, defeated, he has a chance to learn something; he has been put on his wits on his manhood; he has gained facts; learns his ignorance; is cured of the insanity of conceit.' Would you concur?"

"Yes!" the scholar shrieked. "Yes! No! Yes!" The muscular convulsions that rippled his spine only magnified the already unendurable pain.

"Are you surprised how much pain you're capable of surviving? Are you wondering how your consciousness can even contain suffering of this magnitude? It's OK to be curious. The thing to remember is, the human body today is really no different than it was twenty thousand years ago. The circuits of pleasure and pain are as they were. So you might think that there is no difference between the experience of being tortured to death during, let us say, the Spanish Inquisition and the experience that I can offer you. You might think that, wouldn't you? But, speaking as something of an aficionado, I'd have to say you'd be wrong. Our evolving understanding of neurochemistry is really quite valuable. Ordinarily, the human body has the equivalent of a safety valve: when C-fiber stimulation reaches a certain level, endorphins kick in, blunting and assuaging the pain. Or else unconsciousness results. God, it used to piss me off when that happened. Either way, the phenomenology of pain is limited. It's like brightness: you can experience only a certain level of brightness. You maximally stimulate the cones and rods of the retina, and after that point, there's no change in the perception of brightness. But when it comes to pain, contemporary neuroscience changes the whole game. What's in your IV drip is absolutely crucial to the effect, my dear Angus. You knew that, didn't you? We've been administering a substance known as naltrexone. It's an opiate antagonist—it blocks the natural painkillers in your brain, those legendary endorphins. So the ordinary limits of pain can be *pushed past*. Not exactly a natural high."

Another wail of agony—almost a keening—interrupted his disquisition, but Demarest was undeterred. "Just think: because of the naltrexone drip, you can experience a level of pain that the human body was never meant to know. A level of pain that none of your ancestors would ever have known, even if they'd had the misfortune to be eaten alive by a saber-toothed tiger. And it can increase nearly without limit. The main limit, I would say, is the patience of the torturer. Do I strike you as a patient man? I *can* be, Angus. You'll discover that. I can be *very* patient when I need to be."

Angus Fielding, distinguished master of Trinity College, began to do something he had not done since he was eight: he broke down and sobbed.

"Oh, you'll *yearn* for unconsciousness—but the drip also contains potent psychostimulants—a carefully titrated combination of dexmethylphenidate, atomoxetine, and adrafinil—which will keep you maximally alert, indefinitely. You won't miss *anything*. It will be quite exquisite, the ultimate in-body experience. I know you think you've experienced agony beyond endurance, beyond comprehension. But I can increase it tenfold, a hundredfold, a thousandfold. What you have experienced so far is nothing at all, compared to what lies ahead. Assuming, of course, that you continue to stonewall." Demarest's hand hovered near the dial. "It's really most important to me that I receive satisfactory answers to my questions."

"Anything," Fielding breathed, his cheeks wet with tears. "*Anything.*"

Demarest smiled as the black pools of his gaze bore down on the aging don. "Look into my eyes, Angus. Look into my eyes. And now you must confide in me utterly. *What did you tell Paul Janson?*"

# CHAPTER THIRTY-SEVEN

"Lookit, I've got one person watching the entrance," Jessica Kincaid told Janson as they rode together in the back of the commandeered yellow cab. "He thinks it's a training exercise. But if she goes out, decides to head for one of their private planes in Teeterboro, we might lose her forever." She wore a cotton-knit shirt adorned with the logo of the phone company Verizon.

"Did you do the tenant search?"

"Did the whole enchilada," she said.

In fact, with a number of discreet telephone calls, she confirmed what observation had suggested, learning more than she needed to know. The inhabitants of the building included masters of finance capitalism, foundation directors, and old New York types who were better known for their philanthropy than for the origins of the wealth that made it possible. Flashier souls, eager to flaunt their newfound money, might opt for a penthouse in one of Donald Trump's palaces, where every surface gleamed or glittered. At 1060 Fifth Avenue, the elevators still retained the brass accordion doors originally installed in the 1910s, as well as the darkened fir-wood paneling. The building's co-op board rivaled the Myanmar junta in its inflexibility and authoritarianism; it could be counted upon to reject the applications of prospective residents who might turn out to be "flamboyant"—its favorite term of derogation. Ten sixty Fifth Avenue welcomed benefactors of the arts, but not artists. It welcomed patrons of the opera, but would never countenance an opera singer. Those who, in a civic-minded spirit, supported culture were honored; those who created culture were shunned.

"We've got one Agnes Cameron on the floor above her," Kincaid said. "Serves on the board of the Metropolitan Museum of Art, socially impeccable. I called the office of the director, pretending to be a journalist writing a profile of her. Said I was told she was in a meeting there, and I needed to double-check some of the quotes. A very snotty woman said, 'Well, that's impossible, Mrs. Cameron is in Paris at the moment.' "

"That the best candidate?"

"Seems to be, yeah. According to the phone company records, she had a high-speed DSL Internet connection installed last year."

She handed Janson a cotton-knit shirt emblazoned with the black and red Verizon logo, matching hers. "Turns out your friend Cornelius has a brother at Verizon," she explained. "Gets 'em wholesale. His-and-hers." Next came a leather instrument belt to cinch around his waist. A bright orange test phone was the bulkiest item. Rounding out the costume was a gray metal toolbox.

As they approached the doorman at the awning, Jessie Kincaid did the talking. "We've got a customer, I guess she's out of the country now, but her DSL line is on the fritz and she asked us to service it while she's gone." She flipped a laminated ID at him. "Customer name is Cameron."

"Agnes Cameron, on the eighth floor," the doorman told them, in what Janson recognized as an Albanian accent. His cheeks were lightly flecked with acne, and his visored hat sat high on his wavy brown hair. He went inside and consulted with the guard. "Repair guys from the phone company. Mrs. Cameron's apartment."

They followed him into the elegant lobby, which was trimmed with egg-and-dart molding and tiled with black and white marble in a harlequinade pattern.

"How can I help you?" The second doorman, a heavyset man also of Albanian origin, had been sitting on a round cushioned stool and talking to the guard. Now he sprang to his feet. He was evidently senior to the other doorman and wanted it to be clear that he would be making the decisions.

For a few moments, he silently scrutinized the two, frowning. Then he lifted an antique Bakelite internal phone and pressed a few digits.

Janson looked at Kincaid: Mrs. Cameron was supposed to be out of the country. She shrugged, in a tiny motion.

"Repairmen from Verizon," he said. "Verizon. To fix a phone line. Why? I don't know why."

He put his hand over the mouth of the phone and turned to the two visitors. "Mrs. Cameron's housekeeper says why don't you come back when Mrs. Cameron's in town. Be another week."

Jessie rolled her eyes theatrically.

"We're out of here," Paul Janson said, tight-lipped. "A favor: when you see Mrs. Cameron, tell her it'll be a few months before we'll be able to schedule another appointment to fix the DSL."

"A few *months?*"

"Four months is about what we're looking at," Janson replied with implacable professional calm. "Could be less, could be more. The backlog is incredible. We're trying to get to everybody as fast as we can. But when an appointment is canceled, you go to the end of the line. The message we got was, she wanted to have the problem dealt with before she got back to town. My supervisor got three or four calls about her problem. Bumped her up as a special favor. Now you're saying forget it. Fine with me, but just be sure to tell Mrs. Cameron that. If somebody's getting blamed, it isn't going to be me."

Weariness and wounded pride competed in the voice of the beleaguered phone repairman; this was someone who worked for an immense and immensely resented bureaucracy and was accustomed to being blamed personally for the failings of the system—accustomed to it, but not reconciled to it.

*If somebody's getting blamed:* the senior doorman flinched a little. The situation called for blame, did it? Such a situation was best avoided. Now, speaking into the phone, he said confidingly, "You know what? I think you'd better let these guys do their job."

Then he jerked his head in the direction of the elevator bank. "Down the hall and left," he said. "Eighth floor. The housekeeper will let you in."

"You're sure? Because I've had a very long day, wouldn't mind knocking off early."

"Just go up to the eighth floor, she'll let you right in," the doorman repeated, and beneath the impassive manner was the faintest hint of pleading.

Janson and Kincaid walked down the polished floor to the elevators. Though the ancient accordion gate was intact, the cab they entered was no longer manned. Nor was there a security camera inside: with two doormen and a security guard in the lobby; the co-op board undoubtedly had rejected the additional security measure as intrusive overkill, the sort of showy technology that one would expect in an apartment building put up by Mr. Trump. A couple should be able to exchange a chaste peck in the elevator without worrying about gawking spectators.

They pressed the button to the eighth floor; would it light? It would not. There was a keyhole next to the button, and Janson had to massage it with two thin implements for twenty seconds before he was able to rotate it and activate the button. They waited impatiently as the small cab rose and then slowly shuddered to a halt. Given the munificence of the building's tenants, the unrenovated nature of the elevators amounted to something of an affectation.

Finally, the doors parted, directly onto the apartment's foyer.

Where was Márta Lang? Had she heard the elevator door opening and closing? Janson and Kincaid stepped quietly into the hallway, and listened for a moment.

A clink of china, but distant.

To the left, at the end of the darkened hallway, a curving staircase led to the floor below. To the right was another doorway; it appeared that it led to a bedroom, or perhaps several. The main floor seemed to be the one beneath them. Lang had to be there. They scanned the area for fish-eye lenses, for anything that might suggest surveillance equipment. There was none.

"OK," Janson murmured. "Now we go by the book."

"Whose book?"

"Mine."

"Got it."

Another faint sound of china: a cup clinking against a saucer. Janson peered carefully down the staircase. There was nobody visible, and he was grateful that the stairs were of worn marble: no squeaky floorboard would serve as an inadvertent alarm system.

Janson signaled Jessie: remain behind. Then he swiftly descended the stairs, keeping his back against the curving wall. In his hands was a small pistol.

Ahead of him: an enormous room, with thick curtains drawn shut. To his left: another room, a sort of double parlor. The walls were of white painted wood, intricately paneled; paintings and engravings of no partic-ular distinction hung at geometrically precise intervals. The furnishings had the look of a New York pied-à-terre designed, long-distance, for a Tokyo businessman: elegant and expensive, yet devoid of individuality.

In a flash, Janson's mind reduced his surroundings to an arrangement of portals and planes: one representing both exposure and opportunity, the other the prospect of safety and concealment.

Wall to wall, surface to surface, Janson progressed through the double parlor. The floor was a polished parquet, much of which was covered with large Aubusson rugs in subdued colors. The rug did not, however, prevent the soft creak of a plank underfoot as he reached the entrance to the adjoining parlor. Suddenly, his nerves crackled as if receiving a jolt of electricity. For there, in front of him, was a housekeeper in a cotton uniform of pale blue.

She turned toward him, holding an old-fashioned feather duster out in front of her, frozen, and her round face was contorted into a terrible grin—a rictus of fear?

"Paul, watch yourself!" It was Jessie's voice. He had not heard her descend, but she was a few feet behind him.

Suddenly the housekeeper's chest erupted in a spray of scarlet and she toppled forward onto the carpet, the sound muffled by the soft woven fabric.

Janson whirled around and saw the silenced gun in Jessie's hand, a wisp of cordite seeping from its perforated cylinder.

"Oh, *Jesus*," Janson breathed, gripped with horror. "Do you realize what you just did?"

"Do you?" Jessica strode over to the body and, with a foot, nudged the feather duster that remained in the housekeeper's outstretched hand.

It was not a device used for cleaning house, save in the bloodiest of senses: artfully concealed beneath the fan of brown feathers was a high-powered SIG Sauer, still affixed to the dead woman's hand by an elastic strap.

Jessie had been right to shoot. The safety was off on the powerful automatic handgun, a bullet chambered. He had been a split second from death.

Márta Lang was not alone. And she had not been unguarded.

Was it possible she was still unaware of their presence? At the end of the second parlor was another doorway with an ordinary swing door, evidently opening onto the formal dining room.

There was another sound of movement, coming from within.

Janson lurched to the wall to the left of the door frame and spun around, holding his Beretta chest high, preparing to squeeze the trigger or deliver a blow, as was required. A burly man holding a gun burst through, apparently having been sent to investigate. Janson smashed the butt of his Beretta on the back of the man's head. He went limp and Jessie caught him as he went down, gentling him to the carpet silently.

Janson stood still for a moment, composing himself and listening intently; the sudden violence had drained him, and he could not afford to be anything less than focused.

Suddenly, there was a series of loud blasts, and the swinging door was perforated by several magnum-force bullets, spraying splinters of wood and paint. Were they fired by Márta Lang herself? Somehow he suspected that they were. Janson looked at Kincaid, verifying that she, like him, was out of the line of fire, safely to the side of the doorway.

There was a beat of silence, and then the sound of quiet footfalls; Janson instantly knew what Márta Lang—or whoever it was—was doing, and what he had to do. She was going to peer through the bore holes her gun had drilled in the wooden door, assess the damage. She had established a line of fire: surely nobody would remain standing where bullets had just flown.

Timing would be everything, and Janson had very little to go by. *Now!* With all his strength, Janson reared up and threw himself, shoulder first, against the swinging door. It would be his weapon—a battering ram. The door moved too easily at first, and then, with a thud, it *connected,* sending the person on the other side of it sprawling.

It was indeed Márta Lang he saw as the door swung all the way open. The door had slammed into her, knocking her against a Hepplewhite-style dining-room table. The heavy automatic weapon in her hands had been sent flying, too, clattering to the table just a few inches beyond her reach.

With catlike agility, Lang scrambled to her feet, rounded the table, and reached for the black gleaming weapon.

"Don't even think about it," Jessica said.

Márta Lang glanced up to see Jessica in a perfect Weaver stance, holding her pistol with both hands. Her shooting stance said that she would not miss. Her face said that she would not hesitate.

Breathing hard, Lang said nothing and did nothing for a long moment, as if torn by indecision. At last, she stood up straight, verifying the position of her weapon with a sidelong glance. "You're no fun," she said. The lower part of her face was reddened from where the door had slammed into her. "Don't you want to even up the odds a little? Make the game interesting?"

Janson advanced toward her, and at the moment when his body was interposed between Márta Lang and Kincaid, Lang's hand darted out to grab back her weapon. Janson anticipated the move, and he immediately wrenched it from her hands. "A Suomi burp gun. Impressive. You have a license for this toy?"

"You've broken into my house," she said. "Caused grievous bodily injury to my staff. I'd call it self-defense."

Márta Lang ran her fingers through her perfectly coifed white hair, and

Janson tensed for a surprise, but her hands returned empty. There was something different about her; her speech was flatter, her affect more casual. What did he really know about this woman?

"Don't waste our time and we'll try not to waste yours," Janson said, pressing on. "You see, we already know the truth about Peter Novak. There's no use in trying to hold out. He's a dead man. It's *over,* dammit!"

"You poor muscle-bound idiot," Márta Lang said. "You think you've got everything figured out. But you thought that *before,* didn't you? Doesn't that make you wonder?"

"Give him up, Márta," Janson said with gritted teeth. "It's your only chance. They've pulled the plug on him. An executive directive from the President of the United States himself."

The white-haired woman's contempt was magnificent. "Peter Novak is more powerful than he is. The U.S. president is only the leader of the *free* world." She paused to let it sink in. "Getting the big picture, or are you waiting for it to come out on video?"

"You're deluded. He's somehow brought you into his own madness. And if you can't break free, you're lost."

"Tough talk from a goddamn organization man. Look into my eyes, Janson—I want to see if you even believe what you're saying. Probably you do, worse for you. Hey, like the fat lady sings, freedom's just another word for nothing left to lose. You think you're some kind of hero, don't you? I feel sorry for you, you know. There's no freedom for people like you. Somebody is always manipulating you, and if it's not me, it'll just be someone else, someone a little less imaginative." She turned to Jessica. "It's true. Your boyfriend here is like a piano. He's just a piece of furniture until someone plays him. And someone's *always* playing him." Something between a grin and a grimace flashed on her face. "Has it never struck you that he's been three steps ahead of you all along? You're so wonderfully predictable—I suppose that's what you call *character.* He knows just what makes you tick, just what you're capable of doing, and just what you'll decide to do. For all your derring-do in the Stone Palace, he was playing with you like a kid with a goddamn action figure. We had remote surveillance rigged up there, naturally. Kept tabs on everything you did, every move. We knew every element of your plan and we'd prepared contingencies for every anticipated variant. Of *course* Higgins—oh, that was the fellow you sprang—was going to insist on saving the American girl. And of *course* you were going to give up your seat to the lady. What a perfect gentleman you are. Perfectly *predictable.* The craft was wired to blow by remote, needless to say. Peter Novak was practically waving a baton—he could have been conducting the whole goddamn operation. You see, Janson, he made you. You didn't make him. He was calling the shots before, and he's calling the shots now. And he always will."

"Permission to blow the bitch away, sir?" Jessica asked, raising her left hand like an eager cadet.

"Ask again later," Janson said. "You get only so many chances in this world, Márta Lang. Is that your name, by the way?"

"What's in a name?" she said, blasé. "By the time *he* gets done with you, you'll think it's *your* name. Now here's a question for *you:* do you think that if the hunt goes on long enough, the fox starts to imagine it's chasing the hounds?"

"What's your point?"

"It's Peter Novak's world. You're just living in it." She flashed a strangely ethereal smile. When Janson had met her in Chicago, she seemed the very picture of a highly educated foreigner. Her accent was now decidedly American; she could have come from Darien.

"There is no Peter Novak," Jessie said.

"Remember, dear, what they say about the Devil—that his greatest trick was persuading people he didn't exist. Believe what you like."

A memory pricked at Janson. He looked at Márta Lang intently, alert to any flicker of weakness. "Alan Demarest—where is he?"

"Here. There. Everywhere. You should call him Peter Novak, though. It's rude not to."

"*Where*, goddammit!"

"Not telling," she said lightly.

"What does he have over you?" Janson exploded.

"Sad to say, you don't know what you're talking about."

"He *owns* you somehow."

"You don't get it, do you?" she replied witheringly. "*Peter Novak owns the future.*"

Janson stared. "If you know where he is, then, God help me, I will extract the information from you. Believe this: after a few hours on a Versed-scopolamine drip, you won't know the difference between your thoughts and your speech. Whatever comes into your head will come out of your mouth. If it's in your head, we'll extract it. We'll extract a lot of garbage, too. I'd rather you came clean without chemical assistance. But one way or another, you *will* tell us what we want to know."

"You're so full of it," she said, and turned to Jessica. "Hey, back me up here. Can't I get a little feminine solidarity on this one? Haven't you heard—sisterhood is powerful." Then she leaned forward, putting her face only inches from his. "Paul, I'm really sorry about your friends getting blown *sky-high* off Anura." She fluttered her fingers and, in a voice that was pure vinegar, added, "I know you were all broken up about your Greek butt-boy." She loosed a short giggle. "What can I say? Shit happens."

Janson felt a vein in his forehead throb painfully; he knew his face was mottled with rage. He imagined smashing her face, imagined fracturing her facial bones, a spear hand driving the bones of her nose into her brain. Just as swiftly, he felt the fog of fury recede. He recognized that the point of her needling was to get him to lose control. "I'm not presenting you with three choices," he said. "Only two. And if you don't decide, I'll decide for you."

"Is this going to take long?" she said.

Janson grew aware of choral music in the background. Hildegard von Bingen. The hairs on Janson's neck stood erect. " 'The Canticles of Ecstasy,' " he said. "The long shadow of Alan Demarest."

"Huh? *I* turned him on to that," she said, shrugging. "Back when we were growing up."

Janson stared at her, seeing her as if for the first time. Suddenly, a series of small nagging details snapped into place. The movement of her head, her sudden, bewildering shifts of affect and tone, her age, even certain lines and locutions.

"Jesus Christ," he said. "You're—"

"His twin sister. Told you sisterhood was powerful." She started to massage the loose skin beneath her left collarbone. "The fabulous Demarest twins. Double trouble. Terrorized fucking Fairfield growing up. The Mobius morons never even knew that Alan brought me into the picture." As she spoke, her circular movements became deeper, more insistent, seemingly responding to an itch deep beneath the skin. "So if you think I'm going to 'give him up,' as you so artfully put it, you'd better think again."

"You don't have a choice," Janson said.

"What is she doing?" Jessica asked in a low voice.

"We always have a choice." Lang's movements grew smaller, more focused; with her fingers she started to dig at something to the side of her clavicle. "Ah," she said. "That's it. That's it. Oh, that feels so much better. . . ."

"Paul!" Jessica shouted. She made the inference a moment before he did. "*Stop* her!"

It was too late. There was the barely audible pop of a subdermal ampoule, and the woman threw her head back, as if in ecstasy, her face flushing to a purplish red. She made a soft, almost sensual panting sound, which subsided into a gargling sound deep in her throat. Her jaw fell open, slack, and a rivulet of saliva dribbled from the side of her mouth. Then her eyes rolled up, leaving only the whites visible through her half-parted lids.

From unseen speakers, the ghostly voices sang.

> *Gaudete in ilio,*
> *quem no viderunt in terris multi,*
> *qui ipsum ardenter vocaverunt.*
> *Gaudete in capite vestro.*

Janson put a hand on Márta Lang's long neck, feeling for a pulse, even though he knew there would be none. The signs of cyanide poisoning were hard to miss. She chose death before surrender, and Janson was hard-pressed to say whether it represented an act of courage or one of cowardice.

*We always have a choice,* the dead woman had said. *We always have a choice.* Another voice, from decades past, joined it in his memory: one of the Viet Cong interrogators, the man with the steel-framed glasses. *Not to decide is to decide.*

# CHAPTER THIRTY-EIGHT

The console on the secretary-general's desk chimed. Helga's voice: "I'm sorry to disturb you, but it's Mr. Novak again."

Mathieu Zinsou turned to the high commissioner for refugees, a former Irish politician who combined a vigorous style with a fair amount of loquacity; she was currently feuding with the under secretary-general for humanitarian affairs, who had been conducting turf battles with unyielding and unhumanitarian fervor. "Madame MacCabe, I'm *terribly* sorry, but this is a call I must take. I think I've understood your concerns about the strictures coming from the Department of Political Affairs, and I believe that we can address them if we *all reason together*. Ask Helga to arrange a meeting among the principals." He rose and bowed his head in a courtly gesture of dismissal.

Then he picked up the phone. "Please hold for Mr. Novak," a woman's voice said. A few clicks and electronic burps, and Peter Novak's voice came on: "*Mon cher* Mathieu," he began.

"*Mon cher* Peter," Zinsou replied. "Your munificence in even *considering* what we discussed must be honored. Not since the Rockefellers donated the land on which the U.N. complex sits has a private individual offered to—"

"Yes, yes," Novak interrupted. "I'm afraid, though, that I'm going to decline your invitation to dinner."

"Oh?"

"I have something more *ceremonial* in mind. I hope you'll agree with my thinking. We have no secrets, have we? Transparency has always been a paramount U.N. value, no?"

"Well, up to a point, Peter."

"I shall tell you what I propose, and you tell me if you think I'm being unreasonable."

"Please."

"I understand that there will be a meeting of the General Assembly this

Friday. It has always been my fantasy to address that august body. Foolish vanity?"

"Of course not," Zinsou said quickly. "To be sure, few private citizens have ever addressed it. . . ."

"But nobody would begrudge me the right and privilege—I think I can say that without fear of contradiction."

"*Bien sûr.*"

"Given that a great many heads of state will be present, the level of security will be high. Call me paranoid, but I find that reassuring. If the U.S. president is present, as seems possible, there will be a Secret Service detail on the case as well. All very reassuring. And I shall probably be accompanied by the mayor of New York, who has always been so friendly toward me."

"An extremely public and high-profile appearance, then," Zinsou said. "That is not like you, I must say. Remote from your reclusive reputation."

"Which is exactly why I suggest it," the voice said. "You know my policy: always keep them guessing."

"But our . . . dialogue?" Confusion and anxiety roiled within him; he struggled not to let it show.

"Not to worry. I think you'll find that one never has more privacy than when one is in the public eye."


"God*damn* it!" Janson yelled. He was reviewing the tape recording of Demarest's last phone call.

"What could I have done differently?" Zinsou asked, and his voice held both fear and self-reproach.

"Nothing. If you'd been too insistent, it would only have aroused his suspicions. This is a deeply paranoid man."

"What do you make of this request? Bewildering, no?"

"It's ingenious," Janson said bluntly. "This guy has more moves than Bobby Fischer."

"But if you wanted to flush him out . . ."

"He's thought of that and has taken precautions. He knows the forces against him are ultracompartmentalized. There's no way the Secret Service could ever be let in on the truth. He's using our own people as a shield. That's not all. He'll be walking up the ramp to the General Assembly Building with the mayor of New York by his side. Any attempt on his life would endanger a well-known politician. He's entering into an arena of incredibly tight security, with eagle-eyed security details attached to national leaders from around the world. There'll be the equivalent of a force field around him at all times. If an American operative tried to take a shot, the resulting inquiry would probably blow everything sky-high. As long as he's in the General Assembly, we can't touch him. Can't. Imagine it—he'll be thronged. Given all his generosity around the world, it'll be considered an honor for the international community—"

"To welcome a man who seems to be a light unto the nations," Zinsou said, grimacing.

"It's very Demarest. 'Hidden in plain view' was one of his favorite descriptions. He used to say that sometimes the best hiding place was in the public eye."

"Essentially what he told me," Zinsou mused. He looked at the pen in his hand, trying to transform it into a cigarette by the power of thought. "Now what?"

Janson took a swallow of lukewarm coffee. "Either I'll figure something out . . ."

"Or?"

His eyes were hard. "Or I won't." He walked out of the secretary-general's office without another word, leaving the diplomat alone with his thoughts.

Zinsou felt a tightness in his chest. In truth, he had slept poorly since he had first been briefed on the crisis by the president of the United States, who had only reluctantly acceded to Janson's insistence that he do so. Zinsou was and continued to be utterly aghast. How could the United States of America have been so reckless? Except it wasn't the United States, exactly; it was a small cabal of programmers. Planners, as Janson would say. The secret had been passed down from one presidential administration to another, like the codes to the country's nuclear arsenal—and scarcely less dangerous.

Zinsou personally knew more heads of state than anyone alive. He knew that the president was, if anything, underestimating the bloody tumult that would be unleashed were the truth of the Mobius Program ever to emerge. He pictured the prime ministers, presidents, premiers, party secretaries, emirs, and kings of a duped planet. The whole postwar entente would lay in tatters. Throughout the world's trouble spots, scores of treaties and charters of conflict resolution would be falsified, invalidated, because their author would have been unmasked as an impostor—an American penetration agent. The peace treaty that Peter Novak negotiated in Cyprus? It would be shredded within hours, to mutual recriminations between the Turks and the Greeks. Each side would accuse the other of having known the truth all along; a pact that once seemed impartial would now be interpreted as subtly favoring the enemy. And elsewhere?

*Your currency crisis in Malaysia? Terribly sorry, old chap. We did that. The little dip in the sterling seven years ago that caused the economy of Great Britain to lose a few points of GDP? Yes, our exploitation of that made a bad situation much, much worse. Awfully sorry, don't know what we were thinking. . . .*

An era of relative peace and prosperity would give way to one bereft of both. And what of the Liberty Foundation offices throughout the developing world and Eastern Europe—exposed now as an undercover American intelligence operation? Many cooperating governments would simply not survive the humiliation. Others, to maintain credibility among their citizens, would suspend all relations with the United States and designate the former ally as an adversary. American-owned businesses, even those unrelated to the Liberty Foundation, would be seized by governments, their assets frozen. World trade would be dealt a devastating blow. Meanwhile, the planet's embittered and disaffected would, at last, have a casus belli; inchoate suspicions would find a catalyst. Among both official political parties and broader resistance movements, the revelations would provide a rallying cry against the American imperium. The semi-unified entity that was Europe would finally coalesce—around a new shared enemy, with a united Europe squaring off against the United States.

Who could defend it? Who would think to? Here was a country that had betrayed its closest and staunchest allies. A country that had secretly manipulated the levers of government across the planet. A country that would now incur the unmitigated wrath of billions. Even organizations that were dedicated to international cooperation would fall under suspicion. It would, very likely, spell the end of the United Nations, if not immediately, then in short order, in a tide of broadening rancor and suspicion.

And that would mean—what was the American expression?—a world of trouble.

The Caliph reread the cable he had just received, and felt a pleasurable glow of anticipation. It was as if overcast skies had parted to reveal a pure and luminous ray of sunlight. Peter Novak was going to be addressing the annual meeting of the U.N. General Assembly. The man—and he was, ultimately, no more than a man—would show his face at last. He would be greeted by insipid gratitude, by laurels and acclamation. And, if the Caliph had his way, by something more.

Now he turned to the Mansur minister of security—plainly little more than a jumped-up carpet merchant, despite the rhetorical inflation of his title—and spoke to him in tones both courteous and commanding. "This meeting of the international community will be an important moment for the Islamic Republic of Mansur," he said.

"But of course," replied the minister, a small, homely man who wore a simple white head wrap. On matters that did not concern Koranic orthodoxy, the leadership of this spavined, desolate little country was easily impressed.

"Your delegation will be judged, rightly or wrongly, by its professionalism, comportment, and discipline. Nothing must go awry, even in the face of unknown and unexpected malefactors. The very highest level of security must be maintained."

The Mansur minister bobbed his head; he knew he was out of his depth and, to his credit, realized there was no point in pretending otherwise, at least in the presence of the master tactician who stood before him.

"Therefore, I shall myself accompany the delegation. You need only provide the diplomatic cover, and I shall *personally* ensure that everything happens as it should."

"Allah be praised," the small man said. "We could hope for nothing more. Your dedication will be an inspiration to the others."

The Caliph nodded slowly, acknowledging the tribute. "What I do," he said, "is merely what must be done."


The narrow town house was elegant and yet anonymous-looking, a brownstone like hundreds of others in New York's Turtle Bay neighborhood. The stoop was a gray-brown, with raised black grip stripes in diagonals across the steps. They would prevent slippage when the stairs became slick with rain or ice; the electronic sensors beneath the strips would also detect the presence of a visitor. The sun bounced off the thick, leaded glass of the parlor: it was purely ornamental in appearance, but proof against even heavy-caliber bullets. Sterile Seven is what the deputy director of the Defense Intelligence Agency had called it: it was a safe house reserved by the Mobius planners for their occasional use, one of ten around the country. Janson would be protected here, he was assured; equally important, he would have access to the most sophisticated communications equipment, including direct access to the extensive data banks compiled by the joint intelligence services of the United States.

Janson sat in the second-floor study, staring at a yellow pad. Janson's eyes were bloodshot from lack of sleep; a headache pounded behind his eyes. He had been in scrambler communication with the surviving members of the Mobius Program. None was sanguine, or even pretended to be.

If Novak were arriving in the country, how would he do so? What were the chances that border control would alert them of his arrival? An advisory had gone out to every airport, private and public, in the country. Airport officials were notified that because of "credible threats" to Peter Novak's life, it was crucial to report his whereabouts to a special security task force coordinated by the U.S. State Department and devoted to the protection of foreign dignitaries.

He phoned Derek Collins, who was on Phipps Island, where the size of the National Guard contingent had been tripled. In the background he heard the jangle of a dog's collar.

"Gotta say, Butch has really taken to this place," Collins said. "Hell, the sorry-ass mutt's actually growing on me. With all that's been happening, it's kind of relaxing having him around. Of course, the workmen who were here yesterday fixing things up didn't exactly take to him—he kept looking at them like they were food. But I bet you're calling for a status report on other matters."

"What's the word?"

"The good news is, the cobra's en route—we're pretty sure, anyway. The bad news is, Nell Pearson's body was discovered yesterday. The Mrs. Novak of record. Supposedly a suicide. Slit her wrists in her bathtub. So that thread's been snipped off."

"Christ," said Janson. "Think she was murdered?"

"Naw, it was a 'cry for help.' Of *course* she was fucking murdered. But nobody will ever be able to prove it."

"What a goddamn waste," Janson said. There was lead in his voice.

"Moving right along," Collins said bleakly, "nobody's sighted Puma. Zip, nada, nothing. Four reports of look-alikes, quickly falsified. The fact is, our guy might not be arriving from overseas—he might already be in the country. And he'd find it child's play to arrive incognito. This is a large, populous country with more than *five hundred* international airports. Our borders are inherently porous. I don't have to tell you that."

"This isn't a time to talk about impossibilities, Derek," the operative said.

"Thanks for the pep talk, coach. You think every damn one of us isn't working balls-out on this? None of us knows who's going to get killed next. If you want to talk about impossibilities, though, you'll be interested in the latest thinking around Foggy Bottom."

Five minutes later, Janson hung up with an unsettled feeling.

Almost immediately afterward, the silver-gray phone on the green-baize-topped desk rang quietly, the quietness of the ring somehow lending it additional significance. It was the line reserved for White House communications.

He picked up the phone. It was the president.

"Listen, Paul, I've gone over and over it with Doug here. This address Demarest's giving before the General Assembly—there could well be an implicit ultimatum here."

"Sir?"

"As you know, he asked for the control codes to the entire Echelon system. I put him off."

"Put him off?"

"Blew him off. I think the message he's sending is pretty unambiguous. If he doesn't get what he wants, he's going to appear before the General Assembly and set an explosion. Lay the thing out, with the whole world hanging on his every word. That's just a surmise. We could well be wrong. But the more we think about it, the more we think it's a credible threat."

"Ergo?"

"I hope to God he's hit by a thunderbolt before he can stand up and give that speech."

"Now that sounds like a plan."

"Barring that, I've decided to meet with him just beforehand. Capitulate. Give in to his first round of demands."

"Are you scheduled to make an appearance at the U.N.?"

"We'd left it unclear. The secretary of state will be there, along with the U.N. ambassador, the permanent representative, the trade negotiator, and the rest of the tin soldiers we always send. But if we're making this . . . barter, it'll have to come from me. I'm the only one with the clearance and authorization to do this."

"You'd be putting yourself in harm's way."

"Paul, I'm already in harm's way. And so are you."

# CHAPTER THIRTY-NINE

# The New York Times

## U.N. GENERAL ASSEMBLY TO MEET

### FROM AROUND THE WORLD, HUNDREDS OF NATIONAL LEADERS TO ASSEMBLE IN "DIALOGUE OF CIVILIZATIONS"

**By Barbara Corlett**

NEW YORK—For most native New Yorkers, the convergence here of hundreds of foreign heads of state and high-ranking ministers prompts one big worry: will the motorcades make the problem of traffic gridlock worse? In the U.S. Department of State and in diplomatic circles elsewhere, however, loftier concerns are the order of the day. There are hopes that the 58th General Assembly meeting will lead to substantial reforms and a heightened level of international cooperation. U.N. Secretary General Mathieu Zinsou has predicted that it would be a "watershed moment" in the history of the troubled organization.

Anticipation has been bolstered by rumors of a possible appearance before the General Assembly by the revered philanthropist and humanitarian Peter Novak, whose Liberty Foundation has been compared to the United Nations in its global reach and even its diplomatic achievements. The U.N. is owed billions of dollars from member nations, including the United States, and the Secretary General makes no secret of the fact that the consequent salary freezes and cutbacks have made it difficult to recruit and retain high-caliber employees. Mr. Novak, whose munificence has been the stuff of legend, may have concrete proposals for easing the U.N.'s financial crisis. Top-ranking U.N. officials suggest that the Liberty Foundation's director may also propose a joining of forces with the U.N. to coordinate assistance to those regions most afflicted by poverty and conflict. The reclusive Mr. Novak could not be reached for comment.

*Continued on page B4.*

It would all happen tomorrow, and what happened would depend on how good their preparations were.

*One foot in front of the other.*

Janson—officially an outside security consultant hired by the Executive Office of the Secretary-General—had spent the last four hours wandering through the United Nations complex. What had they forgotten? Janson tried to think, but mists kept closing in on him; he had slept very little in the past few days, had been trying to sustain himself with black coffee and aspirin. *One foot in front of the other.* This was the civilian reconnaissance mission upon which everything would depend.

The U.N. complex, extending along the East River from Forty-second Street to Forty-eighth Street, was an island unto itself. The Secretariat Building loomed thirty-nine stories; in the skyline of the city, celebrated landmarks like the Chrysler Building and the Empire State Building were skinny protuberances by comparison—trees beside a mountain. What distinguished the Secretariat wasn't its height so much as its enormous breadth, greater than a city block. On either side of the building, the curtain wall of blue-green Thermopane glass and aluminum was identical, each floor demarcated by a black row of spandrels, its symmetry interrupted only by the irregularly spaced grilles of the mechanical floors. The two narrow ends were covered with Vermont marble—a concession, Janson recalled, to the former Vermont senator who had chaired the Headquarters Advisory Committee and served as America's permanent representative to the U.N. In a more innocent era, Frank Lloyd Wright termed the Secretariat "a super-crate, to ship a fiasco to hell." The words now seemed menacingly prescient.

The low General Assembly Building, which was situated just to the north of the Secretariat, was more adventurous in design. It was an oddly curvate rectangle, swooping down in the middle and flaring to either end. An incongruous dome—another concession to the senator—was placed on the center of its roof, looking like an oversize turbine vent. Now that the General Assembly Building was vacant, he paced through it several times, his eyes sweeping every surface as if for the first time. The south wall was pure glass, creating a light and airy delegates' lounge, overlooked by sweeping white balconies in three tiers. In the center of the building, the Assembly Hall was a vast semicircular atrium, green leather seats arranged around the central dais, which was a vast altar of green marble atop black. Looming over it, mounted on a vast gilded wall, was the circular U.N. logo—the two wheatlike garlands beneath a stylized view of the globe. For some reason, the globe logo, with its circles and perpendicular lines, struck him as a view centered upon the crosshairs of a scope: target earth.

*"Some people wanna fill the world with silly love songs,"* the Russian crooned tunelessly.

"Grigori?" Janson said into his cell phone. Of course it was Grigori. Janson glanced around the vast atrium, taking in the two huge mounted video screens on either side of the rostrum. "You doing OK?"

"Never better!" Grigori Berman said stoutly. "Back in own home. Private nurse named Ingrid! Second day, I keep dropping thermometer on floor just to watch her bend over. The haunches on this filly—Venus in white Keds! Ingrid, I say, how about you play nurse? 'Meester Berman,' she squeals, very shocked, 'I *am* nurse.' "

"Listen, Grigori, I've got a request to make. If you're not up to it, though, just let me know." Janson spoke for a few minutes, providing a handful of necessary details; either Berman would work out the rest or he wouldn't.

Berman was silent for a few moments when Janson finished talking. "Now it is Grigori Berman who is shocked. What you propose, sir, is unethical, immoral, illegal—is devious violation of standards and practices of international banking." A beat. "I *love* it."

"Thought so," said Janson. "And you can pull it off?"

*"I get by with a little help from my friends,"* Berman crooned.

"You sure you're up to doing this?"

"You ask *Ingrid* what Grigori Berman can do," he answered, spluttering with indignation. "What Grigori up to doing? What Grigori *not* up to doing?"

Janson clicked off his Ericsson and kept pacing through the hall. He walked behind the green-marble lectern where speakers stood to address the assembled, and looked out at the banked tiers of seats where the delegates would be congregated. The chief national representatives would fill the first fifteen rows of chairs and tables. Placards were mounted on bars that ran along the curved tables, country names spelled out in white letters on black: along one side of an aisle, PERU, MEXICO, INDIA, EL SAL-VADOR, COLOMBIA, BOLIVIA, others he could not make out in the dim light. To the other side, PARAGUAY, LUXEMBOURG, ICELAND, EGYPT, CHINA, BELGIUM, YEMEN, UNITED KINGDOM, and more. The order seemed random, but the placards went on and on, signposts for an endlessly various, endlessly fractured world. At the long tables, there were buttons that delegates could press to signal their intention to speak, and audio plugs for headphones, supplying simultaneous translation in whatever language was required. Behind the official delegate tables were steeply raked tiers of seats for additional members of the diplomatic teams. Overhead, a recessed oculus was filled with dangling lights and surrounded by starlike spotlights. The curving walls were of louvered wood, interspersed with vast murals by Fernand Léger. A small clock was centered along a long marble balcony, visible only to those at the rostrum. Above the balcony were yet more rows of seats. And behind them, discreetly framed by curtains, was a series of glassed-in booths, where translators, technicians, and U.N. security staff were stationed.

It resembled a magnificent theater, and in many ways, it was.

Janson left the hall and made his way to the rooms that were immediately behind the rostrum: an office for the use of the secretary-general and a general "executive suite." Given the placement of the security details, it would simply be impossible to launch an assault on those spaces. On his third walkabout, Janson found himself drawn to what seemed to be a little-used chapel, or as it had more recently come to be styled, meditation room. It was a small narrow space with a Chagall mural at one end, just down the corridor from the main entrance to the Assembly Hall.

Finally, Janson walked down the long ramp on the western side of the building, from which the delegates would be pouring in. The geometry of security was impressive: the looming bulk of the Secretariat itself functioned as a shield, offering protection from most angles. The adjacent streets would be blocked off to nonofficial traffic: only accredited journalists and members of the diplomatic delegations would be permitted in the vicinity.

Alan Demarest couldn't have chosen a safer venue if he'd retreated to a bunker in Antarctica.

The more Janson explored the situation, the more he admired the tactical genius of his nemesis. Something truly extraordinary would have to happen to foil it—which meant that they were counting on something that could not be counted on.

*What fellowship hath righteousness with unrighteousness? And what communion hath light with darkness?*

Yet Janson saw the imperative for such a fellowship more clearly than anyone. Defeating this master of subterfuge would require something more than the bloodless, calculated moves and countermoves of the rational planners: it called for the unbridled, unslakable, irrational, and, yes, unbounded wrath of a true fanatic. About that there could be no dispute: their best chance to defeat Demarest was to resort to the one thing that could not be controlled.

To be sure, the planners *imagined* they could control it. But they never had, never could. They were all of them playing with fire.

They had to prepare to get burned.

# CHAPTER FORTY

The motorcades started arriving at the U.N. Plaza at seven o'clock the next morning, escorting humanity of every cultural and political coloration. Military heads of state in their full-dress uniforms strode up the ramp as if reviewing their troops, feeling protected and empowered by their self-bestowed ribbons and bars. They regarded the narrow-shouldered leaders of the so-called democracies as nothing more than puffed-up central bankers: did not their dark suits and tight-knotted ties signal allegiance to the mercantile classes rather than to the authentic glories of national power? The elected leaders of the liberal democracies, in turn, viewed such gaudy regalia as the generals sported with scorn and disapproval: what miserable social backwardness enabled these *caudillos* to grab power? Thin leaders looked at fat leaders and entertained fleeting thoughts about their lack of self-control: no wonder their countries had incurred staggering foreign debts. The stout leaders, for their part, regarded their attenuated Western counterparts as colorless and chilly Gradgrinds, sapless administrators rather than true leaders of men. Such were the thoughts that flickered beyond each toothy smile.

Like molecules, the clusters mingled and collided, formed and reformed. Vacuous pleasantries stood in for long-winded complaints. A rotund president of a central African state embraced the lanky German foreign minister, and both knew precisely what the embrace signified: *Can we move forward with debt restructuring? Why should I be stuck servicing loans taken by my predecessor—after all, I had him shot!* A gaudily bedizened potentate from Central Asia greeted the prime minister of Great Britain with a dazzling smile and the tacit protest: *The border dispute we have with our belligerent neighbor is not a matter of international concern.* The president of a troubled NATO member state that was the rump of a once great empire sought out his opposite number from stable, prosperous Sweden and made small talk about his last visit to Stockholm. The unspoken message: *Our actions against the Kurdish villages within our borders may disturb your pampered human-rights activists, but we have no choice but to defend ourselves from forces of sedition.* Behind every handclasp, hug, and back clap was a grievance, for grievances were the cement of the international community.

Circulating among the delegations was a man wearing a kaffiyeh, a full beard, and sunglasses: typical attire among certain ruling-class Arabs. He looked, in short, like any of a hundred diplomatic representatives from Jordan, Saudi Arabia, Yemen, Mansur, Oman, or the United Emirates. The man looked self-possessed and a little pleased: no doubt he was happy to be in New York, looking forward to making a side trip to Harry Winston, or simply to sampling the sexual bazaar of the great metropolis.

In fact, the ample beard did double duty: it not only helped alter Janson's appearance but served to disguise a small filament microphone, activated by a switch in his front trouser pocket. He had, as a precaution, placed a microphone on the secretary-general as well; it was mounted within a small nodule on his gold collar bar, and was completely hidden behind his wide four-in-hand knot.

The long ramp led to a walkway immediately adjoining the General Assembly Building, where seven entrances were set back into the marble exterior of the curving, low-slung building. Janson kept moving among the incoming crowds, always looking as if he had just seen an old friend across the way. Now he consulted his watch; the fifty-eighth annual meeting of the General Assembly would come to order in just five minutes. Was Alan Demarest going to arrive? Had he ever *intended* to?

It was a barrage of camera flashes that first signaled the legend's arrival. The TV crews, which had dutifully recorded the arrival of the great and the good, potentates and plenipotentiaries, now focused their video-cameras, boom mikes, and key lights upon the elusive benefactor. He was difficult to pick out from the tightly huddled group in which he walked. There, indeed, was New York's mayor, with a hand around the humanitarian's shoulder, whispering something that seemed to amuse the plutocrat. To the man's other side, the senior senator of New York State, who served also as the deputy chairman of the Senate's Foreign Relations Committee, kept in step. A small entourage of senior aides and civic luminaries followed close behind. Secret Service agents were stationed at strategic intervals, no doubt ensuring that the area was free of snipers and other potential malefactors.

As the man known to the world as Peter Novak entered the West Lobby, he was swiftly hustled by his entourage into the executive suite behind the Assembly Hall. Outside it, the soles and heels of hundreds of expensive shoes clattered against the terrazzo flooring as the lobby began to empty and the hall began to fill.

This was Janson's cue to retreat to the central security booth, located behind the main balcony of the Assembly Hall. An array of small square monitors surrounded a large monitor; they displayed multiple camera angles on the hall itself. At his request, hidden cameras had also been placed in the suites tucked away behind the dais. The secretary-general's security consultant wanted to be able to keep an eye on all the principals.

Adjusting the control panel, he shifted among camera angles, zooming in, looking for the table where the delegation from the Islamic Republic of Mansur would be seated. It did not take long.

There, seated at the aisle, was a handsome man in flowing robes that matched those of the other men in the Mansur delegation. Janson pressed several buttons on the console and the image appeared on the large central monitor, supplanting the wide-angle overhead view of the assembly. Now he enlarged the image further, digitally reduced the shadows, and watched, mesmerized, as the large flat-screen monitor filled with the unmistakable visage.

Ahmad Tabari. The man they called the Caliph.

Rage coursed through Janson like electricity as he studied the planes of his ebony face, his aquiline nose and strong, chiseled jaw. The Caliph was charismatic even in repose.

Janson pressed several buttons, and the central screen feed switched to the hidden camera in the executive suite.

A different face, a different kind of merciless charisma: the charisma of a man who did not aspire, a man who *had*. The full head of hair, still more black than gray, the high cheekbones, the elegant three-button suit: Peter Novak. Yes, Peter Novak: it was who the man had become, and it was the way Janson had to think of him. He sat at one end of a blond-wood table, near a telephone that was directly connected to a intercommunication system at the high marble dais in the Assembly Hall as well as to the technicians' stations. A corner-mounted closed-circuit television allowed the VIPs in the executive suite to keep abreast of developments within the hall.

Now the door to the suite opened: two members of the Secret Service with curled wires descending from their earpieces made a visual inspection of the room.

Janson pressed another button, switching camera angles.

Peter Novak stood up. Smiled at his visitor.

The president of the United States.

A man normally brimming with self-confidence was looking ashen. There was no audio feed, but it was clear that the president was asking the Secret Service detail to leave the two of them alone.

Wordlessly, the president withdrew a sealed envelope from his breast pocket and handed it to Peter Novak. His hands trembled.

In profile, the two were a study in contrasts: one, the leader of the free world, seeming defeated and slightly stooped; the other, broad-shouldered and triumphant.

The president nodded and looked, for a moment, as if he wanted to say something, then thought the better of it.

He walked out.

Camera angle no. two. Novak slipping the envelope into his own breast pocket. That envelope, Janson knew, could change the course of world history.

And it was only the first installment.


The Caliph glanced at his watch. Timing would be everything. The metal detectors made it impossible for even delegation members to carry in firearms; this was as he expected. Yet securing such a weapon would be an elementary task. There were hundreds of them in the building, the property of the United Nations security guards and other such protectors. He had little respect for them or their skill: the Caliph had faced down some of the deadliest warriors in the world. It had been his personal valor that earned him the undying respect of his ragged and uneducated followers. Mastery of ideology or Koran verses by itself would not have sufficed. They were a people who needed to know that their leaders had physical courage, intestinal as well as intellectual fortitude.

The aura of invincibility he had lost that dreadful night at the Steenpaleis he would regain, redoubled, even, once he had completed this, his most daring act. He would do the deed, and in the ensuing uproar, he would be able to make his escape in the speedboat docked at the East River, just a hundred feet east of the building. The world would learn that their righteous cause could not be ignored.

Yes, getting his hands on a high-powered gun would be almost as easy as taking it off a warehouse shelf. Prudence, however, had required that he wait until the last moment to acquire it. The more time that elapsed afterward, the greater the chance of exposure. Securing the weapon, after all, meant deactivating its possessor.

According to the schedule of events that had been shared with Mansur's U.N. ambassador, Peter Novak would commence his address within five minutes. This member of the Mansur security detail would have to take a quick trip to the bathroom. He pushed out the latch-lever door that led out of the hall, and made his way toward the chapel.

The Caliph walked very fast, his sandals echoing on the terrazzo, until he caught the attention of a square-jawed, crew-cut American Secret Service agent. This was even better than an ordinary U.N. security officer: his weaponry would be of particularly high quality.

"Sir," he said to the dark-suited agent. "I protect the leader of the Islamic Republic of Mansur."

The Secret Service agent looked away; foreign heads of state did not fall within his bailiwick.

"We have received a report that someone is hiding—in *there!*" He gestured toward the chapel.

"I can ask someone to check it out," the American said impassively. "Can't leave my post."

"It's just over there. I myself think there's nobody there at all."

"We had the whole place turned over a few hours before. Be inclined to agree with you."

"But you'll take a look? Thirty seconds of your time? Doubtless there's nothing to the report, but if we are mistaken on this score, we shall both be hard-pressed to explain why we did nothing."

A grudging sigh. "Show the way."

The Caliph held open the small wooden door to the chapel and waited until the Secret Service man walked through.

The chapel was a long narrow space, with a low ceiling and recessed lighting to either side; a spotlight illuminated a black lacquered box toward the end of the hall. It was topped with a glowing slab of glass—some Western designer's notion of secular religiosity. On the wall opposite the door was a mural with crescents, circles, squares, triangles, all overlapping, evidently signifying some amalgam of creeds. So very Western, the conceit that one could have it all, like the trimmings on a Big Mac: needless to say, the spurious harmony was predicated upon the unquestioned dominion of Western permissiveness. At the other end, near the entrance, was a series of small benches with rush seats. The floor was of irregular rectangles of slate.

"Ain't no place to hide here," the man said. "There's nothing."

The heavy, soundproofed door closed behind them, cutting off the noises of the lobby.

"What would it matter?" the Caliph said. "You have no weapon. You'd be helpless against an assassin!"

The Secret Service man grinned and opened his navy jacket, putting his hands on his waist, allowing the long-barreled revolver to show from his shoulder holster.

"Apologies," the Caliph said. He turned around, his back to the American, seemingly captivated by the mural. Then he took a step back.

"You're wasting my time," the American said.

Abruptly, the Caliph whipped his head back, cracking into the American's chin. As the burly agent reeled, the Caliph's hands snaked toward his shoulder holster and pulled out the .357 Magnum revolver, a Ruger SP101 equipped with a four-inch barrel for enhanced accuracy. He slammed the butt down on the agent's head, ensuring that smug infidel would be unconscious for many hours.

Now he secreted the Ruger inside his small valise of tooled leather and dragged the muscle-bound American behind the ebonized light box, where he would be invisible to a casual visitor.

It was time to reenter the Assembly Hall. Time to avenge indignities. Time to make history.

He would prove himself worthy of the title that his followers had bestowed upon him. He was the Caliph indeed.

And he would not fail.


In the executive suite, the light on the black slimline phone started to glow: it was the speaker's "ready in five" notification—standard procedure, alerting him a few minutes before he would be asked to step out in front of the assembled leadership of the planet.

Novak reached for the phone, listened, said, "Thank you."

And as he watched, Janson felt a jolt of foreboding.

*Something was wrong.*

Urgently, desperately, he jammed on the REWIND button and replayed the last ten seconds of video feed.

The light glowing on the glowing phone. Peter Novak reaching for it, bringing it to his ear . . .

*Something was wrong.*

But *what?* Janson's unconscious mind was like a tocsin, wildly tolling its alarm, but he was tired, so very tired, and the fog of exhaustion closed in.

He replayed the last ten seconds once again.

The glowing light of a purring internal phone.

Peter Novak, protected by a battery of security guards but, for the moment, alone in the executive suite, reaching for the handset, for the instructions to prepare himself for his moment in the world's spotlight.

Reaching with his right hand.

Peter Novak holding the handset to his ear.

His right ear.

Janson felt as if his very skin had been coated with a layer of ice. A terrible, painful clarity now commanded his mind as it filled with a cascade of images. It was maddening, faces and voices intermingling. Demarest at a desk in Khe Sanh, reaching for a phone. *These H&I reports are worse than useless!* Holding the phone tight against his ear for a long while. Finally, speaking again: *A lot of things can happen in a free-fire zone.* Demarest in the swampy terrain near Ham Luong reaching for the radiophone, listening intently, barking a series of commands. Reaching with his *left* hand, holding the phone to his *left* ear.

Alan Demarest was left-handed. Invariably so. Exclusively so.

The man in the executive suite was not Alan Demarest.

*Christ almighty!* Janson felt the blood rush to his head, his temples throbbing.

He had sent a double. An impostor. Janson had been the one to warn the others about the danger of underestimating their opponent. Yet he had done just that.

And the stratagem made perfect sense. *If your enemy has a good idea, steal it,* Demarest had told him in the killing fields of Vietnam. The Mobius programmers were now Demarest's enemies. He gained his freedom by destroying his own duplicates, but then he had been planning his takeover for years. During that time he had not only been accumulating assets and allies: he had created a duplicate of his own—one who was under *his* power.

Why hadn't Janson thought of it?

The impostor who sat in the executive suite was not Peter Novak; he was working for him. Yes, this was precisely what Demarest would have done. He would have . . . reversed the angle. *See the two white swans instead of the one black one. See the slice of pie instead of the pie with the slice missing. Flip the Necker cube outward instead of inward. Master the gestalt.*

The man who was on his way to address the General Assembly was the Judas goat, leading them to their slaughter. He was the cat's paw, drawing out their fire.

In just a few minutes, the man, this copy of a copy, this doubly ersatz Novak, would take his position before the green-marble podium.

And he would be shot dead.

That would not be Novak's undoing. It would be their own undoing. Alan Demarest would have confirmed his most paranoid suspicions: he would have flushed out his enemies, would have discovered that the whole invitation had indeed been a plot.

At the same time, they would have destroyed their last direct link to Alan Demarest. Nell Pearson was dead. Márta Lang, as she'd called herself, was dead. Every human vessel that might lead to him had been severed—except the man in the executive suite. A man who must have given half a year of his life to recuperate from reconstructive surgery. A man who—willingly or unwillingly—had sacrificed his own identity to the brilliant maniac who held the future of the world in his hands. If he were killed, Janson would have lost his last remaining lead.

And if he mounted the podium, he would be killed.

The scheme they had set in motion could not be stopped. It was not in their control: that was its great recommendation—and, possibly, its lethal flaw.

Frantically, Janson flipped to the camera angle on the Mansur delegation. There was the aisle seat that had been occupied by the Caliph.

Empty.

*Where was he?*

Janson had to find him: it was their only chance to prevent catastrophe.

Now he activated his filament microphone and spoke, knowing his words would be relayed to the secretary-general's earpiece.

"You have got to postpone Novak's appearance. I need ten minutes."

The secretary-general was seated at the high marble bench behind the dais, smiling and nodding. "That's impossible," he whispered, without altering his public expression.

"Do it!" Janson said. "You're the secretary-general, goddammit! You figure it out."

Then he raced down the carpeted stairs and toward the hallway that bounded the Assembly Hall. He had to find the fanatic from Anura. This assassination would not save the world; it would doom it.

# CHAPTER FORTY-ONE

Janson's rubber-soled feet raced down the white-tiled hallway. The Caliph had disappeared from the Assembly Hall—which meant, presumably, that he was retrieving a weapon he or a confederate had somewhere managed to stow earlier. The South Lobby, brilliantly lit from the expansive glazed wall, was vacant. The giant escalator was empty. He bounded toward the delegates' lounge. Seated on a white-leather sofa, two blond women were deep in conversation: from the looks of them, they were extras from a Scandinavian delegation who found that there was no room for them in the Assembly Hall. Otherwise, nothing.

Where could he be? Janson's mind desperately sorted through possibilities.

*Ask it differently: where would you be, Janson?*

The chapel. A long, narrow space that was almost never used but was always kept open. It was adjacent to the secretary-general's suite, just to the other side of the curved wall that fronted the Assembly Hall. The one room in the building where one was guaranteed to be unobserved.

Janson put on another burst of speed, and though his rubber-soled shoes made little sound, his breathing grew heavier.

Now he pushed open the heavy, soundproofed door and saw a man in flowing white robes bending down behind a large ebonized box. As the door closed behind Janson, the man whirled around.

The Caliph.

For a moment Janson was so convulsed with hate that he could not breathe. He composed his face into a look of friendly surprise.

The Caliph spoke first. *"Khaif hallak ya akhi."*

Janson remembered his large beard and Arab-style headdress and forced himself to smile. He knew that the man had addressed him in Arabic; probably it was an insubstantial pleasantry, but he could only guess. In Janson's best version of Oxbridge English—an Arab royal might well have been educated at such an institution, absorbed its customs—he said, "My dear brother, I hope I wasn't intruding. It's just that I've such a migraine, I was hoping to commune with the Prophet himself."

The Caliph strode toward him. "Yet we would both be sorry to miss any more of the proceedings, having come so far. Don't you agree?" His voice was like the hiss of a snake.

"You make a good point, my brother," Janson said.

As the Caliph walked toward him, scrutinizing him closely, Janson's skin began to crawl. He came closer and closer, until he was just a foot away. Janson remembered that social conceptions of permissible physical distance varied among cultures, that Arabs typically stood closer to each other than Westerners did. The Caliph placed a hand on Janson's shoulder.

It was a gentle, friendly, confiding gesture—from the man who had killed his wife.

Involuntarily, Janson flinched.

His mind filled with a flood of images: a cascade of destruction, the ruined office building in downtown Caligo, the phone call informing him that his wife was dead.

The Caliph's face suddenly closed.

Janson had betrayed himself.

*The assassin knew.*

The muzzle of a long-barreled revolver was jabbed into Janson's chest. The Caliph had made his decision; his suspicious visitor would not be permitted to escape.


Mathieu Zinsou stared at the packed Assembly Hall, saw row after row of powerful men and women beginning to grow restive. He had promised that his introductory remarks would be brief; in fact, they turned out to be uncharacteristically rambling and prolix. Yet he had no choice but to stall! He saw the American ambassador to the U.N. exchange glances with his colleague the permanent representative; how was it that this acclaimed master of diplomatic oratory had become such a bore?

The secretary-general's eyes flicked back to the pages on the lectern in front of him. Four paragraphs of text, which he had already read; he had nothing more prepared and, in the tension of the moment, very little notion of what might appropriately be said. One would have had to know him intimately to notice that the blood had drained from his dark brown face.

"Progress has been made all over the world," he said, his vowels orotund, his message embarrassingly banal. "Genuine advances in development and international comity have been seen in Europe, from Spain to Turkey, from Romania to Germany, from Switzerland and France and Italy to Hungary, Bulgaria, and Slovakia, not to mention the Czech Republic, Slovenia, and, of course, Poland. Genuine progress has been made, too, in Latin America—from Peru to Venezuela, from Ecuador to Paraguay, from Chile to Guyana and French Guyana, from Colombia to Uruguay to Bolivia, from Argentina to . . ." He was drawing a blank: *I'll take South American nation-states for one hundred, Alex.* He scanned the rows of delegations before him, his eyes darting from one national placard to another. "To, well, *Suriname!*" A sense of relief, fleeting as a glowworm's flash. "The developments in Suriname have been most heartening, most heartening indeed." How long could he draw this out? What was taking Janson so long?

Zinsou cleared his throat. He was a man who seldom perspired; he was perspiring now. "And, of course, we would be remiss if we did not single out for attention the progress we have seen among the nations of the Pacific Rim. . . ."

Janson stared at the man who had robbed him of the happiness that had once been his, the man who had stolen the treasure of his life.

He bowed his legs slightly, keeping his feet spaced out at shoulder level. "I have offended you," he said plaintively. Suddenly, he swept his left elbow up over the Caliph's right shoulder and grabbed the wrist of his gun arm with both hands. With a powerful upward wrench, he locked the man's arm. Then he lashed out with his left leg, and the two men landed hard on the slate floor. The Caliph whipped his left hand repeatedly to the side of Janson's head. Yet a protective move would enable the Caliph to wriggle free: Janson had no choice but to try to endure the painful blows. The only viable defense would be an offense. He forced the Anuran's wrist into a lock, twisting it palm upward. The Caliph followed the direction of his pressure, angling the Ruger toward Janson's body.

It would take only an instant for his trigger finger to fire a lethal shot.

Now, Janson slammed the Anuran's gun hand against the slate floor, producing a spasm that caused him to loosen his grip on the weapon. In a lightning-fast movement, Janson grabbed it and scrambled to his feet. The Anuran remained limp on the polished stone floor.

*He had the gun now.*

Immediately, he triggered the switch that activated his lip mike. "The threat has been neutralized," Janson told the U.N. secretary-general.

Then he felt a staggering blow from behind. The cobralike assassin had leaped from the ground and vised a forearm around Janson's throat, choking off his air. Janson bucked violently, twisting and thrashing, hoping to throw off the younger, lighter man, but the terrorist was all coiled muscle. Janson felt bulky and slow by comparison, a bear menaced by a panther.

Now, instead of trying to dislodge the Caliph's grip, he reached around and held him even tighter. Then he kicked both his legs into the air and hurled himself to the floor, landing heavily on his back—yet cushioning his impact with the body of his assailant, who was slammed against the floor as he fell.

He felt an expulsion of breath against the back of his neck and knew that the Caliph had been dealt a serious body blow.

Winded and aching himself, Janson rolled over and began to rise to his feet. As he did so, the Caliph rose, with incredible endurance, and threw himself at him, his hands formed into claws.

If the distance between them was greater, Janson would have ducked or stepped aside. Neither was possible. He lacked the speed. He lacked the agility.

*A bear.*

So be it. He held out his arms, as if in an embrace—and, with a surge of strength, he squeezed the Caliph to his body, locking his arms around the other man's chest. Tight. Tighter. Tighter still.

Even as he squeezed, however, the assassin rained powerful blows on the back of his neck. Janson knew he could not hold out for much longer. In a sudden, convulsive effort, he dropped his armlock and *lifted* the Anuran into the air horizontally, where he thrashed like a powerful eel. In an equally abrupt movement, Janson fell down into a crouch, his left knee bent to the ground, his right knee angled upward. At the same time, he slammed the lithe-bodied assailant down against it.

The Caliph's back snapped with a horrifying sound, something between a crunch and a pop, and his mouth contorted into a scream that would not come.

Janson seized him by the shoulders and slammed him against the slate floor. He did so again. And again. The back of the Caliph's head no longer made the sound of hard bone against a hard floor, for the rear cranial bone had been smashed into fragments, exposing the soft tissues beneath.

The Caliph's eyes grew unfocused, glazed. The eyes were said to be the windows to the soul, yet this man had no soul. Certainly not anymore.

Janson jammed the Ruger into his own shoulder holster. Using a small pocket mirror, he adjusted his beard and kaffiyeh and made sure there were no visible bloodstains on his person. Then he walked out of the chapel and into the General Assembly Hall, where he stood near the back.

For years he had fantasized about killing the man who had killed his wife. Now he had done so.

And all he felt was sick.

The black-haired man stood at the podium, giving a speech about the challenges of a new century. Janson's eyes searched every hollow and contour. He looked like Peter Novak. He would be accepted as Novak. Yet he lacked the sense of command associated with the legendary humanitarian. His voice was thin, wavering; he seemed slightly nervous, out of his depth. Janson knew what the consensus would be afterward: *Very fine speech, of course. Yet poor Mr. Novak was a bit under the weather, was he not?*

"Half a century ago," the man at the podium was saying, "the very ground under our feet, the land of the entire United Nations complex, was donated to the U.N. by the Rockefellers. The history of private assistance for this most public of missions goes to the origins of the institution. If I can, in my own small way, provide such assistance, I would be profoundly gratified. People talk about 'giving back to the community': my own community has always been the community of nations. Help me to help you. Show me how I can be of greatest assistance. To do so would be my pleasure, my honor—indeed, nothing less than my duty. The world has been very good to me. My only hope is that I can return the favor."

The words were vintage Novak, by turns charming and hard-edged, humble and arrogant, and, in the end, nothing short of winning. Yet the delivery was atypically hesitant and tentative.

And only Janson knew why.

The master of escape had escaped again. How could he ever have imagined that he might trump his great mentor? *Your arms are too short to box with God,* Demarest had once told him, half joking. Still, there was an uncomfortable truth there. The protégé was pitting himself against his mentor; the student was testing his wits against his teacher. Only vanity had prevented him from seeing that failure was foreordained.

As the man at the podium finished his remarks, the audience rose in a standing ovation. What his address lacked in style of delivery, it made up for in rhetorical appeal. Besides, on such an occasion, who could begrudge the great man his proper due? Janson, stone-faced, walked out of the hall, and the noise of the resounding applause quieted only when the door closed behind him.

If Demarest wasn't at the United Nations, where was he?

The secretary-general had walked off the dais together with the clamorously applauded speaker, and now, as a twenty-minute recess began, both would repair to the carpeted chamber behind the hall.

Janson realized that his earpiece had been dislodged by his recent struggle; he repositioned it and, crackling, heard snippets of dialogue. He remembered the hidden microphone on Mathieu Zinsou's collar bar; it was transmitting.

"No, I thank *you*. But I *would* like to have that tête-à-tête you mentioned after all." The voice was fuzzy but audible.

"Certainly," Zinsou answered. His voice was nearer to the microphone and clearer.

"Why don't we go to your office, in the Secretariat?"

"You mean *now?*"

"I'm rather pressed for time, I'm afraid. It'll have to be now."

Zinsou paused. "Then follow me. The thirty-eighth floor." Janson wondered if the secretary-general had added the specification for his sake.

Something was up. But what?

Janson made a dash for the eastern ramp of the General Assembly Building, and then lumbered toward the looming Secretariat Building. His right knee twinged with every step he took, and the bruises on his body were starting to swell and smart—the Anuran's blows had been not only forceful but well aimed. Yet he had to put all of it out of his mind.

Inside the Secretariat lobby, he flashed the ID card that had been prepared for him, and a guard waved him through. He pressed the button for the thirty-eighth floor, and rode up. Mathieu Zinsou and Alan Demarest's agent, whoever he was, would be following him within minutes.

As he rode up to the top of the skyscraper, the transmission to his earpiece fuzzed out. The metal of the elevator shaft was blocking off the signal.

A minute later, the elevator stopped at the thirty-eighth floor. Janson remembered the floor plan: The elevator banks were in the midpoint of the long, rectangular floor. The offices of the undersecretaries and special deputies were lined against the west-facing wall; to the north were two large, windowless conference rooms; to the south, a narrow, windowless library. The secretary-general's teak-lined office was along the east wall. Because of the special meeting, the floor was almost entirely vacant; every staff member was doing duty attending to the visiting delegations.

Now Janson removed his headdress and his beard and waited around the corner from where the elevator banks opened. Sheltered by the recessed doorway leading to the library, he would be able to monitor both the hallway to the secretary-general's office and the elevator banks.

He knew he would not be waiting long.

The elevator chimed.

"And this will be our floor," said Mathieu Zinsou as the elevator doors opened. He made an after-you-my-dear-Alphonse gesture to the man who looked, for all the world, like Peter Novak.

Could Janson have been correct? Zinsou wondered. Or was the strain finally getting to the American operative, a man whom circumstances had given responsibilities far greater than any man should have to shoulder?

"You have to forgive us—almost everybody who normally staffs my office here is in the General Assembly Building. Or somewhere else altogether. The annual meeting of the General Assembly is like a bank holiday for some U.N. employees."

"Yes, I'm aware of this," his companion said tonelessly.

As Zinsou opened the door to his office, he startled as he saw the figure of a man seated behind his own desk, silhouetted by the ebbing light.

*What the hell was happening?*

He turned to his companion: "I don't know what to say. It seems we have an unexpected visitor."

The man at Zinsou's desk rose and stepped toward him, and Zinsou gaped in astonishment.

The helmet of thick black hair, only lightly flecked with gray, the high, almost Asiatic cheekbones. A face the world knew as Peter Novak's.

Zinsou turned to the man at his side.

The same face. Essentially indistinguishable.

Yet there *were* differences, Zinsou reflected, just not physical ones. Rather, they were differences of affect and mien. There was something hesitant and cautious about the man by his side: something implacable and imperious about the man before him. The marionette and the marionette master. Zinsou's whirling sense of vertigo was lessened only by the recognition that Paul Janson had guessed right.

Now the man at Zinsou's side handed an envelope to the man who could have been his mirror image.

A subtle nod: "Thank you, Laszlo," said the man who had been waiting for them. "You may go now."

The impostor by Zinsou's side turned and left without so much as a word.

"*Mon cher* Mathieu," said the man who stayed behind. He held out a hand. "*Mon très cher frère.*"

# CHAPTER FORTY-TWO

Janson heard Zinsou's voice distinctly in his earpiece: *"My God."* At the same time, he saw the Peter Novak who was not Peter Novak press the DOWN elevator button.

He was leaving.

In Janson's earpiece, another man's voice: "I must apologize for the confusion."

Janson raced to the elevator and stepped in. The man who was not Peter Novak wore an expression that was startled—but devoid of recognition.

"Who are you *really?*" Janson demanded.

The suited man's response was glacial and dignified: "Have we met?"

"I simply don't understand," said the secretary-general.

The other man was magnetic, utterly confident, utterly relaxed. "You'll have to forgive me for taking very special precautions. That was my double, as you've no doubt figured out by now."

"You sent a *double* in your place?"

"You're familiar with the role played by the 'morning Stalin,' are you not? The Soviet dictator would send a look-alike to make certain public appearances—it kept his enemies on their toes. I'm afraid that there had been rumors of an assassination attempt in the General Assembly. Credible reports from my security staff. I couldn't risk it."

"I see," Zinsou said. "But you know, of course, that the Russian prime minister, the premier of China, many others, also have enemies. And *they've* addressed the General Assembly. The U.S. president himself has honored us with his presence today. This institution has an unbroken record of security, at least on this small plot of land here on the East River."

"I appreciate that, *mon cher.* But my enemies are of a different order. The heads of state you mention could, at least, assume that the secretary-general was not himself conspiring against them. It hasn't escaped me that the first person who occupied your office and position was a man named Lie."

Zinsou's veins were chilled. After an excruciating moment of silence, he said simply, "I'm sorry you think that."

Peter Novak patted Zinsou's shoulder and smiled ingratiatingly. "You mistake my meaning. I don't think it anymore. It's just that I had to be *sure.*"

Beads of sweat had broken out on the secretary-general's forehead. None of this was anticipated. None of this was according to plan. "Can I get us some coffee?" he said.

"*No,* thank you."

"Well, I think I'll have some," Zinsou said, reaching over to the phone console on his desk.

"I wish you wouldn't."

"Very well." Zinsou maintained eye contact. "Tea, perhaps? Why don't I just call Helga and tell her to—"

"You know, I'd rather you not make any phone calls, either. No need to clear your schedule or consult with anyone. You may think me paranoid, but we don't have much time. In just a few minutes, I shall be leaving from the rooftop helipad: all arrangements have been made."

"I see," said Zinsou, who didn't.

"So let's get our business done," said the elegant man with the glossy black hair. "Here are instructions for getting in touch with me." He handed the secretary-general a white card. "It's a number you can call to get a return phone call within the hour. As our plans develop, we'll need to be in regular touch. Your Swiss bank account has, you'll find, already been enhanced—simply an advance on a package of benefits that we can finalize at a later point. And there will be regular monthly payments, which will continue as long as our partnership remains on a solid footing."

Zinsou swallowed. "Very thoughtful."

"Simply to put your mind at rest, because it will be very important that you're able to focus on what truly matters, and not make any errors of judgment."

"I understand."

"It's important that you do. In your speeches as secretary-general, you've often maintained that there's a thin line between civilization and savagery. Let's not put that proposition to the test."

Janson kept a foot in the elevator door, triggering the electric eye and preventing the elevator from moving. "Give me the envelope," he said.

"I don't know what you're talking about," the man said; his Hungarian accent did not slip. If the words were defiant, however, the tone was apprehensive.

Janson formed his right hand into a spear and delivered a crushing punch to the man's throat. As the man fell to the floor in a fit of helpless coughing, Janson dragged him out of the elevator. The man swung at Janson, a sluggish, poorly aimed uppercut. Janson dodged the punch and struck the Ruger against his temple in a controlled blow. The Novak impostor crumpled to the floor, unconscious. A quick frisk verified that there was no envelope on his person.

Now Janson crept toward Zinsou's office, pausing just before the doorway. The sounds came both from his earpiece and through the door.

A clear, tinny voice in his ear: "This is all a bit unexpected." Zinsou was speaking.

Janson turned the knob, threw open the door, and rushed in, the Ruger in his right hand. Demarest's reaction to the intrusion was immediate and deft: he repositioned himself directly behind Zinsou. There was no line of fire that would reach him and not strike the secretary-general.

All the same, Janson fired—wildly, it seemed: three shots high overhead, three slugs smashing into the window, causing the whole pane to buckle and then disintegrate into a curtain of fragments.

And there was silence.

"Alan Demarest," Janson said. "Love what you've done with your hair."

"A poor shot, Paul. You shame your teacher." Demarest's voice, at once rich and astringent, resounded in the room as it had resounded in his memory for so many years.

A cool gust of wind riffled a pad of yellow paper on the secretary-general's desk: it underscored the odd reality of being windowless on the thirty-eighth floor, with nothing but a low aluminum grille between them and the plaza far below. Sounds of traffic from the FDR Drive mingled with the cawing of gulls that wheeled and soared at eye level. There were darkening clouds overhead; soon it would rain.

Janson looked at Alan Demarest peering around Zinsou, who was obviously struggling to maintain his composure and doing far better than most would. Beneath the black pools of Demarest's eyes, he saw the bore hole of a Smith & Wesson .45.

"Let the secretary-general go," Janson said.

"My policy with cat's paws has always been to amputate," Demarest replied.

"You have a gun, I have a gun. He doesn't need to be here."

"You disappoint me. I thought you'd prove a more formidable antagonist."

"Zinsou! Walk. Now. *Get out of here!*" Janson's instructions were crisp. The secretary-general looked at him for a moment, then moved from between the two blood enemies. To Demarest, Janson said, "Shoot him and I shoot you. I will take the *opportunity* to shoot you. Do you believe me?"

"Yes, Paul, I do." Demarest spoke simply.

Janson waited, Ruger in position, until he heard the door close.

Demarest's eyes were hard but not devoid of mirth. "The football coach Woody Hayes was once asked why his teams so seldom threw the forward pass. He replied, 'If you put the ball up in the air, only three things can happen, and two of them are bad.' "

Incongruously, Janson recalled Phan Nguyen's obsession with American football. "You sent me to hell," he said. "I think it's time I returned the favor."

"Why so angry, Paul? Why so much hate in your heart?"

"You know."

"Once things were otherwise. Once there was a connection—something we shared, something deep. Deny it if you want. You know it's true."

"I don't think I know *what's* true, anymore. I owe you that."

"You owe me many things. I shaped you, made you who you are. You haven't forgotten, have you? I never held back. You were my prize protégé. You were so smart and so brave and so resourceful. You were a fast, fast learner. You were made for great things. The way you turned out . . ." He shook his head. "I could have made you great, if you had allowed me to. I understood you the way nobody else did. I understood what you were truly capable of. Maybe that's what really spooked you. Maybe that's why you rejected me. Rejecting me was a way of rejecting you, rejecting who you truly are."

"Is that what you believe?" asked Janson, fascinated despite himself.

"We're different from other people, both of us are. We know the truths that others can't deal with. The Scythian called it right. Laws are like cobwebs—strong enough to catch the weak, but too weak to catch the strong."

"That's bullshit."

"We're strong. Stronger than the others. And together, we would have been so much stronger still. I need you to acknowledge the truth about who you are. That's why I brought you in, had you come to Anura, lead that last mission for me. Look around you, Paul. Think of the world you live in. Face it, you can't stand them any more than I can—the mediocrities, the complacent bureaucrats, the shambling paper pushers who never miss an opportunity to miss an opportunity. Mediocrities whom *we* have permitted to run the world. Do you honestly doubt your own ability to run things better than they do, to make better decisions than they do? You love your country? So did I, Paul. You had to be made to see what *I* was made to see. Just think, Paul. You sacrificed most of your years on this earth to serve a government that took about five seconds to decide to have you killed. I had to show you that. I had to show you the true face of your employers, of the government you almost gave your life for, time and again. I had to show you that they wouldn't hesitate to have you killed. And I did. Once, you turned the American government against me. The only way you could see the truth was for me to do the same to you."

Janson was sickened by the man's smooth prevarications but found himself at a loss for words.

"You're filled with hate. I understand. God forsook his own son in the Garden of Gesthemane. I failed you as well. You were calling out for help, and I failed you. So much of the time we all live out our individual existences, each of us at the center of our own stories, and when you needed me, I wasn't there for you. You were upset. Your learning curve was so steep that I made a mistake: I tried to teach you things you weren't ready for. And I let you go. You must have thought I deserved what I got from you."

"And what was that?"

"Betrayal." Demarest's eyes narrowed. "You thought you could destroy me. But *they* needed me. They always need men like me. Just like they've always needed men like you. I did what I had to do—what had to be done. I always did what had to be done. Sometimes people like me are seen as an embarrassment, and then actions are taken. I became an embarrassment to you. I embarrassed you because you looked at me and saw yourself. So much of you was me. How could it be otherwise? I taught you everything you knew. I gave you the skills that saved your life a dozen times over. *What made you think you had the right to judge me?*" At last, a diamond-hard flash of anger pierced his eerie calm.

"You forfeited any rights you had by your own actions," Janson said. "I saw what you did. I saw who you were. A monster."

"Oh please. I showed you what you were, and you didn't like what you saw."

"*No.*"

"We were the same, you and I, and that's what you couldn't accept."

"We weren't the same."

"Oh, we were. In many ways, we still are. Don't think I didn't keep tabs on what you got up to in later years. They called you 'the machine.' You know what that was short for, of course: 'the killing machine.' Because that's what you were. Oh yes. And you presumed to judge me? Oh, Paul, don't you know *why* you took it on yourself to destroy me? Are you that devoid of self-insight? How comforting it must be to tell yourself that I'm the monster and you're the saint. You're afraid of what I showed you."

"Yes—a profoundly disturbed individual."

"Don't delude yourself, Paul. I'm talking about what I showed you about *yourself.* Whatever I was, you were."

"*No!*" Janson flushed with rage and horror. Violence was indeed something he excelled at: he could no longer run from that truth. But for him it was never an end in itself: rather, violence was a last resort to minimize further violence.

"As I used to tell you, we know more than we know. Have you forgotten what you yourself did in Vietnam? Have you magically repressed the memories?"

"You don't fool me with your goddamn mind games," Janson growled.

"I read the depositions you filed about me," Demarest continued airily. "Somehow they neglected to mention what you'd got up to."

"So *you're* the one who's been spreading that bilge about me—those twisted stories."

Demarest's gaze was steady. "Your victims are still out there, some of them still crippled but still alive. Send an agent out there to interview them. They remember you. They remember with horror."

"*It's a lie! It's a goddamn lie!*"

"Are you sure?" Demarest's question was an electric probe. "No, you're not sure. You're not sure at all." A beat. "It's as if part of you never left, because you're haunted by memories, aren't you? Recurrent nightmares, right?"

Janson nodded; he could not stop himself.

"All these decades later and your sleep is still troubled. Yet what makes those memories so adhesive?"

"What do you care?"

"Could it be guilt? Reach down, Paul—reach down inside you and bring it up, bring it back to the surface."

"Shut up, you bastard."

*"What do your memories leave out, Paul?"*

"Stop it!" Janson yelled, and yet there was a tremor in his voice. "I'm not going to listen to this."

Demarest repeated the question more quietly. "What do your memories leave out?"

The images came to him now in frozen moments of time, not with the fluidity of remembered movement but one frame after another. They had a ghostly surreality that was superimposed over what he saw in front of his face.

Humping another mile. And another. And another. Knifing through the jungle, taking care to avoid the hamlets and villages where VC sympathizers might make all his struggles for naught.

And forcing himself through an especially dense intertwining of vines and trees one morning, where he happened upon a vast oval of *burn.*

The smells told him what had happened—not so much the mingled smells of fish sauce, cooking fires, the fertilizing excrement of humans and water buffalo and chickens as something that overpowered even those smells: the tangy petrochemical odor of napalm.

The air was heavy with it. And everywhere was ash, and soot, and the lumpy remains of a fast-burning chemical fire. He trudged through the burned-out oval and his feet became black with charcoal. It was as if God had held a giant magnifying glass over this spot and burned it with the sun's own rays. And when he adjusted to the napalm fumes, another smell caught his nostrils, that of charred human flesh. When it cooled it would be food for birds and vermin and insects. It had not yet cooled.

From the caved-in, blackened wrecks he could see that there had once been twelve thatch-covered houses in a clearing here. And just outside the hamlet, miraculously untouched by the flames, was a cooking shack framed with coconut leaves, and a meal that had been freshly prepared, no more than thirty minutes earlier. A heap of rice. A stew of prawns and glass noodles. Bananas that had been sliced, fried, and curried. A bowl of peeled litchi and durian fruit. Not an ordinary meal. After a few moments, he recognized what this was.

A wedding feast.

A few yards away, the bodies of the newlyweds lay smoldering, along with their families. Yet, by some fluke, the peasant banquet had been saved from destruction. Now he put aside his AK-47 and ate greedily, shoveling rice and prawns into his mouth with his hands, drinking from a warm cauldron of water that had once awaited another sack of rice. He ate and was sick and ate more, and then he rested, lying heavily on the ground. How odd that was—so little remained of him, and yet it could seem so heavy!

When some of his strength had been replenished, he pushed on through uninhabited jungle, pushed on, pushed on. One foot in front of the other.

That was what would save him: movement without thought, action without reflection.

And when he had his next conscious thought, it, too, came with the wind. The sea!

He could smell the sea!

Over the next ridgeline was the coast. And thus freedom. For U.S. Navy gunboats patrolled this very segment of the shoreline, patrolled it closely: he knew this. And along the coast, somewhere not far from his latitude, a small U.S. navy base had been established: he knew this, too. When he made his way to the shore, he would be free, welcomed by his Navy brethren, taken away, taken home, taking to a place of healing.

Free!

*I think so, Phan Nguyen, I think so.*

Was he hallucinating? It had been a long time, too long a time, since he had been able to find any water to drink. His vision was often odd and unstable, a common symptom of niacin deficiency. His malnutrition surely had brought other cognitive impairments as well. But he inhaled deeply, filled his lungs with the air, and he knew that there was salt in it, the scent of seaweed and sun; he knew it. Liberation lay just over the ridgeline.

*We will never meet again, Phan Nguyen.*

He trudged up a gentle slope, the ground thinning out now, the vegetation growing less dense, and then he startled.

A darting figure, not far from him. An animal? An assailant? His vision was failing him. His senses: they all were failing him, and at a time when they must not. So close—he was so close.

His gaunt fingers fell, spiderlike, to the trigger enclosure of the submachine gun. To be undone by his enemies when he was so near home—that would be a hell beyond imagining, beyond any he had endured.

Another darting movement. He squeezed off a triple burst of gunfire. Three bullets. The noise and the bucking of the weapon in his arms felt greater than they ever had. He rushed over to see what had been hit.

Nothing. He could see nothing. He leaned against a gnarled mangosteen tree and craned around, and there was nothing. Then he looked down, and he realized what he had done.

A shirtless boy. Simple brown pants, and tiny sandals on his feet. In his hand was a bottle of Coca-Cola, its foamy contents now seeping to the ground.

He was, perhaps, seven years old. His crime was—what? Playing hide-and-seek? Gamboling with a butterfly?

The boy lay on the ground. A beautiful child, the most beautiful child Janson had ever seen. He appeared oddly peaceful, except for the jagged crimson across his chest, three tightly clustered holes from which his life-blood pulsed.

He looked up at the gaunt American, his soft brown eyes unblinking.

And he smiled.

*The boy smiled.*

The images flooded Janson now, flooded him for the first time, because these were the images his mind was to banish—banish utterly—the day that followed, and then all the days that followed. Even unremembered, they had pushed at him, weighed on him, at times immobilized him. He thought of the little boy on the basement stairs in the Stone Palace, of his own hand frozen at the trigger, and he grasped the power of the unremembered.

Yet he remembered now.

He remembered how he sank to the ground and cradled the child in his lap, an embrace between the dead and the almost dead, victim and victimizer.

*What fellowship hath righteousness with unrighteousness? and what communion hath light with darkness?*

And he did what he had never done in country. He wept.

The memories that followed were beyond proper retrieval: The child's parents soon came, having been summoned by the gunfire. He could see their stricken faces, yes—sorrowing, with a sorrow that voided even rage. They took their boy from him, the man and the woman, and the man was keening, keening . . . and the mother shook her head, shook her head violently, as if to dislodge the reality it contained, and holding the lifeless body of her child in her arms, she turned to the gaunt soldier, as if there were any words she could utter that would make a difference.

But all she said was, *You Americans.*


Now the faces, all of them, dissolved, and Janson was left with the hard-eyed gaze of Alan Demarest.

Demarest had been talking, was talking now. "The past is another country. A country you never fully left."

It was true.

"You could never get me out of your head, could you?" Demarest continued.

"No," Janson said, his voice a broken whisper.

"Why would that be? Because the bond between us was real. It was powerful. 'Opposition is true friendship,' William Blake tells us. Oh, Paul—what a history we shared. Did it haunt you? It haunted me."

Janson did not reply.

"One day, the United States government handed me the keys to the kingdom, allowed me to create an empire such as the world had never seen. Of course I would make it mine. But however big your coffers are, it's not always easy to settle your accounts. I just needed you to acknowledge the truth about us two. I *made* you, Paul. I molded you from clay, the way God made man."

"*No.*" The word came like a groan from deep within him.

Another step closer. "It's time to be truthful with yourself," he said gently. "There's always been something between us. Something very close to love."

Janson looked intently at him, mentally imposing Demarest's features over the famous countenance of the legendary humanitarian, seeing the points of resemblance even on the recontoured visage. He shuddered.

"And a lot closer to hate," Janson said at last.

Demarest's eyes burned into him like glowing coals. "I *made* you, and nothing can ever change that. Accept it. Accept who you are. Once you do, things change. *The nightmares will cease,* Paul. Life gets a whole lot easier. Take it from me. I always sleep well at night. Imagine it—wouldn't that be something, Paul?"

Janson took a deep breath, and suddenly felt able to focus once more. "I don't want that."

"What? You don't want to leave the nightmares behind? Now you're lying to yourself, *Lieutenant.*"

"I'm not your lieutenant. And I wouldn't trade my nightmares for anything."

"You never healed, because you wouldn't let yourself heal."

"Is this what you call healing? You sleep well because something inside you—call it a soul, call it what you like—is dead. Maybe something happened that snuffed it out one day, maybe you never had it, but it's the thing that makes us human."

"*Human?* You mean *weak.* People always mix those two words up."

"My nightmares are *me,*" Janson said, in a clear, steady voice. "I have to live with the things I've done on this earth. I don't have to like them. I've done good and I've done bad. As for the bad—I don't *want* to be reconciled with the bad. You tell me I can take that pain away? That pain is how I know who I am and who I'm not. *That pain is how I know I'm not you.*"

Suddenly Demarest lashed out, batting the gun out of Janson's hand. It flew clattering to the marble floor.

Demarest looked almost mournful as he leveled his pistol. "I tried to reason with you. *I tried to reach you.* I've done so much to reach you, to bring you back in touch with your true self. All I wanted from you was an acknowledgment of the truth—the truth about us both."

"The truth? You're a monster. You should have died in Mesa Grande. I wish to God you had."

"It's remarkable—how much you know and how little. How powerful you can be, and how powerless." He shook his head. "The man kills the child of another and cannot even protect his own. . . ."

"What the hell are you talking about?"

"The embassy bombing in Caligo—did it shake your world? I thought it might when I suggested it, five years ago. You'll have to forgive me: the idea of your having a child just didn't sit well with me. A Paul Junior—no, I couldn't see it. Always easy to arrange these things through the local talent—those wild-eyed insurrectionists dreaming of Allah and the virgins of Paradise. I'm afraid I'm the only one who could appreciate the delicious irony that it was all brought about by a *fertilizer* bomb. But really, what kind of a father would you have made, a baby-killer like you?"

Janson felt as if he had been turned to stone.

A heavy sigh. "And it's time for me to be going. I have great plans for the world, you know. Truth is, I'm getting *bored* with conflict resolution. Conflict *promotion* is the new order of the day. Human beings *like* battle and bloodshed. Let man be man, I say."

"Not your prerogative." Janson struggled to get the words out.

He smiled. "*Carpe diem*—seize the day. *Carpe mundum*—seize the world."

"They made you a god," Janson said, recalling the president's words, "when they didn't own the heavens."

"The heavens are beyond even my ken. Still, I'll be happy to keep an open mind. Why don't you file a report about the hereafter when you get there? I'll look forward to your MemCon in re Saint Peter at the Pearly Gates." He was expressionless as he leveled the pistol two feet away from Janson's forehead. "Bon voyage," he said as his finger curled around the trigger.

Then Janson felt something warm spray against his face. Blinking, he saw that it came from an exit wound at Demarest's forehead. Undeflected by window glass, the sniper's shot was as precise as if it had been fired point-blank.

Janson reached out and cupped Demarest's face, holding him erect. "*Xin loi,*" he lied. *Sorry about that.*

For a moment, Demarest's expression was perfectly blank: he could have been in deepest meditation; he could have been asleep.

Janson let go, and Demarest crumpled to the ground with the utter relaxation of life surrendered.


When Janson peered out from the secretary-general's antique telescope, he found Jessie precisely where he had stationed her: across the East River, her rifle positioned on the roof of the old bottling plant, directly beneath the mammoth neon letters. She was starting to disassemble the weapon with deft, practiced movements. Then she looked up at him, as if she could feel his gaze upon her. All at once, Janson had a feeling, an odd, lighter-than-air feeling, that everything would be all right.

He stepped away from the scope and looked out with his own two eyes, his face cooled by the breeze. Hunter's Point. The name had become mordantly appropriate.

Looming above his beloved, the enormous Pepsi-Cola sign glowed red in the deepening gloom. Now Janson squinted, saw the reflected light from the neon spilled onto the glistening waters below. For a moment, it looked like a river of blood.

# CHAPTER FORTY-THREE

"I want to thank you for joining us, Mr. Janson," said President Charles W. Berquist Jr., seated at the head of the oval table. The handful of people at the table, mainly senior administrators and analysts from the country's principal intelligence agencies, had made their separate ways to the blandly handsome building on Sixteenth Street, using the side entrance that was accessible from a private driveway and guaranteed that arrivals and departures would not attract notice. There would be no tape, no log. It was another meeting that had not, officially, taken place. "Your nation owes you a debt of gratitude that it will never know about. But I know. I don't think it'll be any surprise that you'll be receiving another Distinguished Intelligence Star."

Janson shrugged. "Maybe I should get into the scrap-metal business."

"But I also wanted you to hear some good news, and from me. Thanks to you, it looks like we're going to be able to resurrect the Mobius Program. Doug and the others have walked me through it several times, and it's looking better and better."

"Is that right?" Janson said impassively.

"You don't seem surprised," President Berquist said, sounding straitened. "I supposed you anticipated the possibility."

"When you've been around the planners as long as I have, you stop being surprised by their combination of brilliance and stupidity."

The president scowled, displeased with the operative's tone. "You're talking about some very extraordinary people, I'll have you know."

"Yes. Extraordinarily arrogant." Janson shook his head slowly. "Anyway, you can just forget about it."

"The question is, where do you get off talking to the president like that?" Douglas Albright, the DIA deputy director, interjected.

"The question is whether you people ever learn anything," Janson shot back.

"We've learned a great deal," Albright said. "We won't make the same mistakes twice."

"True—the mistakes will be different ones."

The secretary of state spoke. "To jettison the program at this point would be to scuttle tens of thousands of man-hours of work, as Doug points out. It would also be like trying to unring a bell. As far as the world is concerned, Peter Novak still exists."

"We can remake him, recast him, with a whole set of additional safeguards," Albright said, giving the secretary of state an encouraging look. "There are a hundred measures we can take to prevent what Demarest did from recurring."

"I don't *believe* you people," Janson said. "A few days ago, you'd all agreed it was a colossal error. A basic miscalculation, both political and moral. You understood—or, anyway, you *seemed* to understand—that a plan that was premised on massive deception was bound to go awry. And in ways that could never be predicted."

"We were panicked," the secretary of state replied. "We weren't thinking rationally. Of *course* we just wanted the whole thing to go away. But Doug here went over everything with us, calmly, *rationally*. The potential upside remains extraordinary. It's like atomic energy—of course there's always the risk of a catastrophic mishap. None of us are debating that. Yet the potential *benefits* to humanity are even greater." As he spoke, his voice grew smoother and more sonorous: the senior diplomat of the press conferences and television appearances. He seemed hardly the same man who had been so frightened at the Hempel estate. "To turn our backs on it because of *something that didn't happen* would be to abdicate our responsibility as political leaders. You can see that, can't you? Are we on the same page?"

"We're not reading the same goddamn *book!*"

"Get over yourself," Albright snapped. "Fact of the matter is, we owe it all to you—you handled things perfectly. You're the one who made the resurrection possible." He did not have to refer to the details: that two men had quickly been removed from the Secretariat Building, each draped with a sheet, headed for very different destinations. "The understudy has recovered nicely. He's been kept in one of our security facilities, subjected to extensive chemical interrogation. Just as you surmised, he's terrified, absolutely ready to cooperate. Demarest never entrusted him with the command codes, of course. But that's OK. Without Demarest around to constantly rescramble them, our technicians have been able to penetrate the systems. We've regained control."

"That was your mistake in the past, imagining that you *had* control." Janson shook his head slowly.

"We've certainly got control over Demarest's understudy," said the gray-faced technician Janson remembered from the Hempel estate gathering. "A fellow named Laszlo Kocsis. Used to teach English at a technical school in Hungary. He went under the knife eighteen months ago. A carrot-and-stick situation. Make a long story short, if he went along with Demarest's plans for him, he'd get ten million dollars. If he didn't, his family would be slaughtered. Not a strong man. He's pretty much under our thumb now."

"As you anticipated," the DIA man said graciously. "We'll be offering him a small island on the Caribbean. Fitting his reclusive ways. He'll be a gilded prisoner. Unable to leave. Under twenty-four-hour guard of a Consular Operations unit. It seemed appropriate to borrow some funds from the Liberty Foundation to pay for the arrangement."

"But let's not get sidetracked by formalities," the president said with a tight smile. "The point is, everything's in order."

"And the Mobius Program is back in business," Janson said.

"Thanks to you," Berquist said. He winked, a show of his characteristic affable command.

"But *better* than before," Albright put in. "Because of all that we've learned."

"So you grasp the logic of our position," the secretary of state said.

Janson looked around to see what the president saw: the complacent faces of the men and women assembled in the Meridian International Center—senior civil servants, senior administrators and analysts, members of permanent Washington. The remains of the Mobius Program. They were the best and the brightest, always had been. From childhood, they had been rewarded with the top grades and test scores; all their lives they had received the approbation of their superiors. They believed in nothing greater than themselves. They knew that means were to be assessed only in relation to their ends. They were convinced that probabilities could be assigned to every unknown variable, that the wash of uncertainty could be tamed into precisely quantified risk.

And despite the fact that their ranks had been decimated by unanticipated vagaries of human nature, they had learned nothing.

"My game, my rules," said Janson. "Gentlemen, the Mobius Program is over."

"On whose orders?" President Berquist snorted.

"Yours."

"What's gotten into you, Paul?" he said, his face darkening. "You're not making sense."

"I get that a lot." Janson faced him squarely. "You know the Washington saying: there are no permanent allies, only permanent interests. This program wasn't your devising. It was something you inherited from your predecessor, who inherited it from his predecessor, and so on. . . ."

"That's true of a lot of things, from our defense program to our monetary policy."

"Sure. The lifers work on these things—as far as they're concerned, you're just passing through."

"It's important to take a long view of these things," President Berquist said, shrugging.

"A question for you, Mr. President. You have just received and accepted an illegal personal contribution of $1.5 million." As Janson spoke, he imagined Grigori Berman guffawing back in Berthwick House. It had been the sort of outsize mischief that pleased him beyond measure. "How are you going to explain that to Congress and to the American people?"

"What the hell are you *talking* about?"

"I'm talking about a big-time Beltway scandal—Watergate times ten. I'm talking about watching your political career go up in flames. Call your banker. A seven-figure sum was wired to your personal account from an account of Peter Novak's at International Netherlands Group Bank. The digital signatures can't be faked—well, not easily. So it sure seems like a foreign plutocrat has put you on his payroll. A suspicious-minded member of the other party might start to wonder about that. Could have something to do with your signing that banking secrecy act into law the other week. Could have something to do with a lot of things. Enough to keep a special prosecutor busy for years. It's looking like a four- or five-column headline in the *Washington Post*: IS PRESIDENT ON PLUTOCRAT'S PAYROLL? INVESTIGATION PENDING. That sort of thing. The New York tabloids will run with something crass, like RENT-A-PREZ. You know those media feeding frenzies—there'll be such a din, you won't be able to hear yourself think."

"That's *bullshit!*" the president exploded.

"And we'll all enjoy watching you explain that to Congress. The details will arrive by e-mail tomorrow to the Justice Department as well as the relevant members of the House and the Senate."

"But Peter Novak . . ."

"Novak? Not an angle I'd want to focus any attention on, if I were you. I don't think either one of you will come away with your reputation intact."

"You're kidding me," the president said.

"Call your banker," Janson repeated.

The president stared at Janson. His personal and political instincts had gained him the highest office of the land. They told him that Janson was not bluffing.

"You're making a terrible mistake," said Berquist.

"I can undo it," Janson said. "It's still not too late."

"Thank you."

"Though soon it will be. That's why you need to decide about Mobius."

"But—"

"Call your banker."

The president left the room. A few minutes passed before he returned to his seat.

"I consider this beneath contempt." The president's hard Scandinavian features were livid with rage. "And it's beneath *you!* My God, you've served your country with incredible loyalty."

"And was rewarded with a 'beyond salvage' order for my pains."

"We've been through that." Berquist glowered. "What you're proposing amounts to nothing less than blackmail."

"Let's not get sidetracked by the formalities," Janson said blandly.

The president rose, his face tight, blinking hard. Wordlessly, he sat down again. He had talked down recalcitrant opponents before, had directed the high beams of his charm at the disaffected and resistant, and had brought them around. He could do this.

"I have devoted my life to public service," he told Janson, his rich baritone swelling with grave sincerity. "The welfare of this country is my life. I need you to understand that. The decisions that have been made in this room have not been made thoughtlessly or cynically. When I was sworn into office, I took an oath *to protect and defend* this nation—the same oath my father had taken twenty years before. It is an obligation I take with utmost seriousness. . . ."

Janson yawned.

"Derek," the president said, turning to the director of Consular Operations and the one man at the table who had said nothing so far. "Talk to your guy. Make him understand."

Undersecretary Derek Collins removed his heavy black glasses and massaged the reddened grooves they left on the bridge of his nose. He had the look of someone who was about to do something he would probably regret. "I kept trying to tell you—you don't know this man," Collins said. "None of you do."

"Derek?" The president's request was clear.

"To protect and defend," Collins said. "Heavy words. A heavy burden. A beautiful ideal that sometimes requires doing some ugly things. Uneasy rests the head, right?" He looked at Janson. "There aren't any saints in this room, make no mistake about that. But let's show some respect to the basic idea of democracy. There's one person in this room who's gone a long way on some scraps of common sense and some common decency. He's a tough son of a bitch, and he's as true a patriot as they come, and, agree with him or not, at the end of the day, this has to be his call. . . ."

"Thanks, Derek," President Berquist said, solemn but pleased.

"I'm talking about Paul Janson," the undersecretary finished, facing the man at the head of the table. "And if you don't do what he says, Mr. President, you're a bigger fool than your father."

"Undersecretary Collins," the president barked, "I'd be happy to accept your resignation."

"Mr. President," Collins said in a level tone, "I'd be happy to accept yours."

President Berquist froze. "Goddamn it, Janson. Do you see what you've done?"

Janson stared at the director of Consular Operations. "An interesting song for a hawk," he said with a half smile.

Then he turned to the president. "You know what they say: 'Consider the source.' The advice you've been given may say more about your advisers' concerns than your own. You really ought to think in terms of alignment of interests. Goes for you, too, Mr. Secretary." He glanced at the now queasy-looking secretary of state and returned to Berquist. "As I said, as far as most of the people in this room are concerned, you're just passing through. They've been around before you, they'll be here after you. Your immediate, personal interests don't really mean a whole lot to them. They *want* you to take the 'long view.' "

Berquist was silent for half a minute. He was a pragmatist at heart, and used to making the cold, hard calculations that political survival depended upon. Everything else was secondary to that essential arithmetic. His forehead gleamed with sweat.

He forced a smile. "Paul," he said, "I'm afraid this meeting got off to a bad start. I'd really like to hear you out."

"Mr. President," Douglas Albright protested. "This is *entirely* inappropriate. We've gone through this again and again, and—"

"Fine, Doug. Why don't you tell me that you know how to nullify what Paul Janson's gone and done? I haven't heard anybody here bother to address that particular matter."

"These aren't comparables!" Albright stormed. "We're talking about the long-term interests of this geopolitical entity, not the greater glory of the second Berquist administration! There's no comparison! Mobius is bigger than all of us. There's only one right decision."

"And what about, oh, a looming political scandal?"

"Suck it up, Mr. President," Albright said quietly. "I'm sorry, sir. You've got a decent chance of toughing it out. That's what you politicians specialize in, isn't it? Cut taxes, launch a decency campaign against Hollywood, go to war in Colombia—do whatever your pollsters say. Americans have the attention span of a gnat. But, if you'll forgive my directness, you *cannot* sacrifice this program on the altar of political ambition."

"Always interesting to hear what you think I can and cannot do, Doug," Berquist said, leaning over and squeezing the analyst's beefy shoulders, "But I've think you've said enough today."

"Please, Mr. President—"

"Put a sock in it, Doug," Berquist said. "I'm thinking here. Doing some deep presidential-level policy reevaluation."

"I'm talking about the prospects of reengineering global polities." Albright's voice rose to a squawk of indignation. "You're just talking about your reelection chances."

"You got that one right. Call me a stick-in-the-mud. I kinda have a hankering for the scenario where I'm still president." He turned to Janson. "Your game, your rules," he said. "I can live with that."

"Excellent choice, Mr. President," Janson said neutrally.

Berquist gave him a smile that combined command and entreaty. "Now give me my goddamn presidency back."

# The New York Times

## PETER NOVAK TO YIELD CONTROL OF THE LIBERTY FOUNDATION

BILLIONAIRE PHILANTHROPIST TURNS OVER FOUNDATION
TO AN INTERNATIONAL BOARD OF TRUSTEES.

MATHIEU ZINSOU TO SERVE AS NEW DIRECTOR

### By Jason Steinhardt

AMSTERDAM—In a press conference held at the Amsterdam headquarters of the Liberty Foundation, the legendary financier and humanitarian Peter Novak announced that he would be relinquishing control of the Liberty Foundation, the global organization that he created and ran for more than fifteen years. Nor would the organization have any foreseeable difficulties in funding: he also announced that he was turning over all his capital assets to the foundation, which would be reconstituted as a public trust. An international board of directors would include prominent citizens from around the world, under the chairmanship of the U.N. Secretary General, Mathieu Zinsou. "My work is done," Mr. Novak said, reading from a prepared statement. "The Liberty Foundation must be greater than any one man, and my plan, all along, had been to delegate control of this organization to a public board, with broad accountability among its directors. As the foundation enters this new phase, transparency must be the watchword."

Reactions were generally positive. Some observers expressed surprise, but others said they had long anticipated such a move. Sources close to Mr. Novak suggested that the recent death of his wife had helped catalyze his decision to retire from the operations of the foundation. Others point out that the financier's reclusive habits were increasingly in conflict with the exposed and highly public position that his work at the foundation demanded. Novak was sketchy about his future plans, but some aides suggested that he planned to remove himself from the public eye entirely. "You won't have Peter Novak to kick around anymore, gentlemen," one deputy told members of the press with cheerful irony. Yet the mysterious plutocrat has long had a gift for the unexpected, and those who know him best agree that it would be a mistake to count him out.

"He'll be back," said Jan Kubelik, the foreign minister of the Czech Republic, who was in town for a G-7 Conference. "Depend on it. You haven't seen the last of Peter Novak."

# EPILOGUE

The lithe woman with the spiky brown hair lay prone and perfectly still, the four-foot rifle braced by sandbags fore and aft. The shadows of the belfry rendered her perfectly invisible from any distance. When she opened her nonscope eye, the cityscape of Dubrovnik seemed oddly flattened, red-tiled roofs scattered before her like colored faience, shards of ancient pottery. Beneath the bell tower where she had been positioned for the past several hours, there was a sea of faces that continued several hundred yards to the wooden platform that had been erected in the center of Dubrovnik's old town.

They were the faithful, the devoted. It was lost on none of them that the pope had decided to start off his visit to Croatia by addressing an audience in a city that had come to symbolize the suffering of its people. Though more than a decade had passed since the Yugoslav army laid siege to the Adriatic port city, the memory of the assault remained undimmed among the town's citizens.

Many of them had stamp-sized laminated photographs of the beloved pontiff. It wasn't merely that he was someone known to be willing to speak truth to power; it was the unmistakable radiance he had about him—charisma, yes, but also compassion. It was typical of him that he would not merely decry violence and terrorism from the safety of the Vatican; he would take his message of peace to the very heartlands of strife and separatism. Indeed, word had already got out that the pope intended to address a history that most Croatians preferred to forget. In the ancient conflict between Catholic and Eastern Orthodox faiths, there was much cause for contrition on both sides. And it was time, the pontiff believed, for the Vatican and Croatia alike to confront the brutally fascistic legacy of the country's Ustashi authority during the Second World War.

Though Croatia's leadership, and much of its citizenry, was bound to react with dismay, his moral courage had seemingly only increased the devotion of his throngs of admirers here. It had also—Janson's suspicions had recently been confirmed by his contacts in the capital city of Zagreb—

resulted in a carefully organized assassination plot. An embittered secessionist movement of minority Serbs would avenge their own historic grievances by murdering the figure whom this predominantly Catholic nation
venerated above all others. In silent collusion was a network of extreme
Croatian nationalists: they feared the pontiff's reform-minded tendencies
and sought an opportunity to extirpate the treacherous minorities who had
taken root among them. After such a monstrous provocation—and no
provocation could be greater than the slaying of a beloved pope—none
would stand in their way. Indeed, even ordinary citizens would willingly
join in the sanguinary business of cleansing Croatia.

Like all extremists, of course, they had an inability to anticipate the
consequences of their actions beyond the immediate realization of their
goals. The Serbs' murderous act would indeed be repaid, ten thousandfold,
in the blood of his ethnic kin. Yet those massacres would inevitably inspire
the Serbian government to intervene forcibly: Dubrovnik and other Croatian cities would again be shelled by Serbian forces, compelling Croatia
itself to declare war upon its Serbian antagonists. A conflagration would,
once more, burst upon this most unstable corner of Europe—dividing
neighboring countries into allies and adversaries, and with what ultimate
results, nobody could say. A global conflict had once been sparked by a
Balkan assassination; it could happen again.

As a gentle breeze filtered through the medieval buildings of the city's
old town neighborhood, an unexceptionable-looking man with short, gray
hair—nobody who would ever get a second look—continued to pace
down the street Bozardar Filipovic. "Four degrees off the median," he said
softly. "The apartment block on the middle of the street. Top floor. Got
a visual?"

The woman repositioned slightly, and adjusted her Swarovski 12×50:
the gunman lying in wait filled the scope. The scarred visage was familiar
from her face book: Milic Pavlovic. Not one of the Serb fanatics of Dubrovnik, but a seasoned and highly skilled assassin who had earned their
trust.

The terrorists had sent the best.

But then so had the Vatican, which sought to eliminate the assassin
without the world knowing what it had done.

The executive security business was only formally a new pursuit for
Janson and Kincaid. For that matter, it was only formally a business: as
Jessica had pointed out, the millions that remained in Janson's Cayman
Islands account were his to keep—if he hadn't earned it, who had? Still,

as Janson had said, they were too young to put themselves out to pasture. He had tried that—tried to run from who he was. That was not the answer for him, for either of them; he knew that now. It was the hypocrisy—the hubris of the planners—against which he rebelled. But for better or worse, neither of them had been made for a peaceable existence. "I've done the small-island-in-the-Caribbean thing," Janson had explained. "It gets old fast." The bountiful cash reserves simply meant that the partnership could be selective in choosing its clients and that there would be no need to stint on operating expenses.

Now Kincaid spoke in a low voice, knowing that the filament mike carried her words straight to Janson's earpiece. "Goddamn Kevlar body armor," she said, stretching her long, loose-jointed body beneath the layers of bulletproof mesh. She always found it uncomfortably hot, protested his insistence that she wear it. "Tell me the truth—do you think it makes me look fat?"

"You think I'm gonna answer that while you've got a bullet in the chamber?"

She found her spot-weld—stock to cheek—as the craggy-faced assassin assembled his bipod, and inserted the magazine into his long rifle.

The pope would be making his appearance in minutes.

Janson's voice in her ear again: "Everything OK?"

"Like clockwork, snookums," she said.

"Just be careful, all right? Remember, the backup shooter's in the warehouse at location B. If they get wind of you, you're in his range."

"I'm on top of it," she said, suffused with the deep, glowing calm of a perfectly positioned marksman.

"I know," he said. "I'm just saying, be careful."

"Don't worry, my love," she said. "It'll be a walk in the park."